PRAISE FOR *THE DEAD WANDER IN THE DESERT*

"Seisenbayev is like Prometheus guarding the fire of . . . the culture and literature of his nation. There are very few creators like him. And there is only one in Kazakhstan. He is utterly unique!"

—Anatoly Kim, Russian-Korean writer

"Yesterday I finished reading Seisenbayev's *The Dead Wander in the Desert*, and I can appreciate what a big thing this is. Oh, this is a universe—this is a novel. A folk epic. A novel as a panorama of being. And the main character here is not a person but the nation."

—Georgy Gachev, Russian philosopher

"Rollan Seisenbayev has powerfully and urgently struck the bell of alarm, uncovered the people's pain, and thrown the spotlight on his nation's tragic fate: the burned steppe, the marsh wetlands, the boundless sand through which the dead wander."

—Gerold Belger, Kazakh translator and writer

"Rollan Seisenbayev is a true creator of spiritual values. There are few enlighteners like him. And he is alone as a creator of such universality."

—Erbol Kurmanbaev, Kazakh philosopher and politician

"Rollan Seisenbayev blazingly and mercilessly shows the limits of human existence. He shouts, 'People, be vigilant. We all stand on the brink of an ecological catastrophe that will bring death to all life on earth.' And yet he still manages to show a way to salvation [in a] . . . return to its origins!"

—Rustem Dzhanguzhin, Tatar author

THE DEAD
WANDER
IN THE
DESERT

THE DEAD
WANDER
IN THE
DESERT

ROLLAN
SEISENBAYEV

TRANSLATED BY **JOHN FARNDON** AND **OLGA NAKSTON**

amazoncrossing

Text copyright © 1986 by Rollan Seisenbayev
Translation copyright © 2019 by John Farndon

Previously published as МЕРТВЫЕ БРОДЯТ В ПЕСКАХ by TAFA in Kazakhstan in 1986. Translated from Russian by John Farndon with Olga Nakston. First published in English by AmazonCrossing in 2019.

Published by AmazonCrossing, Seattle

www.apub.com

Amazon, the Amazon logo, and AmazonCrossing are trademarks of Amazon.com, Inc., or its affiliates.

ISBN-13: 9781542005395
ISBN-10: 1542005396

Cover design by Philip Pascuzzo

Cover illustrated by Philip Pascuzzo

Printed in the United States of America

With sorrow in my soul, I dedicate this book to the fishermen of the Aral, the people of Semipalatinsk, and the victims of the nuclear insanity and ecological disasters of the twentieth century, whose voices sound the alarm, whose souls groan over the planet and plead for sense in the living.

—Rollan Seisenbayev

Water . . . you are the richest treasure in the world, but also the most sensitive. One can die by a spring of magnesian water. One can die two steps from a saltwater lake. One can die even from two liters of dew if they hold traces of dissolved salts. But to us you bring an infinitely simple happiness.

—Antoine de Saint-Exupéry, *Wind, Sand and Stars*

Translator's Preface: The Beauty of Steppe Grass

Working on Kazakh author Rollan Seisenbayev's *The Dead Wander in the Desert* has been for me a truly extraordinary journey into another culture and another imagination.

The culture of the Kazakhs is an ancient one, built on stories passed down orally from generation to generation, and their view of the world grew under vast open skies and rolling steppes, where it is hard not to be awed by your own insignificance.

In Rollan's book, one man strives to avert perhaps the greatest environmental tragedy of the last century: the destruction of the Aral Sea. It is a powerful tale of hubris—a reminder of the folly of forgetting our place in the world, something maybe even the Kazakhs themselves had forgotten. It's an inspirational reminder, too, of the centrality of imagination, of community, of tradition, of spirituality, and of connection to the world and our very humanity. But it is also a story that needs to be told—the tale of the extraordinary sufferings of the Kazakh people in the last century under the Soviet Union.

Once you have read the book, I am sure you will not be quite as surprised as I was at something Rollan told me when I met him for the first time in a Turkish restaurant on London's Great Portland Street over delicious dolma. He had been led directly to me from Central Asia, he announced, by his shaman.

I have never asked just how or why his shaman chose me or had even heard about me. It seems something that is not mine to delve into. But there is no doubt in my mind that I was now being led on a journey, a journey that included a mind-blowing tour around Kazakhstan under the guidance of Rollan and many quite wonderful Kazakh people, so that I could see the key sites of the novel and have these in mind as I worked on the translation.

Of course, the real journey is the book itself and the challenge of bringing it into English—readable yet reflecting its own uniquely Kazakh way of expression and storytelling. I was helped tremendously to ensure the translation is accurate by my sharp translation partner Olga Nakston and by Rollan's equally sharp old friend and colleague Gafura Alimbekova and his wonderful wife, Clara.

But my own task was to render it in English in such a way that I captured the distinctive slow rhythm and lyricism of Rollan's original, the sense of phrase piled on phrase, of awe for words and the sound of words. In this book, Rollan does not simply tell a story of political and environmental tragedy but delves deep into the heart of being. It is a Muslim book, and it is the tension between the godless drive of Soviet plans and the spiritual crisis of the Kazakh people that shapes the narrative flow. Lessons from the Quran and repeated Soviet news bulletins vie for attention as sources of the truth.

A central part of Kazakh culture, even today, is the *dastarkhan*, the many-dished feast with which Kazakhs traditionally entertain guests. The dastarkhan goes on for hours, because as they eat, the men, especially the elders, are expected to deliver monologues to which everyone listens deferentially. Rollan is a master of these monologues, and he can speak extempore for hours, during which time everyone listens with rapt attention—unbroken even while he answers a phone call and then continues!

Another key and linked part of Kazakh culture is the oral tradition of poetry, storytelling, and music. A nomadic people, Kazakhs didn't have printed books until recently, but they are a highly literate people, and oral poetry, storytelling, and music have been integral to their lives for thousands of years. Masters of the art are the most revered figures in Kazakh society.

Poetry is highly formalized, and the *aitys* (poetry contests like rap battles but with much higher status) have been major events for a thousand or more years. The aitys tradition is alive and well today, and the poets, or *aqyns*, are hugely respected—and the prizes for winning contests can be big. There are aitys shows now on TV, like *The X Factor*.

Rollan's prose has a sense of an endless yarn with an ancient, epic rhythm that allows it to switch easily between the modern sections, ancient myths, poetry, and the high seriousness of Muslims schooled deeply in the Quran.

So it was not enough to simply translate accurately for meaning. The English version had to have an aural and discursive quality, like the Kazakh. The prose had to sing, or chant, and the many poems had to have the same rhyme and meter as the Kazakh originals. Even the prose had to have a Kazakh rhythm. To avoid sending the English reader into an unwanted trance, the English text had to be readable, yes, but it had to, I felt, have an unfamiliar sound of ancient high seriousness that is peculiarly Central Asian and sits well with the contemporary narrative.

There are many words that will be unfamiliar to English readers, both Kazakh words such as *aul* and *dombra*, and Russian Soviet terms. I could have simply translated these as "village" and "lute." But because they are key to the flavor of the book and have a particular meaning in Kazakhstan, I have kept these words italicized and explained them in a footnote the first time they appear.

The Dead Wander in the Desert is not a light read. It is not constructed with the same psychological hooks and fast-moving plots that English readers are familiar with. And yet it takes us on a much deeper, and maybe richer, journey—a journey into what it means to be human and what our place in the world is. It's a journey of beauty and resonance and imagination. Above all, the story is very timely in view of the crisis in climate and the shifts in global culture.

John Farndon
London, January 14, 2019

Prologue

1968

Here, close by the village of Karaoi, the Syr Darya grows broad, swirling boisterously and bubbling along its banks into fulvous foam. Anyone standing on its brink can feel the river's joy. Here at last by Karaoi, after long days creeping through the searing sands, suffocating, losing hope of ever reaching the sea, she suddenly senses its distant roar and shakes herself back to life in sheer delight—and dashes on to meet him, loyal and devoted, as she has for thousands upon thousands of years.

Yet anyone standing on the brink cannot fail to notice something else. He will realize that over the years the river has slowly but surely dwindled, her bed shoaled, her banks crumbling. And he might ponder this for a while and feel sadness in his heart.

And so the young geography teacher stood on the brink and gazed sorrowfully at the river. Yes, she was shrinking. Far away in her upper reaches, factories erected along the river's side in recent years had greedily drained her water. And lower down, as she wound through the desert, her waters were splashed out over the vast cotton and rice plantations that spread away on either side . . . If it goes on like this, the Syr Darya will soon be drunk to the dregs. She will fail to bring her waters to the sea. She will die. If the river dies, the sea will die too. And if the sea dies, then the fishermen and farmers and cattlemen who live by its shores will die. The auls, their ancient villages, will crumble to dust.

It was hard for Zhalelkhan to imagine, but it could happen. He was teaching for his third year in Karaoi, where he'd come right after graduation. In those three years, he'd gathered around him a small circle of keen geography students and often took them on field trips. Last summer, they had hiked up the Amu Darya. This year, they were walking along the Syr Darya.

They'd been walking the entire day, and it was only near dusk that Zhalelkhan finally called, "OK, guys. Time to stop." The smoke drifted up from the campfire as the little group prepared supper—prefaced by a mass plunge into the cool river. After dinner, as had become a habit on these walks, someone played a guitar, and some of the children, exhausted from the long trek, fell asleep. Then the teacher, stirring the campfire with a stick, asked, "Did you know that in all history, there have been very few great rulers who have not found themselves by the banks of the Syr Darya?"

The children hushed, expectant. The crimson sun had already dipped behind the dunes, and the gloom was spreading. Gophers flitted about on the steppe, foxes chasing them.

"About two and a half thousand years ago, these steppes were the home of the fierce Saka people. The Persian king Cyrus the Great came here to conquer them. But the Saka's homeland was very dear to them, and they defeated the Persians and took Cyrus captive."

The teacher's soft voice held the children rapt. And not only the children. His young colleague Zhadyra, newly graduated, was listening with the shy, girlish intensity that revealed her growing feelings for him.

"The Saka were a rather amazing tribe. The women dominated everything. The men were ruled by the women and worshipped their spirits. After the capture of Cyrus, their queen, Tomyris, commanded her warriors to cut off Cyrus's head and drop it into a wineskin filled with blood. 'Were you thirsty for blood, Cyrus?' she cried. 'Have your fill of it!' Then the warriors tied the wineskin tightly and hurled it into the Syr Darya. It's worth reading the histories of Herodotus—this legend is in there.

"And after Cyrus, Darius grabbed the throne of Persia. He gathered a huge army and determined to conquer the Scythians, as we call the Saka now. The Scythians fell back, and as they did, they burned everything behind them and destroyed all the wells. Darius challenged them to stand and fight. But instead of replying directly, the Scythian king Idanthyrsus sent the Persians gifts: a swift-winged bird, a mouse, a frog, and five arrows.

"'The Scythians are begging for mercy!' rejoiced Darius. But his wise commander Garil explained, 'Oh, almighty Darius! With these gifts, they are saying,

"Persians, fly like birds, run like mice, hop like frogs across our marshes, away from our land! Otherwise, death from Scythian arrows awaits you!'" And Darius left the Scythians' land at once.

"During that campaign, though, Darius had gouged out the eyes of the brave warrior Imanbek, who had come to ask the king to free his friend from captivity. Imanbek lost his eyes but set his friend free. So Darius understood that such people, such a tribe, would bow their heads before no one. Blind Imanbek lived by the Syr Darya and became a musician, a healer, a prophet, and a poet."

The seventh-form boy Omash, exclaimed, "My granddad used to tell me that the grave of Holy Imanbek still exists!"

"It does. In the past, people used to travel there to bow to the shrine of the saintly Imanbek—which was said to cure the sick. Now it is in Baikonur and impossible to get to."

Omash stared in the direction he assumed Baikonur lay and became thoughtful. A line of crimson sunset streaked the top of the distant dunes, and he imagined it as a vast Persian army, their iron helmets turned copper by the sky. The air rang with the hum of voices, the clanking of swords, and the jangling of spears . . .

"Later, in the third or fourth century, these lands were owned by Turkic Khaganates."

"Sir!" remembered Omash. "You promised to read poems to us."

"By the warriors of the Khaganates? Another time . . ." He fell silent, then asked, "Omash, can you tell me, what is man?"

"Me?" The boy became flustered and blurted out the first thing that came into his head. "Man . . . is proud!"

Everyone started to laugh.

"That's true, of course. But what do you think yourself?"

Omash was silent, unable to find the right words.

"Man is the beginning of intelligent life," said Zhalelkhan. "Only Man has a mind. Yet that is also what makes him dangerous. Man's knowledge can become a terrible destructive force."

"How?" said the children, nonplussed.

Their teacher remained silent, then sighed. "Sometimes, it seems to me that humans are Nature's great mistake."

The children glanced at each other nervously.

"Because Man challenges Nature, the mother who gave him life."

Zhadyra flung her head back and answered with defiant sincerity.

"To subdue Nature, to bend it to our will—isn't that our destiny?"

Zhalelkhan smiled sadly.

"No, Zhadyra. Not principally. Nature should be loved, not subdued and conquered. It can't be done. Nature will take harsh revenge on Man for his interference."

Zhadyra looked at him blankly.

"But this is a subject for serious debate, and we'll talk about it one day. It just came into my head when I noticed that the reeds are rather scraggy and the river shallow . . . Anyway, it's bedtime!"

"What about the poems?" clamored the children.

"Sir, why did our army go into Czechoslovakia?" Omash asked suddenly.

"Because the Czechs wanted to overthrow socialism!" everyone cried.

"What do you think about it, Omash?" Zhalelkhan looked at him, curious. He particularly liked Omash for his candor and his rather grown-up wit.

"I don't like violence," the boy quietly replied.

"Neither do I."

"Do read the poems for us, though, Zhalelkhan," pleaded Zhadyra.

He smiled at her in thanks for easing the tension, whether intentionally or not.

"OK. You've persuaded me."

Be warned, oh you wise men, of this dreadful world, be warned.
Be wary, oh you fools, of the human demon, be wary.
Here, death is sovereign. Here chaos rules.
Oppression is the hero here; duplicity, the master.
Here order is not possible. And justice is invisible.
Goodness here's a rarity; health is ever feeble.
The bat is still at war with day; moths flee candle flames.
You armed barbarians with sword, you mutilated brains,
You gave lions to ants for destruction: Is that your fairness, world?
You let elephants be vanquished by flies: Is that your justice, life?

Omash lay with his eyes open for a long while. How many stars there are in the sky! How close they seem! It seems as if you'd only have to call, and they would rip away and fall to the ground like silvery rain.

In the village, crazy Kyzbala's dog sat in the middle of the yard, lifted its head, and howled. A sinister howl. An omen not just for one dead but for ten. In Karaoi, the dogs that normally reacted to even the faintest sound fell silent, afraid, as if crazy Kyzbala's dog was burying not only people but every living creature in the world.

High on a sandy hillock near the sea, a male wolf lifted his head and howled. A she wolf and her cubs joined in. But soon they, too, fell silent and ran down the hill and off toward far Balkhash . . .

Meanwhile, herds of saiga antelope swept past Karaoi. One . . . two . . . three. Headlong they rushed without glancing back, flying away and heading for Balkhash too.

The people in the aul slept on, unaware of the turmoil on the steppes that was stirring everything into motion. At last, the dogs caught the scent of the agitated night. One after another, they sniffed, and listened, and began to bark. One bark. Then another. Until finally their barks swelled and combined into one vast and dismal yowl. The people awoke and rushed outside, and soon the whole of Karaoi was up.

The old fisherman Nasyr threw on a light *chapan*[1] and went out into the street. Beyond the forge, he saw saiga streaming by and wondered what had frightened them. A sense of foreboding touched his heart. He prayed that nothing had happened to Omash. That Zhalelkhan is a teacher, but he is raw and inexperienced. Look what they've set out to do: to hike all the way up the Syr Darya to Tashkent.

Omash awoke, feeling sick. He tried to get up and walk to the riverbank to throw up. But he couldn't. He could only raise his body part of the way before falling back and losing consciousness.

Zhalelkhan was shivering. He moaned quietly. His head ached with a searing pain that seemed as if it would tear his skull apart. He tried to stand, but his body was like limp cotton. He struggled to turn onto his side and then vomited. That made him feel better. He sat up and looked around.

All seventeen children were there—except for Omash. Day was breaking. The teacher reached for the kettle to take a sip of water, only to vomit again.

Then he saw Omash lying facedown. Zhalelkhan raised the boy's head, but he was out cold. Zhalelkhan hurriedly woke the children. None of them could stand. The children moaned and tried to get up, then fell down as if knocked over. Zhadyra opened her eyes. Zhalelkhan said to her, "I think we've been poisoned."

Fighting the awful pain in his head, Zhalelkhan swayed and staggered toward the *chaban*'s[2] hut a quarter mile away, over the dune. There'll be someone there, someone who can help them . . . If only he could get there, if only he could let them know . . .

Suddenly he saw the snakes.

There were hundreds of them, thousands. The steppe floor was writhing and glittering in the light of the rising sun—a living, sparkling carpet. But the serpents spared no thought for the man who stumbled listlessly among them. The hissing avalanche slithered away from the river, heading for the desert.

Zhalelkhan approached the chaban's hut. Sensing the snakes, the horses whinnied and tossed their heads in fear. The stallion, tied to a post in the center of the yard, dashed around it, snorting and rearing.

No matter how hard he rapped on the door, no one answered. Could the chaban have been poisoned too? And then it dawned on him. It's the river water . . . the water from the Syr Darya.

He reached the stallion. Then his body convulsed, and he threw up violently. The horse backed away from the foul reek. Zhalelkhan stretched out for the bridle, but the horse shook him away.

With a huge effort, the teacher mounted the reluctant horse. "Let them know . . . I must let them know . . . ," he muttered feverishly.

He rode up toward the highway, the snakes scattering under the horse's hooves, hissing and coiling.

Kakharman Nasyrov, the head of the local fisheries, was awake earlier than usual that morning. At this moment, he was speeding toward the regional oblast office.

"What's that!" his terrified driver cried, braking sharply as a giant ribbon of snakes crossed the road ahead of them.

"Let them pass," soothed Kakharman, irritated. He looked at his watch.

"There are so many, Kakharman-aga.[3] Look! It'll take all day."

"What's got them moving like this?" Kakharman wondered.

"Look, a rider!" The driver pointed. The rider was waving wildly and shouting, but they couldn't make out the words. "It's Zhalelkhan!"

"The children!" shouted Zhalelkhan, getting nearer. "The children have been poisoned . . . The children . . ."

Kakharman leaped from the car, helped the teacher off his horse, and carried him into the car.

"To the oblast," he yelled to the driver as he ran back toward the horse. "Tell them in the oblast!"

And he rode off rapidly to the river.

Omash was delirious. He would gain consciousness but only fleetingly. He would open his eyes, see the snakes coming nearer, then black out in terror. Nearby, some of the children writhed in agony, some moaned quietly, while some tried to get up. The snakes did not come near them but slithered quickly toward the sands.

"Omash!"

"Daddy!" Omash whispered, smiling weakly. "I don't want to die . . ."

"You won't die, son . . . You won't die . . ."

Kakharman lifted his son in his arms. He cradled him as the snakes wriggled past. It looked to him as if the river was overflowing its banks, letting loose a flood of these vile creatures to make war upon the human race.

But it was simpler than that. It was all very simple. Though Kakharman didn't know it then, the day before, a chemical plant on the upper reaches of the Syr Darya had released an especially toxic Japanese defoliant into the river. Seventeen children and two teachers from Karaoi, the chaban and his family, became the first victims of the catastrophe of Sinemorye.

Kakharman stood with his son dead in his arms and didn't know why he was dead.

Just as he didn't know that dead fish were being washed onto the banks all the way up the river. That the fish were already beginning to rot. That the smell, the foul stench, was heaving itself from the river, and throwing anyone standing on the bank into despair . . .

1

The old fisherman Nasyr could barely sleep. He turned over in his hard bed, sighing and murmuring unintelligibly. The old sleep poorly and little, disturbed by memories.

But anyone who thinks Nasyr's sleep is disturbed simply by the troubles of old age would be wrong. Nasyr was unusually robust and sinewy—he was an old man who had not aged. Only the wrinkles deeply imprinted onto his swarthy, high-cheekboned face bore witness to his many years in this world. Nasyr's vivid eyes looked at the world with a frank independence. Like many people from thereabouts, he was taciturn, self-contained, and purposeful. But if anyone ever managed to coax him into conversation, he would suddenly reveal himself to be a captivating storyteller. He told folk tales and myths well. His voice took on an unexpected tone of authority. At such times, nobody interrupted him, guessing correctly that this would cause offense.

Soon after the war, the *kolkhoz*[1] fishing collective by Kokteniz-Sinemorye was brought back to life and the fisherman Nasyr made its chairman. The war had left him with scars, but he bravely led the fishermen out to sea again.

What kind of fishermen were they? The maimed returning from the front, war widows, and young orphans.

And the sea answered Nasyr's team with kindness: fish filled the *kolkhozni-ki's*[2] patched-up nets. And although life was hard back then, the people didn't despair. They knew it was just a stone's throw from trouble to happiness. You might be wounded today and healed tomorrow . . .

But now? It's as if fortune and misfortune have changed places. As if the sea has decided to torment old Nasyr as he nears the end of his life. As if it is unwilling to let the man who loved it so faithfully and with such devotion all his life go peacefully. As if it wanted to take revenge on him for the sins of all humanity. The sea was dying. Man has brought it too many sorrows. It was dying, and it would not give old Nasyr a quiet, honest death either.

For some time, the old fisherman's thoughts had been swimming in a circle. He dozed and woke up, closed his eyes and opened them, but kept on thinking the same thing. When nature is damaged, it fights back. How many mountains have vanished from the face of the earth, and how many have risen again since the day of creation? How many seas? What about the rivers and streams? And how many human homes have been buried beneath the ashes and yet have been built again? Nature needs it to happen. Nature, and only Nature, knows why.

What a fool was Man who descended from Adam and Eve! How foolish and arrogant. Long ago, he stopped respecting Nature as a mother and began to force her to his will, attacking her again and again, ignorantly and irreparably, with increasing violence. And even though she was patient and benevolent, like a mother with her recalcitrant child, she was now taking revenge for his folly and cruelty. Indeed, it is said God blessed Man with a life of peace and with intelligence. Did he not create people in his own image and tell them to "live, and your kin will spread across the world"? He said, "Everything is yours—the fish in the rivers, the birds in the skies, the abundance of fruit born by the bountiful earth. Enjoy the earth and its riches." Although God provided well for Man's belly, he gave him too little reason. If we read the Quran very closely, isn't it written that the power of one over another contravenes the law of balance in Nature? Doesn't it mean that in time, the normal working of Nature will eventually break down?

For years now, somber thoughts had plowed endlessly through Nasyr's mind. In public, he remained silent, afraid to pronounce his thoughts aloud. Yet the old fisherman had not lost hope. He believed that man must not abandon the parched sea in its anguish. If man brought trouble to the sea when he drained it, then man must heal it.

Because look, just look . . .

The sandy shore and the ocher steppe—too vast to take in—have become a wasteland, a desiccated desert. Not a drop of rain has fallen in years. As if the sky itself has turned away from man, who torments the earth by pummeling it with concrete, by ripping the guts from its forests, by convulsing its surface with nuclear explosions. For generations, the Kazakh has roamed the steppe, at one with Mother Nature, his flesh and blood a part of her. But now he has wrenched himself from her. Oh, you stupid son! You will get no sympathy from your Mother. She will get her revenge on you, you can be sure. You are foes now. There is no longer peace between you, nor strength or stability—life here is adrift, like the sands that whip across the coast and leave the sea behind.

His sleep was short, like a bird's sleep. But then Nasyr, who slept without bedclothes, felt a surprising chill and fumbled sleepily for the covers. A fresh breeze wafted over him, and he awoke. How wonderful! A cool breeze riffling through the window slot.

Mullah Nasyr threw a light chapan over his shoulders and stepped out the door, and the wind, as if saying hello, tore off the chapan and flung it on the ground. The old man abandoned it and turned his exposed chest to the north wind. He stood like that for some time, reveling in the freshness. Then, hurriedly, bending low as the elderly do, he ran toward the sea, clad only in his vest and pants.

He did not hear the ash-gray mare and her foal neighing anxiously on their leashes or clattering the fence with their hooves. For the first time in years, he saw the sky pregnant with thick rain clouds. The heavy sky loomed low over the land. The north wind was blowing stronger and stronger. And the old man, after trying to run a few hundred yards, realized he would never reach the shore on foot. He turned back, and then stumbling, falling over, and getting up again, reached the paddock. He quickly bridled the mare, leaped unsteadily onto her bare back from the wheel of the bullock cart, and galloped off toward the shore. Whinnying pitifully, the foal scampered out through the gate and raced after its mother. Hearing its cry, the mare slowed down and turned her head so sharply that Mullah Nasyr almost fell from his horse. He cursed angrily and slapped the mare on her haunch with his broad, oar-calloused hand. He should have locked the foal up, but he wasn't going back now.

The wind tossed handfuls of brackish soil in his face, forcing his eyes shut. Covering his face with one hand, he galloped toward the shore, never doubting the horse understood that it must rush him to the sea. He had but one wish: to reach the shore at once.

Only he knew why he was so desperate to get there.

The sea, which for so long had been receding, starved of water, choked by salt, and expiring day after day, was breathing heavily as the wind whipped up

17

its waters and threw waves crashing onto the shore. The fishermen's boats jigged and bobbed choppily on the crests of the waves. Twenty or more already had been swept away from the shore. As Mullah Nasyr tried to dismount, a violent gust caught him and sent him down onto the sand. He felt something crunch in his ankle as he hit the ground, but he had other things on his mind. He hastily began to move his lips in a long, carefully pronounced prayer.

Thunder rumbled as if the sky would come crashing down. Lightning blazed in the cloud-darkened sky. The wind howled like a wolf pack. The old man tried to move crouched close to the ground but was twice bowled over. Torrents of rain assaulted his shoulders.

Is it possible that life is returning to these lands? Is it possible that nature, like a tenderhearted mother, has held out her hand in peace?

Bent low, the old man prayed. Leaning forward, he touched the ground with his forehead and prayed again, his knees sinking deeper and deeper into the soft mud. As he straightened up, his vest turned gray as the water cascaded down on him. But old Nasyr was oblivious to it all. At this moment, he was talking directly to God.

"Almighty Allah! Generous and boundless was your kindness to us, but at last you turned away from us. How many times I prayed to you! What bitter stories I told you about the miseries heaped on our people! You did not respond; well, that is your will. But now you have taken pity on us with this blessed rain! Amen!"

He longed for a flood. Let it all be flooded, utterly inundated, just to fill the sea again! But even for this small downpour, one should thank God. He broke off his prayer and only then felt the sting in his eyes. He blinked and ran his palms over his face. He licked his lips—salty. "The salt is from the soil," he thought. He never suspected the worst. He never realized the saltiness was because the rain was acid. Soon, he and the people of these lands—the cotton and rice growers of Kazakhstan, Uzbekistan, and Karakalpak, and even the herders far up in the Altai and Tarbagatai Mountains, would suffer a new calamity and be vanquished by it.

Unaware, Nasyr continued to pray.

"Oh, Allah! Our people remember many things. They remember hunger and affliction. They remember the hard years of the thirties and the desperate times after the war. But no one remembers such misery as they suffer now.

Prosperity and happiness have fled Sinemorye and its people! The sea was once our source of delight and consolation. I'm not ashamed to say this, Allah: its body and soul were our conscience. Who, looking at its clear, cool waters, could have known it could ever be drained dry? Our fishing nets were never empty. Our boats danced on its smooth surface. Now, there are just salty banks where there once were islands. And those sisters—Amu Darya and Syr Darya—no longer bring their water to the sea. The sea is dwindling, shrinking farther and farther from its old shores, and all that is left behind is dry land, salty and dead.

"I won't say old Sinemorye parts with life easily, but it has been alone in its fight with death. Thanks, Allah, for seeing its suffering."

It seemed as if the downpour would never end. Indeed, it was growing more intense. And so were Nasyr's prayers. Planting his knees deeper into the wet mud, he prayed for the rain to go on.

It was like this at the end of the thirties. The rain had come down for a week. The sea level had risen. Small islands and bays vanished beneath its surface, and water flooded onto the land and into the fishermen's homes. The fishermen were forced to throw up cane huts and live in them the whole summer. In winter, they moved into dugouts. Water gushed down from the mountain gorges of Pamir and Tian Shan through the Amu and Syr. But the people didn't complain or suffer deprivation—there were plenty of fish in the sea in those years.

If this downpour continues a few more days, the two raging rivers will breach their man-made banks and pour into the sea, and the fish, tired of the salty water, will rush toward the sweet fresh water.

And the fishermen will have no catch.

Already the fish were tightly shoaled and reaching for the surface. And the nets were useless, twisted in knots by the turbulent waters. But now the sea had changed! How it had boiled to life! Full-flowing waves were rushing onto the shore. And the sky, roped by coils of black clouds, continued to pour its rains down on the snowy peaks of Pamir and Tian Shan. The perdurable snows were melting, shedding fresh water into the two great rivers in the ancient way pre-destined by God. The stone barriers that people had constructed to divert water onto the rice and cotton fields began to buckle and break, and hour by hour, the sea was filling with fresh water.

A wave washed against the kneeling Nasyr. He froze in shock as fear and hope intermingled in his soul. And when a second wave surged over him, he scooped his calloused hands into the water and drank greedily in great gulps. The salt burned his tongue, but he scooped and gulped again and again.

Sometimes in the past, boats would return to the shore with no fresh water left. But back then, you could just dig into the damp sand and drink straight from the hole. That time is gone. Now, it's twenty-five, maybe thirty miles from the old shoreline to the water's edge. Oh, Water! Of course you remember your old shores, and now you are striving to reach them. But you are too weak. Well, Allah will replenish you with this great downpour. Be patient. The two rivers will save you. And Nasyr is eagerly praying for you.

He's been praying for years, but little has come from his prayers. Over these years, your lush green margins turned into a salt pan. And seeing this, Nasyr became desperate. Once, in a conversation, he had let slip that he believed his prayers would save the sea. The people of the aul mocked him openly and mercilessly. The youngsters thought he was mad and thought he'd make a good match for the crazy old woman, Kyzbala, who lived on the fringe of village. Mullah Nasyr bore their scorn patiently. But now, today, alone in the dawn on the empty shore, he is happy. He had promised to call a downpour down onto the sea. He had promised to save Sinemorye. Let everyone look and see. Allah did not abandon Nasyr. Allah had heard his words and blessed him!

Old Nasyr had lived many years before the people pressed him to become their mullah. People knew him as a good fisherman. He had become chairman of the kolkhoz. He was a strong *paluan*, a wrestler. The old fisherman had retired honorably. But he couldn't bear doing nothing for long. Even now, he often goes into the sea, taking his grandson, Berish, with him.

The sea, though, is not what it was. There are barely any fish, just salt-tolerant catfish and ling. It can now be called dead, truly dead. The eyes see the sea die, but the soul does not believe. The soul can't forget this land was once populous. But when misfortune struck the sea, people had started to leave these lands. Some gave up fishing altogether and moved far away from Sinemorye. The floating factory ships became lodged in the sands. Entire auls and kolkhozes were abandoned.

Now only the occasional saiga strays through their swinging doors, finding shade from the summer heat. The land between Sinemorye and Balkhash has become a desert, filled with feral dogs gathered into packs to prey, wolflike, on deer and saiga. Wolves, too, roam this abandoned land. Last winter, hunters shot them from helicopters. They killed dogs as well. From high up, it's hard to tell them apart. Mullah Nasyr himself had often seen the bodies of the dogs on snow-covered dunes.

Along with many others, the well-known and respected Mullah Berkimbai left his aul. But how can an aul live without a mullah? How can the dead be properly buried? And so, the wily young Kaiyr became a mullah. It is said about people like him that they can worm their way through any hole. It is also said that he studied somewhere—either in Kazan or maybe Leningrad—but never completed his studies and returned to his aul, where he quickly gained Berkimbai's approval. He never left his mentor for a moment, nor missed a single prayer or burial service. He was young but showed himself to be deeply pious. Berkimbai told people that Kaiyr had studied in a seminary in Kazan and knew Arabic well.

"Wasn't it the naval academy?" some people in the aul asked. "And didn't he get kicked out?"

And others shook their heads and said, "We knew his father—he was a con artist, and his son takes after him. Remember how he was at school? Not exactly an Arabic scholar!"

But one day, Mullah Berkimbai came down on the gossip. "It is a sin for a Muslim to judge something that he has no knowledge of. You will only bring divine retribution down on yourself. He was expelled from the naval academy because he was attending a seminary at the time. The young man's devotion to Allah deserves only praise."

So said Berkimbai, looking sternly down on the people from beneath heavy eyebrows.

Nasyr respected Berkimbai. The mullah was fluent in Arabic and could easily explain the canons of the Quran. But then Berkimbai left the aul, and Kaiyr took his place. People say, "When the jackal appears, the raven dies of hunger." In the year Kaiyr became mullah, there were many funerals. Old and young died. It seemed God had decided they must lie in their native land rather than be buried far away. The new mullah was kept very busy. Kaiyr fervently read the burial rites and did not turn away rewards for his diligence, accepting both money and livestock. He quickly became rich. The old people began to urge him to marry, for it is not good for a mullah to be a bachelor.

Then Kaiyr betrothed himself to a young beauty from Bishkek and had a modest wedding. No one from the aul made friends with her. And how could she be friends with them, having grown up in the city, so spoiled by her parents that she didn't even learn her mother tongue? When he was single, Kaiyr had lived with his brother in his parent's house; after the wedding, he moved into one of the abandoned villas in the middle of the aul.

Once, the old *zhyrau*[3] Akbalak from the Shumgen aul became very ill. Akbalak's daughter asked the healer Otkeldy to tend to her father. The zhyrau and the healer were great friends, but along with the healer, Mullah Kaiyr also arrived. Akbalak greeted the swarthy, hook-nosed young man with little pleasure. "Didn't I invite my old friend Otkeldy?" he exclaimed. "What are you doing here, black raven?"

And so Akbalak dismissed the young mullah. And once Kaiyr was out the door, Akbalak said, "This is not a mullah; this is a predator! To spite him, I won't die!"

The people spread Akbalak's words around with glee.

In the meantime, Kaiyr's relatives were leaving the aul one by one. And Kaiyr prepared to go with them to Zaysan.

As a child, Nasyr had studied under the mullah and had learned to read the Quran fluently. People started asking Nasyr to become mullah. He wasn't going out on the sea much now, and so Nasyr decided not to offend them by refusing. He retrieved the Quran from its hiding place at the bottom of an old trunk and became mullah—the last mullah of Sinemorye.

Nasyr listened intently. It seemed as if the storm was dying down, but the sea was still pushing great waves onto the shore. They hit the sand and gasped for breath as they dwindled to nothing, but as each expired, a new wave came flying from behind it. The boom and boom of the waves mingled with the relentless rattle of the rain. Mullah Nasyr was going nowhere. He was still on his knees, soaked through. His left leg was numb, and even the slightest movement made him wince as pain shot through his ankle. So he prayed. Of course, it wasn't the time to be worrying about his son, Kakharman, but the boy was always on his mind, especially when he prayed.

Kakharman, Kakharman . . .

Nasyr had only one son, although Allah gave him children generously, five of them altogether: four daughters besides the one son.

22

Kakharman had left his homeland as well. Suddenly, in a single day, he had packed and left the sea forever with his whole family. Kakharman was the director of the *Koktenizrybprom*.[4] But the Regional Committee had taken against him, and he had to go. He was liked by his subordinates, though, and he had good friends. And when Kakharman up and left his native aul, they began to leave too. Some moved to the Caspian Sea, while others went beyond Kazakhstan to Siberia and the Baltic. The ordinary people took their lead from the educated and moved on as well. Abandoned fishing trawlers, ships, schooners, and boats lay upon the shore. Long ago eaten by rust. Long ago torn apart by the wind.

In the past, Nasyr saw his son often. He still thinks of him every day and can't understand why the authorities got rid of him. It is a crime to banish a man so ahead of others in his intellect, his abilities, and his education. Isn't this just the kind of talented young man that should rise to the highest ranks of government? A man with a clear mind and a desire to be useful to people.

Five secretaries of the Regional Committee had come and gone in this district in the last twenty years. Each one started work in the same way: tossing aside the work of their predecessor. Oh, how they had all messed up! One decided to transform the lands into a bread granary. "Kazakhstan is the bread republic! How can we fall behind everyone else?" And in response to this decree, the already-poor mowing lands of Sinemorye were plowed up.

The next secretary, however, wanted to restore everything to its original condition. "How can such an arid place yield bread in such amounts?" Then the third secretary started irrigating Sinemorye's shore to turn it into a miraculous garden overnight. But his genius was thwarted by the cunning Syr Darya, which slyly refused to deliver enough water for his great scheme.

One thing Nasyr could never understand: Why was there no one here to point out the errors of these secretaries? The secretaries have faded into memory, but Sinemorye's misfortunes are real and lasting. Where is the truth? When will we stop thinking that if something is said from above, it is as if the Prophet himself has spoken? People are not slaves . . . or are they? What became of Kakharman, who told them the truth? He was hounded out. He was forced to leave Sinemorye. That is what happens to people who ache for the cause with their soul.

And these secretaries—why would they worry themselves about the sickness of the sea? They'd only make themselves sick. Of course, they never liked that Kakharman came to Moscow so often to warn them of the danger—to ask, plead, or beg—but to no avail. In Moscow, Professor Matvei Panteleevich Slavikov—Kazakhs called him Mustafa—knew of the sea's fate and suffered it in the depths of his soul. Though he was a world-famous scientist, Slavikov could do nothing to help Kakharman because he had no influence on the bureaucrats. Even back in the 1950s, Mustafa was writing that the sea's death was inevitable if people did not learn to use the water from the two rivers properly.

And then the fish started to vanish. In recent years, the fishermen had been forced to travel to Lake Balkhash and the Caspian Sea from early spring until late autumn to get enough fish to fill their quota. And as disaster struck the fishermen of Sinemorye, so Kakharman opened workshops in the auls and set the women to work in small knitwear factories. He came up with so many little enterprises and looked after people so well that they never went hungry. Yet the authorities still disliked him, and he was sacked for failing to fulfill his fish quota! He was outraged by the injustice, shaken to the core of his soul. And he returned from the Regional Committee office like a thundercloud. He stayed at his parents' house that day. But by the next, he was gone, heading with his family for foreign lands. Neither Korlan nor Nasyr tried to stop him. The only thing they asked was for him to leave their grandson, Berish, with them for the summer. Berish had been brought up from a baby by the old couple—calling his parents uncle and aunt—and the boy refused to leave them.

"My fate," said Kakharman that evening, "has always been bound to the fate of these lands, but to live here and watch the sea die a little every day . . . it is like dying a slow and painful death myself. I'll find work abroad and so will Aitugan. Don't worry; we'll be OK. Are you sure you want to stay yourself? Is there nothing that will change your mind?"

After a long pause, Nasyr raised his head and looked his son in the eyes. "May your path go well. There's no reason for us to go with you. It seems like we were meant to die here with the sea."

Korlan, who'd been getting the dastarkhan[5] ready, sighed. She was a large, white-faced *baibishe*[6] with a soft, pleasant voice. This is what she said: "Kakharman, my dearest son, I love you best of all my children. Maybe it's because I have many daughters and only one son. But I always saw something special in you. Even if I was a stranger, I could see you were the best among your peers. Now you've grown into a fine man. You became Sinemorye's conscience and its honor. Our people love you. They worry about you. You made it into the Bureau of the Regional Committee, and now the door there is open to us. Everyone wants to hear about you. They say that if Kakharman stops work, so will we. Let the first secretary of the Regional Committee get his hands dirty and catch the fish himself, they say! Let them all know what we really do!"

And, at that moment, as if to prove Korlan's words, loud voices could be heard from the inner porch as a half dozen people walked in. They were fishermen, Kakharman's closest friends. Each one shook his hand firmly and sat down.

Kakharman resumed the conversation.

"They sack me and put someone else in my place; it's not worth thinking about! Now tell me," he asked his mother and Berish with a smile, "are you going to come with me, or are you staying with the old man?"

"Your father and Sinemorye are the dearest things in the world to me. That is all I want in this life. May God give you happiness and prosperity," his mother answered with calm decision.

"Then it's true they've fired you?" questioned young Yesen, old Zhanyl's son, bluntly.

"That's the truth of it, Yesen. The simple truth," replied Kakharman. Far from being despondent, Kakharman spoke with directness and energy.

Everyone wanted to say something, but again it was Yesen who got in first. "Why, then, Kakharman-aga, should I go on with the automotive engineering course you arranged? If we have another boss, then I won't go!"

"Do you think that because Kakharman loses his job, life stops?" Kakharman soothed. "We all love Sinemorye, Yesen. And our duty is to give the sea all we can. Learning never hurt anyone. You can fish, Yesen, but why not master machines too? Otherwise, how are you going to support your mother? You should go on studying. And don't worry about me. I'll find somewhere for myself. But the sea . . . the sea may have a tough time without me to look after it."

When it was time to say goodbye, Korlan took her son aside and said quietly, "I imagine the oblast took it badly when your father became a mullah."

"Nothing was said," Kakharman said evasively, surprised by his mother's perception.

Suddenly, the ferocious, raking torrents of rain began to weaken and soon stopped altogether. Yet the sky was still wreathed with dark clouds, though in places brighter patches were peeking through. The yellow sand was swollen, sodden through. In the aul, people waited for the deluge to end, then rushed to the sea, some on foot, some on horses. They were excited, and their voices rang along the shore in the dawn twilight.

Nasyr, still on his knees in prayer, turned and saw crazy old Kyzbala racing toward the water's edge. Just like Nasyr, she was soaked through, her thin gray hair fluttering wildly from beneath her *platok*.[7] She stared out over the waves intently, full of hope.

Kyzbala's only son, her only joy, had been taken by the sea. And if her mother's joy was short-lived, she had but a tiny sip of a woman's joy. She was married for barely a year when her husband went to war and didn't come back. Nurdaulet had been a lovely man. Athletic, kind, and full of laughter, he was known in the aul as one of the best fishermen. The name *Sinemorye* was tattooed on his chest. What wartime soil covered this word? Byelorussian? Baltic? German? Only God knows. And the same tattoo had been on the chest of his son, Daulet. That day, Daulet went to sea with Nasyr. A storm blew up, and his boat turned over, and he drowned.

Daulet was in the boat with Kaiyrgali, the healer Otkeldy's son. They had finished fishing and were on their way to the shore. As they rowed off, Daulet shouted, "We'll lead the way back in, Uncle Nasyr; it'll be easier for you to follow."

Nasyr, pulling his nets from the water, waved his hand. The young men's boat was already far ahead when Nasyr and his crew, Karibzhan and Korlan, headed on home too. But out of the clear blue sky, a whirling dark thread of cloud suddenly appeared, and as if hurrying them on, began to chase them.

"Hey, look how that's moving, Nasyr!" Karibzhan exclaimed. "Just like a ling after its prey!" Nasyr stared at the sky, and his heart trembled with dread.

As a child, he had heard old fishermen's tales about waterspouts that suddenly appeared like dark smoke, whipping around in a spiral that sucked seawater up into a writing column.

Everything went dark. But for a few minutes, the sky directly above Daulet and Kaiyrgali's boat remained clear as the cloud ran over them. Then suddenly the boat was enveloped by a great, ominous shadow. To the left of the boat, the water lifted up in a pillar as if magnetized by the cloud. Inconceivably, the calm sea erupted in a frenzy.

"Oh, God!" Karibzhan yelled in horror. "Their boat's just been pulled into the sky!"

Nasyr looked back and caught a brief glimpse of the stern. In an instant, the entire boat bearing Daulet and Kaiyrgali was whipped into the maw of the waterspout.

Kyzbala met them on the shore. "Her mother's heart senses it," thought Nasyr. Screaming shrill enough to tear her body in two, she grasped Nasyr's shirt. "Where is my Daulet? Where is my son?"

How could he answer?

The years have shown little mercy to her. Once she had been young and graceful. Elegant. Hair flowing from her head, long and glossy. But at her husband's wake, something had changed. Kyzbala frequently fainted or rambled incoherently. She became ill for many months, taking to her bed early in the spring and not recovering until autumn. Yet she was strong-willed and aware that she had a son to bring up. She began to raise him in spite of her frailty.

Men circled the beautiful widow, but she let no one near. There were serious suitors as well, mostly soldiers back from the front. Even matchmakers tried their luck. But Kyzbala would have none of them. She stayed loyal to her first love.

And so she continued quietly as a widow. And each spring, she was ill. The ailment would never leave her. For a few days, she succumbed, her head spinning, her talk rambling. Her relatives tried to persuade her to remarry. "Ah, you can't bring Nurdaulet back, Kyzbala. You have stayed true for years. You gave no one cause for gossip. Your relatives are satisfied. Even Nurdaulet's soul must be satisfied. But think of yourself, dear. You are still young. If you join with another, we will not object."

But the young widow was adamant. "I will not believe you. Nurdaulet is not dead. I don't want to believe it. Never talk to me of marriage. Allah will comfort me. He took Nur away, but he left me Daulet. Or did you forget about him? Tell this to my relations."

Yes, some were shocked by her determination. Others smiled. And the tenderhearted welled up with tears. But there were many relatives to help, and Daulet grew up without ever really feeling like an orphan. He completed his basic education but never went away to further his studies.

Daulet would never abandon his mother. He went to work with Nasyr as a fisherman. And Nasyr would often gaze at the boy, who reminded him so much of Nurdaulet—hardworking, affable, smiling. He left school with a gold medal, and Kakharman was convinced Daulet should go further in his education. He urged Daulet to enroll for distance learning at the institute.

"You don't want to leave your mother; I understand that. So, yes, catch fish but study too," Kakharman advised. Daulet took his mother to the best doctors in Alma-Ata. The treatment did her good: Kyzbala recovered completely. A flush of color glowed on her pale cheeks, and her dark eyes sparkled. She wondered if she should go to teach at the school.

Nasyr stood rooted like an old tree. He hadn't the strength to move away from the sobbing Kyzbala. He had looked in the eyes of death. He had seen what few see in their lives: a terrible waterspout, which can lift a boat and its crew into the air, then plunge it deep into the sea forever—or, as the legends say, bear it far into the sky . . .

The sea! Such beauty and majesty but so blind in its force. What songs were sung on the shores of Sinemorye!

> *Oh my love, my dark-eyed lass,*
> *You brought such joy to me!*
> *Yet all your nights were sadly wracked*
> *When I sailed out to sea.*
> *I wish I could have stolen you*
> *And galloped far away,*
> *And yet I had to bow my soul*
> *To torments every day.*

The love of life runs deep among those whose lives are joined to the air, to water, and to fire. The way they sing their songs. Their bonds with friends and family. Their elemental contact, their closeness to air, water, and fire nurture a different attitude toward life and death. Their lives are spent in a fatal relationship with the caprices of nature. Every minute, every second, may be their last. And maybe that's why their songs are shot through with joy and sorrow, laughter and tears.

Those wonderful evenings! Those evenings when the songs, so dear to the heart of Mullah Nasyr, were shared with such warmth. How often had he waited for them impatiently as the sun slowly sank over the sea. He would wait forever now. The sea has abandoned its shores. Where are the boisterous boys to start a song now? Where are they, the people who once laughed on these shores, who worked and enjoyed their lives? Time has borne their voices far away . . .

The first to reach the sea was the old zhyrau, Akbalak. He was riding a camel, but the camel was scared by the salty cacophony, scared go down on her knees. She shook her head and bellowed, and the old man tried to make her kneel in vain.

Kyzbala moved silently toward her, grabbed her by the halter and insisted hoarsely, "*Shok*, damn you! Shok!" The camel shook her head violently and swayed her bulky body, then obediently went down.

Akbalak became a son-in-law to all the aul.[8] His daughter also lived in Karaoi and was married to a local fisherman. He often came to visit his grandchildren. When the downpour began and people rushed to the sea, the zhyrau could not stay at home. He stood waiting for Nasyr to finish his *namaz*.[9]

Once, zhyrau Akbalak had been a fisherman too, a very good one.

And how beautiful his singing was. The moment the boat cast off from the shore, glorious melodies poured from Akbalak's throat. "*Pai, pai*, what a voice!" people cooed. And the fishermen joked, "The singing of Akbalak from Shumgen charms the fishes too. He leaves for the sea, sings from morning until midday, and when he comes back, his boat is full! And look what it is filled with! What a catch! Not a single small fish!"

Akbalak was brave and independent, too, and in the old days, he had audaciously stolen his wife away from Nasyr's aul.

It happened one evening, when the fishermen had set up nets and were heading slowly home for dinner in the sleepy aul. That is when Akbalak strode in and snatched the beautiful Karashash, the daughter of Mergenbai, the wealthiest fisherman in Karaoi. That night, they sailed out to sea and headed toward the farthest islands of Sinemorye. The thief would have been an utter fool to turn up with his bride in his native Shumgen, just two steps away from Karaoi.

He and Karashash lived several months on those distant islands. Mergenbai dispatched five of his sons to look for them, and a few local *dzhigits*[10] joined in the search. The furious Mergenbai was determined to tear the whole aul apart to find them. But Akbalak wasn't in Shumgen, and the dzhigits refused to take reprisals against innocent people. But Mergenbai was adamant. He approached the *aqsaqals*[11] of Shumgen, demanding that they deliver Akbalak to him and make the thief fall at his feet. If not, he would bring death to all of Shumgen.

Akbalak was already far out at sea by the time Mergenbai had even noticed Karashash's absence. And who would have been able to chase Akbalak's boat, the fastest in Sinemorye? Mergenbai fumed for days. At last, he made an announcement. "I forgive the runaway and the insult she has brought upon me. If she chooses this worthless zhyrau as a husband, nothing can be done—that is her fate, and I have no power to change it. But they shall never come before my eyes. They will live in their Shumgen."

No one heard anything about the lovers for a long time. Everyone decided they must have drowned. But one calm evening, their boat glided onto the shore. How much happiness there was in Shumgen. And not just in Shumgen. The whole of Sinemorye gathered for their wedding. Only Mergenbai and his sons stayed away. The aqsaqals came together and went to Mergenbai. They fell at his feet and begged him to forgive his daughter. But the obdurate Mergenbai could not find a drop of joy in his heart. Not even the tears of his wife could melt his frozen heart.

For five years, the beautiful Karashash lived with her precious Akbalak. In the end, though, Mergenbai destroyed her with his coldness. Increasingly distressed, Karashash threw herself into the sea. Akbalak was inconsolable; he spent the rest of his life alone. They had a son, but the son died in the war. And they had a daughter, too, nowadays a considerable baibishe in Karaoi.

And maybe that memory flooded back into zhyrau Akbalak's mind as he got off the camel and gazed into the sea, waiting for Nasyr to finish his prayers. By now, almost everyone in the aul was heading for the shore.

Suddenly, the demented Kyzbala cried wildly and pointed out into the swelling dark waves. Mullah Nasyr continued praying and bowing. But Akbalak strained his eyes to see through the murk, then froze in astonishment. A fishing boat, its mast snapped in half, was drifting toward the shore. The people on the shore gasped.

Kyzbala ran around, shouting hoarsely and unintelligibly. She tugged at people and pointed at the boat, running desperately from one person to another like a wind-up toy. With her rushed a black mongrel with a pale blotch on its neck and a she goat with its white kid. Nobody could make out what Kyzbala wanted.

Then she ran to the old boat abandoned on the shore. It usually took three strong dzhigits to shift the heavy boat, but the old woman strained every sinew and pulled it right over to the water's edge entirely by herself before hurling herself at it in a desperate bid to launch it into the sea. A few boys rushed to her and pulled her away. If the madwoman went into the sea now, she would drown for sure.

Kyzbala realized they would not let her get in the boat. She screeched and wailed and bit the hands holding her back so hard they were forced to let go. Kyzbala dashed into the sea and was up to her knees when a huge wave overwhelmed her and flung her onto the shore as if she were a grain of sand. The old woman beat her hands on the beach in desperation and sobbed.

"The sea is angry," people in the crowd were saying. "It has borne many insults over the years . . ."

"It has been calm for so long, it began to forget how to rage . . ."

"Our nets are gone."

"And your mother with the nets!" cursed someone in reply.

"What's the point in nets, when all the fucking fish are gone?"

That was one-handed Kadyrgaly, the ex-chairman of kolkhoz. His hand had been bitten off by a huge catfish. People respected Kadyrgaly for his plain dealing and rough, no-nonsense language, always used at the right time.

The boat was nearing the shore. The people stared, frozen in fear.

But zhyrau Akbalak suddenly saw two figures in the boat, Yesen and Berish, and yelled out, "Jump into the sea, you idiots! Jump!"

Earlier that night, Yesen had decided he must go out to sea to check the nets, and Berish insisted on going with him. They had lowered the boat into the water with only the new moon watching. They had rowed briskly yet quietly, enjoying the night calm. How could they imagine that nature would unleash a rainstorm they'd remember for the rest of their lives?

At that precise moment, a powerful wave lifted the boat on its crest and flung it right over, hurling the boys into the sea. Yesen cried to Berish, "Hold on to me! Let's swim!"

Berish swallowed a lot of water. Flailing his arms and legs with all the strength he could muster, he hauled himself to the surface. But the next wave engulfed him again. Yesen turned back, dived, and pulled the weakening Berish to him with one arm and swam with the other toward the shore. A few young men rushed in to help them. And the young girl Aigul, who was in the same class as Berish at school, jumped in too.

The wind gusted fiercely, and the rain came down in torrents. Yesen's boat was thrown onto the shore. It buried its motor in the sand, creaked, and fell apart. The next wave immediately picked up the boards and dragged them back into the sea. And as wave after wave rolled in, even the heavy motor was pulled into the deep.

Exhausted, happy, saved! Yesen and Berish looked at the people surrounding them. They were laughing. Kyzbala rushed to Yesen, hugged him, and started crying again. She stroked his head, touched his face, his shoulders, his arms. Then she realized it wasn't Daulet. She became quiet and walked away, mumbling.

Berish walked out of the circle of smiling people and approached his granddad.

"Ata,[12] let me help you to stand up. It's time for us to go home."

"You can't wait to die, it seems," said the old man sternly. But deep down in his soul, Nasyr was pleased with his grandson. Berish had shown himself brave and decisive.

Nasyr tried to get up. But the pain in his ankle was too much.

"Looks like a twisted ankle . . . Find the mare . . . and bring her here."

Berish and Yesen helped old Nasyr onto the horse. The rain lashed down. Everyone headed back to the aul. Nasyr shouted to his grandson, who was leading the mare by its bridle, "I told them that my prayers will save the sea! They laughed at me. Let them laugh now!"

Berish stayed silent. He was thinking about Aigul. "Ah, she's brave!" he thought. He wanted Aigul to walk next to him. But Aigul was far ahead, with her sisters.

Only crazy Kyzbala remained on the shore, with her mongrel with the white blotch and the goat with the kid.

Between Sinemorye and Lake Balkhash, there is now a vast steppe—a brown, dusty wasteland with only rare patches of green, where scraggy trees struggle to survive in lonely islands of grass. Many saigas and roe deer inhabit the sands, and pilots say they recently saw a tigress with her cub. That would be amazing because Caspian tigers have not been seen here for many years—although in the past,[13] they slunk through the *tugai* among thickets of canes as broad as a man's arm. That's how it was. In the auls, there are many houses with their striped skins on the floor. Musa the hunter has two.

Though the tigers are no more, there are still many feral horses in this steppe. Wary and watchful, they won't let anyone near them. You can see them gathering on sand hills. Their tails and manes grow long and thick, so they look bigger than other horses. They often appear near the fishermen's auls—at least, they've been spotted near Karaoi more than once. There are many young mares in these herds, and they try to lure the tame stallions with seductive whinnies as they stream past close to the auls.

On this night of rain, they appeared again near Karaoi, and this time, they led Musa the hunter's fastest stallion away with them. The moment he discovered the loss, Musa leaped on a horse and whirled away onto the steppe in pursuit. But the wild herd was already far away. All his life, Musa had kept hunting birds, and dogs, and fast horses. How he suffered from this loss, becoming sick with distress! And it wasn't just Musa that was upset; everyone in the aul knew that Musa's stallion had won the district and regional gallops several times. The elders knew the reason for the calamity: this was yet another of God's punishments on the aul.

How many more herds will fly close to Karaoi now? Fast as the steppe wind, stealing souls away like time? Wasn't it you, wild horses, that kidnapped the beauty of Karaoi? Wasn't it you who stole the joy of life?

For two weeks, the rain teemed down ceaselessly. At times it would abate, only to return with renewed force. The cold, sharp wind never slackened, and the sea stayed choppy and gray. Only Nasyr's soul was peaceful and calm, his face glowing with a joyous light the entire fortnight.

11

It turned out that Mullah Nasyr had twisted his ankle badly. He was worried that the bone was broken. For days he lay by a low stove, trying to stay still. The famous healer Otkeldy was long dead now, and people had to go to the local doctor, who fixed dislocations casually and carelessly and packed patients with broken or cracked bones off to the regional center for X-rays. People went to the young doctor reluctantly, sighing and remembering Otkeldy.

The late healer would have rubbed tail fat carefully into damaged areas. He would have worked unhurriedly as he told roundabout stories of the latest fishing trip, a funeral he had recently attended, or something similar. And as he nattered away, he would fix the dislocation entirely without pain. Otkeldy's close relatives were respected healers too.

Otkeldy had several daughters but no son—even though he desperately wanted an heir to pass his skills on to. So when he was forty, he had married for a second time to a woman much younger than himself.

Healer Otkeldy and hunter Musa's people had come to these lands from Sary-Arka long ago. After the Great Jute[1] in the middle steppe, these Kazakhs had headed for the sea. But these meat-loving Kazakhs were not always happy to eat only fish, even though the fish in those times were big and fatty. And they could never get used to the sand. So many kept moving on until they died from hunger and thirst. The Pomors urged them to stay, explaining how sly the sands can be—especially for those new to it—but the refugees waved away their advice, pursuing a dream of vast pastures and meadows.

Otkeldy was a boy then and his father a reasonable man, believed by many to be a seer. The day the refugees reached the sea, the grandfather, a respected healer, passed away. They buried the old man with proper honor on a sandy hill.

But they were shocked by the strange habits of the sea people. "Why don't they have a graveyard?"

An old man from Karaoi, prickling, answered, "We sea people almost never bury our dead on the land; the sea is both our graveyard and the beginning of our lives."

Otkeldy's second marriage was not a success and produced no male heir. So he took two more young wives, one after the other. And although it was hard to support such a large family, Otkeldy was not ready to give up yet. Time was hurrying him along, and with his death, his line would end; his skill would die if he did not have a son.

But the two new young wives failed him as well.

Desperate, he stepped back from all domestic affairs, leaving them in the hands of his baibishe, his first wife, and spent his days lying in a yurt, staring sorrowfully into the distance.

Meanwhile, life went on around him. Messengers kept calling from auls, and he would quietly saddle his horse and go to relieve the sufferers. He didn't rush home, always lingering for a while after dispensing his healing. Fortunately, his patients were always happy for him to stay. He wasn't waited for at home.

Nasyr's injured leg had once been in the soft caring hands of Otkeldy. It had cracked slightly above the ankle, and Otkeldy had healed it well. Nasyr chuckled; it can crack anywhere now except where Otkeldy had been at work.

Well. The *khoja*[2] Dauseit, who lived by the gulf of Moiyndy, once fell off his horse and broke his spine. For half a year, Otkeldy stayed by his side. Back then, many healing herbs grew on the shore, and throughout the summer, Otkeldy went out collecting them. Dauseit's daughter Marziya went with him and learned to love these expeditions. She and Otkeldy collected the herbs together, and she learned how to use them.

Marziya was terrified of snakes, but Otkeldy would deftly catch them and squeeze their venom. Marziya was too timid to come close to the old man at these moments.

All that summer, not a single suspicious glance or spiteful gossiping tongue was aimed at the back of the old man and the young girl. Was it only because on their walks along the shore, the girl's younger brother was always with them?

When at last Dauseit recovered and was able to sit on his horse again, Otkeldy prepared to go home. But before he did, he and Dauseit had an earnest conversation. Otkeldy thanked him for his hospitality, saying that in all the half year he lived in this aul, he had not once felt a stranger. In every house, even the poorest, he had been greeted like a dear guest. Now, Otkeldy asked permission to go home.

Deeply moved, Dauseit replied, "For all my life, I will be in your debt, dear Otkeldy. I heard much about you in the past, and now I've experienced your miraculous cures myself. You've given me my life again. Tell me what can I give you in return? I will not refuse you anything."

Otkeldy stayed quiet for a long time. It was strange to see the old man as shy as a little boy. But maybe he thought Dauseit was too sharp not to see Marziya in his eyes, skipping along the sand in her soft boots, wearing that long silk dress that clung so closely to her slender body? Or maybe old Otkeldy thought it would be tactless to respond when Dauseit asked him the reason for the tears that welled in his eyes as he imagined two little boys tramping behind Marziya, gamboling from foot to foot like puppies?

Otkeldy swallowed the lump in his throat but didn't lift his face.

"Surely you are not asking for Marziya?" asked Dauseit suddenly. He fingered his rosary in agitation.

"Ah, you guessed right, Dauseit!" Otkeldy replied at once.

"Let's hear what Marziya herself will say," Dauseit sighed, and sent for his daughter.

Otkeldy was tense as a hunting tiger. He sat straight, his eyes fixed on one of the patterns on the *symrak*[3] rug. Then he groomed his graying moustache and glanced expectantly at Dauseit. The men's tête-à-tête had put Dauseit's baibishe on her guard. And when her daughter was invited in behind the drapes of the yurt, she was worried and followed Marziya in.

At that moment, Marziya was just going down on one knee to greet her father. Dauseit frowned when his wife appeared, and with a disapproving nod directed her to sit down. The dismayed baibishe did as she was told. Otkeldy glanced at the girl. Marziya was agitated. Her eyelashes quivered as she glanced furtively at Otkeldy. There he was, with his hawklike face tilting toward Dauseit, his sinewy hands on his knees. Marziya knew the dexterity of these hands well. Not a single snake was ever lucky enough to slip away from them.

Dauseit explained Otkeldy's request clearly and succinctly. The stout baibishe moaned and fainted. The servant ran in and splashed cold water on her face. Once she was revived, Dauseit made a sign for her to be taken to another yurt. The baibishe wanted to scream at the top of her voice, but she knew her husband's stern temper. She stomped out of the yurt, leaning on the servant.

"What do you say, Marziya?" Dauseit asked. He was amazed when he heard her simple answer. "If Otkeldy is asking for my hand, Father, then please bless us."

At that, Otkeldy sprang up in delight, strode over to Marziya, and went down on his knees in front of her.

"Thank you, Marziya-zhan!" he said. "Be my wife. Be my young friend for all my life!"

He turned to Dauseit, who was upset and just wanted to leave the yurt.

"I swear, Dauseit, that while I am alive, I will take care of your daughter! Believe me, I am not simply and shamefully wishing to add her to my stable of wives. But I have many daughters and not a single son. The Almighty Allah has blessed our kin with the gift to heal people. There were four of us brothers, but I am the only one left; my brothers died of the plague during the hungry years. Now my dearest wish is to have a son. And I believe that Marziya will give him."

Dauseit waved his hand dismissively and hurried out of the yurt.

Otkeldy brought his young wife to his own aul but kept her apart from his other wives. His old wives, jealous of clever, beautiful Marziya, sniped at the newly wed couple. So Otkeldy sent word to fisherman Nasyr. The next day, Nasyr invited the healer and Marziya to Karaoi, gave them his small hut, and moved himself and his family to a nearby earth house.

Nasyr remembers now how Otkeldy lamented, "Ah, Nasyr, people are laughing at me. You are the only one who understands. They have no idea that this is not for my benefit. They just don't realize that if I don't have a son, there will be no one to heal them. They see only that I married a girl younger than my daughter."

Yet Marziya gave Otkeldy three sons, and so three *tois*[4] were arranged, the likes of which the Sinemorians had never seen. Thrice, Musa's fiery black stallion triumphed in the races. Yes, Otkeldy's prediction that Marziya would give him sons had come true! People started to respect him again. And while their sons were growing up, Marziya learned the skills of healing with herbs and started to treat people for minor ailments.

Otkeldy doted upon his young wife. "My song," he would call her tenderly. But he still remembered people's mockery, and his soul turned away from them forever. Nasyr was the only person he respected and sought advice from—the only one to whom he could confide his deepest secrets.

After Otkeldy's eldest son Kaiyrgali finished medical school in Alma-Ata, he spent two months in practice near Sinemorye. Once, Kakharman went out to sea to find a fish shoal and broke his arm in a collision with another boat. Kaiyrgali quickly and skillfully set the bones, tied sprigs of meadowsweet over the bandage on four sides, and dressed it neatly. Nasyr was amazed at the lad's confidence and skill. "My Kaiyrgali will go far," Otkeldy would say, not without pride. But Kaiyrgali drowned in the sea with Kyzbala's son the summer he returned to the aul with his degree.

Kaiyrgali's death hit Otkeldy hard, and he began to look tired of life. It crushed his clear spirit, and he quickly became a feeble old man almost overnight. Deep creases of pain lined his face, and no matter how well loyal Marziya looked after him, no matter how much she distracted him from bitter thoughts, Otkeldy couldn't fight his grief. It led him inexorably into the embrace of death. Among the few graves in Karaoi, Otkeldy's is the grandest. His lofty mausoleum of red burnt brick was erected with the help of Kakharman.

After the death of Otkeldy, it was hard for Marziya to live with her sons. Otkeldy's wives and daughters were bolder now. So Marziya left Karaoi and went to her relatives in Zaysan. Since then, nobody here has heard anything of her.

What worried Nasyr was whether the father's amazing gift could be passed on to the sons. Surely. How could the children of a clever, wise father grow up as blockheads and wastrels? That's what Korlan would say when she remembered Otkeldy.

"Allah will not allow a good person not to be repeated in his children," Korlan would say. "And Marziya, she is clever, too, and knows Otkeldy's art."

After making breakfast for the old man and her grandson, Korlan lay for hours on a soft rug next to the stove. And still the rain didn't stop. At times, it would quiet down and drizzle monotonously, then suddenly it would gain strength again. At times, thunder rolled and lightning flashed across the sky.

"It's pouring for the seventh day," sighed Korlan, getting more comfortably settled. "And there's no sign of it ending. As long as our roof doesn't leak, let it pour. Right, Nasyr? For so many years we've been waiting for such rain."

Nasyr bandaged his ankle tightly and rose to pray. By the time Berish and Akbalak appeared on the threshold and Korlan started to bustle around them, he was thoroughly calm and sitting with his back against the warm stove.

Akbalak threw off his raincoat, unlaced his boots, and, after the usual greetings, took the seat of honor.

Yesterday, in the pouring rain, Nasyr hadn't had a chance to have a proper look at the old zhyrau but thought he looked noticeably more frail. Now, after a longer look, he realized that he had not been deceived. Akbalak's cheeks were sunken, and there was none of that old liveliness in his eyes. Once dapper, the old zhyrau was now visibly tired. His manner, though, remained as lively as ever.

"It's great to be a mullah," he joked. "But one's bones do become as brittle as old chalk."

He asked Berish to bring warm water and a towel. Twice he soaped his hands, washed off the foam, wiped his hands dry, and spent a long time greasing his hands with sheep fat.

For all the previous night, Nasyr had been in pain. That is when he remembered that Akbalak knew how to heal.

In the morning, he had sent Berish to get the old zhyrau.

"I'd already saddled up my camel ready for a journey when your grandson came running, so I've had to put my trip off for a while." He began to gently probe the ankle. "I need to be quick."

Akbalak started slowly rubbing in fat, stroking the twisted joint. Nasyr, watching the zhyrau's hands, said, "God will reward you for your kindness."

"What God are you talking about?" Akbalak responded. "If you're talking about the one I know, you can't expect anything from him!"

"Aka, you're still impudent as ever," observed Korlan, turning to the zhyrau. "Even though you've already got one foot in the grave."

"Thanks to my prayers," Nasyr said, "we've already had a week of rain. Soon, it will melt the snows on the peaks of Pushta, and the Darya will bring the water to the sea. On the north shores of the sea, too, there are underwater springs, and the rainwater is bound to wash away the salt flats so that fresh water from the springs will pour into the sea. Do you remember what Slavikov used to say? Thanks to the springs and the mountain water brought by the rivers, the sea was always full."

"Yet," he said, turning to Akbalak, "if it weren't for my prayers, how would such rain have filled the springs and mountain streams?"

Akbalak objected ardently. "And you think that your God really exists? Then explain to me: Why did he have to dry the sea out? If he was so clever, he'd have revived our Sinemorye long ago!"

"I prayed," Nasyr insisted, "and he heard my prayers . . ."

"Your prayers!" The zhyrau waved his hands. "If he does exist, then why does he treat us so badly? Surely you remember the past. These shores were rich and well populated. Now everyone's abandoned the old places. What's left of our Sinemorye? You can see it yourself. All there is now are dunes and naked steppe, scraggy fish saltier than the sea, and a lot of destitute people . . . There once was a time when people would sail from aul to aul, singing during the holidays! Now they're scattered across Kazakhstan. And your God doesn't see that? Or is he just letting it happen?"

It hurt the old man to say this, but he had thought all this for many years. And the zhyrau's words echoed in Nasyr's heart with pain.

"I swear," Nasyr proclaimed. "I will pray day and night. Allah will give a second life to Sinemorye!"

"That would be good. I won't live to see it, but may this joy fall on our grandchildren."

At that moment, thunder cracked, and a brilliant lightning flash lit up the room. The afternoon rain streamed down harder.

"Lightning like that can crack anything," said Nasyr, thinking.

"As long as it doesn't crack a man," Akbalak added, rubbing in fat, massaging Nasyr's leg, and gently applying pressure to the swelling. "Hey, Berish, find my *khordzhun* and dig out two small batons for me . . . And, mullah, you're going to have to bear it a little longer; your bones aren't so young anymore . . ."

Indeed, Nasyr was in pain. His face was creased, and he pleaded with Akbalak. "Don't spare the fat. Rub more in . . ."

"Even if we drown you in fat, it won't make it better, Nasyr. You'll have to take it." Akbalak's voice was stern.

"In the darkness of years, you can't tell if my bones are old or your fingers are stiff," joked Nasyr, then suddenly let out a yelp of agony so sharp that his eyes smarted with tears. "Aka, I think the bone is back in place."

Akbalak stroked his fingers along the ankle and nodded. "You're right. The bone is back."

He took the batons from Berish, laid them on either side of the ankle, and bound them tightly with clean cloth.

"In a week, you'll be skipping around like a young man."

The rest of the day passed in conversation. As they sat down for dinner, Akbalak asked about Kakharman.

"Living in Semipalatinsk," butted in Korlan.

"Yes," Nasyr concurred. "He's still there."

"Is he in charge of something?"

"No. He doesn't really want to be a boss," Korlan said quickly, giving Nasyr a meaningful look.

"He's captaining barges along the Irtysh."

Akbalak sighed. "Kakharman's a good man. People in Shumgen remember how many good things he did. And how much he did for me! He never failed to give any of my requests his complete attention. But your God was always against good people . . ."

Nasyr remembered going to see his old friend Uzbek Fuzuli on Darya's bank.

The fishing trade started to vanish when the rivers running into Sinemorye were diverted by dams and reservoirs to supply water for rice and cotton.

"So now the real disaster starts for us," Kakharman had said to his father bitterly.

Nasyr had never seen his son so dispirited.

"They're building a massive dam across the river mouths!" he spat.

"Why?" Nasyr was stunned.

"To kill the sea!" Kakharman retorted.

"But why kill it?" To Nasyr's mind, it made no sense. "What about the fish?"

"The fish will suffocate in the salty water and die."

"And what about our people? What about our nation that lives off the sea?" Nasyr exclaimed.

"The nation will say goodbye to its native land, and the people will scatter to the four winds!" His son was quivering with outrage. Then realizing how much he had shocked and terrified his father, he added, "Don't worry. It won't happen overnight. We can still fight it. But our opinions are different from our country's leaders. I have to go to Alma-Ata. If I don't achieve anything there, I'll fly to Moscow, to Slavikov. Anyway, I won't do nothing . . . Go to Fuzuli, Dad. Talk to the people there. Listen to what they're saying about this."

The next day, Nasyr didn't go to the sea. He left Toshemish in charge and set off on a long trek to the Uzbek cotton growers.

Fuzuli greeted him warmly, flicking his *tubeteika* skullcap to the back of his head as he always did. Laughing, he coaxed his wife from the fire. "Darling, today my old friend has come. Let me cook the pilaf myself."

They began to chop up the fresh, steaming lamb together. But Nasyr couldn't wait. He wanted to share his worries with his friend at once and plunged into his lament. The sea will dry out, he told Fuzuli, if another dam is built on the Syr Darya. The springs will turn salty and clog. He talked about Kakharman's struggles, too, and about what will happen to everyone if the sea dies.

Fuzuli listened without interrupting, then asked his wife to fetch the latest newspaper. As he handed the paper to Nasyr, he explained, "The piece on the second page is on just this subject; read it." Nasyr buried himself in the newspaper while Fuzuli, still preparing the pilaf, said, "Moscow, Tajik, and Uzbek scientists got together and figured out a plan to choke Sinemorye. Kazakh scientists were there too. And even our *tamyr*,[5] Zhagor."

In the article, which took up the whole page, a group of scientists discussed the sea's fate, and all were in total agreement. Zhagor Sharaev passionately argued for the building of the dam, and he was backed up entirely by Uzbek and Tajik scientists as well as by Moscow's specialists in land reclamation.

"But what about the opinions of ordinary people?" Nasyr thought. "What nonsense Zhagor speaks! He says that the disappearance of Sinemorye will do no harm to the environment. No harm? What sort of scientists are they? Don't they understand that the water channeled away from the Amu and Syr Daryas for the rice and cotton will be spilled in vain? It will flood the valley and fill it with bogs and swamps!" Nasyr was confused. He could take these words from someone else but not from Sharaev.

"Have you read it?" Fuzuli asked.

"Yes. I get it," Nasyr replied, folding the newspaper. "These people do not wish us well."

"Nasyr, I understand your worries. We've been friends all our lives, but you can guess why I couldn't answer your questions right away. This bone is too big for us to chew over, I'm afraid. You and I have done a lot of things together, but we are two small people, a fisherman and a farmer. This is a huge government question. I am anxious that the friendship between our peoples is not damaged, Nasyr. You fish and we grow. We both have the proverb, 'It's the blacksmith who chooses where to make handles for pans.' There was a time when the state needed Sinemorye's fish—"

Before he could finish, Nasyr snapped back, "Yes! The government needs cotton and rice more now, so they will trash the sea and let it go to hell together with its useless fish!"

Nasyr was immediately ashamed of his outburst and looked down. "Forgive me for letting go on you, Fuzuli," Nasyr murmured. He moved away from the table.

Fuzuli reassured him. "It's nothing, Nasyr; I am not offended. I understand. Your soul is burning. It would be a sin not to say the words that Allah himself orders you to say."

"Cotton and rice are needed, but the sea and the life of our land is of no interest to anyone," Nasyr said quietly, shaking his head.

Late in the evening, when Nasyr was alone, he spent a long time looking through the pile of newspapers Fuzuli brought out. There was little comfort for the old fisherman. On the contrary, his concerns only multiplied. It seemed to him as if the whole world had gone insane. How else could what he read be true?

SEA CREATURES ARE DYING. ABOUT 75 PERCENT OF SEALS HAVE DIED IN SIX MONTHS in the North Sea from a virus that caused severe inflammation of their lungs.

EVERY MINUTE, TWENTY-NINE CHINESE PEOPLE ARE BORN. AT SUCH A DEMOGRAPHIC RATE, the population of the country, now at 1.096 billion people, will reach 1.3 billion by the end of the century. During the last year, 15.4 million Chinese were born. That is almost equal to the population of Australia.

THREE HUNDRED EIGHTY-FIVE PEOPLE HAVE DIED AND MORE THAN SIX HUNDRED ARE INJURED IN THE WORST RAILWAY ACCIDENT EVER

RECORDED. The passenger train bound from Multan for Karachi ran into a freight train.

"DANGER! CADMIUM!" SEVEN CONTAINERS WITH THIS SIGN appeared in front of the gates of the US embassy in Wellington, the capital of New Zealand. They had been delivered there by the members of the international organization of environmentalists, Greenpeace. The containers hold toxic waste collected in Antarctica near the American scientific station McMurdo.

TASS (THE RUSSIAN NEWS AGENCY) IS AUTHORIZED TO ANNOUNCE THAT PARTY AND STATE leaders of Czechoslovakia appealed to the Soviet Union and other union states to provide urgent help to their brothers in the Czechoslovak nation, including armed forces. This appeal is provoked by the threat to the socialist system in Czechoslovakia from counterrevolutionary powers, which are colluding with alien forces hostile to socialism.

TASS ANNOUNCEMENT CAUSES A WAVE OF REACTIONS. SOVIET PEOPLE ARE WORRIED by the danger to the socialist system in Czechoslovakia.

FRANCE HAS RESUMED NUCLEAR TESTS IN THE PACIFIC OCEAN. Yesterday it exploded a charge of medium power in the air above the Mururoa atoll test site.

EIGHTEEN PEOPLE DIED AND ABOUT FORTY THOUSAND LOST THEIR HOMES AS CYCLONE ALIBERA STRUCK MADAGASCAR. Winds reached 124 miles per hour.

WOLF'S AMBUSH. RESIDENTS OF UVAROVO VILLAGE, THE BROTHERS CHALMAEV, and their guest, Eliseev, were walking from the House of Culture late last night. Near the bridge behind the embankment, a wolf was lying in ambush for them and pounced on Eliseev. Fortunately, although the animal was strong, the three young men managed to beat it off.

THE ANCIENT HUNTERS OF SIBERIA AND NORTH AMERICA HONORED the animals they hunted. Before releasing an arrow into the bear, they spoke to it in a friendly and reassuring manner, calling it "Granddad," "old fella," or "master," and after killing it, they asked it not to take revenge.

TROPICAL FORESTS STARTED TO DISAPPEAR FIRST as the lands on which they were growing and giving natural greenery and clean air were taken over by farms, ranchos, dachas, villages, and whole cities. The ecological healing powers of these forests are equal to the world ocean.

THE TRUE DISASTER FOR MARINE MAMMALS AND BIRDS has turned out to be plastic waste in the sea. The animals die trying to swallow pieces of plastic or getting tangled in plastic fishing nets.

IN AFRICA ATTEMPTS WERE MADE TO ERADICATE THE TSETSE FLY BY TREATING FLOODPLAIN forests with deltamethrin and permethrin in very small quantities. Yet as a result, fifty-five varieties of clear-water fish have vanished, and the tsetse fly remains.

THE WHOLE WORLD IS TALKING ABOUT ACID RAIN. IN MANY WESTERN countries, there are maps identifying areas where acid rain falls frequently. But there are no such maps in our country.

AN OUTBREAK OF INTESTINAL INFECTIOUS DISEASES WAS RECORDED this summer in Kyrgyzstan and Kazakhstan. Water taken directly from the *aryk* irrigation ditches; poor-quality meat, dairy products, and vegetables; and overcrowded hospitals are the perfect breeding grounds for sickness to spread.

ON DECEMBER 7 AT 10:41 MOSCOW TIME, a strong earthquake hit northern Armenia. In the epicenter, the strength of the tremors was measured at more than 8.0 on the Richter scale. This is the most powerful earthquake to strike the Caucasus for over eighty years.

AT 14:30 MOSCOW TIME IN THE SOVIET UNION in the Polygon test site in the Semipalatinsk district, an underground nuclear explosion of up to 150 kilotons was carried out. The test was conducted with the aim of improving military equipment.

"IF ALL ANIMALS DISAPPEARED, THEN PEOPLE WOULD ALSO DIE BECAUSE of unbearable loneliness of the soul, because whatever happens to animals happens to humans. Everything is connected. That is Earth's destiny and the destiny of Earth's children." So wrote the Indian chief Seatl in a letter to the president of the US in 1885.

With a heavy heart, Nasyr went home. Fuzuli could offer no comfort to his friend.

A fortnight later, Kakharman returned from Alma-Ata and Moscow. He was silent and grim-faced. Although he didn't say much, Nasyr understood well enough. Kakharman lamented, "If this goes on the way it's going now, then our trawlers will run aground and simply stick in the sand."

JJJ

As he rode back from Fuzuli's, Nasyr realized he would not be able to bring himself to visit the relatives and friends who knew he had gone to hold council.

He was troubled in his soul. The familiar places he passed on the journey reminded him of all the years he had lived on this land. There on his right was what was once Zhasylbel[1] Island—an ex-island, now that there is no water around it. And then he came to Kazankol,[2] the water long gone here, too, leaving only a thick crust of salt.

Yes, Nasyr knew these places. In earlier times, there had been auls scattered across these lands, and he often came to visit them. The houses were still standing, but their walls had long been washed away by the rain. Time had let wild grass grow thick over the courtyards and farmsteads. And over the next mound, there was the dusty bed of the Shumgen River, white with salt. Tall, sturdy reeds had once grown so dense along its shores you couldn't even ride a horse through them. Birds used to sing here in the mornings, such elaborate flutings and so many different voices joining in.

That was the golden time of Shumgen's zhyrau—the singer and aqyn, Akbalak. He often sang with Karashash, who also had a wonderful voice. No one was left unmoved when they sang together. Their sad songs would make people weep, while their happy songs would turn faces bright with joy. And inspired by Karashash, other women sang too. The ordeal of fishing had fallen upon their shoulders as their husbands went off to war. Maybe the singing helped ease their heavy load.

Karashash told people that she would not change the five years she lived with her dear Akbalak for fifty years of any other kind of happiness. That is how much Akbalak and Karashash loved each other. But the vengeance of her father cut short their happiness.

It happened when Akbalak was away in Alma-Ata for the national festival of aqyns. Mergenbai seized his chance, sending four strong dzhigits to Shumgen to kidnap Karashash. When the men got her in the boat, one began to grope her. Maybe that's why Karashash took a final desperate step. She flung herself forcefully from the boat and pulled with her the man who had dishonored her. Neither was seen again.

The aul was plunged into a deep and mournful silence when they heard of the death of the beautiful Karashash. There wasn't a soul in the aul who did not curse Mergenbai. A telegram was sent to Akbalak at once.

The elders of Shumgen gathered for a council. This is what they said: "Mergenbai has brought us great sorrow and woe. Because of him, tragedy has struck. Is he not a monster? Isn't this deed unbearably cruel? He destroyed his child with his own hands! Let someone go to Mergenbai and say these words to him: he must leave these lands forthwith. We will not live with him on the same shore!"

The elders delegated Nasyr to inform Mergenbai. Nasyr mounted his horse and rode toward Mergenbai's house in the evening as the sun was setting. As he came near, he found Mergenbai shouting at the three surviving dzhigits from Karakalpakstan in the foulest terms. There was not a trace of sorrow in his face, only rage.

"Mergenbai-aga, the people demand you leave these lands at once," Nasyr informed him coldly without dismounting.

"The people?" Mergenbai roared, staring at Nasyr ferociously. "You call these stinking fishermen *people*? I'm not leaving Karaoi! Tell them that! And I will get you too! Now, leave!"

Nasyr remained calm.

"I was asked to give you this message. If you're still here tomorrow morning, you have only yourself to blame for the consequences." Nasyr turned his horse to ride away.

"Heyuu!" Mergenbai yelled in rage. "Tell your aqsaqals and *karasaqals* that if any of them even lays a finger on my relatives, I will shoot everybody in the aul! Tell them that! Now fuck off!"

Nasyr made no reply.

The next morning, the angry villagers assembled in front of Mergenbai's house, but he was nowhere to be seen. Instead, they found Kuliya, Mergenbai's wife, who had been in a stupor since the moment she had learned of the death of her only daughter. Mergenbai's five adult sons were rushing around the farm, desperately looking for their father.

The house was searched. The farmstead was searched. Then the whole aul was searched. But Mergenbai was nowhere to be seen. A few dzhigits leaped on horses and sped off into the sands. But Mergenbai had vanished without a trace.

As he approached Shumgen, Nasyr halted his horse. He still wanted to drop in, at least to quench his thirst. But where could he go? Of course, his heart whispered, he could go to Akbalak's. After Karashash's death, he had stayed a bachelor, though sometimes he came to Karaoi to see his daughter. Akbalak knew he would never find a woman to match Karashash and resolved to spend the rest of his life alone.

Nasyr had no wish to trouble Akbalak with his visit. He clicked his horse to ride on, and then abruptly hauled it to a stop. To pass by Akbalak's house would mortally offend a respectable man. And so Nasyr went back toward the zhyrau's low house.

Near the gate, a huge wolfhound bounded up. Startled, Nasyr's horse backed away as Nasyr lashed out at the dog with a thick whip. The dog flew into a fury. Attracted by the noise, Akbalak emerged and shouted at the dog, his voice strong and sonorous. The dog retreated unwillingly, glaring at the horse and its rider from the back of the yard.

"It's been a long time since anyone stopped a horse near my house! I know you, Nasyr, my brother!" Akbalak smiled, stroking his white beard with his hand.

"Who else would visit an old comrade, abandoned by all?" Nasyr responded.

"It's the first time in ten years I've seen your horse near my house," Akbalak said. Nasyr could hear the hurt in his voice.

They went inside, and Akbalak gave Nasyr a bowl of *shubat*.[3]"I'm sure you're tired from your journey. Sit down and rest. I'll go and sort out a dastarkhan," Akbalak said, going to stand up. "You see, my leg has begun to let me down. Old age."

Nasyr put up his hands and pleaded with the old man. "Aka, for goodness' sake, don't worry. I won't stay long. I just dropped in to see you briefly so you wouldn't be offended. We're not living our last day, Aka. We'll meet again and talk at leisure, but now I must go before it gets dark."

"Don't be ridiculous, Nasyr. Do you really think Akbalak will simply let you go? You'd better unsaddle your horse and bring it into the yard."

Akbalak went outside and called his young dzhigit neighbor and asked him to slaughter a ram. The dzhigit and his wife started to prepare dinner for the guest, and Akbalak sat down next to Nasyr and started to sniff a strong, aromatic tobacco.

He decided to treat his old friend with good food. Akbalak, so long a cherished guest at celebrations and get-togethers, was gradually falling into an elderly indifference to the bustle of life. It's a long time since he had a dombra[4] in his hands.

He began to speak. "I see you've come some way. Where from, if it's not a secret?"

"I was at Fuzuli's," Nasyr replied. He didn't want to say anything about the sad sights he had seen approaching Shumgen, so as not to stir up the zhyrau's feelings.

"How's Fuzuli doing?"

"Very well. We're all getting older, but he looks as if he's gotten younger! It hasn't even been a year since his wife died, and he's already married again to a much younger woman. With a young wife, you seem to get younger yourself!"

Akbalak took his dombra in his hands and ran his fingers along the strings thoughtfully. "So you took a detour through the old places, but now you're happy to be back?"

"As if it was possible to be happy in this situation," Nasyr thought, hesitating. At last, he decided that Akbalak saw and understood as much as he did. Akbalak had long been worried about the fate of Sinemorye. And so with unconcealed bitterness, Nasyr came out with it. "My dear Aka, this trip has given me no joy at all. It has only upset my soul even more."

"Tell me what Kakharman thinks. Will they find a way out of this situation, or will the sea die?"

Akbalak put the dombra aside and turned toward Nasyr as he responded.

"What can Kakharman do? In Moscow, the big bosses convince each other that the disappearance of the sea will harm no one. I read it in the newspaper. I couldn't believe my eyes! And now they're trying to convince us. I think this Soviet government is brainless!

"Allah has not sent me death. The only thing he has sent me are creaking bones. I don't understand what's wrong. I don't think I sinned. But he sent his punishment: getting old and senile."

Akbalak was silent and then asked, "They're probably asking for a plan from Kakharman for the fish catch?"

"Of course they're not forgetting the plan . . . But what catch can there be when there are no more fish in the sea? Aka, there is not a single lagoon, not a single gulf or tiny bay, where there'd be as many fish as there were in the past. It's tough for my son. He argued with the bosses—both local and regional. He's even been to Alma-Ata and still found no support."

"I heard the fish factories will be closed down. What does Kakharman think about that? People say one of the trawlers has run aground . . ."

"What use are the factories if there's no sea? And as for the trawler, they are right; it is stranded. Stuck in the sands like a ghost. What can they do now—haul it to the water with ropes? And that's only the beginning of all our troubles, Aka."

"It would've been hard for people without work if Kakharman hadn't organized the cattle farms and opened factories for women. I heard he'd been here recently to check the farms, but he didn't visit me. Tell him that the old zhyrau is upset with him."

"I'll tell him, Aka. I will. But you should understand him. Do you think he didn't want to see you? He has no free time at all. All he does is work."

"While a man is alive and works hard, he has no time for other things. Let's hope Kakharman has enough time for everything, even for conversations with aqsaqals. Tell him the people are grateful. The women are especially grateful. They had to walk a long way to get water before he had those two wells dug right in the middle of the aul."

Right now, Akbalak had no wish to speak ill of his fellow villagers and kept it to himself that many were leaving their native lands. But Nasyr already knew this.

"It's good you have your own drinking water," Nasyr said. "In Karakalpakstan, both Beknazar's grandsons caught jaundice, and one died. People say that the Syr Darya is now all polluted by 'chymicals' that make people sick."

"Poor children! We had this, too, last year. Maybe you heard? The pesticides they're spraying on the rice fields got into the well. The entire aul almost died. Fortunately, doctors from the town were able to help in time. But what's going to happen in the future? I can't understand it, Nasyr!"

Nasyr did not reply. After a long silence, Akbalak took his dombra and started to sing one of his songs with a quavering voice:

> *Once again in the sea, I'll cast my old net*
> *But the sea, the hard sea, won't give us fish yet . . .*
> *Have I strength to survive, God; am I firm set?*
> *What is in your chest: a warm heart or ice?*
> *My kindred's deserted; they're lost and they grieve.*
> *They're weak and they're sick; they no longer believe*
> *Since their homes and their grave mounds they had to leave.*
> *But the sea, the hard sea, won't give us fish yet . . .*
> *We were driven, and listless; we'd nowhere to go*
> *We were blown by the fates, whither we'd never know.*
> *But wherever we went, we met troubles and woe.*
> *For the sea, the hard sea, won't give us fish yet . . .*

Nasyr understood that this was the old zhyrau's lament for their suffering. It'd been a long time since Nasyr had heard Akbalak singing. What power and yearning in the melody! What despair and bitterness in the words!

> *No, the sea, the hard sea, won't give us fish yet . . .*

Akbalak owed his life to Nasyr. If it weren't for Nasyr, his bones would've been rotting in the undersea domain of King Suleiman. Nasyr-paluan[5] was the only one who had dared to go out that night into the wild sea to look for

Akbalak and Karashash. And even though Nasyr is not as muscular as he once was, everything in him reminded Akbalak of that remarkable strength. The broad, powerful chest, still breathing as freely and easily. Those calloused palms. Those tenacious fingers.

When Akbalak went out to sea to check the night nets, Karashash persuaded him to take her with him. It was early morning, and mist still lingered in patches over the water. But as the mist dispersed, the bright sky burst through, clear and soft azure. The water, too, was soft and calm.

Karashash lay back on her arms in the boat with pleasure, turning her face right to the sun. Its rays were not hot yet. Akbalak feasted his eyes on his young and beautiful wife. As they sailed farther from the shore, they began to sing. Whenever they were alone, they would sing duets. Akbalak's strict mother didn't forbid them singing duets in public, but she wasn't very happy when they did. But here, out in the wide-open sea, there was nobody to bother them—and they, both beautiful, both full of life's energy, sang freely and easily. The slow slip-slapping of the soft blue waves set a gentle rhythm.

Songs sound different at sea. They are loud when Sinemorye is angry and tosses their boats like splinters on the wild waves. "Storm, we are not afraid of you!" the fishermen sang. "Against your blind rage," the fishermen sang, "we will resist with steady hearts and cool minds. You will not subdue us!"

But on those days when little waves flop gently against the boards, another song was born in fishermen's hearts. They sang of how wide and open the sea is, how delightful to a man's eyes, how happy are those who live on its shores. "Sea," the fishermen sang, "let the friendship between us never end. Love us, sea," the fishermen sang, "and we will love you till the end of our days."

Karashash must've thought about it all that early morning. She clung to her husband's chest and said, "The sea is being kind to our boat again. My dear, let's go to our island . . ."

This caught Akbalak by surprise.

"But Korym is a long way," he replied, bending his wife gently toward him and kissing her.

"So what? I really want to see Korym again, to lie on its sunny sands, to have a look at our hut . . ."

Karashash looked longingly at Akbalak. And Akbalak was so intent on hugging and kissing her that he let go of the oars, and the waves swept the boat swiftly on.

"You see," Karashash laughed. "Fate is carrying us there!"

"What about the fish?"

"Who will touch our nets? We'll collect them tomorrow on our way back."

"Let's go, then!" Akbalak smiled happily. He grabbed the oars with his strong hands and turned the boat.

Korym Island had been a good shelter for the young runaways. The koulan horses, saiga antelope, and kiik deer were not used to people and came gently and inquisitively to investigate the dzhigit and his girl. Even so, their first night, Karashash was afraid to sleep on the island, so they stayed in the boat. The night was starry and moonless black. The boat rocked rhythmically on the waves. They dropped off to sleep embracing, and their sleep of blissful contentment was not interrupted even by the light rain that fell gently on the lovers' faces and soon dried.

For three months, they had been children of nature. They weaved a hut from reeds, and a fallow deer fawn started coming to the hut. One night, a sandstorm blew up, and the little fawn ran quivering into the hut. Soon it became clear why he was so terrified. The howl of a wolf rang out nearby. Akbalak walked out of the hut, stared around for a long time, then finally shot—and hit—the wolf! It squealed in despair and then fell silent.

From then on, the fawn followed Karashash everywhere. When the time came to say farewell to the island, the fawn was running along the shore, bleating pitifully. "Aka," Karashash said, "look. Our little friend is crying,"

"And you are crying, too, my darling," Akbalak replied.

"We'll take him with us," Akbalak decided, wiping Karashash's tears. "We will give him to the hunter Musa!" Karashash rejoiced. Akbalak climbed off the boat and waded toward the shore. The fawn immediately swam toward him. Once in the boat, it pressed close to Karashash's feet. Back in Shumgen, they gave it to Musa. Many animals lived at Musa's. After treating them and putting them on their feet, he would usually set them free into the wild. The fawn soon grew up but continued to live in the hunter's yard.

They got to the island toward nightfall. After leaving the boat, Karashash looked around excitedly. Akbalak quickly collected dry brushwood and lit a fire. Their hut was broken down now, but the woven beddings had kept well. Akbalak brought one to the fire, and Karashash sat down on it and squeezed her husband's shoulder. The night was quiet, the only sound the crackle of burning brushwood.

In the morning, Karashash woke first. Right away, she woke Akbalak. "Aka, get up. We should go back now!"

"It's been so wonderful to be here again!"

Akbalak pulled Karashash toward him and kissed her.

After a light breakfast, they got into the boat. They hadn't gone far from the island when they noticed the sky was changing. Dark rain clouds were racing across it. Soon the smaller clouds combined into one giant mass, and rain poured down. A cold and piercing wind blew from the north. When they got to the nets, it was very tricky to bring the heavy load on board, and the added weight made the boat hard to manage.

Waves were soon threatening to capsize the boat. Akbalak didn't fear death. He'd been a hair's breadth from it before, and its threat had long faded.

The northern wind was gaining strength. The mast cracked and collapsed, and Akbalak lost control of the boat. They were heading for the open sea. But fate decided to give another twist. The boat suddenly swung toward a jagged reef.

"Aka, we must dump the fish!" Karashash shouted, her voice almost drowned out by the roar of wind and water. Akbalak nodded in agreement, and Karashash started to throw fish overboard. Akbalak made an attempt to regain control of the boat. His wife's courage lifted his spirits. If they didn't survive, their baby would be left alone. He didn't have a chance to think of anything else before a huge wave crashed right into them and hurled the boat on the rocks, smashing it to bits. Akbalak and Karashash were flung into the water, desperately clinging to boards from the destroyed boat.

Nasyr was one of the last coming back from the sea. He was told that Akbalak and Karashash went to sea the morning before and still hadn't come back. Without a second thought, he lowered his boat into the water. Rowing without rest, he got to Korym Island by the time it was dark. He was certain he would find them there.

Now he was being swept through the same place in the sea that Akbalak had lost control of his boat. Utterly exhausted, Nasyr still managed to gather his last strength and safely guide his boat between the perilous stones. All this time, he was calling loudly, "Akbalak! Karashash! Hey! Hey!" By morning, he was completely hoarse, but the sea had subsided. Only then did he find Akbalak and Karashash, still alive and clinging weakly to the wreckage of their boat.

Their dinner was coming to an end. Akbalak ordered Nasyr's bed to be arranged in the back room. It was clean and cool there. Nasyr lay down and stretched his tired legs with pleasure but couldn't fall asleep. He was thinking about his trip to see Beknazar.

Beknazar was finding it hard to come to terms with the death of his dear little grandson. His unshaven face had become gaunt. He looked old. After the funeral, everybody went to Beknazar's but left quickly after the memorial dinner.

Nasyr and Beknazar were left alone. Beknazar was silent. Occasionally he would tremble as he heard the loud wails of his daughter-in-law from another room.

"Of all my grandsons, I loved Aidar the most," Beknazar sighed.

"I came to you in an evil hour," Nasyr murmured.

"No, Nasyr-aga," Beknazar replied. "A man cannot know Allah's intentions . . . But it wasn't idle curiosity that brought you here, was it? I'm guessing that you want to see with your own eyes the dams that have blocked the Syr Darya."

Nasyr nodded.

"Do you remember when newborns were dipped into Syr Darya? Everybody wanted their babies to become wide and free like this river . . . Those times have gone." Beknazar lost his train of thought, derailed by thoughts of the boy's death. "Just yesterday morning I was sitting with him right here, playing checkers." A lump developed in his throat, and he went silent again.

"How old was he?"

"He was supposed to start school this autumn. I was buying him textbooks and teaching him to read. We went together to Nukus not long ago to choose a schoolbag for him . . .

"In the morning, he went to the river with the other children. At midday, they brought him back on a bicycle frame. He was unconscious . . . The trash they treat cotton and rice with got into the water. No one knew about it. Upriver in Uzbekistan, a factory chucked untreated chemical waste into the river. Everything inside the little boy was burning. We gave him glass after glass of cold water to drink, but he died in three hours. Our local doctor couldn't do anything. The doctors were in high demand that day. There were poisoned children in every house. I've seen much in my life but never anything like this . . ."

"Yes, Beknazar, you've seen many deaths. Do you remember how I saved your life back in the hungry thirties?"

"The hungry times, Nasyr-aga, were different . . . Now it's our children suffering. Why? Has this tragedy hit only the Karakalpak auls? I am sure people up and down the Darya are being poisoned! Why is it happening, Nasyr-aga? Are we enemies to ourselves and our children?"

"What can I say? It looks as if the better we live, the worse it gets! The more black oil we extract, the more we spill. The more plants we build, the more waste we produce. So the question arises: Why do we actually need more? Why this race? Do whatever you like. Break it into pieces. Destroy all nature! Ruin your fellow man! We are all barbarians, Beknazar, simply barbarians!

"You reap what you sow. I even think this way, Beknazar. Why does a man need abundance? Hunger, coldness, and destruction educated the souls of our fathers not to anger, nor to despair, nor to hate of their fellow men. On the contrary, it taught kindness, warmth, and compassion.

"What did our fathers used to say? Do not take what doesn't belong to you. Share your last piece of bread with a traveler. Maybe it is the last time you see him. Respect your father: without him, your home is a home without a blessing. Respect your mother: without her, your home is a home without warmth. Our ancestors had many wise precepts. Our forefathers died, Beknazar, and we are going extinct ourselves. And after us, there won't be anyone to pass on these precepts. A race of barbarians is being born, Beknazar!"

In the early morning, they went to the cotton fields.

"My life is simple," Beknazar began. "I am a waterer. The state pays me money for pouring water onto this field. The more water I pour on, the larger my earnings. Maybe an excess of water will rot the cotton or turn the sands to a bog. The waterer wouldn't care at all. The more water you pour out, the more money gets poured into your pocket. Do you understand how it works?"

"What's not to understand? A man with only half a brain came up with the idea."

"No one cares whether the Darya's water reaches the sea. Our job is to leave as much water as possible on the fields." Beknazar looked silently for a moment at the field in front of them and then continued. "But this is what I think, Nasyr-aga. Water should be poured only on certain days. If water was the price of gold, would I be pouring it so wastefully? No. I would be using it sparingly."

He developed his idea further. "If water was poured only on certain days, then the water in the Darya would be enough for both the rice and cotton fields all along its length without causing any harm for Sinemorye. At least it wouldn't be drying out.

"If the officials of Kazakhstan and the rest of Central Asia had sat at the same table and debated intelligently, they could've come to a decision and saved the sea. But now what? Each republic uses the wealth of the earth as if it's their own property. We are not thinking about our children, not thinking about tomorrow. Everything is today, everything is now, now, now . . . and as many gold medals for your chest as possible!"

It was time for Nasyr to head back, and he began to bid farewell to his friend. "Well, Beknazar, I must be going before it gets too hot. Keep well."

"I'll come with you as far as Kurental," Beknazar offered. "My horse has been ready since yesterday."

"Well." Nasyr did not object. "If you have the time to spare, let's go."

Kurental is a lonely tree among the sands. There is a well under this tree by which tired travelers rest or spend the night in a little hut built for them. Nasyr and Beknazar had linked memories of Kurental from the early thirties when young Nasyr and barefooted Beknazar met for the first time.

During the years of the great confiscations, the Kazakhs were deprived of their only source of wealth—their cattle—and suffered terrible deprivation. Endless lines of wretched, bloodless people stumbled along Sinemorye's shores. They were leaving their homelands, heading for the cities. It seemed they thought the cities could save them from death. Many never made it, dying in the sands of thirst or starvation.

Nasyr's father, Belgibai, had one brother, Sansyzbai, who lived in Karakalpakstan. Belgibai worried often about his brother in those days. "There has been no news from Sansyzbai for a long time. In my heart, Nasyr, I have a feeling that Sansyzbai is in trouble. Go, visit him, and find out how he is doing. And on your way back, if you meet resettlers, lead them to the sea; don't let them die."

Nasyr went on his journey on the tough and sturdy she camel named Oisylkara. The sky over the desert was black with flocks of crows circling human corpses. Nimble foxes and badgers ran wild across the slopes of dunes. It was a feast for predators of the desert.

The next day, Nasyr reached the aul where Sansyzbai lived. It was hardly even an aul now. Desolation and devastation were everywhere, with a glimmer of life only in a few lonely yurts. There were no noisy children. No women sitting by firesides. No small cattle. The stench of rotting flesh was unbearable. Nasyr dismounted, tied the camel to a bush, and headed toward the yurts. In his hand, he held his father's thick *kamcha* whip.

As he got near the yurts, he saw swollen corpses. Two foxes ran from one of the yurts. They sat on their haunches about thirty yards away from Nasyr and watched him. Soon Nasyr was outside Sansyzbai's yurt. Covering his nose and mouth with his hand to protect himself from the stench, he walked in and at once recoiled. Sansyzbai was dead. His body was already decomposing. Nasyr shrieked. Sansyzbai's dead wife was lying nearby. He shot from the yurt like a bullet to his camel, where he promptly threw up. He sat on the camel, grabbed its hump with his hands, and wept. Oisylkara headed away from the aul. Crows were cawing exultantly at Nasyr's back, and as he looked back one last time, he saw the foxes and jackals rush in for another feast.

The next morning, Nasyr reached Kurental. He decided to collect some water. He was in agony because he couldn't bury the bodies of his uncle and aunt. He filled his *torsyk*[6] with water, washed his face, and watered the camel. It looked as if the stove in the hut was lit. A sudden thought occurred to him: Maybe he should look and see if anyone was there? But recalling his father's words to be careful in the desert, he dismissed the idea.

The moment he left the well, the door of the hut swung open, and a naked boy of about five years old ran out. The little boy yelled as he rushed toward Nasyr, tripping over a heap of ashes. He fell and was too weak to get up. A weary, disheveled woman ran out after him. She was holding a knife in her hand. Nasyr turned his camel sharply, held his kamcha tight, and with a loud cry, drove

Oisylkara to block her path. The woman stopped short and plunged back into the hut. Nasyr followed.

A middle-aged man, thin and ragged, was holding a child of around eleven years of age between his knees. He was trying to slash the child's neck with a knife; the bleeding child was trying to tear himself free from the man's grip. Next to the man, a child's severed head. Only at that moment did Nasyr become aware of the thick smell of boiling meat hanging in the air. Nasyr cried out with a terrible voice and belted the man with his whip as hard as he could. The child, a ginger-haired Russian boy, broke free and ran to Nasyr.

"Don't kill us!" the woman cried feebly. Nasyr was shaken to the core looking at these miserable wretches. With the boy under his arm, he dashed out of the hut. The other little boy was already running into the sands. Nasyr called after him, and the child looked back, then turned and ran a few more feet before quickly and weakly collapsing. Nasyr carried both boys to the well in his arms, washed the blood from the injured boy, wrapped both of them in his chapan, sat them on the camel, and then slowly began moving away from this terrible place.

One of those children was Beknazar. The other, the Russian boy, was adopted by Musa, who called him Zharasbai. Musa brought him up, and Zharasbai got married and shortly after that went to the city, where he holds an important post. Beknazar grew up at Nasyr's. After the war, his relatives tracked him down, and he went away with them. Now, so many years later, Nasyr and Beknazar stopped their horses by Kurental and drank from the well.

"And now I bid you farewell, Nasyr-aga," said Beknazar sadly.

"Keep well, my brother," Nasyr replied. "If we stay alive, we will meet again. Don't forget about Karaoi; you haven't been to visit us for a long time. Work is work, but you must still find time."

"That is a justified reproach, Nasyr-aga. I kept thinking that once my children grew up, I'd have less to worry about. That is not how it turned out."

And so they parted.

Toward morning, Nasyr dozed off. But his sleep was at once broken by the dog's desperate barking. In the other room, Akbalak shouted, "Nasyr, something's going on there!" Nasyr peered out the window and saw Akbalak's dog fighting a pack of wild dogs. One of them jumped at the wolfhound from behind, caught him by his leg, and threw him down.

Akbalak ran into the yard in his underwear, with Nasyr following close behind. By the time they were in the yard, stumbling in the darkness, the feral dogs had torn the wolfhound to pieces. The pack flew out the gate, barking loudly. Akbalak and Nasyr were about to chase, when the biggest of them turned back, baring its teeth. The old men froze.

"Did you see?" Akbalak finally said. "It looks like they took a few dogs from the aul with them."

"I noticed something else," Nasyr replied. "There were wolves in the pack. Sad times are coming, Akbalak. Our dogs, our friends, are turning into wolves, our enemies."

"What if they got your horse?" Akbalak suddenly shouted. "Run to the barn, Nasyr!"

Nasyr ran. The horse was fine but snorting in terror and tugging wildly at her ties. Nasyr patted her on the neck, and she began to calm down.

Then he rushed back to Akbalak.

Akbalak had fallen to his knees over the body of the dog. The dawn began to gleam over the desert, coloring the edge of the horizon bloodred.

BOOK TWO

The state perishes when it no longer distinguishes good people from bad.

—Antisthenes, fourth century BC

What do I care about living together when I am suffering? What is the good of genius that lives in the sky when on earth, the mass of people are lying in the mud?

—Vissarion Grigoryevich Belinsky in a letter to Vasily Petrovich Botkin, 1841

All our dignity lies in thought. Let us strive, then, to think well. This is the basis of morality.

—Blaise Pascal, seventeenth century

IV

Nasyr's little house was full of people. Kakharman might have said goodbye, but the fishermen still hung on silently. They were all worried, and each thought that if Kakharman was leaving, then nothing could be done.

Kakharman was their anchor, their hope—and now their hope was leaving.

"That's it, my compatriots," Kakharman declared. "I've nothing else to say."

Slowly, one after another, the fishermen began to leave the house. Kakharman sat with his head bowed. Nasyr wanted to ask his son where he was going, but he had a feeling Kakharman wouldn't tell him, so he stayed quiet. Everything in the right time, Nasyr decided. Kakharman will let them know in his own time . . .

Kakharman stood up, and so did Nasyr and Korlan. Suddenly, he hugged his old parents and put his arm around Berish.

"Look after them, Berish! You are so grown-up, my boy."

Berish nodded and turned to hide his tears.

"Now, now," Kakharman whispered. "No need for tears."

Berish nodded again.

In half an hour, they were high up Karaadyr Mountain. From its heights, the seashore shone brightly, but the dusk hid the dark sea itself, far away now, like the distant, happy past. When Kakharman and Sayat were boys, the sea splashed right up to the foot of Karaadyr, and the shore was a lively place. The older kids competed in *kokpar*,[1] and the younger boys raced horses.

Many years had gone by, but Kakharman felt like it was only yesterday that he was on his horse as it raced, clinging to its flowing black mane and shouting the names of his forefathers at the top of his lungs. Musa would trust him—and only him—with that fiery, raven-black racer. Musa would suddenly appear from Karaadyr gorge just as Kakharman headed for the finish line, then gallop alongside on his mare, cheering him on.

How the raven-black stallion used to catch fire! As if on wings, it hurtled toward the finish line, toward the people in bright outfits, glancing back at Kakharman as if asking, "Are you holding on? Hold on tighter, kid. Don't lose your grip!"

Only at Musa's could you see such magnificent stallions. They were raised by Musa for racing or for gifting to neighbors—Uzbeks, Turkmens, and Kazakhs from Mangystau and Arka. But Musa would not give the raven racer to anyone. He kept it for racing.

"Musa's raven racer is out front again!" they shouted at the finish line. "Pai, Pai! Look, look. It's dancing! It's not even tired!"

People looked at Musa with love and respect, even though he and Otkeldy were the only members of the aul who weren't fishermen. When the fishermen went out to sea, Musa would get on his horse and go hunting while Otkeldy would gather herbs with Marziya. Well, that's the way it should be. The fishermen needed both a hunter and a healer on the shore.

After crowding around the victor and singing his horse's praises, the people would all cram into Musa's house for a party. And what kind of Kazakh doesn't like guests?

After Kakharman's very first win—on May Day, '47—his dad rode up to him on a dun horse. The boys surrounding him went silent with envy as Nasyr sat Kakharman with him on his horse and rode toward Musa's. "You have become a dzhigit, son," said Nasyr loudly. And Kakharman, flushed with pride, pressed his face into his dad's chapan, which smelled of sea and sand.

The sea, in his childhood days, had washed right up against the aul. Now it had receded a wanderer's day away, even from Karaadyr. Back then, they would lower the boats into the water right here. Now, the air was acrid, hot, and infused with the scent of saline that scorches the lungs. Once you could sail all the way from here to Akespe Island, which, in those days, was where Professor Slavikov had his laboratory.

Back then, Slavikov spent every summer here. Sociable and easygoing even with the children of the aul, the old professor quickly made friends with the local fishermen. He'd start at Nasyr's, where the scientist and the simple fisherman would chat away energetically and earnestly. Then Otkeldy and Musa would join them, or Nasyr might send a message to Shumgen to invite Akbalak along. Slavikov could speak Tatar and Kazakh fluently. He had once lived in Orenburg and studied at Kazan University.

In those days, Kakharman adored the scientist. Though it seemed there was nothing in the world he didn't know, the professor never forgot everyday customs, always arriving with gifts and sweets for everybody. "Really? Matvei! Why such extravagance?" Akbalak would object, although he was really rather touched by the scientist's attention.

"It's alright, my friends," Slavikov joked. "It won't kill me." Then he would add, "But now I'm hoping for something in return." He meant that Akbalak should sing.

The professor listened to him in rapture. When Akbalak stopped singing, the professor would often pick up Akbalak's dombra, carved out of solid poplar, and would stroke it lovingly.

"Akbalak-aga, old friend! I often remember your songs when I'm back in Moscow. Believe it or not, they help me relax. Sometimes I even sing them myself! You know, if I use Kazakh enough, my boy Igor might just understand it. The *kobyz*[2] you carved for me hangs in a prominent place at home. It's such a shame I'm too old to learn to play it. If only I were younger."

And he'd smile archly at Igor, who would be murmuring, "I will definitely learn to play the kobyz."

Nasyr was amazed by how much Kazakh Igor already knew, though his father was a hard taskmaster.

"To learn a language well, to speak it fluently, you have to live with it. The summer just isn't enough. I'd love to bring Kakharman and Sayat to Moscow sometime. Then the boys can really get to know each other. Would you be OK with that, Nasyr-aga?"

Kakharman, Sayat, and Igor were thrilled by the professor's idea—they had dreamed of spending the summer together for a long time but didn't know what their parents would think.

"Of course. I've no objection. It'll be a change for the boys, and they can learn Russian from Igor."

Kakharman walked away from the Zhiguli. Sayat lifted the hood and peered at the oil filter by the dim light of a small lamp. He didn't want to disturb his friend's solitude at this moment of farewell.

All was silent. The lights of the coastal auls had gone out. The windows and doors of abandoned houses gaped open; many fishermen had already left for Caspy and Shardara. They knew the two exhausted rivers would bring no succor to the dying sea.

The car bringing his wife wasn't yet in sight—and Kakharman's thoughts raked over the past. Back in the summer of '56, Slavikov had brought a young scientist with him from Moscow after warning Nasyr of their arrival in a telegram.

No one in the aul doubted that the guest must be well treated. "Otherwise, why send a telegram?" Nasyr concluded. Everyone agreed. Times were difficult then—they were still suffering postwar privations—but the people of the aul did all they could to present a good face.

Nasyr and Kambar took charge of finding good fish. Musa and Akbalak were dispatched to hunt for saiga. Otkeldy searched for the best melons, and the young and easygoing kolkhoz chairman Zharasbai went to Alma-Ata for flour.

Musa and Nasyr waited for the Moscow–Alma-Ata express on the small platform at Saryshyganak. The guests' suitcases were loaded on a *telega* cart,[3] and the guests—the professor, Igor, and young Professor Sharaev—were put on horses and set off for Karaoi.

Otkeldy, Akbalak, and Kambar were waiting for them in Karaoi, working out the best time for the dastarkhan. It was growing dark by the time the guests reached Karaoi. As the weary travelers climbed up the slope and saw yurts surrounded by lush, vital greenery, they became much jollier.

"By God, my friends," Slavikov exclaimed, "I was missing your yurts all winter! But Yegor Mikhailovich, the sharpest of the 'young and green tribe' has yet to know this pleasure—to see yurts after the hubbub of Moscow! He will get to know the people, see local life, and—I hope—will love it like I do!"

Sharaev, who had never ridden before, was weary and said nothing. He just smiled weakly. But Slavikov wanted to go to the sea right away.

"Matvei is right," Nasyr insisted. "The sea will lift your tiredness if you swim now."

They were soon on the shore. Nasyr invited Slavikov and Sharaev into his boat and took the oars. A little way from the shore, Slavikov threw off his clothes and plunged deep into the cool waters. He came up again far from the boat and shouted, "Yegor Mikhailovich, I'm waiting for you! The water's amazing! You won't find water like this anywhere else!" He turned on his back and swam off.

"Dive in." Nasyr smiled at Sharaev. "You won't be sorry."

"What about you?"

"What else?" Nasyr laughed, and they began to undress. And from the other boat, Kakharman and Igor jumped in too.

"Well, what did I say!" Slavikov yelled, as Sharaev nodded. "The water heals the lost souls of city folk. Am I right, Nasyr?"

"You're right, Mustafa, as always!"

"The Kazakhs call me Mustafa!" Slavikov chuckled.

"And what will you call me?" Sharaev asked Nasyr.

"It depends on you. If you don't abandon your idea to block the Darya with a dam, then they'll call you Yeginbai," Slavikov said.

"And what does it mean?"

"Tell me. Are you still wedded to your idea of the dam and Karakum Canal? Are you still dreaming of directing water into the sands to grow cotton and rice?"

"Yes."

"Then from now on, they will call you Yeginbai, the sower." Slavikov smiled archly and dived. Soon the sun's last rays had colored the water deep red, and it was time to go back.

After that dip in the sea, Sharaev really did feel well. Back in the boat, he started talking with Nasyr. "If we divert the Darya's water into the canals, what do you think will happen to the sea?"

Nasyr look at Sharaev as if he was crazy.

"How can we block the path of water created by Allah himself? The sea will simply dry out."

Nasyr turned to Slavikov, inviting him to join in, but Slavikov kept his back turned.

"From your mention of God, I guess you're not a Communist?"

"I am a Communist. In '42, I was there on the front lines. I was injured and mistakenly listed as dead, so I joined the party posthumously. Now I vote for both party and God," Nasyr joked.

"Why did I ask?" Sharaev went on. "Well, as the party develops postwar objectives, we need to look at things on a larger scale. There's water in your lands. That's good. But there's no water in the Turkmen deserts. We can't accept that. This desert could be giving rice and cotton to our mother country. Our homeland must grow stronger; otherwise, those Yanks will squash us like flies."

"That's true, of course." Nasyr was stung. "But if you siphon off the Darya, the sea will dry out. And there'll be no prosperity in the Turkmen desert or here." He looked at Sharaev doubtfully. "You say the Yanks will squash us like flies. I met a few American soldiers in the war. I ate with them from the same tins, spoke with them. They're friendly people. They have enough wealth of their own. But if you block the Darya, it won't be the Americans squashing us; we'll be squashing ourselves. The drying of the sea will take its revenge on the people who live here."

Sharaev was still smiling condescendingly, and Nasyr was hurt.

"It's hard for me to argue that I think on a grand scale. I'm just a humble fisherman."

An awkward silence fell, and perhaps to ease the moment, Nasyr began to recite:

> *How can the sea·goose ever know*
> *The beauty of steppe grass?*
> *How can the steppe bustard understand*
> *A sea as clear as glass?*
> *How can the gossip ever see*
> *The quiet man's true worth?*
> *How can those who never roamed*
> *Know the value of the earth?*
> *How can the fool who leaves the yurt*
> *Know where else to start?*
> *How can those who wander aimlessly*
> *Know a nation's heart?*

At once, Slavikov began to translate quietly, while in the other boat, Akbalak took Nasyr's recitative up.

> *The purest and most priceless pearl*
> *Lies still on the ocean bed.*
> *The purest and most priceless word*
> *Stays in the soul unsaid.*
> *Sometimes the pearl in some great wave*
> *Is churned up from the deep*
> *Sometimes that word, with sorrow filled,*
> *Is dragged out of its sleep.*

Igor and Kakharman's boat had reached the shore already. They had lit a fire and cooked dinner and were waiting for the adults. When the adults arrived, the young men deftly served out grilled sturgeon as Nasyr and Slavikov looked on with pride.

While they ate, the conversation continued in the same vein. But now it was the professor, Sharaev, and Bolat doing most of the talking. Bolat was one of Slavikov's students and had come to Akespe to see the professor because he missed him so much. Now Nasyr understood why Slavikov had brought Sharaev with him. He had to show the fishermen the kind of opponent he was coming up against so that they'd realize just how serious a problem Sinemorye faced and how obstinate their foes were in their arguments.

At the start of the conversation, the professor introduced Bolat. "This young man turns out not just to be the brightest of my students but a compatriot too. He's from Orenburg, so he's a Russian Kazakh."

"There was a time when Orenburg was considered Kazakh," Nasyr interjected. "Many Kazakhs still live there. I've a few relatives there myself."

"You're right, Nasyr. The lands of the nomads were widely scattered—they roamed from the Irtysh as far as the Volga. It was only in the eighteenth century that they settled in one area and Russian scholars were able to put Sinemorye on the map."

"You're getting carried away by history, Matvei Panteleevich," Sharaev remarked. "Let's talk about the present."

"Now is a time of trouble for Sinemorye. You can't talk about the now without thinking of the future that awaits it."

"Our future is progress," Sharaev snapped. "The Karakum Canal will prove it. The Darya's water will bring life to the sands. It will transform lives. In the sands, where nothing grows now, gardens will bloom. And trees. Even schoolchildren know that planting trees is the only way to stop shifting sand."

"Yegor Mikhailovich, you're really oversimplifying the idea of progress. Progress is not just irrigating deserts and draining marshes. It's a whole complex of issues. Progress is the battle against erosion and salinification. It is a fight with the winds for the fertility of soil robbed of humus. Just add chemicals. You keep saying the same thing, Yegor Mikhailovich. Just water and reap. That's banal. Nature is not an errand boy. It's dangerous to mess with her. But you're trying to spray these problems away and haven't questioned yourself for a moment."

"You're forgetting, Matvei Panteleevich," Sharaev fumed, "that we need to accelerate cotton and rice production sharply. The party demands it, and we can't fail them."

"I'm not saying we shouldn't irrigate arid places. I'm saying we should live and act in harmony with nature, not fight it. In Central Asia and Kazakhstan, they've made their own progress since ancient times, and they never fight nature; they work with it. You and that academic Krymarev designed the Karakum Canal. You want to squander the water of two rivers. The canal will be a disaster for local people. You can't tell me that the canal will not lead to waterlogging!" By now Slavikov was fired up.

The boys had been sitting away from the adults. Now they looked over. Igor got up quickly and came to sit next to his father. Sharaev looked awkwardly around him.

"Ignore us. Matvei Panteleevich and I often have different opinions nowadays. But clashing views is business as usual for scientists."

"It's been a pointless argument for some time now." Slavikov waved his hand. "Let's just leave it at that."

"You're right." Sharaev smiled. "Let's stop debating and put our arguments to the test."

"What kind of test do you mean, Yegor Mikhailovich? You think nature can be a Polygon[4] for your half-baked ideas. Have you thought what will happen to the people who stay on the shores of a drying sea? Can you imagine how they will live?"

"There'll be jobs for everyone, Matvei Panteleevich. Kazakhstan will become a giant building site. According to Lysenko, we need to plow almost four thousand square miles of unused virgin land in Kazakhstan."

"You know very well," Slavikov retorted coldly, "what I think of Lysenko's ideas. But I'm not talking about him. Man has become greedy and impatient. Now he only has techniques. Like a savage given dynamite. And nobody wants to admit the plain truth that if we conquer nature today, tomorrow nature will fight back, and its vengeance will match the fires of hell.

"I am not exaggerating, Yegor Mikhailovich. This is not a metaphor," the professor continued. "Ask Nasyr. He's seen a great deal in his life. The most frightening day he can remember is the day he saw our Katyusha rockets. These little Katyushas are nothing compared to the latest weapons. Hiroshima and Nagasaki only gave a glimpse of their destructive power. If we are humans, if we are humane, we have to protect nature with all the power we now have. If we take away from nature, we must give back in the same degree. Otherwise, it is suicide. We scientists should understand this better than anyone. The Karakum Canal wasn't thought through. It was just built to keep up the records. Just to keep up the records. Yes, there is cotton. There is rice. There are a million tons!"

"How can you say things like this?" whispered Sharaev, looking around nervously.

"There are no whistle-blowers here. And what have I to be afraid of? It's time we stopped being frightened. We're not slaves. I'm not arguing that the country doesn't need bread and cotton and rice. But before growing them, we need to grow scientists and administrators who are directly responsible for the land they want to dig in. That's why my soul grieves. If not us, then who will look after the future? What kind of scientists are we that can only think about boosting rice and cotton production and cannot consider the hundreds of thousands of people we sacrifice for the sake of that boost? Because we'll turn these people into refugees. We don't need progress like this. And we don't ultimately need this kind of socialism. Science must be humane. It must consider humanity first and foremost. Science isn't worth a kopek if it forgets people."

"Risk is an honorable business," Sharaev asserted calmly.

"Let's just drop it, Yegor Mikhailovich," Slavikov interrupted. "As I said, this is a fruitless debate. You won't really argue your case." He looked at Akbalak and brightened. "Let's just listen to our zhyrau. Akbalak-aga, sing to us!" And he smiled so disarmingly at Akbalak that the old zhyrau took up his dombra without another word. He was already in his fifties then, but his voice was still strong. His hands came down upon the strings with a flourish; it was clear that he would give them a storm.

At first, the dombra rippled gently, as the story told of patches of sunlight tenderly caressing the tranquil waters. But the sea wasn't calm for long. The riffs soon became louder and more agitated. The storm was coming nearer. Several interim chords rolled in, and suddenly it all exploded. Wave after wave. Thick fog. Moaning winds. Water crashing onto rocks. Monstrous waves bursting against cliffs and threatening destruction on anything in their path.

It was the first time Sharaev had ever seen or heard a dombra in his life, and he was stunned by how much this simple instrument could express in the hands of a master. He gasped in astonishment, whispering in Slavikov's ear, "This is just amazing, Matvei Panteleevich! I've no doubt I didn't come here in vain."

The professor nodded.

And when he finished the *kyui*,[5] Akbalak carefully laid the dombra down, wiped the sweat from his forehead, and asked Sharaev a simple question. "Where are you from?"

"I'm from Moscow."

"I'm asking where your roots are. Where is the home of your ancestors?"

"My parents were Muscovites too," Sharaev replied.

"It's probably joyless living in a concrete city, Yekor. Do you know any songs?"

"I've heard nothing better than our old Russian folk songs. But I want to say, as a man of music myself, that your dombra—well, it is an amazing instrument."

"I'm glad you liked my kyui," Akbalak replied. "But it'd be good to hear you sing too. Let's forget our quarrels. Sing for us, Yekor."

While working on the project, Sharaev had traveled much in Central Asia but had never gotten close to the locals before. This was the first time he was among such a warm company of Kazakhs, and he felt sorry it hadn't happened earlier. He liked Nasyr and Akbalak and the ever-silent Otkeldy, with his strong, shaven head.

"Let's sing our favorite," Nasyr announced, clearing his throat.

Black raven, black raven
Why haunt me today?
Don't circle, black raven,
I will not be your prey!

Slavikov began to sing along with Nasyr, and soon Akbalak's dombra joined them.

Fly back to my home now
Help mom understand.
Tell my sweet darling
That I died for our land.

Then Akbalak began to sing too. The strong, resonant voice of the zhyrau gave the song majesty and grace. "All of them here are extremely talented!" Sharaev mused. "That is what life by the sea means: natural freedom among the elements." And he joined in too:

A flaming red arrow
Is heading my way.
I see death, black raven:
I'm yours today.

"They make you sing, even if you don't want to, right?" Slavikov tapped Sharaev on the shoulder and laughed with pleasure.

The sad, thoughtful song flew up into the dark sky, over the silent desert, out across the waves, which were calm and silvery in the light of the moon that had risen long ago over the upturned boats. From time to time, you could hear the low snuffle of the tethered horses and the far-off bark of the dogs from the aul.

Lured by the slow and beautiful song, Ata-Balyk swam toward the shore. It drifted in slowly, found a narrow strip of sand, poked out its head, and began to listen. This wasn't completely safe. Once near Akespe, it was listening with rapt attention and got into a fight with the brown catfish.

Now another song was flowing from the shore, steady and velvety. This was Akbalak, Nasyr, and Otkeldy. But at just that moment, the huge brown catfish came toward the shore, where crazy Kyzbala was wandering with her frail old dog. Kyzbala cared nothing about the guests—not for their campfire nor their songs. She lived her own inner life, and they could not reach her dark mind. Occasionally, she joined other women gossiping, but none ever spoke to her. She'd drink her tea quietly and leave just as she came, without greeting anyone. Kyzbala walked whole days on the seashore in bitter sadness, waiting for her drowned son.

Now she was walking along the shore again. The dog was not far behind. Suddenly it began to whimper pitifully. Kyzbala turned. The catfish opened its great mouth and drew in the poor mutt even as it set its four legs desperately against the sand. But in an instant, the dog had vanished into the fish's mouth. Kyzbala waved her hands furiously and shouted, "Uh, damn you! Watching me, yes? I hope you croak! You hear me? Die!" And she kept on walking.

The next day, there was a wonderful spectacle for the guests: horse racing. As soon as they got the telegram, Nasyr and the other aqsaqals had decided to postpone the race until the guests arrived. Now, the race was on, and as the sun came up, the young dzhigits ambled over to the *kon*, from where the riders would hurtle toward Karaadyr Mountain. Meanwhile, in Karaoi, a noisy crowd was heading to watch the horse games—*baiga*,[6] kokpar, and *tenge alu*.[7] Farther off, the toughest boys were engaged in trials of strength, their dark, sweaty backs gleaming in the sun.

Sharaev, Slavikov, and Nasyr were listening to Akbalak.

> *I'll stay on the horse that's swift in the race.*
> *I'll load up my camel with an old marquee.*
> *I grew up untethered, like a wild kulan—*
> *I need the vast, open steppes to graze free.*
> *I'm a reed in the river on the shifting shoals;*
> *The hard ground's grip I'll never know.*
> *I'm like a poplar among the sands,*
> *And the wildest winds can't bend me low.*
> *I'm like a branch on a wind-broken tree;*
> *My trunk and I will never part.*
> *My chest is iron, my face is steel—*
> *Hit me, but you'll never break my heart.*

When he sang his next song, girls in long dresses with ruffled hems and dzhigits in festive clothes began to gather around him.

"Do the young people listen to Akbalak's songs?" Sharaev asked. "Or can they sing better?"

"Or have they got their own modern songs?" Slavikov wondered. He'd never heard the young ones sing on any of his visits. Maybe there are the same issues here as everywhere? The older people have their lives to live, and there's not enough time for the next generation. And Kazakhs have a lot to pass on, especially a warm hospitality that so touched the professor.

A Kazakh will put aside everything else to help you with any request. They respect the old. The younger ones would never go against someone who had lived, who had learned life's lessons. The Kazakhs must appreciate the strength of their spiritual and moral way of life and never lose it. They must enrich and protect it. Then they won't have to worry about the future. The self-preservation of a people. That is a real issue. Not some idle fiction in our troubled times when culture after culture is washed away by the swelling tide of urbanization and the flood of scientific and technical progress.

These are the thoughts that Sharaev's question stirred up. Akbalak, walking out from the circle of young people, touched the thoughtful professor on the sleeve. Slavikov looked up and smiled. Meanwhile, the dzhigits and girls began to sing. Slavikov and Sharaev listened.

"There's the answer to your question!" Slavikov exclaimed. "Listen how much freedom there is in their songs!"

"There is more sadness and defiance in Akbalak's songs," Sharaev observed after a while. "I like them more even though I'm not so old yet."

"But that's not what matters!" the professor exclaimed. "What matters is that the Kazakhs are an amazing people! Quiet, hardworking, unselfish, always willing to share their last with one in need. They also know how to have fun! That's what we are witnessing now."

And there were things to witness, indeed.

In the baiga, tenge alu, and *kures*,[8] the dzhigits from the neighboring stock-raising auls beat the fishermen. The fishermen weren't too upset at first. But then they lost in *kyz kuu*[9] as well. Their last chance of victory was in the main event: the horse riding.

Slavikov noted, not without irony, "Nasyr-*kurdas*,[10] what happened to the fishermen? All the prizes went to the neighbors. Are their boys better?"

"Heh, Mustafa, you know luck can change." Nasyr smiled, and then suddenly his face was wreathed in sadness. "The best of our dzhigits were swallowed by the war."

The professor realized his joke had hurt his friend. "Don't get upset yet, Nasyr," he said, "We'll have the main prize. Musa's raven racer is in top form!"

Nasyr instantly grew jollier, like a child. "Yes!"

Meanwhile, the crowds were heading toward Karaadyr. There were the racing horses in the distance! The dust flung up by their hooves hung in billowing clouds behind them. As people climbed up the slope and made themselves comfortable, the riders hurtled toward the kon. Musa's raven racer was flying out in front. He shot across the kon line like an arrow.

"The raven-black is first! The raven-black is first!" The fishermen on the hill began to cheer loudly and mobbed Musa, who proudly touched his straw hat with his whip. Then he walked to the rider and tapped him approvingly on the shoulder.

"How's the stallion?"

Slavikov and Sharaev soon came up as well.

"Musa, by God, you're simply invincible!"

"This isn't real racing!" Musa declared, looking at Sharaev quizzically. "I remember the Republican races last year. It was hard for us there, for sure. But still, we won!"

Soon people made for the shore. The time had come for the boat competitions. These boat races attracted everyone. They were invented after the war by Kambar, a fisherman from Zhaiyk.

"Yegor Mikhailovich, would you like to try?" Slavikov asked Sharaev. "You and Bolat, a team of Moscow scientists." Slavikov burst out laughing. "You'll share the prize fifty-fifty!"

"Agreed!" said Sharaev. "I like an active vacation!"

He and Bolat stripped and put on their swimming trunks.

"Wait a moment," the professor said as he remembered something about Bolat. "You have a sports diploma, don't you? It wouldn't be fair for you to compete."

"It doesn't matter," Igor intervened. "You can't win this race with a diploma; you need a little more than that."

Slavikov waved his hand.

"That's true, the diploma is meaningless here. But hurry up. You need to choose a lighter boat."

The young fisherman Zharasbai from Karaoi overheard this conversation and rushed to Nasyr.

"Nasyr-aga, we should be careful. Bolat has a sports diploma!"

Nasyr winked.

"What are you afraid of? He's used to light boats, short distances, and calm city waters. Our boats are much heavier, the distance is almost two miles, and the sea is a sly customer. Don't worry. We have many advantages."

"They will probably shoot forward right away," Zharasbai guessed.

Nasyr was surprised by his naïveté.

"What makes you think that? A real sportsman needs to study his rival carefully. This is what I suggest. About ten minutes after the start, when they begin to think that they've got us figured out, you and Beknazar should accelerate and shoot ahead. They'll chase after you, and your task will be to exhaust them. Take turns with Beknazar—first one pushes while the other rests, then the other way around. Is that clear?"

The boats were moving calmly toward the start. Sharaev and Bolat were side by side. Bolat said quietly, "Yegor Mikhailovich, we should stay together. Try not to fall behind me."

"Good thinking."

"They'll be trying to impose their tempo on us. We have to keep it up as if it's easy. Then, coming up to the finish, we'll make our dash."

"And it's in the bag?" Sharaev laughed.

Soon, everybody was at the start. Nasyr whooped loudly, and the race began. At first, they were all clustered together, but as the race went on, the boats began to spread apart. Nasyr was right; the visitors didn't rush ahead but stayed cautiously in the middle. Then Zharasbai shouted a challenge and energetically leaned on his oars. His long-nosed boat glided easily over the water. He quickly shot ahead of the pack. Beknazar gave a piercing whistle and belted after Zharasbai.

"Shall we continue?" Sharaev suggested. "They'll get away."

Bolat nodded in agreement and began to work the oars faster.

"He rows well." Nasyr admired Bolat. "Beknazar, catch Zharasbai and swap so they won't have a moment's rest!"

With just a few wide, deep strokes, Beknazar had caught up with Zharasbai, and Zharasbai gave way.

"Who's going to win it?" Igor asked Sayat and Kakharman.

"Maybe a bet?" Slavikov suggested mischievously.

"Better not," said Kakharman as they laughed. "Dad will win anyway."

Otkeldy and Musa were of the same opinion: no one could beat Nasyr.

"I remember when Nasyr returned from the front line during the war," Musa said. "He was a mess. His shoulder was irreparably damaged, and he could never be a fighter, so they transferred him into the reserves. But the way he pulled himself together, you should have seen it! For a year, he trained his arm and shoulder relentlessly, and in the end, he made it. He was taken to the front again."

"I didn't know that story," said Slavikov in surprise. "He's a man of an enviable modesty."

"He's seen a lot." Akbalak nodded. "We once even received a death certificate for him!" Akbalak smiled archly. "And he came back to life. Otkeldy was the one who helped him with his shoulder back then."

"I don't know what helped him more, me or his strong will," Otkeldy said.

"Yes," Slavikov responded. "That's what I'm saying; our Nasyr is so modest. He hates talking about himself. I'd like to take this opportunity to thank you all for both this celebration and for yesterday evening."

"What are you saying, Mustafa! It's us who should thank you. When else would we be able to take a break and unwind a little? But tell us this, who is Yekor? Is he your boss?"

The professor smiled understandingly.

"His academic status is lower than mine. But he has power, and many things depend on him. He's not a bad person, but we can talk about him later. I want to ask Otkeldy a question. Tell us, where is our society going? What do the stars tell?"

"You're the scientist, Mustafa. We should ask you!"

"Me? Well, first tell me what you think."

"Tell them, Otkeldy. Don't be afraid," Akbalak encouraged his friend. "Mustafa, you must understand," he explained. "Not so long ago, people from the administration came. They banned him from healing and making predictions. They fined him five hundred rubles and threatened him with prison if he didn't stop."

Slavikov was shocked. "Idiots!" He looked at the healer with deep sympathy. "You mustn't lose your divine gift, aqsaqal; it must be passed on to your children. Life in the land of fools. We cannot do anything ourselves, and we don't allow others to either. We'd rather put them in a prison than let them heal."

The race was reaching a climax. Soon the guests' strength was reaching its limit; both the boat and the oars now were as heavy as lead. It was clear the fishermen would beat them. But there was a twist at the finish. As all the boats sped forward together, Nasyr suddenly took the lead and won. After him came Zharasbai and Beknazar; bringing up the rear were Bolat and Sharaev. Nasyr walked over to console them.

"We fishermen have our little tricks, dzhigits. But well done to you too. You didn't give up. You held on until the end."

Toward the evening, the guests began to leave on horses and by boats for their own auls—back to face the worries of tomorrow. It was also time for the scientists to go. Slavikov addressed Nasyr.

"Thank you again for the celebration; Yegor Mikhailovich will certainly remember it—it's his first time!"

Sharaev quietly extended his arm to Nasyr and smiled.

The next morning, Slavikov and his friends were on the move before sunrise and progressed along the shore for the next twenty days. Kakharman and Sayat traveled with them, gladly carrying out any errands for the scientists and proving bright and efficient assistants. Afterward, Sharaev planned to go to Turkmenistan to visit academician Baraev, but just a couple of days before his departure, the cutter they were in capsized, and his shinbone was shattered. It was too late in the evening to take him to the regional medical center, so Otkeldy was brought to the island. Sharaev bluntly refused the healer's help, insisting on being taken to a town for an X-ray. But in the morning, the sky was wild again and the sea raging, and there was absolutely no chance of a safe journey. That night and the next day, Sharaev spent in agony. At last, in desperation, he agreed to accept Otkeldy's help.

After touching the shin, Otkeldy said, "It has to be reset immediately. Any delay and he'll end up with a permanent limp."

Sharaev relented. Softly, hardly touching the dislocated bone with his fingers, the healer reset it and applied a tight bandage. That night, Sharaev slept well. The next morning, Slavikov bumped into Otkeldy outside the patient's tent.

"How is he?"

Otkeldy drew the professor aside.

"Let's not interrupt his sleep. It went well. In about ten days' time, he'll be hopping around like a young kid goat."

Sharaev woke up toward lunchtime. There was hardly any pain in his leg, but he was afraid to believe it. Otkeldy walked into his tent.

"How is it, Yekor?"

"Not bad at all."

"It will be even better if you do as I say."

"I will, definitely!" Sharaev assured him. He knew Otkeldy would put him back on his feet. "I'm just sorry that I'll have to delay my trip to America."

"America? But what would you be doing there, Yekor?"

"In America? Two lakes have dried out there, and they have invited Soviet scientists to take a look. Tell me, Otkeldy, when will I start walking?" He looked at the healer sadly. "I've only two months to spare."

"Two months? Yekor, don't worry about America. You will go."

Just ten days later, Sharaev was on a plane sent for him by the Turkmenian Academy of Sciences. Bidding farewell, Slavikov asked his colleague, "What do you think about these so-called simple people?"

"They are amazing people, Matvei Panteleevich. You turned out to be absolutely right," Sharaev replied. And he went silent.

Soon Slavikov received a telegram from him: Flying tomorrow New York. Mood cheerful. Leg fine. I even dance. I bow to the steppe magician. Sharaev.

"Ah, Yegor Mikhailovich, Yegor Mikhailovich," Slavikov sighed sadly and began tapping a rhythm subconsciously with his fingers.

After Sharaev's departure, life on the island where the laboratory was situated went on as usual. Slavikov threw himself into his work, and the boys helped him.

Once, they caught up with Nasyr's team on their fast cutter.

"Nasyr, the boys are missing home cooking, so expect a visit today!" the professor shouted. He was suntanned and sprightly, and the boys looked noticeably fitter from their work over the summer.

"They can change their clothes too!" Nasyr smiled. "Go on ahead, Mustafa. Your cutter is fast! Tell Korlan to cook dinner!"

And that is what they did. By the time Nasyr entered the house, everything was prepared. They had dinner and drank tea unhurriedly, and then Slavikov addressed the hostess.

"You have a good son, Korlan. He is clever and quick. I can make him a good scientist. He'll make a good partnership with my Igor. I think he should come to the university. I'd also like to see Sayat as my student."

"That'd be good," Korlan sighed.

"Does that mean we shouldn't wait for you next summer, Mustafa?" Nasyr asked.

"Why is that?" the professor was surprised. "You think that I'll look after them? No thanks. They've got their own beards."

"Yes. We'll get there ourselves!" Kakharman blushed.

"Of course we can do it ourselves." Igor joined the conversation. "But Kakharman and Sayat don't need to go to a university. They want to go to Odessa to become marine engineers. But maybe . . ." Igor hesitated and looked at Nasyr. "Maybe it would be possible for Kakharman to come see me in Moscow right after the school exams. We can work on the entry exams together."

"How can you possibly prepare for exams in Moscow?" Slavikov objected. "It would be better for you to come here for the summer. The air is here. The sea is here. It is much better than hanging around in suffocating Moscow."

And that's what they decided. And when Slavikov and Nasyr were left alone, the professor, happy for the boys, said, "Nasyr, our children are so good. Independent, strong-willed. These are indispensable qualities."

Nasyr rolled a cigarette and asked the professor, "Mustafa, you are a great scientist. You know a lot. You write books. You are the only professor I've met in my entire life. But it surprises me that your relationship with Yekor is so cautious."

Slavikov nodded his head understandingly.

"Surprises you, you say. People like Sharaev should be exposed to better influences. We should try to awaken their humanity, everything good they may have inside. Do you understand? Yekor is the only child of a high-rank family. High rank. Only child. Can you imagine? But Yekor is far from a fool. He's levelheaded and can take responsibility. That is all a scientist needs. The fact that he works in the Krymarev laboratory says a lot, although I doubt Krymarev would've taken him if he'd been, well . . . my son. He is one of the designers of the Karakum Canal, which is now being built in response to the decree to irrigate the steppe. The aim is to erect two dams on both Daryas to water the cotton and rice fields of Uzbekistan. The degree of barbarity and inhumanity in this plan is shocking. It is the most shameful, stupid, and harmful example of socialist planning. That's what I think."

"When it is complete, the sea will have no fresh water!" Nasyr exclaimed. "All the fish will suffocate. How can no one understand that?"

"That's why I invited Sharaev here. To let him see everything with his own eyes. To understand the local people. Understand what the sea means to them. What fish mean to them. Maybe then he will rethink what they are doing in their laboratory."

"You think so?"

"Who knows, Nasyr. Who knows. At least it is an attempt to help him to see sense. As for the Karakum Canal, I'm not completely against it in principle—at least, theoretically. But I just know how it will turn out in reality. The water will be wasted. Marshes and salt swamps will develop around the canal. Then, to wash the salt out of the marshes, they'll need vast floods of fresh water."

"But where will the salt swamps come from?" Nasyr didn't understand.

"Where from? In springtime, the melt water will flood the steppe and raise the level of groundwater dramatically."

"Do you mean that the soil is squeezed between two waters? Then is the land truly set on three whales?" Korlan asked.

"Yes, that's about it." The professor settled down comfortably and began to explain in more detail. "The Sumerians, the ancient people who lived by the Euphrates and Tigris, came up with their own ways of using underground water thousands of years ago. They watered the fields with it and were the first to use it for medicinal purposes. And they wrote a book in Babylon entitled *The Creation of the World*. In this book, Nasyr, long before our Bible and your Quran, they wrote about the end of the world, about the deluge, and about the gods of the water kingdom.[11] People from the earliest times were imagining the presence on earth not just of visible water but also hidden water.

"The scholars of early Islam wrote a lot about underground water too.[12] The works of the Khorezm scholar al-Biruni and the Persian scholar al-Karaji have reached us and influence our thinking still.[13] Lomonosov actually used their ideas for his work. A medieval French abbot wrote a book about how to locate underground waters. That was an amazing book! Many wells of those times were dug by people who took guidance from it."

"Yes, yes!" Nasyr exclaimed. "The ability to find water in the desert is a great art. In our lands, there were several who became famous for finding water where there seemed to be none. Uzbeks, Karakalpaks, and Turkmens used to plead with Musa's father to show them where to dig wells."

"That's right," Korlan agreed. "He was a good man. He died so strangely. He fell into a well."

"He fell into a well?" Slavikov became thoughtful, and Nasyr fell silent, recalling Tektygul, Musa's father. Then Nasyr took his dombra and softly played a kyui called "The Finder." Skillfully and effortlessly, Nasyr painted pictures with the dombra of such expressiveness that the professor was deeply moved.

The steps of a lonely traveler amid the barkhans are heavy. The sun shows him no mercy. The sand tumbles and whispers. The traveler stares joylessly. Suddenly, the faint murmur of a brook reaches his ears. Water! Water! Cool, gentle water! In the ears of the traveler, even a faint trickle sounds like the roar of the sea—water, you are so welcome in the desert!

That is how the kyui was intended—a paean to water, as if composed by the hot and weary traveler. Spilling from the rolling rhythm came the gush and sparkle of mountain waterfalls and the gentle ripple of a meandering brook— maybe one of those that seep out from the cool walls of wells.

"I haven't heard this kyui," Slavikov said as Nasyr put the dombra down.

"Really?" Nasyr was surprised. "Akbalak has played it a few times. You can hear water in all Tektygul's kyuis. It might be water from our sea, or it might be some tiny, unknown brook in the mountains in which he once dipped his hand to quench his thirst."

"Tektygul spent his life alone," Korlan went on. "All his life, he was looking for water. He walked from Pamir all the way to Alatau."

"But how did he end up being Musa's father if he was alone?"

"Musa is the son of Tektygul's older sister," Nasyr replied. "Tektygul brought him up as a dzhigit. But Musa didn't follow his father's footsteps. He can find water, but he gave his life to horses and hunting."

Nasyr walked the boys and the professor to the cutter. It appeared that both Nasyr and the professor were haunted by their recent conversation.

Slavikov continued, "To waste water resources is simply a crime! Because man then harms not just nature but himself.

"Lenin said, 'If man is not becoming more beautiful, more wise, more ingenious, then it's not worth even trying to build socialism.' He warned us that being a socialist is not just about the economy. But we're forgetting it. We love quoting him out of context. Taking snatches for our own benefit. But often we simply play with his words, don't we? And we ruin people's souls. We are not grown-up enough to quote him fully! We won the war, but I'm afraid we're losing the fight for humanity. Tomorrow we will realize what we've done only after we've ruined everything."

"Dad, leave it." Igor tugged his father's sleeve. "Mother asked you to be careful what you say."

"There are no informers here." Slavikov smiled. "Anyway, what would I be afraid of now? I was in prison so long, I've already bored my jailers." He returned to his theme. "There was a time Lenin telegraphed the fishermen of Sinemorye to ask them to help the Volga. I'm afraid that it will soon be worse here than it was then in the Volga. Worse, and there will be nowhere to turn to for help. No one cares for Sinemorye's fate!"

"Mustafa," sighed Nasyr. "I'm listening to you and thinking why people as clever as you aren't sent abroad so that they can spread the truth about us. It would've been better if you went to America instead of Yekor."

"No, thank you," Slavikov replied crossly. "Americans are not stupid; they'll work out what's what. I don't think messages about the leading role of the party in engineering progress will mean much there. I'm needed more here. Anyway, they wouldn't let me go to America, Nasyr, my friend. People like Yegor have correct and clean records, and that is their truth. Do you know how much my own record has been blemished by life?"

After seeing his guests off on the cutter, Nasyr sat on the shore, immersed in thought. He felt the breath of approaching trouble after Sharaev's departure. The trouble wasn't close yet, just a wisp of blue-gray cloud over the sea in the distance. But an hour passed, then another, and soon the whole sky above Kokteniz-Sinemorye turned black.

And Nasyr flinched as he imagined the entire storm.

"There's the car!" Sayat closed the hood and called his friend gently. "Do you hear, Kakharman?"

Kakharman was standing on the brink of Karaadyr with his face bared to the dry, burning wind. The car with his wife and children was already close.

"Sayat," Kakharman said, "you and I don't need to speak. I'm leaving without hiding anything from you. But I think you understand."

"Yes," Sayat responded.

The Zhiguli stopped, and Aitugan and the children climbed up to meet Kakharman. Kakharman hugged her and his sons and then turned toward the sea and said, "Children, there is the land of your forefathers. There is our homeland. There is Sinemorye. No matter where life takes you, never forget it. Because a man lives through his homeland." He had a lump in his throat. "Take a handful of this soil so it will always be with you."

Aitugan and the children each carefully folded a little clump of earth in little handkerchiefs. The native earth!

Kakharman had told no one where he was going. He had left everyone at the dastarkhan, gone and bought tickets, and returned to the table without a word.

The cars left them at the station, and they boarded the train. While the train shunted, Kakharman changed into jeans and left the compartment. After putting the children to sleep, Aitugan followed. They peered through the window at the darkening sands.

"Do you know where we're going?" Kakharman asked.

"It doesn't matter," Aitugan sighed. "I've never stood in your way. I just need you to be alive and well." She rested her head on his shoulder. "You decide, and the children and I will follow. I trust you completely."

"I knew you'd understand." He stroked her shoulders. "We're going to Alma-Ata. You'll live there while I go off and look for work. What matters now is that we get as far from here as possible. It's going to be hard but much easier than watching the sea die, than hearing its last moans . . . I . . ." He unbuttoned the collar of his shirt as he choked from the sadness that swept over him. "I can't . . . Go, you should get some rest. I'll stay alone for a bit."

Aitugan nodded and went back to the compartment. And here, too, she at last let go, burying her face in the pillow and weeping.

Home was behind.

Ahead lay uncertainty . . .

V

The rain poured nonstop for over a month, never easing even for an hour. It seemed as if the snows of Pamir and Tian Shan had entirely thawed in answer to Nasyr's prayer. And they drove their roaring, gushing, frothing waters toward the sea, sweeping away concrete dams on their way.

Five times a day, Nasyr mounted his horse and rode to the shore to shout his gratitude to the merciful sky. And now the sea was within walking distance for even the most elderly aqsaqal. The stranded shore, marks of old bays, and hollows of lagoons were all now full of water. The waves splashed right up to Karaoi. Fish frolicked there too. Large belugas, catfish—even sturgeons. Where had they come from? For Nasyr, it was now a joy to pray.

Yet when he was chosen to become a mullah, he started his new duties with a heavy heart, even though he realized an aul couldn't live without a mullah. Life went on as usual. Children were born. The old died. Sometimes weddings happened. At first, he didn't know by heart any of the prayers to Allah to bless people for their earthly deeds. Korlan took Nasyr's role as mullah completely in earnest, even though he often grinned while praying.

Nasyr and Korlan spent a lot of time studying prayers, poring over the intricate pages of the Quran, trying to understand and memorize everything that a proper clergyman should know. Korlan was unswerving in her demands on Nasyr: "Never miss prayer. You are not allowed! Ordinary people may sometimes forget Allah, but the mullah must remember every single minute."

In the end, Korlan got her way. Although Nasyr didn't wear a turban, he did pray the customary way. Indeed, after Kakharman left, prayer became his support. He often spoke with the Most High about his son and found comfort in these conversations.

And now with his prayers he had achieved something unprecedented. The shore was shining with the mercy of Allah! A fortnight of rain, and the sea has already delivered, unfurling its generous wings along the whole shore. The fishermen's nets emerged heavily laden. And Nasyr walked through Karaoi, telling everyone he met, "There it is! The power of prayer! Here is the sea in front of you, just as long ago. Come out of your house, and you'll see it's here."

"May Allah bless you," people replied. "May God give your children happiness, Nasyr."

Soon the elders slaughtered a ram and thanked both Allah and Nasyr. Toward evening people came to his house with offerings. Someone brought a sheep and tied it to his fence, and someone brought a calf. Another brought half of a saiga carcass. And some people even brought jewelry. They spread a white shawl in the yard and laid everything—gold and silver rings, bracelets, earrings—on it. Then they nailed a pole to his roof and tied a white cloth to it. According to Kazakh custom, that meant that a holy man lived there.

Nasyr, pulling *chiriki* slippers on, was perplexed. "What's going on? Why are all these people here?"

"They are waiting for you, Granddad."

"And what do they want from me?"

Baffled, Nasyr stepped over the entrance and gasped when he saw livestock tied to the fence and a pile of goods in the middle of the yard. "Hey, kind people, what sort of bazaar is here?" he exclaimed. "What more suffering do you want to subject me to, when I've already got one foot in the grave?"

People replied respectfully, "These are the donations we must give any mullah. It would be a sin for you to reject them."

Nasyr burst out again, "But I think I'll take more sins on my soul if I don't reject them. Take everything back immediately! How do you think I could look in your eyes after this, you half-wits?"

He strode right out into the yard, grabbed the oars, and ordered his grandson, "Berish, get Yesen here, and let's go into the sea before it gets dark."

"Look!" Berish yelled, pointing toward the shore. A herd of mares was bowling across the shore, pursued by a fiery sorrel stallion with a long mane and tail. The rippling curve of the stallion's back seemed to burst into flame as it caught the crimson rays of the setting sun.

"What a beauty!" Yesen exclaimed. "It's been a while since they appeared, Nasyr-aga—not since they led away Musa's raven-black!"

Berish stood up, dropping his oars. "I can see him. The raven! There he is. Look!"

But Nasyr was busy sorting out the nets. Berish and Yesen watched silently, until Berish burst out, "Granddad, it looks like he's gotten our ash-gray!"

"Where? Where?" Nasyr shuddered and left the net to look. At that exact moment, a gunshot cracked, and a horseman sped toward the herd.

"It's Musa!"

"Yes," Nasyr murmured. Then he shouted, even though it was unlikely Musa could hear him from such a distance. "Musa, run straight! Drive the ash-gray away! Away!"

When it noticed the riders, the fiery sorrel switched direction, and the herd followed. The ash-gray began to fall behind. Realizing he was losing his prize, the sorrel abruptly stopped, pitching sharply into the ground with his hooves. Then he snorted in anger and moved toward his rival. Musa's double-barreled gun boomed again. The sorrel stallion reared up, held his pose for some seconds, then turned back toward the setting sun and led the rest of the herd away.

"Congratulations!" Yesen cheered. "Musa-aga got your ash-gray back."

Nasyr began to admonish his grandson. "Don't joke about this sorrel. We must never let our mare out of the yard or leave the gate open."

"People say he led Akbalak's mare away right in front of his eyes. How could that happen?" Yesen asked.

"That is what Akbalak said himself," Nasyr answered. "He says he saw it all from the window. The mare was in a hobble, but the sorrel kicked it off easily with his hoof. Akbalak says he never saw a stallion more beautiful or more wild. I asked Akbalak why he just watched. You should've driven the stallion off! But Akbalak said the stallion only bit his mare on her withers a few times, and she followed him as if bewitched. For Akbalak, it was a moment of magic! I understand. Only a poet can sacrifice a mare for the fleeting beauty of her abduction. Could an ordinary man do this?"

After setting the nets, the fishermen headed back to the shore. As they dragged the boat out of the water, Kyzbala walked past them, followed by a goat with its kid. Usually, the madwoman would stare and murmur something unintelligibly. But today she paid no attention to them. The white fustian dress was hanging better on her than usual, and her hair was done up in a neat knot. "Even Kyzbala has changed in these happy days!" Nasyr exclaimed.

"Have you noticed," Yesen noted, "how the wild horses shy away from most people but are not afraid of Kyzbala?"

"Alright," said Nasyr. "Go home, you two. I'm staying here for a while."

As the boys came up to the aul, they saw Zhanyl running toward them. "Something's happened to my mother," Yesen murmured, handing Berish the oars and rushing toward her. "Apa![1] What's happened?"

Zhanyl didn't answer. She just hugged her son and ran with him toward the house.

In the yard, Berish saw Musa engaged in a lively conversation with Korlan.

"Where's your granddad?" Korlan asked.

"He stayed on the shore."

"Run and get him. We nearly had a catastrophe here!"

"It's OK now," Musa said and went off to fetch Nasyr himself.

Korlan gradually calmed down and began to bustle around her grandson.

"Would you like *shubat*, little lamb? Then let's go into the house, and I will feed you."

Berish sat at the table and eagerly ate everything old Korlan put in front of him. At last, she sat opposite him, leaning her cheeks on her hands, and sighed. "I guess you miss your mom and dad?"

"And my brothers too," Berish added.

"Now you'll go home only when it's time to go to school."

"Grandma, you're originally from Semipalatinsk, aren't you?" Berish finished chewing and waited for Korlan to respond.

"Yes, from Semipalatinsk. But how did you know?"

"Granddad told me."

"You'll go there in autumn. We'll be happy if it works out for you all. You should help your father. You're grown-up now. It'll be hard for him in a foreign land. It's a pity none of my relatives are still there. They could've helped. But they all died in the hungry year. I'm the only one who survived."

"Tell me more, Grandma!"

"Your granddad and his mother saved me, may she rest in peace."

"Grandma, where did it come from, this hunger?"

"Where from?"

Korlan considered the question awhile, adjusting the platok on her head.

"Where all troubles come from, maybe? Man creates them for himself. The Kazakhs of Sary-Arka didn't work the land; they made their living raising cattle. But all their cattle were taken away.[2] There was no bread, and then there were no cattle. How were they supposed to live? People headed to the cities in desperation, but it was no better there. Many people didn't even reach the cities, dying of hunger on the way. The steppe was full of corpses. There was a horrible stench . . ."

Korlan forgot Berish, stared into the distance, and then came back to her senses. "But where's Granddad gone? Where has he gone off to?" She stood up, and Berish followed her.

Yesen's heifer was still tied to the fence. "Why hasn't Yesen taken it back? Granddad did tell him . . ." Berish was surprised.

"Untie the animal and take it to them. Zhanyl has other things to worry about, I guess. That daughter-in-law of hers has abandoned them and slunk back to the city. People say she's gone forever. How shameless!"

"Saule has gone?" Berish was astonished.

"So her name was Saule? Then, yes, her. What a silly girl. Women are not what they used to be. She was constantly complaining. Apparently, she couldn't carry water with a yoke. What a *khansha*!"[3]Helping untie the heifer, the old woman told Berish, "Zhanyl should just spit it all out and not grieve. Tell her that Korlan invites her for tea. And you stay with Yesen. It'll be hard on him."

Berish found Yesen sitting by the gate. Berish untied the rope and took the cow into the barn, then sat next to his friend.

"Where's your mother?"

"Why do you need her?"

"Grandma invited her for tea."

"Your granddad and grandma are good people. Apa!" he shouted into an open door. "Korlan-apa has invited you for tea."

Zhanyl didn't answer. A child's cry could be heard, and Zhanyl was saying, "Sleep, little one, sleep."

"She left her child?" Berish was astonished.

"I see you already know," Yesen said. "Our aul is like a wireless telephone network in action."

Zhanyl started to walk out of the house with the child in her arms.

"She's so cruel!" she cursed. "She could at least have waited until she'd stopped breastfeeding! But no, she just dumped her and that's it!"

"It's alright, Ma. We'll bring her up on camel's milk. She'll grow up to be a *bogatyr!*"[4] He touched his daughter on the nose, and the baby began to whine again. Zhanyl rocked her to sleep.

"I didn't bring you up on camel's milk, did I?" she said. "I think I should go to Korlan."

"Why did she run away?" asked Berish.

"Do you think any normal person can live here?" Zhanyl shrugged. "She's from the city. She's used to running water and toilets that flush. I can't say I blame her, but it is harsh to abandon an infant."

"But who the fuck knows?" Yesen exclaimed. "Maybe it's for the best that she's gone. People say that now even our women's milk is poisoned."

"What!" Berish exclaimed.

"In Shumgen, many infants die, and doctors even forbid the breastfeeding of babies. How did we end up here, eh? Mothers killing their own children! Has anything like this happened before? My mother took the baby to our neighbor, but Kuralai also refused to feed her. She recently lost her one-year-old son. She says he was poisoned by her milk."

"And will your girl live?"

"I don't know, Berish. If I'm perfectly honest, I don't know . . ."

The PA in the center of the aul came on with the latest news.[5] WHALE ATTACK. OFF THE SOUTHWEST COAST OF ENGLAND, A YACHT was attacked by whales. Local coast guards managed to save only one of the crew. Experts say such attacks are very unusual.

THE AIDS EPIDEMIC REACHES CRITICAL LEVELS among the young, the poor, women, and many ethnic minorities. In the next four years, 200,000 people in the US will die of AIDS. According to official statistics, 66,493 have died from AIDS in the US since June.

DRUG BARONS THREATEN NOT only Colombian officials but also the US administration directly. Terrorists warn of attacks on President Bush's family if Washington doesn't wind down its war on drugs.

MISSILES STRIKE KABUL. Twenty rockets hit the Afghan capital. The rockets were aimed at extremist-held residential areas. Artillery batteries of the Eleventh Army Corps of the armed forces of Pakistan took part in the bombardment.

THE MOSCOW INTERNAL AFFAIRS MINISTRY releases annual crime statistics. In the city, a total of twenty thousand crimes were recorded. Major financial frauds were more frequent. During the past year, there were 155 cases of racketeering, and 13 armed assaults on foreigners at Sheremetyevo Airport were neutralized.

AT 14:30 MOSCOW TIME IN THE SOVIET UNION, an underground nuclear explosion with a power of 20 kilotons occurred in the Polygon test site near Semipalatinsk. This trial was carried out to improve military equipment.

A JOINT NUCLEAR TRIAL WAS CARRIED OUT on Friday morning on the test site in Nevada State by the US and UK. The strength of the explosion was between 20 and 150 kilotons.

CASPIAN MILITARY FLOTILLA TRAGEDY. A POWERFUL landslide struck a number of buildings in the flotilla's military town. The avalanche destroyed the area in seconds. Twenty-eight sailors were buried alive.

PROTEST AGAINST THE CONSTRUCTION of the Volga–Chograi Canal. "To not allow a new ecological crime was the theme of meetings and gatherings that took place in various towns."

WITH THE LAUNCH OF SPECIAL balloons with machines to create ozone, an English group of environmentalists is hoping to restore the ozone layer over Antarctica.

IN THE HEART OF THE AMAZONIAN RAIN FOREST, fifty Indian tribes that have never seen a white person still survive, Brazilian scientists and anthropologists claim.

AN AMERICAN SPACESHIP WEIGHING 2.5 tons is expected to fall to Earth this month.

DROUGHT AFFECTS WESTERN US. In some states, drinking-water resources declined sharply. In Los Angeles and San Francisco, severe restrictions on water usage were introduced.

THICK CLOUDS OF VOLCANIC ASH COVERED the Japanese city of Kagoshima on Kyushu Island, turning day into night. For over two days, the city has been bombarded by the volcano Sakurajima, five miles to the southwest, one of the most active volcanoes in the Far East.

EVENING DISTURBANCES ROCK THE CAPITAL of Moldova. Between 150 and 200 people were shouting insults and threats toward police and bandied antigovernment slogans and posters. Mass disturbances resulted in harsh consequences. Eighty-three police officers were injured, more than forty of the protesters were taken to the medical institutions, and serious damage was caused to the building of MIA (Ministry of Internal Affairs).

THE PROTEST MARCH OF THE REPRESENTATIVES of the people of Tatarstan against the construction of the Tatar atomic power station enters its third day. The route of the march, which began by the walls of Kazan Federal University, went through Naberezhnye Chelny and finished at the construction site in Kamskie Polyany.

SULPHURETED HYDROGEN HAS BEEN DISCHARGED INTO THE ATMOSPHERE FOUR TIMES IN THE LAST FOUR DAYS by the Orenburg gas processing plant. The result has been mass poisoning of the residents of nearby residential areas.

Nasyr lingered by the sea. The refreshed water was inviting him for a conversation.

A brisk north wind blew up, and soon the sea was flecked with ripples.

"Why are you so thoughtful, Nasyr? Are you troubled by some sadness?" the sea asked quietly.

"There's no sadness in my heart. It was rejoicing for days. And it is rejoicing now. I just decided to take a rest on your shore after the boys and I set the nets."

"They will be full, Nasyr. Don't worry. I will give generously. You gave me my life back with your prayers to Allah. I will never forget. You can pull the nets out. They are already full."

"I know your generosity. Thank you. We have spent our whole lives on your shore, and we could never forget your kindness. We will never abandon you. No matter how far a man is taken from you, all his thoughts come back to you. I will tell you one ancient story. Do you remember the times of the Huns?"

The sea interrupted Nasyr. "Many say it is just a legend. You, I see, believe it. I swear to you there's not a single word of fiction in this legend. All of it is pure truth! And I am a witness to it. Listen!"

The Persians conquered my people to make them slaves. They stole cattle, crossed the Darya, and were already approaching the white-headed mountain when an injured and bleeding dzhigit reached my shore, washed his wounds, donned his helmet, sat on a fiery-maned stallion, and then galloped after the enemy army. In the herd of wild horses that came running to me today, there is a fiery stallion with a white mark on its forehead. This is the sign of a unique ancient breed. Only here in the world will you ever see such a fiery-maned stallion.

So Nasyr the dzhigit mounted a stallion exactly like that and galloped after the enemy army. He soon caught up and announced that he wished to speak to the Persian king. The king was amused to see a warrior riding alone right into the midst of an army one hundred thousand strong. "Bring him to me!" the king commanded. And the handsome warrior with a hawk nose and strong chest was brought before the king. The warrior began to talk to the king boldly, equal to equal.

"King, you brutally attacked a peaceful people and took their sons into slavery. You are a victor. I have only one request: be magnanimous as it befits a victor."

But the king was barely listening to the warrior, so astonished he was by the fiery stallion with a mark on its forehead. The stallion was stamping impatiently and stood on its hind legs, yet the warrior stayed on its back with ease.

"What a fine stallion!" the king exclaimed. "Would you like to give him to me?"

The warrior dismounted, and soldiers rushed to the fiery-maned stallion and brought him to the king.

"Tell me your wish. It will be granted!" the king commanded.

"You have captured my best friend. Grant him life, and in return take anything you wish from me."

"Anything I wish?" The king smiled. "And if I wish to take your eyes?"

The warrior, who had never gone back on his words, replied, "I agree, king!" The king set the captured dzhigit free, and the brave warrior had his eyes gouged.

The two warriors, supporting each other, made their way to me with difficulty and washed their wounds. The fiery-maned stallion refused to give in to the enemy and returned to the sea just a few days later. And he wasn't alone. He brought with him a herd of horses. The brave warrior hugged his loyal horse and asked his friend if the fiery-maned stallion's eyes were intact.

"They are intact," his friend answered.

"If the eyes of both of you are intact, then I have nothing to grieve about, my friends!" the brave warrior said. "Live and be happy!"

The sea went silent and then added, "I can tell many stories. Many amazing things happened on my shores."

"We also remember this legend," Nasyr replied. "That's why we do not want to abandon you, even when we are in trouble. You are vital to us, like a mother! And you are entitled to demand help from us, your people."

By now darkness had entirely covered the shore, so the old man headed home. There, he threw off his rubber boots, washed his face, and sat at the table.

Musa arrived and said from the door, "I was about to look for you on the shore, but I realized that I shouldn't interrupt your conversation." He sat at the table. "You don't know anything. I only just managed to save your ash-gray. The fiery-maned stallion has appeared again in our lands, and he is taking mares away again."

"I saw everything from the sea. Thank you for saving the ash-gray. You still didn't manage to get your raven-black back?"

"It's like witchcraft! The fiery-maned stallion bewitched him like a child. The raven-black follows his every step. He would hear my voice and prick up his ears, but his friend is always right there, rubbing him with his side, and the raven-black forgets about me completely. How bold that fiery-maned stallion is, and how reckless. He even went against me today. My dog rushed to protect me, and the stallion killed it with a single blow of a hoof. That's what he's like! I should've shot him, but I can't take this sin on my soul. I met him for the first time three years ago on the western shore. He had only a single mare with him back then. Now he has a harem!" Musa was talking angrily, rolling his tubeteika cap in his hands and waving his arms.

"Yes, such things are," Nasyr said slowly. After eating, he was tired. He was thinking he should end the conversation and go to sleep if he was to be up at dawn to wake the boys and go out to sea.

"It looks to me," Musa continued crossly, "that we'll know no peace until the fiery-maned stallion takes your ash-gray. She, by the way, is not indifferent to him. I saw it today for myself."

"Ya, Allah!" Korlan, who had been silent until now, joined in. "We'll have to keep her locked up."

"Hold her or not, but this demon will not rest until he takes her away. I swear!"

"I will simply slaughter her!" Nasyr lost his temper. "Then we will see who he'll take away!"

Musa waved his hand. "Why slaughter her? What about the foal?"

The old men went on thinking for a moment.

Korlan lost her temper. "As if it matters, you two fools, when such things are happening to the sea! If he wants to take her away, let it be! Even with the foal, if he's so shameless!"

Musa, in order to cover his own awkwardness, changed the subject. "The day before yesterday, I was in the district center. They say that Kakharman has already left Balkhash. Looks like he's headed to the Irtysh, to Semipalatinsk. Nasyr, what have you heard?"

This was news to Nasyr and Korlan, and Korlan could only stretch out her arms in bewilderment.

"We haven't had any letters from them for a month," Berish responded for them.

"If Kakharman didn't stay at Balkhash, it means that things are not going well there either," Musa suggested.

"Where did you say he headed to?" Nasyr asked.

"People say the Irtysh."

"I've heard that our Hero of Socialist Labor Orazbek also settled somewhere there." Nasyr passed the *piala*[6] to his wife. "I can't get my head around it. How can a man who grew up by the sea swap it for a small river or a lake?"

"That is why Kakharman, my light, my sunshine, struggles." Korlan sighed. "If I could visit him, if only for a day, but you will not let me." She looked at the men with reproach.

"I guess Orazbek also longs for the sea. Do you remember the district chief who came here recently?" Musa looked at Nasyr questioningly. "He was saying Orazbek regrets leaving the sea."

"They run away like cockroaches." Nasyr became melancholy and looked sharply at his friend. "Why are you trying so hard to get your raven-black back? Are you planning on rolling away from here too?"

"How did you guess?" Nasyr's question had caught Musa off guard.

"I saw that you packed up a bit in your yard and around the house."

Musa began to laugh. "You barely have a chance to think about something before they know all about it! But seriously, answer me this: Let us suppose everyone else does leave the shore. Do you think you and I could stay here alone?"

"Yes, I'll stay," Nasyr said firmly. "I don't know about you, but Korlan and I will stay. Our people are ignorant, Musa. I won this downpour from Allah by prayer, and Allah has given us hope to rise again. Why don't they cherish this hope? Why are they like a flock of sheep that keep running and running without thinking? What if everything turns out OK?"

He thought about Kakharman for a long time before he fell asleep that night. Why had his son left Balkhash and headed for the Irtysh? Why abandon his homeland? OK, he hadn't found a way of talking to the authorities here, but why make this last step so quickly? Maybe Nasyr and Korlan should not have given him their permission when Kakharman came to ask for their blessing to leave! And now he'll struggle. God forbid he loses his sanity. Of course, it was hard for him there. His life was not working out. Korlan wants to go to see her son. Maybe he should let her go. Maybe a son will listen more to his mother's words? Maybe he should let them both go, Korlan and Berish, in autumn, and perhaps they'll bring Kakharman to his senses.

Sholpan, the morning star, had already rolled out of the sky when Nasyr finally closed his eyes and gave in to sleep—an unstable and restless sleep. Nasyr felt no satisfaction from his decision to let Korlan and Berish go. He didn't really believe his son would come back.

And he didn't sleep long. Someone was knocking persistently on the window, and Nasyr hurriedly got up.

"It's me, Kambar! Something weird has happened, Nasyr! There's a *sagan*[7] of fish in the bay. Bektemis is already there. He sent me to get everyone. There's at least twenty or twenty-five hundred weight of fish! We'll salt it right here."

Kambar ran off, and Nasyr began to get ready.

Kambar wasn't exaggerating. An immense quantity of fish had built up in the bay. Nasyr tasted the water and wasn't surprised. The water was good. So that's the reason. Fish were drawn toward the clear water and ended up trapped in the narrow creeks.

The fishermen worked energetically. By noon, they'd hauled in a huge load. But then they found they'd need more barrels and salt. They threw unpacked fish back into water with spades. But the fish quickly suffocated, and the water was soon packed with dying fish. The people's joy was short-lived. They berated Bektemis, who had gone for more barrels and salt an hour ago yet had still not returned.

Looking at the lifeless heap of fish, Nasyr suddenly remembered an event that had seemed weird at the time.

It was the year Slavikov came with his expedition for the first time. One chilly autumn day, Nasyr was rowing toward Akespe Island, where Slavikov's laboratory was located. Suddenly, close by the left side of the boat, he noticed a huge beluga. It was behaving very strangely. It swam next to the boat and seemed to look at Nasyr. Then it disappeared, only to emerge on the other side of the boat and ram hard into it. The boat rocked so violently that Nasyr fell overboard.

Nasyr had never heard of a fish attacking a boat before. Nasyr was dressed in thick clothes that grew heavy right away, and he started to sink fast. With a great struggle, he rolled back into the boat, but the beluga rammed the boat again. Nasyr struggled to keep the boat balanced. The big fish stayed with him all the way to the island. Sometimes it would put its head out of the water. As he neared Akespe, Nasyr waited for the right moment, then walloped the fish on the head with a wooden mallet. The fish's inertia took it past him and away. When Nasyr set off for the return journey, he was half expecting it to avenge the blow, but he never did see that wild beluga again.

He told the professor what happened. Slavikov asked one of his laboratory assistants to write the story down. That's when it became clear to Nasyr that something was going on in the sea. "When the level of water decreases," the professor explained, "the concentration of salt in the water begins to increase. Some kinds of fish sense the smallest changes in the water, and their behavior becomes erratic. And that's all there is to it. But with time, the new models of behavior develop." He meant that after a time, fish get used to saltier water.

"What other options do they have?" Nasyr grinned joylessly.

After a short midday rest, Nasyr and the boys set out to sea again. Anxious to see what was happening with the nets, they rowed hard. The nets were completely full! To pull them in, they had to wedge their legs and pull with all their strength. Nasyr joyously shouted to Yesen, who could normally pull the net single-handed.

"Hey, boy, I think you'd better get used to this! It's your turn to work now. No catch all year, perfect for staying home and looking after your wife. You did stay home, but there was no wife, eh?"

"I turned out to be of the wrong rank, Moldeke! I don't have a flush toilet!"

Life was boiling up across the whole coast. Fishermen were rushing in to the shore with a catch, emptying the nets, then hurrying back out again. Farther west, the evening shadows fell sooner, and the fish headed into the nets quicker.

Sitting in the boat and wiping sweat off his forehead, Nasyr was looking calmly over the shore. His gaze fell upon a huge trawler that had been stranded in the sand many years ago. Water didn't quite reach it, stopping short only a stone's throw away. This perplexed Nasyr. "Oipyrmai!" he exclaimed. "It poured for a whole month, yet water still doesn't reach the trawler." Doubt began to creep into his mind. "Is it possible?" He was scared to think about it. "Is it possible that the sea will not come back to its original shores? Can it be out of even Allah's control?"

Yes! That is how it was!

Nasyr looked around sadly.

"Granddad, there's some kind of cutter!" Berish shook Nasyr from his thoughts. "Do you think they are looking for us?"

"Quite possibly." Yesen also began to watch the cutter.

The cutter stopped for a while by the farthest boat, then began to move toward them.

"Who are they?" Nasyr put his hat on.

"Hey, that's Samat!" Yesen guessed. "Head of Progress. He's a funny guy; he gobbles meat like a Kazakh. But he talks to Kazakhs only in Russian and through interpreters."

Indeed, it was Samat Samatovich, the manager of the local Ministry of Progress. There were a few men with him.

"Hello!" Samat Samatovich shouted to them and gave the order to stop the motor.

"*As-salamu alaykum*, Nasyr-aga!" shouted a fair-haired young man whose face looked familiar to Nasyr. "Nasyr-aga, I am Igor Slavikov!" The youth waved his hand, guessing that Nasyr didn't recognize him.

Nasyr's tired face lit up.

"Ikor! Ikor-zhan!" Nasyr leaned toward him. Igor stepped into Nasyr's boat, and they embraced.

"How is your father, Ikor-zhan? Is he alive? Why didn't he come?" Nasyr squeezed Igor warmly.

"Dad sends you a big hello," Igor said in Kazakh. "He salutes you all."

"You forgot us," Nasyr reproached the boy.

"Well, here I am, Nasyr-aga. Now we'll be together. Why has Kakharman left Sinemorye?"

"It's a long story," Nasyr sighed, sat down, and gestured for Igor to sit next to him.

"Igor Matveevich, we have little time," Samat Samatovich urged Igor. "Maybe you two can talk later at home?"

"Wait, Samat, let me talk to the man!" Igor raised his eyebrows, intimating that he found Samat Samatovich a pain.

"Kakharman couldn't stand living alongside people like that," Nasyr whispered, pointing his finger at Samat.

Samat lingered awhile, resting his fat stomach on the cutter's board, then joined the young scientists who arrived with Slavikov.

"These young people are with you?" Nasyr asked.

"Yes. They are eager to fight."

"Where are you staying?"

"Still on Akespe Island. Our job is to map the new coast. Can I request for you to join us if your health permits?" Nasyr remained silent, and Igor added, "It is not so much my request as my father's."

"Well, if Mustafa himself asks, how can I refuse?"

Samat urged Slavikov into action.

"Igor Matveevich, we need to go! In the morning I have the Bureau of the Regional Committee. You have that . . ." He began to search for the right word and clumsily added, "That lethal laboratory. You get me?"

"What do you mean 'lethal' laboratory?" The strange word unnerved Nasyr.

A young woman standing next to Samat answered bluntly, "We are here to observe the death of your sea."

Slavikov glared at the girl and jumped into the cutter. Then turning to Nasyr, who was sitting in shock in his boat, he said quietly, "Nasyr-aga, tomorrow I will come to pick you up."

The motor started.

"Do you have a mechanic here?" Samat shouted out.

"I am a mechanic," Yesen replied.

"Then come with us, mechanic. Help us start the laboratory's engine. It's developed a fault."

Yesen climbed into the cutter. The light boat gained speed quickly and whirled away. Nasyr stood up and looked after it for a long time.

"So Granddad, shall we go home?" Berish said.

Nasyr nodded, still dumbstruck.

Nasyr and Berish pulled the boat onto the shore. Nasyr noticed that there were fewer people on the shore and in the sea. He looked up at the sky. It was getting dark. Heavy black rain clouds were gathering over Sinemorye again. Nasyr absentmindedly took a white platok shawl out of an inner pocket, laid it out, and began the evening prayer. With the whole power of his feeling, with all his thought, he concentrated on Allah. The day had awoken many doubts in Nasyr's soul. But he continued to believe in Allah and now shared all his doubts with him in prayer.

When he finished, he walked to the sea, scooped up some water in his hands, and rinsed his face. He then stood straight and smiled. "I'll show you 'death of the sea'!"

A few large rain drops splashed on the ground. Within minutes, the downpour had become powerful and relentless. It began to overwhelm Nasyr with its sheer intensity. He tore off his clothes and yelled over the roar of the rain, "Pour! Pour! I will show them the 'death of the sea'!"

The rain poured seven days and seven nights without stopping. The sea, tired of salty water, was in a state of bliss—filling again with sweet, fresh water borne by the two Daryas, which were engorged by snows melting on the peaks of far Tian Shan and Pamir. No one on that shore could have been happier than Nasyr!

Well, hello, reviving sea, hello! Aren't you a miracle? You are man's joy and man's grief! For thousands and thousands of years, Nasyr's ancestors bowed their heads before your might. And now Nasyr bows his head, silently listening to your music, hearing in this music the deep and ancient sounds of your mysteries.

VI

The first secretary of the Regional Committee, Kozha Aldiyarov, was unusually irritated. The tea in the white teapot set by his assistant on the polished table had gone cold. He sat back in the soft armchair and thought deeply. Deep thinking did not come naturally to him. Aldiyarov was a party functionary and needed only to think of a few things, mostly dictated by the need for self-preservation.

He ordered a fresh brew of tea.

"That's it. Decided. It's time to end Nasyrov's trips to Moscow! He must be forced to crawl. Little cur! What a fool to undermine Kozha Aldiyarov. You will be destroyed!"

He called for the chairman of the Regional Executive Committee. Galym Erzhanov came in with Aldiyarov's assistant, who was carrying the tea tray. After two sips of tea, Aldiyarov glanced grimly at the chairman and brusquely invited him to sit down.

Erzhanov quickly saw Aldiyarov's mood. "Old Creaky Bones is angry. He's clearly planning some nastiness. I must be careful not to lose my study ticket to Moscow. What if he says I can't go? The old man changes his mind ten times a day. Today, yes; tomorrow, no."

People in the oblast were afraid of Aldiyarov. He was a quick-tempered and petty tyrant. Erzhanov was frequently told that Aldiyarov had a grudge against the whole world due to his many years in exile in the dead-end western oblast.

Old Creaky Bones was as shamelessly harsh on his subordinates as he was obliging to his superiors. An inveterate ass-kisser, he surrounded himself with other ass-kissers. Aldiyarov quickly figured out who had a thick wallet and who didn't. And so all regional positions were sold. The practical and talented team that Akatov had assembled over three years with so much effort was thrown out. And now there was just one of them left: Kakharman.

"Have you heard what Nasyrov[1] is up to in Moscow?" Aldiyarov asked Erzhanov.

"No."

"That's odd. I thought you were in close contact with him." He gave Erzhanov a meaningful look.

Erzhanov looked down.

"A close contact doesn't always mean knowledge of plans and intentions." This answer sounded evasive, so he added, "Kakharman Nasyrovich plays his cards close to his chest and is always so unpredictable, Kozha Aldiyarovich . . ."

"So you don't know? Then listen! During the last meeting in the Ministry of Progress, he insisted that there was no need to divert the Siberian rivers! I found out about this today. I had a phone call from the CC. Is this a joke? Doesn't he understand that without the Siberian rivers, Sinemorye will die? Or hasn't he a clue how much hard work the leadership of the Republic put into this plan? But this is only half of the problem. The real issue is that Nasyrov's words have reached Kunaev.[2] Can you imagine what Kunaev will think about me? His first thought will be that I deliberately sent Nasyrov to Moscow. How will I be able to prove it's not true?"

"Kunaev put a lot of work into the diversion of the rivers, it is true. The situation is turning out to be rather ridiculerrs." Erzhanov's affectation was genuine.

"Ridiculerrs!" Aldiyarov mimicked. "It's a stab in the back for both Kunaev and for me! I have to convene the bureau tomorrow and get Nasyrov thrown out. He should not go to Moscow!"

"Kozha Aldiyarovich! Nasyrov lost his cool from the moment Sinemorye was put in danger. He was fighting Moscow's ministries pretty much on his own for repair shops and a boatyard on the shore after all the local fishermen were left without work and were forced to emigrate to find fish and work. We should perhaps consider Nasyrov's administrative ability. After all, these troubles won't be the last ones. And Nasyrov has the knack of solving the most complicated problems set by Moscow. And, there's no one to replace him right now, Kozha Aldiyarovich."

"What are you trying to say?" Aldiyarov interrupted him impatiently.

"I'm just saying it won't be easy. Nasyrov has influence with the people."

"Maybe you're wrong. People don't care about Nasyrov! They're just waiting for Siberian water! If they find out there's no Siberian water, they'll leave—all of them!"

"They've been leaving for some time now."

"Immigrants are leaving: Russians, Germans, Ukrainians. That's the truth as the saying goes. Nowadays, it's Russians that have become nomads. They're looking for warm places, easy money. But where would a Kazakh go? He doesn't have any other homeland but Kazakhia[3] and won't go anywhere else. That's why we need Siberian water. It's not Brezhnev and Kunaev who dreamed it up. It's a real problem that has been worked through by scientists and is supported by the ministries. The state needs cotton. It may damage the fisheries, I agree. But cotton needs water, Galym Erzhanov!"

"People talk a lot about Siberian water nowadays. In the summer, I was listening to the arguments of Professor Slavikov; they sounded very convincing to me."

"Slavikov has lost his mind, and Nasyrov plays along!"

"It seems he knows Kunaev well . . ."

"Of course he does. Kunaev is a great man. The whole world knows him. And who knows Slavikov? Who listens to his opinion?"

Erzhanov replied patiently, "When I went to Moscow, I learned that he is very well-known in the Institute of Geography and in many ministries. Many are even afraid of Slavikov."

"Everyone should be afraid of that crazy man! He's got voices in his head!"

Erzhanov realized it was pointless to argue anymore. He stood up.

"Think about Nasyrov. Do you understand?" Aldiyarov said.

"That you have decided to revoke Nasyrov's party membership?"

"For the time being, we'll just remove him from his job. We should start tactfully. He is a proud man. He'll understand and will leave on his own accord."

After Erzhanov got back to his office, he tried a few times to pick up the phone and dial Kakharman's number, but he hadn't the nerve. If Old Creaky Bones found out, he'd be in the shit. "So now you've ended up cautious and prudent, just what you despised so much in others," he thought joylessly. Galym hated himself. He admired Kakharman, yet here he was, abandoning him to his fate. Everyone knew people like Kakharman were rare. Wasn't it his duty to save him? Of course it was. What a shame, then, that Erzhanov was going away to

Moscow to study. Otherwise, he would've fought Aldiyarov. But . . . his wife has been sitting on the suitcases for a long time now. She can't wait to live in the capital forever, and family is what truly matters.

But would he have really fought? What's the point of lying to yourself? Kakharman will be kicked out, and Erzhanov will go quietly to study in the KGB Academy. A future general. That is the psychology of his generation, a generation that grew up in fear. It lives with caution. In the bureau, he is destined to be one of those who won't say a word in favor of Kakharman. Each time he is about to stand up and do it, the knocking of his knees and the dryness in his throat stops him, and he sits down with his head hanging low.

The reason for the urgency of the meeting of the Bureau of the Regional Committee was obvious. Fish production was falling well below projections. Nasyrov's report was heard. Kakharman explained candidly why the plan was failing. In his version, the situation in Sinemorye was threatening not just the fish economy of the region but the Republic as a whole. He also said that many scientists who were involved in this grand project of reversing the Siberian rivers from the beginning now rejected their early ideas.

Aldiyarov, who was chairing the meeting at which Kakharman was putting his case, interrupted him. "Comrade Nasyrov, which side do you take yourself? Which group do you support?"

"I don't support any group. I'm on the side of the truth," Kakharman answered.

"And your truth concludes that Kazakhstan doesn't need Siberian water?"

The people in the room held their breath. Everyone had long known that Aldiyarov disliked Kakharman and never missed an opportunity to attack him. For Aldiyarov, it was completely the fault of Kakharman's obduracy, moral assertiveness, and bluntness that there were no more fish in the sea, that the huge factory ships were stranded, and that the catches in the lakes and rivers had shrunk. Yet even those who took Aldiyarov's side in the debate couldn't help but feel sorry for Kakharman.

No one would openly express their views, though. Kakharman had no illusions; he knew he was alone. Such knowledge can sometimes give a man courage and composure, if only because he knows he must rely entirely on his own strength. Maybe that's why he never gave in to Aldiyarov. And he thought, "Eh, old man, what a troubled life you have. Tomorrow you'll have to report to Kunaev and tell him you suspended the idiot who dared to contradict you. Kunaev probably hasn't a clue who I am, but you have to be careful, Aldiyarov, don't you? You're a slave to the marrow of your bones. But you'll have to tell Kunaev you've choked the awkward marmot. And of course, our sea cares nothing for this futile tussling of spiders in a jar!"

"You understand me correctly, Kozha Aldiyarovich. Everyone realized long ago that Siberian water will not save us."

"Utter rubbish! Whose tune are you playing? You do realize, Nasyrov, don't you, that you're acting like a complete anti-Soviet?"

The room woke up. Some tried to shape a wry smile in appreciation of the sharpness of Aldiyarov's tirade, but no one really found it remotely funny to see the little old man lifting his withered finger above the desk and raising his querulous voice to shout the words "anti-Soviet!"

"Scientists and engineers have proven this Siberian water won't be enough to even wet the man-made channels—this water will never reach us. Beyond that, the biological composition of the Siberian water is completely alien to our local soil. This water will bring illness and problems to Central Asia," Kakharman replied coolly, ignoring the accusation.

"What composure," Aldiyarov thought. "He doesn't fall for petty squabbles. He fights for what he believes. He knows his business too. What a shame he's not our man. Pity he's too old for reeducation. Only one thing we can do: pull him out by the roots. But now I need to take this conversation in a different direction, or he'll beat us all. And all because those Moscow scientists, all those Slavikovs, brainwashed him all these years."

"Let's not change the subject," Aldiyarov said. "Enough of your demagogy. You'd better tell us why the half year fish plan is collapsing."

"And the yearly plan will fail as well, Kozha Aldiyarovich."

"Why?"

"Maybe we should ask the fish why it doesn't get caught. Maybe the fish will prove more talkative than me." Kakharman grinned.

Those listening began to smile but quickly bent their heads down as Old Creaky Bones, feeling the atmosphere changing, scowled around the room, searching for anyone on Kakharman's side.

Despite his pigheadedness, Aldiyarov knew very well that the oblast would fail to meet its fish target. Yet he couldn't ever express his thoughts either at local meetings or to higher levels.

Completing the plan was the only way to stay afloat and alive. He never went very deeply into the so-called human factor, leaving such an onerous task to the sentimental or inquisitive types. Nothing beyond the concept of the "plan" existed for him.

He had almost tripped up on Kakharman. He had realized—and just in time—that Kakharman's integrity was dragging him into the abyss too. One of them had to be eliminated. If Kakharman didn't break his neck, Aldiyarov might fall instead.

Their clash began with the fact that the quota for fish had doubled since Aldiyarov came to the oblast. It had been doubled even as it became clear that the real fish catch had only been half of the previous quota. Aldiyarov called for Kakharman and without any preamble, demanded, "Nasyrov, the fish catch has to be doubled. I have already pledged to the higher-ups that the number will be hit." He didn't go into any details. "Just do it!"

In a month's time, he again called for Kakharman. "How is our promise?"

"What promise?" Kakharman asked stiffly. "I gave no promises. Did you think that if you pledged in Alma-Ata that fish production will double, then the amount of fish in the sea will double at the same time? Sadly, that is not the case."

Since that meeting, Kakharman had been frequently excluded from the hierarchy at work. He was usually the last to learn about many decisions and so had no chance to object to Aldiyarov or his plans. Then Aldiyarov's favor fell upon Samat Samatovich, Nasyrov's deputy. Kakharman was stuck out at sea most of the time, and so Samat Samatovich took his place in most meetings. Samat Samatovich became rather smug, grew a paunch to suit his new position, and completely stopped speaking Kazakh. Some alleged that he even scolded his own wife in Russian. "It serves you right," Kakharman admonished himself, looking at Samat Samatovich. "It was you who picked him from the ministry."

At another regular meeting of the bureau, the matter of fish was raised again. Aldiyarov addressed Samat Samatovich with a question. "So Nasyrov insists that our objectives are set too high. What do you think, comrade Tuzgenov? Is this plan realistic?"

Samat Samatovich responded readily and began to explain. "It's very realistic, Kozha Aldiyarovich! That—"

"That's enough. You can sit!" Aldiyarov interrupted him and addressed Kakharman. "Your deputy assures me that the goal is realistic. Which one of you should the members of the bureau believe?"

"That's an interesting question, Kozha Aldiyarovich. They will believe the one you believe." Kakharman grinned bitterly.

"I believe Tuzgenov."

"Then I'm sorry. I don't believe him!"

"Maybe you don't believe me?" Aldiyarov turned white.

"I don't believe you either," Kakharman replied.

Aldiyarov rejoined pointedly, "Then I doubt that we will be able to work well together, comrade Nasyrov. If the oblast can't meet its target, why would we need a fishery at all? Let fishermen do other things. They can graze cattle or work the land since they seem to have forgotten how to catch fish. Am I right, comrades?"

"Many of them no longer go into the sea, and many leave forever."

"Where do they go?" Aldiyarov turned toward the secretaries.

"To Caspy, Shardara, and Balkhash."

"We let our people go, and now we wonder what went wrong?"

Kakharman exploded. "Fishermen will never become farmers. They are forced to leave and go where there is water and fish."

Aldiyarov acted as if Kakharman's comment was insignificant. "If it was known up front that the coast could not be revived, then why were schools, community centers, and repair shops built in almost every kolkhoz? And why are the workers responsible for that not punished accordingly? If everyone leaves tomorrow, what will we do with those schools and community centers? It seems millions were wasted!"

Kakharman looked at the members of the bureau. They were shivering like lambs, each anxious about their party card and their position. "That's the socialism we have built!" Kakharman often thought in despair.

"Comrades!" Aldiyarov barked. "I consider your silence a sign of support for Nasyrov! I have to interpret Nasyrov's intervention as a deviation from the party's norms and principles. Nasyrov is to blame for wasting millions in state funds! And these are not just my words. According to his own words, he goes to every corner of our country to meet people. Recently, the sums he has spent on business trips was added up. It turned out to be a large sum. Even I can't indulge in such journeys at the government's expense!" Aldiyarov smiled acidly. "Maybe, comrade Nasyrov, you will tell us what kind of business connects you to American scientists in Moscow? Who gave you permission to meet with them?"

"What kind of permission is needed for that? I met them at Professor Slavikov's—"

"Slavikov! Slavikov!" Aldiyarov exploded. "Who is Slavikov? And after visiting Moscow, what were you doing in Tajikistan and Turkmenistan? Why did you go to Uzbekistan and Karakalpakstan? I've been warned more than once about you. But, my friend, you should know, I've cut short the careers of people better than you."

"Please don't 'my friend' me. Kozha Aldiyarovich, let's respect each other. I am prepared to give an account to the members of the bureau. You asked who permitted me to meet up with American scientists. Our state has no intention of going to war with America. Quite the opposite. We are aiming to build ties with America to understand each other better. Slavikov is a scientist with a worldwide reputation. His works are used both in our country and abroad. I didn't reveal any state secrets to American scientists. What would I tell them? That our sea is dying?

"And I traveled Central Asia because I wanted to see with my own eyes how the waters of the Amu and Syr Daryas are being used. I traveled the banks of these rivers from Pamir to Sinemorye. I came to the conclusion that the waters are being wasted in many areas because I saw that thousands of square miles of land have been waterlogged and turned into salt marshes. In order to dry those areas out, thousands and thousands of tons of the same fresh river water will be required. I have not seen anywhere the appropriate drainage to regulate the water levels. The wages of the water suppliers are piece rated. That is, they depend on how many times the watering is carried out and on the volume of water used. So the more the water is used, the more the supplier is paid. That's absurd!"

Everybody was listening to Kakharman miserably.

"The corridor of fresh water in the sea, which fish used to follow to the mouths of these two rivers, is now almost gone. During the spring, when the time to spawn comes, fish can't find their way to the rivers. The fish just don't reproduce. I wrote an open letter to the party's Central Committee about my trip across the republics of Central Asia, about the desperate situation on the coast and sea, and about my meetings and conversations with the scientists—"

Aldiyarov interrupted him. "So you shoot ahead to beat everyone! That is the tactic of an upstart! Who asked you to do all this?"

"My conscience, Kozha Aldiyarovich!"

"Do you think we are all without conscience? Not you, but the Regional Committee should've written that letter!"

"It makes no difference who writes it. I did it because it was quicker—"

"There's no significant difference to you, but there is to us, and a very big one."

"Since you began working in our oblast, you haven't written a single letter to the higher authorities about the daily needs of the people."

"Complaints and slander are not my style. I am used to getting things done. And you, comrade Nasyrov, obviously enjoy writing more than I do."

"It's not me who writes them. The nation is writing them. The people. They are in complete despair. But they write in vain. The letters keep coming, but nothing happens."

"Both the Regional Committee and the Republic are waiting for the Siberian water. Without it, all measures are only half measures, and there is no solution in them."

"If you acknowledge that everyone has been put in the position where you and the sea have to be saved, then you should also acknowledge that it's unfair to blame the fishermen for their inability to meet their quota. It is not their fault. That is why they write!"

Aldiyarov was beside himself with fury. "You can write to the president of the United States if you wish, even to the UN, but we are waiting for the Siberian water. Is that clear, Nasyrov? And we will force the fishermen to do their work!"

Their eyes met.

During his life, Kakharman met many officials who cared about nothing but their career and their own welfare. One of them was in front of him now.

Gazing into Aldiyarov's eyes, Kakharman thought: "Two of your predecessors, Kozha Aldiyarovich, declared the campaign 'For the Republican Billion.' Every tiny bit of green land was plowed up. Wheat was sown everywhere. Yet neither of them ever got a decent harvest. Everybody knew it's impossible to grow wheat in our lands. You all wanted to be awarded the Star, but in the end, we were left without meadows and without bread. We were left on ruined land. But that wasn't enough. You've gone on tormenting the land, Kozha Aldiyarovich. Now you've taken up rice. You've diverted the waters that were stopping the sea from dying onto the rice fields, and now there are swamps and salt marshes—and there's no rice and no sea."

"Fine," Aldiyarov sighed as if guessing Kakharman's thoughts. "What do you suggest?"

"I say every day what I suggest. We have to abandon this plan immediately. That is the only solution. We have talked and talked across the world about how we will turn a desert into a flowering garden. Why is a garden needed there? Why is rice needed there? And cotton? If we don't back away from this nonsensical idea, it will all soon be buried under salt from the dried-up sea. And the salt will be spread by the wind for many hundreds of miles. And if only it was just rice and cotton affected! This salt threatens all of Central Asia, Altai, Siberia! We still don't know all the interconnections in nature! Why do we endlessly fight with nature as if she is our sworn enemy. If we destroy this sea, then tomorrow millions of tons of salt will bury vast territories all around! She, nature, is unconquerable. No matter what, she will have the last word, not us! And if today man is destroying Sinemorye, tomorrow the sea will kill man."

But Aldiyarov was determined to find something that might undermine Nasyrov.

"Can you explain to me why Hero of Socialist Labor Orazbek has left his homeland?"

"No, I can't. I can only guess. We took Orazbek with us to Moscow and Alma-Ata on many occasions. Many times, he heard the conversations of scientists and ministry workers about what will happen to the sea in the near future. He probably just lost hope."

"But you personally encouraged Orazbek to leave," Aldiyarov said with quiet menace. Kakharman was not expecting such a bizarre accusation.

"Me? Why? Doesn't he have his own mind?"

"Why? I will tell why. So that you could gossip everywhere and say 'Look, under Aldiyarov, people are leaving their homelands, even such able people as Orazbek!' Why? I'll tell you. To stir things up! Is it still not clear to you, comrades, why Nasyrov was meeting foreigners in Moscow!" And he looked at everyone.

"You have no respect for yourself, Kozha Aldiyarovich. That is a crude, clumsy political accusation!"

And then even Galym Erzhanov couldn't resist a protest. "Kozha Aldiyarovich, for sure, we shouldn't give these issues a political slant. We have enough of problems in everyday work. Let's not go into politics."

Kakharman began to speak stiffly and sharply. "If we look at what has happened to the sea this way, then all of us—you, and Alma-Ata, and Moscow, and the Politburo—are political criminals. So let's not adopt such a tone, Kozha Aldiyarovich. But now that the conversation has gone this way, if you imagine yourself politically literate, then explain some basic things to me. For instance, why are we not permitted to talk and write about our most acute problems? Our letter has been returned from *Pravda* with just a few formal words! Slavikov's letter, which he sent to the Politburo, has lain unanswered for a year. What are they waiting for? Russian writers and publicists speak about the problems of Baikal in nearly every edition of the main newspapers. But we are not allowed to speak about the troubles of Kazakh people? Perestroika has been going on for a year already, but we are still silent. Where is the truth, Kozha Aldiyarovich? And you're feeling very good, because on the sly, you are getting rid of honest people. Now it's my turn, or am I wrong?"

"It's not hard to achieve if you want it that much." Aldiyarov smiled. "But jokes aside, I, personally, have no doubt of your honesty, comrade Nasyrov. As for our shared psychological, so to speak, condition, I begin to wonder. We, the Communists, must care for each other's health. It seems to me, Kakharman Nasyrovich, that lately you are not aware of your speeches and your actions. We, the members of the bureau, are seriously concerned about your health. Where is Maksimov?" Aldiyarov addressed the room.

"I'm here, Kozha Aldiyarovich!" The head of the Department of Health stood up.

"Nikolai Valerianovich, am I right? Do you agree with me?"

Maksimov blushed and replied hesitatingly, "It's hard to tell without an examination."

"Then you should invite Kakharman Nasyrovich to see you." Aldiyarov was angry at Maksimov for not supporting him. "That is our common concern, that we should look after the health of our comrades. You should take a rest. There will be good care, a strict regime. Is it not so, Nikolai Valerianovich? You see, doctors have the same opinion."

Maksimov sat down, feeling spat on.

At that moment, Samat Samatovich asked his question. "Comrade Nasyrov, could you also explain this strange fact? Your father is a Communist, a veteran of war, a well-known fisherman. How come he became a mullah?"

"This is the sort of people that Aldiyarov gathers around himself. They are not wolves but jackals!" Kakharman thought, glancing across at Samat Samatovich. It became clear to Kakharman that the meeting of the bureau was almost finished and that it was pointless to try and say anything further.

He said only these words: "I don't know where you were born, Kozha Aldiyarovich, but I am a son of this damaged and long-suffering land, of this abandoned sea. I will spend my whole life trying to save my land, my sea. And it's pointless to threaten to send me to the nuthouse. I am not the timid kind. Let your rudeness and intrusiveness be on your conscience. So let's assume that we were simply talking about work. I would like to warn you officially that Nasyrov is not one to lay down arms. Poor perestroika, if you begin by surrounding yourself with Samats. The people of our lands are sensible, but, to our misfortune, fools get into government—"

"Nasyrov, remember where you are!" Erzhanov interrupted him but mostly just for form's sake.

"And do not touch my father," Kakharman went on, his voice growing stronger. "Remember, we are all walking under God—"

He suddenly hesitated, looking at the people around him, as if seeing them for the first time. Then, with pain in his voice, he exclaimed, "Have you ever seen how fish suffer when they can't find clear water? How they die? A fish wants to live. It is also God's creation. No, you haven't seen it. You need to see it not only with your eyes but with your heart!" He went silent for a minute and then added, "Kozha Aldiyarovich, I ask to be informed of the bureau's decision in writing. Goodbye."

After the meeting, Aldiyarov called over Erzhanov with a friendly gesture. "Our Nasyrov decided to fight to the bitter end, eh? He says he's not one to lay down arms. Did you hear?" Aldiyarov was visibly worried.

"Yes, Kozha Aldiyarovich. He is very well-spoken. But you shouldn't take his rhetoric too seriously," Erzhanov reassured Old Creaky Bones.

"Let him go and complain anywhere and to anyone he wants!"

"Nasyrov won't be looking for fairness for himself."

"Then that's a wise decision. If he makes trouble for us," Aldiyarov said threateningly, "I'll have him locked away in the middle of nowhere! I'll destroy him!"

"You shouldn't pursue him any further. Don't anger him. It could create bigger problems. I'll talk to him. Just don't do anything for now."

Only much later, when Kakharman lost his path in a dust storm and, exhausted, was rushing around in complete darkness will he recall that meeting and everything that happened. And he will think about Erzhanov with gratitude because he'll realize the peril he escaped from with the help of Galym, who somehow managed to neutralize Aldiyarov's dangerous moods. Only much later, when he held his deceased mother in his arms.

"Yes, talk to him," Aldiyarov agreed. "What's happening with your move to Moscow? Are you going?"

"I'm waiting for the call. It should be anytime now."

"I have a feeling you'll get it tomorrow. And I have the following official assignment for you: to become a general!"

With a folder tucked under his arm, the head of the personnel department, Zhurynbek, was rushing toward Kakharman, who had only just come back from the meeting.

"Kakha, the men from Moscow have been in touch. They ask that the documents of the five boys we are going to send for study be sent to them promptly."

Zhurynbek was over sixty, and they had known each other for a long time. In all that time, Zhurynbek had never addressed Kakharman in the Russian manner, as Kakharman Nasyrovich. "Kakha" sounded warmer, almost brotherly. Kakharman didn't object; he rarely corrected people if their intentions were good. Zhurynbek had returned from the war without an arm. Kakharman respected this quiet, humble man and ignored all the gossip that he was too old and disabled and that it was time for him to retire. "Zhureke will know himself when he can't cope anymore. He is a conscientious man and will not block someone else's place."

"Well, then, send them, Zhureke. Or are there any problems?"

"There's no problem sending them, Kakha. But I am concerned. If our affairs here are up in the air, will the boys end up without work when they come back?"

Zhurynbek was right in a way, Kakharman knew. Kazakh boys don't settle well in foreign lands. He'd realized that while a student himself. And what if the boys have to choose between a foreign land and a homeland where there is no work? And will they agree to go to Odessa now when they can see for themselves the dismal prospects here?

"Have those who wanted to go changed their minds?"

"No. But that is understandable."

"Are many of them children of ordinary fishermen?"

"Quite a few. But there are only five places. The Regional Committee has reserved three of these five places, and one is for the Regional Executive Committee."

"Nice! They shared places wisely."

"That was Aldiyarov's order last year. I objected, but how can you argue with the Regional Committee?"

"Why wasn't I told?"

"It coincided with your trips to Moscow and the Far East, Kakha. When you came back, I decided not to trouble you."

"Do not include any of the 'babies'! We'll send the documents only of those we recommend: the children of the fishermen."

He quickly signed the documents.

"Send them immediately . . . Wait, Zhureke," he stopped Zhureke at the door. "If there are any complaints, refer them to me."

Kakharman missed lunch and stayed in his office. Once again, he went over what had happened today and decided that he had nothing to regret. He had acted according to his beliefs; he had no other choice.

Kakharman's thoughts were interrupted by the ringing of the phone. His old friend Sultan Karimov from Balkhash was calling. They had studied together for five years in Odessa, sharing a room and going on naval exercises all over the Mediterranean Sea.

"Hi, Kakharman! Your fishermen have arrived. I gave them the best jobs."

"Thank you, Sultan. You are always a great help to me. Do you have business for me, or is it just a friendly call?"

"Are you alright there? I saw you in my dreams last night, so I thought I should give you a call to see how you're doing."

Kakharman was touched. What a genuine friend. Maybe he should work for Sultan?

"I'm fine, still alive. What about you?"

"I'm not too bad. But our Balkhash is dying, Kakharman."

"And I had just decided to move to Balkhash."

"Horseradish is no sweeter than black radish, Kakharman. Do you think it's any better here? But you still should come. You know, I'm always happy to see you."

"Then wait for me. It'll happen very soon!"

He took the call from his friend as a good omen. Sultan's voice brought hope. He needed his friends' help now as much as he needed air. Maybe the ancient legend of the brave warrior Imanbek, who let his eyes be gouged out to save his friend from captivity, had a purpose. People say that in Imanbek's clan there were many clairvoyants, many skillful healers, and many inspired dombra players. After losing his eyes, Imanbek took up the dombra and became a famous player. All the best traveling kyuis, it is said, were composed by Imanbek. That was a time when people valued friendship and even foes never lost their human dignity.

Kakharman remembered Akatov. Both of them had started their jobs around the same time. Akatov had supported Kakharman. They were opening sewing workshops in auls to provide women with work and had finally succeeded in getting a canning plant in the fish factory, where small fish arriving from the Far East were canned. The benefits of these modest undertakings were small, but people were grumbling less. It wasn't that they were overwhelmed with joy or believed that from now on their future would be amazing; it simply became easier to cope with hardships, and life on the seashore seemed just a little less grim.

Very soon Akatov and Kakharman were linked in everything. Akatov began to take Kakharman with him to Moscow. And he also invited both Nasyr and Hero of Socialist Labor Orazbek to one of the larger meetings of ministries and scientists. At the meeting, Akatov presented a clear picture of the situation in Sinemorye. Unfortunately, he was ignored because everyone thought that he was exaggerating. Orazbek, who was insulted by their reaction to Akatov, asked to speak. He spoke bravely and confidently, interspersing his speech with witty Russian proverbs. His performance touched many.

Professor Slavikov began to speak next. "The long-suffering sea we are talking about has been abandoned. We have been complacent about its benefits, and that includes the Ministry of Fisheries. The sea has been losing its way ever since fish started to disappear. And in his celebrated article, the academician Baraev suggests destroying it altogether and turning the entire area into cropland. What a strong, inspirational scientific notion, don't you think, comrades? Well, let me enlighten you with a few details of the past activities of this respectable academician, who has spent all his life irrigating deserts.

"You may be horrified, comrades, if you could see the current state of the Karakum Canal, which has been constructed according to his specifications. Go to Turkmenistan and look at the sorrow this canal has brought to the people.

"I can't understand at all why Uzbek scientists are now saying that if the country needs cotton, give us Siberian water! The country doesn't need such amounts of cotton. Think about it. The country doesn't need it! It's only needed personally by Rashidov—and I think you all know why! In a personal letter to comrade Rashidov, I wrote that if Uzbekistan doesn't abandon the idea of growing such amounts of cotton, then the cotton will ruin all Uzbek land and bring catastrophe on the Uzbek nation! A year has gone by, but Rashidov has not responded."

Polad-zade, who was chairing the meeting, hurriedly interrupted. "Matvei Panteleevich, unfortunately, we have a time limit. Your time has run out."

"Maybe," Slavikov responded tersely, realizing the reason for the interruption. "The sea is a gift of nature, and no one—"

Polad-zade interrupted him again. "Matvei Panteleevich, nobody here will agree with your biased statements." The chairman was growing irritated. "The Karakum Canal is the pride of the Republic. Don't attack it! The mother country demands we dry out Sinemorye as well! This sea is an error of nature."

"Nature doesn't make mistakes, Polad-zade." Slavikov looked at the chairman disdainfully. "Only in the minds of disturbed individuals."

People laughed. Polad-zade froze, looking as if he'd been touched on the face with a red-hot poker. He didn't know what to do next. The professor continued.

"The motherland is not an abstract concept. The motherland has to respect people and take care of them. The same is true for the state and government. Nowadays the government and the people—the nation—are foes. The nation is made of many people who work on the land, and government is a bunch of bureaucratic 'clairvoyants' who are fed by the people's work. The fate of this sea troubles ordinary people. But because it isn't the government who has to face this sorrow, they ignore it. All this, comrade Polad-zade, is concealed in your word 'motherland.'"

Everyone at the meeting froze. Only the shuffling of the professor's retreating steps could be heard. Nasyr was the first to applaud, and the young scientists nearby soon supported him. He was so stirred by the professor's speech that he stood up at once and walked to the podium. "Who are you?" Polad-zade challenged him.

"I am an ordinary fisherman," Nasyr replied and began to speak. "I am an old man. I've seen a lot. But I've never, ever come across such nonsense as I have heard in the past two days." He glared at Polad-zade. "And you have stifled the few clever people who offer you a sensible way to save the sea, to save the people!

"Today I realized that we truly will ruin this sea. We'll make the people who live here beggars, and worse still, our children will damn us. They are already cursing us. It might've been better if I'd died near Moscow in '41, embracing my rifle. Did I survive to see this?

"We thought that we'd live well after the war. We built big factories and spared no effort to do it. But there's a new war now, an invisible one. It's impossible to tell who is attacking us. The government? God? Man himself? Show man mercy. Let him live as a man. Don't you think he deserves it? Isn't it enough to shoot at him, freeze him in the camps, lead him by his nose to the birth of communism, only to exterminate him as if he's the most disgusting beast!

"I remember just after the war, when there were fish in the sea. Lots of people lived on its shores: Russians, Germans, Kazakhs, Koreans, Estonians. Now they've all left, and only Kazakhs and Karakalpaks are left to face their misfortune. They will die with the sea; it's their fate. Professor Slavikov is right: no one cares about these unfortunate people!

"The bureaucrats have grown rich from Uzbek cotton, and all the sorrow was left for the ordinary people. And this sorrow will only end when the nations are extinct! The doctors calculated that a hundred newborns die in our region out of every thousand. Where does such misfortune come from? Mother's milk! It turns out that mother's milk is unsuitable for feeding an infant! How do you accept that? What have we done to the earth? Who are we becoming? I now don't believe any of your words! And when I get home, I will tell everybody else not to believe you. Not today, not ever again!"

Nasyr concluded and walked back calmly to his seat. The people in the hall were on their feet, applauding. After the meeting, Akatov hugged Nasyr. "You, Nasyr-aga, have said just what we never managed to say so plainly!" Kakharman was looking at his father proudly. The writer Zalygin from Moscow, who was sitting not far from Nasyr, shook his hand warmly and congratulated him.

Slavikov approached them and introduced the famous writer to Nasyr.

"Do you read a lot, Nasyr-aga?" Zalygin asked.

"I haven't read any of your books, Sergey Pavlovich, but since misfortune befell us, we read a great deal about environmental protection. I don't understand everything, but my son always explains things to me. Russian writers do a lot to save the land, rivers, and seas."

"That's true," Zalygin replied. "But you understand that this is only the beginning of the fight. Hard years lie ahead."

After a short pause, Nasyr spoke. "You write and talk about the rivers and lakes of Siberia, but you haven't said a single word about our troubles. Yet everything in nature is interconnected. Or do you think that if our sea dries out, its death will have no significance for Baikal in Siberia or some lake in America or even in Africa?"

Zalygin nodded in agreement. "You are right, Nasyr-aga. We wrote nothing about your sea. We realized its misfortune too late."

"Yet how many times did I tell you?" Slavikov intervened. "I was buzzing in your ears about it over and over!"

"We will return what we took," said Zalygin. "We will definitely make a start!"

"OK!" Slavikov said. "How about we all go to my place now? What do you say, Sergey Pavlovich? By the way, I would like to introduce you to another courageous and decent man, Akatov Rakhim Akatovich."

"Glad to meet you." Zalygin shook hands with Akatov. "As for the invite . . . Honestly, I'd be happy to, but I'm afraid I can't."

Slavikov appreciated the intelligence and efficiency of Akatov. On numerous occasions from early March until late autumn, Akatov visited the professor in his island laboratory, and they spent ages talking, wrote many papers, and sent many letters to Alma-Ata and to Moscow. Slavikov was annoyed that Akatov had been transferred into one of the derelict ministries. It meant that affairs in the region were left to get rapidly worse. Slavikov said to Kakharman, "Our government demands pliable people who keep quiet. If a man has an opinion, let alone a conscience, he will be moved away as far as possible. You, Kakharman, will run into troubles too. I think you know that yourself. I'd like to warn you not to despair too soon. Stick to your line until the end."

"Matvei Panteleevich, I have not forgotten the words of Vavilov: 'We will go to the fire, but we will not disown our beliefs.'"

They went to the professor's place without Zalygin. At the table, the conversation returned to Vavilov and to true Russian intellectuals.

"Who, in your opinion, Kakharman, could be considered to be an intellectual now? What is an intellectual?"

"I guess it's anyone who has a higher education."

"And you're right, my friend! An intellectual is a modest and cultured man with a sharp mind. Yet in our county, the so-called intellectual class contains millions of people. Just think about it! It's a whole army! But if there are so many intellectuals in the country, how could it sink to its current state? I think, Kakharman Nasyrovich, that an intellectual, most of all, is a conscientious man, a citizen of his country!"

Slavikov liked this kind of evening in his home, when those close to him in spirit gathered at the table and had a chance to speak openly. He received the fishermen who came to Moscow rarely as heartily as they received him when he visited Sinemorye. After the death of his wife, Sofia Pavlovna, the previous summer, he was now living with his son, Igor, and his daughter-in-law, Natasha. Now they were waiting for Igor. He had called from Obninsk just before leaving and was expected any minute.

"He won't be by himself," the professor warned. "A young American scientist is coming with him." He settled in his chair. "So Kakharman, you know a lot of Vavilov by heart. But I'm beginning to forget, a sign of old age. Nikolai

Ivanovich was a great man! But he lived in a wild time. In no other country but ours were as many intellectuals destroyed as in those years! We young ones thought he was a genius. He was handsome and noble, both in spirit and looks. Remember Chekhov's words: 'Everything in a man should be beautiful, the soul and the body.'[4] And that must have been said about Nikolai Ivanovich. Who can I compare him to, to make it clear? Your Saken Seifullin[5] was also a remarkable individual."

"Have you met Saken Seifullin?" Akatov was astonished.

"I shared a cell with him in Alma-Ata. Kazakhs were treated appallingly. They were accused of nationalism and tortured. Saken used to tell me that even in Annenkoff's Death Carriage it was not as brutal as it was in Alma-Ata. Once, at dawn, he was brought back to the cell after a night's interrogation—or rather, he was shoved in and thrown on the floor, unconscious. We lifted him up and laid him on the trestle bed. The Kazakhs began to cry, even though things were rough for them too.

"'Saken, what have they done to you?' they asked.

"A big, strong man called Musakhan, a docker from the Irtysh steamship company, was with us in the cell. He began to kick the door in rage. 'Monsters! Pigs!' The next day, that docker was taken out and shot.

"Saken only regained consciousness toward evening. We washed his face and gave him a drink. He said to me, 'Matvei, I think our cause is lost. You reap what you sow . . .' He said that to me many, many years ago, and only now do I understand how insightful he was.

"And Vavilov was tortured too. I knew people who shared a cell with him in the Saratov prison. They told stories about his nobility. My teacher, Nesterov, was a student of Vavilov, and was shot like him. And I was exiled to Alma-Ata. From there, I was sent to the camps. I met Akbalak in Kolyma."

"I didn't know you've known Akbalak for such a long time, Matvei," Orazbek said, saddened by the story.

"Only Nasyr knows."

"Matvei, what you have lived through would be enough for three lifetimes. Do you like the labor songs by the Kyrgyz poet Toktogul? Remember them?"

"Of course. How could I forget?"

Nasyr tuned his dombra and began to sing in his strong voice:

The pain of hard labor will never stop:
My mind breaks under its load.
Dust and dirt smeared over my face:
Dust of exile, dust of the road.
My dear old aul is far, far away.
There I was, a lark singing free.
My people, my people, do you recall?
Or did you forget about me?
Every one in exile—they all are friends;
They are all wretched like me,
Here is a Kazakh, a Tatar, and an Uzbek.
A Kyrgyz, a Russian, you see.
They were all forced to this hell in the snow;
Their lungs are gasping breath fast.
Hard labor freezes the blood in the veins
And the time of youth is long past.
Can it be I'll never see home again?
Will I be here to the last?

When the doorbell rang, Slavikov turned to Nasyr. "Nasyr-kurdas, that'll be Igor with the American. Please sing for them too. The father of the young man is a famous American scientist. In his time, he refused the membership of the Soviet Academy of Science in protest against Stalin's regime."

Igor introduced the fair-haired young man to the guests. "This is Henry Trimble. Henry, you haven't seen Kazakhs yet, let alone heard their songs. But it looks as if you will now."

"OK!" the American laughed. "You're not quite right, Igor. I have a friend: the Kazakh poet, Olzhas Suleimenov!"

"I would love to be friends with such a man!" Slavikov interjected. "He is one of my favorite poets. I remember his poem."

The Syr Darya teems on through its lazy, yellow bends.
Where now, white town of Otrar, are your lofty walls?
Those walls that flamed for half a year with burning oil.
Two hundred days, two hundred nights, the siege went on.

The canals were blocked. No bread, no meat, no straw,
The city fed upon the dead.
They drank the blood still warm.
One May morning, treason broke the siege.
Then the long winding ditch filled with corpses.
The books! The books were burning! The great old books!
The books without which the East will sag!
Oh, my Kipchaks!
The steppe could never see
Such jolly folk with such pure faces.
Those who would not surrender,
The steppe would quickly snap their spines,
And throw tall stones on their graves.
It was proud of the tall ones,
And soon caressed the boys again.
It raised the short ones,
But the tall ones, it avenged through envy.
That is how I'll be staining, hiding my teeth by the mass graves . . .
I agree to be a Buddha, Sessu, and pagan Savel!
I agree to be a skull,
I agree to be a sabre . . .
That is how we will stand!
We, the Tall, will stand!

Slavikov recited the poem with great emotion. "What poems these are! Your Olzhas is not just a great poet but a great man." He said, "Sing, Nasyr. Your turn again. Let Henry hear the songs of Sinemorye."

Nasyr picked up his dombra. A drawling, guttural sound filled the room, and everybody went quiet.

And the song of sorrow and sadness flowed . . .
Shining surfaces of wide blue lakes
Will never have the breadth of the sea
If their basin contains a canal.
What is brighter than the moon in the sky?

And yet the night always remains dark.
For the moon is devoured by the darkness.
Which sharp-clawed beast beats the lion?
But even the lion is watched by the hunter,
Threatening with death for a careless step.
The wolf lies in bushes in wait for the herds.
Is the shepherd asleep? If he is, they will
Rend to pieces the sheep and the horse!
Doesn't my prayer plead for the dead,
And won't my call be in vain,
If my own brave lion is killed?
I lost both the leader and the people . . .
Swan, left behind, what awaits me?

Nasyr sang all night, alternating between Kazakh and Russian songs. The professor, Igor, and Natasha sang along.

"Igor!" Henry suddenly brightened up and sang, "*Kalinka, kalinka . . .*"

In Nasyr's hands, the dombra picked up the tune at once, and a bold and playful "Kalinka" was sung by everyone, even Orazbek. Henry, who didn't know the words, simply hummed the melody and rocked, hugging Kakharman and Igor.

When the song ended, they decided to go for a walk in the Moscow night. The city was sleeping, and the streets were empty and quiet. Even on the renovated Arbat, there was no one.

Kakharman was happy that he had taken learning English seriously while at school. He could understand most of what Henry said and answered his questions confidently, even though he had barely spoken English in years.

"I want to visit Kazakhstan!" Henry proclaimed. "Will you invite me?"

"Of course!" Kakharman replied.

"Are foreigners allowed to go to Sinemorye?" Igor questioned.

"Ha, who needs perestroika?" Henry exclaimed.

"Henry," Kakharman asked, "what do you think about our lives? It is easier to see from the outside."

The American replied frankly. "I can't tell what sort of future waits for you, but I have always sympathized with ordinary people. But right now, your society is delaying the development of all civilization, and that is a fact."

They walked in silence for some time.

"I'm not saying that we don't make mistakes," Henry said. "Far from it! Nature and man are so closely connected that they depend entirely on one another. But we have made huge mistakes, and many things have been lost forever. Did you know that in Central Asia, in Otrar, I think, they created the most perfect system of irrigation long ago? Unfortunately, what was achieved by your ancestors has been destroyed. The way man treats nature demonstrates the level of a nation's development."

"The Americans say, 'Let the earth be better after us than it was before us.' This is the most humane principle!" Igor joined their conversation.

"We proclaimed the Buffalo River a national reserve. No one would even think damming it or reversing its flow."

Kakharman moaned with envy and despair.

"In America, we have one-third of our lands under public control. The political sympathies of Congress may change, but it always stays on nature's side because Congress will never go against the nation, and it will not risk losing the nation's trust."

"Voropaev, our director of the Institute of Water Issues, thinks Sinemorye is nature's mistake. And he can get away with anything," Kakharman said.

It was pleasant strolling through the quiet lanes. The city's special charm was distilled into its old quarter, which retained the mystery of the past. Igor liked the small streets of Arbat because they were the places of his childhood and youth. Something deeply familiar and intimate spread from the ancient buildings hushed in the darkness of the night.

They walked until dawn speaking of many things and only parted as the sun shot its first rays into the narrow lanes. Kakharman went to the Hotel Moscow. He knocked softly on the door of his father's room. Although it was early, he and his friends were already drinking tea. "It doesn't matter whether you are in Moscow or in the aul," Kakharman laughed.

After their tea, they went out on the balcony. Orazbek confessed to Kakharman, "I didn't like the atmosphere at the meeting yesterday. I could see they crossed our sea out on their maps with a red pencil." Then he added thoughtfully, "But we all have families: children, wives, parents. We need to think of them." That's when Kakharman realized that Orazbek had already decided to get out. And that's just what he did soon after. Orazbek was the first to leave the shore.

Zhurynbek walked in again and distracted Kakharman from his thoughts just as the phone rang. It was Erzhanov. He informed Kakharman that he had been removed from his office and asked him to come to the Regional Executive Committee toward the end of the working day.

"OK," Kakharman said and hung up.

"Kakha," Zhurynbek told him, "I sent off the documents."

"Thanks, Zhureke. Let the young men study. Education won't hurt them, even if they don't come home."

Zhurynbek said nothing. He was confused, as Kakharman could see.

"Zhureke, did you want to ask something?"

"Kakha, Samat Samatovich told me that you have been removed from the bureau. Is it true?"

"Well, if Samat Samatovich is saying it, then it must be true. Tomorrow I will bid farewell to the workers. You should prepare the notice of my dismissal. And, it would be good if you could hurry up with the payment. I'll probably need money."

By the next afternoon, Kakharman was already in Karaoi. He was there to say goodbye to his parents. And by the evening, he was heading to Alma-Ata, along with Aitugan and the children. He left his family in a hotel in Alma-Ata and went on by himself to Balkhash, just as he had planned.

Balkhash greeted Kakharman frostily with a chill and dusty wind. He couldn't find the people Sultan Karimov had promised to send to meet him at the airport. The air in the small airport terminal was stale and echoed with the chatter of Caucasian workers. The sand storm blew stronger by the minute. Kakharman felt like a trapped animal.

VII

Although people agreed with Nasyr that the rain was a gift from Allah, they couldn't bear seeing Nasyr's eagerness anymore. And then Allah decided to stop the downpour after thirty-eight days. The clouds disappeared, and the bright sun glowed down on the refreshed dunes and hollows, already covered in green.

Nasyr went out to the street and walked toward the repair workshop on the outskirts of Karaoi. Inside the workshop, someone was banging noisily on metal, but outside it was almost entirely quiet in the aul. Almost but not entirely. As he walked past some of the houses, Nasyr could hear women's voices and children's laughter through the open windows. He focused his attention on these windows and tried to avoid looking at all the abandoned houses.

Maybe Karaoi will vanish. If the sea dies, the aul will die too. It had survived for many centuries through good times and bad, but now it was disappearing. And no one will answer the simple question: Why did it happen?

"And you, Kakharman, are not here. You would've told me. I understand very little. I'm getting old, Kakharman, very old. Thank you for at least coming to me in my dreams."

Indeed, Nasyr often saw his son in his dreams, but in all dreams, he was the same: gloomy and troubled. He dreamed of the beluga that once attacked his boat. He dreamed of the war. Dreamed of the postwar years. Nasyr was lost. It seemed to him that all these dreams had some hidden meaning. Sometimes in the mornings, thinking about one dream or another dream, he would get confused in his prayers.

He went into the repair shop and greeted the hunter, Musa.

"I was wondering who is working here so early—and it's you."

"Yes. Who else? The boss took everyone else. Have you heard? The bays are full of fish! They've got a real rhythm there now! They'll meet the yearly quota in ten days!"

"It'd be good if you were right. What we need now is a plan. Work without a plan is unthinkable."

"That's why the boss keeps on pestering me. There's even a plan for the repair of vehicles! And it is not permitted to not meet expectations. You just wait, he says, just knock them off, and I'll leave you in peace. Then, he says, there'll be no more plans at all."

"What?" Nasyr was astonished. "How can you work without plans?"

"Nake, I don't argue. You may be caught up on your prayers, but you've lagged behind life, that's for sure. This boss from the oblast—what's his name? Samat, I think. Samatovich? He decreed the other day that soon not just this workshop will shut but the whole aul as well."

"What are you saying?" Nasyr waved his hands at him, unnerved. "Just a week ago, I saw him at the sea, and he said nothing of the kind!"

"Scared?" Musa smiled.

He snatched a red-hot piece of metal from the coals, threw it on the anvil, and lifted the heavy hammer like a toy. Musa had been a blacksmith all his life, but no one called him a blacksmith. To everyone, he was a hunter.

Musa had been right. Just ten days later, some men arrived from the oblast with Samat Samatovich. Samatovich requested an urgent meeting, where he made the announcement that the senior authorities demanded the closure of the repair shop immediately! Its income was too small, its productivity too low—it had grown unprofitable to sustain.

The mechanics were appalled by the decision.

"What about us? What are we supposed to do? Beg?"

Samat Samatovich responded sharply, and in a monotone, that the authorities know what they are doing; only those at senior levels are thinking and solving the nation's problems.

Indignant, Musa shouted, "The senior level for us is you! Give us a straight answer. Stop trying to pull the wool over our eyes!"

Samat Samatovich calmly replied that there were authorities more senior than him.

"They don't like it," Musa exclaimed, "when people say everything is in God's hands. So, then, what is in their hands?" Everyone laughed.

Nasyr remembered Kakharman. Now he realized how far ahead his son was looking. Here they are, the people for whom he worked so hard, angrily shouting questions at this smug fool.

Along with the workshop, Kakharman had organized a craft co-op. In this co-op, women embroidered and wove rugs, and the unemployed fishermen made bracelets, rings, and female accessories under Musa's supervision. All this was taken to the city for sale. Nasyr still remembered how proud Kakharman had been of the first artisanal products. Later, he explained to Nasyr that while this, of course, was a good source of additional income for people, most importantly it was the start of a revival of national culture, national spirituality. Kakharman sent four young men in whom Musa had awoken a special talent off to Lvov to study.

And now this fat fool says that the workshop and the co-op will be closed?! How do you expect to keep people in the aul then? Ex-fishermen came to Karaoi from almost all the coastal kolkhozes! With no fish and even these ways of earnings closed, then how will people live? What will they eat?

"Calm down!" Samat Samatovich said calmly. "We are not closing the workshops today. We will simply start cutting back as of tomorrow."

The cars of the visiting authorities rolled away in a cloud of dust. Nasyr went home. From a distance, he saw Berish and Akbalak's granddaughter, Aigul, standing by the gates, and something heavy moved in his heart. He just wanted to saddle the mare and go to Akbalak. He went into the shed and began to stroke the ash-gray.

Then he hugged the horse's neck, pushed his face against its withers, and fought to hold back his tears.

When Korlan walked by and saw Nasyr in the shed, she called him.

"Nasyr, you'll miss prayer time."

Nasyr turned around, still hugging the horse. Korlan sighed and thought, "You're my hapless one. Hapless . . ."

Berish and Aigul were talking by themselves.

"When are you leaving?"

"Tonight," Aigul replied.

"I guess you're not going to your granddad in the aul."

"No. To Zaysan. Dad's already there and found a job."

"I won't be here either in a week's time. Will you write to me?"

"Where?"

Berish took from his pocket a folded piece of paper on which the address was written. Aigul took the piece of paper shyly, and, almost crying, lifted her face.

"Berish, do you believe that our sea will disappear soon?" Aigul asked sadly.

"How can I believe it? It's rubbish!"

"I would like to come back here, when I am properly grown up."

"I will definitely come back. It's impossible for the sea to disappear."

"But many are leaving. It's not just us going tonight."

"Why are you leaving at night?"

"How could we go during the day? It would be so embarrassing to look people in the eyes. Father says we need to go at night."

"If you're leaving, it makes no difference when you leave. Just don't leave stealthily, like thieves. My father, when he left, gathered the people and bid farewell to them properly."

"Berish, I can't give you an address now. I don't know yet where we'll be living. Take this from me." And Aigul gave Berish a flat and shiny stone, the size of a coin. "I was just a little girl when my father gave it to me."

Berish carefully studied Aigul's gift.

"Do you know what stone this is?"

"I have no idea."

"It is *korolek*—native copper."

"How do you know?"

"Musa-aga carves things from these stones. When you come across a flat and wide one, you can draw or write on it. I will engrave your face on this korolek."

Aigul blushed and quickly replied, "I must go, Berish. Goodbye. I promise to write!"

And off she ran, sinking in sand up to her ankles. She looked back, waved to him, and kept on running.

"I will be waiting for your letter!" Berish shouted. She looked back one more time and nodded.

Soon after midnight, Berish slipped out of the house unnoticed. Someone waved from the porch of the neighboring house.

"Berish, come here!"

"Yesen, is that you?" Berish rejoiced.

"Of course, it's me. I'm going out to watch the people sneak off too."

"How many people are leaving?"

"More than half the village. The first ones are already too far away to see. I've been watching for a while now. It's a desperately sad scene."

"And how upset my granddad will be!"

"He shouldn't be that upset. The people leaving aren't worth getting upset about! He should carry on praying five times a day, like before. What if the sea fills up again? Then they'll come back. You'll see. Then we will look at them, eh? Tomorrow I will talk to Moldeke myself. He mustn't stop praying. If he gets tired, I'll come to the rescue."

"Do you know the prayers?"

"He'll teach me. I'll remember them all!" Yesen went silent. "Alright, I'm going to sleep. Oh, there'll be such a scene tomorrow when people wake up and half of the aul has gone!"

Kyzbala was the first to notice the change. She got up very early as usual, went out into the street with the white goat, and froze. There was house after house with boarded-up windows and doors. It filled her soul with horror.

"A-a-a!" The crazy woman screamed as if it would burst her heart. Then, lifting up her skirt, she ran to the sea. The goat and the kid raced after her. The old woman was really scared. It seemed to her that she was the only one left in the aul.

On hearing the heartrending scream, Nasyr jumped out of bed. Korlan got up too.

"Ya, Allah, what's going on?"

"Kyzbala is screaming. You stay in bed, and I'll go to have a look."

The aul was half-empty. Houses were abandoned. Window shutters and gates creaked in the wind. Nasyr stiffened. He looked pitifully and helplessly toward the sea. The figure of the mad woman emerged from the sea and came closer. Behind Kyzbala still ran the goat with the kid bleating piteously.

When Kyzbala reached Nasyr, she stopped. She was breathing wildly. Suddenly she collapsed on the sand. Nasyr ran to lift her up, and Korlan brought the poor woman water, which she scooped up with a ladle and splashed on Kyzbala's face. Kyzbala soon opened her eyes and smiled quietly and guiltily. It was the first time in many, many years Nasyr had seen her eyes like this, radiant and intelligent. They sat her down on a bench in the shade in the yard. The goat and the kid attacked a heap of grass that Nasyr had prepared the previous night for his ash-gray. "Sit down, Kyzbala, and have a rest." Korlan stroked her head. But Kyzbala did not rest for long. She quickly stood up and walked out of the yard, with the goat and the kid trudging after her.

From that day, people began to leave Karaoi in broad daylight. The damaged dams upstream were repaired, and the sea again grew shallow, each day moving farther away from the aul. Now Nasyr lay at home whole days, rereading the newspapers.

AFTER THE CHERNOBYL CATASTROPHE, A WAVE of demonstrations and meetings rolled across the whole country, protesting the construction of nuclear power plants. Tensions between nuclear scientists and "greens" have become inflamed. Nuclear scientists insist that the greens' arguments are out of date and ignore the environmental damage done by other kinds of energy sources.

ACTIVISTS FROM A RANGE OF PEACE ORGANIZATIONS in Alameda County in California have started a petition calling for the county to declare itself a nuclear-free zone. Two federal departments—defense and energy—have reacted against this initiative. Their irritation is understandable: the Lawrence Livermore National Laboratory, one of the main scientific centers in the United States for developing nuclear weapons, is located in the county.

Attempts to declare Alameda a nuclear-free zone had been made before but with no success. This time, the protesters have a real chance of achieving their aim. To bring this question to a referendum, the petition has to get just thirty-eight thousand signatures. The laboratory's administration is firmly against going nonnuclear and calls the initiative "unreasonable and very aggressive."

AT 08:00 MOSCOW TIME IN THE DISTRICT of Semipalatinsk, an underground nuclear explosion was set off with a power of from 100 to 150 kilotons.

The test was carried out to maintain parity in the Soviet–American nuclear weapons program. The radiation in the area of the trials and outside the Polygon remain normal.

IN THE THIRD UN COMMITTEE ON SOCIAL, HUMANITARIAN, and cultural questions, a resolution was passed to begin a global program to combat drug use.

The FAMOUS TWELFTH-CENTURY MONUMENT OF KHMERIAN ARCHITECTURE at Angkor Wat was damaged by an earthquake. The Cambodian government has launched an appeal for international help with restoration of the monument, the SPK agency reports.

The Cambodian Department of Culture called for international institutions, governments and nongovernmental organizations of all countries to "undertake urgent steps to assist in restoring and protecting this architectural miracle, which is a universal cultural heritage."

ANOTHER GROUP OF CUBAN PEACEKEEPING TROOPS HAVE LEFT Angola. With the recent departure of ten thousand soldiers, the withdrawal of half of the Cuban military contingent is now complete. The phased withdrawal of the Cuban army from Angola is being undertaken in compliance with the southwest African peace agreement signed in New York in December of last year.

LAST WEDNESDAY A YOUNG MAN APPROXIMATELY TWENTY YEARS OF AGE burst into a lecture hall at Université de Montréal, where sixty students were present. He ordered all men to leave the room, then opened fire, killing fourteen girls. The killer then shot himself.

THE SOVIET HIERARCHY ACKNOWLEDGES ACTS AGAINST NATIONS SUBJECTED TO FORCEFUL RESETTLEMENT AS UNLAWFUL AND CRIMINAL AND GUARANTEES THEIR RIGHTS. Today, as part of the revolutionary renewal of the Soviet community, a process of democratization is beginning to eradicate deviations from common humanitarian principles. The people's desire to know the full truth about the past will strengthen the lessons it has for the future.

A memory of exceptional bitterness takes us back to the tragic years of Stalin's reprisals. Their lawlessness and despotism did not spare a single republic, a single nation. The mass arrests; the suffering in prison camps; and the maltreatment of women, the elderly, and children in resettlement zones keep calling to our conscience and insult our moral sense. They must not be forgotten.

One of the worst policies during Stalin's regime was the forced migration of Balkars, Ingush, Kalmucks, Karachais, Crimean Tatars, Germans, Meskhetian Turks, and Chechens from their homelands during World War II. These forced emigrations also had a profound impact on the fates of Koreans, Greeks, Kurds, and the peoples of many other nations.

The Supreme Court of the USSR unconditionally condemns the policy of forced resettlement as a violation of basic international rights and a contradiction of the humanist nature of the socialist system.

THE STATE COOPERATIVE ASSOCIATION ANT IS ATTEMPTING to sell twelve new tanks abroad. It is yet to be determined how the tanks will be transferred from Ural to their foreign destination.

WITH A SENSE OF DEEP SATISFACTION AND PATRIOTIC pride, all citizens of socialist Romania overwhelmingly approved the decision of the plenum to suggest to the XIV Congress the reelection of comrade Nicolae Ceaușescu[1]—the hero among heroes, the outstanding leader of the nation, the architect of socialist Romania, the outstanding personality of our time—to the highest position as general secretary of the Romanian Communist Party.

THE GENERAL SECRETARY OF SOCIALIST UNITY PARTY E. HONECKER TODAY RECEIVED the chief of the general staff of the Armed Forces of the USSR, Army General M. Moiseev, who is leading the Soviet military delegation now in the GDR on an official friendly visit.

IN THE LAST FEW DAYS IN BAKU AND A NUMBER OF OTHER PLACES IN Azerbaijan and also in some areas of Armenia, tragic events took place that provoked great pain in the hearts of the Soviet people. Blood was shed and there were casualties among Armenians, Azerbaijanis, and other nationalities.

BAPTISM, CONFIRMATION, COMMUNION, PENANCE, PRIESTHOOD, marriage, Holy Unction . . . these are the seven orthodox sacraments, and each one is a milestone on the path of a man's spiritual ascent. Today, church ceremonies are openly returning to the everyday lives of the Soviet people. People are once again being drawn to churches, seeing in them a source of kindness, mercy, and hope.

Nasyr had to saddle up his horse now that the sea was too far to walk to. He continued his fivefold *salah*[2] on the shore. Karaoi was falling into decay. Abandoned dogs circled the deserted yards, looking desperately into their empty bowls, then began to go into the dunes to catch mice and gerbils, each day roaming farther and farther away from the aul. Nasyr's dog began to join the other dogs, and he saw it in the yard rarely. Then the day came when his dog never came back.

"Everything is becoming wild," Musa lamented. "You should see it, Nasyr. The dunes are filled with wild dogs and horses. They are roaming there in great packs."

Only Yesen did not despair. In the evenings, he'd start up his generator and then head off to the district center to collect mail, joking, "Now I am the most important person in Karaoi!"

One day, he returned from the district center with news for the aul. "Today they are removing our telephone station and repair shop. They will start transferring the equipment soon."

"I hope they will leave us some diesel and the generator."

"They won't touch it! I stocked up with diesel to last for the rest of my life!"

Nasyr, holding back his anger, pronounced, "While there's fish in the sea and animals in the sands, we will not starve. I will not move from here until the end."

"Me too!" Yesen asserted.

"You are still young," the old men suggested. "You will change your outlook on life."

"It's my mother's will. She will die here."

The old men advised him.

"Yesen, you should go to the city and visit your wife. Have a proper conversation with her—this is a man's duty."

"I'll go," Yesen assured them. "But it will be a waste of time; she won't come back. Why would she care for us, for this dying aul and its old men and women?"

Nasyr had a thought. "Soon we'll need to send Berish to his parents. You will come to see him off, won't you? At the same time, you can visit the *kelin*."[3] With this, they began to go their separate ways, when Yesen remembered something. "Moldeke, I almost forgot: the regional recruitment office demands you visit them immediately."

"I'm already flying!" Nasyr said sarcastically, swishing his gown as if about to take off.

"I did explain to them that you can't come because there's no transport."

"What could've happened?" Musa was surprised. "Are they going to give you another death notice?"[4]Yesen brightened up. "Nasyr-aga, have you had a death notice before?"

Nasyr grinned. "Two of them, while I was in the war. I'll tell you about it some other time."

The young lieutenant was accompanied by Sayat. When they entered Karaoi, the lieutenant began to lament sincerely, "Such a large aul and completely empty. It makes you feel uneasy just looking at it. It must be awful to live here. Maybe we should go to the office first?"

"What kind of office can be here now? The fishermen have gone to Zaysan to fish."

Korlan greeted the guests by the gate. When she saw Sayat, she clasped her hands and began to cry. He reminded her of Kakharman.

"Where is the aqsaqal, Korlan-apa?"

"Where else? He went for the afternoon prayer."

The men got in the car again and headed to the sea. As thick white dust filled the car, they rolled up the windows.

Nasyr was on his knees. He could never be distracted when he was praying, so Sayat stopped the car some distance away.

"There he is, our hero aqsaqal!"

"Is he praying?" The lieutenant was amazed.

"Yes. He's not lost hope that God will give water to the sea."

"Wow, amazing!" the deputy exclaimed. "Does he seriously believe it?"

"He does. Otherwise, he wouldn't be praying."

"There won't be a sea here. Neither God nor the devil will help him."

"I don't know about God or the devil, but men could've helped him, or have they turned into beasts?" Sayat responded sharply. "You yourself, what area are you from?"

"From Ladoga. There is such a lake . . ."

"I know it. I did my first work experience there while I was a student. Our ship was called the *Ortex*."

"Now Ladoga is also hopeless. Phosphor suffocates every living thing in it."

By this time, Nasyr had finished praying. He hobbled over to Sayat and hugged him.

"It's been a while since you were here. How are you? Is your family healthy? How are your children?"

"They're all fine, Nasyr-aga. They send you their greetings. What is Kakharman up to?"

"Kakharman doesn't write. Aitugan doesn't give him ink. She writes herself. She asks us to send Berish. It's understandable; she misses him. I think they are alright."

"I can take Berish with me."

"Eh, that's good! From Alma-Ata to Balkhash is a stone's throw. You can put him on the train. He'll be there in no time."

Nasyr turned to the deputy and greeted him. The lieutenant raised his hand to the peak of his cap and smiled warmly. "I wish you health, comrade senior sergeant of the Guard!"

"*Malades*,[5] lieutenant!" Nasyr shook the lieutenant's hand. "Who is he?" he asked Sayat in Kazakh.

Sayat laughed and translated Nasyr's question to the lieutenant. The lieutenant tapped his finger on his case and pronounced solemnly, "This, Nasyr-aga, has been searching for you for forty-three years!"

"He is a good Russian!" Nasyr nodded to Sayat. "Go to my house, tell my wife to cook *kuyrdak*.[6] Musa shot a deer yesterday. I'll join you shortly."

"Nake, aren't you even going to ask what's in his case?"

Nasyr replied simply, "We can talk business at the dastarkhan."

But Sayat was insistent. "Then I will tell you myself. This lieutenant here is on the instructions of the military office. Nasyr-aga, he came to give you a military award: the Order of the Red Banner!"

"Eh! Couldn't you tell me all of that at the dastarkhan?" Nasyr smiled archly. "Do you think I didn't guess? About two months ago, I received a letter from my ex–regimental commander, who told me about it. But do I need this order now? My sea is in its death throes, and you say, 'Nasyr, slap a piece of gold on your chest and be happy!'" Nasyr spat heartily, sat on his horse, and set off toward the aul.

He did like the young lieutenant. He reminded Nasyr of Semenov, the commander of his gun company in the war. Semenov was right out of military college, a little idealistic, read a lot, and sang beautifully. Songs brought them together. In the first rough days of war, Semenov would sit down next to Nasyr during brief lulls in the action.

"Sing, Nasyr." And he would lay a friendly arm round Nasyr's shoulder. "*The swan is swimming with a she swan . . .*"

During those days in the forests near Moscow, the name of the hero Bauyrzhan Momyshuly[7] was covered in legend. Nasyr kept asking Semenov if he could be transferred to the Panfilov Division. Nasyr really wanted to fight hand to hand beside his fellow countrymen.

"Momyshuly, I guess, doesn't need anyone to sing for him. And who will I sing with? And anyway, we need heroes too."

Nasyr was not a timid soldier. Twice in his life he looked death in the face.

The Germans attacked continuously for two days. On the third day, their tanks broke through close to the gun emplacements, and a long fight began. Many soldiers died during that fight—almost the entire company, together with Lieutenant Semenov. Nasyr was left alone to man the gun. After he had knocked out his ninth tank, he was struck by shrapnel that lodged deep in his chest. The orderlies managed to carry him, bleeding, away from the battlefield and sent him right away to the rear. After that, a death notice was sent to Karaoi with the signature of the regimental commander.

When they sat at the table, the question came up about where to award the order. Nasyr didn't see the need for a special ceremony and thought it could be done simply at a dastarkhan. But Sayat and the lieutenant had their own ideas, and Musa supported them. While they were deciding, Igor Slavikov and the young scientists from the laboratory appeared at the gate. Sayat had already told them the news. Nasyr was happy to see Igor but looked at the rest of the guests coldly.

They went to the clubhouse. It had three hundred seats, but everyone could fit in just the first row. Kyzbala was near the open door. As the lieutenant read the decree, he found the mewling of her goat and kid embarrassing and glanced uncomfortably at the door.

When the order was attached to Nasyr's chest, he shouted loudly, "I serve humanity!"

The lieutenant raised his eyebrows in surprise but decided not to correct the old man.

Then everyone headed to Nasyr's house. Kyzbala, like their shadow, followed them. Everyone entered the house, but not everyone sat down. Igor and his colleagues began to bid farewell to Nasyr since they had to go for night duty.

Igor embraced Nasyr warmly. "I will definitely write to my father about your honor!"

"Igor, you've begun to forget about us, the old people," Korlan scolded him as she tucked the meat of a young lamb in his bag.

The girl who had told Nasyr about the laboratory was looking at the huge bag with genuine fear. Korlan caught her look.

"Are you alright, dear?"

Igor translated the young woman's answer.

"She's worried about the amount of meat and wonders if it's a bit too much."

"It's alright. You should eat," Korlan sighed. "I guess all you have there is canned food."

Toward evening, Sayat and the lieutenant began to get ready to go.

Nasyr made arrangements. "Korlan, get Berish ready for the journey while I talk to Sayat." And they walked out into the yard.

"Sayatzhan," Nasyr began to complain, "we are being left without a telephone station. That's not acceptable. How can we do without a post office and telephone? Let them at least leave the post office. And what if we need to make a phone call to you? To Kakharman? To our fishermen? People are spreading all over, but their parents, wives, children are here. It's unacceptable, Sayatzhan. It's inhumane."

"I'm aware of that, Nasyr-aga. They will leave one switchboard. You'll have a connection to the regional center. And the post office will be in Shumgen. There are more people there."

"Alright." Nasyr calmed down. "Then we don't have any other requests for you."

"Nasyr-aga, I have also decided to leave, like Kakharman."

"Ya, Allah! Where are you going?"

"To Caspy. I'm being given a mothership[8] there."

Nasyr frowned and then said, "There was enough sea to last our lives but not enough now here for your lives. Forgive us, children. I understand you, both you and Kakharman. Thank you for coming by to say goodbye. I hope happiness smiles on you in a strange land! But I am destined to die here. Tell them that." He pronounced the word "them" with meaning. "Tell them that I will not move from here."

"Yes, that's his final decision," Sayat thought. He couldn't bring himself to tell the old man what he was requested to tell him by the regional center: if Nasyr moves to the district, a house will be ready for him.

Berish hugged his grandfather.

"Ata, I will come back next summer! But don't you go anywhere. Yesen also won't go anywhere."

"We have nowhere to go." Nasyr rumpled his grandson's hair and buried his face in it.

It was decided that Yesen wouldn't go with them, so the two young friends said their goodbyes there. Berish was looking with pity at Zhanyl-apa, who was holding the infant, wrapped up in a light blanket, in her arms.

"Yesen, look after your daughter."

The friends hugged, and Yesen said quietly, "I don't know, Berish. I don't know." He frowned. "It looks like we have no chance."

"You have to save her!" And then Berish began to cry.

Sayat gently nudged him toward the car. From the window, Berish saw the small group of people who had come to say goodbye, and a sharp sense of pity suddenly squeezed his chest. He looked at his grandmother and grandfather, who all at once seemed old, crushed by grief. He was looking at Yesen, who no longer seemed as big and strong as in the past, and at Zhanyl-apa with the infant in her arms, a helpless creature betrayed by her mother, condemned to death. And a sense of the impermanence of the world, an inconsolable feeling that everything in this world comes to an end, overwhelmed his young heart for the first time.

And he knew that at that moment, he had left his childhood forever.

After their grandson left, the life of the old people shrank. The days became long and joyless. And they could not find peace at night. Korlan lay awake for a long time, then sighed and tossed in her sleep. Nasyr knew she was worried. Worried about Kakharman, so far away from home. Worried about her daughters in the city, who hadn't written recently.

As before, the old couple sat together at a dastarkhan three times a day, but now they drank tea in silence, then each went their separate way. Even the frequent visits by Musa or by old Zhanyl failed to give their lives the variety they used to have. Yet one kind of silence is different from another. In the fifty years of life together, Korlan and Nasyr had learned to understand each other without words.

Shortly after Berish's departure, men from the Regional Council arrived in Karaoi. They loaded the machines from the repair shop, the post office equipment, the chairs from the clubhouse, and all the books from the library onto trucks. None of them visited Nasyr, or Musa, or Zhanyl—as if they were ordered not to.

There was still no news from Kakharman, and that worried Korlan. Nasyr kept quiet when she complained to him, and Korlan wasn't offended. She was never offended by Nasyr; she knew there wasn't a day in his life—not during the war years, nor later when he chaired the kolkhoz, or even now he was a mullah—when he wouldn't speak to her in his mind. For her, that was enough.

Like any Kazakh woman, Nasyr felt, she was patient. For him, the harmony of a Kazakh family relied on a wife's unquestioning submission to her husband's will and her great forbearance. She tended the hearth, carefully and selflessly, but the man was always the head of the household. That was the unwritten law of the nomads. But the life of the Kazakhs was changing. The nomadic people were once united against the outside world. As Nasyr saw it, a Kazakh wife was an eternal support. But women were no longer willing to completely submit to their husbands. So now a man rarely finds rest in his family, and that support has been knocked from under his feet.

But this is not what Korlan was like. In countless little ways, he understood, she responded to Nasyr's will, Nasyr's wish to rule in the house, and so helped soothe the troubles and worries the surrounding world was bringing to Nasyr's soul.

Nasyr was lucky with Korlan. How many families never knew that deep love or faith in each other, knowing instead the bitterness of quarrels?

Meanwhile, the seashore was becoming drearier and drearier, day by day. Autumn was coming. The evenings were gray and cold. Nasyr now sat on the bench by the house for a long time when he came back from the evening salah. Korlan would bring a warm camel wool *chekmen* and throw it over his shoulders.

Then they would sit together in the dusk, as if waiting for something. It was at this time in the past that the fishermen would come back from the sea. Noisy and jolly, they would amble past on their way home, full of talk and laughter. Now the shore was quiet—so quiet, that sometimes even the silence rang in their ears. Korlan and Nasyr always talked about the same things. Korlan complained about her ailments or about Kakharman and their daughters not writing. Of course, she wanted to live with her son or daughters, in Semipalatinsk or Balkhash or anywhere. She didn't say this to Nasyr out loud, but Nasyr had known for a long time and would answer like this:

"I know you're sad, Korlan. I know. But this is what I say. If a man is to live properly, he cannot be torn away from his native land. He simply can't. Where else can he find true joy but in his native land? Of course, there are jobs everywhere. As long as you're not lazy, you'll always find a way to make a living somewhere. But what if the soul starves in separation? What then? This is what I'm scared of. Or am I wrong, Korlan?"

"You're right, of course. You're right. You're saying the right thing, Nasyr."

And after sighing for a bit, they went into the house: Nasyr first, and Korlan behind, who worried that he might stumble.

BOOK THREE

The difficulty, my friends, lies not in avoiding death but in avoiding unrighteousness, for that runs faster than death.

—Socrates, in Plato's Apology, fifth century BC

Suffering is the privilege of higher natures: the higher the nature, the more unhappiness it experiences.

—Hegel, eighteenth century

What's the point of political theories that promise a brave new world if we've no idea how that world will really turn out? Who can ensure their success? We are not cattle to be fattened. When one unrecognized Pascal appears, it is incomparably more important than the birth of a score of beautiful ideas.

—Antoine de Saint-Exupéry, twentieth century

BOOK THREE

VIII

Towing a barge heavily laden with shingle, the boat chugged across the wide river mouth. As it swung around into a narrow channel, Kakharman clambered up onto the bridge. A dark and haggard look hung on his face, and his eyes were deeply troubled.

It was three years since he had left Sinemorye. In all that time, he had never found a job he warmed to. He was naturally sturdy and resilient, but his soul had found no rest.

He'd been forced to leave his native land out of desperation. But had he found anything to replace the old job he loved? Maybe he should've stayed to carry on the struggle. How could he know? It seemed he was alone in fighting. It was only he, Kakharman, whose whole heart ached for the fishermen. Because the fishermen still lived by the sea and shared its destiny to the full.

One should learn from these people, not teach them. Many hardships had been borne by the shoulders of the fishermen through the years, and the men had been through tough times. Yet never once had Kakharman seen them break under the weight of misfortune. These folks have a kind of steadiness through sorrow and happiness. They stay true to their nature.

The devotion of the fishermen to their native land was amazing. Not for a moment did they falter as people began to leave Sinemorye—at first one by one, then in the tens, then in the hundreds. It was an uncertain and troubled time. Only the old fishermen kept calm. They would still go into the sea, and they would still return with their catch. But they were saddened by the diminishing haul. Chub, barbel, and pike vanished first, then silver carp became scarce too. For a while, perch and pike were still abundant, but in time, they, too, became rare. Catfish were still caught, but in the place of the familiar fish, strange, long, thin fish began to multiply. The fishermen called them fish-snakes.

These new species had been created by scientists in laboratory conditions and raised in the Shardara reservoir. No one could foresee that this uninvited alien would become such a monster, with a gargantuan snake appetite. It gorged on all sea fish indiscriminately, even caviar. The fishing kolkhozes tried to stop them. The fishermen began to build dikes across the estuaries, but the wild fish-snake seemed to get through them all. It even got into the rice fields and sucked around the rice ears. Kakharman had spoken out against the breeding of this predator. But the scientists and ministry officials, who had never seen the sea, ignored him, and the Bureau of the Regional Committee interpreted his opposition as political shortsightedness and issued a severe reprimand. Kozha Aldiyarov, the first secretary of the Regional Committee, had irritably declared, "Comrade Nasyrov, it's me who gives orders here! If you don't like it, we can help you to find somewhere else to work!"

Slavikov, who had kept his silence until then, rose from his seat. He gazed around at everybody present as if trying to work out who would support him.

"Comrade Secretary!" Slavikov began. "First of all, I would like to thank you for permitting my colleague and me to be here."

"Because this meeting has already dragged on," Slavikov continued, "I will be brief. If today you decide to breed this strange fish-snake, in three or four years, there'll be no fish at all in your waters!"

"Why so pessimistic, Matvei Panteleevich?" The first secretary smiled. "I understand it's hard for you to refrain from acting as a prophet, but you seem to imagine there's no other scientists giving evidence here. I will take this opportunity to introduce them." He made an inviting gesture with his hand. "Here they are, comrades Mikhailov and Pavlovsky, scientists from Moscow. They have been studying this problem for a few years both in Moscow and in Alma-Ata. Am I correct?" Kozha Aldiyarov looked at the scientists, and they nodded in agreement.

"Not all scientists are the same," Slavikov noted dryly after glancing at his new colleagues.

"You might ask me why there will be no fish," he continued. "The answer is the fish-snake will destroy them all. You won't have to wait long to test the truth of what I'm saying. I will live to see this catastrophe, although, God forbid—"

"I don't find your answer well reasoned," the first secretary objected.

"Have you ever personally held this fish in your hands or seen it with your own eyes?"

"No, I haven't," Aldiyarov admitted frankly.

"Then how can I talk to you about this problem?"

"I didn't ask you to be here, did I?" Aldiyarov was irritated again. "You came here of your own will."

Nearly everyone cooed approvingly. One of the few dissenters was Galym Erzhanov, the new chairman of the Regional Executive Committee, who had only been in his job a year or so. Before that, he had spent many years working in manufacturing and held a leading position in the party. Erzhanov was both businesslike and well educated and was equally fluent in both Kazakh and Russian. People were never scared of coming to meetings with him because he was responsive to others' misfortunes and had an open heart.

But as life always goes, the honest, decent man has many friends but even more enemies. If ordinary people liked Galym Erzhanov, then hustlers and dealers avoided him. Erzhanov knew it, but he refused to try to please everybody. This certainly rankled the first secretary, who advised him.

"Beware, many dzhigits have broken their necks trying to gain cheap popularity. People are sly! When you're in power, when you're in the saddle, they envy you. But when you fall off, they will gloat, and none will help you up. Is it worth flirting with them and expecting good faith in return?" Aldiyarov smiled and condescendingly patted him on the shoulder. "Think about it, Galym."

Erzhanov guessed what the secretary was getting at.

"I won't disagree with you. But time is the judge of everything."

"Oh yes, you still have time." Aldiyarov chuckled, twitching his small, dry head.

Aldiyarov's chuckle—shallow, voluptuous—pierced Erzhanov's soul. He was amazed by it when closing the secretary's massive doors behind him and amazed again quite a few times on his way home. "Be sensible, Galym. Don't put your head in the mouth of an old lion." That's what it seemed the secretary was saying.

But he was not scared. It was a new day outside, a new time, and Erzhanov considered himself a harbinger of it.

Yet much later, Erzhanov did begin to think about it, even though he was a brave man, little versed in intrigues. As the petty old bureaucrat bade farewell to Erzhanov, he already knew how he might trip the ardent chairman up.

Erzhanov and Slavikov sympathized with each other. They frequently met and exchanged views. During those meetings, Erzhanov came to understand the true depth of Slavikov's scientific thinking, how attractive and unusual his disposition and the sincerity of the old man's love for the sea.

"My friend," the professor used to say, when they traveled the kolkhozes and *sovkhozes*[1] of the region, "you don't need to go far to find out everything about me. Simply ask the fisherman Nasyr, the hunter Musa, or the old zhyrau Akbalak. They will tell you all there is to know. Or here," the professor said, nodding at Kakharman, who was accompanying them. "Although Kakharman doesn't count. He and I, as it's said nowadays, are playing on the same team. We bow our head to anyone we think can help us to protect Sinemorye!"

"Yes, your team is strong." Erzhanov smiled.

"You're mistaken here, my dear friend." Slavikov grew visibly depressed. "If we were really strong, then would we insult ourselves by bowing?" He went silent, then added, "Although good deeds are not easy to do, no matter where you are." And then he cheered up and said half-jokingly, "Oh, you should ask your deputy Zharasbai about me!"

"I cannot talk about you in prose, Matvei Panteleevich. Would you like a poem?" Zharasbai began to laugh, glancing at the professor mischievously.

Erzhanov looked carefully at his deputy. He wasn't at all surprised that Zharasbai was on such good terms with the famous scientist. From the first days of their work together, Erzhanov had felt an involuntary sympathy toward his deputy and was happy to discover that it wasn't misplaced.

"So have you known each other for a long time?" he asked.

"Matvei Panteleevich has said before that we're on the same team, all of us," Zharasbai asserted, smiling again.

Slavikov turned to Erzhanov. "We've known each other a long time, that's true. Guess, Galym, what nationality our Zharasbai is?"

Erzhanov was surprised.

"What do you mean, what nationality? Isn't he a Kazakh?"

Slavikov burst out laughing.

"Believe it or not, he's isn't! When did Kazakhs have blue eyes and blond hair? He's Russian. During the hungry years, Nasyr saved him from death. And Musa brought him up." He shook his finger jokingly at Zharasbai. "He keeps me informed on everything that's happening locally."

The chairman was very pleased by the conversation. Slavikov in turn thought about Erzhanov. "He is young, trusting, and open. I hope he won't get broken before his time and give up."

That is why Erzhanov shuddered at the arrogance of the first secretary of the Regional Committee toward the old man. Aldiyarov, however, could spot the complete array of moods of the bureau members—a habit, or even an art, that he developed over his long years of functioning within the party apparatus. Sometimes it looked as if he was keeping his head down and not paying attention, but with each cell of his calculating soul, he sensed danger. Erzhanov's discontent would not pass unnoticed.

The secretary seized the moment and asked loudly, "Comrade Erzhanov, it looks like you disapprove of our decision?"

Everyone turned toward the chairman of the Regional Executive Committee—and it was clear to all that the first secretary had a reason for his question.

Erzhanov was beginning to shake with anger. "You, Kozha Aldiyarovich, have no right to talk in such way toward this great scientist. I am talking about Slavikov. I find it hard to understand. It is as if he's a stranger in front of us, rather than a man who for thirty long years has worked tirelessly on the uninhabited islands of Sinemorye!" Blood rushed to the chairman's face. "We should be grateful that he is sharing with us his thoughts on the fate of our land, but instead we insult him!"

The first secretary smiled.

"It took us a lot of hard work to learn to talk at meetings briefly, to the point," he observed. "But with Erzhanov, it now looks like the old roundabout style is coming back. Comrade Erzhanov, it's better to get straight to the point. Should we really care for someone else's sensitivities? The business! The business in hand, first and foremost!"

Seeing a conflict brewing, Slavikov stood up.

"Comrades! None of us has time for pointless arguments. Let's be constructive. It would be fantastic if all of us here could come to the same opinion so we could send all our energy into the same channel!"

"That is entirely correct, comrade Slavikov. But in this case, Moscow is deciding the fate of Sinemorye. Am I right?" The secretary was looking intently at Slavikov's face, while still carefully monitoring the mood of the chamber. Sly smiles appeared on many faces, and Slavikov realized what his opponent was getting at.

"Moscow! Do you really think that Moscow is never wrong? Moscow can make mistakes. I would even say it has already made too many. And one of those mistakes is our Sinemorye. This error could be considered a catastrophe—and not just for Kazakhstan but for the whole Union!" Slavikov looked around the hall, in which the buzz of discontent was increasing.

"You are trying to slander socialism," Aldiyarov cut in sharply. "We have seen many slanderers during our time, but as you can see, we stayed strong."

A prolonged burst of applause erupted. Although to him it was all arrant nonsense, Slavikov bowed politely, then quickly left the chamber. Tiredness and pain were written on the face of the old scientist. Bolat followed him.

"The Center, Moscow. They got used to blaming everything on the Center and on Moscow. What is the purpose of local government? And what are the leaders of the Republic worried about? Where are the citizens of their own republic?" Slavikov realized that the word "citizen" now sounded ambiguous in Russian, and he repeated his last question in Kazakh: "Where are the *azamats*?"

"Azamats?" Bolat asked sarcastically. "What kind of citizen, what kind of first secretary is he? He's just a Soviet *bai*,[2] not a first secretary! He's simply a half-wit! And we tried to explain something to him. We must both be mad, to be honest, Matvei Panteleevich!"

"You are right, Bolat. People like us are called 'fools with degrees.'" Slavikov suddenly cheered up.

Only two out of eleven members of the bureau opposed the breeding of the fish-snake. They were Erzhanov and Zharasbai.

Kakharman had other things to think about, other things to remember, as he made his way up to the bridge and looked thoughtfully over to the deserted banks floating by. The ancient, once-mighty Irtysh was now an obedient and submissive river.

How could you not feel sorrow just looking at its crumbling, abandoned banks? The river had now receded entirely and splashed pitifully at their crumbling feet. Rotting timbers protruded above the cracked mud, and the forests that line the banks had entirely lost their old beauty. According to Sasha Ladov, the captain's assistant, everything here was once different, better, and richer—right up to the day the "foot of the reformer" stamped on these lands.

The old ones who used to scare the life out of those who lived on the land with their tales of the Lord of the Local Water are long gone. The old ones used to say that the Lord will punish anyone who sneers at the river or uses its water unwisely. People won't listen to their dark words now, after a century of technology clenching the heart of Mother Earth tighter and tighter with its steel tongs. No one will stop now. No one will look around, think, and be afraid of what has been done to their land. Aren't these people in their masses just like that fish-snake that devours everything? Don't they understand that a time will come when this fish will start to devour itself?

The bow of the tugboat left trails of heavy, foamy waves. And Kakharman saw pike flickering in the waves, big and gray as the old, old stones. This gray—the color of the old stone monuments—was the color of Ata-Balyk,[3] who once upon a time lived in Sinemorye. Is it still alive, then, Ata-Balyk? Has it not been devoured by the savage fish-snakes?

It is the first time Kakharman has seen Ata-Balyk since his dream at Balkhash—the fish that saved him from the catfish when he was a child.

In those times, it was women who ran the business of the auls. Because the men still hadn't returned from war, the women spent whole days at sea, leaving their children to be looked after by the old men and women. But the elderly looked after household chores as well, spinning and plucking wool in the shadows of the houses and yurts, and it was hard for them to keep an eye on their grandchildren. The children made the most of their freedom, running wild down to the sea. There were no adults on the shore. Only crazy Kyzbala would occasionally walk by, muttering something under her breath. Out at sea, the raised sails of the fisherwomen flashed by. During the war, there was such an abundance of fish in Sinemorye that the women didn't need to go far out in search of fish and put their nets close to the shore. Sometimes, a wild catfish would attack the children, who were busy playing in the waves. Once it happened to Kakharman. He was splashing around in the water with the other children when he suddenly felt an invisible force ripping his feet off the seabed and pulling him through the water, as if he was on water skis. "Apa!" he shouted in horror as he saw the gaping mouth of a huge catfish. The other children screamed in terror and ran out of the water. Kakharman was being sucked into the catfish's mouth! But at that moment, another big fish burst from the depth and plunged in between him and the catfish. Kakharman felt his chest thump on the side of this fish. It veered around sharply and thrust Kakharman to the side with a powerful blow of its tail. He was thrown right out of the water, landing on his back on the sand and losing consciousness. [4]Other children later told him that the catfish swallowed half of the fish that had saved him, but it got stuck in its mouth. "But did the fish survive?" he asked.

"How would we know?" the children answered. "Both fish swam into the sea locked together."

After this incident, Kakharman was often frightened in his sleep. He would scream, wake up, and not be able to calm down for a long time. At first Korlan didn't notice. She came back late from the sea exhausted and, after drowsily eating dinner, would collapse into bed and fall at once into a deep sleep. The next day she was up at dawn to take up oars again. But then one night, she heard Kakharman crying out, "Ata-Balyk, save me. The catfish . . . catfish is opening its mouth. Apa! Apa-a-a-a-a."

Korlan lay down next to her son, pulled him to her, and stroked his head to soothe him. Kakharman recoiled and jumped up, staring at his mother with horror in his eyes. Swallowing his tears, barely able to breathe, he begged Korlan, "Apa, is Ata-Balyk alive? Where is it now?"

Korlan had no idea what her son was asking her about but answered, "Of course it's alive, my boy. Calm down." She pulled her son close to her. Only half-awake, she imagined he was worried about his father. She stroked him until she fell asleep herself, repeating over and over, "Your father is alive . . . Of course he is. How can I or your father die without putting you on your feet first?"

It was time to go to sea. Her mother-in-law was already working by the fire, standing a jug of water into the hot ashes. Korlan stopped to share her worries.

"Apa, it seems Kakharman is scared of something. He cries in his sleep. Maybe we should invite Otkeldy-*emshi*[5] to come by."

"Invite him, dear, yes," she replied.

Otkeldy came as the sun was setting. The tall, thin old man was dressed as usual in a long white gown. The healer asked for water, and Korlan brought a piala. Otkeldy bowed his stern, ascetic face over the piala and read a prayer. Then, saying words only he knew, he moved the piala around Kakharman's head three times and splashed water over the boy a few times.

"Tomorrow, everything will be fine," he said, bidding farewell.

After that, Kakharman stopped being scared, even though he often had the same dream:

> *Ata-Balyk, cutting sleekly through the waves, scales gleaming, eyes shining, is swimming next to him. Whenever Kakharman tires, Ata-Balyk lowers its back to him, and he climbs on—and the fish carries him farther.*

He dreamed of the kind fish many years later, long after he became an adult. But this amazing dream comes less and less often now. Now he dreams about the abandoned, rusty ship hulls on the sand and of wild catfish and a swarming mass of fish-snakes.

He has worked for about a year and a half on Lake Balkhash, and it's become clear to him that this ancient lake is in a sad state. Now he must leave Balkhash as well. He doesn't have the strength to accept that this lake has met the same disastrous fate as his native Sinemorye. And he can't risk meeting any fishermen from Sinemorye—this would just be rubbing salt in the wound. And the wound feels like it will never heal. Only alcohol can briefly suppress the pain.

In the past, Kakharman drank only when visiting friends or on special occasions, when it might offend people to stand aloof. If he'd been told then that he'd one day find consolation in drink, he'd never have believed it. But now . . .

Of course, you couldn't call him a lost man, but as soon as anguish washed over him, he'd dilute it with a bottle.

About fifteen fishermen arrived in Balkhash in March. They were compatriots of the old zhyrau Akbalak from the kolkhozes of Shumgen and Karaoi. Their pride was wounded by the fact that they'd been forced to go so far to catch fish, but people can get used to many things.

When they arrived, the fishermen hurried to find Kakharman. Their foreman was Kambar, a close relative of Akbalak. He was a hardworking, practical man, with a great mind. What a shame he never had a proper education—if he had, maybe now he'd be running a major concern. Kakharman believed in him. When he was still a member of the management team, Kakharman had recommended appointing Kambar as a chairman of the kolkhoz, but the district committee said no, citing his lack of education.

Kakharman was living in a three-room apartment on the edge of the city. When someone knocked on the door, he knew who it was at once. Only his compatriots could forget that apartments have doorbells. Aitugan rushed to open the door.

"Hello, Aitugan," Kambar said from the entrance. "I haven't seen you for so long. How are you getting along here in the new place? How are the children?"

Kakharman embraced each of them warmly. Once they were all settled in the living room, out came the table, and symraks were spread on the floor. Aitugan retreated to the kitchen to organize food while Kakharman, who missed his compatriots deeply, studied each face in turn. All he could see there was pain. If Sinemorye has become a bitter salt land, if it has died, how do human souls live? What joy can fishermen get from their labor if they do not work with their hearts? It is just hard labor, no different from slavery.

Their faces distressed Kakharman. He smiled wanly, conscious that the fishermen were reading the same sadness in his eyes. He said as much to Kambar, who at once opened up to him.

"Ah, you know what our life is, Kakharman, as we do. You fought hard to save Sinemorye. We heard you spent two months in Moscow. Did you achieve anything there?" he asked and gently fingered the cracked, irritated skin on his weathered face. Those years, he and his men had wandered far in winter across the Darya floodplain's blank pools, large and small. It was cruel work. You had to smash the thick ice, drop the nets into the chilly waters, and then drag them from the crack of dawn and until the last sliver of light, in strength-sapping winds and biting cold. The catch was meager—so meager they didn't know whether to laugh or cry—but it kept the fishermen alive.

"Moscow," Kakharman said ruefully. "We will talk about Moscow later." Then, seeing his friend's face droop, he addressed Yesen. "Tell us, Yesen, why are you quiet? I remember the days when you couldn't stop talking."

The once irrepressible Yesen now seem wilted, desiccated, and drooping from his bitter life.

"Nasyr-ata and Korlan-apa are both well. But you know how much they worry about you, Kakharman-aga." Yesen pulled two envelopes from his pocket and passed one to Kakharman. "Where's Berish? The second letter is for him."

"He should be back at any moment," Kakharman replied. "He goes very far when he's training. Does your mother complain about her heart?"

"Yes. When it's windy, both Korlan-apa and my mother are glued to the stove and can't even lift their heads up. In such weather, they say, you can really feel the effects of the uranium mines at Baikonur and Shieli. It's hard, Kakharman-aga. It's very hard. And the drinking water is contaminated." He waved his hand.

Kambar added, "That wind is a complete disaster, Kakharman. The air is so thick with white dust that it's like a fog. A few people have already been lost and died in this wind."

Aitugan, who was setting the table, froze and sighed. "It's so tough there for Mother and Father—we know it too well. We urged them to come with us so many times, but they refused."

Then Berish came back. As soon as he saw the guests, he dropped his bag by the door and raced to hug them. Yesen gave him the letter, and he began to read. The fishermen watched Berish's face moving with emotion as he read.

"Do you miss your grandparents, Berish?" one of them asked gently.

A wave of feeling washed over Berish. Tears welled in his eyes, and he bent his head low to hide them. And he kept his head down for a while as he listened to the older men talk.

The conversations continued at the dastarkhan. Kambar did the most talking, being the oldest.

"I can't see what we can live on. The cattle are not giving birth for the second year. There are no crops in the fields. And the hot, salty air burns everything dry. How can we live like this? There's no fish and no cattle. The rice is rubbish, and there's very little of it. Are we the Soviet people or are we enemies?! Why are we being treated as if we are enemies? Why? I don't understand. We fought and died on the front lines. We brought medals back from the war. So why does the government treat us like this? Cancer is on the rise. Cattle are coming down with tuberculosis."

"Kakharman-aga knows that cancer is much more of a problem than it used to be," Yesen interrupted. "But he doesn't know that now cancer has become so deadly so fast."

"Yes, yes. This cancer now develops quickly. Two or three months and then a man is gone. It's nature taking revenge. Khodzha Abusagit was a picture of health. Yet he was ill for only three weeks before passing away, just before we came here. His son was supposed to come with us, but he stayed back for the forty days.[6] And this plague takes no notice of age. Now even young men are dying of cancer."

"Who? Do I know them?" Kakharman asked sadly.

"Bagdaulet, son of Taitoleu; Shokan, son of Sarsenbai; Serik, son of Shomishbai; and Sagynai, son of Idris," Kambar replied with undisguised bitterness.

"And Khadzhimurat's son Zhakup too. He was studying in Odessa to become a marine engineer. You can't even name them all," one of the young fishermen added.

"People say that when Zhakup's relatives went to collect his body, the institute's tutors told them they will no longer accept students from Sinemorye because cancer is allegedly a contagious illness."

As he listened, Kakharman was thinking that the cancer must be more potent if it was killing people in the prime of life. Every person Kambar had named was between twenty and thirty years of age.

Lost in his thoughts, Kakharman had almost forgotten the conversation, when Yesen addressed him.

"We've been talking nonstop about our troubles, Kakharman-aga! Please don't be offended."

"Why would I be offended? That's our reality now. Not a single comforting word comes to my mind; I understand it all, Yesen."

Kambar began to talk again.

"Kakharman, we've shared our thoughts with you and passed on greetings from your relatives. Now you should tell us about your trip to the big aul—to Moscow. Is there a single person there apart from Mustafa who cares about our troubles?"

"What did my father tell you?" Kakharman parried the question. "He went to Moscow too."

"Nasyr-aga came back ill and broken down and shut down as soon as he came back. We went to visit him, but he didn't want to talk to anyone. He said just a few words: 'I have nothing to say about this damned world and about the people who have lost their humanity and honor.' Our case, as I understood, is hopeless. It's the end for Sinemorye.'"

Kakharman grinned. Kambar had precisely mimicked Nasyr's voice and intonation.

"My father exactly!"

Aitugan and Berish looked at each other and smiled too.

Kakharman looked at each of the fishermen in turn, then began to tell them about the meetings in Moscow and the people he had seen and talked to.

"Basically, there are two opinions about it there, and no one knows which will win. Both are flawed in some way. I went to Moscow because of Balkhash too. But I got no joy at all," he admitted.

The fishermen were downcast.

"So this is it for Sinemorye?" Kambar moaned.

"I guess it's time for us to go," Yesen broke in. "Kakharman-aga needs rest. It's late."

"Why not stay here tonight, Yesen?" Berish suggested.

"Yes, you should stay and have a good chat," some of the fishermen urged.

Kambar and Kakharman were still sitting at the table, so no one else moved.

"Aitugan, dearest. I'd like to talk to Kakharman one-to-one. May I?" Kambar asked suddenly.

"You can all stay here tonight. It'll be cramped, but I'm sure we can find room for everyone!" Aitugan insisted.

"Thank you for your kind offer, but I'd like to invite Kakharman to our hotel. We won't interfere with anyone there. Yesen, did you bring the *torsyk* with you?"

"I left it back at the hotel," Yesen answered.

"If you don't mind, Aitugan, we'll take Kakharman with us. And Berish should come too, and he and Yesen can talk as much as they like."

Aitugan knew exactly what was in the torsyk. So she whispered to her husband while he was getting dressed, "Go easy on the drink and come back soon."

In the hotel, Kakharman and Kambar talked long into the night together in private about everything in the world. They had much to say to each other. Kambar was happy to find that Kakharman had taken the trouble to locate a good place for fishing.

"I'll tell the guys about it tomorrow. They'll feel your concern and might be a bit shaken up. We oldsters are holding up OK, but the young ones break very quickly. It's them who lose their jobs first. We are wandering like tramps across all the waters of Kazakhstan in search of fish. It's no joke to be torn away from home for seven or eight months."

Kakharman listened to his old friend without interruption. The alcohol was having its effect. He was feeling relieved. The dark thoughts were sliding away, and even some faint glimmer of hope appeared.

"That's why a simple drink can be a delight to the soul," he thought.

Kambar knew too well the doubts that befall a man torn from his homeland. Yes, yes, Kakharman needed to forget everything, just for a little while. Kambar filled Kakharman's glass again. And Kakharman drank it rapidly. By midnight, he was looking at Kambar with tenderness and hugging his shoulder.

"Yes, Kambar, only a man can understand the pain of another man. Thank you. Thank you for coming here, for visiting me," Kakharman slurred.

It was nearly morning when he got home. Kakharman went to bed but couldn't sleep. As he dozed, he heard Kambar's voice with startling clarity:

"Sinemorye is dying! The land is ruined and moans with pain, but the big people somewhere out there can't agree. Isn't it appalling? Ambition rules everything. They are tormented by envy of each other. They are tormented by greed. They have forgotten that we are all mortal. They have forgotten mercy, and they have forgotten God. No one cares about us! But if even Sinemorye's happiness is betrayed, then what's the point of human happiness? It's just froth—froth washed away by a filthy stream. And can't even sorrow bring people together?"

At last, defeated, he rose from the bed as quietly as he could, but Aitugan had already lifted her head from the pillow.

"What's wrong, Kakharman? Try to sleep. You'll have to get up for work soon. You've been talking to yourself all night."

That night, he didn't go back to bed. He stayed by the window and smoked. Then, when it was time, he began to get ready for work. He didn't do his customary morning exercises and didn't kiss Aitugan before leaving as he usually did.

"Steer right! Steer right!" someone shouted from the shore.

"Stop the engine! Get the barge unhooked!" Kakharman barked.

The whole team went ashore, and Kakharman went into the cabin, unbuttoning his *kittel'* and flopping on the sofa. He was thirsty but couldn't be bothered to go and get a drink. The radio was transmitting the latest news.

MASS DESTRUCTION OF MARINE FAUNA NOTED IN COASTAL WATERS off Norway and Sweden at the junction of the North and Baltic Seas.

OIL TANKER *EXXON VALDEZ* ACCIDENT NEAR ALASKA IS the biggest ecological disaster in US history.

HUNDREDS OF SETTLEMENTS, INCLUDING PARTS OF BUENOS AIRES, are underwater as a result of torrential rain that fell on the coastal areas of Argentina over the past few days.

A STORM OVER WESTERN EUROPE CONTINUES TO RAGE. HAMBURG—the largest seaport of the FRG—has been subjected to the most intense flooding in the last ninety years. In the coastal areas of England, the storm surge has washed away dams and dikes that protect the coast from floods.

FIRE TO END ALL FIRES. THIS UNPRECEDENTED FIRE CONTINUES FOR THE SECOND WEEK. Car tires are burning—fourteen million worn tires—in a dump on the outskirts of the small town of Hagersville, fifty-six miles from Toronto. The cause of the fire is unknown, and the fire has proven almost impossible to extinguish.

IN AUSTRALIA, MICE HAVE MULTIPLIED IN RECENT YEARS. These tiny rodents cause extensive damage to farming. New South Wales, the country's breadbasket, has declared the epidemic a "mice disaster."

A CYCLONE MOVED FROM NORTHWEST TO SOUTH KAZAKHSTAN earlier in the week.

SALINE STORMS ARE RAGING NEAR SINEMORYE FOR THE SEVENTH DAY in a row. According to forecasts, the wind is not expected to slacken anytime soon. Power lines have been broken, railroad tracks have blown out, and traffic has been disrupted. There are problems with drinking water in towns and settlements, and some houses have been destroyed. Members of the State Commission have arrived in the disaster zone by special flight.

Kakharman listened impassively, leaning his shoulder against the sofa, gazing emptily through the porthole at the slow wash of the Irtysh's waters. He could hear the rumble of pebbles pouring into the barge from the crane bucket and the insistent murmur of voices, but it all seemed meaningless.

If such a wind has risen in Sinemorye, it will bring evil. If the storm changes its direction, it could destroy all crops in virgin lands, including Uzbek cotton. And then the salty rains will pass over the Irtysh.

When they had first moved here, Aitugan couldn't believe these unnatural rains could fall here too. But Kakharman could only smile grimly. "Don't you understand, Aitugan? It's Sinemorye sending us gifts."

"The misfortune of our homelands can reach us across thousands of miles?" Aitugan was genuinely surprised.

"Yes, an ailment that happens in one part of the earth can be felt elsewhere. This is a law of nature. It would be good if the same was true for human society! But it doesn't work like that."

"You are still upset about the same thing, Kakharman," Aitugan replied softly. "In the past, I didn't understand Abai's lines: 'Don't be the son of your father but be the son of your nation.' I thought, 'How can that be?' Now I know. There are people like that, and you are one of them." And she had turned away.

The door of the cabin opened, and his first mate, Sasha Ladov, appeared, smiling, at the threshold.

"Captain," he said, "it's utterly scorching out there! Fancy a beer?"

"Why not?" Kakharman agreed absentmindedly. "Bring it in."

He was still thinking about what he'd heard on the radio. It was late August, yet he'd still had no news from Berish. He could've at least sent a telegram. He'd gone to Sinemorye for the summer to visit his grandparents. Kakharman hadn't stopped him. He understood the boy's need. But what if he is in one of those trains stranded on the steppe by the weather? "But," he thought, "the boy is an adult; he can cope with problems."

Ladov returned.

"I was thinking that you might have prepared everything, Kakharman Nasyrovich, and set the table. But here you are, still looking through the porthole as if it's possible to see something good through it," he joked, unloading beer and a bundle of dried roach from his bag.

"Who cares?" Kakharman waved his hand. "What table are you talking about? The newspaper will do."

Ladov began to pour beer, glancing at Kakharman from time to time.

"I see you're out of sorts today, captain."

"There's been a storm in Sinemorye for seven days nonstop, and my parents are there, and my son as well. But you're right. It's silly worrying." Kakharman tried to cheer himself up. "If we're going to have fun, let's do it properly, and it's a payday—you haven't forgotten today is a payday? Today I'll treat you on the shore! What do you say?"

"I am strongly against it." Ladov didn't like being treated.

"I am older than you, Sasha, and I insist. You live among Kazakhs, and according to our custom, you have no right to refuse an invitation."

"But it seems you always invite me. I already feel rather uncomfortable."

"Let's just say we agree," Kakharman insisted. But he couldn't cheer up. He turned again vacantly toward the window and began to drink beer distractedly.

After that night talking with Kambar back in Balkhash, Kakharman had been unwell at work and wanted to take the day off to sleep and recover but remembered that that night in the House of Culture of the Industrial Complex there was a meeting of scientists from Moscow and Alma-Ata. He couldn't miss that.

The hall was packed by the time Kakharman arrived, and he could only find a seat in the very back row. When he sat down, he examined the men on the presidium.[8] All of them—all the scientists, young and old, and the regional leaders, all sleek and neat, sitting sedately at the long table—oh, he knew them all. Academicians Sitnikov, Koshechkin, Baranov, and Sarymsakov; Ministers Vodolazov and Primus; Heads of Farms Itbaev and Sytykh—they were all here. The meeting was chaired by Yerkinov, chairman of the Executive Committee. Kakharman knew many personally. With some he had private, pragmatic conversations; with some he had argued; and with some he had even had a set-to. But he had never found a common language with any. All these people sitting at the table covered with red velvet were behind the politics of reversing the Siberian rivers.

One after another, the scientists spoke. Then the heads of farms took their turns. They expressed themselves disjointedly, often failing to understand each other. The hydrogeologist didn't understand the biologist. The biologist didn't accept the opinion of the economist. The economist didn't understand the head of farms. There was no consensus. In the end, the presidium turned to the audience for help. Silence fell over the hall.

Finally, Siyrbaev, the chairman of the Kazakh State Hydrogeological Administration, rose from his seat. He began on a high note. "It is entirely wrong in these modern times, when science and technology are progressing so rapidly, to criticize us for the Kapchagay Reservoir!"'The strident voice sliced into Kakharman's ears.

"We've been saying for twenty years that we need to save the Balkhash. Forgive me, but what do we need to save it from? Was anyone harmed by the creation of the Kapchagay Reservoir? You catch fish in Lake Balkhash, like you always did. You grow rice in the fields. And the Kapchagay Hydroelectric Power Plant is an important and powerful source of electricity. The city of Balkhash is flourishing and developing on the lake's shore. It's wrong to constantly bother the men at the top with unfounded complaints."

Now Kakharman began to see the purpose of this meeting. The scientists and leaders of the Republic were puzzled by the rising public discontent with the Kapchagay Reservoir. The unrest was becoming all too obvious—as this meeting proved.

After Siyrbaev, a stocky little man asked if he could add something. He introduced himself as a professor from the Institute of Marine Studies attached to the Academy of Sciences. His opinion was that the western part of the lake had to be preserved and the eastern part destroyed. The dam in the straits of Uzun-Aral must be built at once, he insisted.

Another scientist, a professor from the Institute of Hydrogeology, challenged the stocky man right away. "Yes, but the problems that could arise during construction have not been properly investigated."

Then Minister Vodolazov took the floor. "We must take notice of what has already been achieved. Water resources from Ili-Balkhash are being used very well. We have implemented the Council of Ministers' program, which envisaged the filling of the Kapchagay Reservoir. We also cut down the number of farms growing rice in Akdala. These efforts have been made to improve the situation in Balkhash. I don't understand why anyone objects to the construction of this large canal. I consider it my duty to point out that one day—if not now, then tomorrow—we will have to build the dam in the Uzun-Aral straits. We can't avoid it!"

When the floor was given to Igor Slavikov, Kakharman suddenly leaned forward. "How did he get here?" Kakharman hadn't see him arrive. Maybe Slavikov had wanted to keep his entrance quiet.

Young Igor looked at the hall quietly. He looked tired, haggard, and older than his years.

"Dear comrades!" he began. "One can only be happy that the scientists and heads of farms have come here to share their thoughts with the people. This meeting is a dialogue, and we are all trying to see the problems with more depth and from different perspectives. I'd like to remind you that my father, Professor Slavikov, dedicated almost all his life to the problems of the Aral and Caspian Seas and Lake Balkhash. And now I am trying to make my own contribution. I'd like to bring a strange fact to your attention. Those who brought the Ili River and Lake Balkhash to today's catastrophic condition still hold the waters' fate in their hands. It was those men who refused to listen to those who voiced opposition to the construction of Kapchagay Reservoir. It was clear to anyone who cared to look that Lake Balkhash has long been fed by the Ili's waters and, if denied this water, it would be condemned to death. And many scientists argued that the dropping water level in the lake would cause fish and ondatras[10] to disappear, just as we have seen.

"Today we see many other things as well. We see the diverted Ili's water going to waste in the sand. I fundamentally disagree with many of the scientists who spoke here today. Their views are based on institutional ambition, not honest observation. They have forgotten that the duty of a scientist is to protect the interests of nature, to protect humanity in general—and not the gilded uniforms of the department heads! If we allow such treasures as the Balkhash and Aral to be ruined, we'll commit a crime against the whole Kazakh nation. That is why the Balkhash must live! That's all I have got to say, comrades!"

His last words were drowned in a storm of applause.

Siyrbaev took the floor again.

"Comrades! A false impression of economic managers is being presented. It may seem as if the scientists are looking after natural resources while economic managers oppose them. That's not true. We economists also care about today and tomorrow. But we believe that man has a right to use the wealth of nature for his own interests. Yes, the Kapchagay HPP harms fish and other living creatures of Lake Balkhash. But let's make a simple calculation! All the costs of the loss of fish and ondatras in Balkhash will very soon be more than balanced by the rising income from agricultural products. Don't think that anyone in Moscow or Alma-Ata is unaware of these problems."

Agitated, Bolat took the floor.

"Whoever planned the construction of Kapchagay HPP remembered the Ili and Balkhash only after the design was completed. I would like to tell you about the impropriety of the academician Satkynov. More than once, he approached me with a request to confirm the 'expediency' of Kapchagay HPP for our region. He even promised to reward me well. Naturally, I didn't go along with it. I kicked the man he sent out! And here I declare openly, I will fight for the survival of the Balkhash and Aral till the end of my days! With equal frankness, I would like to declare, comrades, that the program for the revival of Pribalkhash[11] exists only on paper. It's nonexistent. It doesn't have a scientific rationale. There's not even any scientific dialogue on this major issue. There is no public discussion."

"Great performance!" An elderly man sitting next to Kakharman nudged him. "That man is terrific!"

Cries rose from the audience.

"You tell them, son!"

"Be brave!"

Bolat addressed the presidium.

"The scientists sitting here should remember well that a long time ago, Professor Slavikov opposed the construction of the dam at Kara-Bogaz.[12] No one listened to him. But he advised us that the level of water in the Caspian would rise again."

"Nonsense. The water's been dropping in the Caspian for years!" Professor Baranov exclaimed.

"That is old information! The waters in the Caspian are now rising, just as Slavikov predicted."

"But where is your proof?" Itbaev shouted. "What's the point of speaking without facts?"

"Proof? I have proof. Now you're trying to insist on the necessity of the construction of the big Aral scheme, completely ignoring the negative experience of the past years. I would like to quote for you some statements made by Slavikov, which, although dating from the fifties, still resonate today."

Bolat pulled papers from his chest pocket, unfolded them, and began to read. "'Water in Kara-Bogaz-Gol will eventually dwindle to nothing. The loss of water will greatly damage the area. Deliveries of Karabogazsulfat's products and agricultural products will cease. Pastures will be impoverished. The soil will become saline.'

"Back then, no one paid any attention to his words, but they were prophetic! We will spend millions building the Akdalinski channel, and Balkhash will repeat the fate of Kara-Bogaz. Can anyone guarantee this will not happen? No one! So let's finally leave this ruinous and thoughtless practice of winning in a small way only to lose in a big way. Can it be called a socialistic construction? This is idiotist and not socialist! I am categorically against the drive of the party and farm economists for endless growth, against useless gigantism. I am against it both as a Communist and as a citizen! To destroy the Balkhash is to destroy a nation. Kapchagay Reservoir must be discharged, and the water returned to Lake Balkhash! There is no other solution!"

"Comrade Abiltaev!" Satkynov jumped up from his seat and began to wave his hands angrily. "You'll damn well answer for your slander! Do you think that if your Balkhash disappears, then all life will stop? Pessimists like you—in one word, dissidents—are the enemies of socialism! You spread chaos among the people!"

People began to stand up and head for the exit, refusing to listen anymore to the head of the Republic. Those who stayed in the hall shouted, "Let the ordinary people speak!"

A tall, strongly built man climbed out of the third row and headed briskly toward the panel. It was the well-known Balkhash metallurgist, Nurahmet. Those leaving the hall decided to stay, seeing that Nurahmet-aga was going to speak. After a pause to gather his thoughts, Nurahmet addressed the presidium.

"Sirs. The ordinary people would like to know just one thing: Will you give Balkhash a chance to survive, or will you strangle it until it's dead? I am not against any ideas, not against arguments. But if you're interested in our opinion, then I will say this: we want the truth to prevail. And the truth for us is a healthy, normal life for Balkhash. Balkhash is the land of my forefathers. I am saying this because the blood of my umbilical cord is mixed with Balkhash's water. Our ancestors also left these words about lying: 'When a lie ends, humiliation begins.'

"Kapchagay Lake has turned out to be a humiliation for Balkhash and for all of us. This is shameful. We were told that a man-made lake is being created! Just go outside Alma-Ata—and here you go! Swim, and bathe in the sun! But fertile lands were drowned beneath this lake! The graves of our fathers and grandfathers were drowned beneath this lake! Do you think such barbarism can pass without leaving its mark on a man's soul? No!

"The graves of our forefathers are defiled by our soullessness and give us no peace. Alright. Let's say that all of this is just empty words for you, but, please, answer us a simpler question: What did we get from pouring water from the Ili into a single hole near Alma-Ata? Now there's no carp in the Balkhash. Nothing. Spawning grounds dried up long ago. Ondatras have vanished. Sheep die of disease. Instead of fresh water in Balkhash, there's only brine. Our town is only alive thanks to the wind from the lake. If not for the wind, it would've burned in the heat long ago. You already ruined the Aral. Is the Balkhash next?

"Listen to me. I'll tell you what you're doing. My friend from the front lines at Auezkhan used to live in Sinemorye. The war spared him, didn't even touch him—but his native Sinemorye killed him. He died after being ill for not even twenty days with stomach cancer. I recently came back from there. I saw the shores abandoned by water with my own eyes. I still have the taste of salt in my mouth. Salt penetrates a man. These horrible illnesses are because of it. Would you like to know its flavor? Then go to Sinemorye and carry on with your meeting on the salty shores. And while you're there, look how people live there. They don't live. They die like flies!"

The whole auditorium, as if following a command, stood up and headed for the exit.

"Where are you going?" the chairman of the Town Soviet cried. "We haven't finished yet!"

Kakharman was the only one left in the hall. The chairman of the Town Soviet was flustered.

"What do we do now, comrades? You see for yourself how ill-disciplined our people are."

The men on the presidium sat down together in confusion. Some shrugged. Some sat and kept their eyes downcast.

"You can carry on talking!" shouted Kakharman angrily from the last row. "As you can see, there is still one fool in the hall prepared to listen to you."

The next day, Kakharman went with Igor and Bolat to the west bank of the lake to visit Kambar and his men. Igor and Bolat were happy for this opportunity.

It'd been a while since they last saw Sinemorian fishermen, and it was evident they missed them. Not a word was said about the previous day's meeting. Once they had left the city, Bolat addressed Kakharman.

"You should move to Alma-Ata."

Kakharman realized that Bolat and Igor had already spoken about it, because Igor supported Bolat right away.

"That makes sense. You should settle in Alma-Ata. It'd be better for us if you were there."

Kakharman began to laugh.

"I'm like Ichtiander.[13] I can't live without water. That's why I declined so many invitations to move to Alma-Ata. I am who I am. Alma-Ata looks to me like a scorching concrete trap."

Igor had picked up on Kakharman's spiritual dissonance in Moscow. As he saw his friend to the plane, he decided to speak to him frankly.

"Kakharman, I see your despair. I won't tell you that it's not right for a man to lose heart. You know that better than I do. But what else can I say to console you? I know this feeling too. But at times like this, I always remember my father. He fought all his life for what you and I are fighting for now. He hasn't achieved much in his life, but if he'd been broken, he wouldn't have achieved even the small things he did. So it's up to you." Igor, wanting to encourage Kakharman, decided not to tell him that a new expedition to Sinemorye was being prepared. The purpose of this expedition was to give a scientifically based picture of the sea's condition. "To record its disappearance" is how Igor thought of it. He had been appointed as leader of this expedition.

Kakharman listened to Igor sympathetically. But how could he just recover in a moment? His despair had been growing for years, slowly deepening as he wandered from one official's office to another. No matter which official he met, empty promises, feeble excuses, and shaky assurances were thrust on him.

Of course, there were the occasional flickers of promise. In Moscow, he had persuaded the navy ministry to permit the opening of repair shops along the shore in areas where fish had disappeared. He'd had to wait for two weeks to be seen by Minister Buslaev. Nasyr, who came with him, felt outraged and humiliated. "For a cat, it's fun, but for a mouse, it's tears," he kept repeating. Eventually, Nasyr bade farewell to his son and Igor Slavikov at Kazan rail station in silence.

Buslaev had received Kakharman at ten o'clock that evening. The minister greeted Kakharman warmly.

"I heard you came with your father. Where is this distinguished fisherman?"

Kakharman explained that his father couldn't stay for so long in Moscow and had returned to the aul.

"So the old fisherman was cross with me?" It seemed to Kakharman that the minister was really upset by this. "Was he really upset?"

Kakharman was rather surprised that such a busy man as the minister was asking about his father.

"Well, I won't pretend he didn't go home offended. But I don't think this is what matters now; I need to tell you about the disastrous condition of our land, our sea and our people."

It seemed to Kakharman that the minister couldn't be a bad person if he was so personally interested in the feelings of an old man completely unknown to him.

"It's a shame we upset the old man," the minister said thoughtfully and pointed at the heaps of papers and folders piled on his desk. "We are busy developing yet another five-year plan. I have read your notes, Kakharman Nasyrovich. Believe me, I didn't know that Sinemorye was in such a sad state. I and my comrades in the department consider your notes important and timely. Today, I called the State Planning Committee,[14] Ministry of Health, Ministry of Water Resources, and the Academy of Sciences and introduced the problem explained in your notes to all of them. They all seem to agree with me that the situation is disastrous and agree that something must be done urgently, but you know how hard it is to get our bureaucratic machine whirring. We'll have to wait. I called Kunaev. Yesterday Rashidov called me. I know their opinion, but I can't agree with them. According to them, we just have to wait for the water from the North. But if we keep waiting, then we will destroy Sinemorye! The achievements of Kunaev are measured by the amount of bread the Republic grows and the achievements of Rashidov, by cotton. What comes from that? Each one is pulling the bedclothes toward himself. Oh well. Yes, please, describe briefly the nub of the problems again."

In just twelve minutes, Kakharman succinctly and scrupulously described what was going on. Buslaev listened to the director of the fish factory from Sinemorye without interrupting.

"Viktor Mikhailovich, sir! It would be so good if you could come to our region and see what is happening there with your own eyes!" Kakharman finished.

"But you don't even have any fleet left there. There's nothing to see," the minister replied dismissively.

"You can gaze upon its ruins." Kakharman smiled, then added, trying to mollify the sting of his facetiousness, "In Kazakhstan, almost all our natural waters are in trouble, even the smallest streams and ponds."

Buslaev looked worried as he listened, but it was hard to tell if he agreed with Kakharman or not. He understood how Kakharman felt and even admired him for his strength of feeling. "He's certainly right," the minister thought. "The ocean has given us millions: millions of tons of fish and millions in financial returns. Why would we care for one-kopeck lakes and rivers? And now it's becoming an ecological disaster."

He recalled his late mother's oft-repeated words more and more frequently now: "How can a nation," she would say, "that doesn't value its land and the wealth laid in it be considered a nation at all?" Buslaev's mother lived till the age of eighty-six. He kept meaning to have a heart-to-heart conversation with her, kept meaning to spend an evening or two with her, but she had died suddenly. He was just having a lunch break when he received the call, right in the ministerial cafeteria. The deputies lunching with him expressed their condolences. He called his wife and asked her to go to his mother's at once.

"Aren't you coming?" she asked.

"I can't!" he replied sharply and in despair. Then, damping his flash of anger, he added softly, "I'm going to the Kremlin for appointment with Leonid Ilyich.[15] I'll try to get there later. Take someone with you. I'll send a car to pick you up." Then he had returned to his office and stretched his legs tiredly in the armchair. "Your mother died, the dearest person on earth to you, yet you can't just leave everything and go," he had thought bitterly.

Despite her age, his mother kept a clear mind till the end. She was quiet but stubborn. No matter how much Viktor Mikhailovich tried to convince her to move to Moscow, she never would. So she lived until she died in her native village in Bryanschina, honoring the modest graves of her parents. She would visit Moscow to celebrate her son's birthday and might stay a week or two. But even this short period of separation from the village was hard for her.

Once, Buslaev returned from work upset and angry. Later in the night, he suddenly woke and clearly heard his mother's voice: "Vitya, you're not looking after yourself at all. You shouldn't get so upset over such trivialities." Agitated, he put on his slippers and, taking care not to wake his wife up, headed for the kitchen in the darkness. He opened the fridge and downed a glass of Borjomi.[16] His agitation didn't go away. Then he decided to give Slavikov a call, despite the unsuitable time.

The professor's voice was clear and pure—of course Slavikov was still awake. Viktor Mikhailovich hesitantly explained the vague reason for his late call, then asked, while lighting a cigarette and searching for an ashtray, "Did you listen to my speech?"

"I did. You were calling for ministers, who've forgotten about God, to show a sense of duty and care. But God speaks to you with your mother's voice and keeps you awake. Think about it: How can a man be or become a director if he has at least a drop of conscience remaining?"

"Matvei Panteleevich, forgive me, I lost my temper then."

"I've already forgotten about it. To wake in the middle of the night, call, and ask for forgiveness—that's quite a feat for a man as important a person as you. Oh well, you won't be able to sleep now anyway. You may as well come round to my place if you want to talk properly."

"In the middle of the night? What will Sveta think of me?"

"I have no idea what your Sveta will think about you. She will tell you tomorrow herself. Don't worry. Ministers' wives, unlike scientists' wives, sleep deeply. She probably won't even know you went out in the middle of the night."

Viktor Mikhailovich's mother had quickly found a common language with the professor. She admired him and called him a God's man. Whenever she visited Moscow, Slavikov would always invite mother and son to visit him. At first it seemed strange to Viktor Mikhailovich that his poorly educated mother could talk so much with the great professor, about pretty much anything. "Possibly all the troubles and misfortunes that fell on all their generation make them closer," he thought, watching the very famous scientist turning into an ordinary old kolkhoz man in front of his eyes.

When in the village with Viktor Mikhailovich, the professor would habitually get up early and go for a long walk. By the time he got home, the old woman and Viktor Mikhailovich had already finished breakfast. One day, they stayed at breakfast longer than usual. The old woman was complaining to her minister son about the impassability of roads and was saying that the fields are befouled with chemicals, and the soil is impoverished. Viktor Mikhailovich acknowledged it all with a hoarse, sardonic cheerfulness. "Mom, you shouldn't worry. We can see all the bumps and ravines of Russia from Moscow."

The mother refused to accept the joke. "If you can see everything in Russia from Moscow, then sort everything in Russia out! People have left the villages. Kolkhozes are falling apart. Folks are going God knows where and scattering all over the country. Our boys and girls have gone. Some to Kazakhstan, some to Siberia. But I don't believe they're building a beautiful life there. My neighbor's son Petka read a book about Siberia. Do you know what they call those who arrive in Siberia? Argali! And they fear them like the plague! Did we Russian women give you birth, bring you up from poverty and hunger, so you could ruin yourself and others by drink?"

Buslaev didn't interrupt his mother, seeing the depth of her resentment. And then the professor appeared.

"I heard what you were saying, Elizaveta Svyatoslavovna, so forgive me for intruding into your conversation. I personally think that man is the greediest creature of nature. Man destroys everything—birds in the sky, animals on the land, fish in the water. Now only one thing remains: to eat each other."

The old woman nodded in agreement. The learned professor began to give examples of the evil man does to nature. He touched upon ancient tales about Christ and Muhammad and began to talk about the revolution of 1917.

"May God give you a good journey, Matvei Panteleevich," she thanked the professor. "I, myself, am a little dim; I see everything but can't express it in words." She looked into the distance thoughtfully and said something that Viktor Mikhailovich remembered for a long time. "Matvei Panteleevich, man is weak, which is why devilry pushes him toward pettiness, meaninglessness, and cruelty. These men, sitting in their armchairs as if on satanic thrones—are they strong or wise? All their wisdom is in their backsides. Because their backsides can think of only one thing: how to protect their seats! They should bow to nature, to Mother Earth, then maybe they'd be less stupid."

Slavikov only laughed.

When Viktor Mikhailovich told Leonid Brezhnev his mother was dead, he asked how old she was. "Ninety-three," Buslaev replied.

"Well, she had a life, then," said Leonid Ilyich. He sighed dutifully. "May God let us to live to such age." It became clear the personal moment was now over, and he returned to his businesslike tone. "Time, we hardly have any time!" he kept saying over and over again.

Buslaev had to go to the funeral in secret. It was humiliating and insulting. He was a large man—so large that whenever he got into his black Volga, it would lean noticeably to the right—and it was strange to see tears well in the eyes of this bear, when, after pulling the door closed, he quietly said to the driver, "To Sosnovka. To my mother." Annoyed with himself, he banged his giant fist on his knee. "'She had a life.' So much indifference in these words!"

Buslaev's mother was buried early in the morning because he had to get back for the selection meeting.

"It will be hard for me to get to Sinemorye, believe me, Kakharman Nasyrovich. But I already gave my orders. And all your demands," Buslaev said warmly, "will be met. I can guarantee you. And I ask your father for forgiveness. Tell him that and bow to him."

The next day, after finishing his business with the department head, Ivanov, Kakharman sent a telegram to the aul. In their depressed state, with people still leaving in droves, this telegram was a great boost for the fishermen.

The small black Gazik was bouncing wildly along the bumpy steppe road. The driver was chatty and entertained Igor and Bolat with stories from his life while Kakharman napped. But Kakharman woke with a start when the Gazik, straining up a steep ridge, suddenly stalled, rolled backward, and stopped. Its rear wheels were stuck in sand. As Kakharman opened his eyes, the driver jumped out of the car, loudly slamming the door behind him.

"Have we arrived?" Kakharman rubbed his eyes.

"We just got stuck," Bolat laughed.

"It's nothing. We'll all push!" the driver said as he got back behind the wheel and stomped on the clutch and throttle. He was torturing the poor car, but it still wouldn't move.

"OK. Let's push." Kakharman got out, followed by Igor and Bolat. They heaved against the back of the car, groaning under the strain. But the car only dug in deeper.

"Do you have a spade?" Kakharman asked the driver.

"I have both a spade and an ax. We'll need to chop some branches and put them under the wheels." He got out of the car, then leaped back in. "Everybody in the car! Quick!"

Kakharman, Bolat, and Igor looked around in surprise.

"Wild dogs!" the driver shouted. "Quick! Everyone in the car!!"

A large pack of dogs had appeared on a mound around a hundred yards away. When the dogs caught sight of the men, they rushed toward them. Kakharman slammed the door just as the first dog reached the car. Soon the pack was swarming over the hood and climbing on the roof.

"Do you have a gun?" Kakharman asked the driver. He was now wide awake, focused, and energetic.

"As luck would have it, I left it behind." The driver cursed.

"This doesn't look good," Kakharman said. He was thinking feverishly of what to do.

Meanwhile, one of the dogs began to stare at them. Saliva was dripping from its mouth and onto the windshield.

"These dogs have pretty much turned into wolves," Kakharman said, recoiling in surprise.

"Look, Igor. Their eyes are like gimlets. It really plays with your mind."

A dog that had jumped onto the car's hood bared its teeth, growled, and pounded the metal with its paw. Two lean and ragged dogs stood on their back legs and peered through the side window from the driver's side. A ginger bitch was snarling wildly, battering the glass with her muzzle until the whole window was splattered with saliva. Kakharman pressed the horn.

"Turn on the engine," he ordered the driver. "Step on the gas. I've seen a lot in my life, but it's the first time I have ever been in a situation like this!"

The dogs weren't scared by the roar of the engine or the blast of the horn.

The ginger bitch looked familiar to Kakharman. "Whose dog is that? Where have I seen her?" he was thinking. All the dogs, one by one, lifted a leg and urinated on the windshield. Kakharman spat with anger. Spurts of urine were heard on the roof. Then they all jumped from the car and loped off to the steppe. "Isn't that Syrttan?" It dawned on Kakharman. "Of course! It's Syrttan, my father's dog!"

Kakharman lowered the window a little and yelled after the pack.

"Syrttan! Syrttan!"

The ginger bitch stopped for a moment, then ran after the pack. The unbearable smell of urine hung heavily in the car. The men jumped outside.

"They bit through both tires," the driver said, bending down to look at the wheels.

Kakharman was nauseated by the stench and walked away, worried that he might throw up. Igor and Bolat had difficulty recovering from what they'd just seen.

Kakharman wiped his face with a handkerchief and said angrily to the driver, "Who cares about the tires, after the humiliation we've just been through? Even dogs piss on us now!"

Igor and Bolat began to laugh, and Igor slapped Kakharman on the shoulder.

"Would it have been better if they had torn us into pieces?"

"Don't you care that in broad daylight, mangy wild dogs pissed on the heads of four men?" Kakharman was getting seriously angry. "If anyone ever finds out, people will turn their backs on us!"

The driver, who had already forgotten about the ruined tires, was now laughing with Igor and Bolat.

It was late evening by the time they reached the lake bank, and the fishermen were already setting up the tents and getting ready to sleep. As the luckless travelers told the fishermen about their adventures, the fishermen, of course, couldn't help but laugh. Yesen added brushwood to the fire, and the flames flashed up fiercely into the dark, spreading a flickering glow across the faces of the fishermen and their guests. The moon drifted from the clouds and shone its pale light silently far over the sleeping steppe.

"Let's sleep," Kambar suggested. "We have to be up early tomorrow."

They all flexed their stiff joints and got up to go to their tents. Suddenly, a distant chorus of eerie wails pierced the silence. Kakharman stared out into the gloom and saw the steppe moving like a sea as numberless ondatras scurried away under the moonlight.

"They are looking for a new place," Yesen observed.

"Do they always scream like that when they are on the move?" Kambar was surprised. "I wonder if they sense some kind of danger."

Kakharman recalled his conversations with the head of the Balkhash fishing sector, who was complaining bitterly that ondatras were vanishing from the lake as the water level dropped with the building of the Kapchagay HPP.

"When the water becomes shallow," the driver suggested, "the ondatras move in large flocks to new places, but they don't usually do it as feverishly as they're doing it now."

Soon the barking of wild dogs could be heard, and the barking was getting closer.

"Yesen, get me the gun," Kakharman ordered.

Yesen dived into the tent and pulled out a five-shot rifle for Kakharman.

"It's Musa's gun; it can't miss."

The terrified squeaks of the small, helpless muskrats penetrated the men's hearts.

As they neared the fishermen sitting by the fire, the animals first turned back, then rushed toward them as the barking pursued them. The ondatras jostled in terror around the fishermen's feet, looking for shelter and protection. Kakharman felt the quivering of their little bodies against his calves. Just beyond the light from the fire, dogs were tearing the ondatras apart. Kakharman took aim at one of the dogs, pulled the trigger, and missed. The dogs froze for a moment but then continued their bloody pursuit.

"They are not easily scared," Kambar said.

"They are not afraid of much," the driver said, joining the conversation. "I saw with my own eyes in Kalmykia how they killed a herd of saiga."

Kakharman was carefully watching the veteran dog he'd missed with his first shot. It wasn't pushing forward like other dogs but lurking behind. "It's cautious; maybe it's the leader," Kakharman said to himself. The ondatras were pressing against the men's legs and had no intention of leaving. There were about 150 of these poor creatures.

Now the pack leader was running in behind the fishermen. Suddenly it crouched, ready to pounce. Kakharman lifted his rifle, paused for a moment, and pressed the trigger. A shot cracked through the dark. The leader, meeting the bullet in midair, somersaulted and dropped facedown. The pack was confused after losing the leader. The fishermen began to shoot them almost at point-blank. The pack quickly scattered. A few dogs were dead; others were wounded and dragged themselves away, whimpering. Kakharman and the fishermen rushed after them to drive them farther away. The pack disappeared onto the steppe. Feeling safe now, the ondatras continued on their way.

In the morning, the fishermen found the area around their tents strewn with the bodies of the little animals and dogs. Kakharman walked to the dead leader and knew at once it was one of the dogs that had urinated on the windshield. The ginger bitch, lying a bit farther off, was wounded but still alive. She opened her eyes slowly and looked at the people.

"But this is Nasyr-aga's dog!" Yesen exclaimed.

Kakharman had known it before Yesen. The dog looked at Kakharman, whined, then crawled to the leader and tried to lick its paw. "Syrttan!" Kakharman called. The dog dropped her head and, without opening her eyes, snarled.

"We should shoot it. It shouldn't just suffer," one of the fishermen suggested.

Kakharman nodded weakly, walked away, and waited for the shot.

Once the barge was unloaded, Kakharman gave the order to turn back. They must return to the quarry on the other bank, as they did day after day. The loaded barge was towed with the flow and then went back empty against the flow. There were no strong winds, like Sinemorye has, on the river. There were no huge and perilous waves. And there was no ruthless secretary of the Regional Committee insisting on meeting the fish targets.

The once-powerful Irtysh wound its way through shallows now, living an inconspicuous life, never waking any strong feelings in men, whispering in its ripples as if to say, "Everything has passed, everything has passed . . ."

Kakharman struggled to adjust to the monotony of his days, to the monotonous routine of work.

"Are you bored again, Captain?" Ladov's voice woke Kakharman from his thoughts. "For you, the sea wolf, the river's ripples must seem like useless toys." Ladov, who was ever cheerful, smiled and said, "Let me take the wheel."

"What can compare with the sea?" Kakharman exclaimed warmly. Then, rather embarrassed by his earnestness, he gave the wheel to Ladov.

In the evening after the last trip, the team went to the office to get paid. Ladov and Kakharman headed for the beach. They waded into the water, then Ladov, throwing his arms wide, swam toward the middle of the river and shouted, "The water is amazing, Captain!"

Kakharman slowly swam after him. After immersing himself in the water, he began to feel the river differently. Yes, the Irtysh may have been shallow and narrow, but its flow was still strong. Small, silvery fish were softly touching Kakharman's legs.

Sinemorye. It used to be called the Great Sea, but what can you call it now? The Dead Sea? Maybe Irtysh's own Ata-Balyk is still alive. But not everyone can see Ata-Balyk. It can appear before the eyes only of that person whose conscience is clean, whose thoughts and actions are beautiful. Will Kakharman ever see it again? Who knows? But to his father, Nasyr, who lived all his life by the sea, it probably showed itself many times—and maybe even spoke to him. It probably told him of its loneliness.

He and Ladov returned to the barge only when the dinner prepared by the boys was ready. Sitting at the table, Kakharman couldn't stop thinking that his life had gone awry. And his need for alcohol . . . Here it is, freedom! What, God, but drink can give a man such freedom? There was a time when drinkers in his homeland weren't even considered to be people! How has this nation gotten sucked into this disastrous funnel of drink? Shame and disgrace. No one nowadays remembers the rare and brave example of the hunter Musa. Once Musa said to Kakharman, "If I drink even a sip of that muck, the horse feels it; it snorts angrily and won't let me near it. So I have to dodder home on foot since I can't mount, even if I try to be clever and approach the horse from downwind. It makes me think this wretched water is probably damned by God! Your father Nasyr keeps saying there's no bigger tragedy in this world than the war. But I think alcohol is worse. Whoever alcohol pulls in dies a painful death. No, I won't even let it near my mouth!"

The sailors long ago noticed that the captain was often miserable, taciturn, and lost in his own thoughts. They didn't try to distract him; they simply started their own slow conversation.

The empty barge was now going up against the stream on its return pass. Captain Maltsev's boat came up level with them, and the voice of Vysotsky[17] flew through every crack in the boat:

> Drenched through with blood under the leaden rain,
> We accept our fate: well, it won't go away again.
> The heat of our bellies melted the frozen snow.

It was man though, not God, who brought this slaughter down,
They fly away—they shoot, they run—as they go.

"Maltsev is so monogamous." Ladov smiled. "He doesn't embrace anyone but Vysotsky."

"Everybody should love Vysotsky. He is our conscience."

"People have to adore someone. Yesterday he was in a cage; today he is an idol."

They could not help listening:

You wretched gang of dogs, don't you dare chase my pack!
In a fair fight, be sure, madam luck would have our back.
We are wolves; our life is good. We are wolves with every breath!
You are curs, you are dogs, and you will meet a dog's death.

Maltsev's barge was going farther down the stream, taking with it Vysotsky's voice. Ladov said, "I just can't understand this, Kakharman Nasyrovich. Why the hell are we transporting these pebbles? Well, we'll dig it up now, but who will return it to the river?"

Kakharman slowly lit a cigarette and, after a long silence, began to talk.

"It is theft. These pebbles will never be returned to the river. It's crazy to even think about it. In a country of fools, there are very simple answers to the most difficult questions. Our department is busy with theft and piracy. The shipping company has to transport twelve million tons of these pebbles a year. A ton of it now costs twenty-two kopeks. So today, we are stealing it at twenty-two kopeks, but tomorrow it will be impossible to restore it even for twenty-two million. This damage will be astronomical. Each year we rake out millions of tons from the riverbed. The level of water has dropped two yards. And these are just the flowers; the berries are still to come.[18] There's not a single decent beach or a boat station on the Irtysh now. It's all sludge.

"There won't be a name for this tragedy, Sasha. We'll simply lose the power of speech when we see it in its entirety!"

Turning an empty glass in his hands, he mused, "And then, when the state finally realizes the danger, it'll be too late. We will have no excuses to give our children. God will never forgive us our dreadful sins. Nothing awaits us but a curse! I already feel this curse. That is why my days now are so grim, but the future will be even worse.

"I won't stay here for long," Kakharman said. "I hung around for a couple years on Lake Balkhash. Ah, what's going on there, too—oh, my God! The same as in my homeland. I came here to get away, and what do I find! The Irtysh is barely alive. Soon only a pathetic brook will be left, and travel guides will say, 'Here, comrades, ten years ago, the great Siberian river Irtysh used to flow, though you can't see it anymore!'" Kakharman hit his fist on the table. "I've got to go!" After another long silence, he smiled sadly and slurred, "With each year, I become more and more absurd, like Korkut-baba."

Ladov had heard this legend of Korkut[19] from Kazakhs before.

Korkut-baba was an extraordinary man, they say. No one loved life as much as he, nor played the kobyz[20] *so well. And no one was so naïve. Just think about it! He thought people die only because there are gravediggers and graves that need filling. And when he asked any gravedigger who they were digging for, they all would answer (maybe as a joke or maybe not): "People say there is a musician with a kobyz—it's for him." Korkut traveled far and wide, and everywhere the gravediggers told him the same: It's for you.*

Then he laid a rug on the waters of the Syr Darya and floated on the rug far downstream. He was very sad, and he realized that he could never return to people, never return to the land, because it's on the land among people that gravediggers live. Day and night, he played on his kobyz beautiful, magical melodies about life, love, and happiness. And people along the banks listened with delight and waved at him sadly. Finally, the rug was swept into the sea. His shining songs became loved by fish, by seagulls—and even Ata-Balyk itself listened to them with delight. For many years, as soon as the sun rose over the horizon, Korkut would take his kobyz and start to play. And Ata-Balyk would rise to the surface and ask, "There is a lot of sadness in your music, Korkut. Where is this sadness from? What troubles you?"

"Eh, Ata-Balyk," Korkut would usually reply, "life is sadness. How can I be happy if I know I was born just to die one day?"

"So there are no pleasures in life?"

"There is little pleasure but a lot of suffering."

"Then why are you afraid of death? Will it not free you from sufferings?"

"No matter how bitter the sufferings are, Ata-Balyk, I want to live, and I'm scared to die."

"Then don't die, Korkut! Your music is needed here, in this world, even though it's full of pain."

Ata-Balyk once asked the musician, "I am being told that you sleep neither during the day, nor during the night, Korkut. Is it true?"

"The Almighty is watching me. He is just waiting for me to fall asleep. The moment I fall asleep, he will steal my soul out of me and will take it to heaven."

And this is how Ata-Balyk replied: "While I am with you, don't be afraid of anything. Have a sleep, and I will guard you." And Korkut believed the mighty fish and began to sleep.

"What a bliss it is—a sleep!" he thought admiringly.

But everybody knows, no man in the world can avoid his fate. Death was following him, even though it was very sad about it. Yes, yes—the fact is that death felt very sorry for Korkut and delayed the moment when it would have to wave its wing over him with all possible means. Often, the Almighty reproached the angel of death Azrail for his excessive kindness toward Korkut, but Azrail couldn't help himself. He followed in Korkut's footsteps and enjoyed the playing of his kobyz. Azrail explained it to the Almighty in this way: "If I take the soul of this genius, what will happen to his magical music?"

"Isn't his genius my creation? Isn't it me who disposes of his life?" the Creator answered.

"But why did you create him different from other people? Why didn't you give him two life terms? Doesn't genius deserve it?"

"I do not make exceptions, even for geniuses. In the end, he is not a god but only a two-legged creature. You should quickly fly to the earth and deliver his soul here!"

And Azrail flew to Korkut.

Korkut woke up on his rug in cold sweat and realized that the conversation of the Creator with the angel was only in his dream. But he was already at an age when people no longer easily dismiss their dreams.

"Korkut-baba," he told himself, "your death is walking somewhere near, so meet it with dignity."

That is what he told himself as he washed his face with seawater, read the morning prayer, and took the black kobyz in his hands. The kobyz began to cry the moment Korkut's fingers touched the strings. And the musician's eyes began getting moist, too, but Korkut held back the tears so that Azrail wouldn't see his weakness. Ata-Balyk was swimming nearby, pushing the red rug.

The kobyz was singing about how weak and feeble a man is but how immeasurable and infinite the life he leaves behind. Korkut, who didn't accept Islam and until his last day worshipped only fire, suddenly saw a bright light. But he didn't realize what kind of fire was calling him— he didn't guess that this is not a fire lit by a man but the face of the sun, rising over the horizon. And then he thought, "Today, when the heavenly body touches the waterline as it goes down, my old body, which has enjoyed life ninety-six years, will become a cold corpse."

But here's the odd thing! The more hysterically the black kobyz cried, the lighter the face of the old man became. His heart, seemingly insensitive because its joy was so often displaced by the sadness in it, was getting more and more warm, and his soul, which quickly warmed, began to rush toward the sky by itself. His heart was saying, "You should be embarrassed! Do not humiliate yourself with such ungrateful love for life because life is so transient! Aren't you tired? Don't you want to rest? Don't be sorry about life because there is an eternal happiness in front of you—when you will never think about death, when you will be forever happy. Time is ruthless on earth; everyone is equaled by it. But there, it simply doesn't exist. Isn't that bliss: to never think about time! Speed your earthy death, Korkut, for its arrival will let you be reborn to this new life."

And then Korkut, raising his hands to the sky, whispered through tears of joy: "Death, come to me!"

At exactly the same time, the snake sent by Azrail crawled onto his chest and injected its poison into the old man's blood. The kobyz fell from his hands, and Korkut died. Azrail greeted him with sadness.

"Welcome, holy Korkut! May your soul find peace in heaven!"

A dark mist swept over the waves. A black wraith fell upon the sea. The sea was raging, piling up gigantic waves. Ata-Balyk was crashing in the depths as the sadness pierced its heart. It rushed through the dark water in search of a red rug, in search of its friend, but the soul of the holy old man was already resting in heaven.

Since then, it's said that the sad Ata-Balyk often calls out longingly for Korkut's soul, and they say that sometimes Korkut's soul comes down from heaven and has long and profound conversations with the mighty fish.

"Yes, I shall leave Irtysh. Korkut-baba used to run from death, and I will run from dead water. But I'm afraid this carrion will follow me everywhere," Kakharman said.

"And where am I supposed to go?" Ladov answered. "They say it's better elsewhere, but looking at you, Kakharman Nasyrovich, I think even if I leave my homeland, what will it change?" He hesitated. "Please, don't take my words personally."

"You are close to the truth, though I don't like hearing it." Kakharman stood up. "Let's get ready. And tell the boys to get ready."

Maltsev's barge was coming their way again. Again Vysotsky's coarse voice tore Kakharman's soul apart:

> *I'm fed up to the teeth, choked up from my spleen.*
> *I'm even tired of songs now; what's that all about?*
> *I should dive down to the bottom like a submarine,*
> *And lay there in the darkness and not send a signal out . . .*

Aitugan and the children were waiting for their father to start dinner.

"They don't want to eat without you." Aitugan smiled, sensing that Kakharman was gloomy again. He stank of alcohol. At such times, she tried to distract him from his mood and often succeeded. A clever woman, Kakharman thought, can make a man feel that he is master of the house—a master whose thoughts are listened to, whose inner world, seemingly invisible but fragile and vulnerable, seems as important as the trials of the external world.

But it was hard for Aitugan too. She patiently bore all the ills of life, but inside, in her soul, she was restless and worried. They'd been living in Semipalatinsk for a year and a half already in a small room in one of the barracks. Once, Aitugan reminded Kakharman, "You said that by this summer, it would be sorted out with the apartment. Have you asked about it?"

"I'll find out," Kakharman replied half-heartedly, and Aitugan understood that he would not beg or grovel for it. Since then, she hadn't mentioned it. The children helped her carry water from the well. After Sinemorye and Balkhash, she couldn't get used to the frosty winters and penetrating winds. At the bus stop, the chill wind cut through them, and she and the boys jumped like rubber balls in order to keep warm. Then they got in the freezer of a bus and sat for an hour in bitter cold as they came home from school, the only Kazakh school in all Semipalatinsk, which was located at the other end of the city. They didn't have any relatives here or friends. And although she had good relationships with her colleagues, she hadn't gotten close to any of them. Besides, all her colleagues lived in the center of the city, and she couldn't go all the way from Zaton to visit them very often. And she couldn't really invite them to visit her—how can she ask people to this tiny room in a barrack? She talked to only one person, Yakubovsky's wife, Mariya. However weary and close to despair Aitugan got, though, she knew that if she fell apart, then they wouldn't have any life with Kakharman.

But Kakharman couldn't get used to Semipalatinsk either.

After the vastness of the sea, the Irtysh seemed rather feeble. Only gradually did he realize that he shouldn't compare a river with the sea. The sea will seem as lifeless as a puddle if it's not his motherland, and a river may seem like an infinite sea if he was born there. Kakharman recalled his mother's sad sighs. "It'd be so nice to see the Irtysh again, my dear son, because I was born there. It'd be nice to go to Chingistau, set up a yurt at Zidebai,[21] and live again like many years ago." Back then, he thought resentfully, "How is it possible to abandon our sea?" Now he understood many things.

Once, Yakubovsky, going to Chingistau on business, invited Kakharman to join him, remembering his words that it was his mother's homeland. Kakharman happily agreed.

The trip was in the autumn, at the time when a traveler gazing over the vast, monotonous landscapes of a withered steppe could fall into despair. Only in the mountains of Orda were Yakubovsky and Kakharman smiled on by a little greenery spared by the scorching sun, and it cheered them up. In the distance, the pale-blue peaks of Chingistau soared over the green meadows. Soon they were at Zidebai by the Abai[22] monument.[23] "This is where my mother was born," Kakharman said quietly.

How bleak and barren it all looked then, especially compared to that distant time when Abai lived here. They say that back then, Zidebai was richly verdant, its luscious meadows and green pastures rolling away into the hills. Kakharman spent a long time standing by the monument and by Shakarim's grave. Autumn. Silence. Desolation.

In Zidebai, they were met by District Committee Secretary Gafez Mataev. He saw that Kakharman looked depressed and tried to reassure him. "This is the area where Abai used to spend his winters, his *dzhailyau* (summer pasture) was farther up the mountains. Those are heavenly places! You can go up into the mountains now and stay in a yurt, but it's cold this close to the winter. You should visit Chingistau in the summer."

"Does that mean you're inviting us to come next summer?" Yakubovsky asked.

"Yes! But now I want to show you something. Have you heard about the Konyr-Aulie cave?[24] It's considered sacred. Invalids stay here for one or two nights and, they say, are healed miraculously."

"Is that the cave described in Mukhtar Auezov's novel, *Abai*?" Kakharman asked.

"Exactly!" Gafez replied. "Let's go!"

They traveled to places linked to Abai for three days. They listened to the beautiful and haunting stories of the people of old. They heard lovely songs and listened to kyuis. It was an extraordinary corner of Kazakhstan, rich in ancient customs.

Gafez tuned an ancient dombra and began to sing a sad Abai song in his deep, melodious voice. Sorrowful words merged together with a poignant melody.

Oh, I'm weary and weak—deceived by them all,
Betrayed both by friends and foes great and small.
It's hard to see anyone, in the distance or here
Who would not bring down on me suffering and fear.
Each has his agenda and can never be straight.
If you fall, he'll abandon you to your cruel fate.
Then he will say, "Well, I'm just the same."
No, he won't stand by your side in this one-sided game.
There are thousands of liars for each honest soul,
Yet when you fight by yourself, there's a terrible toll.
Drunkenness and debauchery swarm everywhere,

And no one thinks now of friendship or care.
There's no respect for achievements, or even the old.
The grasping step forward, ever more bold
And only money earns honor or shame.
You just alter your colors, and go on the same.

In a shepherd's yurt not far from Konyr-Aulie, Kakharman yielded to the moment and sang, for the first time, a *zhyr*[25] that he'd heard many times before from Akbalak:

How oft 'neath a saddle, patchy and worn,
There's a horse that to racing might have been born?
Or among some old arrows, you might find too
Just one that can pierce steel armor clean through.
Yes, meet those who come to you with a soul that is free,
But remember among them there's one who will be
Enjoying your troubles, spoiling your peace.

Gafez was extremely moved. "Kakharman, I'd never have thought you had such an expressive voice!"

Yakubovsky was also touched. He said ardently, "What a broad and incisive folk language, whether it's Kazakh or Russian."

"It'd be great if you would explain it to our bureaucrats." Kakharman grinned, recalling the loud bark of the instructor at the meeting of the Republican Central Committee when Kakharman began his speech in Kazakh.

The shepherd and his wife began to prepare the bed for the guests, so Kakharman stepped outside with Gafez. It was night in the mountains. The air was cool, and stars glittered, large and bright. A wind began to blow up from the west. Kakharman was feeling good from these three days. Thanks to Gafez, he had managed to restore the peace of mind he had lost long ago.

The shepherd's voice came out of the yurt—the bed was ready. At that moment, a huge explosion boomed out through the night. The ground under Kakharman's feet began to shake. "It's that Polygon!"[26] Yakubovsky spat angrily. "People were protesting at the meeting of Nevada Semipalatinsk[27] just a while ago!"

"The authority that ignores the people should be sent to hell!" Kakharman swore.

The shepherd said, "They always make their explosions at this time. Not so long ago, about three miles away from here, after the explosions, a small lake appeared. After drinking water from this lake, three flocks of sheep died—right at the watering place, right on its shore. And all my sheep lost their fur by evening! I was told to send them for meat. But I thought, 'What will they do with this meat? Would they really dare to feed people with it?'" The shepherd turned toward Yakubovsky.

"So we'll be eating lamb, and the lamb will eat us?" Ivan answered angrily. "Who else would they feed animals to? Man will eat anything, whatever you give him. That is how we are brought up."

The shepherd shook his head. "Once after that, wolves killed three of my sheep and then died themselves. I went to visit my neighbor and saw them over that hill." The shepherd pointed into the darkness. "And would a single crow sit on them? No. They circled around but wouldn't settle. They sensed the poison."

"That's nothing!" Mataev exclaimed bitterly. "You'd better tell people about your family—let them know what is happening here!"

The shepherd stayed silent for a bit and then said, "What is there to tell? Who can help me in my trouble now? The government? God?" He looked at Kakharman. "Didn't you see my children? They're sleeping in that outbuilding. My eldest son finished school this year and"—his voice cracked—"and hanged himself. In our district, it's not the first suicide. It's mostly young people, hanging or shooting themselves. My daughter is fourteen years old, but she's only about three feet tall. She just doesn't grow any taller. There are many like this in the sovkhoz and about a hundred in the district. The youngest is seven years old. He was born with his legs joined together. He is mentally damaged."

The chaban lowered his voice so that his wife, who had just walked out of the yurt, wouldn't hear. Kakharman was shocked by the story. "That's awful!" he gasped. "We are barbarians if we're damaging our people so cruelly! Hello, bright future; hello, communism! We are crawling toward you on all fours, bringing with us all the freak dwarfs, the mental defectives with fused legs, and all our poisoned children. Hello!"

He couldn't sleep in the two hours before dawn. They left early. But the shepherd's children were already awake. Kakharman didn't have enough courage to look at them. The two of them were busy in the back of the yard, making odd noises. He quickly looked away, his eyes full of tears, and rushed to get into the car.

"What are you thinking about, Kakharman?" Aitugan distracted him from his thoughts.

"Do you remember that I told you about that shepherd from Chingistau?" Kakharman replied. "I thought about him again."

But Aitugan knew that wasn't the only thing troubling Kakharman. She was patient and didn't pester him with questions. She hoped her husband would share things with her when the time was right.

There was a knock on the door. Yakubovsky walked in, and the small room, filled with the large man, became even smaller.

"Aitugan, I'll only stay for a minute. I still have lots to do. I brought a letter from Sayat. For some reason, he sent it to my address." He gave an envelope to Kakharman. Kakharman was soon absorbed in reading, and Yakubovsky stretched his arms out regretfully, "Aitugan, dearest! I just can't find the apartment. They keep dragging it out, the devils! City hall hasn't allocated a single one to the shipping company. Honestly, I don't know where to hide my eyes from you."

"It's OK, Ivan. We'll wait," Aitugan reassured him. "The only thing that's not good is that the Kazakh school is very far, but the rest we can cope with."

"That's for sure." Yakubovsky smiled guiltily. "If there's nothing else . . ." He suddenly slapped himself on the forehead. "I completely forgot! Next to the school, we have three barrack rooms that will soon become vacant. Would you like to move there? The rooms are small and a bit run-down, but at least there are three of them."

"That's fantastic!" Aitugan blushed with excitement. "Of course. We'll move there, no question!"

Kakharman inserted the letter he just read into the envelope.

"My assistant Sasha Ladov is getting those three rooms. Have you forgotten?" he asked.

"He can move in here!"

"No, Vanya. It wouldn't be right. He also has two children."

"For Ladov, it'll be more convenient. It's closer to his work, the nursery is just across the road."

"Have you spoken to Sasha?"

"It only just dawned on me! I'll talk to him."

"You just don't have the whole picture. He was going to bring his mother-in-law from Ryazan'. In that village, there are only six old women and one old man. It's hard for her there. An old man used to look after them, but he died recently."

Aitugan turned away. Kakharman gently put his hand on her shoulder:

"Let's not climb up on other's backs. Done this way, any happiness will turn into trouble. I've been working in the shipping company only two years, and he's been waiting eight years. And you, Vanya, don't waste your time on trifles. We can see that not everything in the world is up to you." And then he changed the subject in order to smooth over the awkwardness between them. "Greetings from Sayat to you and a bow to you, Aitugan. Our Sayat now is a head of a large floating base. He invites us to come to him at the Caspian." He made a sign to Yakubovsky to go outside. The driver of the blue Volga, who was waiting for his boss, turned the engine on.

"Hold on. Not yet." Yakubovsky waved to the driver, then addressed Kakharman. "Our quota on pebbles has been increased to eighteen million until next year. And we've been allowed to open our own mothership. I'm thinking of appointing you head of it. Write a refusal to Sayat so he doesn't think too highly of himself!"

"And do you think I will agree? Don't you know what I think of this theft?"

"No, I don't think I do!"

"That's because you've never asked! We are on the verge of destroying this river! Of course, you don't need to be clever to use its riches barbarically. No counting, no troubles—just rake the rubles! But what will happen tomorrow? Tomorrow we'll be spending millions of rubles to return everything the way it was! And only if it is possible. But what if it turns out that we can't restore it?"

"Do you think I don't understand this?" Yakubovsky was upset.

"You stand in front of your management with your arms by your sides. I don't believe you do understand!"

"As it happens," Yakubovsky objected, "our shipping company earned hundreds of millions of rubles!"

"Forget these millions. I don't want to hear about them. It makes me sick! It's paper wealth and not real. Tell me, what use is it to our shipping company?"

"No use. Almost everything goes to the state budget."

"Exactly! The ministry officials like to eat—and not that stinking twenty-kopek sausage you and I see once a month. Wouldn't it make more sense, though, to spend half of the money restoring the river? Who will pay the debt to the river? Look at it! It is almost entirely destroyed!"

Yakubovsky grew gloomy again.

"As it happens, these pebbles are being extracted without any purpose at all. It's just, the more the better."

Kakharman was stunned.

"Why are you surprised? It's the same along the Irtysh's bank and in Omsk, and in Tomsk, and so on! Everybody steals what they can."

"But you don't steal, comrade Yakubovsky!" Kakharman said quietly, choking with anger.

"It's not me who steals; it's the system!"

They sat down on a bench, turned away from each other, and stayed silent for a long time.

"I'd better go," Yakubovsky said weakly. "I've got an evening planning session."

"Wait, Vanya." Kakharman held Yakubovsky back. "I have made a decision. I can't stay here any longer. You have a great area, the boys are good, and the city is not too bad, but I can't live like this any longer. I am not such a brainless brute that I can turn a blind eye to what I am doing here!"

"Where are you going? To the Caspian?"

"I don't know yet. I'll let you know when I decide."

Yakubovsky left, and Kakharman stayed sitting in silence on the bench. He leaned back against the barrack wall, still warm from the day's sunshine, and closed his eyes. The boys were running and kicking the ball without paying any attention to him, and their cheerful voices flew into the sky and dissolved. Aitugan sat next to him.

"School term begins in three days, and we still haven't heard from Berish. I'm beginning to worry."

"Berish will be here." Kakharman smiled warmly for the first time that day. "I dropped the knife twice—that's a certain sign he'll be here soon." And he hugged his wife gently.

It was getting cooler now. The blue twilight was thickening.

"Call the boys to dinner."

Aitugan stood up and went into the house.

"Dad, look who's coming!" the youngest one shouted and rushed out.

And there was Berish, striding across the yard with a backpack on his shoulders.

"Koke! Hello!"

"My dear son! Berish!" Kakharman embraced his son warmly and caught the familiar scent of Sinemorye on him. The younger ones clung to his arms and shouted over each other. Aitugan ran out of the house and hugged him tightly.

"How about something to eat, Mom?" Berish said, finally freeing himself from her embrace. "I'll just go for a quick swim . . . I missed the Irtysh . . ."

The younger ones followed him as Aitugan began to prepare the table.

"How about something to eat?" She kept repeating his words through happy tears. "He's so grown-up now, oh, my God." A misty smile spread across her face. "The way he says it in such a deep voice, 'How about something to eat?'"

Soon they were all seated and eating. To each of his father's questions about his grandparents, the sea, and life in Karaoi and Shumgen, Berish replied carefully and in detail, which Kakharman found rather amusing. But Aitugan looked at her son with reverence, mute admiration written all over her face.

"Grandma is often ill," Berish told him. "Aunt came, and she'll take her to the city hospital again. There's barely anyone left in the aul, Koke." Berish went silent, collecting his thoughts. "The wild horses have enticed Uncle Musa's racer. And our ash-gray almost left with them, too, but luckily Uncle Musa saw what was happening, fired his gun, and brought her back."

"How is he getting on without his racer?"

"Not great. He's gone a little crazy. He follows the herd and tries to bring it back. But I doubt he'll succeed. People say these herds have now gone beyond Balkhash. His baibishe comes to us every day, sighs, and says, 'Who cares for that damned gelding? I just wish my Musa would come back.'"

"How's Granddad? Is he well?"

"Yes, Granddad is well. But he is not the same as he used to be. He's always quiet and lost in thought. He prays five times a day. He keeps saying there'll be water in the sea! Dad, isn't it impossible?"

"Of course it's impossible. But let him believe. This faith helps him to live. Faith is a great thing, Berish. Is there any other news?"

"There is this news. Now we have a laboratory. Uncle Igor runs it. And Professor Slavikov sent Indian tea and sweets for Granddad and Grandma."

"What sort of laboratory is that?" Kakharman bristled, sensing something bad.

"They call it the Laboratory for Observation of the Death of the Sea."

"So our government has signed the sea's death warrant!" Kakharman exclaimed and went silent. Then, hiding his wet eyes, he walked out of the house.

It was time to sleep. Kakharman, lying in bed, kept turning from side to side. The news that Berish brought wouldn't leave his head. "Vandals!" he thought. "Utter vandals! They think they live on the earth for its last day. Just wait. The sea will have its vengeance on you!"

Finally, his tired mind fell into sleep. He again dreamed about the sea. He dreamed about Korym Island, where large fish used to gather.

He sees Ata-Balyk at once. It is moving heavily and is extremely emaciated. Next to it is the Ana-Balyk—fish mother—also thin and exhausted. A shoal of fish follow in their wake. And the closer the shoal gets, the more scared Kakharman becomes. The shoal aren't fish but monstrous creatures, and they are heading toward him. Creatures with two or three heads, with conjoined tails, slithery bodies without fins, and with bulging eyes and lumpy bodies. But it is unclear where the shoal is heading. It is unclear whether Ata-Balyk is really leading these creatures or if Ata-Balyk is being driven by them. Ata-Balyk's eyes are red, feeble, and sunken. Maybe these are the last minutes of its life, because suddenly, as Kakharman's heart trembles ominously, it slowly, slowly begins to sink. The fish following it suddenly begin darting to and fro anxiously, and the mouth of the brown catfish appears for a moment . . .

He also dreamed about his father.

Mullah Nasyr, down on his knees on the pale dead shore, whispers prayers. He is as thin and exhausted as Ata-Balyk. And his hair is entirely gray. "Father . . ." Kakharman calls to him. "Father!" But the old man, down on his knees, doesn't turn. "Father! Sinemorye! Father!"

Aitugan began to stroke her husband's arm, whispering quietly, "Stay calm, Kakharman. Stay calm . . ."

"Father," Kakharman keeps murmuring and sobbing. "Why are you praying? What God do you pray to? Everything is lost, Father. Do you hear me? Answer me, Father!"

"Be quiet, son!" Nasyr whispers sharply without turning his head, and in that whisper is a fury that startles Kakharman. "Don't call for misfortune. It's already at the doorstep! Pray! Pray to Allah!"

"But where is he, this Allah?" Kakharman shouts. "Why would I need him if everything is lost?"

"To stay a human being, my son!"

IX

The fishing settlements along the Sinemorye coast were falling into decay. Nasyr and hunter Musa were almost the only people still living there. There was nowhere else for crazy Kyzbala and her loyal dog to go. Zhanyl and her son Yesen wouldn't move either. It was a strange life for the fishermen. There were hardly any fish left in Sinemorye, and many didn't want to go on long expeditions to catch fish, like Kambar's team did. Some began to graze livestock, while others began farming. That was better than abandoning the graves of their forefathers and moving away.

In Shumgen, everything was relatively stable. Only a few households had left so far, and the main settlement looked in much better condition than others. The Shumgen fishermen made the trek to the Caspian and Balkhash regularly. They also went to Shardara, Torgai, and Yrgyz. In this way, little by little, they managed to meet the target, which was still relentlessly demanding. But in winter, they could catch fish at home in the ponds behind the weirs built by Kakharman. It seemed the fishermen were getting used to their grim life, since it had been going on for almost ten years already.

The old zhyrau Akbalak was too ill to think much about it as he was lying by the hot stove. His daughter had come from Karaoi with her husband to look after him, but he stayed sick.

At night he was cold even next to the stove. During the day, he wouldn't come out into the sun and spent all day by the stove. He warmed up and slept, slept and warmed up again. He would often jump up fearfully, then sit down. When he slept, it sometimes seemed to him that he had already died. In moments like those, he would quickly pick up the dombra and begin to play, jumping from one tune to another, bitterly realizing that he could no longer play even a single kyui from beginning to end.

Something had happened to Akbalak that stirred his soul. He once had one comfort: a young ginger mare that he cared for like a mother cares for her child. But not so long ago, the wild horses had taken the mare away.

One evening at dusk, that fiery stallion had cantered boldly into the yard and, as if sensing that the feeble owner wouldn't resist, danced brazenly up to the ginger mare and ripped away the leash with his teeth and began to circle playfully.

Akbalak had watched this strange romance in awe, rooted to the spot. The stallion beckoned her away. As they moved beyond the gate, he stamped his hoof triumphantly. The herd neighed in answer and galloped off.

Caught barefoot, Akbalak ran around the house in search of his shoes. By the time he found them, the horses were already out beyond the edge of the aul. Their backs shone gold in the setting sun, and their manes and tales tossed like waves on the wind. Akbalak began to call the mare, yelling her name. The mare looked back, slowing down. But what was the voice of her feeble owner compared to the new, free life now waiting for her? The stallion began to gently nudge her forward. She neighed loud and long, and old Akbalak's heart cracked as his lonely soul rushed toward her. "Goodbye! Goodbye!" he murmured and began to cry as he watched his beloved mare and the scarlet stallion disappear into the distance, framed by the large red disk of the sun.

And the sounds of a new melody he had long felt suddenly began to ask for its freedom. Akbalak rushed home and quickly tuned the dombra. In a moment, the whole melody appeared up to the last sound—as if it had always been living somewhere and only now had found Akbalak.

Yes, Akbalak had wanted to tell this story for decades. Often in his memories, he had seen the sea's rollers, challenging each fisherman. Often, he had heard their menacing roar. And often, so often, he remembered the caress of the wind on Korym Island, that tender cradle of love for him and Karashash. Play, dombra, play! Like Akbalak, you can never forget your darling Karashash. And there she is! Young, happy, stepping into the boat! There she is, turning her head toward the baby she's breastfeeding! All Akbalak's life, the entire span of its earthly burdens, all its earthly happiness, were poured into this last melody of the old zhyrau. Play, dombra, play! Akbalak is not dead yet. His heart still beats. His eyes still see. But today he has received a sign. It wasn't the young mare bidding farewell to him; it was life. That was what the dombra in Akbalak's hands was singing: goodbye, life; goodbye, life . . .

Exhausted, Akbalak rested the dombra on his knees and sat back and closed his eyes. Yes, goodbye, life. It's sad to bid farewell, but what can one do? Lately, he had often thought it would be nice to invite old friends Nasyr and Musa to visit him to brighten his loneliness. At last, he sent his son-in-law to get them, but only Nasyr came. Musa wasn't at home. He was away, scouring the desert for his raven-black racer.

As soon as he saw Akbalak, Nasyr understood that his days were numbered. He clasped the old zhyrau's hand firmly. Bitterness and regret were written on his face, and Nasyr thought about the fact that fate seems more willing to separate people than to bring them together. After the customary greetings, Akbalak's daughter set the table while Akbalak explained why he had sent his son-in-law to fetch Nasyr.

"Nasyr, I don't have long left. Don't be upset that I tore you away from your affairs. I don't have anyone left but you and Musa. Just listen to my request. It is my last. Tomorrow, I want you to take me to Korym Island. I want to be on the sea one last time."

He looked at Nasyr's face pleadingly and, reading the doubts on the old man's face, said, "Don't worry. I won't die on the way. We'll leave early in the morning, and we'll be there by sunset. We'll stay there overnight, then we'll come back. I have words I've been preparing a long time. I'll tell you them on the sea."

When they saw how set the old man was, Akbalak's daughter and son-in-law, Tobagabyl, realized it was pointless to try to dissuade him.

Nasyr thought a while, then said, "I can't refuse your wish, Aka, though I haven't been to the island for a long time. We'll go tomorrow."

Early the next morning, they met on the shore. Tobagabyl wanted to go with them, but Akbalak insisted. "You'll meet us in the car when we're back. And Shortanbai will come with us."

Shortanbai pushed the boat out and jumped in. Back when Kakharman was a director, Shortanbai was one of the boys he had recommended to the institute. The boy studied in Odessa and now was on holiday before going off to the Caspian for practice. He'd often heard about Korym Island but had never been there, so he was grateful the old men had invited him.

As the boat moved out, Shortanbai pointed at the water.

"Look, the water is completely still, Nasyr-aga. It's as flat as a mirror. Yet the wind is blowing. Why?"

"Too much salt in the water, son. It's as heavy as lead."

Nasyr pointed the boat toward Korym Island. When they reached the open sea, he handed the tiller to Shortanbai and adjusted Akbalak's pillow and asked if he needed anything.

"How easy it is to breathe out here, Nasyr!" Akbalak exclaimed. "I missed the sea air so much! Scoop me some water. I'll wash my face."

Nasyr listened to the rustle and slap of the seaweed against the bottom of the boat. Rank and unnaturally green, the weeds irritated him. But as they moved farther out to sea, the rustling died away. The water became clearer, and soon the seabed was visible. Suddenly, Nasyr glimpsed the shadow of a large fish flashing beneath the boat. A moment later, a large, gaunt fish swam near the boat. Nasyr thought he could see a scar on its head.

"Shortanbai," he ordered, "slow down a little."

Yes, the scar stood out starkly. And Nasyr knew immediately that this was the fish that had capsized his boat long ago. He grabbed the oar and prepared to beat it off, but the fish dived under the boat, only to reappear on the far side. Nasyr saw its wretched backbone so bare of flesh, it looked like a skeleton with scales. Its eyes and mouth were half-shut.

Shortanbai exclaimed, "Nasyr-aga, is that a beluga?"

Nasyr looked. Yes, there was a beluga with its brood. The brood were horribly deformed, with just one eye on top of their heads staring accusingly up into the sky. "Even fish are now mutants," Nasyr thought and spat angrily.

Akbalak's eyes seemed to be shut, and he was quiet. The sun was burning fiercely. Akbalak opened his eyes but turned away from Nasyr and looked intently into the water.

For years now, both Daryas, polluted by chemical waste, had swept their toxic waters into the sea. And the sea was unable to rid itself of this poison, as powerless and defenseless as Akbalak was in the sunset of his life.

"Nasyr," Akbalak said, "you're a mullah. You're a man who talks with God. You've been talking to him about our poor sea. Yet the water is no better."

Nasyr was silent for a while, then answered thoughtfully.

"Aka, you've been gently making fun of God, mullahs, and hajji all your life. We've never really had a serious talk about the Creator. I don't think we'll be able to have one now."

Akbalak laughed quietly.

"People have pushed your God aside, Nasyr. He stepped into one boot with both feet. He sits there in the sky and doesn't see anything. Yet people fly into space, without asking him whether it's allowed or not."

Nasyr, who prayed five times a day, who knew the Quran by heart, also had doubts. Yes, if Allah has eyes, doesn't he see Sinemorye is dying?

But he said, "Let's not blaspheme. No matter how much man flies into space, he'll never push God aside."

"If God really exists, then I'd like to give him a few strong words for giving such misfortunes to humanity."

"No, Aka. Let's not touch God. Let's talk about people. They fully deserve your sharp tongue. I have no doubt that misfortunes on earth are created not by God but by people. Let's assume there's no God. Then can you explain that devilish force that pushes people toward bad actions and knocks them off the path of truth and justice, of goodness and reason?"

"Three forces fight inside of a man. The first one is kindness and humanity. The second is the lion, ready for a fight, for an attack. And the third force is abomination, the tendency to lie. This force is like a pig."

"And that pig—isn't it the devil, Aka?"

"Maybe. People often turn into brainless pigs. I became convinced of that long ago. Animals are much kinder in their souls and more reasonable."

"True, Aka," responded Nasyr, roused. "I've been waiting to hear you say this for a long time." A huge warmth toward the old man welled up in Nasyr's heart, and he wanted to talk about something simple and humane. "Tell me, Aka, how did the young stallion take your mare away in broad daylight?"

"It wasn't in broad daylight. It happened in the evening," Akbalak said with a rueful smile. Then he coughed until large veins appeared on his forehead. He dabbed his eyes with a handkerchief as tears began to flow. Catching his breath, he took a sip of water, then handed the piala back to Nasyr. "Horses treat each other with understanding and tenderness. I didn't try to chase them. Their hearts grew together in an instant, and their love was impossible to destroy.

That fiery stallion was beautiful, marvelous! What mare could resist him? And I thought, let them love each other for a long, long time. And I blessed them. Like children."

They were getting closer to the island. Akbalak peered eagerly at the widening strip of land, and soon the shapes of trees were visible. But as they moved closer, Akbalak was plunged into despair. The trees were scraggy and thin. The island looked threadbare. Yes, you could still call it a green bowl in the middle of a blue sea—but only with your eyes closed. The sea was dying, and that meant there was an end to all things in this world. Akbalak knew it and felt it like no one else; he himself was dying. Now, in the sunset of his life, Korym Island has faded too. Even the familiar saxaul bushes, which he and Karashash had so admired for their sturdiness, looked like they had drooped and become frail.

Ah, Karashash, beloved Karashash! You've been gone so long! Akbalak has little time left to walk the paths of this earth. Karashash's body sank to the bottom of the sea, and Akbalak's will be buried in the ground. But his soul will fly over the sea with the gulls that swoop and swirl. And, who knows? Maybe Karashash's soul is flying over the sea, too, hovering in anticipation of Akbalak's soul. Maybe her soul has already found shelter here . . . Why not?

Then . . . then . . . Akbalak was deep in his thoughts when it suddenly struck him. He shouldn't be buried on land! His body should go into the sea, with Karashash. Yes, yes! Why didn't he think of it before? Here it is, his final wish, which he'll tell to Nasyr, to his relatives. And it is Nasyr who should give his body to the sea. He will understand without explanation that only in this way will Akbalak be able to find Karashash in the other world.

These thoughts settled Akbalak's soul. He closed his eyes, and the melody he had played on the dombra the day before drifted back. And although yesterday it seemed done, now he understood what was missing, the final perfect phrase it needed for completeness—the phrase he now purred to himself. He mustn't forget it, this melody. He sang it two more times, hardly moving his lips, nodding his head to the beat. Only then did he calm down. He will not forget it now . . .

As they approached the island, they began to see dead fish. And more dead fish drifting slackly on their sides. And soon the corpses of gulls and other birds bobbed past. The stench of death filled their nostrils. Two gulls that had been following the boat suddenly screamed and dived toward them.

"Shortanbai, watch out!" Nasyr shouted, waving his oar in the air. But one seagull managed to nip the boy sharply on his shoulder. The second seagull veered away as it saw Nasyr's oar. Shortanbai looked up, shocked. His shoulder was covered in blood.

"Don't stop the engine!" Nasyr ordered. "I'll clean your wound."

Now the birds attacked them from the front. They swooped around the bow and hurled down toward them. Nasyr yelled and carved the air with his oar, but the bigger of the two birds batted its wings right over Nasyr's head, completely unafraid. Akbalak banged loudly on a bucket, and Shortanbai roared and waved a boat hook.

"Careful!" Akbalak shouted. "Don't kill them. There's no need to kill them."

Nasyr and Shortanbai nodded quietly. But the bigger gull swerved past Nasyr's oar to catch his sleeve with its beak, pulling a long tear in the fabric. Nasyr gripped the steering wheel and pushed the throttle.

"Oh, God, what's happening?" Akbalak cried. "Are these the friendly gulls that took bread from Karashash's hands?" Then he called to Shortanbai, "Come here and show me your wound."

Shortanbai tore his shirt from his shoulder and sat next to Akbalak.

"It really gashed your shoulder! I won't waste drinking water washing it. Be patient, and once we're past this stinking place, I'll get water from the sea."

"It's still bleeding," Shortanbai said a while later. So Akbalak took a small sack from his pocket and untied the braid, then took some herbs out of paper bags and spread them over the wound.

"That really stings, Granddad!"

"It's an astringent herb. That's why it burns. Just bear with it."

Then Nasyr said in surprise, "Hey, it looks like we've got a welcoming party. There are people on the island."

"I guess Father must have informed them over the radio." Shortanbai shrugged.

"Was he scared that we'd get eaten by the wolves or picked off by the gulls?" Akbalak wasn't happy. "Why bother people for nothing."

"Ikor is there. He's always happy to talk to you."

"I wouldn't mind talking to him either." Akbalak's irritation lifted instantly.

And then the screech of gulls was back. Nasyr turned toward the sound, but the sun was shining into his eyes. As he shaded his eyes, he saw a whole flock rapidly approaching. He let go of the steering wheel and rushed to pick up the oar, but the gulls had fallen on the men and were now mauling them. Nasyr and Shortanbai flailed around with their arms as they tried to protect their eyes. On the shore, Igor ran to his motorbike to get a gun. The boy and girl with him began to shout and wave their arms wildly. The birds paid no heed. At last Nasyr grabbed the oar and Shortanbai, the boat hook. Nasyr swung the oar fiercely and managed to strike three birds. But the other gulls didn't let him swing the oar again. They dived toward his back and pummeled him and Shortanbai with their wings and beaks. Nasyr collapsed onto the bottom of the boat. Shortanbai lost his balance and plunged overboard into the water.

"Keep down!" Igor shouted and pulled the trigger. The shot hit a few gulls at once. The surviving gulls shot into the sky, shrieking. There was uproar all around. Horrible squawks as the wounded birds fell in the water. Shortanbai tried to clamber back into the boat, but one of the wounded gulls nipped his pants and yanked him back.

"Nasyr-aga!" Shortanbai shouted. But Nasyr was still lying facedown at the bottom of the boat. Akbalak hit the gull on the beak with a ladle. But his strike was too feeble. The gull glared at the old man angrily. Akbalak dropped the ladle in shock. Just at that moment, Nasyr came to his senses and yanked Shortanbai into the boat.

"They're coming back!" Shortanbai shouted as he pulled on his shirt.

Igor also saw them too. He raised his gun and fired. Again a few gulls plummeted into the sea. But still the flock came. They dived toward the boat, completely unafraid of Nasyr's oar. This time, though, they didn't attack the men. They simply came in low over them and doused them in shit.

Aghast, Nasyr spat overboard as they ran up onto the shore. "I have seen a lot in my seventy-three years, but I have never been so insulted and humiliated."

Shortanbai looked at Nasyr, who was looking at himself with disgust, and Akbalak, who had covered his head, and then burst out laughing.

Grunting, Akbalak took off his cape and allowed Nasyr and Igor to lift him under his arms and help him walk to a large tent, where they laid him on the straw Igor had prepared for him.

"Thank you," Akbalak said. "But Tobagabyl shouldn't have troubled you." Akbalak was very touched that so many people were looking after him.

"No thanks are needed, aqsaqal. I am always happy to see you and Nasyr-aga."

"Nasyr, give me some water," Akbalak said thickly. As he stretched out on the aromatic straw, he suddenly felt broken and exhausted. By the time Nasyr got to him with a piala full of camel's milk, he was already asleep.

Meanwhile, Lena treated Shortanbai's shoulder with iodine and bandaged it. The sun was setting, and a warm darkness settled softly over the island. Soon the fire they had prepared was crackling into life next to the tents. Nasyr left the young people by the fire and lay down next to Akbalak to sleep.

The young people were murmuring quietly so as not to wake the old men up. Lena threw her braid behind her back.

"I never thought gulls would attack people! Shortanbai, your wound is very serious."

Akbalak's deep sleep soon turned to that familiar delirium between dream and reality. Akbalak began to mumble through his chapped lips . . .

"My precious Karashash! Here I am, returned to Korym Island. Our hut is nearby. Tomorrow Nasyr and I will go there. Karashash, my dear! I am now a frail, old man, and soon I'll die. You would not recognize it if you saw my body now! But our souls, dear Karashash, never age. They are completely different from our bodies, I swear. That must be, because otherwise people couldn't find each other in the other world. No, in the other world everything is thought through properly . . ."

Akbalak went silent for a moment and then began to talk again.

"Back then, in '37, when I was trying to get to you, that melody was already forming inside me. The song about you. And yesterday that melody finally matured. It has at last been given to me from above. And today I am happy like never before. Because I realized what has saved me. For nineteen years at Kolyma, loneliness and cold tormented me, but your love rescued me. And now I have finally completed the song of our destiny. I have found the right ending for it!"

Akbalak fell quiet again. Karashash's face appeared vividly now in his unsteady slumber, and Akbalak reached for her with his entire being.

She said, "We are going to Allah, Akbalak. Our daughter, Almagul, is staying on earth. I cannot forget her. How can I forget our only child? How is her life going, Akbalak?"

"She doesn't have much happiness, dear Karashash, but let me finish my story. I had only one comfort: to look into the fire and talk to you, to hear your melodious voice. And once in Itzhekken-Siberia, where people travel on dogs, I . . . I . . ."

A lump rises in Akbalak's throat.

"What happened in Itzhekken?" Karashash asks.

"I killed you. Or rather, that's how it seemed. I saw death coming over you, and I couldn't do anything to stop it. Don't you become an accomplice in murder if you don't prevent a death?"

"But how did you kill me, Akbalak?"

"It was a cold autumn evening. We were cutting down the forest, sitting by the fire to warm up from time to time. I'd put my gloves in my pocket and was adding branches to the fire. As always, I was looking at the fire and talking to you. You often used to come to me in the fire. For some reason, this time I just couldn't picture your face, your arms, no matter how many times I asked you to come. You weren't there. I was already tired from looking into the fire when I suddenly saw you. You were falling from the boat. You shouted, and it seemed like you called to me. I rushed into the fire. But what could I do, Karashash?"

"Yes," Karashash replies. "I did call for you. I saw how you jumped up. I saw the fire . . ."

"Is it true, my precious?"

"Yes," Karashash answers simply.

"In the evening, when we prisoners were returning to barracks, my Tuvan[1] friend warned me, 'Akbalak, don't look into the fire so long. You can die of melancholy.' And I stopped looking into the fire. But not because I was afraid of dying of melancholy. No . . ."

"You were worried about me," Karashash says.

"Yes," says Akbalak. "You ask me about Almagul. If she's destined to know happiness, then you and I will be happy with her happiness. We will be happy for our grandson Shortanbai's achievements too. But I doubt they'll be happy. Bad times have come, Karashash. And sadness will not skip them."

"I have to go," Karashash whispers.

"Stay a little longer," Akbalak pleads.

"Goodbye, goodbye . . . ," Karashash murmurs softly.

Her face begins to dissolve, and Akbalak, stretching his arms out, shouts, "Karashash! Karashash!"

But his hands touched only Nasyr.

Nasyr stirred but didn't wake. The sleep of the two old men of Sinemorye was not a calm one.

"What do you think of Odessa, Shortanbai?" Igor asked. "How are your studies going?"

"I'm getting used to it," Shortanbai answered, waving away mosquitoes. "Next summer, we're going abroad for practice."

"But aren't you swimming in the Black Sea?" Lena asked.

"The boys from the fourth year go to the ocean to practice."

"So you'll go to old man Santiago?"

"Who's Santiago?"

"Oh, that's your dad!" Lena also smiled and put her head on Igor's shoulder.

"I'd be proud to have a father like him," Igor said.

Shortanbai couldn't understand a word they were talking about and just looked at them in surprise.

Slavikov added wood to the fire and asked him, "Have you ever read the phrase, 'The old man dreamed about lions'?"

"The young people don't read anymore," Lena intervened. "They don't know anything and don't want to know anything. Am I right, Shortanbai?"

"Old man and lions? It's Hemingway. *The Old Man and the Sea.*"

"That's it precisely." Sergey smiled.

The moon appeared and began to climb through the sky.

"We completely forgot about the fish," Lena gasped. "Maybe it's already done?"

"Not yet," Igor reassured her. "Peel some potatoes. We should wake the old men up."

Shortanbai, suddenly serious, asked, "Igor Matveevich, what will happen to our sea, to our shore? What do the scientists think? What will they do about it? It's frustrating. We have our own sea, but we have to practice on the Caspian."

"Yes, you'll have to travel a bit. How many of you are studying in Odessa?"

"Five. If I'd known how hopeless things were, I'd have thought twice about going to college."

Nasyr had been awakened by the voices and listened to the zhyrau's breath. He was sleeping steadily now. Grunting, Nasyr clambered out of the tent. He saw the bright ring around the full moon and guessed there would be fog in the morning. It would be hard for Akbalak if they couldn't get back to Shumgen tomorrow. Igor and Shortanbai went on talking in low voices. Nasyr walked over to them. He felt the heat from the fire and only then realized he was cold.

"Did you have a good rest, Nasyr-aga?" Igor smiled.

"Yes, thank you."

"You traveled far, so you must be tired."

Nasyr frowned. "Those gulls! The gull is a predator, but that was the first time I saw it attack men. But there's not much point in being upset. People probably deserve such treatment."

"Should I wake my granddad up, Nasyr-aga?" Shortanbai stood up.

"No. He'll wake on his own. Old people don't sleep long. Prepare a nice soft seat for him by this tree so that he can lean against it."

Igor and Shortanbai began to prepare a comfortable seat for Akbalak.

"You said," Nasyr addressed Igor, "that you saw Kakharman in Balkhash."

"Yes. He looks well, but his mood is not great."

"Has he given up?"

"Given up? No. Kakharman is not that type. He's strong. His job is good, and his wife, Aitugan, is a rock."

"Yes, my daughter-in-law is wonderful. My old woman reads her letters and cries with happiness. Aitugan knows just how to hide her husband's shortcomings and highlight his accomplishments!" Nasyr was silent for a while, then said in a different voice, "I hear gossip that Kakharman has begun to drink. No need to hide anything from me, Ikor. I'm not an old woman who needs to be protected."

Slavikov was confused; the directness of Nasyr's question put him on the spot.

"It's hard to say, Nasyr-aga. But, yes, Kakharman drinks. But is that the whole truth? You always need to know the causes too. And the causes are in the community and in the state. How can you respect the order that doomed Sinemorye to death? That's why someone might drink. Who doesn't drink these days? I drink. How can anyone who is not indifferent survive without drinking? The question of who drinks more and who drinks less is a very different question. But Kakharman won't destroy his mind or his soul with drink. Try not to worry about it, Nasyr-aga."

"If I could've found a barrel of wine at Kolyma, I would've probably drowned in it!" Akbalak's voice came from behind them.

"Go and help your granddad," Nasyr told Shortanbai. The time of the night hunt was coming. An owl hooted not far away.

Igor studied Akbalak's face. The old man was once a muscular, strong, and handsome man, but now he had withered and lost height. And how he used to sing! Igor's father often used to say that Akbalak's voice was unique, that Kazakhs don't have any more singers like him. He is the last singer of the steppe. "You should listen to Kazakh songs more often," his father used to say, "and then you will learn the Kazakh language."

When he was packing to go to Korym, Igor had found the portable tape recorder his father had used to record Akbalak singing. Akbalak was already old then, but his songs were astonishing. They resonated with rich harmony and the deep philosophical thought of a wise man. The professor himself could listen to Akbalak endlessly. Sometimes he thought it was these songs that first made him fall in love with Sinemorye and the Caspian. When he was a head of the Institute of Geography of the USSR, Slavikov often organized expeditions to study flora and fauna of lakes and seas across the country. But each summer, he would go by himself to the shores of the Caspian and Sinemorye and stay there until late autumn. The professor was now ill and could no longer visit, but in each letter, he insistently asked his son to send information about the Sinemorian laboratory, which Igor always did regularly, properly, and carefully.

"Bring me my dombra, dzhigit," Akbalak said to Shortanbai.

Akbalak took his dombra and began to softly pick out that ending of the melody that had come to him. Then he played the whole melody from beginning to end.

After starting light and joyfully, the melody began to fill with quiet sadness. Gradually more and more minor chords edged in among the bright majors, began to flesh out and take over the body of the melody, and move into a resonant sound—tragic, high, and mournful.

Yes, Akbalak was bidding farewell to life, Nasyr realized. Akbalak could express many things in music. Out of his dombra rumbled the heavy groan of a falling tree, a tree that seemed to have trapped a human soul, a human soul frozen in Kolyma hell. And with the falling of the tree, the dombra cried with such piercing solitude that Nasyr's heart ached. Nasyr heard in the strings the clatter of rifles, the shouts of pursuit, the barking of sheepdogs, and the clank of chains. For a moment, the melody lightened, maybe as Sinemorye, which Akbalak had been apart from for so long, appeared in his mind. But even by the sea, Akbalak's heart never stopped suffering, and Nasyr heard clearly the sad roar of the dying sea. It didn't want to die. It begged the heavens and mankind for mercy. But what was that? Over the sad roar, a heartrending cry shivered, flying closer and closer, a cry so piteous it must tear your heart apart! The voice of his precious Karashash. Goodbye, Karashash! Goodbye, my beloved.

Akbalak finished playing, laid the dombra on his knees, and wiped the sweat from his forehead. Everybody sat in silence for a long time. When a true dombra player stops playing, the listeners usually stay silent for a while. The melody resounds in their ears from start to finish, as if the listeners were experiencing again what they've just heard.

When an owl hooted nearby, Lena, who was the first to return to her senses, began to clap in admiration. A warm, fragile smile appeared on Akbalak's lips as he looked at the girl gratefully.

"What we just heard was amazing!" Lena exclaimed. Sergey nodded in silent agreement.

"I call it 'Farewell to Korym,'" Akbalak explained to Nasyr. "I want you to remember it for a long time. I want it to remain after I'm gone."

Nasyr knew that it wasn't just a farewell to the island but to life.

Shortanbai brought a piala with shubat to Akbalak's lips. Akbalak took a few sips and peacefully closed his eyes.

Suddenly a rabbit screamed. An owl must've fallen on it like a stone and snatched the poor thing with its talons. Soon all went quiet. The soft splish-splashing of the waves became clearly audible, and the sea glimmered matte silver in the milky light of the moon. It used to be at this time that fish would play, but the sea's deeps had dwindled with the years.

But the firelight attracted a brown catfish, and it was now swimming slowly toward the shore, thinking miserably about the twists and turns of its life. It had already been hungry for a few days, and it had almost been hit by a horse and rider in the shallows, only diving into the depths in the nick of time—a moment later and it would have been floating belly-up! Yes, it's losing its alertness and growing old. The sea is no longer a fortress but a trap. It's empty and uncomfortable, and the water is not what it used to be.

The catfish lifted his head out of the water and stared at the people by the fire. Then it swam close to the shore, lifted its head again, and moved its whiskers. It could sense the fresh meat lying on top of a box and began to crawl up the shore toward it. Before anyone noticed, it had snatched the meat and was slithering back toward the water. But its tail caught on a line with a twang. The campers turned at the sound, and Shortanbai got up to see what could've fallen over there. The catfish was already nearly in the water.

"Catfish! Catfish!" Shortanbai shouted.

Everyone but Akbalak rushed toward him. But the catfish, swinging its huge tail vigorously, was already sliding away into the water.

"Ah, that's our old acquaintance." Igor smiled.

"The famous criminal," Lena laughed. "It must've gotten hungry again!"

"It's certainly got a wild appetite," Igor added. "It drags everything it finds on the shore into its mouth!"

"There's a big catfish living in Karaoi as well. It's very curious. It waits for me when I start praying. And as soon as I begin to pray, it lifts its head from the water and stares."

Akbalak spat. "Now every living creature revenges itself on man. Or am I wrong, Igor? Maybe you can explain what is happening to our sea. It doesn't have long left. And with its death, we'll also die. The sands will bury us. Every year, the sandstorms become stronger and angrier. The more the sea recedes, the worse the sandstorms get. I've been living here eighty years, but I've never seen such sandstorms."

"Yes, Akbalak-aga, you're right. Meteorological observations show the strength of winds has doubled in the last few years. And the salt dust is ruthless. It buries everything, destroys everything."

"What a fog!" Nasyr said, looking around. "Aka, see it around the moon. I doubt if we'll be able to sail back tomorrow."

Akbalak studied the moon carefully, then said, "It should disperse by the morning."

Lena was doubtful.

"The weather station said the fog will be thick. Our equipment indicates the same."

"The fog will disperse by morning, dear," Akbalak repeated. "Look at the moon. Can you see the reddish rim? That's a sign."

"But our equipment says differently!" Lena responded stubbornly.

"Do you think your boxes of metal are more sensitive than my bones?" Akbalak asked and began to cough. He was too out of breath to talk freely.

"Lena," Igor gently reproached the girl, "young people don't object when listening to their elders. That is the Kazakh way."

"I understand." Lena smiled. "But what if the elders are wrong?"

"The elders can't be wrong."

"It's called an advection fog,"[2] Igor explained to the young people and then turned to Akbalak. "Fogs happen now four times more frequently than they used to, Akbalak-aga."

Gradually, they all began to retire.

Lena asked quietly, "I wonder who will turn out to be right: our equipment or the old men?"

"What are you talking about?"

"About the fog."

It wasn't the first time Sergey had come to Sinemorye with Igor. He knew the local aqsaqals and the unerring precision of their predictions well.

"The old men will be right, Lenochka, I'm sure." He went briefly silent, then said thoughtfully, "We should send our greetings to Musa and try to invite ourselves to hunt with him. What better than a hunt with eagles? Have you ever seen one?"

"A hunt with eagles? Oh, I always wanted to see that! Will he take us both?"

"I think so. Now, go to sleep." And he kissed her on the cheek.

Nasyr added wood to the fire. He and Akbalak were alone. Nasyr scrutinized Akbalak's sunken face and said, "Aka, you're looking tired. Maybe we should go to sleep?"

"Don't hurry me to rest. I'm still alive, I think, and not quite ready for eternal peace. What's the news from Kakharman? Is he still in Balkhash?"

"We haven't had any letters from him for a while. I'm beginning to wonder if something's happened."

"Our fishermen are very pleased, though. Since Kakharman went to Balkhash, Kambar has been getting some good sites. And the catch is decent. But I don't know if I'll be able to thank Kakharman myself, so do pass on our gratitude."

"Of course. I will. Don't worry." But Nasyr's thoughts were returning to the familiar anxious, unresolved circle, and he said, "Yes, Aka, nature has risen against man. It doesn't have the strength to tolerate our barbarity. I remember Otkeldy liked to say that the world is like a fragile bird's egg, and if you accidentally break it, it'll be a doomsday. You know, he used to study every leaf, every blade of grass, and say, 'Look after it, look after even the tiniest bit of nature.'"

"But did we listen? You, Nasyr, pray to Allah," Akbalak rejoined. "Answer this question. If Allah does exist, then why didn't he redeem man? Why didn't he say, 'Enough! Stop! Look what you're doing!' I just can't understand a God like that! So I simply think there is no God! Or that he is a damned bastard if he can't stop and redeem such a bastard as man himself."

"That's right," Nasyr encouraged the old man. "Let's talk about man rather than scold Allah. It's a sin to swear like that! A terrible sin!"

"I don't want to talk about either man or God!" Akbalak flared up. "And I don't feel sorry for man! I'm waiting for him to destroy himself. The sooner the better! I just want to ask you one question: Does man have a right to live if he's such a brute?"

The moon was heading toward the horizon. The fog was noticeably thicker. The fire was dying away, and the old men could hardly see each other.

"I hope you won't be blushing in front of the young woman in the morning," Nasyr said. "The fog is really thick."

"Yes, we'll see at the dawn who was right, but I really don't trust their equipment. The fog will soon dissolve. I'm telling you."

Akbalak began to cough. Corrosive chemical fogs like these were making people ill.

Nasyr gave Akbalak a fresh handkerchief.

"Aka, cover your mouth. It'll be better for you."

Lena was the first to wake. Her mouth felt sticky. The fog was still thick. The equipment was right, and the old zhyrau was wrong. She nudged Sergey.

"Serezhenka, hey!"

Sergey opened his eyes sleepily and yawned.

"What's the matter?"

"See the thick fog. It's like broth. You can't even see your own hand. Science has won!"

"Congratulations." He turned over and fell back to sleep.

Nasyr laid out a clean shawl in front of him for the morning prayer. He could barely see the shawl in front of him. Yet by the time he finished the prayer, the colors of the shawl were beginning to glow. He shook it, folded it neatly, and put it in his pocket. Then he turned to Akbalak.

"How are you feeling, Aka?"

He didn't really want to wake Akbalak and spoke just to hear him.

"OK, Nasyr. Thank you," Akbalak responded. Nasyr could tell from his voice that Akbalak was no worse, and he was relieved. He got up and headed inland for a little walk.

In the meantime, the fog was thinning.

"Serezha, wake up!" Lena sounded concerned. "The fog is dispersing. Look!"

"Oh no! Hold on to it. Don't let it go!"

"How can I hold on? Have you lost your mind?"

"With your hands, of course!" And Sergey burst out laughing, "So then, shame to science?" He kissed Lena, murmuring gently, "Of course, shame, terrible shame."

Soon the fog over the island was just a few drifting patches, though it still hung over the sea like a thick curtain. Igor and Shortanbai fetched the firewood that they had stored under a tarpaulin the day before, and the fire was soon crackling joyously. When Nasyr returned from his walk, Igor offered to show him the laboratory.

"I'm worried the old man may become really ill after such a foggy night," Nasyr said to Igor. "We must get him back to Shumgen safe and sound. Thank you for your kindness and care. May Allah bless you!"

"I understand, Nasyr-aga. It'll be OK to leave in half an hour."

"Let's go right after breakfast. It's a long journey. And the fog will disappear very early if Akbalak's predictions come to pass."

"By the evening, it will come down again, like yesterday. It'll be the same for the whole week."

"It looks like it. I know from experience."

"Our equipment is beginning to gain some experience too." Igor smiled.

"I respect science. I never distrust it. But it'd be good if it harmed nature and people less! Then it could reach toward God and turn Earth into a blooming paradise." Nasyr went quiet for a moment. "Long ago, after my compatriots asked, I took the Quran in my hands and became a mullah. From that day, I have continuously asked Allah to return water to our sea. Our lands were once a paradise on earth. I am not exaggerating, Ikor. Let science take the place of

God. I am not against it. I'll pray to it like I pray to God, only let it free people from sorrow and trouble. Let it add to man's joy. Let it give people happiness!"

Their conversation was interrupted by the voices of Lena and Sergey. They had laid a tablecloth on the ground and were calling them for tea.

"Nasyr-aga, I need your advice," Igor said, taking an audiocassette from his pocket. "This is a recording of Akbalak's songs my father made. And yesterday I recorded his new kyui. What will the old man think?"

"You don't need my advice! Everybody will be very happy to hear his young voice, and he will be happy too."

"His voice is not that young. The first record was made about fifteen years ago."

"That doesn't matter! His voice was great even then! Just turn it on without warning. He'll be really surprised! His soul will rise!" They headed toward the fire.

Shortanbai was looking after Akbalak. He poured warm water over his hands and gave him a soft, fresh towel.

Akbalak turned to Nasyr.

"Have you already taken your postprayer walk? I don't have the strength anymore for the morning walks. But I would've liked to say goodbye to Korym." There was a melancholy bitterness in his voice.

"You can't really enjoy a walk in such fog," Nasyr comforted the old man.

"We should be getting ready for our trip. I'm not feeling very well, Nasyr."

"We will go right after tea."

When the sounds of the dombra came from a box little bigger than a matchbox, Akbalak turned in surprise. He recognized his dombra, and he recognized his voice. But he quickly suppressed his first emotions and began to listen critically, slightly frowning. But when the kyui that Igor had recorded the day before poured out of the recorder, he couldn't control his emotions anymore. The aqsaqal's eyes filled with tears, and the old man, embarrassed by his tears, lowered his head.

Right after breakfast, they began to pack. Akbalak was still overcome by emotion and at times looked as if he didn't understand where Shortanbai was taking him. He stared at the island with longing. He was crying, bidding it goodbye. And when the boat took off, he leaned toward the shore, toward the people who were waving, with all his body. Yes, his heart was dragging him back to Korym. It hadn't had enough time to say goodbye! It was still whispering, "Goodbye, Korym!"

When they got back to Shumgen after midday, the coast was clear and sunny. But by evening, the fog had fallen again. Everything around them quickly became gray, and in barely half an hour, a thick darkness had fallen over the entire shore. In such a fog, you could not see the hand on your arm.

Nasyr realized he couldn't stay any longer with Akbalak and rushed off to get back to Karaoi. Akbalak didn't ask him to stay, knowing he was thinking about Korlan, who was probably worrying about him already.

It was after midnight by the time Nasyr got home, and he went straight to bed. But he was up early the next morning for his prayer. After prayer, he gave straw to the mare and remembered the big net he'd been meaning to fix for a long time. The fog was still thick, but he found a ladder in the yard and began climbing onto the roof. Indoors, Korlan woke up.

"What are you up to, Nasyr? Are you trying to break your neck?"

When he dragged the net into the house, grunting with effort, she was surprised.

"*Oiboi,* are you going to mend it?"

"The fog will be here at least a week. If we're mending the nets, the time will go quicker."

"Who needs these nets now?" Korlan sighed.

"Don't talk like that! There are many useless things in the world. Who knows what might come in handy?"

Then the light flashed a couple of times and went out. The house was plunged into darkness.

"What a nuisance. The lamp is in the pantry." Korlan groped her way toward the door. "Get the matches from the table and give me some light."

Nasyr followed her.

"I hope there's still some kerosene in the lamp."

"Musa has probably already guessed that the generator should be fired up." Nasyr got ready to leave. "I'll go and help him."

"He went to Shumgen to see Akbalak yesterday. Didn't you see him there?"

"He must've gone there the other way." Nasyr was perplexed. "Even more reason for me to go. It won't be easy to mend the net in the darkness."

Nasyr poked at the engine, walked around it on one side and then the other, and came back with nothing. He angrily undid the belt and threw it.

"Damn it!"

Back home, he lay down and turned away from Korlan. But he didn't lie down for long. He spat, got up, and began to mend the nets. Korlan, who never went against her husband, sat at the other end of the net. Then old Zhanyl dropped by with her granddaughter in her arms, and Musa's old woman was not far behind. With four of them, mending the nets was a joyful task, and they almost forgot to stop for lunch. Then after lunch, even crazy old Kyzbala came by. She never normally visited. Kyzbala greeted them, then froze timidly in the doorway. She was invited in and offered a soft *topchan*[3] to sit on. All the women were scared of being alone in the dark, so they made their way to Nasyr's house. That's how it was for a few days. They spent their days with Nasyr and Korlan and went home at night.

Two boys, led by Kaiyr, who knew the terrain well, were hurrying to Karaoi. They were in trouble.

On the train, two Kazakh men had walked into the carriage where Kaiyr and the boys were sitting. Kaiyr knew then they were being watched. He recognized one of the men from the Shymkent police. And there were other young men in the carriage from the Baltic States who were also going to look for *anasha*.[4] They all needed to be warned. But how? Kaiyr decided he must give a sign to Petr and Arno at least. On his way through the tambour door, he winked at Petr. After a little while, Petr followed him through for a smoke. Kaiyr told him brusquely, "Those two who just got on—police. Be ready for anything. We may have to jump off the train. I'll let you know."

On the third day, the fog began to lift, although it thickened again in the evening. In the brief daytime brightness, Nasyr saw shapes moving on the aul's farthest slope. Were they people? Or animals? It was all too vague. Probably wild horses, he thought.

After washing himself for prayer, Nasyr looked back as he returned to the house. But there was no one. Yet as he knelt on the prayer mat and began to pray, the strange figures wouldn't leave his head! Maybe there was nothing strange about it at all. Maybe he had just imagined them. His blood pressure always shot up on foggy days, so he'd spent three nights almost without sleep, waking with a headache and noise in his ears. Everybody else felt the same.

Yet maybe he didn't imagine it. When he finished praying, he didn't stand up right away. The shifting apparition on the hills resonated strangely in Nasyr's soul. Nasyr turned his gaze into himself, into his long memory, shrouded by a fog as thick as the fog on the shore. Now in the fog of his memory, the old man saw the shadowy figures moving through the murk like the figures on the hills. There are many of them. They've been walking through the sands for a long time now—from the east to the south and to the west, into the cities, where they hope to escape starvation. Wretched, hungry, and thirsty, many fall and cannot get up. But nobody stops. Nobody pays attention. The dying don't plead for help. They know there's no help for them.

When Nasyr was eighteen, he was bursting with energy. He was only just starting to go out fishing with the venerable aqsaqals and karasaqals.

The Pomors[5] used to share bread and fish with hungry nomads and invited them to stay on the coast, trying to convince them that only death awaited them in the sands. But very few heeded the warning. They were probably afraid of the Pomors' way of working. They were herders and had never held a *ketmen*[6] nor caught a fish. Who knows how many died in the sand.

Once, when Nasyr was coming back from the sea, he found a boy of about thirteen not far from the aul. The boy was too weak to stand. But when he saw Nasyr, he pulled himself to his feet with an effort, just as the girl bending over him collapsed. Feebly gripping his kamcha, the boy glared warily at Nasyr. Of course, they had been through many troubles and encountered many who would not balk at taking someone's last scrap of bread—who would even eat human flesh. Nasyr talked to the children gently. "I see your sister is not well. Come with me."

"Water, water . . . ," the girl whispered.

"There's no water, Korlan. No water." The boy's lips were black and cracked with blood. His legs shook like the legs of a newborn foal.

Nasyr dropped his oars, strode to the girl, and lifted her in his arms. "Follow me," he ordered the boy. The boy bent down to pick up the oars. "Leave them. I'll come back for them later." The girl was as light as a feather. When he opened the door, his mother gasped in surprise. Otkeldy was called at once, and the healer gave the children an herbal mixture.

As he left, he warned, "Give them only fish broth in the morning but no food, or it will make them ill."

Within a month, Korlan was completely changed. Her cheeks glowed, and her eyes shone. She turned out to be so handy and quick with housework that Nasyr's mother could only gasp. Very soon, the house was clean, warm, and cozy. Nasyr really liked this lithe girl of fourteen years for her cleverness and spirit. His mother observed, "These children must be from a good family. Have you heard Korlan sing? A shame you didn't. Ask her to sing for you one day. They probably had a musical family. Not everyone can sing the songs from Semipalatinsk that Korlan sings." Nasyr's mother loved Korlan until she died.

By the autumn, Korlan's brother was going to sea with Nasyr. But each day, he grew ever gloomier and more thoughtful, until one day, he just vanished. Nasyr asked Korlan if she knew why, and she replied, not daring to look up at Nasyr, "He probably went to look for our uncle. Thank you for everything. I must go too."

Blushing to his ears, Nasyr declared, "I won't let you go anywhere!"

Korlan bowed her head and ran shyly into the house. How much time has passed since that day?

His praying and thinking done, Nasyr wiped his face with his hands and said, "Amen!"

"Amen!" came a voice from behind him.

He turned around. Three men were standing by the door, their faces black with dust.

"*As-salamu alaykum,*[7] Nasyr-aga!" said the man closest to Nasyr.

"*Waleikum assalam!*" Nasyr replied. "Who are you? I don't know you."

Nasyr looked closer and guessed that these were the people he saw on the hill.

"I am Kaiyr, Nasyr-aga. You might remember me. I was mullah in Karaoi before you."

"My goodness! What brings you here?" Nasyr relaxed. "Go clean the dust off your clothes, wash your faces, and then we'll drink tea. I'll go organize something."

The travelers settled in quickly and sat at the table. By the time Nasyr had finished making the tea at the stove, the loaf of bread and the butter on the table had vanished.

"Take more bread from the box." Nasyr pointed to Kaiyr. "You seem to be starving."

"We haven't eaten for two days," Kaiyr answered, cutting the bread. "Where is Korlan-apa?"

"She went to visit the old women. They all fell ill at the same time. You can see for yourself what's going on here."

"And there's no light?"

"Everything's fallen apart. Yesen is with his team in Balkhash, so there is nobody here who can fix the generator. I poked it a bit, but what's the point? I know nothing about it. And here we are, sitting in the dark. And where are you coming from and where are you heading?"

Kaiyr didn't answer right away. Knowing the old man's sharp temper, he didn't want to lie. The old man would see through it and kick them out. But the habit of fabrication prevailed, and he began.

"His name is Petr. He's from Moscow." Kaiyr pointed at the boy with curly blond hair to the right of him. The boy looked intently at Nasyr, and Nasyr felt uncomfortable. "What a sharp look!" he thought.

"And this is Arno. He's Estonian. His mother is seriously ill. We came to collect some poppies for her. Arno's mother is amazing, so how could we not? I visited them in their house and ate her homemade bread!"

"May Allah bless you! We've plenty of poppies here. Just walk to Moiynkum; it's not far." Nasyr sighed. "There's nothing worse than the suffering of the ill. It'd be better if the police thought more about the fact that our lands are dying, the sea is dying. But they've found something else to do: catch idiots who come here on the railway for poppies."

"Exactly. That is what I'm saying," Kaiyr agreed, then changed the subject. "Have many people left here recently, Nasyr-aga?"

"There's only a few houses left that—"

Nasyr didn't finish his sentence. Petr suddenly began to cough violently. Nasyr looked at him with pity and addressed Kaiyr.

"Your friend has breathed in too much salt and sand. Take him out."

Kaiyr and Petr stood up.

"Let him drink two or three ladles of water. Maybe it'll make him throw up."

Nasyr and Arno were left alone.

"How old is your mother?"

"Sixty-five."

"Still young. It's good you don't abandon her when she's ill. You can't call those who leave their old folk human. I know your country. Estonians are good people, hardworking and neat. During the war, a few families evacuated from Estonia were brought to our aul. I became good friends with a young man called Rain. He stayed on here a long time after the war. He was a good fisherman. Then his grown-up children found him and took him back with them. And they were right to do so. Have you been to Kazakhstan before?"

"No. We were exiled to Siberia. But I was born and grew up in Tallinn." He suddenly felt embarrassed by his broken Russian. "Granddad, sorry. Do you understand? Do you understand what I'm saying?"

Kaiyr, seeing that Nasyr and Arno were talking, took it as a good sign.

"What are you talking about?" he asked, sitting with them.

"I'm telling him about the Estonians who used to live in Karaoi. Did you meet them? I'm saying there is no bad nation, just bad people. There's people like this in any nation." He turned to Petr. "Feeling better?"

Petr nodded.

"Thanks, Granddad."

"When guests visit, I should slaughter a sheep, but I don't have one. Kaiyr, explain to our guests. When the old woman comes back, we'll have kuyrdak made from fresh saiga."

"Thank you for your hospitality, Nasyr-aga, but we don't need much."

"I'll go and give the mare some straw," Nasyr said, standing up. "I haven't had a chance to walk her for two days now."

"That ash-gray mare is all you've got," Kaiyr observed, not without malice. Nasyr pretended he didn't hear. He wrapped his face with a damp cloth and walked out.

"A wise old man," Arno said.

"Rather hapless. The others realized right away, dumped everything, and left. But this one decided to be stubborn."

"Khan!" Arno proclaimed, as if offended for Nasyr. "We don't understand him, so why should we condemn him?"

"Arno is a philosopher," Petr intervened. "Just give him an excuse. You should be grateful to God you're alive. Don't forget about Tallinn. You owe your life to the khan."

Kaiyr motioned Petr to be quiet.

"So the aqsaqal has said that there'll be no proper feast and has asked us not to be offended with him."

"We should be killed rather than treated," Petr said gloomily and threw his jacket over himself. "Let's go and have a look at the generator. Maybe we can thank the old man for his hospitality by fixing it."

Petr quickly found the problem with the generator.

"The engine is clogged with salt dust, and the pump needs cleaning. Somewhere here there's got to be fuel; let's look. Watch with the matches, or you'll blow us all up."

"I think I've found it," came Arno's voice from the darkness. "There're lots of barrels here!"

Kaiyr found a stick, wrapped a cloth around it, and created a torch. He put the match next to it, and the cloth burst into flame. Petr laughed.

"Look for a toolbox."

They soon found the toolbox nearby.

When Nasyr returned, he found the guests had gone. While he had been out, Korlan had returned and had begun to organize things.

"I see you're hungry. I'll put the kettle on now."

"Hurry up. We've got guests."

"Ya, where did they come from? Fell from the sky?"

The old man didn't like Korlan's tone and changed the subject. "Has Musa come back?"

"Not yet. So where are your guests? Who are they? Did they get lost?" Korlan asked again.

"I don't know. I went out to feed the mare, came back, and they were gone."

"Could you have imagined them, by any chance?"

"You're such an idiot!" Nasyr flared up. "Can't you see the dastarkhan? They were sitting right here! One of them is our old mullah, Kaiyr." Then Nasyr triumphantly found the key evidence. "And whose bags are these, then?"

Korlan looked at the backpacks in surprise.

And then suddenly, the lights flashed on, and the old people had to cover their eyes because it dazzled them.

"Bismillah! It's them, no one else! Well done, boys!" Nasyr exclaimed happily.

The guests soon returned. Tired and hungry, they had a quick dinner, and Petr and Arno went to sleep right away. Kaiyr decided to spend some more time with Nasyr. They drank another cup of tea while the wind whistled behind the windows, throwing sand against the glass.

Nasyr listened carefully and said, "I think it's calming down. Don't you think?"

"About time. It's been too long already." Korlan began to clear the table, but Nasyr stopped her.

"Wait. Let our guest bless the dastarkhan."

"Everything is Allah's will," Kaiyr said, carrying out Nasyr's request. Then he lay back on the cushions carelessly and, as if forgetting who he was talking to, continued on pompously, "A mullah doesn't have much to do: name a newborn, carry out a marriage ceremony, and send the deceased to the grave. Quite a good life! Read the prayers and collect the money. You're not very lucky, Nasyr-aga. You became a mullah when the life on the coast has gone quiet. People are no longer born here, don't get married, and don't die."

Nasyr looked at Kaiyr coldly.

"Do you think I became a mullah to get rich? It's you, you were young once, who live like this. You think only about your own belly! But the moment there's a sign of trouble, you run away! I am not a kite or a raven to wait for someone's death!"

After this cold rebuke, Kaiyr pulled himself together. "Devil pulled my tongue! I spoke without thinking. Forgive me, Nasyr-aga."

But Nasyr-aga's face was already dark with rage.

"I am not a mullah! It's you who is the mullah! Nasyr was born a fisherman and will die a fisherman. Do you get it, man?"

Arno woke up because he heard Nasyr's loud words. He looked at Kaiyr questioningly.

"Go back to sleep," Kaiyr muttered. "Nasyr-aga and I are reminiscing."

Nasyr felt uneasy that he'd woken the guests and said more accommodatingly, "It's not your fault. It's the times that are upon us."

It seemed as if the old man had simmered down. And Kaiyr, feeling grateful, said, "Yes, Nasyr-aga. A mullah is Allah's envoy on earth. I can't say the same about myself. I am too erring, but you. It is very good that you don't miss any of the five daily namazes. It brings a lot of good—if not to us, then to those who follow us."

"If only," Nasyr sighed. "Explain to me the words of the Prophet Muhammad. For the last two years, I've been praying day and night, but I couldn't convince Allah to save Sinemorye. He heard me only once and sent rain. The downpour lasted for thirty-eight days. A lot of snow melted on the peaks of Pamir, and both Daryas overflowed and flooded toward the sea! If you could have seen what a celebration there was; how fish rejoiced in this fresh, clean water; how the fishermen jumped for joy! And then what? This celebration turned into a new tragedy. The water level went down again, and all the fish were stranded on the shores. The sea died. I wish my eyes hadn't seen that! Why is he punishing us, Kaiyr?"

"No matter how well you follow the Quran, Nasyr-aga," Kaiyr said after a silence, "you won't achieve forgiveness from Allah. For you personally, maybe, but not for this land, not for the people who have destroyed it. I don't know if anyone could do that."

"And I can't find an answer to this question: When did man stop listening to nature? Why does he not see that nature is ill and that the illness was created by man himself? He deserves to be damned!"

Arno lifted his head from the pillow and asked Kaiyr to translate the old man's words. Kaiyr translated. Arno joined the conversation.

"I can't understand it either. We consider ourselves civilized people. We read a lot. We know a lot. We achieve great technical progress. But we don't have wisdom. We don't have prudence. We're just the same barbarians we used to be, and that's appalling!"

"You're right, son! That is what people are lacking: prudence."

"The problem is the country doesn't want people with clear and straightforward minds because they contradict 'developed' socialism!"

"Bureaucratic socialism," Kaiyr clarified.

"Man is strange! But can he be any different? Is his flawed nature inevitable? Must the short-lived dictatorship of the proletariat turn into the lifetime power of officials? You, Nasyr-aga, maybe think someone up there cares for your district. Why would they? It's much easier for them just to say, 'In place of the sea, we will plant gardens and sow wheat.' If I could do things in my own country, then I wouldn't be wandering in the sands like a jackal, collecting poppies!"

"But you do it for your ill mother." Nasyr was confused. "I used to think that only my fellow countrymen fight for the truth. But it turns out it's the same all around the Union! And our leaders don't like it. They look at their own people as mortal enemies."

"You're right," Arno agreed joylessly.

The guests slept until midday and probably would've slept even longer if it weren't for Nasyr. He walked into the yard, and as he looked down the valley, he saw a green *bobik*.[8] Nasyr quickly woke Kaiyr.

"It looks like police are here. All of you into the pantry, quick! Just in case!"

The boys grabbed their backpacks and rushed through the barn and into the pantry. By the time Nasyr walked out of the house, the car was already there.

An elderly captain got out and, after greeting him, asked, "Are you aqsaqal Nasyr?"

"Yes, that's me," Nasyr replied, shaking the captain's outstretched hand.

"Sad news from Shumgen, aqsaqal. I was asked to let you know that Akbalak-zhyrau is in a bad way. He has asked for you and Musa. Be ready; a car will come to pick you up."

Nasyr listened to the news sorrowfully.

The captain asked, "Aqsaqal, did you see any strange men passing through here?"

"It only just cleared up. We had really thick fog. Where are you from, yourself? You don't look like you're from our local police."

"I am from the railway police. If you've seen no one, then I should be off. Goodbye."

"Be healthy." Nasyr said his goodbye, then remembered. "Son, Musa has not come back yet! If you come across the hunter, tell him about Akbalak." Nasyr smiled. "He should really get out of the wolf's burrow now that the storm is over."

The captain was surprised.

"How can he live in a wolf's burrow?"

"Easily! Whenever he has an argument with his old woman, he gets on his horse and off he goes to the wolf's burrow."

Once the policeman had left, Nasyr opened the pantry and called his guests to lunch. After lunch, they got ready to leave. Just then, a truck stopped by the window.

"Has our Berish come for a holiday?" Korlan clasped her hands. "I rubbed my eye for two days, and it turned out to be for joy!" She was looking out the window impatiently. Nasyr also peered out.

"Your eye didn't twitch for nothing! Our little lamb has arrived. Our dear Berish has come!"

It was strangely touching and funny to see Nasyr so affected as he rushed around the house like an old woman, mumbling, "Our little lamb has come! What a joy! What a joy!" Then he had an idea.

"Talk to the driver," he suggested to his guests. "He may be able to take you to the station."

Berish walked in and embraced his grandparents.

"He came! He came!" Korlan was crying and gazing at the face of her grown-up grandson. Nasyr was walking around Berish like an excited dog.

The driver agreed to give the guests a lift, but first they had to unload coal from the truck. Kaiyr, Arno, and Petr grabbed the spades, and it was soon done. When they came in to bid farewell to the old people, Kaiyr took Nasyr to the side and handed him some money.

"Put this paper away." Nasyr was cross. "Don't insult me!"

Early the next morning, Nasyr went to Shumgen.

He found Akbalak lying on high pillows. The eyes of the old man were shut. Musa was already there. Almagul walked toward her father's bed, went down on her knees, and took his hand in hers.

"Father, you have visitors."

Akbalak's eyelids twitched, but he didn't have enough energy to open his eyes. Nasyr and Musa walked out of the house and sat on the bench. Almagul and Tobagabyl also came out.

"Who else have you told?" Nasyr asked.

"We sent telegrams to everyone he asked us to." Tobagabyl pulled a piece of paper from his pocket. "Here's the list."

"Are there many men in Shumgen?" Musa asked.

"They're all away," Almagul replied. "Some in Balkhash, some in Torgai."

"Yesterday, Father called for me and asked me to call for you, Nasyr-aga. He hasn't opened his eyes since."

Nasyr gave the list to Musa.

"He remembers everyone who was close and important to him. He hasn't even forgotten Matvei from Moscow. But people say that Slavikov is also seriously ill now. So better not to worry him. But we should inform Igor. Is the radio in working order?"

"I will send everything today," Tobagabyl answered.

"And we should send a car to Karaoi to pick up the old women and think how we will accommodate everyone. Tell your neighbors to get ready. We'll stay with Akbalak for now."

Then they walked into the house. Musa stood, deep in thought, looking at Akbalak's face, at his gaunt cheekbones barely covered with skin. The sea was dying before his eyes, and now Akbalak was dying, too—decrepit, exhausted, and disfigured by illness. Akbalak, who was once handsome and strong, the pride of this land. Where could he escape these relentlessly bitter thoughts that followed him every day, just like Nasyr. If only he could hide in a wolf's burrow and close his eyes.

Musa really had been staying in a wolf's burrow these last days, finding refuge from the raging storms that caught him between Karaoi and Shumgen. He had quickly tied up the horse, found the hole, and, grunting, squeezed into the burrow. Only then did he realize his mistake. A she wolf with a cub was hiding in the depth of the burrow. Musa froze. He couldn't retreat, but he couldn't fire his gun either. His gun was behind him, and he was so tightly squeezed in the burrow that he just couldn't reach it. The wolf's eyes glittered, and she growled. Then Musa shouted so piercingly that the startled wolf shrank to the ground. Musa lay still, with his hunting knife ready. The wolf looked at him but stayed completely still. Two or three hours passed like this. And Musa understood that the wolf wouldn't touch him as long as he didn't make any sudden moves. And so, he lived like this in the burrow for a few days. He slept only in brief, wary naps, waking with the slightest rustle. But always he saw the same two green lights of the she wolf's eyes.

When the storm began to quiet down, the she wolf began to growl quietly. She was letting him know: "It's time for you to go your own way now, man, or there'll be trouble." Musa realized that staying in the burrow was now dangerous.

At any minute, the male wolf could come back. As he gently massaged his leg muscles back to life, the she wolf growled louder and shifted forward a little. Musa slid backward frantically until he could jump out of the burrow and into the air. The hot wind hit him in the face. And right away he heard a wolf's howl not far away. Limping slightly, he ran to the hollow where he had left his horse. The she wolf emerged from the burrow, sat down, and listened to the howl for some time. Then she howled herself, raising her muzzle high. Musa hurriedly mounted the horse. Now he was safe. The she wolf set off toward the male. They met on the slope, sat down, and began to howl together.

Akbalak wrinkled his gray eyebrows, and his eyelids slowly lifted. He looked at Musa and Nasyr but quickly closed his eyes again. Nasyr sat closer to him and took his hand to check his pulse. Akbalak began to rave.

"What is he saying?" Musa asked.

Nasyr listened carefully. At first, he couldn't understand anything, but gradually it became clear what he was trying to say.

"It's hard for me to die," Akbalak was saying, "but I won't regret leaving this world. This world will be punished. Remember my words! Today man consumes everything greedily and destroys the wealth of his land, but tomorrow the mutilated and impoverished earth will consume him. She has no other choice! The devil controls man now, and God has turned away from him, clutching his head. God has lost! Man should be destroyed by the earth that gave him life. That will be his punishment and also his salvation."

That is what Nasyr understood from the broken and rambling speech of the old man, and he shuddered to see how much despair and anger Akbalak was suffering.

Akbalak went silent, opened his eyes widely, and with bony, weak fingers shook Nasyr's hand.

"You're here. I decided not to die until I saw you."

He got his dry, quivering lips under control and moved them slowly and deliberately with great difficulty. His yellow face expressed suffering and struggle.

Almagul whispered, "My father has refused water for two days now."

"Nasyr!" A cold sweat broke out on Akbalak's face. "Give my body to the sea. That is my request. The rest decide yourself. I want to be with Karashash . . ."

Nasyr was scared by Akbalak's request. Hadn't he just been taken to the open sea for the last time? He glanced at Musa, who also seemed surprised. So many fishermen drowned in the sea, but they hadn't wished for death.

Tobagabyl, guessing Nasyr's and Musa's anxiety, said, "Father told us about this last wish long ago. We are not surprised."

"We must fulfill the last wish of our older brother," Musa said. "We will do what he asks."

And, imagining how they would lower the old man's body, wrapped in shroud, into the sea, he thought, "His life was different from that of other people; let his death be unusual as well."

Akbalak heard Musa's words, and the expression of his eyes and movements of his eyebrows showed that he was pleased. Then he stretched his arm toward Nasyr as if asking, "And what will you say, brother?"

"We have never yet failed to obey to you, Aka." Nasyr said, "Your wish will be fulfilled."

By evening, Akbalak couldn't speak anymore. With a weak flick of his fingers, he called for Almagul and whispered something to her. Almagul fell on her father's chest in tears. A neighbor helped her away. Akbalak put Nasyr's hand on his heart and looked at him one last time, then passed away.

Nasyr closed his friend's eyelids and began to cry bitterly.

All those who came to mourn his death reacted to Akbalak's last wish with horror. But Nasyr made it clear that they could not fail to fulfill the old man's last wish. And so Shumgen busied itself with preparations for the departure of Akbalak, the most famous zhyrau of the whole shore. Igor and his colleagues arrived from Korym. And on the next day, Akbalak's friends began to arrive from everywhere.

"My father might be offended he wasn't informed," Igor said, and a telegram was quickly sent to Professor Slavikov. A reply came back the same day.

The deceased was carried into a big yurt erected for the occasion. A white flag hung on it.

"Why white?" Lena asked.

Berish explained, "When an old person dies, a white flag is hung, and when a young one dies, then it's red."

The last to come to Shumgen that day was the fisherman Khodzhanepes from the Turkmen coast of Kara-Bogaz. After he arrived, everyone gathered for dinner, and Nasyr announced that the next day they would all go onto the sea in four large boats. Akbalak's oldest friends, who had come from the far corners of Central Asia, broke into subdued conversation and nodded in agreement.

Kumbek, from Kyrgyzstan, took off his soft hat and said, "I had to come when I found out about Akbalak's death."

"We didn't really expect to see you," Uzbek Fuzuli replied. "We heard you were ill."

"Everyone's ill at our age. My legs barely move. But I came anyway, and I don't regret it. I've a chance to see you all again. Only Allah knows if we'll see each other again."

"You're right, Kumbek." Khodzhanepes nodded. "Each of us thought the same. Long ago, we were quicker moving."

Beknazar from Muinak stroked his beard thoughtfully. "Yes, old people have a short life. You know, today you're alive, but tomorrow . . ."

The honored aqsaqal, zhyrau Kadyr from Balkhash, changed the subject. "Khodzheke, tell us what's happening with the dam in Kara-Bogaz. How many are they planning? Have they given it the go-ahead?"

"Why wouldn't they? They don't think with their brains. Now Kara-Bogaz doesn't care anymore, and these dogs have completely ruined it. The water has gone, and only salt marshes are left, and the winds blow sand and salt all the time. People are getting ill, children are dying. But why am I telling you—here it's the same!"

"And do you think it's different in Balkhash?" Kadyr exclaimed bitterly. "They should all be brought here to live for a while."

"Oh, if you could bring them here! One of the first ones to ruin Sinemorye and Kara-Bogaz was our great 'scientist' Babaev," Khodzhanepes said.

"Babaev wasn't alone!" Fuzuli interrupted him. "What about Rashidov? And Kunaev?"

Nasyr, finally freed from his duties as organizer, sat next to Kadyr but wasn't taking part in the conversation. He had spent the whole day on his feet, and now his lower back was hurting. He pulled one of the pillows prepared for the guests toward him and lay down.

There was no point in hiding it. Nasyr was alone now. So how had he come to this? He had nothing to blame himself for. He never rushed. He never chased the petty pleasures of life. And although he would sometimes give his body rest from toil, his spirit was tireless. His thoughts knew no respite; his soul never slept. His soul was like a loaded camel, sinking in the sand, bearing the burden of its own destiny under the divine sky.

His eyes closed by themselves, and he fell asleep. He was woken by Fuzuli, who, touching him on the shoulder, said cheerily, "Our Nasyr-aga definitely got old. The moment he lay down, he fell asleep."

The sleep hadn't refreshed Nasyr at all. His head was still heavy, and his lower back hurt. He walked into the yard to wash his face. Lena and Sergey were helping the women. Igor, giving Nasyr a towel, said, "Nasyr-aga, you're very tired. Go to sleep early, and we will take care of everything."

Nasyr nodded toward Lena and Sergey.

"Thank you and thanks to your friends, Ikor. May Allah bless you!"

The next day, people who'd heard about Akbalak's death kept arriving in Shumgen, especially from Balkhash and Torgai. Igor, Sergey, and Tobagabyl greeted them warmly and took care of things.

After breakfast, Akbalak's body was carried out of the yurt with due honor, laid on a cart, and carried to the sea with a long line of mourners walking behind. The sky was blindingly blue, and the sea sparkled in the distance. The body moved toward the dead sea.

As the boats began to move out, the women left on the shore cried piteously. Almagul gripped her face and threw herself toward the sea, but the women held her. Soon the boats stopped. Nasyr read the prayer. Then he and Kumbek carefully lowered the body, shrouded in plain white, into the water. Weighed down by a large stone, it quickly vanished into the deep.

"Goodbye, Akbalak!" Nasyr wiped his face with his hands.

"May the sea waves be always gentle to you!" some old men cried. "Goodbye, the people's favorite!"

The boats stayed still for a long time, and the people in the boats didn't move. Igor touched Nasyr on his shoulder.

"What if we listen to Akbalak's last kyui? Is it permitted?"

Nasyr nodded in agreement, then stood up and addressed the people.

"Before his death, Akbalak asked me to take him to Korym Island. There he played his last kyui to us. Igor managed to record the music. Maybe we should listen to it?"

The suggestion was approved by silent nods.

The strong, unfettered chords soared. The heavy sighs of loneliness and frailty were all too audible in Akbalak's kyui. The voice of a tired old man saying goodbye to life. It cried. It sobbed like a child. And it whispered, "Goodbye, life! Goodbye! Much remained unknown in you. Many things I had no chance to appreciate. But leaving you now, I say, 'You were beautiful, oh life!'"

Nasyr turned around to look at the spot where he and Kumbek had lowered the body. For a moment, it looked as if the water was seething, ready to boil. The head of the familiar brown catfish appeared where the water seethed. It looked toward the boat, then disappeared back into the water.

The next day, the old men got ready to leave, and Turkmens, Tajiks, Uzbeks, and Kyrgyz, who lived apart for many years, came together to bid farewell to Akbalak.

"May Allah let us meet again soon for a different reason!" the hunter, the farmer, the fisherman, and the shepherd vowed. Kumbek and Fuzuli decided to stay another week. At the last moment, Kadyr decided to join them. They sat in a small circle and began to talk about the past.

"Would you like me to tell you about Akbalak?" Kumbek asked and soon began his tale. "I've known Akbalak since 1915. We met at far-off Talas.[9] Aka was handsome then: tall, slender, and broad-chested!

"The occasion was a wedding. The famous manap[10] of Talas Batis was marrying off his only son. And what a wedding it was! It was lovely! And the singing prize was won by Black Asan. He was a good singer, I'll grant you.

"Batis was known as a connoisseur of fine words; and it wasn't surprising that aqyns[11] and zhyraus came often to his aul and stayed long. Akbalak was specifically invited to the wedding. Everybody liked Akbalak, but Batis especially admired him, particularly when he sang terme[12] with his strong, powerful voice.

"Batis looked at the other manaps sitting around him and exclaimed, 'There is not another zhyrau in Kyrgyz equal to Black Asan. Be generous with him!'

"A raven-black agamak[13] was presented to Black Asan and a glorious chapan thrown over his shoulders. Asan bowed.

"'May your happiness, Batis, be as big as the Ala-Too mountains![14] May your children have luck in everything they do!'

"Smiling into his moustache, the manap said, 'And where's zhyrau Akbalak from Sinemorye? Call him here!'

"Akbalak was called for. Batis addressed all those present, 'How about a competition between the two zhyraus: the Kyrgyz and the Kazakh? Whose mind will be sharper? Whose word will be finer?'

"The other manaps made approving noises.

"'If Asan-zhyrau agrees to it, I am ready!' Akbalak responded.

"'If you're ready for it, then so am I!' Black Asan glared. I remember that he was rather full of himself.

"They sat facing each other. I forget their exact words, so I'll tell you what they sang in my own words. Asan was laying it on thick about how powerful Batis was, how rich he was, and how handsome—all that kind of thing.

"But Akbalak had always been brave and frank, so he took a bold line. He refused to sing praises to Batis. Instead he praised the Kyrgyz land and its people. And he hinted that his generous host became rich and noble thanks to the hard work of the people. There was admiration in his songs, but it wasn't admiration for Batis but the great friendship between ordinary people: Kazakhs and Kyrgyz. The song left no one unmoved. And manap Batis was touched by the sincerity and cleverness of Akbalak's song and said to him, 'You've won. You're a nightingale among poets! Please accept some gifts from your Kyrgyz brothers!'

"The gifts were very generous! A six-part yurt, the white-legged golden eagle Ala-Too, a fast horse, a golden cradle . . . and, most importantly, he was given the jewel of Issyk Kul—the lovely Meruert. Magnificent gifts indeed!

"Akbalak bowed quietly and with dignity. When the horse was brought to him, Batis himself came and helped Akbalak into the saddle. Then Akbalak headed for home. The young Kyrgyz—me among them—rode out to send him on his way. But I had another reason to bid him farewell. I sincerely admired him and wanted to show him respect, but I was also head over heels in love with Meruert. She loved me, too, although we had not yet talked about it.

"It was on the second day of our journey that the hour of separation from her homeland came. We were on the bank of Issyk Kul. Meruert asked if she could wash her face with water from the lake of her homeland for the last time. She washed her face and stood for a long time, looking into the distance. Then she began to sing the song of farewell. After she sang, Akbalak called for me.

"'Kumbek, you're looking very sad. What troubles your soul?'

"Meruert was sitting by the fire. Yet I couldn't tell Akbalak of my love. I was too proud. So instead, I decided to express myself in the language of the dombra. Akbalak gave me his. You all know the famous kyui of Temir, 'In Love.' It begins lightly and playfully but ends with the powerful, sad sounds of the pain of unfulfilled love. I played this kyui so tenderly that Meruert wept. Temir created this melody when he was a middle-aged man in foreign lands and met a wonderful woman, the wife of a rich *bai*, and he recognized at once his first young love. All these years, she had kept loving Temir. And when the time came to leave, he played this kyui to her. And she understood! And when they said goodbye, she said, 'Be happy, Temir! You did not forget me. And all these years, you, too, lived in my heart and you still live there. But women cannot make a choice.' And she cried bitterly for many days . . .

"When I finished playing, Akbalak put his hand on my shoulder.

"'No one has yet played Temir's kyui so well!' he exclaimed. Then he looked at Meruert, who was wiping her tears with a silk handkerchief. 'Don't cry,' he said. 'I could not refuse my gift because of the customs of the aitys.[15] But my beloved wife, Karashash, is waiting for me at home. So please let me consider you as my Kyrgyz sister. You're free! You can go home, Meruert! And let me give you this cradle to rock your children in.'

"'Oh, honorable Akbalak-aga!' Meruert joyfully replied. 'I don't know how to repay your generosity. Yet I am scared to go home. I will be given away as a gift again or sold. I ask you to bless me and Kumbek's marriage.' He blessed us right away, and since then, we have lived in harmony."

And so Kumbek finished his story.

A week later, Fuzuli suddenly grew anxious to leave. He needed to stop in Semipalatinsk on his way home. Nasyr was about to ask him to visit Kakharman but changed his mind. It wasn't his way to bother people with requests.

"Why do you have to go to Semipalatinsk?" he asked.

"It's not good," Fuzuli replied. "My brother has been arrested. I'll pull his arms and legs out, the son of a bitch!"

"What's happened?" The old men were dumbfounded.

"There's a whole gang of them. They were taking children from orphanages, pretending they were going to foster them—"

"And then what?" Nasyr interrupted him, worried.

"What can one do with orphans? They used the orphans as slave laborers in their houses."

"Ya, Allah! How could that happen? Why did the government let them do something like that?" Nasyr shouted.

"The government!" Fuzuli said back. "The government doesn't care at all whether children are in an orphanage or being used as slaves. This year alone, those bastards took two hundred children from Semipalatinsk."

"Were they recorded officially as Uzbeks?"

"Of course. How would a child know what nationality he is? Uzbek or Kazakh? They think this way: it'd be better for Kazakh children to be handed over to Uzbeks than to go from one state-owned house to another. They don't have Allah, Nasyr. They don't!"

Nasyr was shocked and couldn't say a word. What an appalling story! What sort of nation are you, Kazakhs? What has happened to you? Where is your will? Where is your pride? Don't you see what's being done to your children?

Almagul came in and laid a soft, aromatic pilaf out for the old men. Nasyr stretched his hand toward the dish, then froze, looking at the fluffy rice. Each grain seemed to swell before his eyes until they weren't grains anymore but children's heads. They went on swelling until they were whole children. The children came alive and began to move. They filled the room, the whole house . . .

A strange mist fell over Nasyr's eyes. Barefoot, half-undressed children were walking over the sand, struggling to move their thin, weak legs. How many were there? And now many were dropping silently to the ground. They lay there in the sand, dead. Black birds circled over them. And dark clouds of carrion crows swirled down from the sky onto their small corpses. And then they whirled around the living, knocking them off their feet with their wings. And these children also fall on the fiery sand, too weak to even lift their hands to protect their young faces, their heads, their little necks.

"Poor, poor children." Nasyr began to cry. "Poor souls—"

But he didn't have a chance to finish. His mouth was foaming, and he fell face-first into the pilaf.

"He's poisoned. He's been poisoned." He heard Korlan's voice from afar.

The black bird, maybe one of those picking at the children, circled and circled over his head.

X

Kakharman found it puzzling that destiny had brought him to Lake Zaysan. Who'd have thought it? He had traveled the country widely and had seen many rivers and lakes, but he never imagined that this little pond in East Kazakhstan would end up as his shelter. People here greeted him warmly; they paid attention to him and offered their sympathy. As soon as he arrived, Kakharman had demonstrated his expertise and knowledge.

In Semipalatinsk, no one wanted to see a man like Kakharman go. And when he finally handed in his resignation, Ivan Yakubovsky was bewildered. He invited Kakharman to sit down. He put cigarettes on the table but didn't take one.

"Maybe you're upset with me?" Yakubovsky said. "Just tell me honestly. I am more than prepared to apologize."

"You have done nothing to upset me, Ivan."

"And where will you go?"

"I haven't decided yet." Kakharman paused, then continued thoughtfully. "I want to visit Sayat on the Caspian. I'll look at how his life is working out there. I'd like to finally settle down. Do you understand? I still can't find my place. Don't take it the wrong way. You have nothing to do with it. I'll never forget your kindness. That's all I can say. Please just sign my resignation, and I'll go."

"I won't do it." Yakubovsky folded the paper in fourths and put it inside the desk.

"Ivan!"

"You go to the Caspian. That is an order. Is that clear?"

"No, it's not," Kakharman laughed. "Are you suggesting I go at state expense?"

"Yes, but you'll be part of an official mission. As soon as you complete your mission, I'll sign your resignation. Deal?"

Kakharman could clearly understand Yakubovsky's concerns. He had said the same himself, thinking, "Kakharman, it's not hard to leave your job but think first what you'll do afterward. Measure seven times, as the saying goes. And Yakubovsky needs people . . ."

"OK. Have it your own way." Kakharman agreed to go on the trip.

"Done. Give my regards to Sayat. I've heard he's not doing so well. I hope that by the time you come back, you'll have forgotten about your resignation."

Kakharman returned from the Caspian depressed. It all began when he didn't find Sayat there. He had gone away. "Why the hell did I come here?" he muttered to himself, lying in a bed at the hotel. He was irritated with the squeaky hotel bed, the dirty state decanter, the three piss-colored glasses on the table, and the dreadful picture on the wall that was painted no doubt by a local amateur. He drank for two days. On the third day, Sayat came back. He found his friend unshaven and with big bags under his eyes. Kakharman didn't recognize him. He was standing in the middle of the room unsteadily, staring bleary-eyed at him. He asked rudely, "What do you want?" Sayat was confused. Kakharman sat at the table and bowed his head. The rest seemed more like a bad dream. Someone seemed to sharply pull the bottle from his hand as he tried to fill up the glass. Someone dragged him into bed. He lifted his head and shouted, "Leave the bottle, man. Don't mess with me. Do you hear me?" As he was drowning in his own mumbles, the figure bent over him and roared, and Kakharman saw it wasn't a man at all but a wild wolf dog. And the dog grabbed the bottle with its teeth, poured the contents on the floor, and began to stare at Kakharman with its glowing eyes. Kakharman was scared, began to scream, covered his head with his hands, and hid under the pillow. But the great, cruel muzzle kept coming at him—first from the right, then from the left. He could find no place to hide from its evil grin.

Sayat had a relative who lived on the outskirts of the city. Sayat asked him to prepare a good dinner and went to the hotel to fetch Kakharman toward evening. After two cups of hot broth, Kakharman began to feel better. "You should eat more, Kakharman," Sayat suggested. He knew what was making his friend so depressed. Kakharman felt the pain of their homeland personally. He had traveled the country to tell the world what was going on in his homeland. He had knocked on the closed doors of official after official. But he had achieved nothing. And now he was broken. It was all too obvious.

Trying to distract Kakharman from gloomy thoughts, Sayat asked, "So what have you decided? Will you move to the Caspian? Think about it. At least it's closer to our homeland. We could visit Karaoi more often."

Kakharman answered quietly, "What difference does it make where I watch the death of our land, of our sea? The farther I look from, the safer my sanity is."

"You're not really going to travel from place to place your whole life," Sayat objected. "Are you Korkut-baba? He was frightened of death and traveled from one place to another. No matter where he went, he'd meet gravediggers, and he'd ask, 'Who are you digging the grave for?' And they'd reply, jokingly, 'For Korkut.' Then he decided that people can die anywhere because there's land everywhere so a grave can be dug anywhere. So he sat on a rug with his kobyz and floated down the Darya. 'Who can dig a grave on water?' he thought. He floated on the Darya for a long time and was overjoyed that he had outwitted death! He was carried into the sea, and he rejoiced, 'Now I am immortal!' Then he decided to have a nap, and while he was sleeping, a poisonous snake crawled onto the rug and stung him to death."

"Why are you telling me this? Are you trying to say that the fate of Sinemorye is predestined from above? You should know it's not God but man that brings our sea closer to death each day!" Kakharman's voice cracked, and his face sagged with exhaustion.

Sayat realized that they wouldn't have a proper conversation that day. "OK, Kakharman," he sighed. "I'll ask them to prepare a bed for you. You look tired. We can talk more tomorrow."

"I can't talk calmly about Sinemorye. Please understand me. Will you help me with a ticket tomorrow? I'm going back."

"So soon?" Sayat was surprised.

"Yes," Kakharman replied firmly.

Sayat saw that there was no arguing.

The plane to Semipalatinsk flew via Alma-Ata, so Kakharman decided to spend a few days in the capital. Sayat called ahead to Bolat. "Tell him not to meet me at the airport," Kakharman said. "I'll call him when I land."

Sayat nodded. "Keep in touch, Kakharman. Don't disappear. And most importantly, keep yourself together. Don't get discouraged. Keep being an example for us. Give my greetings to Aitugan."

"Stay healthy yourself. The boys you've got with you are good boys. They look up to you and value your humanity, Sayat. Remember that."

They stayed silent for a bit.

And when boarding was announced, he gripped Sayat by the hand and said earnestly, "Hey, friend! I have some kind of awful apathy and don't know how to escape it. I feel I'm falling into a deadly spiral, and only my old parents and my family hold me back. I look at Moscow hoping that they get new leadership. Surely there's got to be a change? Then what? Can you imagine a time when we're told, 'Sayat! Kakharman! We have something for you!' And we'll be needed everywhere, eh? We just have to wait, Sayat. Just wait." And Kakharman embraced his friend tightly. It was hard to say goodbye, and they didn't even know that this would be the last time they would ever see each other.

Bolat met him at the airport. According to Kazakh custom, the welcomed guest would've stayed in Bolat's home, but Kakharman flatly refused. He knew that Bolat, who had a newborn baby, rented just two rooms in the big house of an old Volga German, and he didn't want to trouble his friend. So Kakharman asked him to get him a room in the Hotel Kazakhstan. He took a cold shower, put a fresh shirt on, and stood in front of the mirror for a minute. His face looked refreshed, and his mood was better. He grinned and teased his reflection: "Stick to your guns. We'll break through!"

He found Bolat had set the table—and there was Kakharman's favorite beer. "Bolat, you treat me well!" Kakharman laughed. "I don't envy anyone who doesn't have a brother like you."

Bolat shrugged shyly.

Kakharman did not hide his troubles, laying them all out plainly to his friend all at once. Bolat listened unquestioningly because he knew that, through all his restless and troubled life, through all the struggles, Kakharman was doing what needed to be done. He had a clear mind and firmness of thought because every statement he made was supported by observation. Kakharman's way of thinking could be simplistic, but it was human wisdom. Kakharman's motto was "to watch life and say what mattered." That's what Bolat felt, listening to his friend. He understood why Professor Slavikov respected Kakharman and Nasyr.

Slavikov loved them not only because they had been kind and hospitable to him when he was living among them. He respected them for their clear minds. He was not joking when he said, "If Kakharman had devoted himself to science, he would've achieved much."

"That's enough of my complaining," Kakharman said. "You better tell me about yourself. Have you been able to get an apartment?"

"I am a truth seeker, and truth seekers don't get apartments."

"It must be hard on your wife," Kakharman sympathized.

"Of course. I am still like a bachelor. I spend six months in a row away from home on expeditions, but she . . ."

"Have you grown tired?" Kakharman asked, noticing Bolat's haggard face.

"I got back from Sinemorye three days ago," Bolat began. "Nasyr-ata and Korlan-apa are both well. They struggled during the winter without Berish."

"And how is Kyzbala doing?" Kakharman asked, suddenly curious.

"As well as her goat! Last summer, the goat had a kid that was taken by a catfish. People say she came to Nasyr-aga to find a male for her goat, saying that both she and her goat need a kid."

"Her loneliness is over. Now there will be two of them crying on the shore. She for her son and the goat for the kid."

Bolat had no wish to embark on a tricky conversation about his work observing the death of the sea. So Bolat suggested, "Can we now go to my place? You'll see how I live. We can continue our conversation there."

After the dusty winds of Guryev,[1] Alma-Ata looked like paradise to Kakharman. It was nice to see people here dressed more elegantly and walking around without troubled expressions on their faces. They were greeted by the landlord, Khorst Bastianovich, in the yard under an apple tree. When Khorst Bastianovich was young, he had fished at Sinemorye, then moved to Alma-Ata with his grown-up sons. They bought a house, and once Khorst Bastianovich and his wife were settled, their sons went off to earn money.

How did Bolat end up at Khorst Bastianovich's? When Bolat's son was born, their previous landlord asked them to move out. Bolat tried to get the landlord to allow them to stay until the spring, but the landlord was adamant, insisting he had just two weeks to get out. It wasn't easy finding another place in the middle of winter. One evening Bolat was wandering, tired and depressed, and absentmindedly said to an old man, who was clearing his yard of snow. "May God help you, aqsaqal!"

"That'd be good." The old man turned out to be rather chatty. "Why are you so gloomy?" he asked.

"I have nothing to be happy about," Bolat replied. "I'm trying to find a place to rent, but I'm not very hopeful."

"Are you single?" the old man asked.

"If only. I have a wife, a schoolboy brother, and now a newborn son—he's not even a month old yet."

"Good for you!" the old man laughed. "You're rich." Then he stopped laughing and rested his forearms on the shovel's handle. "And are you a student?"

"I finished at the university. I work." The old man took his hat off and began to wipe the sweat off his forehead. "Just wait here for a bit. My old woman should be back from the shop soon. We'll talk about it."

Bolat's heart skipped a beat, and a little hope bubbled up and floated in the chilly air. Then he suggested, "Aga, give me the spade, and you have a rest."

The old man waved his hand. "It can wait. I'll finish clearing after lunch."

But Bolat took off his coat and began to clear the snow.

Their new landlord's wife, Irina Mikhailovna, really liked the attentive young man. And she liked Mariyash, too, and treated her like her own daughter from day one. The old people must've really missed their children. "Bolat, you're very lucky with Mariyash," she used to say frequently. "You should really appreciate her, boy."

The landlord, Khorst, had trouble with his eyes. He only noticed Kakharman when they were close to one another. "Oh, Kakharman-zhan, it's you, dear friend!" And the old man embraced Kakharman in accordance with Kazakh custom, touching Kakharman's chest with his.

"Hello, Khorst-aga! How are you doing? Where is Irina Mikhailovna?"

"My old woman is in the hospital. She got sick in the winter, and she's still there. And I just sit here and wait. Mariyash was telling me all morning: Kakharman will come, Kakharman will come. And here you are."

Mariyash called for Bolat, and he disappeared into the house. "I've heard you're now in Semipalatinsk," Khorst said, watching Bolat leave. "Tell me what life is like there."

"To be blunt, life there is crap."

"I am getting old, Kakharman, and keep thinking I will die in a foreign land. How did it turn out this way that all our people are spreading out far and wide, like cockroaches? Who would've thought this could happen? That is why I'd like to praise your father, Kakharman. He didn't leave! Orazbek visited me recently. You probably know him. We're chatting away, and all of a sudden, he tells me that he thinks we can't condemn those who try to live their lives well. That it's much better to live near the capital because it's easier to educate your children there. But what is there in that hole? So I told him, 'Orazbek, I used to say you are a true *batyr*,[2] but allow me to take my words back.' 'How so?' He was thrown off balance. He was worried, you know. He probably thought I'd attack him with the fact that he bought a Volga for his son on the backs of heroes or something like that. 'OK. I'll explain,' I say. 'You have a medal. It was put on your chest not for your personal achievements but for your labor with other people. Am I right, Orazbek?' 'You're right,' he replies. Then, I say, 'If you're a hero of Sinemorye, then why did you abandon the people who were working with you? Why didn't you share their fate, Orazbek?' He had nothing to say, and when we said goodbye, he begged me to keep this conversation just between us."

Kakharman saw that Khorst was unhappy. A man loses much when he bids farewell to his native land and traditional way of life. City life is slow-moving, and your circle of friends is small. A man quickly withers in the city, and old age comes to him sooner. What if Khorst were to return to Sinemorye now?

Bolat came out of the house. He had a fresh towel over his shoulder and a jug of warm water and a basin in his hands.

"Let's wash our hands and go to the table!"

Khorst rinsed his hands and face and asked Kakharman, "So how is it in Semipalatinsk? Do they follow Kazakh customs? Probably not. They seem to be more Russian there. But I think people should preserve their customs wherever they are. Thank you, Bolat-zhan." And he passed the towel to Kakharman.

Mariyash greeted Kakharman warmly by the door.

"I haven't seen you for so long, Kakharman-aga. Come in."

She moved aside to let him through, but Kakharman invited her to go first.

"I see, Mariyash, that you and Bolat are doing well. And how are your children? Are they well too?"

"Glory to God, yes. I haven't prepared anything special, Kakharman-aga. I was visiting Irina Mikhailovna in the hospital and only just came back. Forgive me. Everything was prepared very quickly."

The old man looked tenderly at the young couple and said sadly, "I just can't imagine how my old woman and I are going to get by when you get an apartment. We've gotten so used to you."

As Kakharman looked around the room, he couldn't help noticing all the packed boxes. Kakharman could see that Mariyash and Bolat were troubled by something.

Bolat stood up. "Dear Kakharman-aga, welcome to our home."

But Kakharman sensed this wasn't what he really wanted to say. As Kakharman looked at him questioningly, Bolat waved his hand.

"Kakharman-aga, you know my brother Kadyr. He used to come to Karaoi and visit Berish at your father's house. He got into a university, but after the first year, he left and went to the army. Three days ago, his wife gave birth to their son, and she's now living with us. We sent a telegram to Kadyr at once because we knew he'd be so happy. But when I came home from work, I found Mariyash and Khorst-aga in tears. They had just received a telegram from Afghanistan." Bolat fell silent, tears suffocating him. "Kadyr fought until the last bullet. He was awarded a medal. He already had two. But who needs them, these pieces of metal? Tomorrow his body will be delivered."

Mariyash began to cry. "We don't know how to tell his wife. I visited her this morning, and she asked if we'd heard from Kadyr. I just can't bring myself to tell her. She's so happy. We called for her relatives to come."

Kakharman was stricken. He was so distraught, he couldn't speak even a single word of sympathy. He was amazed at Bolat's strength. He had spent the day with Kakharman and yet managed to keep his sorrow to himself.

Kakharman knew he couldn't stay silent any longer and began to speak. But the words were forced and bland. He felt awkward. Suddenly all his troubles appeared trivial before this real sorrow. It wasn't him who needed sympathy and support but Bolat.

Khorst-aga whispered to Kakharman when he found a moment, "You should spend some time with him. The boy is having a really hard time. When he heard about your arrival, it took his mind off things. He was really looking forward to having you here."

In the evening, relatives came and picked up the new mother from the maternity hospital. The next day, Khorst and Irina Mikhailovna stayed with Bolat all day. For days, there was much crying and moaning in the house. The young woman was inconsolable, but Kakharman, seeing her clutch her newborn baby to her breast, found new strength. "There'll be no peace in parents' houses until our military pulls out of Afghanistan," Kakharman thought. "Who knows how many young men have died in that foreign land? And who will ever tell us what it was for?"

After a few days, Kakharman and Bolat went to buy a ticket for Kakharman's return flight to Semipalatinsk. In the center of the city, near the ministries, they bumped into Akatov. Surprised to see Kakharman, Akatov called out to them from across the street.

"Kakharman, how did you end up here?" He smiled and embraced Kakharman warmly.

"And who's this with you? The face is familiar, but I can't quite remember."

Kakharman reminded Akatov where he might have seen Bolat before.

"So you're Slavikov's student." Akatov shook Bolat's hand. "Nice to meet you. How are your parents, Kakharman?"

Kakharman said they were both well.

"Only to be expected. Nasyr-aqsaqal is a strong man. May Allah save him. Next time you see them, pass on my greetings and bow low for me."

"He frequently speaks of you," Kakharman said warmly. "He still grieves that we came back from Moscow with nothing. Even your decisiveness and bravery didn't help."

Although Kakharman was talking with warm sincerity, the conversation was taking an unpleasant turn.

"Let's not talk about it. The aqsaqal thinks too highly of me. How's everything in Sinemorye?" he said, turning to Bolat.

Bolat quickly brought the minister up to date on the poor state of affairs: that many fishermen's auls were disintegrating, that many Sinemorian fishermen had left in search of work, and that many had turned to other means of making a living, such as rearing cattle and growing rice. Akatov listened unhappily.

"No, I don't wish well on the people who destroyed Sinemorye. May a similar fate await them! Surely the time has come now to fight people like that with everything we have, yet we're holding back for some reason. It's the same everywhere! Everywhere, we are forced to act with caution by the old slave in us. Why, I don't know. We've been waiting for this time for so long. We had so many hopes! Yet here we are now. Maybe to root out the cowardly pathetic old slave in us, we have to be destroyed?"

He went quiet, moving his gaze from Bolat to Kakharman, then said more calmly, "Why are you quiet, Kakharman?"

"I haven't lived in those areas for a long time now, so what can I say?" Kakharman smiled.

"I know that's not out of choice. I know the secretary of the Regional Committee forced you out. That fool! I wouldn't even hire him as a stable hand, yet he is the secretary! It's not easy to deal with him. He is a sly operator. But I just can't understand, Kakharman, why didn't you get in touch with me? You could've at least given me a call."

Kakharman blushed, and Akatov smiled and waved his hand.

"I understand. We find it easier to die than to ask a favor. Where are you now? What are you doing?"

"I'm in Semipalatinsk Port. Before that, I worked in Balkhash. Now I'm coming back from the Caspian. I was thinking about staying there, but I realized that horseradish is no sweeter than radish. It's the same everywhere. I look at my life and can't understand it: Is it because I am so depressed that I can't find a place for myself, or is it just that the world around me is so depressing . . ." Then he added in an apologetic tone of voice, "I wanted to visit you."

"You can do that today or maybe tomorrow. We'll talk. But now I must dash off to the Central Committee." Akatov stretched out his hand to bid farewell. "Gorbachev is coming to Tselinograd,"[3] he added.

"When's he coming?" Kakharman was excited.

"In the next few days. I don't know the exact date."

Akatov touched him on the sleeve, guessing his thoughts.

"I doubt you'll be able to meet with the highest authority. It's practically impossible. It may turn out to be a lot of effort in vain."

"Effort doesn't worry me. I've already worked so hard; it'd be nothing to give it another try."

After they said their goodbyes to Akatov, Kakharman announced, "I'm not going to Semipalatinsk anymore. We'll take tickets to Tselinograd. Maybe we'll be lucky enough to talk to Gorbachev personally." And he strode off energetically.

Kakharman was transformed—the indifference and insularity were gone. Bolat was filled with hope as he saw the change in Kakharman.

"If I don't get a chance to talk to him personally, then at least I can pass a letter to him. What do you think? Go home and bring all the relevant documents. We'll write the letter now." Kakharman almost pushed Bolat out the door. Then he had a shower, sat down in the armchair, and began to think.

He knew this opportunity could decide many things. To give the sea back its clear water, to fill it to its old shores. Suddenly he realized that he could spend the rest of his life doing just that.

Bolat came back, and they worked through the night to write the letter. They finished it early in the morning and then drank hot tea in silence.

Bolat stretched and joked, "We can sleep in Tselinograd."

"Yes, we'll get some sleep there. But leave your beard in Alma-Ata. Go shave! Don't you think the letter is a bit too long? Maybe we should make it shorter?"

"We can leave it till Tselinograd."

"Fine. We are short of time. Use the bathroom; I'll go after you."

On the plane, they fell asleep as soon as it was at cruising altitude. Kakharman dreamed about his home and his father.

Nasyr is sitting on the bench by the house and asks Kakharman, "Tell me, who are you upset about? The pathetic group of officials who forced you out? But people still respect you. So why is it you never come to your home aul?"

His father's short moustache and neat beard are completely white, and his eyes shine with tears on his thin, dark face.

A wave of tenderness—distant, almost forgotten, from his childhood—washed through the sleeping Kakharman's breast and made him weep.

His old mother ponderously carries the samovar into the house and calls his father. His father is sitting so still, it is as if he hasn't heard her.

"Nasyr, your tea is getting cold," his mother repeats. "Why do you sit there every day, staring at the sky like an idiot? Allah is not sending any rain. What can you do? Do you hear me?"

"You see how old your mother has grown," Nasyr scolds. "We thought that after going to the Caspian, you'd come visit us, stay for a few days. We were looking out the window constantly. But you didn't come. All the old men and women . . . they pray for your well-being. They wish you luck in all you do. You should've seen how they prepared for your visit. Musa even slaughtered a lamb. Then when it turned out you weren't coming, he came to me and said, 'Kakharman's heart must have grown hard. It's a stone's throw from the Caspian, yet he didn't come and see us. If a person like Kakharman acts like that, it means all people will go downhill.' And he also says this: 'It means Kakharman has forgotten our distress. It means that like the others, he went away to search for a better life.' 'A sting on your tongue,' I reply. But I can't prove he is wrong. I am so embarrassed. Gaziza read the cards about you; she says there is a serious obstacle in your path. And Musa invited all the neighbors to his home and fed them the lamb that was meant for you. I can hold myself together in front of the others, but my soul is aching for you. I see you always in my dreams. You walk in torn clothes through a burned forest. You are walking alone, and I always think when I see this dream: Where are your friends when you had so many? I sense you're walking through the desert, and you've been walking for many days already."

Then he hears his mother's voice. "Oh, Nasyr, how long must I wait for you? I don't enjoy drinking tea by myself. Why are you staring at the sky? If God was willing, the rain would've come long ago. He has turned away from us—you should've realized that long ago."

Nasyr turns toward her voice, mumbling something. Then he picks up the jug of warm water next to him and rinses his mouth. "I must go, Kakharman," he says. "The old woman is calling . . ."

And then Bolat nudged Kakharman's shoulder, and he opened his eyes. The plane had just landed and was taxiing along the concrete runway. Kakharman closed his eyes again, but neither his father, nor mother, nor their old brick house, nor their familiar voices appeared again.

There were no rooms in the hotel at all. It was clear from the fact that the streets were spotless and all the fences and houses newly painted that the big guest was due to arrive soon! Bolat called a friend, who was happy to let them stay since his wife was away. They stayed in Tselinograd for three days and rewrote their letter several times before giving it to a typist to type up quickly, paying twice the normal price. On the night before everybody believed Gorbachev was arriving, Kakharman woke up many times, worried he'd oversleep. He stepped out onto the balcony early in the morning, began to smoke, and decided not to go back to bed again. He had very high hopes for this day. He was convinced that he wouldn't be able to see Gorbachev personally. Akatov was surely right. Yet a strong hope, once rooted inside a man, can make him obsessed. There was at least still a tiny chance that he could pass the letter to him. "May the spirit of my suffering sea support me. May the spirits of my ancestors support me!" he said out loud as Bolat joined him on the balcony.

"Get ready, and we'll go to the square." Kakharman was fired up by their one slim chance.

But the miracle didn't happen. They kept seeing the general secretary from a distance, behind people's backs, and over their heads and between cars. Kakharman pushed forward, which clearly looked suspicious to one man in civilian clothes. He sharply and discreetly pushed Kakharman in the chest. It wasn't an unskilled hit, Kakharman realized when his whole rib cage spasmed in pain. At the same time, two pairs of strong hands grabbed him by the elbows and yanked him out of the crowd.

"What's up, boys?" Kakharman asked, trying to turn his head to see their faces. They were strong men, a head taller than Kakharman. They said nothing and passed Kakharman to some policeman who had come up to them. Then they went quietly back to their original places in the crowd. Bolat had no idea what was going on, so he just ran after the policemen and Kakharman.

"Where are you taking him? What has he done?"

For his questions, the policemen pushed Bolat into the car as well. As the car pulled up outside the police station, Kakharman realized they would be prosecuted for a "disturbance of the public order." The detainees were taken to different rooms on the second floor. A young man, who was talking on a phone, motioned Kakharman to a chair. He was wearing a new suit, a snow-white shirt, and a narrow tie. When he put the phone down, he looked coldly at Kakharman.

"So you behaved disgracefully on the square?"

"I haven't done anything wrong."

"That's odd. If that's so, you wouldn't be sitting in front of me now."

"Does it mean I am not allowed to talk to the general secretary?"

"You are not."

"And who is allowed?"

"Is there no one else in the Republic you could talk to?"

"No—and that's the problem! They've taken no notice of me for many years now!"

The young man stood up, walked around the table, and bent toward him confidentially, laying his hand on the back of the chair. "You're a brave man. I'd even say too brave."

"Not brave. Desperate," Kakharman replied.

The young man picked up the letter, which the policemen had seized from Kakharman, and began to look through it.

"What is this—a statement?"

"Can't you read?" Kakharman couldn't hide his irritation.

"Tell me the basic premise of your statement, please." At that moment, another policeman came in and handed the young man a document. "I'm waiting," he said, glancing at the document.

"The statement describes the appalling state of affairs in Sinemorye. Have you heard about it?"

"I have. But I never had a chance to go to the sea."

"Well, at least you've heard of it."

"Are you really a desperate man?"

"Yes. A broken man who lost hope." Kakharman's anger was rising.

"And yet, you're a brave man," the young man repeated. "You have changed many jobs recently. You have resigned from Semipalatinsk Port. What is going on with you, eh, Kakharman Nasyrovich?"

Kakharman wasn't surprised that the document the officer had brought in contained the details of his life. He even liked the efficiency of it. "Ah," he thought, "if only all people worked with such speed." And he expressed his envy. "What fast and precise work. I like it."

The young man nodded in agreement, recognizing what he was talking about.

"You haven't answered my question."

"I'm sorry. I don't even know your name or how to address you properly."

"Sergey Petrovich," he said, offering Kakharman cigarettes. "You can smoke, if you'd like."

"Thank you, Sergey Petrovich." Kakharman began to smoke with pleasure. "At moments like this, smoking is a joy. Where are you from, if that's not a secret?"

"You better tell me about yourself," Sergey Petrovich replied, tapping ashes into an ashtray.

"What's the point, Sergey Petrovich? Who am I in comparison to the disaster that's fallen upon our sea and our land? You're right. I have changed jobs often in the last few years. I used to wonder if it really matters where a man lives. I was young. I didn't understand many things. I can't live in Sinemorye. I cannot bear watching the sea perish. I left, hoping that I could fight for it. But I am losing the fight. I'm just banging my head against a wall. I came to Tselinograd with the hope of having a conversation with the general secretary or at least giving him this statement. But thanks to your boys, that hope has perished as well!" he said bitterly and fell silent. The cigarette died as he spoke, so he squashed it and dropped it in the ashtray. "This was probably my last try, Sergey Petrovich. It wasn't meant to be. Now my old thoughts have come back to me. I know that the sea will die. That is all I wanted to say. And any information you need about me is on your piece of paper. If you're interested, read it."

"Where did you come from to Tselinograd?"

"From Alma-Ata."

"And now you'll go there again?"

Kakharman grew thoughtful. Should he go to Semipalatinsk or go and visit his parents? He had almost run out of money, and he didn't want to go home empty-handed.

"Why are you asking?" Kakharman asked.

"You and your friend must leave Tselinograd today."

"Why? I don't understand."

"There's nothing for you to understand. Just do as you're told. So where will you go?"

Kakharman suddenly wanted Aitugan there with him. He would've buried his head in her lap and cried and told her about all his failures, about the humiliation he was experiencing. He didn't respect men who cried or complained about life, but at that moment, he could understand them. Neither the policemen nor this Sergey Petrovich cared for Kakharman, or some doomed sea, or the sorrow of the people dragging out their miserable existence on its salty shores.

"So what have you decided?" he was asked again.

"I'll go to Semipalatinsk."

Sergey Petrovich walked out of the room.

"There's an evening plane to Semipalatinsk," Sergey Petrovich said when he returned. "My officers will walk you to the plane."

"But where is my friend?"

"He'll fly to Alma-Ata. The plane to Alma-Ata is also tonight. You can spend some time together. He is waiting for you outside the station." Sergey Petrovich paused, then added softly, "Don't be upset with us, Kakharman Nasyrovich. I wish you a good journey." He offered his hand to say goodbye. "And your statement will stay here."

"Goodbye, Sergey Petrovich."

"Wait," Sergey Petrovich called after Kakharman as he reached the door. "I can tell you this. You are an honorable man. If the opportunity arises, your letter will be passed on to the person it is addressed to."

Kakharman was dumbfounded; he believed and he didn't.

He just mumbled, "You are also an honorable man. Be well."

A lieutenant went with him. He bought two tickets and asked Kakharman and Bolat not to leave the airport.

Soon, despite a coffee, Kakharman began to doze off on the bench. The night without sleep was taking its toll on him.

Bolat asked him, "Kakha, what are your plans for the future?"

"I don't know," Kakharman admitted sincerely, looking at the empty paper cup. "I've done all I could. Is there a place in Moscow or Alma-Ata where we haven't been yet? We have spoken at meetings and at many plenums. We are powerless."

The plane to Alma-Ata was leaving two hours before the plane to Semipalatinsk. It was painful for Bolat to say goodbye to Kakharman. Kakharman hugged him, pulled him to his chest, and whispered, "All the best. Be healthy!"

"I'll wait for Kadyr's forty days, then head to Sinemorye. We'll spend summer and autumn there," Bolat said. Kakharman felt that Bolat was holding something back.

"You're hiding something from me. That's not right. Tell me what it is."

Bolat went silent.

"Back in Balkhash, Igor and I didn't tell you, Kakharman, but there is to be a laboratory created at Sinemorye to observe . . . How do I describe it?"

"To observe the death of the sea."

"Yes, basically that's it."

"I heard about it from Berish." Kakharman hugged Bolat again.

After saying goodbye to Bolat, Kakharman returned to the same bench, sat back, stretched out his legs, and closed his eyes. He was alone and abandoned, like a traveler in a desert who has fallen into a dried-up well. Who will hear his screams from this hopeless hole?

Kakharman fell asleep and had a dismal dream where he had not fallen in a well but into a rocky abyss. And as he fell, he knew he would never get out again. Yet, strangely, he felt no pain. Touching his head, arms, and legs, he found he was unharmed. Yet horror gripped his soul in an icy chill. It seemed to him that he had been falling for an eternity, that was how far away the top of the abyss was. He began to scream with fear.

Kakharman woke in a sticky sweat. The airport speakers were announcing boarding for the Semipalatinsk flight. He quickly finished his vodka, and half-asleep and half-drunk, joined the hurrying people. Once on the plane, he reclined his seat right away and fastened his seat belt, assuming he'd fall asleep. Yet for some reason, sleep didn't come, so he began to flip through old newspapers.

THE WHITE DEATH IS ON THE DARK CONTINENT. SPECIALISTS SOUND THE ALARM. Drug use is becoming a widening problem in Africa. The continent mostly avoided this twentieth-century evil until recently.

IN THE FEDERAL REPUBLIC OF GERMANY, SIX PEOPLE HAVE DIED AS A RESULT OF THE STORM THAT HAS RUN THROUGH THE COUNTRY. The wind, which reached a top speed of 124 miles per hour, felled thousands of trees in the southern and western FRG.

ON SATURDAY THE UNITED STATES CARRIED OUT another nuclear test on the Polygon in Nevada. The power of the explosion, code named Laredo, was measured at between 20 and 150 kilotons. The current test was the 679th since the opening of the Polygon in Nevada in 1951.

TRAGIC NEWS OF AN ACCIDENT ON THE US BATTLESHIP *IOWA*,[4] not far from the coast of Puerto Rico. It was caused by a powerful explosion, and the news was received by the American people with great regret. When reporting on the catastrophe, the American and world press note that even in peacetime, naval activity can result in unexpected tragedies.

AIDS VIRUS THREATENS CHINA. AN UNEXPECTED RISE OF THE NUMBER OF DOCUMENTED carriers of AIDS virus in China leads to demands for a decisive response.

PASSENGER TRAIN NUMBER 159, *AURORA*, EN ROUTE FROM LENINGRAD TO MOSCOW, crashed near Bologoye station. Twenty-five people were killed in the crash, and 107 people were injured and taken to the hospital, 3 of whom died later.

TWENTY-THREE PEOPLE DEAD AND MILLIONS OF DOLLARS OF DAMAGE has been done by a storm that passed over France on Saturday. Wind speeds reached 105 miles per hour. Hilly Montmartre in Paris suffered badly.

Century-old trees here were pulled out by their roots. The Bois de Boulogne was blocked by fallen trees.

A FIRE IN CANADA HAS LASTED SEVENTEEN DAYS. The Canadian firemen have finally managed to put out the fire on the gigantic dump of car tires in Hagersville.

AT 06:57 MOSCOW TIME IN THE SOVIET UNION in the area of Semipalatinsk, an underground explosion of between 20 to 150 kilotons was carried out.

The newspapers also reported on high child mortality in Africa.

Kakharman smiled grimly. As if mortality were lower here! Who would acknowledge that in many areas of Central Asia, child mortality was twice the average for the whole Soviet Union? When Professor Slavikov said angrily that the Soviet Union led the world in child mortality, Kakharman didn't believe it at first. But as everybody knows now, Slavikov was right. Yet again, he was right!

The air traffic controllers at Semipalatinsk wouldn't let the plane land, and it was diverted to Ust-Kamenogorsk, about sixty-two miles away. "Troubles don't come alone," thought Kakharman. He didn't have any relatives or people he knew in Ust-Kamenogorsk. He went outside for a smoke. The night was soft and gentle and felt cool after the stuffiness of the airplane. A shiny white Volga pulled up outside the airport building. Three long-haired men jumped out, dressed fashionably. They moved confidently, and it was easy to see in them people who don't know need, who are never denied anything.

They kicked opened the door and headed toward an administrator. The administrator wasn't at his desk, but a beautiful young woman came out and walked toward them. It was clear she was expecting them. The woman and the young men greeted each other warmly. Kakharman watched them through the glass doors. They were talking and gesticulating animatedly. Kakharman observed them for a while, then lost interest. He finished his cigarette and headed back into the hall. The boys were coming out just as Kakharman came in, and they almost bumped into each other at the exit. Then he realized one of the boys was Kaiyr. Kaiyr was overjoyed to recognize Kakharman.

"What has brought you here, Kakharman-aga? My greetings . . ." Kaiyr stretched both his arms toward him. He was slender and fast in his moves, and his face glowed with joy, and his eyes sparkled. The two boys who were with him went off to smoke.

"How come I'm here?" Kakharman replied. "Well, you know, I got lost . . ."

Kaiyr couldn't figure out if he was joking. He began to laugh, interpreting Kakharman's words in his own way.

"Well, if you, Kakharman-aga, got lost, what can we mere mortals do? It means that Allah himself ordered us to wander in darkness. You talk in enigmas, Kakharman-aga."

"Am I not supposed to stray?" Kakharman became interested by this turn of the conversation.

"No! Your life must be error-free. Don't forget, if something were to happen to you, it'd be the end for Sinemorye."

Seeing Kakharman's confusion, Kaiyr said in a different tone. "I remember! Four years ago, I borrowed some money off you back in Moscow, and now in Ust-Kamenogorsk, I'll pay it back. How strange, eh?"

He pulled 150 rubles out of his pocket and gave them to Kakharman.

"It's rather late, but here it is. I know, you gave them to me for my beautiful eyes. But for me, it was a loan." Kaiyr pushed the money into Kakharman's hand.

Kakharman knew Kaiyr as a clever wheeler-dealer and didn't like him for that, but he began to see him in a different light. And Kaiyr, detecting that little warmth in Kakharman's heart, smiled winningly.

"Hey, Kakha, why are we still standing here? Let's go have some fun. Today you're my guest." He pointed toward the boys. "I'm flying with them to Moscow."

"My plane wasn't allowed to land at Semipalatinsk, so we had to land here and are waiting for a plane that can take us to Semipalatinsk."

"No plane is going to fly before morning, I guarantee you. Come with us."

"But what if there is a plane?" Kakharman was doubtful. "Then I'll miss it. I'm pretty tired of wandering across the Republic. I'm exhausted, and I miss home."

Kaiyr asked one of his friends to ask about the Semipalatinsk flight.

Kakharman asked Kaiyr about his life.

"You're studying somewhere. But where do you live? Here in Ust-Kamenogorsk?"

Kaiyr deftly flicked the butt of his cigarette away, and Kakharman smelled anasha. Now he understood the unnatural glitter in Kaiyr's eyes. Kaiyr didn't answer directly.

"A smart man can always find a place in life. Life goes on, people are born, and people die—but they can't be without a mullah. Most often, I visit Zaysan. By the way, there are a lot of fishermen from our homeland in Zaysan. Do you remember Berkimbai-khoja?[5] He died not so long ago. We've observed the seven days, but before the forty days, I'm flying to Moscow to unwind and do a few things."

Kaiyr's friend came back, confirming that no planes were expected before the morning.

"Let's go, Kakharman-aga." Kaiyr took Kakharman by the arm and drew him toward the car. "We'll have a great time, and you'll have a chance to relax properly."

They let him sit in front as a sign of special respect. Kaiyr introduced him to his friends. The strong scent of cannabis lingered in the car.

Kakharman turned to Kaiyr. "Are you into smoke?"

"Kakha, people say cannabis[6] smells but money doesn't. That's why I have to deal in it. But let it be just between us."

"Alright. It's your business."

The Volga stopped in front of a big house. The light was shining through two windows on the top floor.

Kaiyr livened up.

"Kakha, we have arrived. We are expected!"

"Is it alright?" Kakharman was doubtful. "They must be asleep."

"Everything is alright."

Kakharman was surprised by the size of the apartment.

"Let me introduce you to everyone!" And Kaiyr began to introduce Kakharman to the fashionable youths as his brother and a ship's captain.

The youths raised their glasses in salute.

"Please, Kakharman-aga, here's the table." Kaiyr showed him a place at the table. "Take off your jacket and relax."

"I'd like to wash my hands."

"Sasha, please help my friend," Kaiyr said.

The boy who had driven the car walked Kakharman down a long corridor to a bathroom plastered with photographs of naked women.

"You can use any of these towels."

Kakharman looked around curiously, then washed himself with cold water. The tiredness was gone. He was reenergized. When he returned to the room, Kaiyr and the two boys from the car were already sitting at the table. A girl in a long dress with an open back climbed on Kaiyr's lap. She asked with mock sadness, "You leave tomorrow?"

"If we survive till tomorrow," Sasha replied. He had a girl on his lap too.

"It looks like they're not taking us to Moscow, Marishechka," she said to her friend archly.

"Do men go to Tula with their own samovars?" Marina came back.

"Kakha, what would you like to drink?" Kaiyr asked, leaning across the table.

"Something strong."

"Whiskey!" Marat shouted. "Let's 'dumbfound' our guest!"

Kaiyr grinned. "You're so naïve, Marat! This man was drinking whiskey while you were still crawling under a table. Back in his time, Kakharman-aga was dealing with American scientists. And they were surprised by his Oxford accent. And you talk about dumbfounding . . . Hau doo you doo! Nice to meet yoou!" He said in mock English.

After he gulped down the whiskey, a vitalizing fire spread through Kakharman's veins. He could see the kind of people he was with, and at first, he had barely suppressed his habitual contempt for such lowlifes. But now, after a whiskey, he tried to see them differently. In turn, they accepted him as one of their own. They walked him to a room with the *vidak*[7] and burst out laughing loudly when he backed right out after he saw naked bodies on the screen. At the table, Kaiyr was discussing business with one of the others. Kakharman caught him saying, "Two K—no less. For less, no." He turned to Kakharman, surprised.

"Kakha, didn't you like the movie?"

"I'm past the age when that sort of thing does much for me!" Kakharman sat back down at the table.

Kaiyr's friend stood up.

"Goodabyee! You have until tomorrow to decide. I'll come to see you off."

"I have nothing to think about. I will not repeat the offer. The price on poppies rises each day. It's getting more and more dangerous to acquire it. I offered it to you at two K as a friend. In Moscow or Riga, I could sell product this good for six K," Kaiyr said firmly.

His friend thought for a bit.

"Alright. I'll think about it. See you tomorrow."

Kakharman addressed Kaiyr. "Do you have cold water, by any chance?"

"What are you talking about, Kakha? Marat, bring my friend some cold water. And a bottle of champagne for me!"

Marat, who was sitting in a dark corner with a girl, jumped up right away and, to Kakharman's surprise, returned almost instantly with water and champagne.

"All done, chief." He lowered his head in mock deference.

"Call Moscow. Maybe Georgy is back."

Marat sat the phone on his lap and dialed the number.

"Are you going to talk to him yourself, Kaiyr?"

Kaiyr shook his head.

"What am I to tell him?"

"Tell him that today I'm flying out from Ust-Kamen, and I have two idiots with me. Tell him to bring a car with a trailer. I have a lot of luggage."

"Kakha, would you like a drink?"

"Kazakhs say instead of asking, it's better to give."

"You're right, Kakha. Apologies."

"Are you not drinking yourself?"

"You're like Stierlitz.[8] I have things to do in Moscow. I don't drink before doing business. If I start drinking, I can't stop for a lo-o-ong time. That is all."

"I have the same problem," Kakharman sighed. "But it's better not to drink at all. In the past, I never drank, but now I'm getting the habit. That is how I drown my sorrow. I treat venom with poison."

Kaiyr had seen many people who had lost their way after leaving Sinemorye, going around and around in circles. He imagined Kakharman lost like this for a moment and shivered. His fate and pain would be hard—harder and more tragic than that of a more ordinary man.

And then Kaiyr recalled the last days of Berkimbai-khoja. One morning, the khoja called to Kaiyr from his deathbed. Almost inaudibly, he asked Kaiyr for *kumys*.[9] Kaiyr held the cup to his lips, and the khoja took a sip, then rested for a long time. With an effort, he began to talk. Not all his faint words were audible, but Kaiyr, who hadn't left his bedside for a long time, could guess them from the movement of his lips.

"Common people speak truly. 'It's better to be a servant in your homeland than a prince in a foreign land.' I never thought properly about these words, but now that I'm eighty years old, I understand them. Too late, unfortunately. So I will be buried in a foreign land. I should've stayed by the sea, no matter how hard. Nasyr has proved wiser than me, more dignified, more courageous—and I am far from him."

"Dear khoja," Kaiyr reassured him, "don't be upset. We will bury your body in the sands of Sinemorye, no matter how hard it may be."

Berkimbai livened up, gratitude on his face.

"Thank you, Kaiyr. I had many hopes for my sons, but you have been closer to me than them."

"We will put your body in a zinc coffin and bring it to the motherland on a plane. Anything can be done for money, if only there was money."

The reassured khoja made a sign with his weak hand.

"Close the door."

Kaiyr quickly closed the door, guessing Berkimbai's intention.

"I have a small package under my pillow. Get it out."

Kaiyr pulled the money, wrapped in a clean shawl, from under the pillow.

"There are five hundred rubles. Will that be enough?"

"No, dear khoja. It's not really enough. Nowadays it would cost around a thousand."

Berkimbai delved under the duvet, his face covered in sweat with the effort. He pulled out another bundle and gave it to Kaiyr.

"Here's another five hundred. If that's not enough, you pay the rest."

The door was opened, and the baibishe came in with a jug of warm water and a basin. She helped the khoja wash his face and wipe it with a soft towel. Then she brought breakfast in. Berkimbai couldn't manage even a cup of tea, he was so weak. He lay still and then lost consciousness. He didn't come around for the whole day. Toward midnight, he passed away, very quietly, without saying anything more.

In Zaysan, the khoja, who was respected by everybody, was carried on his last journey with honors. Those who washed his body received generous gifts as a sign of gratitude. Kaiyr, who read the burial service, received a young mare and foal. Of course, he didn't mention the money Berkimbai had given him. Did the khoja ever imagine that he'd be a victim of a lie from his trusted student on his deathbed?

What has Kakharman achieved in this life? He, Kaiyr, hadn't finished college, and didn't have any qualification. But he had that most basic thing in this life: money. And if you have money, you have everything: a car and a table filled with good food. So what if the business is dangerous? That is what makes it so thrilling! He's a hunter. He travels light. He lives exuberantly, with style. And that is how he'll always be.

Kakharman interrupted his reverie. "You say some of our fishermen work in Zaysan?"

"Yes. Zaysan is rather remote, and our people like that."

"I would like to see Zaysan!" Suddenly, Kakharman felt decisive. "I'll go and see my fellow countrymen, talk to them. Why not? Or am I wrong, Kaiyr?"

He had finished the black bottle of champagne by himself, and that and the whiskey he had drunk earlier were having a very strong effect.

"Do you seriously want to go to Zaysan? The car that brought us here is going there in the morning. I'll talk to the driver."

"Please do."

The driver had no objection to giving Kakharman a ride. Early in the morning, Kaiyr and Kakharman said farewell. Kakharman fell asleep right away in the back seat. That was hardly surprising, since he hadn't slept at all the night before.

He woke up when the driver poked his shoulder.

"Aga, wake up. We'll take a short break here."

Kakharman opened his eyes. Pain from the night of heavy drinking split his head. He got out of the car. An elderly man was sitting by a spring and after laying a shawl on the ground, cut bread over it. Kakharman vaguely recognized him as the man who got into the car this morning.

"Nobody goes past this spring without stopping," the driver said. "Wash your face. Uncle Semeon is waiting for you."

"Your uncle has a stern look," Kakharman joked, looking at his fellow traveler.

"It's only first appearances. His soul is golden."

After washing his face with water so cold that his fingers hurt, he walked to the old man.

"Sit down," he invited Kakharman. "Let's get to know each other. My name is Semeon Arkhipovich. Come on, have some food. You must be hungry."

Kakharman sensed the good in him in his kind, soft voice. Kakharman introduced himself. They ate slowly. When they'd finished, Semeon Arkhipovich folded the shawl and sent the driver to the spring to rinse the cups. Then he turned to Kakharman.

"It looks like you've had a rough night, son. It wouldn't hurt to have a drink to ease your hangover. What do you say? Don't be shy," Semeon Arkhipovich encouraged him, searching through the car. "It's normal."

He returned with a bottle, filled up a glass, and gave it to Kakharman.

"Thank you, Semeon Arkhipovich. That's very good timing. What about you?"

"I drank enough in my life. A year ago, I stopped drinking altogether."

Kakharman downed the glass and squawked. Semeon Arkhipovich rejoiced and also squawked, looking at him mischievously, then gave him some soft sheep's cheese. "We won't be in Zaysan until tonight, so you'll have plenty of time to sleep."

As soon as the car moved off, Kakharman dropped off to sleep again. He slept for two hours. Semeon Arkhipovich was happy when he woke. Understandably. A long silence on a long trip tires a man and provokes sad thoughts. And in the Kazakh tradition, he began to ask Kakharman where he was from and what he did. Kakharman told him about his difficulties over the last few years. As he spoke, he painted a picture not only of the dismal life of Sinemorye but also the sad, sad path the Republic had followed in the last twenty years. Kakharman's impassioned speech made the driver turn around toward him several times with respect and sympathy. Semeon Arkhipovich listened carefully and quietly, sighing frequently. When Kakharman had finished, a heavy silence descended on the car. Semeon Arkhipovich, who had experienced a lot in his life, was shocked. Kakharman, for the first time in the past few years, finally felt the relief of sharing his pain without withholding anything.

"I've heard a lot about you and your father, Kakharman," Semeon Arkhipovich finally said. "In Zaysan, we have families from your lands. They tell us a lot about you, Kakharman. They often talk about your father, Nasyr. We already have an impression of a person prepared to sacrifice his own life to save the sea, to protect from ruin the lands where he was born and where he lived for so many years. We also admire Nasyr. To stay behind when many have left their homes, to hope to fill the sea again with prayers . . . one must either be insane or a saint! And I consider him a saint. You know, Kakharman, people with such strong character are very rare. I, in my turn, would like to tell you about my father. He's of the same kind as yours, a strong man. He was shot as an enemy of the people. He was taken from work. We weren't even able to say goodbye. My mother was a teacher. She was taken during the night. She was marking homework. Only much later was she told that my father had been arrested. Twenty-seven years later, I found my mother here, in Zaysan.

"And I was sent to so many places! At first, I lived in a boarding school, where the children of the enemies of the people were brought up. How many times did I try to run away! But each time, I was caught and returned. They would shave a cross on my head, the sign of a runaway. Then the war started. During the war, I realized that if that place couldn't kill me, then neither would a bullet. I didn't value my life, but I made it all the way to Berlin without a single scratch. Yes, it does happen! I was considered brave. I finished the war as a commander of the Order of Glory. Well, I thought, if death spared me, then God himself has ordered it. I already knew by then that my father had been shot. And to find out something about my mother, I went home. I got out in Bryansk. Kakharman, if you only saw our postwar people! Thin, drooping women and the half-naked, hungry children with them. I made my way to my native village. When I got there, it was almost night. Only half-burned walls remained of our house. I have never cried as bitterly as I did then, even when my mother was taken away."

Semeon Arkhipovich went quiet for a moment. "Have I tired you out, Kakharman?"

The car shook suddenly, and Semeon Arkhipovich looked at the driver disapprovingly.

"Look where you're going, or you'll turn us over! What a boy—likes to listen to everything. That's why you're still single. Girls don't like boys like that."

And he continued his story.

"So there I am, crying. A man always has a little beacon of hope in his soul, like a small candle. I never quite believed I had lost my mother and father forever. But now I was sitting in the snow, clutching my gun—and my parents' house kept appearing before my eyes. Here's my father walking by, coughing and making the floor creak. Here's my mother bent over her notebooks. I had faith still . . . I was sitting on the ruins of my parents' house. It began to rain, and I was soaked. But I didn't leave. I just sat next to the ruined chimney and kept saying to myself, 'You should remain human, Semeon. No matter what happens to you, how much sorrow hits you, keep a human face, Semeon!' That's easy for me to say now. But back then . . . back then I had a gun. I could end it all with a single bullet. I took courage and thought, 'My body will be found with a gun next to it. People will say, "What was he doing here?"' Back in those days, people valued honor, not like nowadays . . .

"Then I heard some shuffling steps and looked up—and I see Marfa! And she said to me, just as if all those years had never passed, 'Senya, poor little one!' 'Auntie Marfa, dearest!' I jumped up and hugged her. And she was hugging me and crying. We just got into her house. She had nothing to put on the table, so I got out my provisions. When I left the next morning, I asked her to keep a note for my mother to tell her that I had come back, that I was alive.

"I went to the Far East and found a job as a sailor. I spent twelve months at sea without setting foot onshore. That time was happy—I understand that now very well. For twelve months, I was surrounded only by the quiet ocean, with only the quiet company of fishermen. Each day, the sun gives place to the moon, and the moon gives place to the sun. A good life for a son of an enemy of the people!

"But then I went and finished college and got married. Then there was the Twentieth Congress.[10] They started to look at us traitor's children in a different way—Aha, here's Zaysan . . . A little farther is Priozerskoe, our aul!" Semeon Arkhipovich pointed out the distant lights through the window. Kakharman's eyes were drawn to the brightest light of all: the light of a lighthouse.

"Just take me to a hotel," Kakharman said. The driver began to laugh.

"Hotels in a fishermen's aul! Where are you going, Sake?"

Semeon Arkhipovich explained.

"That's what they call me—the people here don't like to use my patronymic. Come to my place, Kakharman. I can't guarantee much. I've been living as a bachelor for a long time! I just think: as long as I have a roof over my head. I was divorced while in the Far East. While I was at sea, she got involved with someone on the shore, so I kicked her out! I have a daughter. She's at a university, studying. I married again. She was a wonderful woman! But she died here, in Zaysan."

"Does your daughter visit frequently?"

"Not really. There's nothing for her to do here. It's not Moscow or Leningrad."

He spoke without a trace of bitterness. In the meantime, the driver stopped the car outside a small, run-down house. They walked in and turned the light on.

The driver said, "Sake, I'll go to Balziya and tell her you've arrived."

"Don't worry. It's very late. We'll manage by ourselves. And thank you. Give my greetings to your father and mother."

After saying goodbye, the driver left. Semeon Arkhipovich started to light a fire in the stove.

"I do have gas, but I like cooking on the stove. There's no comparison to a real fire."

He crouched in front of the stove and began to blow on the kindling.

"You should take your coat off. By the time we've refreshed ourselves, tea will be ready." As Kakharman looked around this modest bachelor dwelling, he could see how spare it was.

But if Kakharman was staring at his host, it was because Semeon Arkhipovich had been sitting on the front seat in the car, and Kakharman hadn't seen his face properly. Now, seeing his fellow traveler in the light, he was surprised by how piercing his gaze was. It was the look of someone decisive and courageous.

After washing, they sat at the table. At that moment, the front door opened, and a young woman walked in.

"Brother, you're already here! We didn't expect you today," she said warmly. Then seeing the guest, she became shy.

"*As-salamu alaykum*, brother!" A tall man appeared in the door behind her. "I told her you had arrived, but she just couldn't wake up."

"What a life you have," Semeon Arkhipovich laughed. "Normally Balziya can't wake you up, but now . . ."

Kakharman was surprised. Semeon Arkhipovich began to speak in clear Kazakh.

"Anyway, you should praise yourself less, and don't spoil Balziya. I can't stand men who spoil their wives." He hugged Balziya. "So how are you? How are your children?"

"What can happen to children? I prepared meat for your arrival; I'll go and warm it up. Duisen, let's go." And she tugged him away by his sleeve.

"Don't be shy! Kakharman, these are my relatives. Balziya is my sister. Duisen is my brother-in-law."

"Do you speak Kazakh?" Kakharman was still astounded.

"Why are you so surprised? I've been living in Kazakhstan for the last twenty-five years—enough time to learn."

"There are many Russians in Kazakhstan, but hardly any speak our language. Although that's not true in all of Kazakhstan. In Sinemorye, you'll rarely come across a Russian who can't speak Kazakh. But here in the east, even Kazakhs consider it shameful to speak in their own language; they prefer Russian."

"You shouldn't confuse me with other Russians. I am special. I have Russian bones but Kazakh meat!"

As they talked, he pulled a few bottles out of his bag. He put one on the table and the rest on top of the wardrobe.

"And here's the food!"

Balziya appeared in the doorway. The saucepan was wrapped in a towel and steaming. Balziya emptied the meat into a large dish and set it in front of the men.

"Thank you, Balziya! You see that bag? There are presents for you in there. Take it and go home to sleep now. I know you have to get up early tomorrow. Duisen can stay with us."

They stayed up late. Kakharman heard about life in Zaysan. He asked how many vessels the Zaysan Rybprom had, what volume of catch they needed, and what was the water level in the lake, and made some conclusions for himself. He thought maybe he could find work in Zaysan as an ordinary engineer but then grew doubtful.

In the morning, he decided to go for a walk through the aul. Placid Zaysan reminded him of his home. This upset Kakharman. He'd thought perhaps here he'd find comfort—a little support to help him pull himself back together. But he saw Aitugan in his mind and remembered her tears: "We are so tired of constantly moving from place to place. We are exhausted, and so are you. Will there ever be the end to it, Kakharman? You're already forty years old. Settle down. We can't spend our whole lives like this."

The chairman of the local fishery kolkhoz received Kakharman warmly. He was a sound and careful man who weighed his words. It was obvious they didn't get many visitors to this remote aul. Semeon Arkhipovich left Kakharman with the chairman and went to continue with his own business, promising they'd meet later back in the house.

"So you're a visitor here? If you have any requests, we'll be happy to see to them."

"I'm not just a visitor, aqsaqal. I am looking for work."

"What qualifications do you have?"

"I am a fisherman."

"We desperately need fishermen!" the chairman exclaimed but then looked doubtfully at Kakharman. Kakharman didn't look like an ordinary worker. Seeing his confusion, Kakharman introduced himself and outlined his recent jobs.

The chairman was dismayed.

"Oh! I've heard about you—thousands of times! I can offer you any position, even as my deputy." He went silent and then added despondently, "I don't know if you'll be working here with us. Maybe it'll be better for you to find something in the Zaysan Rybprom management, eh?"

"Dear Zhomart-aga! No matter what position we hold, we're fishermen first. I've no more interest in working in the management than you, I imagine. Let me work in the kolkhoz as an ordinary fisherman. Then you can see for yourself what I'm worth."

The chairman liked this answer. But he decided to press Kakharman on his decision.

"It's not hard to take you in the kolkhoz as an ordinary fisherman. But won't your fellow countrymen laugh at you?"

"Laugh at me or at you?" Kakharman grinned slyly. "Zhomart-aga, people will gossip anyway. But as they say, a caravan sorts itself out during the journey."

"Then it's your choice. If you want, I'll give you a vessel. Or if you'd prefer it, you can start as a foreman."

"Thank you, Zhomart-aga. But I'll not change my mind; I just want to be an ordinary fisherman."

"But what about somewhere to live! I'll only be able to get you a flat next summer. I can't get you anything any sooner! No offense."

"No offense!" Kakharman stood up and offered his hand gratefully to the chairman. "I'll be back in a week's time." And he headed toward the door.

"Wait," the chairman stopped him. "Can't you stay here another day? A girl is getting married today. She's from your homeland, Kakharman. The boy is one of yours, too—one of those who settled near Alma-Ata."

The event, which had little to do with Kakharman, made his heart flinch. Suddenly everything became dark in front of his eyes. A weakness came over him, and he had to lean against the doorway. He felt as if he would faint. But the chairman was completely oblivious.

"If people still get married, maybe life is getting better? It's still nice that your fellow countrymen join each other. They clearly want to stay together, closer. You know, it helps you through when you are away from your homeland. Why am I saying this? It's just that a similar thing happened here, although not on the same scale as in Sinemorye. Here we had an awful drought from '74 to '79. The water in the Irtysh, Zaysan, and Bukhtarma dropped ten to thirteen feet. Fish disappeared; the kolkhoz had no income. People began to leave. But in the end, people stayed and survived. Please, God, let this never happen again. Now there is plenty of water in the Zaysan and enough fish. Those who left are returning rather sheepishly. I should not have taken a single one of them back into the kolkhoz, but I can't take this sin on my soul. How can one separate a man from his homeland?"

"Who are the young couple getting married?" he asked.

"The bride is Baiten's daughter. Do you remember Baiten from your homeland? But I can't remember the groom's name. People say the main matchmaker is a Hero of Socialist Labor who is coming from the Alma-Ata region."

"Is his name Orazbek?" Kakharman was surprised.

"That's it. Orazbek! I remember now," the chairman replied.

Kakharman shook his head and began to say goodbye.

"Thank you, Zhomart-aga for treating me as a human being. I was beginning to forget how that felt. It's hard for me, as you probably guessed. So, yes, may God protect Zaysan from the fate of our sea." Kakharman turned to go and was already in the yard when the chairman called out again from the window.

"I'll pick you up tonight. You're staying at Semeon's, aren't you?"

272

On his way back to Semeon Arkhipovich's, he heard the distant ringing of hammer on anvil from down the road. At once he guessed who the blacksmith was. Semeon Arkhipovich was sitting in the yard, his back to the gate, hammering metal lightly over the anvil. When he noticed Kakharman, he put the hammer down and got up to greet him.

"Are you back already? Go and wash your hands. Balziya is waiting. She and Duisen live just over there." He nodded at the neighboring house. "Have you agreed to something with Zhomart?"

"I think I have . . . But it's difficult to arrange a place to live—he says he can't get anything until the next summer."

"You can live at my place for now, and I'll move to Balziya's."

He said it with such confidence that Kakharman understood immediately that it had been decided.

"Balziya is a teacher. Duisen is a fisherman. They have two children. They moved here to be closer to me." He opened the door for Kakharman. "It's a long story. I'll tell you another time."

Balziya greeted them warmly, "Come in. Duisen is at work, so you, brother, must look after our guest."

"Kakharman, what will we drink?"

"Maybe better not to drink?"

"Balziya will be offended." He winked to Kakharman. "Am I right, sister?"

Balziya blushed. "You men are your own masters. If the guest doesn't want to drink, why force him?"

"That's true. Good news: Kakharman is going to move here, to Zaysan. He had a conversation with Zhomart. If we could only have another five or so people like Kakharman here!" He opened the bottle. "It's not good to drink cognac during the day. Let's have a little vodka." He filled their glasses. "I'm very glad I met you, Kakharman!"

Kakharman began to lift his glass, then put it down right away. Semeon Arkhipovich looked at him with surprise.

"Please don't be offended," Kakharman explained. "I'll drink later. Yesterday I heard of the death of the khoja Berkimbai. This is the first grave in your land of a man from my land. I'll visit the graveyard and have a drink afterward."

"You're right," Semeon replied. And when he heard steps approaching, he quickly put the alcohol away, winking at Kakharman.

The door opened, and a woman in her fifties with snow-white headwear appeared in the doorway. She had a small boy with her who was gripping the hem of her long dress.

"Hello, dear Kakharman! How are your parents? How's Aitugan?"

Kakharman recognized Otkeldy's widow, Marziya, right away. Time had not spared her beauty, but her posture and manner were as noble as ever.

Kakharman stood up and stretched his arms toward her.

"And how are you, Marziya-apa?"

She smiled with her full, beautiful lips, and they hugged.

"So people haven't forgotten me yet! God!"

Pulling Kakharman gently to her, she kissed him on the forehead. Tears shone in her eyes. Kakharman walked her to the head of the table and helped her sit down on soft blankets.

"I think about our sea every day. I must be getting old. No matter how much I get used to living here, I still can't say I made it my home. In my mind, I am always in my homeland."

Kakharman nodded respectfully, and then she addressed Semeon Arkhipovich.

"I heard you visited your mother's grave. May she rest in peace."

"May your words become true, Marziya!" Semeon Arkhipovich thanked her. "In Ust-Kamenogorsk, I came across your fellow countryman and delivered him here."

"May Allah bless you! And it's good it worked out this way. People say a nation is glorious with its best sons. Kakharman has done everything he could to save our land." Marziya sighed, then said, "How are my sister and brother-in-law doing?"

Kakharman listened to Marziya and realized that no matter how far life sent people from his land, their souls stayed in Sinemorye.

"Kakharman," Marziya asked, "what will happen to our land in the future?"

Kakharman played with the edge of the tablecloth. What could he say?

"It won't be easy to revive our land, Marziya-apa. But have the people who took its life thought about that? We ordinary mortals must simply wait. That's how it is. I don't want to give anyone false hope."

Semeon Arkhipovich joined the conversation, saying bleakly, "We are sitting here, waiting, but catastrophe is drawing nearer."

"What will happen," Marziya asked mournfully, "to ruin such a treasure as our sea?"

After that, she went quiet. But when Kakharman said he would like to visit the house of Berkimbai, she sighed, "Let's go. I'll walk you there."

"How is Nurlan?" Kakharman asked Marziya as they walked.

"Nurlan was weak and frail, so I decided not to send him to study in a city. And anyway, he didn't want to leave me alone, and I had no money to educate him. We've been together since we arrived here. He completed a medical course in Ust-Kamenogorsk and now works here as a paramedic."

"Paramedic," Semeon Arkhipovich interrupted. "Why do you have such a low opinion of him? He is a healer. Can you believe it?" He looked at Kakharman with delight. "Last year, I broke my collarbone, and Nurlan straightened the fracture right away!"

"That is a gift he got from his father. Here we are. This is Berkimbai's house. It's only his widow in the house now. Poor dear. She couldn't find comfort in her children. Her eldest son was killed in a fight, and the youngest is in prison." Marziya began to whisper. "People say money corrupts people.

"It was hard for Berkimbai. Who could've met his last wish when he had children like this? An old woman? His desire was to be buried in his homeland. That rogue Kaiyr began arranging it but returned from the city with nothing. He said he couldn't find a zinc coffin. What sort of time are we living in! You die but can't be buried in your homeland."

Kakharman was doubtful that such an operator as Kaiyr couldn't buy a zinc coffin in town. Of course he had pocketed the money. He hadn't been sitting by the bed of the dying khoja for nothing. "A snake warmed on the chest! Jackal shit!" Kakharman swore quietly. He was totally disgusted by Kaiyr, although why should he care if one mullah ripped off another?

Women were forbidden from going to the graveyard, so Semeon Arkhipovich and Kakharman went on together. There, by the grave of his fellow countryman, who was buried in a foreign land, Kakharman became thoughtful again. If the sea will die soon, what is the point in taking the dead there? They won't hear the splashing of its waves, and they will lie in solitude and neglect. Would that not be an abuse to their memory?

He shivered. Whenever he was agitated, he trembled. Though he considered himself strong, he just couldn't get rid of these shakes. What strong nerves you need to cope with this crazy life.

He stood by the grave of his fellow countryman without a single reassuring thought in his mind. Berkimbai was dead. Kakharman will die. Many more of his countrymen will die. All in a foreign land. And their descendants won't know what Sinemorye is. All that will be left on the map is a salty white stain.

Kakharman looked disconsolately at the marble plaque in the brick wall. There in a brass script were Berkimbai-khoja's dates of birth and death. What can these numbers tell the local people? If only this grave were in a thriving homeland. Then anyone who walked past might say, "The khoja Berkimbai rests here. He was a good man. He read prayers well. He knew the ancient scripts. There was no better educated man in all our land."

Semeon Arkhipovich touched Kakharman on the shoulder.

"Kakharman, let's go home. I have a headache. The bombs are going off in Semipalatinsk again—I can tell that better than any seismograph. If I have a hellish headache, that means that the explosions are happening again."

Kakharman looked at the pale, drooping face of Semeon Arkhipovich and became alarmed. It looked as if his new friend was about to fall. Indeed, if Kakharman hadn't caught him in his arms at that moment, Semeon Arkhipovich would've collapsed.

Semeon Arkhipovich whispered, "Go . . . Find a car . . ."

Kakharman laid him on the ground, folded his jacket under his head, and ran toward the aul. By the time he came back with the car, Semeon Arkhipovich's eyes were closed, and he was delirious. With the driver's help, Kakharman picked the old man up carefully and carried him to the car.

"Where should we go? Home or Balziya?" the driver asked. "Don't forget your jacket."

"Don't worry about the jacket. Drive as fast as you can. Then get a doctor!"

The driver put his foot down.

"I'll bring Nurlan. The moment they begin to test bombs in Semipalatinsk, Semeon-aga is stricken. On test days, nearly everyone in our aul is like sleepy flies—the old people can't even get out of bed. Our people are like space dogs: all the experiments are carried out on us!"

As he waited for the doctor, Kakharman laid a cold wet towel on his friend's head. The driver brought Nurlan quickly. A thin young man in a white gown walked briskly into the house and gave Semeon Arkhipovich an injection.

Handing Kakharman his jacket, the driver mumbled, "Nurlan knows Semeon-aga's illness well. You can put the kettle on, and by the time it boils, Semeon-aga will be back to normal."

"It's nice to meet you, Kakharman-aga," Nurlan addressed him pleasantly. "I've heard a lot about you."

Looking at the smiling young man, Kakharman saw the familiar features of Otkeldy's face. They shook hands.

"Kakharman-aga," Nurlan suddenly addressed him. "Please sit down. I'll check your pulse."

Kakharman obeyed, and Nurlan asked, "Semeon-aga probably had a little to drink this morning?"

"Just a little . . ."

"On days like this, it's enough to send his blood pressure shooting up. And you're overtired yourself, Kakharman-aga. Your nervous system is extremely fatigued. You should rest."

"Here in Zaysan, I realized that my nerves are really not in great shape," Kakharman admitted. "Thanks for your advice."

By the time the kettle had boiled, Semeon Arkhipovich had indeed come around. He sat up and looked around.

"Nurlan, you brought me back to life again," he joked tiredly. "Kakharman, did I scare you?"

"Don't get up," Nurlan warned him. "You should lie down a little longer."

In the evening, Zhomart came to get Kakharman as promised. Kakharman didn't want to leave Semeon Arkhipovich, who was still unwell, but Semeon Arkhipovich winked at him cunningly, tapping Balziya's son on his shoulders.

"He will stay with me, so don't worry. Sarsen, will you read to me?" Then he teasingly wagged his finger at Zhomart, warning, "Just deliver my guest back safe and sound."

"I can get back by myself. I can still walk, I think. I won't be late," Kakharman said, mildly offended.

"Yes, right. Do you really think your countrymen will let you go before morning?" Semeon waved his hand.

He was, of course, right. The people who had so long considered Kakharman their protector kept him at the wedding until the morning.

Conversations went on through the night, and the young people sang noisily. The wedding was on a Friday, so they had all the weekend to recover. Like weddings everywhere, it was lively and full of joy. But if it had been in Karaoi or Shumgen, then there would have been horse races, there would have been fighting competitions, and there would have been all kinds of other things in accordance with Sinemorian customs. Kakharman realized with sadness that he might never see another Sinemorian wedding.

The news of Kakharman's arrival had spread across the aul quickly, and everybody was waiting for him at the wedding. The old people were first to greet and bless him. "May luck always be with you, Kakharman. Forgive us for leaving our homeland and finding shelter here in Zaysan. You are a reasonable man; you will not judge us. What else could we do when the fish vanished from the sea?"

Then he was surrounded by young people who paid their respects and listened intently to his stories about his trips to Moscow and Alma-Ata. At some point, Kakharman was left alone. And a young, school-aged girl took the chance, blushing with embarrassment, to ask, "Kakharman-aga, where is Berish now?" Her question both surprised and pleased Kakharman. In Karaoi or Shumgen, it would've been entirely inappropriate for a girl to ask openly about a boy. But the question happily reminded him that Berish had grown up! He was fourteen years old!

Not long ago Aitugan had told him, "Berish has decided to go to a boarding school, not far from Karaoi. He'll still spend his summers with his grandparents. He hasn't told you yet because he's a little nervous; he asked me to talk to you first." Kakharman had not been very happy with his son's decision. "Don't forget," Aitugan warned him. "He is as stubborn as you are. Once he's decided something, he will not change his mind."

In the end, Kakharman didn't object, seeing in the decision a love for his homeland. He decided to talk to him about it eye to eye. "Your mother told me of your request. You are grown-up enough to make your own decisions, but in the future, come straight to me without a middleman. I agree to your decision and respect it. In winter, you can stay in boarding school, and in the summer, you go to your grandparents. I believe in you, Berish. I respect your independence!"

"I also believe in you, Koke!" Berish shouted and ran straight out of the room, maybe feeling that otherwise he would have succumbed to the impulse to give his father a tender hug, which would have been too embarrassing for a young teenager.

That's what Kakharman thought about when the unknown girl stood in front of him, awkwardly waiting for an answer to her question.

But what was it Berish wanted to express to him when he said, "I believe in you"? Was he hinting that he was drinking too much, rolling down toward the bottom, suffering and trying to climb out, but Berish believes he can save himself?

People began to encircle Kakharman again. The girl was looking into Kakharman's eyes, waiting. Her cheeks were red with embarrassment, and she was now so confused, she looked as if she was about to start crying. Kakharman, worried she'd actually weep, quickly answered, "Berish has returned to Sinemorye. He studies in a local boarding school. But he spends his summers in Karaoi with his grandparents. I haven't seen him for a year now."

Kakharman wanted to ask the girl whose daughter she was, but she had already gone. Meanwhile, the wedding continued.

"Let Kakharman speak!" came a call from the table.

"Yes! Yes!"

Everybody looked at him. Kakharman took a glass of champagne. A silence descended. The bride and groom stood up to hear his blessing.

"My dear friends! I am rejoicing with you on this unforgettable day. Be happy! Never forget, you are children of Sinemorye! May God let us all return to our homeland, return to our sea!"

For that brief moment, they all believed it might happen one day.

The time came for new dishes. Many got up to stretch their legs. The manager of Zaysan Rybprom came over to Kakharman. Kakharman had known Rakhimbek for a long time. They had met frequently in the ministry in Alma-Ata, were of a similar age, and addressed each other as "ty," so Rakhimbek began the conversation without the exchange of courtesies.

"Kakharman, I'll come straight to the point: I want you to be chief engineer."

Rakhimbek was sincere, and Kakharman was touched by such a genuine offer.

"Thank you, Rakhimbek, for thinking of me." Kakharman smiled softly. "But I think you may be an idealist. My candidacy won't even make it to the Regional Committee—it will be blocked right here in the department."

"Are you afraid of Karabai? Is he a brother of the secretary of the Sinemorian Regional Committee?"

"I've never been afraid of anyone. But you're right. They are related; Karabai is his cousin. I don't expect them to be nice to me."

"I'll talk to the first secretary of the Regional Committee. Protazanov is a decisive man. If he meets you, the outcome will be positive. I need decisive, practical people, Kakharman. In those times when we were scared to open our mouths, all the main posts were occupied by sycophants and careerists. But now a different time is coming, and it calls for a different mind-set!"

"What will you do? Explain to Karabai that you're hiring me for the common good?" Kakharman grinned. "No, it won't work. Don't even hope. You'll just get yourself in trouble. I'll go to Zhomart in the kolkhoz as an ordinary fisherman. It'll become clearer then what I should do next."

"I'll talk to them anyway," Rakhimbek began to insist.

"Don't do it. That's my personal request to you." Kakharman put a friendly hand on Rakhimbek's shoulder. "OK?"

By the morning, only Kakharman's fellow countrymen remained in the house. The tables were put away and the rooms tidied up. In accordance with custom, dastarkhans were laid on the floor, and people sat around with their legs folded. The master of the house put alcohol out. Kakharman, who hadn't had a drink all night, addressed his fellow countrymen.

"Maybe it's time to stop drinking? At least for today."

"Indeed," Orazbek agreed. "Let's have green tea instead."

The young people didn't dare object to the older ones, but it was clear from their faces they were disappointed. When Kakharman noticed, he spoke to the host.

"The boys were looking after guests the whole evening and are tired. It'd probably be better to set them a table in another room. Let them enjoy themselves. We won't be in their way then."

The young people brightened up and set a table in another room. Soon the sound of conversation, laughter, music, and the rattle of glasses echoed throughout the house.

Orazbek, who looked well for his sixty-five years, was sitting up straight, looking at his guests. He knew them all. He knew their family trees back to the seventh generation. Unlike the fishermen, who quietly concentrated on the food, Orazbek was chatty and charming. In Karaoi, people thought only Nasyr could outdo him for eloquence. He had a kind and soft character—sometimes even too soft. And anyone would envy his looks. He was tall and handsome, with beautifully carved cheekbones. It so happened that Orazbek was to be the first and last Hero of Socialist Labor in Sinemorye.

In the midfifties, Nasyr was also nominated for the medal, but it didn't come through for some reason. Slavikov used to joke, "Eh, Nasyr, it's me who spoiled your career. If you weren't friends with me, you would've had a star on your chest." When Orazbek returned from Moscow with the golden regalia, Nasyr met him at the station, took him to his house, slaughtered a cow, and invited the whole aul for a *toi*. Nasyr made a sentimental speech, saying that Orazbek's success was a success for all fishermen, his glory the glory of the whole of Sinemorye—now he was responsible not only for himself but for the whole district! Be healthy, Orazbek! May God protect you! Amen!

Later, when dark days came upon Sinemorye, Slavikov, Nasyr, and Kakharman frequently took the golden-auraed Orazbek with them to Moscow and Alma-Ata. Orazbek was the first to recognize that it was going to be impossible to get any sympathy for the dying sea—and the first to leave its shores, ahead of many Russian and German families. When he came to bid farewell to Nasyr, Nasyr wouldn't even look at him. "Dear Nasyr-aga! Before I go, I want to say goodbye to you," he said. But Nasyr interrupted him crossly, saying, "Very well! Have a good journey. Goodbye!" before he turned away.

"Of course, we are all good sons of Sinemorye," Orazbek began pompously.

"All good sons of the sea, you say?" Nasyr burst out. "Who has called you that, you son of a bitch! Why do you, 'good son,' abandon your frail and dying parent? Are you human? Why won't you share the bitter fate of your homeland? You are a traitor, that is what you are! You'll be eating nice food, you'll protect your body, but your soul will be spat on by those contemptuously looking at you as you leave! Get out!"

Orazbek left hurriedly.

And Nasyr stayed, sitting in the same place, not moving, until the evening. He was in a state of shock. Women came to say goodbye and cried, the whole aul was caught up in the predeparture bustle, but Nasyr saw and heard nothing of it. He then went to bed and spent two days lying facing the wall, refusing food.

Kakharman hadn't seen Orazbek since then, and his name stopped being mentioned in publications.

Kakharman was looking at Orazbek with curiosity. He was surprised to see that his hands, once worn and rough, were now smooth and well treated. Orazbek caught his gaze, took his hands off the tablecloth, and began to talk to Kakharman.

"People say if the Almighty decides to knock a man off the righteous path, he first takes his mind."

Orazbek was trying to guess the mood of his listeners. There were no young people in the room, and the elders nodded in agreement. Orazbek continued.

"We had to leave Sinemorye, my dear countrymen. I won't say we have a bad life now, but we don't have peace. We are all slowly getting old, and when a man is old, he thinks about his homeland, his home places. I often have our sea in front of my eyes, my dear countrymen. It is dying, and it is calling me."

"Ya, Allah!" the old women sighed. The old men went quiet.

"Today Kakharman said everything each one of us feels. The sea didn't rely on God. The sea relied on man. And although there's not another creature in the world more ruthless than man, it is in man's power to save the sea. That is what I'm thinking now. I am thinking I could've been one of those men. But I haven't become one. My dear countrymen! I am indebted to our sea. We all are. Let's not forget that. Let us pass this obligation on to our children and grandchildren. Who knows? If not us, then maybe they will be able to repay our debt to the sea. I'm not saying this because I'm more intelligent."

He went silent as he tried to find the right words but got confused because from the corner of his eye, he saw Marziya looking at him disdainfully. She took Orazbek's speech with a pinch of salt.

"You're right there, Orazbek," she said.

Then everybody began to laugh.

"You're talking well."

People were laughing from the heart, without bitterness. And Orazbek smiled, too, making it clear he was not offended by his *zhenge's*[11] joke.

Orazbek looked around at the gathering sadly and then said, "When will we gather again, my dear countrymen, to sit and converse like this and give our souls a rest? I invite everyone to the toi I'll have near Alma-Ata. But I doubt you'll come. You're all busy and have things to do."

"You should not have left Sinemorye, Orazbek," Marziya said. "What example did you show to your fellow countrymen?"

"You're right," Orazbek sighed bitterly. "I doubt people will forgive me now, even if I crawled back to Karaoi."

Soon people began to leave. Marziya turned to Kakharman.

"I'll be waiting for your visit today. Come and have lunch with us and the matchmakers and guests."

Going out into the yard and deeply breathing in the cool morning air, Kakharman began to feel a pleasant dizziness. The sun was already rising. The sky was pale pink. As he passed the dancing young people, he saw the bride and groom sitting on a bench.

Kakharman said to Nurlan, "You must be tired. There's no need to walk me home. I will find my way."

"Kakharman-aga, stay with us," the groom said. Kakharman nodded, and he and Nurlan sat down next to the newlyweds.

"What a beautiful wedding!" Kakharman said. "Tamila, Seikhun: be happy!"

"Thank you, Kakharman-aga," Tamila responded shyly.

Seikhun began to talk excitedly. "You should visit us in Alma-Ata, Kakharman-aga. You can stay with us, see how we live."

"Why aren't you dancing?" Kakharman asked.

"Seikhun is tired," Tamila replied.

Nurlan discreetly nudged Kakharman, and Kakharman realized that he may have said the wrong thing.

Seikhun, noticing Kakharman's discomfort, said calmly, "Kakharman-aga, I lost a leg in Afghanistan. I have a prosthesis. I spent five months in the hospital in Moscow. The doctors struggled to fix the blood circulation. Even when I returned to Zaysan from the hospital, I couldn't walk for a long time. But Tamila and Nurlan got me back on my feet."

"Where did you meet Tamila?" Kakharman asked.

"We've known each other a long time. We were friends in Sinemorye."

"They're childhood sweethearts." Nurlan smiled.

"If it weren't for her"—Seikhun smiled gently at Tamila—"I don't know if I would've survived. I didn't want to live. I came back from Afghanistan changed.

If you only knew how many of our men were killed there! And how many of our wounded made it home, only to die here! I shared a hospital room with fifty others, and only a few of us survived. Only much later did I learn that I was also expected to die, but the doctors didn't tell me that. Can you imagine what it's like for them? They treat the wounded, yet they know that the days are numbered for many of these boys. One morning, I hobbled to the veranda with difficulty to warm up in the sun. Beneath the veranda, they were unloading zinc coffins from a truck. And I realized they were for us. We were doomed. Even though we still lived, our coffins had already been made. I fainted, and for a few days I was delirious, but then Tamila walked into the ward, and I ordered myself, 'No, you won't die. You'll live.'" Seikhun gently hugged his young wife.

"A friend of mine from Alma-Ata just lost his brother in Afghanistan," Kakharman said.

"If you could only see the graveyards of our soldiers along the road from Kabul to Salang[12] and all the way to the border. It's just awful. You can't look without shuddering! Nineteen-year-old boys. Why did they have to die in a foreign land?" Seikhun struggled to suppress his emotions. "Why has it happened? Who will answer?"

"Did you win any honors?"

"Yes, he has two orders of the Red Star and several medals. But he doesn't wear them," Nurlan replied for Seikhun.

"And I won't wear them," Seikhun said stubbornly. "Kakharman-aga, you haven't had a drink all evening. Maybe you can have one with me for all the boys who died in Afghanistan?"

"I will have one drink," Kakharman replied and repeated firmly, "For this cause, I will! Pour it, brother!"

"Seikhun, what plans for the future do you have?" Kakharman asked. Seikhun was drawing on the ground with a stick and hesitated before answering.

"To be honest," he began, looking quickly at Tamila, "I don't want to stay at the reservoir near Alma-Ata. Many of our people are there, but I still feel we are not on our land. When I see our people raising fish in a pond to catch, I feel sorry for them. Of course, for boys it's better to study in Alma-Ata. People are fed and dressed. But I couldn't live there. I just can't get used to it. I want to return to Sinemorye this autumn. I haven't spoken to my father yet, but Tamila and I are in agreement on this." He hugged his wife.

"But what if Father is against it?" the bride asked.

"We will slip over the border. And if we can't slip, we'll fight our way through. Or we'll have to spend winter by the pond." Seikhun laughed mischievously. "Kakharman-aga, you're right. Without your homeland, there's no life and no happiness. I won't be a great fisherman without a leg, but it doesn't matter. I'll be good at something else as long as I am by the sea. I'll enroll in a distance-learning course, and we'll survive somehow. Right, Tamila? If it weren't for this leg!" He banged his fist on his prosthesis in frustration.

Kakharman pulled the boy toward him. He didn't say another word to Seikhun or Tamila, but his feelings were clear even without words.

He arrived in Semipalatinsk during the night. Aitugan was still awake. They embraced tightly by the door.

"You're back . . . fit and well, thank God!"

Kakharman went to have a shower as Aitugan prepared the table. Coming out refreshed and in his favorite casual shirt, he began to feel as if the weight of the two-week trip had finally fallen from his shoulders. The tea was nice, but he praised it so much, it was as if he had never drunk anything more beautiful and aromatic in his entire life. Innocent Aitugan just looked at her husband with eyes full of love and didn't notice the excess. Kakharman, meanwhile, was considering how to tell his wife that he'd agreed to go to Zaysan to work as an ordinary fisherman. Aitugan had never objected to her husband and obediently followed him everywhere, but she couldn't really understand him, and he knew she was getting tired of a life of constant traveling and living out of suitcases. So Kakharman told her first about the trip, about the great man Semeon Arkhipovich, about Marziya, and about the wedding.

Aitugan sighed. "The explosion had its effects here too. The day before yesterday, in the middle of the day, I felt sick. I was sitting in the teachers' room and couldn't get up. My head felt as if it was made of rock, and my legs wouldn't hold me up. When she saw me, one of my colleagues just calmly said that they must be testing again. And, of course, here's the newspaper from yesterday, with an announcement from TASS."

"What can be more terrifying," he thought, "than the fact that in a county as immense as Kazakhia, there is not a single place where the fear of destruction doesn't follow you! In the 1930s, four million people died of starvation. The current catastrophe will destroy everybody! Yes! Yes, by the beginning of the twenty-first century, the Kazakh nation will be exterminated! It will become a crowd of two-headed and three-legged freaks who will crawl along the scorched and ruined land!"

"Aitugan, do you have anything to drink?" asked Kakharman, feeling that something had squeezed his heart again, feeling that if he didn't have a drink now, he would simply die with anguish.

"I do, but is it worth it?" But after looking at her husband, she brought a bottle right away, though she did reproach him. "You have become completely dependent on alcohol lately, Kakharman. That's bad."

"Vodka is the only cure for radiation poisoning," Kakharman joked sullenly. "But it's nothing in comparison to what you and I have been through, Aitugan. So is it worth even talking about this?"

He filled his glass.

"Without you, Aitugan, I am weak and lost. That is what I've realized lately. I want you to always be healthy. That is the only way for us to keep our home and our family. I drink for you!"

"Thank you, Kakharman, for needing me!"

And their little son began to murmur something in his dream, quickly and feverishly.

"The children have missed you. Why didn't you visit Sinemorye on your way? I am so worried about our Berish. Every now and then, I'm frightened for him."

"I didn't want to open old wounds. It would be torture for me."

"Did you know that Kambar-aga has passed away?"

"Yes, Bolat told me. It's no surprise—he had cancer."

Aitugan went quiet, although she also had good news for Kakharman. Yakubovsky had managed to find a two-bedroom apartment for them in a comfortable house near the Kazakh school. The children were thrilled and persuaded their mother not to tell Kakharman yet. They wanted to tell him themselves. And now, remembering about the apartment, Aitugan began to glow with joy. Kakharman, knowing nothing about it, looked at his wife in surprise but decided to leave the conversation about Zaysan till tomorrow.

In the morning, the children rushed into Kakharman's bed with cheerful squeals and, interrupting each other, told him about the new apartment. Kakharman responded awkwardly.

"Dad doesn't seem to be happy at all." Aitugan lifted her head from the pillow and looked at her husband, beginning to guess that Kakharman was hiding something.

After breakfast, the children ran to play outside, and Kakharman was left alone with Aitugan.

"Ivan asked you to visit him as soon as you can," Aitugan recalled. "He said that you'll have to go to the first secretary. I prepared a suit for you. You should get dressed and go there."

"I won't go anywhere." Kakharman's face was shadowed with gloom.

Aitugan was overwhelmed with foreboding. Seeing her husband frown, she knew he had bad news for her.

"You've decided to do something, I know. Tell me honestly."

"I want to leave Semipalatinsk, Aitugan. That is my news. I'll find some work in Zaysan. I've already spoken with the local chairman there."

"What work?"

"I'll be an ordinary fisherman. They promised to get us a place to live by the next summer. For now, we'll live in an apartment. I've already agreed to this with Semeon Arkhipovich."

Aitugan was devastated. A week ago, she couldn't believe their luck that the housing situation was finally resolved—it had been so unexpected. But even more unexpected was the news that they'd lose that apartment before they even got it. Of course, she knew well enough that if Kakharman had decided something, nothing could stop him. If he'd promised in Zaysan he'd be back soon, then that was exactly what he'd do, no matter what. Her whole life, Aitugan lived as if she had no will of her own. In the end, everything happened as Kakharman decided it.

At last, Aitugan said, "Still, you should go to see Yakubovsky. Don't refuse the apartment for now. And we can continue the conversation when you're back. Alright?"

After Kakharman left, Aitugan thought for a long time. Maybe there was still hope. Zaysan is the same as the Caspian. Who will be waiting for them there with an open embrace? Does Kakharman really want to live in the dirty little shacks of the local shipping company? And the climate! Bora winds and burning sun can be hell for a person not used to them. Even if he doesn't think about himself, he should at least for once in his life think about his wife and children!

Aitugan gradually calmed down. She began to think her arguments were so undeniable that everything would end well. They'll stay here. They'll settle and begin to live like human beings.

While Aitugan was arguing with herself, Kakharman made his way to the shipping company offices. Upon arrival, he went to the accounts department and gave a report on his business trip. There was no one waiting to see Yakubovsky, so his secretary nodded toward the door, and Yakubovsky, who was talking on the phone, smiled at Kakharman and gestured for him to sit down.

"Nice to see you, Kakharman! How was your trip? Has Sayat comforted you?"

"Sayat sends his greetings. He's OK."

"Did you know Minister Akatov visited us the other day? I think you know him?"

"Yes, from back when I was at Sinemorye. He was chairman of the Executive Committee there."

"It turned out he had a conversation with our first secretary of the Regional Committee, Bozganov, about you. He was interested in my opinion of you and asked to see your personal records. When he found out you didn't have decent housing, he made an order to the city Executive Committee, and they found an apartment for you right away. It's a good apartment! I can finally look Aitugan in the eyes. She has struggled so much in the shack you live in now. I am so happy for you! My Valusha says, 'As soon as Kakharman is back, invite their whole family to visit.'

"The first secretary wanted to meet you, so I'm going to give him a call and let him know you are here." Yakubovsky picked up the phone.

Bozganov invited them to come to his office before lunch. He was a lean, dark-skinned man. He introduced himself courteously and invited them to sit down.

"Akatov has told me a lot about you, Kakharman Nasyrovich. The same is true of you, Yakubovsky."

Bozganov asked Kakharman about how things were in Caspy.

"What can I tell you?" Kakharman asked. "Do you want to know what I saw or what I heard?"

"Let's be sincere, Kakharman Nasyrovich, as perestroika demands of us. Tell me about both."

"I can't see perestroika yet. I see it only on paper." Kakharman became gloomy when he heard the word. It was used everywhere, and it attracted him, but it also irritated him because at that moment, he had nothing to do with perestroika, just as perestroika had nothing to do with him.

"You're right. The speed of perestroika is unsatisfactory. Perestroika should be coming not so much from above as from below. It's foolish to rely on our bureaucratic apparatus, which will never start perestroika by itself."

"I can see that myself. I used to spend a lot of time in Moscow. I told everyone about the disastrous situation in our land and tried to get some sympathy at the very least. I've been in every office at the State Planning Committee. I've seen some very charming women there! And I saw well-fed, well-groomed men! They come at nine and leave at six, and all they do for the whole day is drink tea. When people come to see them, they say to come back tomorrow, the day after tomorrow, in a month's time, or even better, in a year. But what they mean is: never come back, just disappear or die. And what specialists they have there! They'd struggle to even find Kazakhstan on a map, no matter how much I talk to them about it!"

Kakharman then told him everything he had seen at the Caspian and elsewhere during his fifteen-day trip. When the conversation came to the wedding and Afghanistan, Bozganov stood up abruptly and began to pace about the office. Kakharman guessed that he, too, had lost someone in the war, and regretted bringing it up.

They sat in silence for a few long seconds before the secretary spoke.

"Last year, my brother was killed in Afghanistan. He was a military man. Recently at the Central Committee, I inquired how many Kazakhs have died in this war. But no one knows—no one even keeps count."

"Count?" Kakharman exclaimed bitterly. "What count are you talking about? Who needs to count in a country where another number has become a refugee!"

"And if you look," Bozganov continued, "you will see that we have reached extreme levels of poverty. The same applies in the culture of the mind! It would be right to erect a monument to the victims of Afghanistan, but just look at how this kind of initiative is treated. It took ten years to get the monument to Mukhtar Auezov[13] erected! In Semipalatinsk, this Mecca of Kazakh culture, everything is falling apart. It was very different when I was young. I remember beautiful little merchants' houses of red brick. They had wonderfully ornamented facades. I remember the ancient fountains. I remember the gardens. But what now? They have been replaced by vile and lifeless concrete boxes. The streets have boring names. There's nothing to look at, nothing to rest your gaze on."

Their meeting was coming to an end. When they were at the door, Bozganov spoke to Kakharman in a serious tone.

"Entirely by accident, I discovered that my predecessor was collecting compromising evidence against you. I closed the file. You should know that he was a clever and ambitious man, so I don't think he was doing it on his own initiative. I would guess that someone above was putting pressure on him to do it. But I closed out the file, so you can work now without worrying about anything, Kakharman Nasyrovich. Let's stay in touch."

When they left the building of the Regional Committee, Kakharman addressed Yakubovsky.

"Did you know that compromising evidence was being collected on me?"

"I did. But I didn't want to upset you. He was collecting compromising evidence on me too."

Kakharman spread his arms as he sat in the back seat of the car. "What a scumbag!"

"Let's end this conversation." Yakubovsky slammed the door, and they moved on. "I'll give you a lift home. After lunch, go to city hall and find out what documents are needed to get an order for the apartment. I'll pick you up in the evening as we agreed."

Kakharman nodded absentmindedly. The thought that someone was collecting compromising evidence against him would not leave his head. It was certainly at the behest of the seaside "little czar," Kakharman was certain.

He received the order for the apartment the same day. He had time before the evening, so Kakharman decided to show it to his wife and children. Aitugan couldn't hold back the tears when she stepped through the front door. The boys, not paying any attention to their parents, frantically ran around the apartment. They ran to the balcony, slammed the doors to the bathroom and the toilet, and jumped joyously in the entrance hall. Then they rushed to turn hot water on, and Aitugan rushed after them, worrying that the children might burn themselves. Kakharman, looking at his happy family, began to doubt that he could go to Zaysan.

"We will move tomorrow!" Aitugan proclaimed decisively, wiping her tears.

"To where? To Zaysan?" Kakharman joked feebly.

"No. Here," Aitugan replied softly but decisively and looked at her husband with love.

When the Irtysh was covered by ice and the vessels were brought in for maintenance, the old angst got hold of Kakharman. Even his summertime work didn't seem so grinding compared to the winter refurbishment of decrepit barges. But at the moment there was no other work for him.

He began to drink more again despite Aitugan's reproaches—only drinking would drive away the anguish. It was a respite, though. For the long-term effects of alcohol had so damaged his nervous system that he suffered many sleepless nights. Long winter nights would often find him sitting silently in the kitchen, chain-smoking and staring at the wall through bleary eyes. Sleep might only come toward morning. He slept restlessly, tossing and murmuring—and sometimes sobbing like a child.

One of these nights, he dreamed of Ata-Balyk.

How long since he was in the sea? A thousand years maybe. That is why he's so happy to plunge into its deep waves once more. He has fresh, pink lungs now, and he can breathe freely and deeply. He has lithe, strong arms and slender hips. And it takes so little effort to glide through the waves now that the burden of the years no longer weighs on his shoulders!

Swimming past, Ata-Balyk recognizes him and turns toward him. It swims next to him, gently lodging its head under his elbow.

"Where are you coming from, Ata-Balyk?" Kakharman asks.

"Don't you know?" The fish looks distrustfully at the son of Nasyr the fisherman.

"No."

"From the millions of spawning eggs left in the Darya, I raised the fry, and now I am leading them to Sinemorye."

"Have a good journey, dear Ata-Balyk!"

"May your words become truth, man!"

And although its way to the sea is a long one, Ata-Balyk looks strong. Kakharman looks back. An endless river of fry streams out behind Ata-Balyk. Suddenly the great fish turns sharply away from Kakharman. It has caught sight of a huge catfish and its greedy, gaping maw to gulp in masses of the helpless fry. Ata-Balyk dashes toward it and thwacks it with a swish of its mighty tail. The blow flips the catfish right over. Recovering, it rushes at Ata-Balyk, only to suffer another blow.

The hungry catfish retreats toward the shore, where it hunts for the old woman with a goat on the shore. A dog that never leaves the old woman's side and a goat that barks desperately in warning as it sees the catfish. The goat leads its kids away from the water. The catfish watches for a long time but realizes this time it won't be lucky. It swims right to the shore, lays its large head on the sand, and sighs as the goat and kids walk away. Kyzbala is wandering along the shore, oblivious. The catfish knew her of old, and Kyzbala knew the catfish. She had seen it swallow a rider and his horse whole.

Whenever she sees the catfish, Kyzbala always has the same thought, "What terrible power is in this fish? Not a net can catch it. I first saw it when I came to Karaoi as a young bride. That young bride long since became a decrepit old woman, but the catfish lives as before."

Of course she isn't thinking so clearly, because Kyzbala is crazy—but perhaps the thought flits through her mind like a passing cloud. And the catfish in turn maybe thinks, "Why is this woman still alive? What's the joy? What's the point of her life? Man is an odd creature. He keeps hoping and believing until the last days of his life. But the sea answers his hopes less and less each year. And that is how it should be. Man showed no mercy to the sea. So, you, Kyzbala, should not expect the sea's mercy."

So the catfish surely thinks, remembering that it had once swallowed Otkeldy's son, Kaiyrgali, and her son, Daulet. It seems Kyzbala guesses this. She meets the catfish's eyes with her own piercing gaze. Sometimes the catfish would swim up very close to Kyzbala as she sat at the water's edge, looking for her son. But every time it went to snap its great jaws over her, she turned so sharply toward it and gave it such a merciless stare that it beat a hurried retreat.

But it is trying its luck again now, hoping to catch her unawares, when she turns and waves her arms angrily, yelling, "Get away from here! Get out of my sight, old fool!"

The catfish sighs and heads into the sea. It soon comes across a shoal of fry, but then, remembering the beating from Ata-Balyk from which its sides still sting, the catfish skirts warily around the fry. The shoal stream on, unperturbed. Ata-Balyk slips from under Kakharman's arm, looks back, and says, "Goodbye, Kakharman! See you next time!"

And with that, it disappears.

Kakharman stays in the sea. He suddenly feels that familiar loneliness that descends on him in times of deep, hopeless depression. This chill fills his body like an avalanche with catastrophic speed—and he looks back and understands what caused this loneliness and horror. The brown catfish is looming behind him. It opens its jaws, and Kakharman is being pulled into its mouth. Nothing can save him now, but he thrusts his arms forward and . . . wakes up to the sound of shattering glass.

He was covered in a cold, sticky sweat. He got up and went to the bathroom, wet a towel, and rubbed himself all over. He had made his decision: he must move to Zaysan, and he must do it without delay!

The next day, he went to Yakubovsky.

Kakharman began to talk without preamble.

"Do you still have my notice? Take it out and sign it. I can't spend another day here! Every night, I dream about the sea, I dream about fish . . ."

"You should drink less, Kakharman," Yakubovsky tried to joke. "Otherwise, the devil himself can visit you in a dream."

"Will you take it out, or should I write a new one?"

"Just wait a moment. Don't rush me. Give me a chance to think. It's so sudden."

"Vanya, you always understood me. Let's not play games!"

"Alright. You can go. I won't try to hold you back, I know it's pointless. But first pay a visit to the first secretary. He is looking for a new job for you. You must explain everything to him yourself, since I don't feel comfortable doing it."

Kakharman put his hand on Yakubovsky's.

"There's no need for it. He'll understand. He is a clever man."

"To hell with you!" Yakubovsky waved his hand.

And the next day, Kakharman left Semipalatinsk.

The snow was already deep when Kakharman's car slid into town, and the lake was thick with ice. Kakharman got out of the car and walked to Semeon Arkhipovich's house with a small suitcase in his right hand. Semeon Arkhipovich did not recognize him in his winter coat and hat. Semeon Arkhipovich had been hammering on the anvil. He looked briefly at the newcomer and went straight back to work.

"Come in. Take your coat off."

Semeon Arkhipovich's voice was warm and friendly.

"You may be a guest, but I must ask you for a small favor. Fill the kettle with water and put it on the stove. I'll just finish work, then we'll have tea."

Kakharman dropped his small suitcase in a corner, hung up his fur coat, put the kettle on the stove, and added more coal.

"Go into the other room," the master of the house urged. "Relax."

Kakharman went through, into the second room. He had noticed a good library in the flat on his first visit but hadn't had time to look through the books. Looking through them now, he found a battered collection of all ninety volumes of Leo Tolstoy's complete works. On a table by the window, there was a bookmarked copy of Dostoevsky's *A Writer's Diary*.[14] He began to read from the bookmarked page, paying attention to the places underlined in pencil.

Take our railways for example. Understand our space and our poverty. Compare our capital with the capital of other great powers and think: how much would our railway network, which we need as a great power, cost us? And note: their networks were established long ago and over a long time. But we must do it in a rush: and their distances are small but ours are like Pacific Ocean . . .

It's not so much to do with a sum of money but the entirety of the nation. There'll be no end, if you itemize all our needs and all our squalor. And at last, take education—namely science—and see how far we have to go to catch up with others. In my humble opinion, we must spend each year on education at least as much as we spend on the military if we want to catch up with any great power. If we consider how much time we've already lost, and how little money we have, then, in the end, it will have to be a shove, not a normal process—a mighty shake up, not a gentle learning . . .

But let's assume that not only teachers will be created with money but scientists too: and then what? You can't make people. What's the point in being a scientist if he doesn't understand that essence? For example, he'll learn about pedagogy and will be teaching pedagogy well from a cathedral, but it won't make him a pedagogue. People, people are most important. People are worth more than money . . .

The nation began to drink—first with joy and then with habit. Was anything better than sleaze shown to them? Were they entertained, were they taught anything? Now in some places there are pothouses not for hundreds of people but only for tens of people: even fewer—for low tens of people. So how are they paid? They are paid in immorality, theft, concealment, usury, robbery, destruction of a family with the shame of the nation—that is what they paid with!

"How forcibly the thoughts and feelings of Dostoevsky are echoed today!" Kakharman thought.

Mothers drink, children drink, the churches are emptying, fathers steal: a bronze hand of Ivan Susanin was sawn off and taken to a pot house: and it was welcomed in the pothouse! Just ask medics what kind of generation can be born from such drunks?

If in the next ten-fifteen years the inclination of the nation toward drunkenness does not decrease but stays steady, then won't the dream come true? . . . The people had to save themselves before! They will find a protecting force in themselves they were always able to find: they will find in themselves the beginnings of redemption—beginnings which our intelligentsia just can't find in them.

They won't want the pothouse anymore then: they'll want labor and order, they'll want honor, not pothouse!

Recently I suddenly came to a thought that here, in Russia, in the intellectual classes, there cannot be a man who wouldn't lie. That is because here even completely honest people can lie. I am convinced that in other nations, in the majority of other nations, only scoundrels lie: they lie for the sake of practical gains, in other words they lie with criminal intentions.

But in our nation even honorable people can lie and for very honorable purposes. Many of our people lie out of hospitality. What Russian lying hints at, is the fact that we all are ashamed of ourselves . . . It was Herzen who said of Russians abroad that they can't behave in public: they talk loudly when everybody else is silent, and can't say even a single word properly and naturally, when it's time to talk.

The kettle began to boil. Semeon Arkhipovich laid the hammer aside and stood up. Kakharman came in from the other room. Semeon Arkhipovich was genuinely surprised.

"Is it you, Kakharman?" They hugged. "I'm sorry. I took you for someone else. I have so many visitors."

Kakharman began putting presents on the table.

"That's for you . . . that as well . . . I have presents for everybody: for Balziya, for Duisen, and for Auntie Marziya."

He soon began to feel good. During tea, he relaxed and thought again that Semeon Arkhipovich was the only person that he could be completely frank and open with. Life was not completely hopeless when people like Semeon Arkhipovich still existed. He was always attracted to people with difficult and complicated fates. Kakharman could learn something from them, kindness and humanity in particular. He was very interested in the life of this Russian man who made his home in a Kazakh family and who was both a father and a brother to Kazakh children.

Semeon Arkhipovich got ready to go to Balziya's.

"She should be back from school. I'll ask her to make dinner for us."

Kakharman carefully touched him on the elbow.

"Maybe we shouldn't trouble them? There's enough food here."

Semeon Arkhipovich considered for a moment.

"What if they get offended?"

"They are not small children who get offended because of such nonsense."

Nevertheless, Semeon went out and came back very quickly.

"Balziya is home. We can have a drink while we wait for dinner to be ready."

He filled their glasses. Soon the drink's pleasant warmth was spreading through Kakharman's body. It was getting dark. Semeon turned on the electric lights.

"Are you tired? Maybe you want to lie down before dinner?"

"Better not. When will you tell me the story about how you ended up here?"

"It's a long story," Semeon Arkhipovich began. "What a life our generation had, Kakharman! How mightily the millstones of life ground us. Sometimes I close my eyes and wonder what our life was for. I already told you the story's beginning. My father was arrested, then my mother soon after, and I was sent to a boarding school for the children of enemies of the people. After that, I searched long for my mother but couldn't find her. I went to the Far East as a sailor . . ." Semeon Arkhipovich knitted his thick ginger eyebrows. "I thought I'd forget about my mother when I left my homeland. But a man cannot forget his mother. I could never stop thinking about her, so I always felt lonely. And that loneliness became a torture for me. Whenever I was back on the shore, I would drink heavily in order to forget myself.

"I can't say I quite got to the DTs, but I was often visited by the big and small devils. Do you remember the devil that visited Ivan in *Brothers Karamazov*? These devils became my friends. I would return to my fishing barrack three sheets to the wind, sprawl on the straw on the floor, and let my head fill with colorful dreams. The devils would jump into my head in different colors: sometimes red, sometimes green, sometimes in other colors. The green ones were the most talkative and the slickest at seduction. The strangest and vilest I called Azgyr.[15] Oh, what a siren he was! I only needed to shout, 'Azgyr!' and he would appear right away, saying, 'What is it you want?' He would bow with a sly little smirk wandering over his lips. 'I'm bored, but I've nothing to say,' I'd reply. 'But I know what to say, my friend. I'd like to ask: Don't you think you drink too much? You drink and don't eat.' 'Have a look in my pockets. They are empty. I have money only for vodka.' 'Oh, my dear, if you go on drinking without eating, you'll wreck yourself and will die.' 'Leave it, Azgyr. Death won't take me no matter what I do. Death doesn't need me. I realized that long ago.'

"'Fool! It's us who want to give you death.' 'You? Why would you do that?' 'Don't you understand? We are not interested in seducing weak and worthless people, but if we can mislead people like you, our life gets extended by a century. Do you understand, Semeon Arkhipovich? In days like these, God is in mourning. He closes the windows and doors and weeps all day long, Semeon Arkhipovich. He weeps because there is no joy in the world—the world he created with his own hands! We devils were the first to betray him, and then humans followed our example. When we seduce a man, when we turn him into an animal, God bites his elbows in despair.' And I thought, What can I do, a small and sinful man? What can I do if even God himself is engulfed in sadness? 'You are right,' Azgyr said, reading my thoughts. 'And so you know the answer: drink, love women, lure them into darkness, let yourself be seduced, and never think about the next day!' 'Go away! Go away!' I would shout to him when conversation went this way. 'Why are you so rude to me?' he would ask, hurt. 'I will let you in on a secret: conscience is a contagious illness. Many devils become stricken by conscience by stealing it from people. Sometimes you send one of them on a sinful mission—but he refuses, saying his conscience will not permit him.'

"'Azgyr!' I would interrupt him. 'Show me at least one devil with a conscience. Or are you lying to me? I have never come across one.' 'Hee! They are in the madhouses. The best doctors are draining the conscience out of them. Soon they will become normal devils, their hearts will blacken again, and they will return to their work. That red brother of mine who visits you sometimes is one of those treated in the hospital. They are colored red to avoid confusion.' 'He wasn't completely cured.' 'Why?' 'He always encourages me to start a revolution. What a weirdo! Seventy years have passed since our revolution. Everything is screwed down so firmly that no one will be able to start another revolution ever again.' 'It will be that red devil who ruins you. Because you are afraid of him.' 'No!' I would rage. 'Maybe you have seduced man, but you will never be able to beat God, you jackals.' And then I'd throw a boot or stool at him.

"But I have other addictions too. I joined a library and started to read hungrily. I would not stop reading, even out at sea. I'd take books with me. Our captain Maksimov also liked books, and we grew close. He never avoided me when I was drinking too much, and he never scolded me. I think he felt sorry for me. When on shore leave, he often invited me to visit him. He had an amazing wife, a very intelligent woman. Russian women like that are impossible to find nowadays."

He went silent as he gathered his thoughts.

"Russians . . . don't judge Russian people who lost their roots too harshly, Kakharman. It's not always their fault. And not all are bad. I made my life among Kazakhs, but I am Russian to the marrow of my bones. But sometimes it is useful to see your nation from the outside. And I'll tell you this about Russia: it desperately needs a merciless critique. Tomorrow may be too late. Sometimes it seems that Russia has led the Russian man astray deliberately by telling him he is part of a great nation, by exalting him too highly. You know, I'm sixty-two years old, but I feel less and less pleasure each time I hear the words 'Russian nation,' or 'Russian people.' Yes, the Russian nation gave birth to great men, to geniuses like Pushkin, Tolstoy, Dostoevsky, but what does it look like now? I think I read in Chaadayev[16] the words 'all nations are like other nations, but only Russians need to terrify the world.' And even Pushkin, the greatest exponent of our Russian spirit, often exclaimed, 'Why the hell was I born in Russia!' Who can give the nation these words of caution nowadays? How much longer will we be stuck in this swaggering complacency? The whole world points its finger at us and smiles slyly: look, the king has no clothes!"

Semeon Arkhipovich went to the other room and came back with an open book.

"Now listen to what Abai said about his nation." Semeon Arkhipovich put on his glasses and read. "'The ignorance inherited from their fathers, absorbed with their mother's milk, makes its way through the meat and reaches the bones to kill the humanity in them. Between themselves, my fellow countrymen have grimaces and antics, whispers and ambiguous hints, but nothing interesting comes to their minds. They try to think, but they have no time to focus their thoughts. You talk to them but they can't even listen with attention. Their eyes roll and their thoughts scatter. How can you live like this? How can we carry on?'

"Abai was great because he just spoke the brutal truth! Today, we Russians don't like quoting anything like that from our classics. We like to beat ourselves on the chest and repeat, 'We are great! We are great!' No other nation says anything like that about themselves! God! But with all our morbid narcissism, Pushkin's 'we are lazy and disinterested' says it all!

"In the sixties, I came to Zaysan for the first time, searching for my mother, and I was astonished when I met this one old man. He was head of the shepherding family Dauletkerei. He played the dombra wonderfully and knew so many folk legends—I could've listened to him forever. What a deep knowledge of native history, and what a great understanding of his roots! And he was fluent in Arabic, too—just a plain chaban! But look at us Russians. Arabic? Do any of the Russian leaders in the Republic even know Kazakh? It is simply boorish to live among the Kazakh people and not know their language! Back in the fifties, people were embarrassed by it. There were many Russians and Germans in Kazakhstan who knew Kazakh well—including my mother, who often exchanged letters with Mukhtar Auezov."

Kakharman was listening to the story with interest.

"Maksimov's wife was Anfisa Mikhailovna," Semeon Arkhipovich continued. "After a while, she began to nag me. 'It's not good to live as a bachelor, Semeon. There's a pretty girl at the house next door, but you give her zero attention. I can introduce you, if you'd like. And if you like each other, maybe you could marry?' I was shy, of course. And an idealist when it came to love—probably like all teachers' children, at least back then.

"And here was Anfisa Mikhailovna suggesting I just marry a girl from next door without suffering for my love! How far from my ideals! I could fall in love with only one thing back then: books!

"All the same, the next time I visited Anfisa Mikhailovna, I saw a pretty girl there. It was her, of course. She was the librarian Masha. And Anfisa Mikhailovna whispered to me, 'What do you think about Masha?' 'She's a nice girl,' I replied. 'She's in love with you, you know. You should value that, Semeon.'

"Soon Anfisa Mikhailovna began to arrange the wedding. I didn't feel comfortable about it because I had no money. But she reassured me, saying we could celebrate the wedding at their place and that she would organize the table. All I needed to take care of were the wedding clothes. 'Just borrow money from someone,' she said. 'We would've given you money ourselves if we could.'

"I had a good friend, Volodya Anchishkin, a Khakas,"[17] he said, "and I decided to borrow some money from him. He was a kind old man. He had had a hard life, but it didn't make him bitter or angry. Only later, after I served my ten years in the camps, did I find out that he wasn't a Khakas at all but a pure Kazakh by the name of Kudaibergen. In '24, he was accused of banditry and counterrevolutionary activity and was arrested, but he escaped and went into hiding in Siberia and ended up in the Far East.

"The next day, I went to Kudaibergen. The old people greeted me kindly, sat me at the table, and fed me for a long time. Finally, I made my request—or rather, I babbled it. Kudaibergen asked me how much I needed, and I said one hundred and fifty rubles. 'But will that be enough?' he asked, unconvinced. 'It'll be enough,' I said, waving my hand.

"'No, Semeon,' Kudaibergen insisted. 'A man has a wedding once in his life. You shouldn't skimp. You're a good man, and you should have a good wedding. Take three hundred but with one request. Let the money be a present to you from us.'

"'No. I'll only borrow!' I resisted. I was proud. Then the old man decided to change tack. 'OK,' he said, 'you can borrow one half, but the other half is a present! And you will return your debt when you are rich.' I agreed. Masha and I got married, and we had a daughter. It seemed that my restlessness had gone, and a new phase of life had begun. But Masha turned out to be a shortsighted, often frivolous woman and had a great weakness for jewelry and money. God will forgive her. And our child was never neglected. Masha loved our daughter and looked after her well.

"When I came back from a long voyage in 1951, I found a letter. It turned out my mother was alive, and there was her address—in a camp, of course.

"I sat down at once to write a letter back to her. I filled the whole notebook. I wrote everything I'd been through. My little daughter woke up in the night and asked, 'Dad, what are you writing?' I kissed her and said, 'Sweetheart, your grandmother is alive. Do you understand? She's alive! Soon she will be freed from the camp, and we will all live together. Do you even know your grandmother's name? Do you? Her name is Nadezhda too. I gave you my mother's name, Nadenka!'

"But I never had a chance to mail that letter. Early the next morning, I was taken away. I was not allowed to speak to my wife, even though I only wanted to ask her to mail my letter. The NKVD had quite a bit of information on me. They knew my mother was in a camp and that I was the son of an enemy of the people. But I was taken in because I once stupidly said to someone, 'We won the war with blood—we pelted the fascists with corpses.' I really could only have said something like that after a lot to drink. I admitted it. The investigator squinted. 'Trofimov, the war has been won by comrade Stalin. Stalin! Why all this gibberish? You yourself would go into an attack and shout: For Stalin! Have you forgotten, scumbag?' 'I did go charge in an attack,' I replied. 'And we all shouted, "For Stalin!" I am a Russian soldier. A Russian soldier fighting for Stalin and dying for the motherland.' 'That's right!' The investigator grabbed me by the collar. 'You're singing beautiful songs!' I tried to push his hand away and received a heavy punch to my face. Blood splashed, and when I saw the blood, I went a bit crazy. I jumped up and slapped the investigator with the edge of my hand, and he fell. Of course! I was one of Stalin's soldiers. I could kill a man with a single blow—a fist, knife, pistol's handle, or a rifle butt. I am not so proud of that now.

"The inspector came to his senses and ran from the room. I knew he'd be back and that he wouldn't be alone.

"I was right. Two of them jumped on me. I hurled them away. They didn't get up. I turned toward the inspector, preparing to kill him, but more men rushed into the room. Some ran behind me and shoved me to the floor and pummeled me viciously. I don't know how long they were hitting me for—a minute? An hour? A day? I woke up on the stone floor. My whole body was one giant bruise. I lost consciousness again. When I regained consciousness, I could tell that my ribs were broken, and my right leg was broken too. It wasn't until the next day that I finally managed to lift my head and look around. I was lying in a small isolation ward. My lips were matted with dried blood. The door opened with a screech, and the investigator and the warden entered. 'Water!' I began to wheeze. 'Give me water, animals.' 'Maybe you'd prefer a cold beer?' The investigator hit me, and I lost consciousness again. I came around when the warden splashed water on my face. 'So, Trofimov, who won the war?' the investigator swaggered. 'Did the corpses win it? Why so quiet now? I am not letting you out of this place alive!'

"In the end, I was given ten years. I was allowed one meeting with Masha. I asked about the letter. 'I mailed it, mailed it.' She nodded, crying. 'May our daughter be happy!' I said to her. After that day, I never saw her again. She didn't wait for me. She got remarried and moved to Novosibirsk. I saw my daughter twice in Alma-Ata. I send her money every month. Nadiya doesn't refuse the money, but she doesn't want to see me."

"Why not?" Kakharman was surprised.

"How could it be any other way? Her position doesn't permit her: her father-in-law is in the higher echelons of the party, people say. If you open any celebratory newspaper, he's there, standing on the platform."

"In Alma-Ata?"

"Yes . . . So . . . What happened next? Ah, yes! My education wasn't great. I finished only seventh grade. I served my ten years and went to Sverdlovsk to enroll in the technical school. The director of the school was impressed by my knowledge. 'Son,' he said, 'you can go right to the final year!' So I finished technical school in a single year. You're surprised, Kakharman, but there's nothing odd about it. If you only knew what kind of men I served my sentence with! People from the Academy of Sciences and the Writers' Union—the whole of educated society ends up in the camps! I wasn't too lazy to listen to them. My mind soaked up their knowledge like a sponge. Everything I learned there has stayed with me since—that's what's amazing! In mathematics and physics, for example, I was trained by Professor Konrad. 'Young man,' he would encourage me, 'all of this will be useful when you're free. You should get more education.'

He himself was fluent in twelve languages. People like that had to suffer humiliation from idiot wardens. People like that were taken in to be mauled by the prison lice!

"I returned to Vladivostok and discovered that my Masha had got married and left the city and that Kudaibergen had returned to his homeland. He said that his soul was longing for his home aul and couldn't bear to be away anymore, that his old bones must be buried in his native land.

"With nothing to keep me in Vladivostok, I went to Zaysan to find my mother. It took me twenty days to get there! In Zaysan, the kind people explained to me that they had a Russian woman who lived with chaban Dauletkerei. I asked them to point the way across the dzhailyau, and I went on foot. I walked for two days across the steppe. I walked and exulted! The rough steppe soared vast around me. It was green and ringing! Freedom roared out afar in every direction! There was no end to my happiness, just as there was no end to this steppe.

"And the Altai sky! Nothing can be compared to the Altai sky! And the Altai mountains!

"When I climbed up yet another green hill, I fell on the grass, lay on my back, and spread my arms freely. A white-winged Altai *berkut*[18] flew far above me. Gazing up into the blue sky, I began to think, 'Semeon, this year, you'll be thirty-eight. Where is your life? How have you spent it? What have you achieved?

"'You were born in 1924.

"'In 1937, your father was pronounced an enemy of the people and executed. But you learned that only in the seventies.

"'In 1938, one late night, when your mother was working on her pupils' homework, men walked in and snatched her away. She was the wife of an enemy of the people and so an enemy of the people herself. She ended up in the Karaganda mines[19] for nine years! You were sent to a boarding school with many children whose parents were declared enemies of the people.

"'In 1940, you began to earn your own bread in Penza.

"'In 1941, you volunteered for the army. Did you get to the front line right away? No. You spent eight months in a paratroop school near Moscow.

"'In 1946, you came back from the war. Traveled across the whole Russia searching for your mother. Didn't find her. Went to the Far East. Lived there until 1952. Almost killed yourself with drink. Met Masha, married, and daughter Nadiya was born.

"'In 1952, you were taken.

"'Now it is 1962. You're free. Now you're lying on the Altai grass and look-ing at the sky. It's simple math: you've been free only six years. The rest are your years of suffering, years of restlessness. Isn't it too much, isn't it?'

"After a little rest, I went on walking. I was told that by the evening, I should see the Dauletkerei's flock. And that is what happened. As the sun came down, I saw a flock on one of the hills. I couldn't see the chaban or his dogs yet. But I pushed aside the juniper bushes, and there, there I saw a tree, and a little old woman under it. I walked closer and recognized my mother immediately. How much she'd changed! In my imagination, she was completely different—just like she was when I saw her last, when I was still a boy and she was a young woman with long, girlish plaits.

"I kept looking at the tiny old woman. I devoured her, as if to absorb even the tiniest details. And in those minutes, I realized who had protected me from death. It was her! She had prayed to God to keep me alive. It was she, who, when I was within a hair's breadth of death in solitary confinement, walked in, washed the blood from my face, and gave me water. It was she who whispered to me, 'Don't die, dear son. Let me see you alive at least once more! Don't resist these animals. They have power. They can easily kill you. I protected you from the fascists' bullets on the front line, but I am powerless before these butchers. Endure the humiliation again—it's nothing new for you—but do not resist. Let me please see you alive!'

"That is what she told me then. But having grown old before her time with the sorrow of separation, she was sitting against a tree, reading a book. 'Mama . . .' I barely squeezed her name from my lips. The book fell from her hands. A dog rushed toward me, began sniffing me, and then barked. Mother turned toward me and straightened her small, round glasses. 'Mama!' My legs gave way, and I fell on my knees. 'Son!' my mother whispered and ran toward me.

"That was the scene Dauletkerei saw when he came out of the *yurta*, attracted by the dog's barking. He was a masculine man of a middle height with a long beard. I will never forget his kindness for all these years he had looked after my mother!

"The next day, he informed all local auls that Nadezhda's son had been found, and he organized a proper toi. Many people gathered and everybody hugged me, but nobody asked where I'd been all this time.

"Dauletkerei was sitting in the shade of a yurta on thick duvets. It was clear that he ruled the feast. And it was him who had told everyone not to trouble me with too many questions. My mother's face flushed, and with sadness I noticed in her eyes a cold light that later used to make me shudder, a light that stayed with her for the rest of her life.

"I stroked her hand. 'Now everything will be fine. Now we'll be together.' 'Yes. Yes,' she replied. 'May God give us strength, and may God let me die before you.' 'What are you saying, Mama! We will live long—our life together only just began! We will go to Penza, to our native Nikolsk!' 'Alright, dear son,' she sighed. 'It would be nice to have at least a glimpse at our homeland.'

"Dauletkerei had eight children, five sons and three daughters. Three of the sons didn't return from the war. Two made it all the way to Berlin. The eldest, Bokai, died in Magadan[20] camp. Tokai would've been forty-two years old. In accordance with Kazakh customs, he married the widow of his older brother. It was a good custom, not to abandon the widow and not to give her to someone else's family. Nurzhamal had two children with Bokai and then ten with Tokai! I was amazed. She was a beauty, just over forty years old and with twelve children! The older ones were just beginning school, and the younger ones were still breastfed. It was in this vast family that chaban Dauletkerei lived. And a place was found for me, too—the Kazakhs accepted me warmly.

"I spent the whole summer with Dauletkerei, but I couldn't bring myself to ask him about his son Bokai. But Dauletkerei's grandson Sailau, who now works as a director of a sovkhoz not far from here, told me about his father's arrest.

"'In 1949, your mother fell seriously ill, Uncle Semeon. Nine years of camps had a terrible effect on her health. After the mines, she came here to Altai completely exhausted. And if it wasn't for Granddad, to whom she was sent as an assistant, she would've died. During the spring, two KGB officers came to our winter hut. Auntie Nadiya, as soon as she was free, had started to send letters to different departments, searching for her husband and for you, Uncle Semeon. It looked as if someone really didn't like that. They came down and shouted at her violently and then began to grab her and twist her arms. But there was no one home apart from us children, since all the grown-ups were in the *koshara*.[21] Auntie Nadiya was screaming with pain and crying. But then Dad came back. "What are you doing?" he yelled at them. "She's ill—leave her alone!" "Get lost!" was their response. Dad went out silently. I can't remember now what they were asking Auntie Nadiya, and I can't remember her answers. She must've given the wrong answers. They stripped her and took her outside, barefoot and half-naked. It was still freezing, the snow only just beginning to melt. They forced her to run around the yurta while they smoked. We were looking out the window. Little Balken suddenly became hysterical. And we all began to cry too. Grandfather and Grandmother and Uncle Tokai were running toward the house from the koshara. They saw the agents, and Granddad began saying something to one of them. The agent grabbed Granddad's beard and pulled him to the ground. I rushed to Granddad; I just jumped out of the house, ran to him, and hugged him. Auntie Nadiya yelled, pleadingly, "Don't touch them. They haven't done anything! Ata! Go home, I beg you!" Then the one who was holding my grand-dad by the beard shouted at her, "Keep running, bitch! Move your legs faster!" Then Dad came up to him. "Why are you doing this to an innocent woman who is ill?" "You think she's innocent? Did you know that she's an enemy of the people?" the lanky, acned guy shouted. "Run faster, I said!" And he fired his gun in the air, then turned to Dad. "Are you protecting this wretch? We will add you to the list as an enemy of the people. Do you understand, idiot?" "Me, an enemy?" My father was appalled. "Do you know my brother and I went the whole way to Berlin! And where were you, jackal?" Auntie Nadiya fell down and didn't get up again. Mom ran to her, but one of the two KGB bastards kicked her in the chest. Mom gasped and fell to the ground. Her eyes were wide open, but she couldn't breathe. Dad was so mad, he knocked the bastard who kicked her down. Then Dad picked up the revolver and hit the second agent on the head. The agents ran to their horses. Dad raced after them. Granddad shouted, "Stop, Son!" but my father heard nothing. In the morning, the two returned and, of course, they weren't alone. They took away my dad, and we never saw him again. We don't even know where he's buried.'

"That was the story Sailau told me."

Semeon Arkhipovich sipped cold tea. "He found it hard to tell this story, unbearably hard," Kakharman thought. And as if guessing his thoughts, Semeon Arkhipovich spoke.

"Yes, Kakharman, how many horrors people lived through in those years! And it's still unclear whether we have drunk everything from the cup or not. What awaits us tomorrow? I don't have much faith in people today. They remind me of animals. Back in those years, the bastards acted more openly, but nowadays their fangs are hidden behind a mask of decency.

"My mother's illness got worse. Dauletkerei's wife stayed by her side as if she was her own daughter. Mama told me later how she had suffered. But she suffered not so much because of the illness but because the innocent Bokai suffered because of her. She told me she begged God to return Bokai. 'God, who am I? It is better to take my soul but return Bokai. He has elderly parents, a wife, and children. I am not guilty before you, God, so answer my plea and return him!' But God didn't return Bokai. The agents proclaimed him an enemy of the people, sent him to the camps, and left him to rot there. And she lived with that heavy stone on her neck for the rest of her life!

"By that time, Marziya had moved to Zaysan. All of Zaysan was filled with rumors of her healing skills. Dauletkerei brought her to us, and it was she who put Mama back on her feet. She recommended kumys for the tuberculosis. Then Marziya took all the children in the house to the mountains to gather the herbs she needed. In the next few days, she kept saying to my mother, when checking her pulse, 'Nadiya, you have too much heaviness on your heart. You must let it go. Think only about getting better, and then my herbs will help you.' Marziya made Mama drink a concoction of these finely powdered herbs three times a day. After a week, she began to feel better, and the illness began to let her go.

"One day, Marziya cast beans[22] and said, 'It won't be easy for you to recover, Nadiya—but you will, and you will have a long life. I can hear the voice of a young berkut, and you will have great joy. But it won't be soon.' 'May God see your words come true,' Mama replied. 'A young eagle—so my dear son is alive?' 'He is alive, Nadenka. He is. Beneath him is blue water, in front of him a long path, but it is a path that is clear and leads to you.' And Marziya gathered the beans. 'And is my husband alive? Tell me, Marziya!' 'I can't hide it,' Marziya said sadly. 'He's not among the living.' 'My heart felt that!' Mama acknowledged. 'But you must get stronger,' Marziya comforted her. 'You must recover, if you want to see your son. Don't forget; you must survive to meet him.'

"And Mama did recover. Soon, she was going outside to sit in the fresh air and sunshine. Sailau and Balken became very fond of her. She read many tales to them in both Russian and Kazakh. Balken could already read and write in Russian by the time she was three! Mama also taught them to play chess. One of Tokai's sons is now a chess master and lives in Alma-Ata. And Balken is a women's regional champion.

"They were told of Bokai's death. Tokai went to Siberia to collect his brother's body. But of course, he didn't get the body, and the camp officers refused to even talk to him.

"After two years, I was fluent in Kazakh, thanks to Tokai. I not only spoke but could sing Kazakh songs too. I didn't have a great voice, so I preferred singing when I was alone.

"Dauletkerei was an expert blacksmith and taught me his trade. When it was Tokai's turn to tend the flock, I would stay at home and help Dauletkerei. He had a small smithy on the outskirts of the aul, and we spent a lot of time there. Dauletkerei's father was a famous local *zerger*—a master in gold and silver.

"I had a good life at Dauletkerei's, but I was still drawn to the city, to people, to a busy life. I suggested to Mama that we move to a city. I could find factory work that would support both of us. Mama was recovered by then but didn't want to leave Dauletkerei. She was rather attached to the old man. And she always had to drink kumys for her health—and where would we get kumys in Russia?

"Just how deeply she had put her roots down in Kazakh land I found out only later, after we went to Penza, our homeland. Virtually nothing was left of our village; just three old women were living there. Baba Marfa had died long ago. Mama and I looked sadly at the boarded-up houses and the yards overgrown with weeds. It was the same across the Penza district. My heart ached for our Russia. It was even tougher on my mother. She kept sobbing and sighing heavily. We went to Nikolsk. It was a small town, but it was once famous across Russia for its glass. We couldn't find her parents' grave, so we went to the local glass museum. Mama cheered up there and stood for a long time by each exhibit. She knew the history of each object. I wasn't surprised, because her father had been a famous glassmaker. There was a curious exhibit titled 'A Glass with a Fly.' Mama told me the story.

"'Old prince Bakhmetiev, the owner of the glassworks, was sad that his only son had taken to drink. The prince was afraid that after his death, the business would fall apart and that his son would spend all his inheritance on drink. So he gathered his master glassmakers and shared his worries with them. No one dared to give advice to the prince, but one suggested molding a drinking glass with the image of a fly. The genius of this object was that if you fill it with liquid, the fly moves its legs as if alive, making its holder not want to drink its contents. Unfortunately, the young prince didn't quit drinking, and Bakhmetiev left the glassworks to his nephew Obolensky.'

"As she told me these stories in the museum, she visibly changed before my eyes—her face grew happy, and even her wrinkles seemed to disappear. That is how someone's soul can soar when they speak of the beautiful past!

"But I wasn't happy for long. As soon as we emerged from the museum, we slammed back into our troubled life. Like coming out of a wonderful feast into the plague. And it was a plague. The streets of Nikolsk swarmed with drunks, even though it was a workday. There were drunks by the shops, on the streets, in the gutters, and on benches. I thought even the town itself was drunk—it was gray and disheveled, its houses carelessly staggering down the slope at odd angles. And the railway station was packed with brazen, reckless drunks. Horrible to look at! Mama and I waited for the bus to Penza as these drunks reeled back and forth, clutching beautiful crystal vases, sparkling salad dishes, and even little chandeliers! Wonderful glasswork given away for a bottle of vodka! There were Caucasians buying it all—rushing to their cars to deposit their loot, then coming back to fill up their arms once again. One of the men walked up to my mother, saying, 'Mother, just a fiver! Take it. You won't regret it!' 'I am ashamed to buy someone else's honor, especially so cheaply,' Mother said coldly and turned away. She was very upset. 'This is not mass produced; I made this by hand! And I can sell my work for any price I like.' He pushed the vase to me. 'I don't want to give it to these mountain rabble. I only want it to go to someone who shares my soul—I will only sell to a Russian. The Caucasus is packed with our crystal! We sell for a fiver, but there, it's sold for five hundred. They are buying us, you can say, with their scraps.' He swayed heavily. 'And I need a drink. Do you understand, brother? Take it. You won't regret it.'

"Indeed, that vase did look unusual. It had light, clear lines and an extraordinarily vivid pattern that created a mood right away. I gave the man a tenner and put the vase in my bag. 'Wait here,' the man said and disappeared. He returned quickly with a long box. In the box, there was an exquisite female figure in crystal. I was amazed how familiar the hand of the craftsman seemed—a familiarity that I couldn't understand yet it enriched my soul. The man could see that I liked the figure. 'Give me another fiver and take it.' I gave him the fiver he asked for and an additional three rubles. The extra rubles surprised him, and he almost threw them in my face, saying sharply, 'I am a master of my work, not a beggar!'

"Mama came back from the trip to our homeland very depressed. 'There's no more Russia!' she repeated. 'Where is it heading, God?' she kept saying. We had this conversation. 'Go by yourself, Semushka. I will stay with Dauletkerei. It's hard for the old man without me, and I struggle without him. You shouldn't have taken me to Nikolsk and Penza. I finally understand that I'm afraid of Russia, even though I feel sorry for it. But you're still young. You should go. Maybe you'll get married, and I will not be in the way of your life.'

"I went to Ust-Kamenogorsk, and at the airport, I began to think about where I should go. I decided to go to Ural, far away from my homeland. I chose Sverdlovsk, the biggest town in Ural. I worked in a factory, finished technical school, and did indeed get married. She was a good woman, jolly and energetic. Tonya—Antonina—that was her name. She was divorced, and I loved her two daughters like they were my own. Now they are both married—one lives in Alma-Ata, and the other one went to Karaganda.

"A man is an odd creature, Kakharman. I should've just gone on living in Sverdlovsk. Everything was going well there! But no. I began to think about Zaysan. I began to worry about my mama. It was as if I had abandoned her. Tonya guessed my turmoil, and I told her what was on my mind. It was decided that I would take time off from work to visit my mother. I began to praise Altai to Tonya and suggested maybe we could go together rather than me going by myself. And this is what she said. 'With you, Semeon, I can go anywhere. Maybe even for good—why not? Liuda is about to finish school. She can enroll in the technical college. We'll leave her the apartment and go.' 'Are you serious?' I asked. I never thought someone could love me that much. 'Of course!' she replied, laughing, and kissed me. 'What would I do without you in this life?'

"I went ahead to Zaysan. When I got there, I found Mama had gone to live in an apartment in Ust-Kamenogorsk. Dauletkerei was very weak, but he came to the table organized to mark my arrival in Zaysan. Sailau and Balken, who had grown up and enrolled in the university, were living in Ust-Kamenogorsk with Mama. 'Who gave her the apartment?' I asked, surprised. 'What sort of miracle is that?' 'Miracles do happen sometimes,' Dauletkerei said. He smiled mysteriously and told me this story.

"Last winter, they had been visited by the first secretary of the Regional Committee, Protazanov. He met Mama and asked how she had ended up there. Mother told him the story of her life. 'My father was a master glassblower,' she told him. 'In the small town of Nikolsk, there was a glassworks, once famous across Russia.' 'Why do you use the word "was"?' Protazanov asked, surprised, 'It still exists.' 'Indeed, it just exists,' Mama replied. 'Not so long ago, my son took me there. But everything is in ruins: the people and their morals. There are no old-school Communists.' 'What's the difference between the old and the new?' Protazanov asked, probably not without an ulterior motive. 'They were pure. Mud didn't stick to them. That is why they were executed or sent to the camps. My husband was a chairman of the kolkhoz. He was shot in 1937. And so my whole life, I have lived with the title of the wife of an enemy of the people.'

"Protazanov learned a great deal about her life. He was completely won over by the great courage with which she had born the calamities of her life. But most of all, he was amazed at her mind. 'I had nothing else left in life,' Mama replied, 'but to read books.' She smiled wryly. 'Everything was forbidden in this life but reading.' When Protazanov was leaving, he asked if she had any requests for him. 'I feel guilty before you, Nadezhda Pavlovna. I would really like to do something good for you; you deserve it.' Mama replied, 'What do I need? I am already old and ill; my life is coming to an end. I've been living with Dauletkerei's family for a long time. I became a daughter to him, a sister to Tokai, and a grandmother to his children. I owe my life to these people. Dauletkerei has grazed cattle since he was young. His children died during the war, and one son, Bokai, died in a camp. Tokai carries his work on. During the war, he was awarded an order of the Red Star, but during the thirty years of his honest life as a chaban, he wasn't even acknowledged with a piece of paper. These are deserving people! These are people who need to be noticed!' Protazanov said thoughtfully, 'The problems of today are difficult, that's for sure, and to think about tomorrow is harder. I was appointed here only recently. We will sort things out in industry, first, and then we'll look into farming.'

"As he said goodbye, Protazanov spoke to Mama again. 'Still, Nadezhda Pavlovna, I see something troubles your heart. Tell me what it is. Who knows? Maybe I'll be able to help somehow?' 'I wouldn't want to trouble you,' Mama said. 'Nonsense! What sort of Communist would I be if I won't listen to people's troubles?' So Mama decided to tell Protazanov her request. 'I would like to thank these people by giving their children a good education. But I don't know how can it be done without moving into a town—at least to Ust-Kamenogorsk? If I am to ask a favor of you, it will not be for myself but for the children of these lovely people, to whom I owe my life.' 'I understand you, Nadezhda Pavlovna!' Protazanov smiled. 'Write an application right now. I will take it with me and will be in touch shortly.'

"He kept his word. My mother was given a three-bedroom apartment in Ust-Kamenogorsk, and she moved there with Balken and Sailau.

"I headed to the district center to go to Ust-Kamenogorsk to see Mama at once. Dauletkerei gave me a pacer to ride, and that thrilled me! I was rushing across the wide steppe rejoicing! This is where I should live! Why on earth did I go into town?

"Mama could see far and didn't try to keep me against my will. She knew that sooner or later, I would choose between the town and the steppe. Soon the lake appeared. Zaysan! My heart quivered. And I realized that if I'm drawn to water, I should stay in Zaysan. I could be a mechanic, build a house, bring Tokai's children with me, bring them up, and give them an education. Why not? I reached Mama and asked her advice. My decision excited her. She was very happy. It was decided! The next spring, I moved there and began to build the large house I dreamed about. From the beginning, Dauletkerei and Tokai's children helped me. We erected it in just three months! My wife and daughters came. We organized a great toi. Dauletkerei kissed me on my forehead like a father. 'You have golden hands, Semeon! Your home is one of the best ones in Zaysan! May this house be filled with happiness and children. May Allah help you. Amen!'

"Antonina also liked it here—the clear Altai air, the unspoiled nature—who could not? There was only one thing she couldn't get used to at first, and that was the fact that I spoke Kazakh. 'Maybe you're a Kazakh yourself, Sema?' she would ask doubtfully, and I would joke, 'Whichever you prefer.' She was also accepted into Dauletkerei's family. Mama liked her too. In those years, there were many Russians in Zaysan, and Antonina wasn't bored. She was happy to be friends with Kazakhs as well. Then the troubles began on the Chinese border. I look now and think in the past, Kazakhs were called nomads, but now we Russians are the nomads. No other nation abandons their fathers' graves as easily as we do!"

"But where is your Antonina now, Semeon Arkhipovich?" Kakharman asked quietly.

He pulled a cigarette from his pack and tapped it on the table.

"Brother, Kakharman . . . I buried all my dearest ones at almost the same time: Dauletkerei, Mama, and Antonina. They all died of cancer in the last three years. I see you're not drinking. Have a drink for the peace of their souls. They were good people, and it's hard for me without them . . . Dinner should be ready now. Balziya will be waiting."

They walked out of the house. An icy, stinging wind was blowing.

"Don't be in a rush to get a job," Semeon Arkhipovich said. "We can go to Tokai's winter hut tomorrow. You need some time alone. You need positive emotions. And we can do a good job for him cleaning kosharas! Tokai will be pleased!"

"I've never cut *kizyak*[23] before. I'm ready!"

But the next day, a strong wind blew up. It wasn't safe to travel, and they had to delay their trip. So Kakharman had time to think things through. His fellow countrymen in Zaysan would not like it if he became an ordinary fisherman. Kakharman understood that. They wanted him to be a local leader. They wanted to feel his care and involvement, so they could feel better themselves. But they'd no idea how tired Kakharman was, how tired he was of being a so-called leader. He'd been defeated so many times. He no longer had faith in fairness. What was the point of fighting if there was no truth?

On one of the days of the blizzard, Marziya visited Semeon Arkhipovich. Semeon Arkhipovich was working metal, and Kakharman was reading a book. Marziya sat down.

"Kakharman-zhan, I come to you on business. People want you to be one of their leaders. Don't listen too much! I understand them, but I understand you too. Life has battered you a lot, and to lead for you now is like rubbing salt on open wounds. Do you want to clear your doubting soul? Then do what your heart tells you. And your heart is tired. It needs rest."

Kakharman hugged Marziya in an outburst of emotion.

"You guessed all my thoughts so well, Marziya-apa! Thank you, *apatai*!" He began to feel better at once.

"I came to invite you and Semeon for dinner. We can talk more then."

"Our Marziya is a person of a rare sensitivity," Semeon noted thoughtfully after she left.

BOOK FOUR

Dear God, don't let me lose my mind.[1]

—Alexander Pushkin, nineteenth century

God is what you have in your soul.

—Leo Tolstoy to his daughter on his deathbed, 1910

Don't let me go through birth pains

Yet not give birth, mourn but not weep;

Think but not lament;

Travel but never arrive.

—Narekatzi,[2] *tenth century*

XI

In autumn, the cold came especially rapidly on the coast. And Nasyr's camel, which Karaoi relied on to bring drinking water, fell ill and died. Nothing else could be done but to use Yesen's gawky, dumb calf, which would bolt from the harness like a devil from frankincense. On a few trips, the calf would smash the cart to pieces, and old Zhanyl would return home without water, sobbing. Musa stepped in. The calf became compliant as soon as it felt his firm hand, so Musa became the water carrier.

It took Nasyr a long time to get over Akbalak's death. He was taken to the regional hospital, but even after treatment, he remained so depleted that he merely lay by the stove, groaned, read last year's newspapers, and browsed his well-worn Quran. But even the Quran failed to heal his soul! The more he read its yellowing pages, the more lost he felt. How could he go on living? What could he do? The book gave him no answers, so he'd put it away carefully in a canvas bag and go out to sit in the yard.

Nasyr lay almost prostrate in the regional hospital for two months. His daughter, seeing her father's despair, wanted to send a telegram to Kakharman, but Nasyr objected. "Don't trouble him. He has enough worries already." Nasyr considered his illness a trifle next to the spiritual turmoil of his son.

Toward the middle of November, when the first sharp frost hit the coast, when the piercing sand winds blasted from the steppe, the fishermen returned from Balkhash, and it became much jollier in Karaoi.

The wives and children were so happy to have the fishermen back. The fishermen had a fortnight's rest before going out to cut the reeds. In January, when the lakes and ponds are under ice, they brave the chill to go ice fishing right through until March. Finally, in the spring, their summer migration across Kazakhstan begins, and they leave their homes behind again.

On the day after their return to Karaoi, the fishermen took Musa to visit Nasyr. They were all on their way to Shumgen to commemorate Akbalak.

Nasyr sent them off with kind words. "You are doing a good deed, dzhigits. It's a shame I can't go with you. I'm still so unwell."

It was decided that when they came back from Shumgen in the evening, they would come to Nasyr's for dinner.

Nasyr told Korlan at once, "Get two or three young women to help you prepare a good meal. The fishermen will come with their wives and children."

"There'll be so many people!" Korlan began to panic.

"It's nothing compared to the old times. How many are there left in Karaoi?" Nasyr reassured her.

"That's true," Korlan agreed. "And it will be good for everyone to get together. The fishermen are away half of the year."

Nasyr began to read the Quran like he used to.

Behold! In the creation of the heavens and the earth; in the alternation of the night and the day; in the sailing of the ships through the ocean for the profit of mankind; in the rain which Allah sends down from the skies, and the life which He gives therewith to an earth that is dead; in the beasts of all kinds that He scatters through the earth; in the change of the winds, and the clouds which they trail like their slaves between the sky and the earth; (Here) indeed are signs for a people that are wise.

O ye people! Eat what is on earth, that is lawful and good; and do not follow the footsteps of the evil one, for he is to you an avowed enemy.

For he leads you to what is evil and shameful, and tells ye that ye should say of Allah ye have no knowledge.

The parable of those who reject Faith is as if one were to shout like a goat-herd to things that listen to nothing but calls and cries: Deaf, dumb, and blind, they are void of wisdom.

And they fear the Day when ye shall be brought back to Allah. Then shall every soul be paid what it earned, and none shall be dealt with unjustly.

To Allah belongeth all that is in the heavens and on earth.[1] Nasyr put the book away and, as so often now, sank into thought, repeating in a whisper the last words: "*belongeth all that is in the heavens and on earth.*"

The evening came, and Korlan and the young women sat exhausted at one of the food-laden tables. The fishermen's wives and children began to gather at Nasyr's house and were dressed in their best. Soon the fishermen themselves returned from Shumgen and wearily took their seats next to their wives. Kyzbala came in, too, and sat next to Korlan. Nasyr looked at the guests. Times were when the village on the seashore had been a large and bustling community. Now the entire population could fit into the three small rooms of Nasyr's house.

Nasyr began to address his guests.

"My dear countrymen! Allah has been merciful to us again. Our fishermen have returned to Karaoi alive and well. Amen!" Nasyr was quiet for a moment. "It's fine to say amen, kind people, but it looks to me that it has nothing to do with God. God has been lonely and powerless for a long time now, and he probably doesn't care whether we are alive. He abandoned us and turned away from the sea. That is how things are, my dear fellow countrymen. But let's not complain. Though poor, we have laid out a meal for you. So, tonight, let's be thankful for what we have and ask Allah to make sure things don't get worse. Amen!"

"The same is happening to Lake Balkhash," Kambar added. "All the fish have gone. I'd be happy to blow up that Kapchagay Reservoir before it completely ruins the lake! But it looks as if our leaders just don't get it. When will we all come to our senses, eh? And, who'll bring us back to our senses if Allah leaves us too?"

"Spit in their eyes, and it'll be divine dew!" Yesen said bitterly.

Nasyr decided to redirect the conversation. "Let's raise our spirits with a song. What do you say, friends?"

It was as if Nasyr had been personally addressing Kyzbala, who was sitting impassively next to Korlan, because at once she began to sing with a strong and clear voice.

The fire you lit in my heart died out,
Light of my soul, I will never love anyone again!

The fishermen were amazed. Then they remembered that when Kyzbala was young, everyone used to invite her to weddings for her beautiful voice.

Nasyr grinned, looking at Korlan and Zhanyl. "Why are you not joining in? You also used to sing nicely."

"My God, we have forgotten the words!" Korlan clasped her hands.

"We forgot everything!" Zhanyl was upset. "And do you remember Kyzbala-kelin? No one could pass her by without stopping to look at her—she was so beautiful!"

Korlan sighed. But she began to sing along:

If you're a river, then I'm your gray duck—
Float on your water and drink.
Shili is a river with reeds,
Think about us too, my dear . . .

But her voice was quivery in comparison to Kyzbala, who, finishing the song, then began another, her eyes slightly closed, her body rocking slightly from side to side.

Recall Zhilal, in the summer dawn,
When you saw me go.
"Don't spare the enemy," you said.
"Show no mercy or pity toward him."

While listening to Kyzbala, Nasyr thought of her husband, Nurdaulet. He could sing well, too, and the singing at a feast would so often be started by Kyzbala and Nurdaulet together.

When both riverbanks
Are overgrown by thick forest,
The dzhigit dreams of one thing:
For his beloved to come out to him . . .

Nurdaulet would begin the song with his rich, soft voice—a voice even Akbalak admired. Akbalak used to lament that if Nurdaulet had stayed alive, his children would've been fine singers. Heroes die first, as the saying goes. And that is exactly how it happened in that far-off, stupid war. Nurdaulet died the death of the brave. And not just him. Many sons of Sinemorye didn't come back from that war.

And now Kyzbala was singing after so many years . . . It was as if she were with Nurdaulet again and answering his voice:

From my childhood, I grew with you, my beloved,
So why am I parted from you now?

Looking at the crazy woman, Nasyr understood that she found no special meaning in the words, but she led the melody so finely, it was as if it flowed from her heart and soul. Then she stopped singing as unexpectedly as she began. She threw a very old soldier's jacket that she had kept since the war over her shoulders and went out. As usual, the goat followed her. Nasyr followed, hoping to stop her so that she could spend more time with the guests, but she didn't respond to Nasyr's voice and walked off to wait again on the shore for her lost Daulet. Who knows if she actually remembered him? Who knows if she would've recognized him now if he walked out of the sea and approached her?

With Kyzbala gone, the tension vanished from the gathering. Kambar looked at Yesen enthusiastically.

"Come on. Let's have Nartai's[2] song, Yesen! Let's shake things up!"

"You're on!" Yesen picked up his dombra and began to play Nartai's *tolgau.*[3] But a watchful eye would have seen that Kambar's liveliness was not entirely sincere. In fact, he was very worried. He had lost a great deal of weight during the summer and knew that illness had descended on him and that he was coming to the end of his life. Back in Balkhash, he'd already thought about going to a hospital but kept delaying. Today, when he coughed up blood, he knew he was beyond help. He tried to stay positive and energetic—and could just about manage.

After midnight, people began to leave. Eventually, only Musa and Kambar were left with Nasyr. And only then Kambar frankly admitted his illness to his two friends.

"I won't keep it from you, aqsaqals. I have decided to move my family to Shumgen. I am not like others. Don't think that. I have a serious reason for this. And the local government says that everyone in Karaoi will be relocated sooner or later."

Seeing Nasyr looking harshly at him, Kambar continued hurriedly.

"Now I'll tell you the most important thing, my dear friends, what I meant when I said I had a serious personal reason." He lowered his voice and murmured, "While in Balkhash, I realized I am seriously ill. I haven't said anything to anyone, but my team noticed and took me to see a doctor in Alma-Ata. The doctors said I have a tumor in my stomach. You know it's become common here. If I survive another half a year, that'd be good, but everything might end even sooner. So I decided to move my family to Shumgen while I'm alive."

A terrible silence descended when Kambar finished speaking. Nasyr was devastated. He lowered his head to hide his tears. Musa fell silent.

The weather outside intensified. The winds were growing angrier. Pitiless Karabas winds. With the moans of the dying sea filling Nasyr's head, they seemed like the evil harbingers of new troubles.

As the wind howled on, Nasyr plunged into thought again. Not about Kambar but Kambar's father. He'd first met him in 1939, when he was called up to join the army. The secretary of the District Committee stepped forward to talk to the recruits. He was only a little older than they were but spoke eloquently, finding telling comparisons and allusions that made it sound as if there was no more honorable or dutiful thing these young boys could ever do than join the army. That speaker was Zhabar, Kambar's father. Zhabar was the first true Communist Nasyr had seen and remained an example to him for the rest of his life. But he was executed in 1940 as an enemy of the people.

Kambar suffered all the hardships and privations that fell on those branded a member of the family of an enemy of the people. Kambar's mother, Guldari, spent many years in the camps near Karaganda and only managed to meet her son in the 1950s. She was the first to come back to Karaoi from the camps, very thin and much aged. She never told anyone what she had been through; she just sighed heavily and coughed when someone asked. There was gossip that she was nearly shot, then kept in a cell on death row for three days. When she came out, they said, her hair was snow-white.

Nasyr would often visit Guldari for a friendly word and ask if she needed any help. He was already the director of a kolkhoz then. She never asked for anything but thanked him. "A low bow to you, Nasyr, for your kindness to me. My soul was scorched. I saw so much violence and humiliation. But don't worry about me. I'm alive and well, so all is good. But it would've been nice to find my children, Kambar and Altynshash. Are they alive? Ah, to see them once more."

Soon after Guldari's return, Nasyr gathered people for a toi. Not a big one, he said, very modest but still a toi. He invited Slavikov, who was working in his laboratory on Akespe Island. At the toi, the professor talked with Guldari. They spoke for a long time, and the professor named many people, hoping some would be familiar to her. Then he said, "Your Russian is very good. Did you learn to speak so well in the camps?"

"We are Orenburg Kazakhs. Before going to the camp, I spent three years in Moscow with my husband, when he was studying there." And these two people, who had both suffered, became friends.

Slavikov often visited Guldari, and they always had something to talk about. And then her son, Kambar, was found. He was living in Siberia as a fisherman. But he brought the sad news that his sister, Altynshash, was dead. And Guldari at last gave freedom to her tears.

Shaken by her sobs, Slavikov left the house, followed by Nasyr and Kambar. "There's nothing more bitter," the professor muttered quietly, "than the sorrow of a mother." He looked at Kambar. "Look after her. You need to leave Siberia and move here."

"Yes," Kambar replied. "I decided it as soon as I got here."

The professor laid his hand on Kambar's shoulder. "I understand, Kambar. Life has denied you many things as well. But now we have some hope. It's time to start living! No matter what!"

"I didn't have a chance to get an education. I began to work right after the orphanage. We children of the enemies were given the hardest work. People looked at us with hatred. There was nowhere to run away, and no point in running—you would only be shot. It happened a few times. In the orphanage crosses were cut into our hair," explained Kambar. "That's how local people could catch us if we escaped. In Vladivostok, I met a girl who was in the orphanage my sister was being taken to by chance. It was she who told me my sister was shot on the way there. But please don't tell this part of the story to my mother. It would be better if she doesn't know."

Of course, neither Nasyr nor Slavikov said anything to Guldari. And Nasyr liked Kambar right away. He lived up to Nasyr's expectations and proved hard-working and decisive. The girl in Vladivostok that Kambar had mentioned soon came to Karaoi, and they got married. In Karaoi, people began to call her Bakyt, which meant "happiness." And she did indeed bring a lot of happiness to Guldari's home. Everyone in Karaoi rejoiced to see such joy and peace in the family. When old Guldari was dying, she said these touching words to Bakyt: "You have become a daughter to me. You have replaced my Altynshash for me. May God give you happiness, my dear daughter. It's easy for me to die because I know I leave Kambar in your kind hands."

Remembering this, Nasyr thought about Allah's lack of mercy toward good people, people like Kambar, as he sat by himself late into the night. If God exists—if, as people believe, he gives his blessing to those who stay on the righteous path in this life, no matter what hardships they endure—why is he so merciless to his servants?

Nasyr barely noticed how his inner conversation about God had become a prayer: "Great Allah! I don't have the courage to doubt your existence, but when will you show yourself with a good deed? Don't take Kambar to join you. Prolong his days on earth. Your faithful servant Nasyr asks you. Haven't I deserved your trust? I pray to you five times a day. There's not a minute in my life when I don't say your name. So listen to my words and give a helping hand to Kambar. Have mercy on him, oh Great Creator! Who else can I ask for help, if not you."

"Oh, Nasyr, you still haven't come to bed!" Korlan said, getting up. "Who are you praying about so earnestly? Tell me."

It was already growing light outside, and the wind had calmed a little, but a dull and dusty gray pall still hung over the morning.

Korlan went out to get water. It was time to put the kettle on.

"You should lie down and get some sleep."

"I'll feed the cattle first and then lie down."

Nasyr dressed slowly, went out, and took hay to the barn, muttering, "It's only hay by name! How can it be a food if it is packed with salt? It's poison!"[4] He poured oats into a bag, hung it from the neck of the gray mare, and patted her on the shoulder. After the death of the old camel, Nasyr needed less food for his farm yet he was still short. That was true even though the cattle had stopped producing offspring ever since the salty winds started bowling in. Nasyr couldn't decide if he was sad for the loss of the calves or comforted that they at least wouldn't die of starvation. And is it really time to worry about cattle when people are dying?

Nasyr lingered, thinking, by the mare and stroking her withers absentmindedly.

"Why are you sighing? I find it so hard without the camel. Now I only have you, so listen to the old man and keep nodding to everything else he mutters. Nod that you understand. I always believed you could understand. The camel was no fool; he listened to me, too, and understood."

The mare interrupted Nasyr, urgently pressing her head in his hand, asking for more oats.

"Do you think I would've kept any from you? I'd be happy to give you more, but I don't have any. But here's hay . . . No, you can't be deceived; it smells of salt, and that is why you turn your muzzle away. Oh well. I'll feed it to the sheep. And the goats will be fine eating it."

"You just listen what our old woman demands. She said you should be slaughtered before you're taken away by that wild stallion who had his eye on you. But I ask her, how will I live without you? The camel died, and now they're slaughtering mares. But I have decided that I won't let anyone get you."

Korlan was waiting for him by the samovar, and breakfast was on the table. "He should go to sleep," she thought as she looked at her tired husband. "His eyes are red from insomnia."

As if guessing her thoughts, Nasyr, without eating anything, lay down and covered himself with two duvets. He was feeling feverish. "Maybe I'm getting ill?" Nasyr thought. "Ya, Allah," he murmured, then turned on his side and dropped off to sleep so quickly, he had no chance to regret that today, for the first time in many days, he had missed the morning prayer.

He woke up after midday as he heard the murmur of men's voices in the kitchen. It was Musa, Igor, and Bolat—though it was Musa doing all the talking and the young scientists just added comments from time to time. When they saw Nasyr emerge, they got up to greet him.

"Such dear guests have visited me!" Nasyr rejoiced. "So where are you heading to?"

"Our season is coming to an end, Nasyr-aga," Igor replied. "We're preparing to leave. I'll go to Moscow and Bolat, to Alma-Ata. We came to say goodbye."

"That's kind of you, Ikor. It's good you and Bolat still remember the old people."

Igor took a heavy envelope from his pocket.

"Here's a letter for you, Nasyr-aga."

"Who from?"

"From my father. He requests that you personally give this envelope to Kunaev. My father already phoned him, and Kunaev promised to receive you."

"Could I help you, Nasyr-aga?" Bolat looked at Nasyr and waited for his answer.

"Should I get ready to go with you?"

"The sooner Kunaev reads this letter, the better it will be for the matter involved."

Nasyr picked up the envelope.

"When do I need to go to Alma-Ata? I am ready to go now! Woman, put together some clean clothes for me." He looked at Korlan with touching severity.

"Oh, Nasyr," Korlan began to protest. "Why are you going so late in the day? Let's all have dinner instead. Then tomorrow you can go."

Nasyr realized that his fervor was out of place and laughed.

"I normally don't put off things until tomorrow, and this letter has given me wings! Your father writes so well, Igor, so well! That is how a clever man should talk. Matvei, will no one listen to you when you say our sea is dying? How deaf must people be not to hear you? How blind? If our sea died quickly and only we died with it, it wouldn't be so bad. But no! It's been dying many years, and its slow death tortures our souls. And the salt spreading on the wind will kill everything far around! Ah!!" Nasyr clutched his head in despair, then waved his hand. "I'm fed up with it! I'm fed up with talking about the same thing over and over again!"

When Korlan found a good moment, she whispered to Bolat, "I'm scared to let him go. He's only just recovered from his illness. I'm worried he might cause you problems on the way."

"When we're in Alma-Ata, I'll take him to the doctor," Bolat reassured her. "Nasyr-aga, what do you think about visiting a good hospital?"

"Don't hold him up in Alma-Ata." Korlan was seriously scared. "What will I do here all by myself? The New Year is almost here."

"I'm fine visiting doctors, but I won't swallow their pills. I recently had a letter from Beknazar's brother. He's promised to bring Sakbolat, their local healer. He's got a clear head, and people say he's got golden hands. I'll wait for him. I trust in herbs. We've been using healers and their medicines all our lives. Without them, I would've been dead a long time or walking through Karaoi with Kyzbala." He grinned and then looked at Korlan tenderly. "Don't worry. I won't be long. I know it won't be easy for you to look after the cattle by yourself."

But they couldn't leave the next day. The wind strengthened overnight and by morning had turned into a storm. The aul was cloaked once more in filthy gray darkness. They were forced to wait in Karaoi four days for better weather, holed up in Nasyr's house. As they talked—and they had ample time for talk—Igor and Bolat admitted that all the signs that accompany a dying sea were all too visible. They also explained in great detail what the laboratory was for, even though it was painful for Nasyr to hear. It wasn't the first time Nasyr had heard about the laboratory, but his face still darkened, and he looked ashen when he heard what they had to tell him.

By the time the storm eased up on the fourth day, Karaoi was almost out of drinking water. Yesen harnessed his camel and headed toward the well, then began to go from house to house with flasks of water.

"You are the only true man we have left," Nasyr encouraged him when he appeared by the door. "Don't forget it."

"My mother will always remind me if I forget." Yesen wiped the white dust off his forehead. "She forces me out of the house. Man, man! I'm thinking about making another trip just in case."

"Are you going by yourself?" Bolat asked.

"There's no one else. I don't want to bother our fishermen. They need to rest—they've been away from their families for half a year and have missed their wives." He smiled. "And I, being single now, am far too busy to be bored."

"We are also single." Igor rolled along with joke. "Bolat, shall we help him? We'll be a team of bachelors."

Yesen scratched the back of his head. "That's not quite right. You're guests after all. You should stay. And come visit me in the evening. Let Korlan-apa take some rest. She's probably tired from cooking for four people."

"What sort of guests are we?" Igor protested. "We are one of you."

"OK. Let's go, then," Yesen agreed. "It'll be more fun with three of us."

By the morning, the storm was completely gone. Nasyr woke because it was unusually quiet and found Korlan already up. He got dressed and went out into the yard. The sun was rising. The breeze seemed as if it had just taken a break after rounding up the clouds and was now sending its fresh breath up into the deep blue. All Karaoi was buried almost up to the chimneys with snow and sand. Nasyr's good mood departed abruptly. "It's a warning," he thought gloomily. "The sea will die. It will happen very soon, maybe in the next couple of years! And these low houses will stay buried beneath the sand forever."

He walked behind the house, relieved himself, washed up, and approached Korlan, who was sitting on a bench, wrapped in a warm shawl with her eyes shut. Nasyr sat next to her, and Korlan opened her eyes.

"I dreamed of Kakharman. I have a bad feeling."

"It's not easy for him in a foreign land. He is proud, ambitious; he never got used to bowing to others."

"Nasyr, maybe we should leave everything and move to our son?"

"What are you saying, old woman?"

"I just can't do it anymore. Whenever I see him in my dreams, there are dark clouds over him. I am scared of this cloud. I wake up right away and then can't fall asleep again."

Nasyr stayed silent for a moment, then replied flatly, "No, I won't go anywhere. I will die here. I decided it long ago."

Korlan closed her eyes again and stayed silent as if she hadn't heard Nasyr's words. Kakharman appeared again in her vision, and Korlan's heart tightened when she thought of his sad fate. Nasyr stayed with her a little longer, then went into the house to put the kettle on. As they sat down for breakfast, a Volga pulled up outside the house. Inside was Chairman of the District Executive Committee Zharasbai and Musa.

"Hello, Father and Mother!" Zharasbai hugged Nasyr and Korlan, looking warmly into their eyes. "How are you doing here? I missed you a lot." He had been addressing Nasyr and Korlan as "Father" and "Mother" for a long time, for Kakharman and Zharasbai had spent all their childhood years together.

Old Korlan spread her arms wide for Zharasbai and kissed him on the forehead.

"My dear ones, may God give you health."

Zharasbai sat between the old people. Nasyr put his hand on his shoulder.

"We are fine. And how are you? How's your family? You're probably so busy, you never see them!"

"I am very busy. We were about to start visiting auls, but the storm forced us to stay in Shumgen." He accepted a piala with hot tea from Korlan's hands.

"Even if it takes a storm to bring you here, it is good," Nasyr said very strictly. "We never receive visits from senior management here."

But his censure was feigned. Nasyr was proud that the boy he had saved from death in the sands long ago was now an important man in the region.

"Father, I understand you're displeased. But this time I deliberately came to Karaoi to seek you and get your advice. We are now gathering people together for the kolkhoz management meeting. We can talk about everything and discuss our sad business there." He looked at Igor and Bolat. "I'd also like to invite you, dear friends."

But the kolkhoz management meeting didn't take place where it was supposed to because the building was smothered right up to its windows by snow and sand. It was decided to hold the meeting at the post office. Zharasbai opened the meeting with a short speech.

"My dear fellow countrymen! Life in our country changes rapidly. The time for perestroika and glasnost has come. I don't want to say that perestroika will bring change in a single day. We will have to rake away for years to remove all that has heaped up with stagnation during the past decades."

"And what about our sea? Will perestroika forget about it?" the fishermen asked, interrupting Zharasbai.

"Tell us clearly," Kambar said. "When will the torture of our sick sea stop? Will perestroika heal it?"

Zharasbai went silent. Everything the fishermen were saying was true, and he knew that the situation was worse than they thought.

"Calm down!" Nasyr intervened. "Let the man finish what he was saying!"

"The whole world knows about the tragedy that's happened here. Right now, I cannot tell you anything reassuring. The catastrophe is worsening but is no longer in the hands of regional authorities. All decisions about it must be taken at the government level, at the level of the Union." Zharasbai paused; it was clearly hard for him to acknowledge his own helplessness. Then he said quietly, "Let's talk about Karaoi. The situation here is very sad. We, you, and everybody else knows that. Taking this into account, the Bureau of the Regional Committee has made the decision to leave Karaoi and move to Shumgen. I think you understand why this decision was made. We are struggling to provide you with electricity and telephone connections; it's hard to deliver fuel to you. The kolkhoz has practically disappeared in Karaoi. There are not enough people here even for a single kolkhoz department."

People began to protest again. Not many were willing to move to Shumgen.

Then slowly Korlan got up, and the fishermen went quiet.

"Dear Zharasbai! You have a good soul, and you care for us. There's no doubting that. But Nasyr, who you respect like your own father, and Korlan, who you regard as a mother, will never leave Karaoi. We were born here and will die here."

Korlan spoke with such quiet dignity that Zharasbai could do nothing but wave his hand. He knew that no one would leave Karaoi, since only the toughest remained.

"We won't force you," he replied softly, "but it will be increasingly hard for us to look after you. That is what I needed to tell you. It will be hard for us, but it will be even harder for you, friends!"

"We will look into it, then!" the fishermen laughed in mockery of Zharasbai.

"Very well." Zharasbai also laughed in response. "I have news, by the way." He drew an envelope from the inner pocket of his jacket and opened the letter. "Do you remember Nurdaulet? We thought he died during the war. Well, he's alive! And now he addresses you."

"Ya, Allah!" the people gasped.

"Alive! He's alive?"

Zharasbai began to read.

"'My dear fellow countrymen! Do you remember me, fisherman Nurdaulet? I have dreamed of seeing you for so long. But after being wounded in 1945, I was left without arms and legs, and I didn't have courage to return to you. I asked myself who would need someone like this. Here, in the asylum, there are many poor men like me. My life has gone by, and I am now a withered old man. But I still dream of being buried in my homeland—as I have dreamed all my life. I want my body to be cast into the water, into the sea. I deserve it because I was born a fisherman. Please carry out my request, my dear fellow countrymen! If you agree, I'll write a statement to the management that after my death someone will come to take my body. Is my dear Kyzbala still alive? Is my son alive? Kyzbala must have another family, other children. If so, don't tell her anything about me. I saved three hundred rubles and would like to leave them to my son. That is all I want to write, my dear fellow countrymen. You know when I think about Karaoi, I keep crying, and I cannot stop. I await your reply.'"

Everybody was astounded. In the resonant silence, Zharasbai could hear the ticking of his watch. Everybody was thinking about Nurdaulet and those dismal forty years in an asylum on some distant island they'd never heard of before.

Who has damned this life so cruelly that even an invalid without either arms or legs must suffer for forty years before he comes back to his homeland and family? Who has damned this life so much that poor Nurdaulet was too ashamed to return to Karaoi so as not to be a burden on everyone? Why did he think that? Did the people who loved him seem so callous to him?

Everybody turned to Nasyr. It was customary in the aul that the old fisherman have the last say. Nasyr stood up. He was on the verge of tears, and his lips trembled.

"We . . . we . . . are we animals? He didn't dare to write to us for forty years. Only toward the end of his life has he brought himself to ask for such a small favor. There are no other people left now who knew Nurdaulet. Not even Kyzbala. But I can say on behalf of those who did know him that he was an honorable man. And he has stayed so. We must bring Nurdaulet here at once while he is alive, not wait until he is dead! He must spend his final days among us." Nasyr paused, admiring Nurdaulet's honor. "What dignity. He doesn't want to be a burden for us while he's alive. He asks to bring him here only after he dies! But don't tell Kyzbala about Nurdaulet yet. Who knows what effect it will have on her."

"We need to choose who we send to bring Nurdaulet home."

"Send me, Nasyr-aga!" Yesen volunteered.

"Let Yesen go," the fishermen agreed. "We'll collect money for his trip. He should go as soon as possible!"

Zharasbai wasn't at all surprised at the response of these villagers, so dear to his heart. He had known since his childhood how they would give everything to the last bit to a person in need.

As he ate with Nasyr and his friends later, Zharasbai explained. "It's getting harder and harder to deliver mail to you. The most often it can be done now is once a month."

"That is enough." Musa moved the plates toward Igor and Bolat. "We don't have any young people left, so who needs the newspapers? Friends, have some more to eat. Don't be shy. You have a long trip ahead of you, and you'll get hungry."

Musa was looking at the young men happily, almost tenderly.

Musa never had children of his own. Three years in German captivity had taken their toll. When he and his wife complained to Otkeldy that they didn't seem to be able to have children, Otkeldy examined Musa and told him, "You can't have children. You have poison in your blood, Musa." And Musa realized the effect biological weapons can have on a man—the ones they tested on him in the concentration camp.

Nasyr answered Zharasbai. "Musa and I nowadays talk only with God. Why would we need your newspapers? They all lie anyway."

Zharasbai asked the young scientists, "Where are you heading to, if it's not a secret?"

"The season has ended, so I'm going back to Moscow; Bolat's going to Alma-Ata. I'll pay a visit to your regional center. I have something I need to talk about. By the way, I have something to talk to you about personally as well."

"We'll work out what we can tell you so the meeting will be useful."

"My father has spoken to Kunaev, who asked for the calculations to be sent. I have the calculations. Bolat and Nasyr-aga will take them to Kunaev."

"It would be good for us to have a copy as well."

"Yes, indeed."

Igor and Bolat left Zharasbai alone with his parents and began to walk along the shore, their feet sinking deep in fine white sand. In the distance, the sea sparkled in the sun like a polished silver blade. As always, Kyzbala was on the shore.

"I wonder," Bolat said thoughtfully, "if the news that Nurdaulet is alive will reach her mind?"

"Maybe the powerful emotional shock might bring her back. Things like this can happen. Who knows? But what a tragedy! They both are so unhappy!"

The two young men's car hadn't arrived yet, so they all decided to go with Zharasbai.

"I'm worried you'll get sick during the trip." Korlan was running around Nasyr. Igor and Bolat helped Nasyr into the back seat of Zharasbai's car. The fishermen came to see them go. Nasyr, remembering Kambar's illness, had a word with Zharasbai.

"Listen, son. I won't go to Shumgen, but Kambar definitely needs to move there. Help him get a good house—and a good hospital in Alma-Ata. He's come back from Balkhash seriously ill."

"Don't worry, Father," said Zharasbai. He took Kambar by the hand. "I'll go to Alma-Ata and talk to the doctor soon, Kambar-aga. I'm going through Shumgen now. I'll arrange for them to send a car for you."

"Thank you, Zharasbai!" The fisherman was very embarrassed. "I didn't ask Nasyr. I just shared things with him, and then you came here. Thank you again. What else can I do but say thank you?"

Nasyr protested in irritation. "What can be more valuable than saying thank you?" And he began to hound everyone to get moving. "Zharasbai, let's go! We must make sure we're not late for the train!"

Zharasbai and Igor dropped Nasyr and Bolat by the crossroads at Barlyktam. After waving goodbye, Igor went to sleep. Zharasbai let him doze. Staring out across the monotonous and miserable steppe, which stretched endlessly in all directions, he began to think about his own problems.

Zharasbai pulled out a cigarette and began to smoke. The driver turned on the radio, and sounds of a dombra came out.

"Leave this music," Zharasbai told him.

It was the kyui of Asan-kaigy,[5] who spent all his life wandering across the earth in search of a blessed land. The great bard traveled far and wide but could never find this land. Zharasbai smiled grimly. If even Asan-kaigy couldn't find it on earth, then modern man definitely won't be able to.

Zharasbai came to the area where his mother had taken him when he was five years old. His mother had taken him and his brother on a search for their father, who had trekked from Samara to Karaganda to find work and money. They lived in Karaganda for a year before his father was killed when a mine caved in. Mother refused to stay in Karaganda and took the children across to the auls. Zharasbai could only vaguely remember it. The Kazakhs used to give them bread and fish and let them stay overnight. But his mother's health was ruined; she was pregnant, and in one of the auls she became seriously ill. The master of the house—a tall, quiet man—put up a hut for them in the yard, where they lived for six weeks or so. Zharasbai quickly became friends with the master's children, and soon his blond hair was the only difference between him and them. He quickly learned Kazakh. His mother, Zharasbai remembered, was unable to get up. She would press him to her chest and repeat frequently the word "Tashkent." Only after many years did he realize why she didn't stay in Karaganda: she wanted to take them all to Tashkent. She either had relatives in Tashkent or someone had told her that it was possible to survive in Tashkent.

His mother died giving birth, along with her baby. Zharasbai remembered clearly how he used to sit for hours on a small hill on the outskirts of the aul. Sometimes, he would wake frightened in the night, run to his mother's grave, and cry bitterly with his face on the dry, lumpy clay. The master's kindly wife would often send her oldest son to fetch him. "Don't go to the grave so often, even if it's your mother," she would say to him. "It's not good." And now, when he hears the Kazakh proverb, 'A child attracted to graves will die early,' he always remembers that kind lady, though he can't remember her face or the face of her husband, or the faces or names of their children.

He lived in the master's house for a year. No one asked him to leave. He probably would've stayed there forever. But a terrible famine came to the Kazakh steppe. After the great confiscation, there were no cattle left,[6] there was no bread, and people began to leave their homelands. Those who stayed survived by catching mice and jerboas on the steppe. And some ate human flesh. If it hadn't been for Nasyr, Zharasbai would have been boiled in a cauldron. Nasyr saved him from a man who had lost his mind with hunger.

Zharasbai began to smoke again. And suddenly for the first time in his life he thought that now—today, tomorrow, as soon as possible—he has to remember these people who looked after his mother and her two children. He must recall their faces, their names, and the faces of their children, he must!

Memory . . . What is it: a human memory? Why does it retain for so long the voices of hundreds of people and countless sounds and colors, sometimes maddeningly brief and accidental? Who will explain why it works like this? Sometimes it opens its secret chambers to us by itself, and we gratefully take strength and new hopes from it. Zharasbai tried to compare memory to the flashing screen of a TV. But on this TV, you can't switch channels. Zharasbai closed his eyes . . . and the screen lit up. In those terrible days, this quiet man, the master, would go out to hunt. But there were no animals on the steppe left to hunt. And if he did come across something, that creature would quickly vanish. And what could he do without a horse? The master felt their death was coming. So many in the aul had already died. And those who could still move joined a long trail to the city so desperate and slow-moving, it looked like a funeral procession. Death went before them, borne in an invisible coffin. Soon the man and his family joined the trail too. Where were they going—to Tashkent? To Karaganda? Zharasbai couldn't remember. Everyone used to say, "City, city," but what city no one would say. And although people tried to stay together, many fell behind. And these stragglers were attacked by others driven mad by hunger. They would be killed and eaten; only their bones would remain on the burning fires. The man and his family walked for a long time, and eventually there was no one either in front or behind them. The stony road dwindled to dust, and they found themselves among the sands, and now thirst hit them on top of the hunger. By dusk they came to an abandoned old well. Two riders were already circling. The master tried to scare them off with a shot of the gun . . .

After the shots, the screen of Zharasbai's memory jumps from one image to another randomly. Then suddenly the most appalling picture of all flashes.

At dawn, Zharasbai was woken by a shot. And then another shot cracked. The master's exhausted wife, her arms crossed over her bloody chest, was looking with horror at the master, then staggered backward and fell into the well. The master collapsed over the well and wept piteously. Zharasbai started to run but tripped and fell. He lay there, shivering with fear. The master was still crying at the well. There was no one else. And Zharasbai suddenly realized that the master had killed his children as well! He froze. His legs dissolved into cotton and would not move. But the master paid no attention to him as he lay there, sobbing quietly for hours. At midday, the master woke up, looked at the boy with bleary eyes, and came toward him. Zharasbai opened his eyes, but he had no strength left and just shrank.

"Don't worry. I won't touch you," the master said with dry lips. The five-year-old boy understood that the master was saying goodbye. The master hugged the boy, kissed him, and then let him go. Then the man took off his shoes, sat on the edge of the well, rested the trigger of his rifle next to his big toe, and put the barrel in his mouth. Zharasbai was left alone, completely alone. This picture had stayed in front of his eyes all his life. But only now, when he is over fifty, was he beginning to remember what happened before this tragedy.

"They won't leave us alone," the woman said when the master fired shots in the air, as the riders came close.

"I hope they choke on our meat!" the master said angrily.

"They are following us."

"Let them. I still have the ammunition," the master replied. The baby tied to the mother's back was sobbing awfully, desperate for food after sucking its mother's breast until blood came out. The eldest son, Dauletkali, wasn't looking at his mother. Earlier that day, they had shared the last pieces of bread equally between them: two for the parents and three for the children—him, his seven-year-old younger brother, and Zharasbai. He no longer looked for hope from his mother like his innocent brother. Zharasbai understood everything.

His father whispered, "Quiet!" Everybody froze. A jerboa appeared at the top of the sandy slope. The man lifted his gun and aimed. Dauletkali could see his father's hands were shaking, his eyes watering. He pulled the trigger. Crack. The jerboa rolled down out of sight. "If I didn't kill it, then I definitely wounded it," the master said and began climbing the slope. At first, the children tried to follow but were so weak they fell back down. This time they were out of luck. Shooting jerboas had been their salvation, but this time, the master came back with nothing . . .

When did they reach that fatal well? After half an hour? Or the next day? Zharasbai doesn't know. How many days had passed since they left the stone paths of Arka to walk on the sand? Zharasbai doesn't know that either. But as soon as they reached the well, the mother and children fell asleep with the sleep of the dead. The master laid his chekmen over his wife and children. His wife kept moaning in her sleep for water. The master was silent: he had no one to ask. He breathed through his nose, as if to let the cold night air through his mouth would make his thirst worse. He was scared to fall asleep: terrified they might be attacked and eaten by people even hungrier than them. The thought that his wife and children could die without being buried stirred a dreadful, impotent rage in him. The master looked at the sleeping children—and he realized that they would never get up again. And yet he had no strength to carry them either. Yes, yes, that was exactly what he thought—otherwise how else could he have come to the decision to kill them himself rather than give them to those who hunt human meat? Zharasbai remembered that the master and his wife comforted the children by telling them, "If we get to the sea, we'll have fish, and we will survive."

Now the master probably thought bitterly that they wouldn't make it to the sea. Where was it, that sea? Would it ever come their way? Would it help them to find the path? No. Nobody will help them. They believed in their own strength, believed that Allah would help them. Now it was clear they didn't have enough strength to even get up, and Allah was far away in the sky and forgot about them long ago. The master realized he was falling asleep. He shook himself, trying to get rid of the sleep. Everything was quiet. A lizard darted past close by. No matter how hard he fought, he still dozed off, his face pressed against the barrel of his gun. Then he was woken up by a hoarse cough. It was already light. He crawled to the children and listened carefully. Then he rushed to the younger one. A narrow trail of blood was oozing from little Ulan's mouth. He put his ear to the child's chest; the child was dead. The master hugged the little body, which was already growing cold, as if trying to restore it to life with his body. His wife was still asleep . . . Yes, yes, that must be the exact moment when the thought was born in him, the exact moment he realized clearly and irrevocably they would not make it out of the sands. The master took four bullets from a small bag and wiped them carefully with a cloth . . .

What happened next? After that he hears only voices.

"Do you want to kill us with your own hands?" his wife asked.

"And myself too."

"Kill me but don't touch the children."

"None of us has any hope—not you, not me, not the children."

"I beg you in the name of the God: don't touch the children!"

"What God are you talking about? Where is this God? Do you want to go mad? Do you want some skunk to eat them in front of your eyes? Or do you want to see two more deaths after Ulan's?"

"Find the strength to get the children out!"

"I have no strength!" the man shouted in rage. "None! Everything is pointless. Do you understand?"

"Don't touch them! They are my blood!"

"And mine too!"

They kept talking for a long time. Finally the woman understood she could not talk him out of his decision.

"Then kill me first. I cannot see my children's deaths," she said quietly.

After the shot, the master ran to his wife and lifted her head. Her hair was completely white, drained of its color in a single moment.

He remembered what happened more clearly from then on—from the minute he saw a man on the camel. It was young Nasyr. He lifted the hungry, exhausted children, Beknazar and blond Zharasbai, up onto the camel. People in Karaoi wept when they saw the children. No one believed that they would survive. Musa asked Nasyr to give Zharasbai to his care, and Musa carried him from Nasyr's house. The boy asked, struggling to move his lips, "Is this Tashkent?"

"He speaks Kazakh!" Musa's mother was amazed.

"Then," Musa exclaimed joyously, "he will be a brother and a son for me! No, boy, it's not Tashkent. It's Sinemorye."

"Son?" Musa's mother shook her head. "You are still a child yourself."

"I'm already a teenager," Musa replied with dignity.

Zharasbai kept kneading the cigarette until all the tobacco fell under his feet.

"Yes, Sinemorye is a sacred area," he thought now. "How many people were saved by the sea? Those who actually reached it! The kind local people helped everyone; they would share their last piece of bread. How many souls they saved by their warmth and kindness! Long ago, they shared their land with hungry Koreans, and the area has become a homeland for resettled Caucasian-Karachais, Ingush, Balkars, Chechens, Estonians, Lithuanians. And now the land is dying—it's dying in front of everybody's eyes."

After settling in the carriage, Nasyr lay down right away. He had to prepare himself for the upcoming conversation. Such was the weight of responsibility he felt that he would not permit the conversation to even leave his thoughts, and so he began to think about the letter.

Yes, he was carrying an important letter, a letter so important that the soul of Matvei screamed with pain in it. In the book he wrote back in the fifties, Matvei warned that the sea would die if the two Daryas were cut off. So even then, Matvei understood that someone was developing plans to extend cotton production using these waters, although Nasyr hadn't heard Matvei even mentioning it then. So what will Kunaev say after reading this letter? All the newspapers are announcing that perestroika is progressing across the country—but where is it, this perestroika? Nasyr didn't see anything like it around him.

And with the regular rattling of the wheels, his thoughts became unrushed and steady. The old man's deep thoughtfulness was understandable. This word "perestroika" promised so much, and yet life to Nasyr seemed unchanged. Was he the only one not to see results from perestroika? Was it just yet another campaign slogan? The words, the incitements, the renewed calls—they have all happened before! And it was so easy to destroy the good built only yesterday by hard work.

What wheat there was in the past! Golden stems with grains as thick as your finger! Where did the snow-white rice go? Rice you could gorge on with your eyes alone? Yes, they decided they must boost production, and meadows and pasturelands were plowed. The food that sustained the cattle was destroyed, and with it, the cattle. Now dust rules vast areas. Matvei wrote, "Seven hundred tons of dust falls on every square mile here in the maritime territory." Just think about it: seven hundred tons! What sort of country is that! What sort of people live in it? For seventy years, they were obsessed with only one idea: conquer, conquer, conquer! Industrialization, mechanization, automatization: nothing in this country was done with care. Everything was abandoned and warped, and the warriors disappeared in the thickness of time after each campaign, and nobody knows who's guilty, what caused it, and why it was all needed. "The country of slaves," Nasyr thought bitterly, "in which nothing is done for the benefit of the people, but everything is done to their detriment! Now we cannot be called a nation. Now we are just a crowd, we are trash—we've given our lives into the hands of ignorant men who are scared of people like Kakharman!"

When his thoughts brought him to his son, Kakharman, Nasyr thought bitterly, "Yes, yes, people like Kakharman. And during the course of my life, I saw a lot of those worthless office fellows, who look into the mouth of their superiors waiting to be told what to do. After five o'clock, they go to their tall stone houses, and there they don't care about anything."

As usual, Nasyr woke up early. He slowly washed himself and sat on the small folding stool opposite the partially opened door to the compartment. He was cross. Bolat soon woke up. He could see that the old man was sitting sternly, puffed up like a berkut before a hunt, and greeted Nasyr as indifferently as possible.

"It's good that you're up," the old man said brusquely. "We're approaching Alma-Ata."

Yesterday he'd wanted to talk to Bolat about Kunaev, but he had decided to wait until he felt fresher. And now, when Bolat returned to the compartment with his face washed and hair brushed, Nasyr asked impatiently, "People say that Kunaev is leaving his position. I'd like to know if that is true or not."

Bolat smiled. "I haven't been in the capital for half a year, so I haven't heard the gossip. We'll find out when we get there, Nasyr-aga."

Nasyr frowned, then said, "I won't go to your place now. Take me to a hotel."

"But Khorst-aga will eat me alive for taking a guest to the hotel!"

"Khorst will understand. Right now I need a telephone." Nasyr suddenly began having doubts. "I have a feeling, Bolat, that we won't succeed."

"Are we asking for alms? If Kunaev receives you, you just tell him everything as it is, and don't spare his feelings."

"But what if he won't receive me? What if he assigns it to one of his assistants?"

"Also tell the truth. Only the truth! That's the only option."

Nasyr cheered up.

"I will insist that Dimash see me himself. And I won't leave until I speak to him—that is what I'll tell them."

From the railway station, they went to the Hotel Alma-Ata, where Bolat arranged a single room for the old fisherman.

"Go home and see your wife, then come back to me," Nasyr told him. "I'm going to a hairdresser. Don't tell Khorst I am here for now. We'll finish our business first, and then we'll visit him."

Bolat was delayed. So Nasyr decided to call Kunaev's assistant himself. The person who answered told him, "I've heard about you. Go to the Central

Committee and leave the letter there." The assistant explained how to get there and which policemen to give the letter to.

Nasyr objected, saying that he needed to meet Kunaev personally. The assistant went quiet for a bit, then took his full name and asked him not to leave the room but to wait for a call back.

Nasyr stayed in his room for three days. Bolat took the letter to the Central Committee, and Nasyr spent all three days watching TV. He especially liked the Kyrgyz channel, which featured old Kazakh and Kyrgyz songs. But he was getting worried that they had forgotten about him. Several times, he was on the point of calling again but stopped himself. They couldn't have just forgotten. Dimash must have enough of worries—as soon as he gets some spare time, then he'll be in touch.

Finally, the phone rang. Nasyr hurriedly picked it up. It was Bolat, who promised to visit him during his lunch break. Nasyr was scowling and gloomy when he greeted Bolat.

"I'm tired of sitting by this damn phone. Let it explode! Matvei and I are two old men who must've lost their minds. We thought we'd meet Kunaev himself! I should go home before I make a complete fool of myself."

Bolat tried to calm the old fisherman down.

"No, Nasyr-aga. That is not how things are done. Even if Kunaev cannot receive you himself, then at least he should inform you about it."

"It's not only me and Matvei who need the sea!" Nasyr was getting worked up. "Mustafa is right when he writes that the sea is important for the whole world! To destroy it is a crime against humanity! That is what we need to tell Kunaev!"

"Let's go downstairs and have lunch, aqsaqal. You haven't eaten any hot food for three days now."

"But what if they call?" Nasyr worriedly looked at the phone, although he really wanted to eat something hot.

"They are probably having a lunch break now as well," Bolat said, which convinced Nasyr to be led downstairs to the restaurant.

"Oh, what a lot of people!" Nasyr exclaimed. "Don't they work?"

"It's a lunch break now." Bolat began to laugh. "And most of these people are here on a business trip like you and me . . ."

"Let's hurry up," Nasyr said, agitated. "It will be seriously embarrassing if they call, and I'm not there. They'll think I am not an aqsaqal but a light-weight. Oh, I wanted to ask you about one more thing. I would also like to see Kakharman. Maybe I should go and visit him in Zaysan. It's not that far from here, is it?"

"Indeed!" Bolat rejoiced. "Why didn't I think of it sooner? Let's do the following, Nasyr-aga. Let's call Kakharman and tell him to fly here right away. It will be easier than for you to fly there."

"That's a good idea!" Nasyr was noticeably happier. "I just want to talk to Kunaev as soon as possible!"

"We can send a telegram to Kakharman today. By the time he's asked for leave from work, and gets a flight here . . ."

The phone finally rang on the fourth day, early in the morning.

"Come to the Bureau of Passes at six o'clock this evening precisely. You will have fifteen minutes with Dinmukhamed Akhmedovich."

Nasyr didn't even have a chance to thank whoever it was because he had already hung up.

Kunaev met the old fisherman by the doors of the office. He invited him in, offered him a seat, and sat opposite Nasyr. This courtesy pleased Nasyr. "So how old are you, Nake?" Kunaev asked respectfully. Nasyr deliberately answered in accordance with the eastern calendar.

"I was born in the year of the horse, Dimash."

"So you're eighty-four, Nake," Kunaev understood quickly, and Nasyr was pleased. He said in his mind, "Ya, Allah, give me luck!" The satisfaction of the aqsaqal didn't go unnoticed by Kunaev. Nasyr in turn studied the leader of the Republic, who was sturdy and still young.

"I've read the letter from Matvei Panteleevich," Kunaev continued. "I'd like to thank him for his contribution. We are preparing a response letter to him, and it will be posted in the next few days." Judging by the tone of voice, Nasyr understood that Kunaev didn't really like talking about Slavikov. "Have you known him for a long time, Nake? Ah yes, probably for many years, since he was in exile in your lands. And has he learned Kazakh from you? I can detect a southern pronunciation."

"He is a clever man. He learned the language in one summer! And he knows more proverbs than any Kazakh!"

342

It felt as if Kunaev was not paying any attention to what Nasyr had said.

"Nobody can avoid the errors of his time," Kunaev announced slowly. "They don't always reveal themselves right away but maybe as years go by, Nake. Back in my time, I also fought with Slavikov for our sea not to die. But now I see that none of us succeeded in bringing the matter we started to an end. We didn't manage to turn the Siberian rivers."

Nasyr exclaimed, "Dimash, did Slavikov ever fight for turning the rivers? It's just childishness, and Mustafa is a serious man!"

Kunaev didn't expect this kind of answer from Nasyr. He looked sharply at the old fisherman and then turned away. After that, the conversation took on a formal character, and with a few slick words, Kunaev diverted Nasyr from the essence of the matter. And he did it so subtly that Nasyr came to his senses only in the fifteenth minute, when it became clear the meeting was coming to an end.

Walking down Furmanov Street, Nasyr tried to pin down his impression of the meeting. It hadn't been productive—the high official had given him no hopes, hadn't said anything on the matter—yet at the same time, it seemed to Nasyr that despite the small, unpleasant hitch about Slavikov, the conversation had been warm and trusting. Even if Kunaev was deluded, then his heart was sincere, and he didn't wish ill to Nasyr, or to Slavikov, or to the sea, or to the nation that inhabits its poor shores. But what Nasyr couldn't understand was that without wishing any evil, he was nevertheless bringing evil to the sea and to the people of the shore, and to Nasyr personally, and to Professor Slavikov . . . No, it wasn't evil, but there was something else that the old fisherman couldn't comprehend.

As he reached the hotel, he caught sight of Bolat and Khorst. When they saw Nasyr, Khorst came over, and the old friends hugged and looked at each other for a long time.

"Now it's time to go to my place!" Khorst urged. Irina Mikhailovna had a plump, skillfully prepared carp ready on the table. As they sat to eat, Nasyr began to tell them about his conversation with Kunaev.

"Nasyr-aga," Bolat asked jokingly, "did you notice any signs?"

"Signs?" Nasyr remembered. "No. I didn't see anything. It doesn't look like Kunaev is intending to give up his comfortable chair yet. Basically, he told me that the problems of our sea and the distress of our people are being considered at the highest levels. We must not despair, but we mustn't think that a way out of this dead end has been found. All of us have ruined the sea. He also said that the sea people should remain active. That is all he said. He is a clever man, so he didn't give empty promises. That is what I understood. He said they are preparing a response to Matvei—an official answer," Nasyr finished importantly.

Bolat and Khorst nodded approvingly as they listened to Nasyr, and Irina Mikhailovna crossed herself.

"May God see to it. May he take care of your sea from the heavens, and may there be on earth honorable people who will not abandon you in your troubles."

"There was a telegram from Kakharman," Bolat said, passing Nasyr the form. "He will come; we must just wait for him."

"That's good. I haven't seen him for a while. How happy Korlan will be! I'll tell her everything." Nasyr was smiling. He was in a good mood and decided to stay in Alma-Ata for a few more days to wait for Kakharman.

The next day at midday, Nasyr and Bolat called Professor Slavikov in Moscow. Slavikov picked up right away. His voice sounded weak, since he was still not entirely well after his heart attack. But he spoke clearly and was very happy to talk to Nasyr.

"It's good that Kunaev received you. Is he going to cancel the turning of the rivers, then? Fantastic! So there'll be no mutual grievances between us. I should stop lying in bed. Time to get back on my feet. I'm planning to visit you by the sea in spring before I die! But you have made me very happy, Nasyr! Do you sense that the times are changing? Even Kunaev has begun to speak differently. Well, well, if we could carry on like this, Nasyr! I also wrote the same letter to Gorbachev, yes, yes! So we will keep hoping. But goodbye for now, Nasyr. See you soon! Oh, I almost forgot! I received a telegram from Kakharman saying he'll be in Moscow soon. If you see him, tell him that we are expecting Igor tomorrow."

Nasyr was sad saying goodbye to his old friend. Nasyr's heart ached, and he suddenly felt like it might be their last conversation. The professor probably also felt the same way. His voice cracked at the last minute.

Kakharman arrived the next day. Bolat picked him up during his lunch break. Nasyr looked with curiosity at the elderly Russian Kakharman had with him, then impulsively hugged his emaciated son.

"Dear son, you have made your old man so happy!"

Kakharman said shyly, "Semeon Arkhipovich, let me introduce you to my father." Then he addressed Nasyr. "I am staying with Semeon Arkhipovich. He has kindly helped me while we're waiting for an apartment."

Nasyr shook the kind man's hand with pleasure.

"You have very good pronunciation. Not every Russian can speak our language so well."

"He's been living in Kazakh lands for a long time and has many Kazakh relatives," Kakharman explained. "But I also keep being surprised, Father. Kazakhs themselves forget their language readily, and to meet a Russian man who speaks Kazakh so well . . . What is it?"

"It's a sign of respect," Semeon Arkhipovich replied, "to the nation among which you live. How can it be any other way? Kakharman is right. I've been living in Zaysan for many years, so it'd be embarrassing not to learn the language!"

"And I, Semeon Arkhipovich, am especially happy today, as you can see. I met my son. I've got some extra money with me. Bolat can take us to a restaurant, and we'll have lunch. What do you say?"

"Show the way, Bolat!" Kakharman replied, laughing. Nasyr and Semeon Arkhipovich were looking at each other warmly as they all walked out. If someone said these two simple men liked each other from first sight, they'd be right. Soon Khorst joined them, and they made room at the table for him next to Nasyr.

An hour and a half passed in lively conversation before Bolat and Khorst left, since Bolat had to get back to work, and Khorst needed to go home. Nasyr, Kakharman, and Semeon Arkhipovich then went up to Nasyr's hotel room. Nasyr was disturbed by how reserved Kakharman was. Kakharman was naturally taciturn, but now his reserve infected them all as he sat listening absentmindedly and dropping in brusque, often unnecessary comments now and then. Nasyr understood that some serious changes were taking place in Kakharman's soul.

When they sat in the deep, soft armchairs, Semeon Arkhipovich said, "You have a joy today, aqsaqal, but I have sadness. I came to bury my closest friend. Grigory was the best person I've ever known. And I am not exaggerating, Nake. With his death, an ache has come back to me, an ache I was beginning to forget, the pain of loneliness and abandonment. It's hard to experience the death of close people."

"We meet at a sad time for you, Semeon. May the earth be an eiderdown for him."

"Long ago, Grisha revived me. He was one of those people who think more about others than about themselves. The world depends on people like this. I remember what he told me when I lost the will to live: 'Sema, it's easy to die, but it's hard to survive. If you're just afraid of difficulties, then yes, of course, go ahead into the coffin. But if you still respect yourself, if you consider yourself a man, then keep living, no matter what.'"

"To decide to die is not easy either," Kakharman objected. "After all, people don't kill themselves for no reason. Every death is a protest against a life that hasn't worked out. A protest against savagery and obstructions. Is it not?"

"That's also true," Semeon Arkhipovich replied. "But I was going through something different, more despair than protest. Death would not have made me look any better. And if you want to protest, then it's much easier to do it alive than dead. Maybe not as beautiful but much more courageous."

"Kakharman, how's our Berish doing?"

"He sounds cheerful in all his letters. He wants to become a dzhigit."

"Good for him. I approve! And how are you doing with housing? When do they promise to provide you with some?"

"I'm hoping to get it this winter. Then I'll finally be able to bring Aitugan and the children. I keep thinking, too, about bringing Berish back from boarding school. What sort of life is there? He can stay home in the winter and live with you in the summer."

"Alright. We will talk to him too. Why are you going to Moscow?"

"Here in Zaysan, we have issues with equipment. I'm going to try to sort it out in Moscow with the help of my old and new friends."

Then Nasyr said with pleasure, "I am so happy that Dimash received me. We had a good conversation. He knows all our issues well and always keeps them in his head."

When Kakharman heard Kunaev's name, he sprang to his feet as if he were stung.

"Father, do you believe him? Amazing! You haven't spent much time going from office to office if he deceived you so quickly! 'Go back to your middle of nowhere, Nake. We'll fix it all, and you just hope and wait.' And he probably tapped you on the shoulder approvingly. Ah, Father! These gentle, trustful conversations have been going on for thirty years. For thirty years, they've been tapping us on the shoulder. Yes, yes, we'll sort it all out. Don't worry. For thirty years, hiding behind the name of the nation, they have robbed people, plagued the land—the precious land people live on—and keep the best sons of the nation behind bars or exile them!" Kakharman clenched his teeth. "Dear God, how sorry I feel for these trusting people! I feel sorry for my poor nation, deceived many thousands of times!"

"Ya, Allah!" Nasyr thought fearfully. It was the first time he had seen his son in such despair. "So this is what is happening in his heart! This is the pain he carries in his soul, my poor son!" Tears welled in Nasyr's eyes. Kakharman sat down and turned away.

Nasyr came to him and awkwardly put his hand on Kakharman's shoulder.

"You should go home, Father," Kakharman said quietly.

"That's right; that's right," Nasyr began to murmur. "My old woman is waiting for me. That's right. I should go home."

After arranging for business leave with the department, Kakharman flew on to Moscow on a night flight.

Nasyr also began to get ready. In the morning, he and Khorst went to the market. Nasyr decided to get some presents for his fellow countrymen. Soon their bag was full.

"How will you carry it?" Khorst asked. "It's so heavy."

"Who said that I will carry it?" Nasyr smiled. "The train will carry the bag!"

"And what about the distance from the station to the aul? Will the train carry it there as well?"

"Someone will meet me there. It only looks like a lot. But as soon as Korlan gives things away, there won't be enough for everybody. As you may remember, she is very generous."

"Don't forget that my Irina Mikhailovna prepared a few things for you to bring back."

"There'll be space for everything. Don't worry."

News flew across the market. Kunaev was removed and a Russian appointed in his place. Nasyr was shocked by this news and stopped still in the street. Khorst was walking ahead, then saw Nasyr and ran back with a box.

"You don't look well! Have a seat. And then let's go home. We can buy the rest in the shops; I'll sort it out myself."

Khorst took the shopping bags and helped Nasyr to the hotel so he could lie down. The news devastated him. Kakharman was right! And he, old fool, had just kept listening to the gentle speeches!

Toward evening, crowds of young people were spreading across the central streets. They were heading toward the Government House, and soon the whole square was filled with a noisy throng. From his room, Nasyr could see they were mostly Kazakhs. He had a bad feeling about it. Were they going to protest? Who of them would like that a Russian has been appointed as first secretary in Kazakhstan?

He put on his warm coat and went outside. There were hordes of people by the entrance, and it was noisy. Nasyr moved with the crowd. Soon he was in the square and was swept right into the midst of the crowd, unable even to turn. The young people around him were shouting slogans demanding that the first secretary be a Kazakh. It got colder, and the young people shuffled to stay warm. Though the occasional argument rippled through the young protesters and the curious spectators—like Nasyr—everyone agreed one thing: Kazakhstan should be governed by a Kazakh! And the young people were writing banners right there on scraps of cloth and lifting them high above their heads.[7]

"This is not good," Nasyr thought. He couldn't understand why they would let this happen. Nasyr also thought that Kunaev's place should be taken by a Kazakh, not a Russian, but dzhigits have hot blood and sharp tempers. How would it end? Nasyr couldn't say.

Next to Nasyr, a short man in glasses began to talk.

"Does a Russian stand at the head of the Soviet Union? Yes. There's nothing special about wanting to be governed by a person of your own nationality! That's how it's been since ancient times. There's nothing wrong with it!" He looked at Nasyr. "Am I right, *aga*? We keep saying 'socialism, socialism.' But is it in line with socialism not to trust another nation? I can understand it only in this way: they don't trust the Kazakh nation!

"Why did these people come here?" the man continued. "They came to express their resentment. Their faces were spat in! They were told, 'You need to be managed from the Center, from Moscow.' What?! Haven't we got our own sons to take the place of Kunaev? Who can believe that this Russian will care for the interests of the Kazakhs? He'll be controlled from the Center. I have nothing against Russians. I have many Russian friends. They are great people, but I would like to ask you: Did a crow ever bring up a berkut, or did a berkut bring up a crow? Kunaev was Brezhnev's sycophant, that's for sure, but can it be said with certainty that this Russian will gather around himself the best, most honest and decent Kazakhs? The true core of the nation, the real nation? Will we have a future? Are we not threatened by extinction?"

"You're right, son!" Nasyr agreed. "These are true words."

In the meantime, the square had been surrounded by police cars, soldiers, and policemen. Next to the policemen were vigilantes with red armbands who were clutching metal bars in their hands.

Somebody said, "Vodka is being given away. Some of the boys have snatched a whole truckload already."

"But why is vodka needed at a time like this?" Nasyr was aghast. "This is not good at all: the dzhigits' blood is hot enough, and they'll go completely crazy if they drink!"

His companion shook his head. "Vodka and cigarettes are being given away. It'll all end in trouble. There are many already high on anasha here too."

A tough-looking man butted in.

"Let the boys warm up a bit. There is a saying: when the temperature goes down, the drinks go down." And he began to laugh.

"What are you so happy about?" the man in glasses sullenly responded. "All the drinkers will get mown down like chicks!"

"Yeah, right!" the tough guy retorted slyly. "How else do you deal with them? That's the idea!"

"Nonsense! How could trucks with vodka be brought in through the police cordons?"

Then a young boy shouted at him.

"Hey. If that's the way you're thinking . . . fuck off!" And he would have lunged toward the tough guy if his friends hadn't stopped him. The tough guy quickly disappeared into the crowd.

Some people climbed onto the stage. Nasyr couldn't see their faces clearly, but it didn't matter. Nasyr, just like many of the students present, knew only what Kunaev looked like.

When Nazarbayev[8] appeared and began to speak, someone in the crowd began to shout, "Brother Kazakhs! They're arresting our best people illegally already!"

Everybody turned to where the shouts were coming from. A young man with a cigarette in his teeth shoved Nasyr in the shoulder. Nasyr smelled the strong aroma of anasha.

Nobody was listening to the speakers on the stage. Nobody believed the words they were saying. Even when the singer Bibigul,[9] beloved by everyone, appeared onstage and burst into tears, the noise did not abate.

More soldiers and policemen arrived, protected by plastic shields and armed with rubber truncheons. They looked exactly like the Ulster policemen Nasyr had seen on the television. He was horrified.

Everyone was waiting for the newly appointed leader to appear on the stage. "He needs to appear soon because the mood is in danger of boiling over," Nasyr thought. "What is more stupid than sending in armed and impatient soldiers and policemen and vigilantes with metal bars against unarmed students?"

All the megaphones began to amplify the same chant: "Leave! Leave!" The armed soldiers drove in toward the students in a tight wall. But the students were moving toward them. Powerful jets of water erupted from the police water cannons. In the freezing air, the coats of the young people quickly crusted with ice. The students shivered with cold but would not leave. A jet of water caught Nasyr in the back. The old fisherman fell—first on his knees, then facedown onto the ground.

A young man helped him up.

"Aga, go home. They may kill you." The young man smiled sadly. "We will need aqsaqals tomorrow to collect our corpses." He looked into Nasyr's face and rejoiced, "Wow, Nasyr-aga, how did you end up here? Did all the people from our land move here now?"

"Whose son are you?" Nasyr looked at him closely.

"Sarsengali's, from the seventh junction!"

"Yes, I think I know you. Thank you for helping me. But you shouldn't stay here either. It will not end well. Do you study here, in the capital?"

"No. I work in a factory."

They moved to avoid another powerful jet of water.

"Where are you staying, aga?"

"In a hotel. There it is, nearby."

"Let's go. I will walk you there."

They began making their way through the crowd, trying to avoid the icy jets.

"What is your name, son?"

"Makhambet. Aga, let's hurry. I don't want you to catch a cold. We should get in the warmth quickly."

They began to walk faster. Makhambet kept shaking ice off Nasyr's soaked coat.

"Don't go back to the square, son. Better go to your dormitory."

"Why would I care, aga? I don't really have anything against the government."

"Was it all organized or what?"

"No. It was completely spontaneous. A union of hearts, as they say. An impulse. Only thieves and hooligans organize."

"Is it because you are all against the fact that a Russian has been appointed instead of Kunaev?"

"I personally don't care who. As long as he's a decent person and not a criminal."

"Come home, Makhambet. What are you doing in Alma-Ata?"

"What sort of work can I get there, aga? I decided not to take the last piece of bread from my father but to come to the city to get a job. People from our lands went all over the place."

"You are all questions, young man," Nasyr joked mirthlessly. His teeth were chattering with cold.

"I won't argue. Young people nowadays live as if in a garbage dump. Troubles come from every direction. They've piled up for seventy years, and now they're stinking and writhing with worms."

Nasyr didn't know what to say.

"The whole year after Afghanistan, I was in a hospital in Tashkent," Makhambet continued. "I had plenty of time to think. I will never forget the hell of it. Who were we there? We were meat for the cannons. Afghanistan has opened my eyes to many things. We were cannon meat there, but who are we here? Nobody feels like a human being in his own country. Everyone feels like cattle. All are spat on. Why, aga?"

Nasyr again didn't have an answer.

"A deep grievance sits in every man. Take today's demonstration, for example. Kazakhs were protesting against national inequality, of which we have had plenty already. And now with the appointment of a Russian, there'll be even more."

Makhambet opened the front door of the hotel and began to say goodbye to Nasyr.

"I should go, aga. My friends are waiting for me. If you ever go past the seventh junction, visit my father, give him my greetings, and tell him everything you saw today."

"Thank you, son! You are a good dzhigit. You have good people with you: proud, honest, and brave! I will pray for you—Allah will surely help you."

"Well," Makhambet said, smiling, "if Allah joins our side, then everything will get sorted out."

And he was gone. The old man went up to his room and was very, very cold. What's the difference between what is happening in Ulster and here? Nasyr couldn't tell anymore.

He took off his coat, hung it on the back of a chair, and moved the chair toward the radiator. "Just one command," Nasyr thought indignantly, "and all those thugs with metal rods will attack unarmed youth." Nasyr naïvely thought that the nation's leaders wouldn't allow a slaughter. Then he suddenly froze: What if it did happen? And he began to reassure himself that it couldn't.

The old man got undressed and went to bed. He had a dream. Furious thugs with rods attacked the students. There were shouts and moaning, and the blood flowed. The young woman who had said there should be no drinking or smoking fell down. Blood poured from a wide wound on her forehead. She tried to get up but received a kick in the face from a canvas boot and fell again. Canvas boots began to stomp on her. An old woman rushed toward her, yelling, "What are you doing to the child? I curse you!" But she, too, was knocked over . . .

Nasyr woke up and jumped out of bed. The piercing voice of the old woman was ringing in his ears. The gray light of dawn oozed through the window. Worry settled in the old man's heart again: Why had he dreamed something so horrid? Could it be true?

He rushed toward the window. People were still walking toward the square. Everyone was going together: policemen, students, soldiers, and hired toughs. The old fisherman had calmed down and felt relieved. "If they are all going together, then everything is fine . . ."

Any person might have thought the same thing when looking at that scene, any person who didn't know just one thing: late the night before, the leaders of the Republic had made a fateful decision to clear by force any young people that hadn't left the square by morning.

Nasyr washed himself, spread a towel on the bedside rug, and began to pray. He prayed for a long time and finished his prayer saying, "Bismillahi, ar-Rahmani, ar-Rahim! Ya Rabbim, the Almighty Creator! We believe in your power and beg you for mercy! Show us the true path, Allah, the righteous and irreproachable path. Direct our thoughts toward righteous deeds, and save us from sin and temptation!"

He stayed for a while on his knees after the prayer.

When he prayed on the seashore, he often saw a light over the water—a light or a half-transparent cloud that took on an almost human shape. Nasyr assumed that it was the Creator making himself felt. In minutes like this, the old fisherman's heart filled with quiet joy and reverence. A clarity would shine through his thoughts, and peace would settle on his soul. A deep sense of bliss would flow down from the back of his head through his entire body to the balls of his feet. It seemed the Creator appeared before Nasyr to let him know: I accept your prayer; keep praying; be faithful to me, God's slave, and I won't leave you. If the prayer gives you bliss, you know you won't be abandoned. Your soul will rest in paradise, Nasyr! The soul of any person who faithfully prays to me will go to paradise.

And, in that moment, he badly wanted to see that cloud again. But only a voice came. And that voice said to Nasyr, "God's son, don't give in to the devil's temptation! Beware of the devil, who will appear before you in human form. Love the person nearest you. Do no evil to him. Know: to let evil in your mind is a sin. Don't try to outdo others in strength or in wealth. It will only bring disappointment. Steer your desires, my son, to the path of truth. Only then can you and those around you avoid misfortune."

Nasyr was grateful for this voice. Here, in the frantic capital, he hadn't even hoped for that. "Ya, Rabbim, ya, Rabbim, I bow before your omnipotence, Allahu Akbar!"

Bolat and Khorst came to see him after lunch. They told him what was happening outside, and then all three of them rushed to the window. Nasyr gasped. The vigilantes were hitting the young boys and girls on their heads. They chased them as they tried to run. And with the help of the soldiers and police, they shoved them into cars. Many students were lying on the ice-cold asphalt. Some lay flat or crouched where they fell. Others tried to get up or crawl away.

"Savagery! Shame! Shame!" Khorst exclaimed.

"They decided to clear them by force." Bolat had gone deathly pale.

"I have never seen anything like this!" Khorst exclaimed again.

Nasyr was appalled.

"How will they look their people in the eyes tomorrow? Today they beat their own people up, and tomorrow they'll get onstage and smile at them again?"

He went quiet, shocked by one thought: a nation that will attack its own people will never save its sea! Why didn't he realize it sooner? There's no strength of thought in these people, only an uncontrolled wildness. It's not a nation that listens to God—and God turned away from them long ago.

Darkness suddenly descended over Nasyr's eyes, his ears were ringing, and his heart drove all his blood into his head in strong, arrhythmic pulses. He swayed. Khorst caught him as he fell and dragged him to the bed.

"Water! Bring some water quickly!"

Bolat rushed to the bathroom.

"Everything went dark for some reason." Nasyr struggled to talk. Khorst gave him a glass of water, and Nasyr took a few sips.

"Now put this pill under your tongue." Khorst placed a validolum pill in Nasyr's mouth.

"My blood pressure shoots up, I know. It should go back down now . . . Eh, Khorst, I got old. Nothing can be done about it."

"Of course. Seventy years is not a joke."

"The sea is hurrying me up . . . It wants . . . to take me with it . . . If it was still alive, I would also live until I was one hundred years old . . . But not now . . . I can feel it calling me . . . We will die on the same day. That is how it is."

Nasyr soon began feeling better. Then the phone rang. It was the taxi garage letting them know their car would arrive in ten minutes. Nasyr put on his coat. It was still damp and began to feel cold as soon as he was outside.

When the taxi arrived, Bolat and Khorst put the bags with the presents in the trunk. A vigilante charged up next to them and gesticulated angrily at the bags with his metal rod.

"What's in there?"

"Don't you have anything else to do?" Nasyr erupted.

"Maybe I don't," the man said threateningly.

"You, dzhigit, should be a bit more polite when talking to an aqsaqal." Khorst tried to shame him. "He could be your grandfather!"

"If he is, then he should answer me properly!"

"Are you an inspector?" Bolat couldn't help but insert himself into the argument. "Why do you care for someone else's belongings?"

"Today we are all inspectors!" The man looked at Bolat rudely.

"Alright. Stop holding people up." A police sergeant approached them.

"You should be embarrassed, dzhigit!" Nasyr said to the vigilante angrily. "Why are you beating up young people? Are they animals to be beaten with your metal rod? Just think: you could kill a man if you hit him with that. How would you look that man's mother in the eyes after that?"

The vigilante didn't have a chance to answer. One of his fellow thugs called out to him, "Vanya, quickly, come here! We are being called!"

He ran off, yelling back, "I have no time to deal with you; otherwise I would've made you dance!"

"Fascist!" Khorst exclaimed, looking at the hefty fellow now running away.

"Everyone in the car!" the taxi driver begged. "Let's get out of here quickly."

At that moment, two girls appeared around a corner, spattered in blood. The vigilantes became aware of them and started to move toward them. The girls were followed by a crowd of boys running away from the police. But now they were in a trap—behind them the police, in front the vigilantes who formed a chain right away. The students huddled together.

"They'll kill them!" Nasyr rushed out of the car.

"No one leave the car!" the taxi driver ordered.

A vigilante hit one of the girls on the head with his iron rod. She fell instantly, and blood splashed across the asphalt. The other vigilantes moved in on the boys and began to beat them with their rods. The students fell right away, and blood poured everywhere. Then they dragged the students to the van and flung them in as if they were logs.

Bolat jumped out of the car and ran to intervene. A tall vigilante hit him on the jaw. Bolat collapsed. Khorst and Nasyr rushed to Bolat. As they were lifting him up and pulling him to the side, they, too, were hit by the vigilantes. The same sergeant who had intervened before approached them, took both old men under their elbows, and walked them to the taxi.

"You'll be late for your train," he said tiredly. "Just go."

Bolat was dragged to a bus.

"Where will he be taken?" Nasyr asked.

"To the police station," the taxi driver replied.

"We can't leave him!" Khorst looked at Nasyr.

"Is he alive?"

"He was. But who knows what may happen later." The taxi driver shrugged.

"Do you know where the police station is?"

"I do, but I wouldn't recommend going there. You've got blood on your head, aga."

Nasyr wiped the palm of his hand over his forehead. When he looked at his hand, he saw it was covered in blood.

"No, son. You'd better take us to the police station." Nasyr looked at Khorst. "Are you alright?"

"I think I am. But they knocked out all my remaining teeth, and I only had four of them left."

"As long as your head is intact, you can get new teeth," Nasyr joked.

"You are such heroes, aqsaqals!" the taxi driver added.

There were many cars in front of the police station. The students were unloaded and forced toward the doors.

"There he is, your friend!" the taxi driver pointed to a bus.

"Bolat!" Nasyr shouted from the taxi window.

Bolat began to turn, but a policeman pushed him forward, and he couldn't turn to see them. After a few steps, he managed to turn toward Nasyr. Nasyr saw that there was not an unbruised place on the bloody face of their young friend!

Khorst got out and turned toward the police station. "Nasyr, you go to the railway station. I'll get Bolat out. I know a few people here."

The policemen walked a man past them, someone who looked familiar to Nasyr and Khorst.

"That's—" The taxi driver was startled as he recognized a famous Soviet artist, a world-renowned producer.

"Dear sir!" Nasyr addressed him. "Thank God you are alive. Where are they taking you?"

"Probably to the CC," the producer replied, trying to smile with his smashed and bloody lips. "And you should go away from here, aqsaqal. Otherwise, they'll pull you into this mess too."

They headed to the railway station. The taxi driver carried Nasyr's bags into the carriage. Kind people offered the fisherman the bottom shelf.

"Take care of the old man," the taxi driver whispered to them. "He is not well. Where are you going, yourself?"

"To Moscow," a tall man with a moustache replied. "We won't leave the old man on his own. Don't worry."

Nasyr sat by the window and soon dozed off. The man with the moustache woke him up by touching him on the shoulder.

"Grandpa, your coat is soaked. Take it off, and I can hang it here."

Nasyr took off the coat, and the young man quickly put it on the metal hanger. Nasyr went to the toilet and washed the blood off his head. He looked in the mirror. The wound stung. Nasyr examined the deep-purple bruise on his temple. While Nasyr was away, his friendly traveling companions had put some food on the table. Nasyr added some boiled chicken and opened some pickles that Irina Mikhailovna had prepared. Vasily, the man with the moustache, went to the conductor to get some iodine and began to apply it to Nasyr's temple. The other man was Nikolai. When Nasyr's wound was treated, Nikolai delved into his bag.

"And now we'll have some real medicine!" he said as he pulled a big bottle out and poured three glasses.

"It's strong liquor," Vasily explained. "Will you manage?"

"Ask the man from the front lines!" Nikolai snorted. "You probably had a lot of this hooch during the war. Am I right, Grandpa?"

"I won't lie. That is how it was. But today, I'll abstain."

"We won't force you." Vasily opened his arms in a gesture of tolerance.

But Nasyr considered the offer for a bit and said, "You know what? I've been through a lot in the last couple of days. And I've also caught a cold." He waved his hand. "Give me the glass!"

"That's right, Grandpa! By the morning, your cold will be completely gone!"

For a moment, the liquor made the inside of Nasyr's mouth go numb, but soon the warmth spread throughout his body. Nikolai also drank and snacked.

"Well, Grandpa, now tell us what is going on. People say Russians are getting beaten up."

"Everybody is getting beaten up, not just Russians."

"That is what people at the railway station were saying."

"That is just gossip. I saw everything with my own eyes."

"Tell us what you saw."

He related what he had witnessed slowly and in great detail. He told them how he ended up in Alma-Ata, about Bolat, Professor Slavikov, and the events on the square. The two men listened quietly.

During the night, Nasyr screamed in fear and woke up. He had been dreaming about the same girl again, with blood pouring out of her head like a fountain. Oh, dear God!

He was sweaty and thirsty. He got up and poured himself some water. Nikolai was awake.

"What are you scared of, Grandpa?"

"I dreamed about that girl . . . the one I told you about . . . poor girl."

"Ah, Grandpa, it's just the beginning. I agree with you, it does look like God has turned away from the people. You say they ruined the sea, ruined the rivers . . ." Nikolai went quiet, collecting his thoughts. Then he waved his hand. "Would you like more liquor, Grandpa?"

Nasyr shook his head.

Nikolai poured a shot for himself and downed it.

"You should have some food with it," Nasyr recommended. "It'll go down better."

"If there is one demonic force that can take over a Russian man, it's vodka. Only vodka can beat him. A Russian would sell his own father and mother for vodka. And it has spread from Russia across all our 'Roman Empire'—drinking nonstop and taking bribes. If Kazakhs don't get back to their senses, then they'll become drunkards. I tell you with authority. I learned from life itself. And I do see it. I do not just sit."

"Where do you sit?" Nasyr didn't understand.

"In the zone,[10] where else? In total I spent twenty-two years behind the wires. Do you think I regret it? Not really . . . But we're free now, thanks to Gorbachev and his amnesty."

"Were you both in prison?"

"Vaska only for three years. It's nothing. He was sent there for theft, although he didn't steal anything. And now that he's out, he says he has only one wish: to steal! He was just in prison for it in advance."

"Can someone be sent to prison without stealing anything?"

Nikolai whistled. "Yes, Grandpa! Although you are a wise old man, you are naïve like a child. When I was eighteen, according to the police, I killed a man. It would've been alright, except for one tiny detail: I never met the man I supposedly killed."

"What are you saying?" Nasyr was terrified.

"It often happens like this. I was given eight years. I came out of the prison as a genuine thug. They made me this way . . . Tell me, aqsaqal," he suddenly asked, "do you believe in perestroika?"

"Me?" Nasyr asked sourly. "Not really."

"That's just it. I will tell you about the zone. There's no sign of perestroika there. Everything there needs changing—everything! Everything down to the roots! And now in the zones, everybody is trying to hide the mess, trying to force this illness deep out of sight . . . Eh, what am I talking about? It's the same in society. Everything is done halfway—half propaganda, half truth. I've a feeling there are no people left who would tell the whole truth. There was one, but he lost his usefulness: Solzhenitsyn.[11] Do you know this writer? No, of course you don't. You might consider him a modern Tolstoy. The politicians used to tell me that in his Gulag, he didn't sin against the truth. If you look at the Russians, it's a nation God was generous to when he gave out talents. But there is no man who can lead their lost people now! The party keeps boasting, 'We will take the country out of stagnation.' Liars! And we follow along: first into stagnation, now out of stagnation. We vibrate together with the party because that is how it's supposed to be. Oh well. I'll go for a smoke."

Late in the morning, the train stopped for ten minutes in Dzhambul. Nikolai sent Vasily to get newspapers. He skimmed through *Pravda* and then gave it to Nasyr.

"*Pravda*—Truth. For some reason, your story doesn't coincide with what's written here."

"That's why it is true," Vasily observed sarcastically. He took the newspaper from Nasyr and began to read. "'Yesterday evening and today in Alma-Ata, a small group of students, spurred on by nationalistic elements, came out on the streets to express disapproval of the decision of the plenum of the CC of the Communist Party of Kazakhstan.' So you see, it's just a small group—about ten, fifteen people, the newspaper reassures us . . . And then in the best traditions of the Soviet press: 'Meetings, which took place in factories, workshops, higher education institutions, and other work collectives'—and also in all auls and *kishlaks*[12] across all Kazakh and Turkmen lands, across all the towns and villages of the Soviet Union and the entire earth, and also on the moon and even across the universe, basically— 'favored decisive measures against the hooligans.' That is how it is, aqsaqal."

"This kind of lie will bring no good," Nasyr sighed.

"Arrests will begin. As soon as people in the zone find out that Kazakhs are exterminating Russians in Kazakhstan, then the carnage will begin in Kazakhstan. One hundred and sixty million Russians, thanks to this newspaper, will now consider eight million Kazakhs their enemies. There's not a single word in here about how soldiers, policemen, and vigilantes were beating up unarmed students with shovels and steel rods and hunting them with dogs. Who will believe your word, aqsaqal? Not a single nation has yet stood up against the party and the government. Now the people in power will take their revenge on you to set an example for others."

When the train stopped for two minutes at Barlyktam station, Nikolai and Vasily helped Nasyr carry his luggage off the train.

"Dzhigits, if things don't go well for you in Russia, come to me in Sinemorye! You know the way now. About nine miles directly north from here, you'll find Karaoi. So don't be shy. I'll always be happy to see you. But for now, goodbye."

There were no cars going to Karaoi, so Nasyr stayed overnight with a railway worker he knew. Remembering Makhambet's request, he decided to visit Sarsengali at the seventh junction on his way home. From there, he could get to Karaoi on a camel. After lunch, the railway worker put Nasyr in the car of a freight train machinist, and Nasyr soon reached Sarsengali's home. He was just harnessing a camel to a cart when Nasyr arrived. "Are you doing that for me?" Nasyr asked, as they exchanged greetings.

"Who else?" Sarsengali smiled.

Then Sarsengali told him that the previous night, Kambar had passed away, and someone had been sent from Shumgen to call for him, since with Nasyr away there wasn't anyone to prepare the deceased for burial. "They'll be really surprised that they sent for me, but Nasyr-mullah himself will arrive!"

"No. If they sent for you, then you should prepare the deceased." He sighed. "It's a shame I didn't have a chance to see Kambar before he died. He was a good man. God doesn't rush to take a shithead up to heaven, but he doesn't delay when it comes to good people . . . That is your will, Allah!" Nasyr wiped his face with his hands.

Sarsengali's kind wife, Meiz, was sitting quietly in front of the house without joining in the conversation, just topping up their tea from time to time.

Nasyr addressed her. "Kelin, darling, we have met each other at a sad time. Now is not the time to talk about everyday life. But are your children well?"

"Our eldest is in Alma-Ata and the young one in Afghanistan. God willing, he'll be back in autumn. And here is our daughter-in-law with her son." Meiz smiled.

Nasyr stroked the boy's head, then untied his bags and put presents on the table. The little boy reached for the treats eagerly. Nasyr wanted to tell them about Alma-Ata, about Makhambet, about the bloodshed, but he held back because he didn't want to upset them.

Kambar was buried the next day with all of Shumgen and Karaoi gathered to send him off. The same day, Yesen was with Nurdaulet. Hearing there was a funeral in the aul, Nurdaulet followed ancient custom and entered the aul crying and moaning. As the cart rolled up, there was strong, young Yesen easily carrying in his arms the stump that remained of the man they once called Nurdaulet. Everyone rushed to the cart.

Kyzbala was also led forward, and people loudly called, "Nurdaulet! Nurdaulet!" But her mind didn't wake. The poor woman didn't understand anything. Life-weary Nurdaulet looked into her face with eyes full of tears, hope, and happiness but in vain. His once-beautiful wife no longer knew him.

By the time Nasyr returned to his home, thick ice had set across the water. The hungry wolves from Barsa-Kelmes Island came over as always and rushed into the sands in search of prey. But the times were different, and the sands were different. Now the only prey the wolves could find to eat were badgers.

The gazelles and onagers that were once such easy prey for the wolves were few and far between. Deprived of access to fresh water, they survived by drinking salt water. But the salt affected their offspring dramatically. Now gazelles and onagers gave birth only to male offspring. And when they grew up, the males were much harder for the wolves to catch.

And as they ran into the sands, the wolves came face-to-face with a ferocious pack of wild dogs. The wild dogs were bold and tough. And with good reason. In the last few years, they had grown strong by interbreeding with local wolves.

But this winter, the wolf pack was led by the sinewy white-browed wolf, Beloloby.

The pack met the wild dogs not far from Karaoi. Immediately, the packs tore toward each other. Beloloby could see the dogs had numbers on their side. So he looped around to launch himself on the dogs' flanks. In seconds, he had ripped several dogs to shreds. Yet he was quickly surrounded. Beloloby realized it was time to back off. He dashed off to the side to lead the pack away.

In a helicopter[13] high above, the pilot spoke to the hunters with him.

"It seems marauding wolves are fighting with the local dogs."

"Go in lower," one of the hunters said. "Shoot only wolves."

On the ground, a dark, whirling mass of yelping, snapping, snarling dogs and wolves bowled into Karaoi and flew past the people returning from Kambar's funeral. The wolves were fighting back. But Beloloby knew he had to keep his pack apart from the dogs if they were to survive. And now bullets flew from the metal bird! A few wolves were soon dead in the snow. The dogs stopped and vanished into the dunes, as if knowing the wolves were now at the mercy of the guns of the metal bird. Desperate, Beloloby turned back right into the aul to get his pack away. A few bullets snapped into the sand right next to him. But the helicopter wheeled away.

"Those snipers are savages," Musa noted as he stared up at the helicopter.

"Go after the leader!" yelled one of the hunters in the helicopter.

"But he's in the aul!" the pilot shouted in warning. "We can't risk injuring people."

Below, the villagers ran from the wolf. But Musa reassured them, "He won't touch anyone. He's now seeking our protection."

The men now surrounded Beloloby, and the wolf realized he was now safe from the steel predator.

"In here," Musa urged, opening the barn door and making an encouraging gesture to the hard-breathing wolf. "C'mon. Don't be shy, big wolf."

The helicopter was now hovering directly above.

"They won't have Beloloby," Musa muttered grimly.

Beloloby wouldn't go into the barn. He just crouched under the canopy, licking a wound on his leg.

The helicopter flew in very low.

"They'll blow the roof off!" Kyrmyzy shouted, running out of the house and shaking her fist at the helicopter. "What are you doing?"

"Bring me my gun," Musa ordered his wife. Seeing the gun, the wolf watched his every move.

Above, the pilot spotted Musa loading his gun. "Musa will shoot him. He won't miss, you can be sure!"

Musa fired two shots into the air.

"Hey, he's aiming at us, not at the wolf!" The pilot was shaken. "Shit! Let's not argue with this nut." And the helicopter began to fly away.

As Nasyr came up next to Musa, he realized he, too, admired the wolf. And then he remembered his fellow traveler, Nikolai. There had been something wolf-like in Nikolai, the same wariness as if about to pounce. "There can be wolves among humans," Nasyr thought, then suddenly said out loud, "Some wolves are like humans, like this Beloloby."

Musa nodded in agreement.

"Let's go into the house, aqsaqals. He is scared of us, scared of my gun."

Everybody followed Musa into the house. When Beloloby was left alone, he loped cautiously out from under the canopy. He was free. He ran toward the dunes, then slowed his pace, stopped, sat down, and began to howl. And only then did he slowly trot and vanish into the sands.

Musa watched him go from the porch. Then, wiping a tear away, he murmured, "Ah, wolves, wolves . . . even you can't live here with us anymore."

XII

When he arrived at the hotel, Kakharman had a shower, then sat down to give Slavikov a call. Natasha picked up the phone, and Kakharman learned that Matvei Panteleevich had been ill. He'd been in the hospital for some time, but Igor had just gone to the hospital to bring him home at long last.

"We are waiting for your visit," Natasha said warmly. "Will you be able to come tonight?"

"I will be there!"

Then he called Yegor Ushakov, his old acquaintance from the State Planning Committee. They agreed to meet in his office after lunch.

Kakharman decided to fill the time before his meeting with a slow walk along Gorky Street. As he walked, he realized that his whole attitude toward Moscow crowds was very different from what it once was. Gorky Street no longer seemed friendly and exciting. The lines looked worse and the people queuing gloomier. There was gossip that the price of gold would go up, and the rumor whipped people into a panic. Kakharman had never understood the attraction of the "yellow devil." Long ago, while he was young, he had given Aitugan a small ring for her birthday—and he hadn't bought gold since. Fortunately, Aitugan was equally indifferent to gold and toward luxury generally.

Women on the coast wore silver earrings, bracelets, and rings. The local silversmiths, or zergers, had been famous for their skill since ancient times. Every object they created was a work of art. The ancient zergers, who used to live in towns along the Silk Road, embellished their creations with extraordinarily beautiful ornaments and colors. But as people began to leave the sea, the zergers disappeared too. Eventually, Musa was the only man by the sea who knew how to make things, having learned when he was young. Many beautiful things created by the zergers of Sinemorye survive, but most of the makers' names are already forgotten. Only one name is still revered: Islamgaiyp.

Islamgaiyp died the year Kakharman was born. Islamgaiyp, even as a mature master, used to travel to Istanbul and Baghdad, Mecca and Medina to pick up new skills. He lived in Mecca for three years, supported by Kunanbai.[1] As he worked as a silversmith in Mecca, Islamgaiyp studied Arabic ornamentation and in return shared some of the secrets of Kipchak ornamentation with the masters of Mecca. He also took a liking to Zukhra, the young daughter of the esteemed master Alid-din. Zukhra was very skilled in weaving carpets and *ala-sha*.[2] Islamgaiyp and Zukhra got married, and soon Islamgaiyp returned to his homeland with his young wife, who was warmly welcomed on the Sinemorye coast. Kakharman never got to meet the great master, but as a little boy, he would often stare at the intricate decoration on his mother's silver necklace. Islamgaiyp had given this necklace to Korlan on the day of her marriage to Nasyr. It was created by the master at the sunset of his life, when he was becoming infirm. Yet every single detail of the pattern—each curl, each intricate embellishment—was unique and exquisite.

It was bustling in front of the offices of the *Moscow News*. There was a lively trade in newspapers and books. Arguments were breaking out here and there among the people crowding around. Kakharman had heard about these unofficial publications but never read them before. He bought a dozen or so and tucked them away in his briefcase. He still had time before his meeting with Ushakov. He returned to the hotel and laid them out on the table. He lit up a cigarette and went to the window. Moscow was getting dirtier and dirtier every year. Each time he came here, he found it harder to bear the streets of the capital—they looked dispossessed, rubbish strewn, and crammed full.

Ushakov embraced Kakharman warmly when they met.

"Yegor, I have no one else to go to. Try to understand. It's really hard for the fishermen there."

"Alright. Leave your submission here. We'll come up with something." He looked at the papers. "That's a long list! You'll be lucky to get half of what you're asking for."

"Whatever you can get. I'll be happy to receive anything."

"I'll try."

"Don't let me down."

"Do you have any plans for tonight? Come to my place! I am a bachelor. Marina is away on a business trip, so we can have a wild time!"

"Better on Friday. Today I'm going to the Slavikovs."

"People say the old man is a lost cause—cancer."

"Are you serious? Damn it! He was the only person I could rely on in Moscow, and now this . . ."

"It may be just gossip. You'll find out for yourself today." Ushakov changed the subject. "You better tell me. Is it true that oil was discovered in Zaysan? A friend of mine called me. He read about it in ministerial reports. Now the robbery will begin! They will ruin Altai, the last unspoiled area of Kazakhia! Kakharman, you need to raise your people. They must not drill there! This oil won't do any good to Kazakhs or the Union!"

"And what do you think about it here?"

"Do you think anyone in the State Planning Committee cares about it? Our big men have other things to do."

"Oil . . . in Zaysan . . . Who would've thought?" Kakharman's mind was in turmoil as he walked out of the building. The evening was still far away, so he walked up Herzen Street to the Zoological Museum. He stopped by the small fish exhibit and studied it for a long time. He remembered how, long ago, he and Igor enjoyed coming here. In the hall next door, the crowds were thronging around an exhibition of seashells from Australia given to the museum by the eminent biologist Adilya Kotovskaya. The whole gallery was filled with their varied and fantastic shapes. Nature never repeated itself in any shell, not in color or shape, but in each shell, there was a key idea—a frozen symphony, multifaceted and grand.

Igor opened the door to Kakharman. They hugged and looked at each other closely.

"Did you bring him home?" Kakharman asked quietly. Igor nodded.

"He's in his room. He can hardly walk. He insisted on being taken away from that damned hospital. Take your coat off. He's waiting for you. We are watching the party conference."

Slavikov was sitting in bed with his back against a high pile of pillows. If Kakharman had met him elsewhere, he would not have recognized him. The professor was emaciated, little more than skin and bones! Not so long ago, he had looked like a bogatyr from a fairy tale: well built, light haired, blue eyed.

"It's so good you came!" Slavikov leaned toward Kakharman and touched Kakharman's brow with his own hot, dry forehead. This was the ancient custom of fishermen: when meeting someone close, they touched chests or brows or drew the friend's palm to their forehead. Slavikov made all three of these ritual gestures. The skin on his face, Kakharman noticed, was an alarming shade of yellow.

Kakharman looked away and asked suddenly, "How are you feeling, Matvei Panteleevich?"

"Are you serious?" The professor's eyes sparkled mischievously. "Note to Mustafa . . . *Memento homo, quia pulvis es et in pulverem reverteris!*"[3]

Kakharman looked at the old professor with respect. He has so little fear before death.

"Here we have our own rapid developing cancer. It's a bit like yours—the same trash. But I just think it's time. I have lived my life; now it's time for others to live. I regret only that I had so little happiness in this life. I had great ideas and dreams, but few of them came true. Why am I telling you this? You know it all yourself. Ah, what slogans the French Revolution had! Freedom! Equality! Brotherhood! I carried this inside me my whole life, even though my hands were tied. What freedom? What brotherhood? These are just empty sounds for them. They don't believe in God or in the devil or in the French Revolution. We rejected God for seventy years, fought with him as our mortal enemy! We decided that it's easier to declare him an enemy of the people than live the way he demands." The professor began to laugh dryly. "How didn't I understand it sooner? They decided to fight God, but each now carries the stamp of Satan."

The professor went silent and fell back on the pillows. With sadness, Kakharman identified his own thoughts and feelings in the professor's words.

"Dad, would you like tea?"

"Please . . ."

The professor took a syringe from the bedside table and gave himself an injection. "Morphine," Kakharman thought.

"It works for two hours, and then I need another injection. Have you seen your parents recently? How are they doing?"

"I haven't been home for a while. I get all my news through letters."

The professor said nothing because the phone began to ring. He was about to reach for it but changed his mind. Igor picked up the phone in the other room.

"Who's that?"

"It's Viktor Mikhailovich. He's asking for permission to come around."

"Now he is so polite! When he was a minister, he'd come without permission." The professor grinned. "He's gotten a little nervous since he retired. And he now asks for permission to visit old friends! Do you know him, Kakharman? Buslaev. He was a minister not so long ago—you probably know him. He's actually my distant relative. But that is not why I love him. He is a good man even though he is a minister and even though he once used to go to the Kremlin."

"He didn't go there very often," Igor noted with irony. "He could've gotten two stars. Then he would definitely have had a monument erected in his homeland."

"It wasn't quite in him, I will admit. But it all ended up very comically. As soon as his mother died at his home in Sosnovka, Sosnovka fell apart. Our ministers are fools. They should have kept at least one village warm! Where else are they going to put their statues?"

Natasha put the kettle on the table and looked questioningly at the professor.

"No, I don't want to take the medicine!" Slavikov understood her. "Pour some cognac for me and Kakharman, about two ounces each. I'll have a drink with him for the last time!"

Igor poured the drink. Slavikov raised his glass.

"People say a good dog leaves the house before it dies. But I think it's more dignified for a man to die in his home. That is why I came home!"

"Dad, don't start again."

"Don't interrupt me. I know exactly what I'm saying. I'm sad to say goodbye to Kakharman. He is an honest and honorable man. But it's good that you're in Moscow now—God knows, we may not have seen each other if you'd come later. Bow to Nasyr and Korlan from me. And you, young ones, be healthy! And make sure you don't lose touch!" Slavikov took a little of his drink. "Life has to come to an end one day. But it completely went out of my head . . . I completely forgot . . . that is how it is." He smiled. "It's a shame we have no Nasyr or Akbalak here. I would've enjoyed listening to your songs before dying."

Kakharman admired the professor more than ever. He was captivated by the old man's wisdom, his ability to joke in the face of death. He felt deep sympathy for the professor. "I've known Matvei Panteleevich since I was a child," he thought. "Almost forty years."

Igor adjusted the pillows and helped his father sit more comfortably. Then the doorbell rang. It was Buslaev. He came in and sank into the wide armchair at the head of the professor's bed. Kakharman knew Buslaev right away even though they had met briefly only once, six years earlier. The minister was cheerful and in the pink of health. The professor introduced them all and reminded Buslaev that he had once sent Kakharman to meet him about the situation at the sea. But Buslaev couldn't remember.

"Kakharman, please don't be offended. A minister meets so many different people each day! How can I remember everyone?"

"No offense taken, Viktor Mikhailovich! Especially because you satisfied my request then."

"It's very possible," Buslaev replied, half-jokingly. "After all, I was a good minister." He turned to Slavikov. "We've been criticizing our youth, but they seem to be more educated and more clever than we were."

"During the sixties, the party apparatus and ministers shat upon anyone who mentioned the word 'ecology.' What is this damn ecology? Give us a plan, a plan! It was from your offices that the orders to trample Mother Nature were coming. To take everything she's got," Slavikov said, irritated.

"Matvei Panteleevich, we've been arguing our whole lives. Let's make peace at least in our old age!"

Everybody smiled at the joke. But the professor continued harshly.

"They are idlers, those who protect nature! They slow down our progress! That is what ministers used to shout. And they go on shouting—those who are still alive. Can't you see that we've reached a dead end? You, yourself, still live on concessional terms! Good for you! You have special food, special prices, special cars. Your children work abroad in the West. How good it all is! But you have robbed your people. You took their shoes and clothes away. And then you abandoned them. You spat into their souls, you, people's servants!"

"My daughter came back from New York long ago," Buslaev objected weakly. "Are you scientists any better than us?"

"It depends. Some scientists were directly involved in the destruction of rivers and sea, in the extermination of the forest, in the construction of nuclear weapons and power stations. Were they really scientists? No—forgive me, Natasha—they were whores! There are few scientists who didn't sink so low. You can count them on your fingers. There was also a third type of scientist whom I feel genuinely sorry for. At meetings there were appeals to the hall, 'Are there Weismannist-Morganists[4] among us, comrades?' and everybody would cringe, including talented and decent people."

"Didn't you cringe?" Buslaev asked the professor testingly.

"No, my friend. I didn't cringe. I would raise my hand and say, 'I am a Morganist.' I was one, and I will remain one."

"That explains your journey to Kolyma."

The room was quiet. The professor drank the rest of his tea noisily. Natasha took the empty cup from him.

The professor began to talk wistfully.

"My dear friends! We can listen only to our own bellies. We cannot even guess what great happiness it is to truly listen to nature." After considering for a while, he growled crossly, "And we, throughout history, were listening to the rumble of revolutions and wars. The whole of human history is wars. If you think about it, is that not savagery? The history of humanity should go a different way."

"What way?" Buslaev asked cheerfully. He always felt better when Slavikov left ministers alone and talked about humanity.

"In the end, we must learn reason."

"Dad, that won't happen for another hundred years."

"How can we wait a whole century? By that time, people will have exterminated themselves! I can't believe that we will do that. People must survive. They must step into the third millennium as rational people, not as barbarians." He began to cough heavily. "I am talking about you, young people, not about myself. Both I and the sea that died in front of my eyes are the yesterday. We are leaving, disappearing." He began to cough again, then continued. "How does a

Kazakh feel without the sea, ah? The death of the sea will be a great disaster for the whole of Central Asia. Back in the seventies, I warned Kunaev and Rashidov that the sea must be preserved, that nature's treasures must not be treated so irresponsibly. And back then, they had real power—they could've done something if they'd wanted to. But they did nothing. They were and remained little czars. They were thinking about one thing: how to please Moscow. How else could they stay on the throne?

"They thought I was crazy. I don't hold any personal grudge against them. One is already in his grave, and to Dimash I wish a long life. When I die, I certainly won't be thinking of them. I will be thinking of those Kazakhs, Karakalpaks, Turkmens, and Uzbeks that my words reached, who helped me at least a little in this life—even though we achieved nothing." The professor looked at Kakharman. "Poor Kazakh people! What an awful fate! If I were asked who in our country has suffered the most from the imperial rule of the Center, I would say Kazakhia! But nobody asks me. Maybe they are exterminating the Kazakh nation to put our whole army on the steppes? The fewer Kazakhs in Kazakhstan, the more military units and military sites appear there. And who is Minister of Defense Yazov going to fight with?"

Slavikov, growing tired, leaned back on the pillows.

"Viktor, you probably don't understand why they got agitated in Alma-Ata in December and protested in the square?"

"You know, if I'm honest, I don't. Why would they care who's the party leader?"

"People do care," Kakharman replied.

"They have enough sheep," an offended Buslaev grumbled. "What else do they need? I don't understand."

"Here is one of them, Kakharman. If I tell him now that Kazakhs never had enough freedom, equality, and brotherhood, would he understand me?"

"Dad, conference!" Igor turned up the volume of the TV.

"Take out my Dictaphone. But don't record everything, only the interesting parts!"

During the course of two hours, Igor turned the Dictaphone on only six times—each time the ecological disaster at Sinemorye was directly mentioned.

"People are beginning to talk!" the professor lamented. "If only they'd started fifteen years ago!"

The phone rang again. Igor answered it. Someone wanted to talk to the professor.

"He only returned from the hospital today . . . Yes, yes . . . No. He doesn't answer the phone." Igor's face dropped. "When? Last night. What a loss!" He put the phone down. "Dad, Sakharov[5] died."

After a pause, the professor said dejectedly, "He didn't die his own death. We killed Andrei Dmitrievich. The only man who spent his whole conscious life fighting those in power. What are we in comparison to him? Pygmies . . . He rose among us like an impregnable rock." Then he began speaking in Latin: "*Libertas alicui pecunia non potest vendi.*[6] He did not retreat a single step . . . Natasha, do we have candles?"

He gave himself another injection. Natasha turned the lights off and lit the candles. The professor closed his eyes.

"Dad, would you like us to leave you?" Igor asked quietly.

The professor nodded.

"Yes, please. I never knew him personally, but I always admired him. He did not kneel before shamelessness, lawlessness, or ignorance."

Slavikov passed away three days later. Not many people came to his funeral, just his closest relatives and friends and some colleagues, who, like him, never strived for power or wealth. Matvei Panteleevich was buried in Vagankovo Cemetery, next to his wife, Sofia Pavlovna.

When they returned from the cemetery, Igor turned the tape player on and played the last kyui of Akbalak, the one composed just before he died.

"That is what my father wanted," Igor said. "It's a requiem. Akbalak was saying goodbye to the sea with this music. Now let the sea say goodbye to my father."

Ust-Kamenogorsk wasn't accepting planes. So Kakharman sat in Moscow airport for a second day and was watching the party conference. During one meeting, candidates were suggested for the post of chairman of the Ministry of Water Resources. One suggested candidate was Polad-zade. Kakharman was horrified.

"Are they on drugs?"

Then he stood up and shouted across the waiting lounge at the screen. "Have you gone mad? Who are you suggesting? He is the very devil."

Everyone in the lounge turned toward him. They all probably thought he was crazy.

Kakharman really did feel as if he was losing his mind. And he began shouting loudly, "He is a murderer! It was that man who killed Sinemorye! And now he will kill Balkhash too. Do you hear me? He'll kill it!"

But Polad-zade was already standing on the stage, answering questions, a smile on his face. "They are also possessed by the devil, that's for sure!" Kakharman thought feverishly. "They are all bound by Satan!" He remembered that in his briefcase were those unread religious newspapers he bought outside *Moscow News*. They were filled with biblical quotes—some unfamiliar, some half-familiar, and some familiar through his father's Quran, which Kakharman had sometimes looked through when he had nothing else to do . . . But no . . . The people who were shown on the TV weren't holding a white Bible in their hands. They were holding a black Bible. They were nastily winking at small devils, who were looking from behind the members' shoulders . . .

"Get this murderer off the stage!" Kakharman was shouting. People moved away from him. "Polad-zade is a murderer!"

"Sir, what's going on?" a sergeant said very gently, touching Kakharman on the shoulder.

"Just leave him." A young blond woman moved between the sergeant and Kakharman. She pulled Kakharman toward her. "Sit down."

"Is he your husband?" the sergeant asked.

"Yes, he is!"

"Your husband," the sergeant replied doubtfully, "looks as if he had too much to drink. You should look after him better if he's your husband. It doesn't look good when he screams across the hall when there are families trying to rest."

"It's my fault; he's just a very emotional person. Have a look for yourself!" She nodded toward the screen. "Anyone would howl looking at that."

"Polad-zade did not get enough votes!" People were talking loudly.

Kakharman couldn't believe his ears. Was perestroika really happening?!

The woman poured some lemonade for him.

"He missed out! He missed out!" Kakharman whispered.

"And I think they should all be prosecuted—Polad-zade and Vasilyev and Voropaev!"

"We might be very like-minded!" Kakharman hugged her. "Thank you!"

"Where are you flying to?"

"To Ust-Kamenogorsk."

"I'm off to Alma-Ata. I've been sitting on my suitcases for almost an entire day."

"Are we fellow countrymen? I'm sorry. I was screaming like a madman."

"I doubt we're fellow countrymen." She touched her hair with her hand. "I'm from Saint Petersburg."

"I'm sorry, but do you drink?"

"I do."

"Shall we celebrate this occasion?"

They walked outside and settled in a quiet corner.

"To the destruction of the Ministry of Water Resources!" The woman raised a glass, and Kakharman generously filled it with cognac from the bottle in his bag.

"For the people to always stay people!"

"We haven't introduced ourselves yet."

"Kakharman. I'm from the shores of that troubled sea everyone is talking about. I'm a fisherman."

"And my name is Lyudmila. I am . . . a poet."

"Very nice to meet you!"

Lyudmila didn't reply. She began to declare:

Why did the Creator make all, yet never
Managed to let us live forever?
If we are perfect, then why should we die
If we're not perfect, who was it screwed up? say I.

At that moment, to the annoyance of Kakharman, a flight to Alma-Ata was announced.

"Already?"

"Already!" Lyudmila laughed.

He kept waving to her for a long time. From the distance, she shouted to him some impromptu verses, but he only heard the first lines clearly.

May Allah protect you,
And good luck in all you do!

Where is he—is it Czechoslovakia? Yes, it is Czechoslovakia. How
could he forget? The field he and Salyk are running across is stuffed
with mines. As long as Salyk endures, then he, Semeon, is fine. He's a
tough guy . . . The edge of the forest is close . . . Just as long as Salyk
endures . . . The Alsatians are wheezing very near . . . Knife . . . Get
the knife out . . . The knife is in his hand . . . "Get your knife out!" he
shouts to Salyk. "That's it! Strike!"

He turns around and raises his left arm, and as the wheezing dog
jumps, he sharply plunges the knife right in its heart. He kills the second
in the same manner. He can hear the guns but can't yet see the Germans
behind the slopes. "Just need to make it there . . . to the edge of the for-
est . . ." Two more Alsatians yelp piteously under Salyk's knife. They've
made it! The Germans are on the hill and, swearing, send a few rounds
at their backs, but the bullets slam into the trees . . .

Semeon Arkhipovich opened his eyes. He often dreamed about the war, he
often dreamed of that day, those Alsatians that he hated so fervently that whenever he saw one, he would instinctively grab a knife . . .

The weather got much better. He fired the stove and put the kettle on. Someone
knocked on the window. He turned on the lamp and went out onto the porch.

"It's me, Kakharman, Semeon Arkhipovich!"

"Glad it's you," the old man rejoiced. "Very good timing. I am struggling
here with insomnia."

Kakharman walked in and began to take his coat off.

"The frost isn't easing . . . How are you feeling?"

"I'm well, thank God, and so is my family. I only just returned from the lake
yesterday . . . so I have no food in the house."

The kettle boiled, and Semeon Arkhipovich began to make tea.

"Yesterday I bought some new books. I've been reading Yuri Kuznetsov[7] until late and keep asking myself what we were dying for. Listen."

He went to the bedroom and returned with a book. He put his glasses on and began to read quietly.

The country read his memorial long ago
With all of its steel voices,
But Mother Earth won't accept his body,
And the heavens reject his soul.
Twice a year, his soul yearns for release,
His tomb becomes a stage.
The stream moves on devotedly,
Portraits of him flow past
Yet the people on the stage have no clue
Whose ashes they trample with their feet.

XIII

The snow fell heavily that winter, and the frosts were bitter, but eventually spring crept in among the sands. The snow melted, rivers and lakes were freed from their icy shackles, and the fishermen prepared to return to Balkhash. The team chose Yesen to be their skipper in place of Kambar. "Experience will come," the fishermen decided. "The most important thing is that he's quick and clever." They consulted Nasyr, and he concurred.

So Yesen became a skipper in the same way as Nasyr once became a mullah. Yesen didn't argue with the elders' decision.

Karaoi, which was always fairly quiet, became empty again. On the day after they left, Nasyr couldn't settle. There were as few signs of life in Karaoi as there were in the desert that stretched monotonously far into the distance. "How can this be called life?" Nasyr would sigh. "It's a paltry existence."

After saying goodbye to the fishermen, he lay down and didn't get back up for the whole day. He didn't get up even when Musa came. It looked like Musa was having trouble settling as well. He groaned with helpless frustration when he saw Nasyr and left without even touching the tea Korlan put in front of him. Nasyr got up only when it was time for the evening prayer. He did his ablutions, threw his jacket over his shoulders, and headed toward the dunes. The dusk was growing thicker and the air cooler, which cheered him up a bit. Once he was walking, his legs warmed up, but he still felt sad.

And now until the next frosts, life would continue its miserable round for the small collection of old men and women who remained in the aul. No news ever seemed to reach Karaoi—and with the mail coming just once a month, there was little to get excited about. Nasyr didn't read newspapers now. Whether it was just old age or something else, he had lost all interest in them since his visit to Alma-Ata. He felt sick just at the sight of a newspaper.

The first stars began to glitter softly over the sands. Nasyr stared into the dark distance and thought maybe the great Abai had had the same dismal thoughts when alone in the night. Maybe Abai, too, had been tormented by the idea that less and less truth remained on this earth, that people have become shallower in their thoughts, swapping the beautiful impulses of the soul—honor, conscientiousness, civic spirit—for bustle, greed, vanity, and their own well-being. "Poor Abai!" Nasyr said out loud. "You were doomed to a premature death. You were powerless to make your accusations against us Kazakhs heard—nobody was listening to you."

Abai became Nasyr's sounding board in his old age. Nasyr found an echo of his thoughts and his doubts and disappointments in those of the great poet. At the sunset of his life, Nasyr understood why Abai had been so lonely. The more he read the great poet's work, the deeper he felt the poet's words. He knew much of Abai's work by heart and could quote whole paragraphs like a prayer:

A proof of the existence of a single and Almighty God is the fact that for many centuries people talked about the existence of God in numerous languages—and no matter how many religions there are, all think God is characterized by love and fairness. We are not creators but mortals who learn about the world through the things he created. We are servants of love and fairness. And we differ only by how much each of us comprehends the creations of the Most High. But by believing and worshiping, we have no right to say what someone else should believe and worship. The core of humanity is love and fairness. They are present in everything and decide everything. This is the crown of creation by the Most High. Love is manifested even in the way a stallion takes a mare. In whoever feelings of love and fairness prevail—he is a wise and well-studied man. We are not capable of making science up; we can only see and feel the created world and understand its harmony with our minds.

These thoughts of Abai came to Nasyr's mind as the night came down on the dunes.

Nasyr headed slowly back to the aul.

In the morning, he was up at the crack of dawn. As always, Korlan was already awake, preparing something on the stove.

"Why aren't you sleeping?" she scolded Nasyr. "Why are you up so early?"

"We'll have plenty of time for lying down soon enough."

Korlan didn't respond. She merely adjusted her head scarf. Nasyr went out to the barn and gave the mare her oats, then came back and began his morning prayer. He prayed a long time, as if trying to catch up on what he missed the day before.

During their morning tea, Korlan began to sigh. "I keep thinking about Kakharman. My heart feels—I need to see him . . . I think I should go to see him: my heart aches."

"Why not? You should go," Nasyr agreed. "You'll hug them all, and it will make you feel better."

Old Korlan began preparing for her trip to distant Zaysan that very day.

Spring in the sands turned quietly into summer. And very soon, the summer heat was blazing its way along the shore. This was a time when if you forgot a jug of water outside, it would almost be boiling by the time you remembered. In such sizzling heat, no one moved in Karaoi, no animals would tread even gingerly on the scorching sands, and no bird would brave the air to fly.

Yet this was the time Korlan set off for Zaysan. Nasyr stayed with Berish, whose summer holiday had already begun. Korlan entrusted her neighbor Zhanyl to feed the men, and she began to cook for them once a day. She would wash dishes once a day, tidy up the house, and sweep the floors. But often Zhanyl would just invite them to her place for lunch and dinner. Nasyr and Berish had nothing against this.

Zhanyl was a good woman. No one had a bad word to say about her. Zhanyl was now a widow, and although her life was poor, it was a life full of dignity. People in Karaoi treated her with respect. Life on the coast was always tough, and people worked hard. Yet Karaoi was exceptional among the coastal auls in that the majority of people had a complete lack of interest in luxury. The people of Karaoi were happy with simple food, simple clothes, and modest decoration in their homes. What was truly valued was industriousness, human understanding and kindness, and heartfelt openness. Who knows? Maybe that's one reason Karaoi produced many scientists, famous healers, and skillful masters.

Since ancient times, the fishermen of Karaoi had worshipped only the sea, and for them there was nothing richer than the sea. For centuries, they were happy to have the sea in their souls and in their hands. The fishermen were happy there was a sea, and the sea was happy there were fishermen. That's how it was from time immemorial. So you can only imagine the depth of sorrow drowning the few coastal auls. It wasn't wealth and possessions they had been robbed of. It wasn't even their livelihoods and daily bread. It was their very souls.

When handing the plates to Nasyr and Berish, Zhanyl smiled gently and said, "Eat, eat . . ." Her granddaughter—a thin girl with a pale face—was sitting next to her, staring at the boy and the old man. Sometimes Berish, while waiting for lunch, read tales to little Marzhan. Marzhan would listen carefully and then try to tell them to her grandmother. Nasyr stroked the bright girl on her head and said, "And who do you get your brains from?" And Marzhan answered with certainty, "From Grandma!"

Of course, Nasyr didn't approve of Zhanyl's daughter-in-law leaving, but to see it another way: how hard life is for young people in Karaoi. Even water has to be brought from God knows where. And they have to go out and collect wood in the sands just to keep warm. What young woman could happily live such an arduous life?

And so the girl went back where she came from, and Zhanyl brought up her innocent child, feeding her goat's milk, which Kyzbala shared with her. Every morning, Kyzbala brought a half-gallon jug of milk. It was hard for Zhanyl, but she didn't complain and didn't cry. She was scared for Yesen, scared he would break down if she didn't show how to hold up in this difficult life. And so Yesen didn't lose his heart—it would be shameful when he looked at his mother and at her strength. He did try approaching his wife a few times, but she refused point-blank to come back. And neither would his mother agree to move to the city.

Then one day, out of the blue, Yesen's young wife arrived in Karaoi with her brothers and aunties. Her plan was to take Marzhan back with her. Zhanyl kicked them out of her house. The brothers were going to take the child away forcefully, but old Musa and Nasyr were a match for them. As for Marzhan, as soon as she saw this strange woman in makeup, she was so scared, she began to cry.

After Korlan left, time in Nasyr's house, which already ran slow, ground to a halt. After breakfast at Zhanyl's, Nasyr and Berish would return home and sit with books. Nasyr would look through the Quran, and Berish would get absorbed in adventures and fiction. Often, Nasyr would raise his eyes, look into the distance, and think. He never imagined that separation from his wife, after living side by side for so long, would be such anguish. Of course, there were sometimes quarrels and family disagreements between them, but now with life heading toward the sunset, Nasyr realized that they had had an amazingly good life, despite moments of hunger and sorrow.

One day while Korlan was away, Nasyr opened the prayer book and began to mumble:

> *Bismillahi, ar-Rahmani, ar-Rahim! Thanks be to Allah for the sky that sends rains to the earth; thanks be to Allah for decorating the earth with fruits, herbs and trees; thanks be to Allah for the springs that come from the ground in accordance with his powerful will; for creating life on earth together with water in the ground, rivers and seas . . .*

In the past, when Nasyr addressed the Almighty with his gratitude, a cloud would appear before him resembling a human figure. Nasyr used to think it was Allah himself acknowledging the fervor of his prayers. But lately he hadn't seen the cloud, and it felt as if Allah had turned away from the old fisherman. But there had still been the voice, the same enchanting voice he had heard when he prayed in the hotel room in Alma-Ata. But today he couldn't even hear that.

Nasyr was afraid. He stayed motionless over the prayer book, listening, but there was only an echoing silence. "It's not a good sign," he decided.

He rose from his knees. He knew what he needed to do. He pulled his and Korlan's clothes from the chest. Something told him he must give these clothes to those who needed them more. He must also slaughter a ram, keep a fast for three days, and beg Allah in his mercy to send the rain, for lack of which the seashore is drying out. From the same chest, he took a large knife, sharpened it, washed it with warm water, dried it properly, and headed to the barn.

"Pour water in the jug," he ordered the surprised Berish. "Go and get Zhanyl."

When he got to the yard, he regretted that he hadn't put anything on his head. The sky was breathing with heat like a smithy. In the barn, he caught a black sheep by its leg, pushed it to the side, and tied its legs up with a rope. "Bismillah, there is no fault of yours in it," he murmured and slashed the sheep across the neck. By the time Zhanyl came, he had already skinned the sheep and cut it into pieces.

"Bring a lot of salt; otherwise, we won't be able to preserve the meat in this heat. Berish, show her where we keep the salt. And bring a pile of logs; we need to smoke it properly."

"Why did you slaughter it in such heat?" Zhanyl asked once they had finished with the meat. "Are you expecting guests?"

"What guests would come now?" Nasyr replied. "Now you couldn't force anyone to come here even with a stick. No. I decided to make a sacrifice for Allah. I will fast and pray, and maybe he'll send us rain. Don't you remember, I once managed to persuade him to send rain?"

"How could I forget! But that was a long time ago. And during the summer after your downpour, there wasn't a single drop of rain."

Nasyr frowned and thought, "She is right." His cheerful mood quickly vanished. He sighed. "And now there's no one to even give alms to. No people are left here—neither rich nor poor. I put some clothes on the chest. Could you please adjust them for Nurdaulet?"

"It's not your fault, Nasyr, that we don't have rain here," Zhanyl said, trying to cheer Nasyr up. "You should keep praying. Allah has ears; he is listening to you."

"Of course he is. Who else can we believe in now, if not in God?" He began to take pieces of meat from Zhanyl and skewer them on a stick so that the meat would smoke evenly.

For three days, he stayed at home, adhering to a strict fast. On the final day, Nurdaulet visited him. He had struggled to get to Nasyr's house in his wheelchair because its small wheels kept sinking in the sand. In the yard, Berish took Nurdaulet in his arms, carried him in, and sat him at the table. Nurdaulet had only come to visit Nasyr once before, and that was to request that Nasyr take him to Korym Island.

Nasyr had understood this request in his soul and accepted it. He couldn't look at the invalid without tears. He was so shredded by life that only a small piece of the once-cheerful dzhigit remained.

Since his return to Karaoi, Nurdaulet had only once talked about his life and had never returned to the conversation again. And no one bothered him with questions.

Nasyr, scraping a thick saxaul stick, nodded to him. "What, brother, missing Korym? I remember your request. I haven't forgotten about it. Just wait another day, I'll finish *oraza*,[1] and we'll go. It would be nice to wait for good weather too. What do you think? It's been baking hot for a month already. If it carries on like this, there'll be fires on the sands."

Nurdaulet said nothing and just looked out the window at the incandescent white sand. What was he thinking about? Since he had come back home from the distant island Valaam, his face had become so tanned, it was almost brown. His thick eyebrows hung over his eyes so that his face looked stern. Nurdaulet was living in turns with either Musa or Nasyr, so Korlan had a lot of work to do. Zhanyl and Korlan visited Kyzbala a few times and talked to her about Nurdaulet, but it all was in vain—Kyzbala's insanity was irreversible. Eventually, Nurdaulet asked Nasyr and Musa to take him to her. "We will live together for a little. Who knows? Maybe she'll get used to me and remember me. Nasyr-aga, if you'd only known how much I hoped it'd happen! At this point, I'd be happy to exchange just a single word with her in this life!"

"If our healer Kazhygaiyp was alive," Nurdaulet said to Nasyr before moving to his wife's, "he might've helped Kyzbala to recover. Please take me and Kyzbala to the grave of his father, Abutalip. Maybe it will help. I've heard that if you read prayers and incantations over the grave of the holy Abutalip, it can bring someone's mind back."

"I've heard that, too, but his grave is long gone—our builders leveled it to the ground . . . the builders of communism." Nasyr went silent in frustration. "I thought about the grave of Abutalip long ago, as soon as we received your letter. I also thought about the grave of Imanbek, but there are issues with that as well, brother. It is now behind barbed wire in a military zone."

Nevertheless, he and Nurdaulet got ready to go. Nasyr decided that the poor invalid could at least touch the ground where Abutalip's grave once was. They decided the kind spirit of the holy man must still hover over that place—and what if a miracle happened?

Nasyr loaded a black ram into a cart, put Nurdaulet and Kyzbala in, and headed to the place where the grave of the holy Abutalip once was. They sacrificed the ram, prayed three times, and turned back. After that, Nurdaulet moved in with Kyzbala. But Abutalip's spirit didn't help these poor people. And Nurdaulet decided he had no hope left.

Nurdaulet frequently thought about his son. He thought that if Daulet was alive, then Kyzbala might wake up. And he was thinking this as he sat next to Nasyr, looking out the window. And he saw the same thing in the hot haze that he has seen before: a young *dzhigit*—Daulet—emerging from the sea. He rushes toward his father, hugs him and says, "Hello, Father! We were away from here for forty years. Now both you and I are back . . . Let's go quickly to Mother. She's been waiting for us for forty years. Let's go . . ."

Thoughts of his son and wife tormented his soul. Sometimes, such severe despondency would come over him that he could only think one thing: "How come I am still alive if I don't have even the tiniest hope?! And a man who has no hope can turn into Satan. People feel for you, and sympathize with you, but in your soul, you have only bitterness and bile. It travels through your blood." In moments like these, Nurdaulet didn't want to live—he was prepared to kill himself. But he probably would not have succeeded even at this. He didn't have the physical ability to do it. Now at the end of his life, he, like Nasyr, realized that it's just as hard to die as it is to live. At war, when he was between life and death, he fought for life. Now caught between life and death, he sometimes asked God to end his days, but it seemed like God had decided to torment him right till the end.

Nurdaulet spent all that day with Nasyr. Berish gave him a pile of magazines and newspapers, which Nurdaulet was reading till the evening, and then he stayed overnight.

THE MONUMENT TO DZERZHINSKY IS DEMOLISHED. MANY CURIOUS people gathered in the center of Warsaw on the square, which until recently bore the name Dzerzhinsky Square, after Feliks Dzerzhinsky. The square has now given back its original name of Bank Square.

THE MEDITERRANEAN SEA HAS BECOME ONE OF THE DIRTIEST IN THE WORLD. EACH YEAR ABOUT two million tons of petroleum, one hundred and twenty thousand tons of mineral oil, and sixty thousand tons of pesticides get into the sea. Some experts predict that if the rate of pollution remains the same, the Mediterranean Sea may die within twenty years.

IN THE NAKHICHEVAN ASSR[2] UNDER THE LEADERSHIP of a group of extremists, unprecedented barbaric actions were carried out with the aim of destabilizing the situation on the Nakhichevan section of the Soviet-Iranian border.

THE CURFEW IS CANCELED AND THE SITUATION IS NORMALIZING. THE DAY has come that the people of Tbilisi have been waiting for and that they brought nearer by their will and hard work. With a resolution passed by the Presidium of the Supreme Soviet of the Georgian SSR, the curfew in the city has been abolished on April 18 at five o'clock in the morning. When people heard this news, they kissed each other and cried. So much has been experienced, so much thought of, and so much rethought during these days.

"I AM SEVENTY YEARS OLD," SAYS A DISABLED WAR VETERAN, "AND I HAVE NO LEGS AND ONE ARM. AT MY AGE, I have had to discover how soulless bureaucracy is. I have received no pension for the last eight months. No one cares how I survive or afford to go on living. If I had a gun, I would fire across the line of bureaucrats without giving it a second thought."

MORE THAN TWO THOUSAND YOUNG PEOPLE GATHERED BY THE LENIN MONUMENT IN NOVA GUTA. They were from Krakow, Poznan, Wroclaw, and other towns and threw jars of paint and bottles of fuel at the monument and set fire to the plinth. Water cannons and tear gas were used to disperse the angry crowd. There were wounded on both sides.

FOR FOUR DAYS ALREADY, MEETINGS AND DEMONSTRATIONS ARE TAKING PLACE in the squares and streets of Czechoslovakia. According to estimates by the media last night, about two hundred thousand people took part.

THE EVENTS THAT TOOK PLACE IN BULGARIA OVER THE LAST TEN DAYS could fill up months and maybe years with their scale and dynamic. The party took the country's development in a new direction, with the majority support of the Bulgarian nation.

THE WORLD-FAMOUS MONUMENT TO SOVIET SOLDIERS AND LIBERATORS in Berlin's Treptower Park has been desecrated. A spokesman for the government of GDR Mayer denounced the anti-Soviet action.

MONGOLIA: IT WAS DECIDED TO REMOVE STALIN MONUMENT.

THE BERLIN WALL IS BEING SMASHED UP WITH HAMMERS, AND PEOPLE ARE GRABBING PIECES OF THE CONCRETE to keep or to sell. The border guards have begun its deconstruction and replacement by a mesh partition.

CUBAN LEADER FIDEL CASTRO SUGGESTED THAT MORE people in his country should study English instead of Russian.

AT THE POLITBURO MEETING OF THE CC OF BULGARIA, IT WAS DECIDED to suggest to Soviet ministers that they stop providing villas, currently in state ownership, to the members of the party leadership and use these buildings in line with the interests of society.

THE SITUATION IN DUSHANBE IS ESCALATING AFTER AN ATTEMPT BY THE PROTESTERS to enter the building of the CC of the party. The security forces fired warning shots in the air and used a special "bird cherry." The attackers carried out an arson attack on the CC building and rioted and looted on Lenin Prospect, injuring 108 people, including 39 law enforcement officials, with 6 civilians dead. The exact number of casualties is still being established.

AT 07:01 MOSCOW TIME IN THE SOVIET UNION, an underground nuclear explosion with a power of 150 kilotons was carried out in the Semipalatinsk area.

GORBACHEV AND BUSH WERE DECLARED THE LEADING PERSONALITIES OF THE YEAR, making news in 1989.

A MYSTERIOUS EPIDEMIC IS RAMPANT AMONG SEALS INHABITING the Northern and Baltic Seas. During the last three months alone, waves have carried to shore six thousand bodies. This number is rising each day. Experts are trying to establish what illness haunts the seals but do not know at the moment. The people are powerless to help the dying animals.

The morning that Nasyr ended his fast, he got up as soon as it was light outside and was surprised to discover that Nurdaulet wasn't even in bed yet. "You should get some rest," Nasyr said, putting the kettle on.

"I'll have plenty of time to rest." Nurdaulet lifted his tired eyes to Nasyr. "Soon I'll go to eternal peace, and there I'll get plenty of rest."

"That's true," Nasyr mumbled.

Nasyr had planned to get a ride for himself and Nurdaulet in the car bringing food and fuel to Karaoi. Once at the shore, Nasyr hoped to find someone willing to take them to Korym. Nasyr would spend three days praying, asking Allah to send rain. But, when Nasyr opened the door, the burning air made him gasp and rethink his plans.

"The weather is not changing."

As they ate breakfast, Nurdaulet again talked about Kyzbala and asked Nasyr the question that he had asked him before, "Do you think if Kazhygaiyp was alive, he'd be able to cure Kyzbala?"

How could Nasyr reply?

"Of course, he would've done! Holy people are given an amazing soul and golden hands. He would've definitely cured her—don't even doubt about it! Even Otkeldy would've been able to bring her back to her senses if he was alive. When your Kyzbala found out that you went missing, she fell ill. That is when she got confused in her head for the first time. But Otkeldy got her back on her feet. There are no more healers like him."

Nurdaulet didn't ask another question. He finished his tea and got into his wheelchair with a great effort, then went out quickly, pushing with his stumps.

"Wait for a bit!" Nasyr shouted to him when he was already over the threshold. "As soon as it cools down, we'll go to the island!"

Nurdaulet nodded.

"If God wills! Thank you for your kindness, Nasyr."

Hot tears were streaming down Nurdaulet's cheeks. He was pushing down the road vigorously, not noticing the chair was about to capsize, which is exactly what happened. Nurdaulet fell awkwardly in the sand. Sand stuck at once to his face, which was wet with tears. But he had neither the strength nor the will to move.

Toward the end of the week, the wind began to get weaker, and the weather got cooler. And after two months, the minibus the people from Shumgen and Karaoi were waiting for at last appeared, bringing mail, food, and fuel. There was a letter for Nasyr too. Kakharman had written that his mother had arrived safely. This comforted Nasyr. Berish also received a letter but read it alone.

The driver Asanbai didn't miss a chance to tease him. "If you're hiding it from your granddad, then it must be a letter from a girl."

"What's with this nonsense?" Nasyr interrupted, considering the driver's comment insensitive.

"Aqsaqal, you really are lagging behind in life! So what if he receives a letter from a girl? He's a grown-up—it's about time."

Berish went to read the letter from Aigul in the corner of the yard.

The letter said:

> *I managed to convince my parents to let me finish my studies in Shumgen. My grandma was upset since it is against her will. But in the evening, she forgets about it—and she caresses me and says she has come to terms with it. So in the autumn, I will be in Shumgen again! I can't wait for that day! Now I get what you were saying about betrayal, Berish. I don't want to be a traitor, but I'm not that guilty—right? No parents want to part with their children. But do you think they could be embarrassed themselves? The sea will never forgive them for abandoning it . . . And maybe it won't forgive me either. What do you think? I am waiting for your letter. I want to know what you think of me. But be frank— please. I received the stone on which you carved my face. It's lovely! I carry it in my handbag so that at any moment I can look at it and think of you. That's it. We'll soon see each other and discuss everything. Your Aigul.*

Berish put the letter on his lap and began to think. He loves her—that is why he has this longing in his heart. "Your Aigul," Berish whispered, and his soul was burned by the heat. Every word of the letter seemed reasonable and touching to him. He folded the letter and hid it in his pocket. He was carving her face for a long time—he wanted it to look alive, glowing with sweet and jolly laughter.

And he eventually managed it. But for a long time, he hadn't dared send the stone to her. He was shy. He brought himself to send it at last only at the very end of the academic year. He realized that it couldn't be any other way—he can't lie to his heart. Like other people from Karaoi, he was always direct and honest.

Suddenly, a frantic Zhanyl hurtled into the yard.

"Turagul's house has collapsed, Nasyr! It was standing, then just collapsed. Oh, God!"

"Is everyone alive?" Nasyr jumped up from his chair in the shade. "Are they alive?"

"Yes, yes! The children, thank God, were outside. But the kelin has a broken leg—a stone fell right on her leg."

Berish ran to Turagul's house, and the rest hurried after him.

"Oh, God, soon we will all be gone, that's what my heart feels." Zhanyl, short of breath after the fast walk, pulled her granddaughter toward her and took her in her arms. "No one needs us here, and Satan felt it right away. He is beginning to destroy everything."

There was a great commotion from the women and children around the ruined house. Turagul's wife was sitting on the sand, wailing loudly, her broken leg splayed out. "Great Allah, you sent troubles upon my poor head again! What sins have I committed to deserve it? Have mercy on your servant. Do you hear?"

Some people turned away; it was so hard to hear her piteous cries.

"Kelin!" Nasyr approached the woman. "Remember the children are alive. Don't enrage God with your curses."

When she saw Nasyr, the woman began to cry with new energy.

"Ata, I just can't do it anymore! We have to get away from here."

Other women began to support her.

"In Shumgen, at least people are leading human lives. Why are we left to suffer here?"

"Didn't we have enough grief here? And now everything's gone. We have to move."

"But what will our husbands think? Let them come back first, then we'll decide."

"Autumn is so far away! Today Turagul's house collapsed. Whose will be next?"

"And when they come back, they'll find only our corpses. Why are we even talking about it? We have to go to Shumgen!"

Nasyr realized that Asanbai was right. Nothing would hold these women here anymore.

"Bring the minibus closer," Nasyr ordered the driver. Turagul's wife was put in the front and the children in the back. "To Shumgen. And straight to the doctor!"

The women, careful to ensure that Nasyr couldn't hear them, were whispering to the sighing kelin to pass on a request in Shumgen to get them away from here as soon as possible.

Nasyr turned away. "You are defeated, you foolish man! People don't want to stay here, and they are right to want to leave."

"Are you feeling sad, Nasyr?" Nurdaulet called to him.

"Yes." Nasyr nodded and came up to him. "And you will have to move as well."

"I have nowhere to go, only back to the asylum."

Nurdaulet sighed and looked up at Nasyr despairingly. "He's right," Nasyr thought. "Where would he and Kyzbala go? Who needs these frail old people? They don't have any relatives—they have no family other than this dying sea."

The district leadership was pleased that the women were prepared to move to Shumgen. No one wanted to keep delivering food and fuel to God knows where—to send out a truck just for a handful of people. But they quickly sent one truck after another as the families of the fishermen began to move to Shumgen. Nasyr arranged for one of the drivers to take him, Nurdaulet, and Berish to the sea the next morning. There, by the water, Nasyr would pray.

In the evening, he went to Nurdaulet to tell him about the trip.

"May God give you health, Nasyr!" Nurdaulet was overjoyed.

The old man covered him with a light jacket that Zhanyl had made for him.

"What is the occasion of this present?"

"Zhanyl prepared it especially for our trip. And this is a dress for Kyzbala."

"I'll put it somewhere obvious. If she keeps seeing it, she may put it on. When are we going?"

"If God wills, tomorrow morning. I arranged it with a good driver."

Nurdaulet's sleep that night was broken. He woke up frequently, and then toward dawn, he began to listen for Nasyr coming to collect him. But Kyzbala slept remarkably well. Usually she would get up and walk through the house during the night, but this night she slept soundly.

From the day Nurdaulet had moved to her house, she had slept by the window in the front room. She never forgot to feed him, just as she would never forget to feed her goat and the dog. She would leave food for Nurdaulet in the wooden dish he had carved long ago. At first Nurdaulet would smile bitterly that his wife made no distinction between him, the goat, and the dog, but he soon accepted it and even thanked God for it! He knew that it wasn't Kyzbala's fault. But he felt more and more guilty and sinful—not generally but in relation to Kyzbala. He understood that a man's fate is out of his control. The pillow that Korlan gave him was often wet with tears, and his thoughts followed the same vicious circle. "Haven't I brought enough grief to my wife? And my son Daulet wounded her heart forever by his death. Why have we done it to her—to our Kyzbala? Did we wish her ill? Why, Allah, have you made all three of us so unhappy? You've left me without arms and legs. Why? I never angered you. I was your faithful and obedient slave—and how did you answer me? I begin to think more and more that you yourself don't know what you're doing to your slaves. How many times did I address you, how much have I begged you? But you have remained deaf, and you have not given me even a grain of happiness. That is why I cry. Why do you pummel a man so mercilessly? Where is your mercy? In every morning prayer, your slaves repeat to you: please be merciful, please be merciful. But where is your mercy? If you do not distinguish between a man and an ant, then what are these prayers for; what are these teachings for?"

It wasn't the first time Nurdaulet had had conversations like this with God. During his forty years on Valaam Island, he had renounced God and cursed him over and over again, then returned to him, feeling guilty and asking to be forgiven. And Allah, as if forgiving him his human weakness, would send him quiet and meaningful hours and days of clear and unshaken faith. And then Nurdaulet would think, "He is merciful after all!"

Listening to his wife's sighs and muttering from the far room had become an unexplainable need. Sometimes Nurdaulet could hear his own name in Kyzbala's ramblings. Korlan would frequently comfort Nurdaulet by telling him, "She has never forgotten you and your son, Daulet. She still remembers your names. Sometimes I've heard her saying, 'I won't die until I see Nurdaulet.'" Korlan would add, "Only a woman who truly loves could say something like this."

Nurdaulet couldn't understand how Kyzbala could remember his name but not recognize him. Oh, if only her head would clear for just a second. If only he could hear her say at least one time, "You're back, Nurdaulet. I did say that I won't die until I see you!"

Nurdaulet listened to Korlan's stories greedily while he was living at Nasyr's.

"After Daulet's death," the kind woman would begin, "your wife fell ill and lost her memory. Marziya helped her back on her feet. If it weren't for her—who knows?—Kyzbala might've died."

"Why tell him!" Nasyr would interrupt at first. "The time will come when he'll find out everything for himself."

"How will he find out if we don't tell him?" Korlan asked. "Even though he's come back an invalid, he's still a man. He should know the truth."

"Keep telling it, Korlan. As you say, who will tell me if not you? And Nasyr, don't be afraid of telling me the truth. I have been through sorrow just as you have. No matter how horrible the truth is, I need it. Every single word of truth is important to me. She can't be brought back to her senses now . . . My son cannot be brought back . . . so let these stories flow at least . . . Please, keep talking, Korlan."

"When Kyzbala received her husband's death notice, many men proposed to her. Don't be offended by them—she was very beautiful and respectable, and Allah had gifted her with a bright mind. It's rare for such beauty and mind to be combined in the same woman. Usually if God gives beauty, he stops short on intelligence, and if he gives intelligence, then he won't be very generous with beauty. But it also happens that he gives both, then takes away the third: a kind character.

"Apart from intelligence and beauty, God also gifted Kyzbala character. She didn't allow a single man to hold her hand. Maybe she's holy, people began to say. And for sure, such clarity is only given to holy people. But I can explain it more simply: she was waiting for you, Nurdaulet, only for you . . .

"And who knows? If those idiotic demon wives of Otkeldy hadn't forced Marziya away from Karaoi, maybe she would've been able to cure Kyzbala with herbs . . . Maybe! Only Allah knows . . .

"Once I brought Kyzbala some soup. She was delusional. Marziya was checking her pulse. I sat next to her, and Marziya said frankly, 'Otkeldy would surely have cured her. But I cannot do it myself.' I told her what I thought. 'If Nurdaulet was to walk into the house now, do you think her mind would come back?' 'It's possible. Strong shocks may be good to people like this—it has happened before, Otkeldy told me. You can help the body with herbs, but herbs don't heal the soul. Kyzbala is one of those people who love only once. People like this have a unique psyche.'

"Marziya and I hadn't seen that as we talked, Kyzbala had raised her head. Her sweet face was bright red. She looked at us carefully and moved her lips soundlessly. And then she began to speak, 'God took my husband and my son to heaven. But they'll be back.' She went silent, gathering her strength, then exclaimed, 'And I won't die until Nurdaulet is back!'

"Marziya and I were struck by how clear her words were. But after crying these words, she fell back on the bed.

"Many years have passed since then. And then we received that letter from you, Nurdaulet. All of us in the aul were surprised and happy. And I remembered Kyzbala's words and thought maybe she's a clairvoyant?"

When it became known that the nursing home on Valaam Island was going to be closed, its inhabitants became very thoughtful. And for good reason. For the disabled people who had spent most of their lives on the island, it was home. Where could they go now? The place was soon rife with gossip and wild rumors. Nurdaulet and his friend Ivan Dergachev, who lay on the farthest beds by the wall, were the only ones not to join in. Ivan had fought in the Bauyrzhan Momyshuly division as a regimental commissar. He was reserved, even a little secretive. He, too, had lost his legs in the war. His wife had married someone else, and he had moved to the island. He had a son who sometimes sent him birthday and New Year cards. That son was already grown up, but Ivan didn't have the courage to meet him. When his son finished studying, the young man sent Ivan a letter. He wrote that he was coming to visit him. Ivan was ecstatic with happiness and pride and sent his son money to buy the ticket. The long days of waiting began to drag on. Every day, the ex-commissar would take his chair to the fence and peer greedily into the distance. But the road was always empty! He and Nurdaulet spent a whole month by the gates, but in vain. Their friend Sidor expressed his view on what had happened bluntly, "He got your money, Vanya, and spent it on drink. Be thankful if he drank for your health. He won't come, so don't wait for him."

The commissar said nothing.

Soon he received a second letter from his son. His son wrote that his plans had changed, and he had to go to Siberia as part of his studies. "Please don't be offended by me, Father," he apologized at the end of the letter. "I will return your money from my first paycheck."

"Return the money? What is he talking about?" The commissar was perplexed. "Are we strangers to return money to each other?" But he did cheer up a bit and began to explain to everyone that his son would come as soon as he sorted out his business in Siberia.

But Sidor laughed again. "He won't return any money. Don't worry. He will never return it to you, like a true relative . . ."

Nurdaulet lost his temper. "Listen, Sidor. You are a clever man, but you've never learned to spare someone else's feelings!"

"I am indeed a clever man. I became clever during those five years I had to spend among my shit family right after the war. Money, money, and nothing but money—they'd sell their mother and father for money. In the past, there was a God, and people were afraid to sin before him. Then there was Stalin, and people were afraid of him like they are afraid of a stern father. But now there's no God or Stalin, so they are not afraid of anything. They are free." Sidor turned his angry face toward the commissar, as if it was all his fault. "Try not to be too offended, Vanya, but your son, in Russian words, is a scoundrel, and that's it!"

It seemed as if the commissar had had a stroke. "You . . . are you . . . ," he stuttered hoarsely. "You are . . ."

After this conversation, he didn't recover for a long time. He wanted only to be alone. His last hope had died. Nurdaulet drew a bitter lesson from Ivan's experience: that he should tell no one that he was alive and shouldn't try to force himself on anyone—they would only spit into his soul without a second thought.

Soon after, a parcel arrived for the commissar. No one ever received parcels, so the invalids were astonished when a small wooden box was brought into the room. But when the commissar read the return address, he lit up. "Bauyrzhan!" he exclaimed. "Do you know who this parcel is from? It's from Bauyrzhan Momyshuly!" They opened the box right away, and the room was filled with the delicious aroma of Alma-Ata aport apples![3] When other invalids heard about the parcel, they gathered in the room. About a month before, the commissar had sent a letter in which he wrote about the Kazakh Nurdaulet to the legendary Colonel Bauyrzhan. The colonel considered it his duty to respond to the letter and sent Ivan and Nurdaulet each a book and accompanied his gift with a short letter. The book was *Volokolamsk Highway* by Alexander Bek. The book went from hand to hand until practically everybody in the nursing home had read it.

And with the parcel, the commissar forgot the offense caused by his son and felt more sympathy for Nurdaulet.

The commissar later said to Nurdaulet, "Nur, you should write a letter to your fellow countrymen: tell them about yourself, about this life. They are not animals—their hearts will beat. It's hard for you here. You are the only Kazakh here, and you should be with Kazakhs. Even I want to go to your sea, to that aul—what's it called? Karaoi? You should die and be buried in your native land. Your wife and children can visit your grave. What do you have here?"

"Do you think they'll greet me in Karaoi with open arms? I am 'missing.' It would be better for me to die like a dog and never show myself. What did your son do for you? Mine will do no more. They've been brought up at the same time."

"You shouldn't compare them! I am Russian, and you are Kazakh. We praise our own exceptionality to disguise our shortcomings. I think the Russian man is transformed only by war. In war, a Russian is prepared to give everything he has for his comrades. But in peacetime, he forgets everything—apart from vodka, of course.

"Kazakhs are not like this—yet. They have still managed to preserve something of themselves. So you should write to them, or you will indeed go 'missing.'"

By morning, Kyzbala was laughing loudly in her sleep with a laugh full of joy. The laughter woke Nurdaulet, who looked at his wife in surprise. She walked past him in her nightgown, got dressed quietly, and left the house. It was light, and Nurdaulet got ready to go to Nasyr's. Outside, he heard the thudding of a helicopter hanging over Karaoi.

Nasyr was sitting in the yard, whittling a stick. The helicopter landed not far from his house. "What's going on?" Nasyr asked himself. "Or have they decided to move everyone left by helicopter?" He looked at the men who had jumped down from the helicopter and were heading to his house. "Oh! That's Ikor!" Nasyr exclaimed. It was the first time Nasyr had seen Igor since Mustafa's death. Igor had grown broader in the shoulders and put on a little weight. Nasyr stood up, hugged him, and began to mutter through tears, "Mustafa died . . . Ikor, he died."

"Shall we go into the house, Nasyr-aga?" Igor asked gently.

"Yes, to the house, to the house." Nasyr nodded, inviting the others with a gesture. "Your auntie Korlan is visiting Kakharman. She missed him so much. She said, 'Let me go to see my dear son. My heart is worried.' So she went. I couldn't come to the funeral, may Mustafa forgive me. I was ill myself and spent two months in the hospital."

"I've heard that the whole of Karaoi is being relocated to Shumgen, Nasyr-aga."

"But I refuse!" Nasyr frowned. "Musa and I will stay here."

"That's not good," Igor objected. "You should move; you two can't stay here by yourselves. What if something happens to you? Who will help? The weather is changing every day in the region—it's hard to predict it, and it's still unclear what dangers may wait for you here."

In his soul, Igor was screaming, "Aga! You have to get away from here as soon as possible! And not just to Shumgen but all the way to Zaysan, to your son!"

But knowing how stubborn the old man was, he knew that no reasonable arguments would change his mind.

"But what are you doing here?" Nasyr asked.

"We are taking aerial photographs. Pictures of the sea from above. It's been a while since I saw you, so I decided to drop in for a visit."

"How are Lena and Sergey?"

"They are fine. They got married."

"May God give them happiness and health. Tell them Nasyr will pray for them."

At that moment, Nurdaulet appeared in the doorway in his chair. Nasyr introduced them. Then he suddenly remembered.

"Ikor, can you give us a lift to the sea? Nurdaulet hasn't seen it for forty years! Let him see the sea again at the end of his life. Let the sea bless him."

"No problem at all, Nasyr-aga!" Igor smiled. "But you have to promise to visit us in Akespe. Deal?"

"May Allah bless you!" Nurdaulet rejoiced.

"So why are we still sitting here?" Nasyr began to get ready. "Let's fly! Berish, hurry up!"

"Nasyr, please take me as well," Zhanyl begged while pouring tea for the guests. "I haven't seen the sea for a hundred years now . . . It'll take me only five minutes to prepare my granddaughter."

"Then let's all go to the helicopter!" Igor ordered.

From the sky, Nurdaulet saw that the sea was there only in name. A lump came to his throat. Here it is, then, the inexhaustible evil done by men!

The helicopter came right down to the surface of the water. The sea, now just a salty mud, didn't stir.

They flew past the dried channel of the Syr Darya. "How long ago did water from this river stop flowing into the sea?" Nurdaulet thought. "And how long has its precious water spilled uselessly into the sands from the Shardara reservoir?"

"What have they done?" Nasyr shouted over the roar of the helicopter. "Mustafa kept saying for so many years that we don't need this reservoir. We don't need it! If someone would've just listened!"

"There are similar reservoirs in Uzbekistan, Turkmenistan, and Tajikistan!" Igor shouted in response. "And there, too, water goes into the sand uselessly!"

Nasyr nudged Nurdaulet and motioned for him to have a look to their right. A bright crescent on the dome of a tomb glittered in the sun. Nurdaulet lifted his stumps toward his face in prayer.

"It's the tomb of Holy Imanbek!" Nasyr shouted. "It'd be nice to get closer, but it's impossible! It's a military zone. And beyond there is the Cosmodrome!"[4]Zhanyl was whispering and stroking her face with her hands. The helicopter began to turn toward Akespe Island.

"Nasyr, tell me," Nurdaulet shouted over the noise, "what is this new custom of leaving baby cradles on graves? I don't understand it."

"Child mortality has increased dramatically of late," Nasyr explained. "When people bury a child, they don't want to leave the cradle in the house for the next child to die in."

Soon the helicopter landed on Akespe Island. Nasyr and Berish put Nurdaulet into a light boat, and all three of them went out to sea.

"Hello, sacred sea! The moment I see you again has finally arrived! Nasyr, sprinkle some water on my face! More. Don't worry!" Nurdaulet whispered.

Nurdaulet's face was flushed, his eyes were partially closed, and seawater was streaming down his face. Nasyr picked up the stick that he had carefully whittled over the previous days, rested his palms and chest against it, and began to recite a prayer.

Bismillahi, ar-Rahmani, ar-Rahim!

Ya, Rabbim! We bow before you, believe in your power and humbly ask for your mercy. Make our thoughts clear, our deeds righteous and direct us to the path of the truth, so we will not be lost in the future! Ei, Rabbim-the-Most-High! You created the sky and decorated it with clouds, rain, clear air, and wind; you decorated the land with various herbs, flowers, and gardens. With your mercy, water has seeped through the stone core; water has turned into steams, lifted above the ground and poured down as rain so that grass can grow again, fruits ripen, and everything on the earth is brought to life again: dried trees open their buds anew and from them, leaves will come again, which rustle on the wind, sent by you. Lord of heaven, sun, and moon! I believe in you infinitely, and I beg you: send us a downpour, send us water, save the land and people from thirst. Don't forget about us, your slaves, free your people from suffering, bless us and forgive us, send us your mercy. Hear our prayers and have mercy on us, God!

Keeping his gaze fixed on the sky, Nasyr wiped his sweaty forehead with a handkerchief. All three in the boat—the young boy and the two old men—all stared at the sky in silence, following Nasyr's prayer with their eyes.

The whisper of the sand brushing against the bottom of the boat interrupted Nurdaulet's thoughts. The boat bumped onto the shore, and Nurdaulet uttered solemnly, like an incantation, "Let Allah's mercy to us be like it used to be!"

Lena and Sergey greeted Nasyr as warmly as if he were their own father. They began bustling around him, laying food out on the table near the shore.

"The young people here honor you so much, Nasyr!" Zhanyl was surprised.

Sergey had a present for Berish. He dived into his tent and got a guitar out. Berish was shy. Sergey pushed the guitar into his hands.

"Everyone in your boarding school will be jealous. C'mon, show me what you can do."

The young people sat in a circle, and Berish tuned the instrument. Nasyr went to the shore to read the evening prayer. Kneeling there, he wiped his eyes with a handkerchief for a long time. His eyes seemed to be watering all the time.

Zhanyl approached him quietly from behind. "Everything has decayed here. I remember when I was young everything here was so green, so alive . . ."

"Everything is dying here, Zhanyl—both man and the land."

"Yes, if the sea was alive, we would've had a good life as well."

Nasyr stood up and gazed at the mute water's surface.

"What will you do, Nasyr? Move away?"

But the old fisherman didn't hear her question, and she left him to his thoughts. He was looking at another sea, the sea of his youth. The rumble of the surf that he used to wake to every morning then hit his ears. "Oh, blessed waves," he thought, "will I ever hear your boom again? Will I survive until that blessed day? How sweet and treasured my life would be if I could wake up once more with the sound of the surf!"

Nasyr woke from his thoughts, prayed, and returned to the young people. He looked at Berish, who was plucking the guitar strings and singing quietly.

> *Why, oh my dombra, do you sing about dying?*
> *Why in your strings must such black thoughts keep flying?*
> *Have you no pity for a good and loyal friend*
> *Who is sad yet must stay on the earth till the end?*

Later that day, shortly after Nurdaulet, Zhanyl, and Nasyr climbed into the helicopter again, something happened in Karaoi that finally convinced Musa to move to Shumgen.

As he rode up to his house, Musa heard the wailing of an old woman in the yard.

"They took her! They took Nasyr's mare! They knew no one was at home and took the ash-gray! Look behind you, Musa! There is the herd! Do you see her?"

Musa urged his horse on toward the herd. He could see the leader. Nasyr's mare was standing next to him. "I've been waiting for you for a long time!" Musa murmured, taking the shotgun off his shoulder. "I'll get you now!" Musa flew up the hill after his horse. The herd was standing a little way off from the Fiery, stamping their feet impatiently. The stallion was lovingly courting Nasyr's ash-gray. But Musa wasn't looking at him. He had seen his cherished racer, which was taken away long ago. And the racer, it seemed to Musa, was standing undecided between the loving pair and the herd, looking at Musa. Musa's heart rushed toward the racer, and the racer, as if guessing his ex-owner's feelings, whinnied plaintively. The Fiery left Nasyr's mare and turned toward the hunter. Musa slowly lowered the gun. The Fiery watched the hunter with a bold defiance. "He's so beautiful and so proud!" Musa admired him. And the Fiery hated the hunter. Maybe he was thinking, "Ah, my old foe, we have met again." His eyes were aglow with rage. But Musa's soul filled with sympathy. "Why must I take vengeance on him just because he took my racer? If you put a halter on him now, what will you do with him? Slaughter him for your own use and send him for meat?" Musa couldn't answer his own questions. "Come to your senses. You don't need the racer. You don't know how your own life will unfold. You should leave Karaoi and make a home in Shumgen."

Meanwhile, the Fiery stamped his hoof on the ground and trotted toward the hunter.

Musa's racer whinnied a warning. The Fiery came sharply to a halt.

And then something strange happened to Musa; his ears were ringing, and he heard a voice say, "Musa, who knows better than you what freedom means? You should let him go his own way. Soon you will leave for the town. You will go to your son Zharasbai, and you'll die there. What else do you want? Why do you need a racer in town? He won't come to you anyway. He understands what freedom is and will not exchange it for anything! Go your own way, you silly man . . ."

Musa could've sworn it was the Fiery talking to him. The hunter's head began to spin, everything in his eyes darkened, and he couldn't remember what happened. Did he fall off his horse? Or did he get off by himself? He woke for a moment as he removed the silver saddle of his horse and took off the bridle. "What is happening to me?" he thought, falling down slowly onto the hot sand. "Maybe I've got heatstroke?"

His racer came to Musa and touched first his ear, then his naked neck with its soft lips. The Fiery began to lead the herd away over the sand dunes. He neighed triumphantly, saying goodbye to Karaoi forever, as if he knew that from that day there were no more horses in the aul and there'd be no reason to ever bring his herd back again.

"Eh, Musa." The hunter heard a voice. "You didn't have the courage to shoot the handsome stallion. You've lost, Musa. Life is leaving you, and your strength is melting." "No!" another familiar voice joined in. "You've won, Musa! For the first time, you listened to God. You heard him in your heart! From now on, stay forever pure!"

Musa discovered to his surprise that he was talking with himself out loud.

He struggled to open his eyes, with no idea how much time had passed. It was already dark. He heard a clatter of hooves come and stretched out his arms to find his gun, scaring off a lizard. The silver saddle was lying next to him. Then Musa remembered what had happened and felt sick. He stood up and walked a little way, then began to throw up. His head spun, and his body was burning. The clatter of hooves came closer. And he realized it was a herd of saiga antelopes. If he didn't move out of the way, they would trample him. He pulled both triggers. The herd swerved to the side, avoiding the old hunter. Musa walked slowly toward the aul, dragging the gun through the sand behind him. It was pitch-black. Suddenly the moon shot out from behind the clouds and shone its pale light on the glittering silver saddle.

> *Goodbye, silver saddle! We will remember you! We will keep looking through tears into the distance of time—hopelessly, hopelessly! The future will explain to us: by leaving behind this glittering treasure under the moon to the mercy of the sand, we are breaking down the chain of time. Musa, you're a father! But you haven't passed this saddle to your son. The white sand will cover it, and from that minute, it'll become clear: the nation has died. And then there'll be no one left to answer for this monstrous crime! Goodbye, silver saddle, goodbye!*

Musa and Zhanyl were the last ones to leave Karaoi. Nasyr went to say goodbye to his old friend. They didn't say much. No words were needed.

"In the past, children sought protection in their parents' home." Musa sighed. "Now parents are inviting themselves to their children's homes—that is the confusion, Nasyr . . . I wanted to be buried here, but it looks like it won't happen. I don't have the strength left to stay here. I'm tired. You live and slowly turn into an animal, looking at this dead sea, these hungry creatures in the sand . . ."

Nasyr nodded; he understood Musa. Karaoi was now completely empty. Only Nasyr with Berish and Nurdaulet with Kyzbala remained. And they were only waiting for the minibus to come for them too.

On his way home, for some reason, Nasyr began to walk toward the smithy where Musa had hammered his anvil. Now those sounds would never ring out again. The smithy was silent. The unhearing, dead aul was silent. Only in Kyzbala's house can sounds be heard. But does it matter now?

The sky had turned ominous by the time he reached home, and he began to close the windows firmly. Outside, the withering wind was whistling already. It was the time for the Karabas—the Black Head storm that rages across the coast for weeks on end, burning everything in its path with its deathly breath.

"Oh, Allah, save us lonely people in the sands," Nasyr murmured, looking out the window and listening to the howl of raging nature. "Be merciful to us!"

XIV

More than a month had passed since Korlan had arrived in Zaysan, but she still hadn't managed to have a long conversation with her son. She sighed and lamented and sometimes even grumbled, yet she understood her son. He was spending all his days at work, and when he had a free day, he would spend it with Semeon refurbishing the house given to him by the kolkhoz. And Aitugan kept pushing him in her letters, writing that she and the children were tired of being lonely and unsettled.

Kakharman himself was tired. Really, he was fed up with everything. The debilitating feeling that his life wasn't working out wouldn't leave him. There had been a time when the life stretching before him seemed beautiful.

But now he was drained. Shame burned him inside when he thought about himself. He was a loser, a weirdo—or maybe just a fool. His life seemed lost, and he could die with the burning shame that tormented his pride. He could disappear from the face of the earth without a second thought. The sea, without which he cannot imagine life, had disappeared from the face of the earth, and his people had scattered across the world. What was his life in comparison to this tragedy?

Even the sensitive Korlan understood very little about her son. She sensed something was not quite right and begged God to take care of him. But if some-one asked her what it was that distressed her son and what could possibly make him happy, Korlan could not have answered.

Once all there was left to do on the house was paint the windows and floor, Korlan began to get ready to go to Semipalatinsk. She wouldn't listen to Kakharman, who tried to convince her that it was him who should help Aitugan move. Korlan was determined to go, even though she had only just recovered from an illness. There had been nuclear tests near Semipalatinsk, and Korlan had spent the three days after them in bed with high blood pressure. Marziya's herbal infusions, with which she often treated Semeon Arkhipovich, helped Korlan as well.

Kakharman eventually consented to let his mother go instead of him.

"OK, but I'll take you to Chingistau first, Mom. You've been asking me to take you to your homeland for a long time. And then you can go to Aitugan."

Korlan nodded in agreement, as did Marziya. After that, both women went to drink tea. They had been friends since Otkeldy brought Marziya to Karaoi while she was still a young girl. Here in Zaysan, they spent their days in intimate conversation. They spoke long and keenly about the people they knew and the times they had known. There was no end to these conversations. Whatever Kakharman didn't tell his mother, she could find out from Marziya. From the start, she tried to steer the conversation so that Marziya would tell her what local people thought about her son and whether or not they were spreading rumors behind his back. A kind smile touched Marziya's lips when she saw these little tricks of this direct and honest woman. And she would reply, "Korlan, dear! Kakharman is a very good man. And people value him in this area. He is not a stranger here. The people accepted him right away; he was treated very well. Semeon can confirm that. Semeon let him into his house from the moment he arrived. Everybody values him a great deal, both ordinary people and the high-ups. He's done so much for the kolkhoz through his friends in Moscow."

And Marziya told Korlan about all the good things her son had done, but Korlan stopped her, knowing the truth of Marziya's words.

"But people say that Kakharman has been drinking. Yes, the gossip reached us as well."

She was looking at Marziya. Marziya realized at once that any hesitation would make the conversation even harder. "Eh, Korlan! The dog barks, but the caravan keeps moving. There'll always be gossips and envious people who snipe at a good person. It's hard nowadays to meet a man who doesn't drink."

"As if you don't understand what I am asking you!" Korlan interrupted her irritably.

"Korlan," Marziya replied, "I'd like to tell you as a person who knows what it means to wander, to leave your home, to lose the job to which you gave your soul, that a person's heart is not made of stone. If you knew just how much I cried at night thinking about Karaoi. Another person would've gone crazy long ago, but we are alive, although we deserve to die!"

She was looking into the distance through tears and said very calmly, "Yes, die. The fate of our poor sea gave us no choice. Do you know how much pain he is in, Korlan? Do you know how many years he's been carrying a heavy black stone in his heart? How can he not drink?"

That is what Marziya told her, and they did not speak of it again.

Marziya's strange words stuck in Korlan's head. It was a clear and sunny morning as she helped Aitugan pack in Semipalatinsk. As she stood in the shadows at the back of the room with a dish in her hand, she mused to herself, "The fate of our poor sea gave us no choice!" She understood vaguely that this unnerving, even threatening phrase, was directly linked to Kakharman, but she couldn't understand how.

As she moved over to the window, she was caught in a shaft of sunlight. The sun seemed to burn right through her, and she suddenly screamed. She saw it. She knew at last. She understood Kakharman! She understood everything about her son!

The sunlight struck her full in the eyes, and her eyes went black.

"Apa!" Aitugan rushed to her. "Apa, what's wrong?"

She helped Korlan to the sofa.

"Don't worry, my dear. I'm just not feeling well." Korlan stroked her daughter-in-law's hand. "It'll pass . . . I just need to lie down . . ."

Aitugan put a pillow under her head. Korlan closed her eyes and began to think. "It would've been good to take the herbs . . . the ones that Marziya gave me," she thought, and then fell into darkness.

No, not into darkness but into the dazzling sunlight that exists only in childhood, into the scent of grasses waving under the bright-blue summer wind.

She is striding through the high grasses of Zidebai. She sees the horses cantering through the green sea, toward Karaul River. The foals are chasing after them, and their anxious whinnying flies high, high into the sky. Little Korlan is striding, striding through the grasses of Zidebai . . . The sky arches far above. The steppe stretches far into the distance . . . This world is so immense! How vast, she thinks. What freedom!

And just before the morning in the small aul near Bakanas, shouts ring out through the chilly air, "Shakarim[1] is killed! Shakarim is killed! Get up!" Frightened people rush out into the lanes. And in the center of the aul, a bullock cart rattles to an abrupt halt. People are weeping. Their favorite poet is dead. He is lying with his face up in the bullock cart, his eyes wide open. Karasartov, the chief of the local NKVD, stands in front of the cart and raises his revolver. People cower. "Scared?" Karasartov laughs. "You shouldn't be! You shouldn't be scared of me but of scoundrels like this!" He pokes Shakarim's corpse with his revolver. "Do you know who this is? He is the leader of a faction that stirred up people in the auls!"

"Granddad!" Korlan exclaims.

"They didn't even close his eyes. What shame for him to lie like this!" her mother whispers.

"Shakarim the leader of a faction?" her father asks in surprise. "He never even heard what was happening here in the auls. He lived entirely alone with his books in the mountains . . . What faction? Or has this mlisa *lost his mind?" Korlan's mother hugs her tight and whispers to her father, "Be quiet, or you may bring trouble on us too."*

"Someone should step forward and close the eyes of your beloved charlatan. Who's brave enough?" Karasartov is enjoying himself. The rifles of the policemen and soldiers, sent to support the chief of NKVD, are directed at the small group of people huddling together in fear.

Nobody moves. One step would surely mean a bullet in the head. Everyone knows that.

"Are you scared?" Karasartov continues as he fires several shots into the air. "Come on!"

407

And Korlan's mother, gently holding Korlan in front of her, edges toward the cart. The thin gray face of her beloved granddad is getting closer and closer.

Very recently, just a week ago, he had come to collect provisions from them.

Korlan had sat on his lap, and he had buried his face in her hair, murmuring, "My granddaughter smells so sweet. Like golden honey . . . like honey . . ."

Her mother gently nudges her forward. Korlan carefully closes each of Shakarim's eyes. "Sleep, Granddad . . ." She thinks she can hear her granddad whisper, "Thank you, my dear granddaughter . . . my golden honey."

Karasartov pushes the girl off the cart. She falls on her back in the dust. The young blue-eyed soldiers begin to laugh loudly. She can't understand what they are laughing about . . .

Karasartov makes a sign, and the cart begins to move. For thirty years, no one knew where the body of the dead poet was left. People only found out in 1961 that the murderers had dumped his body in a dry well, far on the steppe.

The mountains of Bakanas . . . The great famine in the Kazakh steppe . . . The plain of Zidebai filling with corpses . . .

If it weren't for Nasyr, who brought her to the sea, if it weren't for the sea, in which there were plenty of fish, she would not be alive. She grew up on the coast of the sacred sea. During those days, the waves could be heard from the window of Nasyr's house. And on their wedding night, when it had only just begun to get light in Karaoi, Nasyr had taken her to the sea . . .

Barefoot, they stepped hand in hand onto the soft, wet sand, the quiet slap of their feet almost inaudible as they moved toward the water's edge. They heaved the boat into the sea, and Nasyr began to pull on the oars. He had decided to take his young wife out for a row at this quiet and beautiful dawn hour. Soon two large fish joined their boat. These fish were Ata-Balyk and Ana-Balyk, there to protect the newlyweds on their nuptial voyage.

"How wonderful!" Korlan thought, and she couldn't understand whether this is what she thought back then as a little girl or whether she's thinking this now after so many years have passed, and she's standing with one foot in the grave.

"Apa . . . Apa, what's wrong?" She heard the voice faintly as if from far away. It sounded familiar . . . painfully familiar because it connected somehow to Kakharman . . . Kakharman . . . "How wonderful!" she thought again. "Don't wake her up. Why are you trying to wake her up? She feels so good; there is no pain . . . She is now that slender young girl looking from the boat to the infinite blue sea and thinking, 'How wonderful!'"

"Apa!" Aitugan shouted again, beginning to get scared. She put her ear against Korlan's chest. Korlan was breathing heavily and unevenly. Aitugan ran to the neighbors—she must call for an ambulance.

> *In place of that beauty, there's now saline land. It's just as infinite as the sea once was. A bright-white wraith whirls around it. Something can be seen, a human figure—it looks like Kyzbala. She wanders through this landscape like a shadow and mutters something quietly . . . How many years has she been wandering? Fifty? A hundred? A thousand? What is she looking for in this wraith? For her son? For her husband? Or is she looking for herself—the one she was when she was different, happy?*

A young female doctor quickly measured the old woman's blood pressure, and fear flashed across her eyes. She quickly opened the leather box she brought with her.

"Do you have disposable syringes? No, why would you have them. Just quickly boil two needles!"

Aitugan rushed to the stove with a saucepan of water.

"We've been rushing around like crazy for the second day in a row," the doctor complained. "There's no medicine, no disposable syringes. But they keep on with the testing!"

"Have they been testing again?" Aitugan got scared.

"Give me the syringes!" the doctor ordered rudely. She hurriedly made injections into a vein. "But what can I do? I have another twenty calls."

The blue waves . . . The sea is leaving. Helpless and defiled, it looks as if it is trying to shrink into itself, curling up quietly. And while shrinking, it divides into two—two big tears . . . And the endless white dust flies over these tears, and the endless saline land wraps around the tears, and nothing lives . . .

Korlan opened her eyes.

"Apa, how are you feeling?" Aitugan asked shyly.

"I'm still alive, my dear." Korlan struggled to move her lips.

"I'll bring some tea." Aitugan stood up. "Not a very strong one, right? And a lot of milk?"

A small, slender girl is walking across the meadow and stooping to pick flowers. The bouquet in her hands is growing bigger and bigger . . .

Chingistau, I am so close to you! But I have no energy left to get to you. Forgive me!

The small girl keeps stooping and stooping, a big bouquet in her hands . . . in her hands . . . a bou . . . a bou . . . quet . . .

Kakharman sent a telegram to Zharasbai. He asked them to inform his father of Korlan's death. He put his wife and children on a plane and carried his mother's body in a zinc coffin on the train. Ivan Yakubovsky went to see him off—they spoke little and said goodbye hurriedly. If they only knew that they would not meet again in this life!

Kakharman found it hard to deal with his mother's death. He was so angry with himself that he hadn't found time to talk to her properly. He took this sin heavily on his soul. And his mother had waited. She had come specifically to spend time with him. He should've realized that she didn't have much time left!

And Kakharman couldn't forgive himself for failing to take his mother to Chingistau as he had promised. He already didn't live up to the old people's expectations, but he could've at least done this—he could've! Soon he began to think about his father and how the old man would cope with the news. They had lived their life in harmony and love. Now he would likely go downhill rapidly. And what should be done with him now? His father definitely will not come to Zaysan. Yet he cannot be left alone to die a slow death in these barren, saline lands.

The train arrived in Alma-Ata during the night, and Kakharman decided not to go out onto the platform. He listened to the voices outside his window, looked at the scurrying crowds, and thought that he should've sent a telegram to Bolat; a man really needs his friends and relatives when he is grieving. Both Bolat and Khorst will be offended that he hasn't informed them.

The platform began to float away. Kakharman lay down, closed his eyes, and saw himself sitting on the small bench by his father's house, crying.

He turned the light on, sat up, and began to look gloomily through the pile of newspapers he bought before his departure.

IN RECENT DAYS IN BAKU AND IN A NUMBER OF OTHER SETTLEMENTS of Azerbaijan and also in some districts of Armenia, tragic events have taken place that echo with pain in the hearts of the Soviet people. Blood was shed, and there are casualties among Armenian, Azerbaijani, and other nationalities. We express our deep condolences to the families of the dead and sincere sympathies to all the victims.

HUNDREDS OF THOUSANDS TOOK PART IN A MEETING TO SUPPORT THE PLENUM OF THE CC OF BULGARIA. The plenum excluded Todor Zhivkov and his son Vladimir from the party and also Zhivkov's close supporter, Milko Balev.

THE SOCIAL AND POLITICAL SITUATION IN CZECHOSLOVAKIA remains difficult following an emergency plenum of CPC that ran through the night from Friday to Saturday. The composition of the new leadership of the party has not satisfied many people, including the Communists.

FROM THE BEGINNING OF THIS YEAR, ABOUT EIGHTY-FIVE THOUSAND PEOPLE have permanently left GDR for FRG and West Berlin. On some days, the number of immigrants reaches three thousand.

THE ATTORNEY GENERAL OF GDR INITIATED A CRIMINAL CASE AGAINST ex-members of the leadership of SED, E. Honecker, Mielke, Stoph, Kleiber, Axen, and Krolikowski. They are accused of corruption and abuse of power, which has led to great damage to the national economy and their own personal enrichment.

TODOR ZHIVKOV IS BEING ARRESTED. THE CHIEF PROSECUTOR OF NRB HAS BEGUN a preliminary investigation of Zhivkov's case, who is being accused of inciting ethnic hatred and misappropriation of public property on an exceptionally large scale.

ON THE POLYGON IN THE STATE OF NEVADA, A NUCLEAR EXPLOSION OF 120 to 150 kilotons has taken place. It's the first nuclear test this year, and the seven hundredth in the thirty-nine years of the existence of the Nevada testing ground.

ARRESTS ON POLYGON. ON SUNDAY NIGHT, THE POLICE ARRESTED six people who took part in the protest against the continuing American nuclear tests. The group of six people penetrated the testing ground in the state of Nevada on January 29 in an attempt to prevent the first nuclear explosion in the USA this year. The arrested activists face jail terms of up to six months.

They passed Dzhambul at dawn. Kakharman got up at midday, shaved, and went to the restaurant car to have some food. There was no one there but a young woman sitting in the corner with a glass of mineral water and a tall, thin man telling jokes to bored waitresses. He recognized that young man—it was Kaiyr. Kaiyr recognized Kakharman, too, and made a sign to the girls.

"My darlings, set the table! It's my brother!" It was obvious Kaiyr was happy to see Kakharman. But Kakharman realized at once the cause of his liveliness. His eyes were sparkling, and Kakharman could smell anasha.

"Where are you coming from?" Kaiyr asked as he ushered Kakharman to the table.

"And where are you coming from and heading to?" Kakharman countered.

"I got on the train in Dzhambul, and I'm going to the white-walled one.[2] It's been a while since we met, Kakharman-aga. The last I saw you was in Ust-Kamenogorsk."

"That's right. But where are your rich friends?"

"Ah, those idiots? They are all in jail. Their dads didn't have enough money to bail them out. It's hard times now. Everyone is lying low. They're wary about accepting backhanders. Tonya!" he called for a waitress. "I hope you understand that my brother and I want to spend our time in a civilized manner? Kakha, what are we drinking? White? Red? Cognac?"

"Whatever they give us. They're quite strict in restaurants now."

"They'll give us whatever we like!"

"You can order whatever you like. I'm on the wagon right now."

"Are you undergoing treatment?" Kaiyr didn't understand.

"Am I an alcoholic needing treatment?"

"Yes, yes." Kaiyr smiled sympathetically. "Back in Ust-Kamenogorsk, I thought, 'He must be going for detox.'"

"If you lived through what I did," Kakharman interrupted him harshly, "through what fate has dropped on me, you would be an alcoholic too."

"I'm sorry, Kakha," Kaiyr said quietly. "I'm only joking."

"I don't have time for jokes now. My mother died. I'm moving her body."

Kaiyr's smile faded from his lips. After a moment, he said, "May Allah rest her soul . . . I will read a prayer now for the peace of her soul." And he quickly took the bottle off the table.

They had lunch and then stood up; Kaiyr went with Kakharman. Kakharman began to feel surprisingly warm toward this "businessman" for his prayer.

"And here are our home sands," Kaiyr noted, when they settled in the compartment.

"This is not sand—it's all salt."

The hot wind swept white dust past the window. After they passed Dzhambul, the curtain of dust grew thicker and thicker.

"In the past, Karabas winds blew once every ten years. Now they blow every year," Kaiyr said, looking pensively out the window. "I remember last year, we were stuck here for a whole week just because of this Karabas. While we were held up here, three people died—blood pressure, heart attack."

"What sends you to Moscow?"

"I'm carrying anasha."

"The punishment's tough, I think."

"I know. But I hope you won't rat me out to the cops?"

"I never did anything of the kind in the past and certainly won't be doing it now. I can't be bothered. Does it really matter who ruins our land, crooks like you or the government? Both you and they are criminals! I will not forgive anyone for the death of my sea and of my land!" He pointed his finger at the window. "Whenever could such a thing happen before? Salt being carried across the land!"

Kakharman was nodding off with his head against the wall of the compartment when Kaiyr slid out of the compartment. He stood in the corridor for a while, wondering whether to go to the restaurant and chat with the girls or to Brigadier Karaulbek. He had known Karaulbek since childhood, when they had gone to the same school. Whenever he was going to Moscow, Kaiyr would usually get on Karaulbek's train. The brigadier was reliable and would always hide Kaiyr from the officers, though that in no way meant that he approved of Kaiyr.

Karaulbek was in a meeting with the train's conductors when Kaiyr found him. They all looked worried, and Karaulbek's face was darker than a thundercloud.

"What's up?" Kaiyr asked. "What's happened?"

"Don't you see?" Karaulbek nodded toward the window. "The Karabas is coming from the sea. It looks like we'll be stuck here for a week." He looked nervously at the loudspeaker. "TASS will be announcing something important now. We were warned at the connection, and now we're waiting. It's not good. If we get stuck here for a week, we'll have to get by without water. Those stupid buggers sent the train off in too much of a hurry."

"And Kakharman is transporting his mother! What will he do?"

And then came the expected message. "The launch of the spaceship *Buran*[3] has been delayed because of the strong winds raging in the area of Baikonur. The cosmonauts are nevertheless in a good mood. The temperature in Moscow is eighteen to twenty degrees, and the time is eight minutes past four in the afternoon. And now some music . . ."

"We are definitely stuck!" Kaiyr spat.

But Kakharman heard nothing. He was still sleeping.

"Are you tired, my dear son?" his mother's voice asked him.

"Me?" Kakharman replied, raising his eyes. "No, not at all."

She was sitting in front of him, wearing the jacket of blue velvet she often wore in her last days.

"Yes, you're tired. But why so suddenly?"

"You're imagining it."

"You can deceive most people but not your mother. My heart felt it long ago, dear son. We all know what you were fighting for all these years. And now you should rest. Don't tire yourself out. Look at yourself. You've aged before your time. I came to see you. I wanted to comfort your heart, but I couldn't. You kept secrets from me . . . And I was confused—how could I approach you? And everyone told me to be careful with you. So I was careful, and then the time was gone."

His mother went quiet and put her hands on the table. Kakharman studied her familiar face. Gray hair was poking out from her pure, snow-white platok. Big, deep wrinkles wreathed her skin. God, she looks tired herself!

"Apa, you look exhausted."

"It's the grave pulling me, son. It's time, I feel. It's time . . . People tell me that you drink a lot."

Kakharman understood. This is what his mother wanted to say more than anything while she was living there in Zaysan. "She couldn't reproach me during life, and she has finally brought herself to it after death . . . What death?" he was surprised. "She is alive. She is sitting in front of me . . . Mom."

Indeed, she was sitting next to him. There was food on the table and an open bottle of Kazakhstan cognac. "When did I open it?" Kakharman thought. "No, it wasn't me, I stopped drinking. It's nonsense! She is not dead . . . There she is, sitting next to me, waiting for my reply."

"Apa, it won't be vodka that will ruin me. That is not what I'm scared of. I wander across life, and I know that I will be brought down by people's cruelty and indifference. Sometimes I think there are no people left. Everyone has turned into Satan to do evil to me, to each other, and to nature. To do evil and only evil. Satan has won man to his side."

"Ah, son. No, it's not just Satan. People can be taken over even by a little devil. And taken over so completely that it's hard to tell whether it's a devil in front of you or a man."

"People are terrifying now, apa. Have you ever seen those people even the devil is scared of?"

"I've heard about them . . ."

"Our people are very spoiled, apa. And there's no light. We keep building a grand society, but we don't care about individual people! Our people were deformed long ago. So what harmony can there be? A man without God in his head or his heart is an animal! Satan himself is afraid of a man like that! There's not a Kazakh now who wouldn't steal, drink, or lie. How can we live like this, apa? How?"

After thinking for a little, his mother said, "You are not thinking about your father at all . . ."

"Ah, apa, it's no matter: fathers and sons . . . We all kick and torment each other because we are imprisoned in a paddock! And it is a burning hell." He raised his eyes and fell back in shock. His mother wasn't in front of him at all. Just a wrinkled, unshaven old man, with a tatty and discolored cloak thrown over his naked body.

"Salute!" the man in the cloak said.

"Hello!" Kakharman replied after fighting back his terror. No matter how carefully he looked at this strange man, he couldn't remember where they had met.

"I'm sorry. I don't know you." Kakharman looked at the stranger warily. "Who are you?"

"Who am I?" the stranger laughed. "You and I have known each other for a long time. But every time we meet, you ask me this stupid question. And you used to ask it because you were drunk whenever I came. I'll introduce myself again." He stood up, waving his cloak. "I am djinn. For all these years, I've been sitting on your shoulders. Sometimes on the right one and sometimes on the left. I wanted to leave you in peace long ago, but I can't—we are also being watched. I would've left it all, wished you all the best, and gone. But you won't be happy. I know this for sure. You don't like money, so you won't steal. You won't become a sycophant or try to climb up the career ladder—"

"What do you want from me, Zhyndybai?"[4]

"If it was up to me, I would've fried the whole wretched human race in hell's fire. You have destroyed everything on earth that can be destroyed. God will send you all to hell for your sins, and he will order us devils to come to earth. He will command us to bring back to life all the brooks and rivers, all the lakes and seas that idiot man has ruined! Bring back to life the animals and all the other living things with which I once filled the earth! Because of you, we'll have to do it all! Do you think it'll be easy? We will drown in blood, and we will suffocate when we start clearing up the mountains of shit after you are gone! People are animals, my friend. God won't give them any mercy. Remember that . . ."

"Kakha! Kakha, wake up!"

Kakharman struggled to open his eyes. Kaiyr kept shaking him on his shoulder. There was no one in front of him.

"We're stuck! We'll be here at least a week."

"Why?"

"We're right in the center of a big storm that started in Sinemorye. Just now they announced that the launch of the *Buran* is being delayed."

The howling of the wind behind the window of the carriage and the fast-approaching dusk confronted Kakharman with an agonizing dilemma. What should he do with his mother's body?

"It's ridiculous to sit here for a week!" Kakharman exclaimed.

"Today or tomorrow, your mother should be buried, Kakha. Otherwise, her body will start to decompose."

Kaiyr made a decision.

"The seventh junction is not far from here—only about three miles! Sarsengali will help us. We must take the coffin out right away and get going. We'll get it there somehow, even if we have to drag it. I'll go and speak to Karaulbek."

"Ask him for a rope!" Kakharman shouted after Kaiyr. "A strong one!"

He left his bag in the compartment. The wind almost blew him off his feet as he jumped down onto the sand. His face was covered by white, salty dust right away. The three of them carried the coffin from the carriage, laid it down on the sand, tied the rope around it, and began to pull.

"You'll get there along the track!" Karaulbek shouted to them.

"Thank you, brother! If we're alive, we'll meet again! We'll have a seat and a good chat."

"May your mother rest in peace!"

The hot wind was burning their faces, and they struggled to move forward. The rope rubbed their shoulders until they bled. Kaiyr, having weakened quickly, fell on his knees.

"Get up, brother. You mustn't sit down. If we sit, we'll be buried under the sand!"

"Kakha, just a little . . . little rest . . ."

Kaiyr began to get up, helped by Kakharman. They slung the ropes over their shoulders again.

"May God forgive us for dragging the coffin. The junction is not three miles away. We've already walked five."

"Ten—no more than that!" Kaiyr shouted, turning his face away from the wind.

"Ten! Five!" Kakharman thought angrily, but he was at once embarrassed by his irritation. "If you hadn't come across him, how would you have managed?" Kaiyr tied his bags to the coffin with belts. Though angered and offended, Kakharman came to terms with it and just thought, "Forgive me, Mother. That is how it is. It hasn't been done with bad intentions, as you can see yourself."

"There's the junction," Kaiyr said with dry lips. "Do you see the roofs, Kakha?"

Kakharman nodded. Sarsengali wasn't home. But kind Meiz met them with her daughter-in-law. The women washed Korlan's body and wrapped it in white cloth. Kakharman and Kaiyr dug a hole and lowered the body into it. Kaiyr read a prayer over the burial mound. By the time they had finished, it was dark, and the searing wind was even stronger. Kakharman was kneeling by the grave, frozen in place. His mother's eyes stared at him from the darkness. Kakharman was weeping silently, his chest and shoulders trembling.

"It's alright, son. It's alright . . . You'll get used to it," his mother's voice said. "My last request is that you bury me in Karaoi . . . I'll feel better there . . . There, I'll be able to rest."

"Her soul has not departed yet," Kakharman thought happily. He felt that his mother's soul was now touching his face and chest, bringing a moment of invigorating coolness. Yes, he must rebury his mother in Karaoi.

"I will fulfill your wish, apa," he replied quietly. "And now I need to apologize, Mother. I have not lived up to your and Father's expectations."

"That's enough, dear son. I never had to blush for you. I was always proud of you. I will pray to Allah. May he protect you. And I also ask of you, dear son, not to leave your father. I didn't see him before my death. Please ask him to forgive me for leaving him alone. It wasn't my will."

The more the wind howled, the more gently Korlan looked upon her son. They had never been as close as they were now, had never spoken with each other as deeply and tenderly as they were doing now. A refreshing coolness brushed his face again. It was his mother's spirit.

Kaiyr returned.

"Kakharman-aga, let's go into the house." He helped Kakharman up. Kakharman leaned against Kaiyr, and the two walked toward the house, bowing their heads against the wind. Kakharman's steps were feeble. He looked back. His mother's eyes were following him. Kakharman screamed, covering his face with his hand.

"Don't be afraid, son. It's me," his mother's voice said. "I'm watching over you."

At the door, Kakharman looked back again.

"I can't go any farther. Goodbye, son! Please ask Nasyr to forgive me. And don't forget: I should be lying in Karaoi . . . only in Karaoi! Goodbye . . . Goodbye . . ." Her eyes began to fade back into the steppe, leaving only a lingering, pale light.

Kakharman slowly returned to his senses. The women's faces were covered in tears. He looked at the young boy of three or four playing with a cat by the stove. The silence of the house was occasionally interrupted by the boy's happy laughter. But there was something unhealthy in the child: heavy breathing and a cough that would shake his whole body.

The dying sea was taking its toll on children. Out of a thousand newborns, a hundred will die—either while still in the mother's womb or shortly after birth. Others refused to take the breast, or the mother's milk would be so poisoned that the children would be sickly, their growth stunted. Yes, this small child is ill. He won't live long on this earth.

Kakharman had known Sarsengali and his wife, Meiz—who was a distant relative on his father's side—for a long time. Kakharman thought that he should thank these people somehow for their help with Korlan's burial.

"I didn't think I'd have to trouble you, apa," Kakharman said. "But I had no other choice. Believe me."

"May the ground be as soft as down for her!" Meiz replied. "It will be hard for Nasyr without Korlan." She sighed. Kakharman realized that the cause for sorrow in the house was more than Korlan's death.

"Where's Sarsengali?" Kakharman asked.

Meiz's daughter-in-law Gulbarshin stood up quickly and walked out. Her sobs could be heard from the other room. The boy left the cat and ran, crying, after his mother.

Meiz wasn't crying, but her chin was trembling. She told them Sarsengali was now in Semipalatinsk and that Makhambet had been given a six-year sentence for taking part in the December disturbances. Only two days earlier, they had been informed by the administration of the correctional labor colony that their son had hanged himself.

Meiz handed an envelope to Kakharman. Kakharman pulled a letter from the envelope and began to read.

"Mama," Makhambet wrote, "I do not regret anything, and I don't feel guilty. If the people I went out into the square with are spoken about badly, don't believe a single word of it. We wanted a different life, a better life—that is the only thing we are guilty of. Don't believe anyone who says that we rebelled against Russians. They are lying.

"I once believed that we would achieve our aim of a better life, but I don't believe it anymore! But you should forgive us, Mother! Forgive Mukhtar for his death in Afghanistan and forgive me . . ."

Kakharman couldn't read any more. He clenched his fist so tightly his knuckles became white. In the far room, Gulbarshin kept crying, and her ill child was crying with her.

On the same day that Kakharman and Kaiyr were dragging Korlan's coffin to the junction, Igor was trying to convince the senior pilot to stay on Akespe Island to record from above the precise moment when the smaller Sinemorye separated from the larger.

"You're joking, Igor Matveevich!" the pilot objected. "We'll be smashed to pieces the minute we take off in this Karabas wind! No, I won't. You do what you like, but I won't."

Then Igor promised to pay the pilot three times his usual pay. After considering for a while, the pilot assented.

"But it has to be done as soon as possible," the senior pilot said. "I don't like the sound of this wind. If it turns into a storm, we are done for."

"We're ready. Serezha, let's go!"

The helicopter took off and, banking to one side, turned toward the smaller Sinemorye.

Strong winds were whipping up sand over the saline expanse, but the sea surface was relatively calm. A herd of saigas were racing down the dried riverbed of Syr Darya. Lena touched Sergey's arm and pointed at them and said, "Take a picture!"

And Sergey, aiming his camera, wondered what could've scared them.

A herd of horses suddenly appeared from behind a long sand hill—they, too, were running in terror. "What are they running from?" Sergey thought anxiously, but at that moment, the wind became ferocious and tossed the helicopter into the air as if it were a toy.

Down on the ground, Igor shouted over the radio, "Turn back immediately! Do you hear me? I order you to turn back!"

But it was too late. In the few minutes since they had taken off, the wind had transformed into a storm of incredible strength. Only then did Sergey understand what the saiga and horses were running away from—they were trying to outrun a horrible white whirlwind, a raging mixture of salt and sand.

Lena was in the helicopter with him and was now checking the camera equipment. Everything was fine. The fiery stallion was flying at the head of the herd, hardly touching the sand with his hooves. Lena was so mesmerized by the scene that she completely forgot about the danger as the helicopter was thrown around violently. Another minute in this storm, and it would be torn apart. Suddenly, the helicopter was buffeted so powerfully that its motor stalled, and the rotors stopped. But it didn't fall. Instead, it was hurled this way and that, like an empty bag on a windy street.

The monstrous tornado roared over the ground in a circle approximately five miles across. Then, with a ghastly whipping motion, it snatched up horses, saigas, wolves, foxes, and the few trees that still remained in the dried riverbed of Syr Darya. It dragged them up into the air, then hurled them back to the ground, then lifted them once more and began to spin them and the helicopter together as if in a giant cauldron. The living and dead creatures were being spun around and around in the air, smashing into each other and crashing against the helicopter panels with their unwilling hooves . . .

An old gray she wolf who had crawled out of her burrow only moments before this horror struck pricked up her ears and began to howl. She was waiting for her male to return from hunting. She pushed her curious wolf cubs back into the burrow. The male, sensing the danger, was quickly dragging a dead corsac by its withers. When he heard his mate's howl, he began to move quicker. When he returned the burrow at last, the she wolf didn't even look at the prey thrown down before her. She simply gently bit the male and tried to urge him desperately into the burrow. But he insisted on dragging the prey in with him. If he had delayed a moment longer, he would have met the same fate as the fiery stallion who was tearing past not far away. In a split second, the stallion was pulled off the ground; the wolves heard his long, terrible neigh as he whirled into the air. Poking his nose from the burrow, the wolf began to howl with such an appalling desperation that the cubs clung to the ground in terror. He howled for a long time, and then the old she wolf joined him . . .

A creature hurtled past the oval windows of the helicopter, upside down, legs up, back to front. Suddenly, a piglike beast cannoned against the window.

"Megafauna! Megafauna!" Lena exclaimed in horror.

"An indricotherium!" Sergey shouted into the microphone.

But the pilots didn't give a damn about any megafauna. They were holding the helm with but a single aim: to bring the machine down as safely as possible on the dunes. But they had barely any control and were entirely at the mercy of fate.

"You've lost your mind!" Igor yelled. "Indricotherium died out thirty million years ago!"

"Then not all died!"

The great beast smashed against the window again, and the glass shattered.

Thirty million years ago, where the Turgay region is now, thick forest grew, and huge, thick-skinned indricotherium used to live. It seemed to Sergey and Lena as if this monstrous storm had dug into the depths of time and hauled these creatures to witness the end of Sinemorye, the end of the world . . .

The fiery stallion hit the side of the helicopter again, and his ribs cracked.

Later, when the remains of the destroyed helicopter were found, Igor discovered the film that Sergey had been using to take the pictures. When the film was developed, Igor saw the fiery stallion, saw close-up that his eyes were filled with blood and insane with fear. He shivered, realizing that this beast had sent them to their deaths.

The storm raged for five days, not weakening for even a minute. Day replaced night, night replaced day—but there was no one to notice. In the lonely house on the seventh junction, the inhabitants were living without morning, without evening, without day or night. The windows were closed, but dust still made its way into the house. From time to time, the women would wipe it from the walls, beds, tables. Before long, there was a big heap of dust by the door. On the fifth day—maybe at midnight or maybe at midday—everyone in the house was awakened by an awful crash. Everyone in the house sat in wary silence, as if talking would bring the ceiling, which must be holding on to its last weak link, crashing down.

Only a person who lives on the sands can know how much Karabas winds oppress a man's soul. It's as if the elements are trying to prove to man how worthless he is, how small he is before the powers of nature.

Kaiyr also woke up feeling thoughtful. He sat with his legs dangling off the bed. "And well, it seems like here's the end of the world, damn it! And what have you done but run around? You kept running around, trying to save some money. What for? And that was the meaning of your life, of the risks you took. Take Kakharman . . . What has he achieved—a good, clever, and honest man? He's wandered around. He has never settled anywhere and has no money. He is utterly alone . . . But imagine we had people like him everywhere—then life wouldn't be that bad, even if it was socialism. It'd be OK. Yes, socialism wouldn't be too bad. But we don't have many people like him. In fact, there are hardly any! So let's assume this house now collapses, and we all, well, die. We will be equal in death, under its dirty remains. Me, a rogue criminal and wheeler-dealer, and Kakharman, a clever, honest, and heroic man."

Just then, sand began to pour on him. Kaiyr swore as he ducked away from a torrent of sand.

Kakharman also sat up. The sand had started to fall on him too.

"We're in trouble, Kakha."

"Maybe the roof's gone."

"It's very apocalyptic, Kakha. I know you don't read spiritual books, but that is what they say: 'How many settlements became too arrogant to listen to their God and his messengers: we made them pay and punished them with severe penalties. And they tried the ill of their deeds and the end of their deeds were a loss to them.'"

"The Quran?"

"Yes. Novelists don't write things like this."

"I can't understand you. You read spiritual books, you know the Quran, but you don't live by it. You drink vodka, smoke anasha—you even seduced me into trying this muck."

"And what do you think about this 'muck'?"

"It makes me feel like I'm floating on the air. It's quite nice. I won't lie."

"Anasha is a good thing! It's salvation! If it weren't for anasha, I would've gone crazy long ago."

"There is something in that." Kakharman didn't want to argue.

"Would you like some cognac, Kakha? It'll make things more bearable."

"Why not?"

They lit an oil lamp. Kaiyr fetched the bottle he had opened on the train and poured them drinks.

"Let's drink to staying alive for a little longer."

"Amen to that!" Kakharman raised his glass.

More sand fell, and the lamp went out.

In the room next door, Meiz sighed sorrowfully. "It must be hard for her," Kakharman thought, "to lose both sons. I hope she doesn't break, like poor Kyzbala . . . The woman grew old so quickly! The stronger the emotional torment, the quicker you approach the end."

He smelled the bitter scent of anasha in the air.

"Would you like a smoke, Kakha?"

"Better not. But tell me, wouldn't you like to enroll at an institute and get an education? Why hang around purposelessly?"

"You're so naïve! Do you know how many degrees I have?" Kaiyr giggled. "Three! But what use are they to me? They're just paper. People say you're nothing without a piece of paper, but the only papers that matter are the ones that have a picture of Lenin on them."

"Oh! Where did you get so many degrees?"

"Can't you guess? I can buy ten if I want. I can even buy a man's head!"

"Now you're exaggerating!"

"I used to not believe it either, but when I was told how much it would cost in Uzbekistan to become a member of our glorious party or, forgive me, a member of parliament, then I began to believe. I was also shown people . . . I can't believe that you don't know anything about it, Kakha."

The storm raged on over Karaoi. It seemed as if it intended to wipe the aul from the face of the earth. It kept pushing houses over, lifting ramshackle shacks and sheds into the air and tossing them far into the sands. The roof of Nasyr's house, which the storm kept lifting and flapping like the wings of a night owl, was finally ripped off. It rolled down the road until it was swept into the air and vanished forever in the raging white wraith. When it happened, Nasyr was sitting in the house, fingering his rosary and repeating from time to time, "Ya, Allah, save us. We are sinful; have mercy on us."

The day before the storm hit Karaoi, the mail had reached Nasyr's house. Trapped inside their house, Berish sat by the lamp and read it all. He read out loud, but Nasyr, listening to the howling of the wind, looked absentmindedly at his grandson without hearing any of it. Berish knew it but kept on reading determinedly, finding it harder to cope with the silence. Anyway, what else was there to do?

YESTERDAY FOLLOWING THE SOVIET-HUNGARIAN AGREEMENT to withdraw the Southern Group of the Soviet Army stationed in Hungary, the first troop train headed back to the motherland.

THE FIRST TROOP TRAIN OF THE SOVIET ARMY LEAVING CZECHOSLOVAKIA with tanks, infantry fighting vehicles, and other machinery has arrived at the boarder station in Chop.

IN THE CENTRAL STUDIO OF FRENCH TV'S CHANNEL FIVE a solemn ceremony announcing "The Man of 1989" took place. "The Man of 1989" was awarded to Mikhail Gorbachev.

DOWNPOURS OF UNHEARD-OF STRENGTH have fallen on the most densely populated Chinese province, Szechuan. According to preliminary data, no less than 50 people were killed as a result of the disaster, and more than 150 people were injured.

THE RESIDENTS OF BUCHAREST COULD NOT SLEEP ON SATURDAY NIGHT due to the roar of explosions and the heavy crackle of machine guns and rifle fire.[5] Thousands of citizens left their houses and joined the soldiers who took the side of the people to protect the freedom they paid for with their lives.

EX-ROMANIAN LEADER NICOLAE CEAUŞESCU AND HIS wife, Elena, have left Romania, Radio Bucharest reported.[6]

EGON KRENZ,[7] NOT SO LONG AGO THE LEADER OF A COUNTRY and Secretary General of the SEPG, is now unemployed. "It's hard to find another job. I think I'll become a writer," he said to the newspaper *Bild*.

THE NEW PRESIDENT OF CZECHOSLOVAKIA, VÁCLAV HAVEL, HAS SPENT ABOUT FIVE YEARS in prison. He celebrated his arrival at Prague Castle as new leader of the country with a wide amnesty. At the beginning of the New Year, there were approximately thirty-one thousand prisoners. More than twenty thousand will be freed. Listening to Havel's speech, criminals cried.

AT 05:30 MOSCOW TIME IN THE SOVIET UNION, in Yakutiya, an underground nuclear explosion of up to 20 megatons took place. The explosion was carried out in the interests of the national economy.

AN INTERNATIONAL DAY OF FIGHTING AIDS IS TAKING PLACE UNDER THE GUIDANCE of the World Health Organization (WHO). This year it's taking place under the slogan "Young People and AIDS." According to experts from WHO, in the past decade alone, about six hundred thousand people have become ill from AIDS and five million turned out to be infected by its virus.

LATE AT NIGHT, FREE ROMANIAN TELEVISION ANNOUNCED that the trial took place in the case of N. Ceaușescu and E. Ceaușescu. They are charged with the genocide of more than sixty thousand people, undermining state power through armed actions against the people, undermining the national economy, and attempting to escape from the country with the use of funds held in foreign banks totaling more than $1 billion.

AT 07:01 MOSCOW TIME IN THE SOVIET Union, an underground explosion of up to 20 kilotons took place on the test ground near Semipalatinsk.

Along with all this news were speeches from the party conference—and many were talking about the disastrous situation of Sinemorye.

But these speeches had no effect on Nasyr now. Where were these indignant speakers before?

The previous day, Nasyr had tried to get out of the house to check on poor Nurdaulet and Kyzbala. He struggled to open the front door, which was almost buried in sand. And he had barely put one foot over the threshold before he was almost blown off his feet by the wind. He had no choice but to go back. "The end of the world must be here," Nasyr thought.

Seeing that praying wasn't much use, Nasyr stopped praying. And when Berish reminded him about prayer time, he pretended that he didn't hear.

"How are Kyzbala and Nurdaulet getting on?" Nasyr kept sighing. "I hope they survive."

During these days, he missed Korlan even more. Who knows? Maybe his heart knew Korlan was no longer alive. If she had been with him, she would've worked out a way to help Nurdaulet and Kyzbala. If she had been with him, he would not have felt so helpless and pathetic.

As he thought about Korlan, a profound sense of perplexity came over him. Now, at the end of his life, he realized he could not understand who Korlan was to him—or rather, she meant so much to him, that if he was asked what is Korlan apart from him and what is he, Nasyr, apart from her, he could not answer. Yes, this deep mystery of mutual existence comes to old people only near the end. And it will not be solved—no! It comes to fill the hearts of two humans with sacred awe. It comes so that two poor humans can move hand in hand along the final earthly path, touched by divine inspiration, by a soft, golden light.

"Granddad!" Berish lifted his head from the newspaper. "Ceaușescu was executed!"

"Who is this Ceaușescu?"

"The Romanian president!"

"I completely forgot the newspapers," Nasyr reproached himself. "All these things are still happening in the world."

"Granddad, what will happen now? Is it the end of socialism in Romania?"

"Maybe. Who knows? Their president was probably no good, and people won't tolerate it. People want honesty and fairness. They don't want to be treated like animals. Just think, whether we live under socialism or communism, people will in the end not let us, ordinary people, to be robbed."

"Under socialism, we all are ordinary people," Berish replied uncertainly, not even knowing if he agreed or disagreed with his grandfather.

"Granddad, will there be life on earth after the apocalypse?"

"Of course. Life never ends."

"And is it true that there is a soul?"

"The soul exists. That's for sure. Do you remember Otkeldy? His grandfather and father were holy people. Otkeldy frequently spoke with the souls of the dead people. He was able to call them."

"And can you call them?"

"When I talk to God, I see things. It was him who sent us rain. Do you remember, when it poured for forty days in a row?"

"But why aren't you praying now, Granddad?"

"Allah doesn't help us anymore. He is offended by man. We have fraternized with Satan, and he can't forgive us for it. Man has to live without God's help. And what did he command us?"

"He said to be fruitful and multiply!"

Nasyr corrected him.

"'I created you, and I bless you! Be fruitful and multiply, let your descendants take over all the solid earth, and you will be masters of the fish in the water, the birds in the air, the seedlings of the earth, and all the treasures in its depths will be subjected to you!'

"That is what Allah said. But how did man carry out his wish?"

Berish was happy that his granddad, who had grown introspective, had started talking. Worrying that the thread of the conversation might be lost, he asked hurriedly, "And how did he carry out this wish?"

"He carried it out badly; he achieved nothing. He started a savage and remained a savage. Since the Stone Age, people have done just one thing: exterminate each other in endless wars. I am offended with man. But I am also offended with God!" Nasyr said daringly, raising his angry eyes to the sky. "Why did God leave man to his own devices? He could see that man is unreasonable and sometimes simply stupid. He should have helped him! Why is he turning away? Is that godly?"

With that, the old fisherman went to the lumber room and grabbed four planks of wood, a pile of screws, and some pieces of metal. He had gotten it all from the smithy a few days before the storm. He had decided to create a new cart for Nurdaulet, one that was comfortable and easy to move. The sand kept falling from the ceiling, but Nasyr was planing away and fitting the wheels without paying any attention.

Toward night, the wind, already fierce, became wilder still. The roof had been torn off the long room of Kyzbala's house on the first day of the storm. She herself had been unwell since that day and stayed in bed. So Nurdaulet had to do all the work around the house. Three times a day, he made tea and boiled rice. Nurdaulet struggled to feed Kyzbala. He tried as hard as he could, but Kyzbala refused to eat and only drank tea. But Nurdaulet was not so unhappy even with that. These tasks weren't too difficult for him—firing the stove, boiling the water, and washing the rice—but they took Nurdaulet so long it was a nonstop process. One task ran into another without giving him a single minute's rest, but this homely life filled his impoverished existence with meaning, and the realization that Kyzbala needed him warmed his heart. By the evening, completely exhausted, he would fall on the duvets and fall into a deep sleep. He woke up each morning to the sound of the wind howling. All day long, the walls of their old house shook, and the ceiling beams creaked. Nurdaulet would often look at his wife's face in the feeble glow of the oil lamp. Sometimes he couldn't tell whether she was asleep or just lying there with her eyes closed. He would've given a great deal to find out what she was thinking about if she was not asleep.

The day before Nurdaulet was supposed to leave for the front line, the couple had walked all night along the seashore. It was impossible for Nurdaulet to remember how often he hugged his slender and dark-haired wife; it was impossible to remember all the kisses she gave back to him. During those nights, the golden coastal sand was their bed . . . and now, so many years later, that sand was their enemy, ready to bury them alive.

Kyzbala began to moan quietly. Nurdaulet understood that she was thirsty. Lifting her head with his stump, he put the piala by his wife's lips. After drinking, Kyzbala looked at her husband blankly and closed her eyes. Her lips began to move; she was trying to say something. Nurdaulet strained his ears, but he couldn't make it out.

Yet big changes were going on in her soul. These changes had begun the day Nurdaulet moved into her house, but they were unnoticeable to the people around her and even to herself. But that day, for the first time in decades, she realized more or less consciously that she remembers things.

The sea—blue, infinite, just the way it was when she saw it in her youth—appears before her. A boat sways on the waves . . . Yes, yes, it is a boat . . . It's called a boat . . . She can now repeat the words, "boat, boat . . ." And her head is resting . . . her head is resting on her husband's shoulder . . . She remembers! In ten days, he will leave for the front . . . They have finished building a house. They spent the whole spring and summer building it . . . And finally it's ready . . . They finished it today, and now they are on the sea . . . Soon they'll swim, but for now they are sitting in the boat . . . She is hugging her husband and moving her finger across his tattoo and reading its letters out loud: Si-ne-mor-ye . . .

"Why did you do it?" she asked.

"I was born here."

"And was it painful to have it done?"

"Of course. Don't you like it?"

"Why not? I like everything about you, Nur!"

"Nur . . . Nur . . . daulet . . . ," Kyzbala whispered.

One of the beams creaked ominously, and sand began to cascade in. Nurdaulet couldn't hear her whisper above the creaking of the timber and the swishing of the sand. Kyzbala was scared of the noise and raised her head from the pillow. She saw the invalid rushing toward her and thought, "Who is he? What is he doing in my house?" For the first time in many, many years she asked herself a question consciously and consciously began to search for an answer.

She looked around. There was a storm outside the house. Sand streamed from a crack near where the beam had failed. How can she block the crack?

And the invalid was looking up at her with a face filled with numb surprise. Such a familiar face . . . so familiar . . . That chest . . . That tattoo. Kyzbala bent forward. There was very little light, and the oil lamp only glowed faintly. "Sine . . ." She bent even lower, already beginning to see something. "Mor-ye." . . . Sinemorye! Nurdaulet . . .

"Nur!" Kyzbala shouted and leaped toward the man. "Nurdaulet! My love!"

Nurdaulet was speechless with amazement.

"Nur! I did say it, I did! I said that I wouldn't die before I saw you again!"

"Kyzbala . . . Kyzbala." Nurdaulet wept.

"I didn't protect our son . . . Forgive me."

And then the central beam collapsed under the weight of sand that had been falling on the house for so many days. A moment later, the entire ceiling collapsed, and the ruins of the house were quickly buried under the sand.

"Nurdaulet!"

"Kyzbala!"

In this double scream, there was a hopeless despair. The screams were muffled by the howl of the wind and then died under a mountain of sand . . .

"No, it isn't easing up," Kakharman thought. "How much longer will we have to sit here?"

"Why the rush?" Zhyndybai said cheerfully. "Salam!"

"Hi!" Kakharman greeted him joyfully. "At least I can talk to you in my boredom."

"Boredom is an unreliable thing," Zhyndybai muttered. He looked at Kakharman testingly. "Have you messed with anasha?"

"I just tried it out of curiosity . . . And boredom . . . Why are you so gloomy? Would you like a smoke yourself?"

"I'm exhausted from the last few days; the storm has tired me out."

"And I thought devils couldn't tire."

"How much do you know about devils, Kakharman? Not as much as I know about you . . . I know a lot about you."

"Aren't you a little cocky?"

"Why would I be modest? I'm not human. For a human, it's no good. I agree. But luckily for us, there are not many people as modest as you, Kakharman. It's easy for us to mislead the rest of humanity. We whisper to them, 'You know a lot. You know so much!' And the fool begins to shout, 'I know! I know more than others!' And shortly after, he breaks his neck. And it's a triumph for us—we won another one!"

"And do you have unemployment?"

"Of course! Everybody values his position and works nonstop—otherwise, you get kicked out. And it's your people's fault, by the way!"

"What have we to do with your unemployment?"

"What do you have to do with it? The political fights, the nuclear tests, the atomic stations, the army, the camps—so many victims! You don't have to look very hard to find examples. By your sea, children die shortly after they are born. There are plenty of devils, but fewer and fewer people on the earth. And how many madhouses are there in the cities? We can do nothing with insane people. We are even a bit scared of them, since they follow neither God nor the devil. In a couple more years, you won't even need devilry anymore. We ministers will all be made redundant since you will destroy yourself. Satan knows how to count money. He won't let there be more of us than the world needs."

"Hmmm . . ." Kakharman shook his head. He had perked up at the word "minister." Maybe he should ask Zhyndybai what departments they have there and what heaven's bureaucracy is like. But then he decided he didn't want to talk about departments anymore. Remembering his earthly business and his pointless visits to bureaucratic offices made him feel sick.

"And the overseas devils live better than our Soviet ones?"

"What makes you think that?" Zhyndybai giggled again. "There are fewer temptations there. People eat as much as they want, wear what they like, have a calmer temperament, and smile more—how on earth can you tempt a man there?"

Zhyndybai went silent and listened.

"Now while I'm chatting away with you, the wind has weakened! That's no good!"

And with that, Zhyndybai dived into the stove and flew out the flue. Ash and soot billowed out of the stove behind him, right onto Kakharman's face, and he woke up. It was just as dark as when he fell asleep.

"What time is it, Kakha?" Kaiyr asked him.

"My watch says eight, but I don't know if it's day or night."

"It's more likely to be eight in the morning. Heaven's war seems to be calming down now. The end didn't come."

Kaiyr lit the lamp and began to smoke. The smell of anasha filled the room. He was thinking, "It's good that it's calming down. Another day and the hut would've collapsed, for sure. And we all would've died a heroic death here under the wreckage and the sand. And each of us would've received a Gold Star of Pointless Labor posthumously . . . Huh . . . I wonder how Karaulbek is getting on there? How's the train? The train was probably blown over long ago and buried under the sand."

Meiz called them for tea. Kakharman felt uncomfortable. He and Kaiyr had forced themselves on her hospitality, lived there, and eaten her food for six days.

"Apa, forgive us," Kakharman said. "We'd no idea it'd work out this way."

"It's alright, Kakharman." Meiz reassured him. "It could have happened to anyone. If we had turned you down, then it would've been a different matter."

Kakharman began to feel better. That is exactly what one would expect from a respectable baibishe.

"But I would like to ask you dzhigits something. We need water."

"We'll get water!" Kakharman replied quickly.

By midday, the wind was much calmer. Kakharman pushed open the door and walked out. The lean-tos and sheds around the house were destroyed. A dog, barking joyously, ran to him and began rubbing his head against Kakharman's feet. "You've been through a lot, poor thing," he murmured, gently stroking it. The wind was still strong but not strong enough to push him off his feet. Gulbarshin and Kaiyr harnessed the old camel into the cart. They put two flasks into the cart and headed toward the well.

He looked at the blown-off roof, which was lying some way off and was partially covered by the sand. It will take at least a year for Sarsengali to build things back up again, that's for sure. And one can only imagine what's happening in Karaoi. How were his father and Berish? As long as they survived. How will he tell them that his mother was dead? And how will his father cope?

The night before, Kakharman hadn't been sure if he'd survive himself. He should have been happy to have made it through the storm, but he wasn't. What if he had stayed alive just to step into the wild cruel world again, to feel his heart ache again and curse this world's absurdity once more?

He sighed, deeply, but the wind threw dust in his face, and he began to cough. He went back to the house, and Meiz was already tidying the house and sweeping the floor.

"How much sand there is—it's awful. And here we are, breathing this salt every day. How unhealthy it is. I think we all will die of cancer; we haven't much longer." She smiled as if apologizing. "Just stay outside for a little while I'm tidying up."

Kakharman nodded hurriedly and walked to his mother's grave. The small hill was clearly visible. He kneeled down and did not move. The wind struck his back. Just as on the day of the funeral, tears began to suffocate him.

He sat by the grave for a long time. When he returned to the house, it was clean, and Meiz was making tea. Kakharman realized that if she lent him her camel, he could be in Karaoi in an hour and a half. But the trip was still too risky, so he decided to wait until the next day.

Kaiyr brought in the full flasks, wiped the sweat off his forehead, and sat down.

"And where's Gulbarshin?" Meiz asked.

"She's in the yard," Kaiyr answered vaguely.

Meiz took the scarf from Kaiyr's face and went to the door to shake the dust from it. The door opened, and Gulbarshin, her face wet with tears, ran in and slapped Kaiyr frantically on his head.

"What's happened?" Meiz shouted. "Explain to me what's happened. Oh, God!!"

Gulbarshin grabbed the iron poker from the stove and struck Kaiyr on the head a few times. With blood dripping from his wounds, Kaiyr wrenched the stick from her hands.

"Have you lost your mind?" he shouted, grabbing his head. His hands were soon covered in blood.

"Tell us why you're so angry?" Meiz ran to her daughter-in-law.

"Apa . . . Apa," Gulbarshin cried with new energy, and only then did Meiz see that her dress was torn. "He's a dog, apa . . . a shameless dog." And she threw herself at her abuser again.

Kaiyr hit her in the chest. Gulbarshin gasped and slowly began to slide to the floor.

"Who have you brought into my house?" Meiz turned on Kakharman. "Don't we have enough grief here already? I just buried both my sons. Now it's time for me to die. What have we done to you to shame us like this? Shame, God, what shame!" She turned toward Kaiyr. "You will not live. Remember my words!"

"She's not dead! Why are you all screaming as if you have never seen a man before!"

The sobbing child rushed to his mother.

"You will not live!" The kind old woman was beside herself. "You will pay for our honor!"

She rushed to the wardrobe and came back with her husband's large hunting knife.

"What honor are you talking about! You are just two stupid women! What is the point of honor if there's only a few days left before the end of the world?"

"Bastard!" Kakharman growled. "Bastard! It's only you who needs no honor! It's you who doesn't need a conscience."

With a single powerful blow to the jaw, he knocked Kaiyr off his feet. Then he jumped on top of him and, growling like an animal, closed his strong, sinewy, work-hardened hands on Kaiyr's neck.

"What have you done, son?" his mother's desperate voice asked. "Why did you do it?"

Yes. It was too late. Kaiyr was dead. It was strange to have killed a man, but Kakharman didn't regret it.

He stood up. The women hugged each other and began to cry out loud. The hunting knife fell out of Meiz's hands and clanged on the floor.

On the same day, a lonely traveler rode a camel across the hot sands. The traveler was tired. A white scarf was drawn over his face up to his eyes to protect his mouth and nose from the dust so he could breathe. He was looking with deep anguish at the endless sands that were scorched here and there by fire. Tamarix and other small bushes were still burning, small islands of grass smoldered here and there, and a blackened saxaul stump smoked nearby.

The traveler was Kakharman. He had decided to travel along the shore so that his native Karaoi would be to his left. What used to be the seashore was lying some way off. The sea was far in the distance, a narrow blue strip sparkling near the horizon, shimmering beneath a thick haze.

The camel ran lightly down the slope. Its feet padded on what used to be the seabed. Here and there, the sand yielded a mass of decomposing bodies of saigas and horses, half-burned bodies of wolves and foxes, and birds with scorched wings. In among them were seagulls. They should be flying over the sea, but instead they were lying with their strong beaks in the sand. When was Kakharman here last? Three years ago? Or four? He had returned to a graveyard—a vast graveyard. The steppe, buried under the sand, had died. Any day now, the sea itself would disappear, and with it, the fishermen houses of Kazakhs and Karakalpaks.

He stopped the camel and suddenly thought, "Will the time ever come when people live differently? But does man make mistakes—even such cruel ones!—then look back in horror and begin to live differently? Well, it doesn't matter for us. But our children? Our grandchildren? Looking at what we've done, won't they begin to see? It just can't be—it can't! They'll be better than we are! They'll be clearer than we are! More clever! More conscientious!"

"You're right, Kakharman, that is how it will be. I'm glad your heart has warmed up . . ."

He heard this voice so clearly that he turned around, thinking he wasn't alone.

"Who's that?"

"I'll give them everything again, the land and the sea! I know they'll be different— your children, your grandchildren . . ."

"I pray to you! Let them be happy!"

"You're talking about happiness again. Do people live on this earth to be happy?"

"What else?" Kakharman shouted.

But the voice said nothing. It had already gone.

Soon Kakharman was by the water. The camel walked in up to its knees and began to urinate.

"You're such an idiot," Kakharman muttered. "The place you chose. Or have we not desecrated the poor sea enough?"

The camel reluctantly walked out of the sea. Heat hung over the water. Suddenly, through the haze, Kakharman could make out a large animal coming closer to the shore. "Can it be the dragon Daut?" Kakharman thought sadly. "Legend says that this creature can drink the whole sea all at once." But it wasn't the dragon. A huge brown catfish jumped from the water onto the white sand. It was in its death throes, its jaws gaping wide. Kakharman couldn't move. And after the catfish came another large fish, throwing itself on the shore close by. And Kakharman knew it was Ata-Balyk! Both the catfish and Ata-Balyk were committing suicide. But while the catfish kept flailing, throwing up sand with its fins, Ata-Balyk lay entirely still. It looked at the man standing next to the camel with its big sad eyes. There was no call for help in the look, as if it knew he wouldn't be able to help.

Ata-Balyk recognized in Kakharman the boy that it had saved many years ago from certain death.

"And where's Ana-Balyk?" Kakharman whispered.

"She died," Ata-Balyk replied. "She couldn't bring the shoal . . ." Ata-Balyk was hardly moving its lips. "Ask Nasyr to forgive me. Once, a long time ago, I almost overturned his boat . . . I did it out of despair . . . I did it in a rage against people . . ."

Ata-Balyk continued moving its dying lips.

"In the spring, we began to bring the shoal to the sea along the Syr Darya . . . But it turned out that the river doesn't go into the sea anymore . . . There was saline land between us and the sea already . . . then she . . . also . . . threw herself out." Ata-Balyk lay on the sand with its mouth and eyes closed forever. Soon the catfish stopped moving as well. Death reconciled these two eternal enemies.

Fish kept jumping onto the sand from the water. They were suffocating in the salty water. They were in pain and driven so insane by the pain that they were jumping out to find a certain, but quick, death on the shore. Soon there was no place for Kakharman to step; the whole shore was covered in dying fish. And then a macabre feast began. Snake-like creatures rushed to the shore and with incredible agility began to devour the fish. Hosts of these bug-eyed creatures with big heads and slimy black bodies slithered among the corpses. And the largest launched themselves on Ata-Balyk, gutting it in seconds, ripping the great fish's remains to pieces.

Kakharman recoiled in disgust. With a shivering hand, he gripped the camel's harness and urged it into a run. Away from here . . . away . . .

He headed toward a gathering of rusty fishing vessels—what once was a flotilla of glorious Sinemorye! The first love of his youth! His first joy! Even from the distance, he could see some people pottering next to them, swarming over them like ants. Gas cutters were glowing brightly. One of the trawlers, *Kazakhstan*, had already been completely cut to pieces. Kakharman came closer.

"Good work! Who are you?"

"Cooperative Sea," one of the men responded readily.

"Why are you cutting them up?"

"We'll be selling it abroad! The country needs money, so the country will have money."

"But will they pay money for this trash?"

"That's not our problem! Let the management deal with it."

"And who is your manager?"

"Samat Samatovich! Maybe you know him?"

"Ah, it's that glutton who speaks Russian but stuffs himself like a Kazakh."

"That's him! Exactly!" The man grinned.

And go away from here . . . away from here as well . . . away from the earth altogether. Do you hear, Kakharman? Away . . .

Nasyr pushed at the sand-covered front door. But the door wouldn't budge. Berish took a spade from the lumber room, climbed out the window and began to shovel the sand away. Half an hour later, Nasyr walked out of his house for the first time in days. Only a few houses in Karaoi had survived the storm—the rest were buried beneath deep drifts of sand. The wind was easing up, but the sun was burning mercilessly. Nasyr put his boots and a light chapan on. Berish stood in the yard, looking sadly at the destroyed aul.

"You should cover your head. The sun is burning."

Indeed, it seemed that Allah had not finished punishing people with this awful storm and had now decided to scorch them instead. Nasyr had lived here all his long life but had never experienced such heat before.

As they walked down the road, they saw a traveler entering the aul on a camel.

"*Ayee*, who is that coming to see us?" Nasyr was overwhelmed. "Berish, have a look. Who's that?"

"I can't really see from here, ata."

He walked forward. Kakharman got off the camel and took the scarf from his face.

"Dad!" Berish ran to him.

439

Kakharman hugged Berish. And then his heart sank, knowing he was seeing his son for the last time. Then he turned toward his father.

The old man, crying and muttering, hobbled up after Berish. Now you could hear what his shaking lips were whispering.

"Son . . . Kakharman . . . Finally . . . Allah has heard me."

With shaking hands, he touched Kakharman's face and shoulders, and they hugged and stood like that for a long time without speaking.

Kakharman was the first to see the police car sliding into the aul slowly but relentlessly. Kakharman knew. A terrible shivering wracked his body briefly but was soon gone. "It's too late . . . too late . . . ," he thought again and calmed down.

Well, he has to say goodbye, he has to say the final words while he still has time. How much time did he have? Two minutes? Three?

"Son! I just want to tell you one thing: don't give up! If there's no road, go off road! As long as you have energy, keep going!"

Berish raised his eyes in surprise, not understanding why his father was suddenly talking like this. He stepped back.

"Dad . . . Are you alright?"

"We are slaves from the moment we are born, and our generation will remain being slaves. But you! You should be people—do you hear me, son?"

The police car stopped a distance away. Kakharman headed toward it. Nasyr, not realizing what was going on, hobbled behind. Kakharman heard his father's steps and sped up to leave him behind. He could not say to this old man, tired of this savage life, the simple words: Father, our mother has died. Let Zharasbai and Aitugan do it; the storm has settled. They will be on their way already.

A captain and two sergeants jumped out of the car. And although Kakharman didn't resist, they clamped his hands anyway.

"Hey, what are you doing?" Nasyr shouted. He came up to the captain. "Son, don't you see? It's Kakharman! Don't you know Kakharman Nasyrov?"

The sergeant with the narrow and handsome face that Kakharman knew began to tie his hands. He tied the knot gently and asked sympathetically, "Is that alright, Kakharman-aga? It doesn't hurt?"

"What can hurt more than this?" Kakharman said as he looked at the endless white saline land around him, and added: "But it doesn't matter. We all had our things to do . . . But we, comrade captain, should've saved human souls. But we didn't. And Satan took them."

"Comrade captain, maybe we can untie his hands?"

"Tie them in the front. He seems well-behaved enough."

"Thank you, captain. Instruction is not a law; the law is not God."

Nasyr thrust himself between the sergeant and the captain. "Son, what are you doing? Don't you see—it's Kakharman!" he kept repeating.

"Captain, permit me to change my clothes in my native home?" Kakharman turned toward Nasyr. "Father, calm down. I'll explain everything to you. I'll explain to you myself. Just wait a minute."

"Where's your mother? Is she alright?" Nasyr asked suddenly.

"I'll tell you that as well!" Kakharman shouted as he disappeared behind the door, followed by the sergeant and Berish.

The air in the house was stuffy. Nasyr's careworn Quran was lying on a low table by the window. Yes, it was Nasyr's favorite place. Since he had retired, he spent most of his time there, at the table, bent over the great book, thinking a great deal. How many years had flown over his parents' house since he, Kakharman, was born? Here's the stove on which he slept so often, snuggled up safely between his parents. Here's the room in which his eldest son, Omash, was born. And that's the corner where Berish's cradle used to be. Yes, the great disaster of his sea and his homeland began the day Omash died, poisoned by Syr Darya's water.

And here they used to spread symraks. Slavikov loved lying on them, listening to Akbalak's songs.

> *So that the truth prevails*
> *The whole earth is washed with blood . . .*

Eh, Akbalak-ata! That is what it's all about. That is what it's all about. The blood will always be there, but you have to wait for the truth . . .

Goodbye . . . goodbye, everyone . . . He suddenly realized exactly what he was doing now.

"Sorry. What's your name? I forgot," Kakharman asked the sergeant.

"Victor," the sergeant answered pleasantly.

"It's a good name." Kakharman smiled. "A winner. Listen, Victor, bring me my *khurdzhun*."[8] Kakharman sat tiredly on the chair.

"Would you like me to untie your hands, Kakharman-aga?"

"Ask the captain for permission first. And you"—Kakharman nodded to his son—"take the Quran to your granddad."

"Why would Granddad need the Quran now?" Berish didn't understand.

Kakharman smiled at him sadly and at the same time said lightly, "Just do it, son."

The sergeant and Berish left the house. Kakharman immediately rushed to the inner porch, grabbed a can of gas, and began to splash it around the corners feverishly. The dregs of the gas he poured over himself. Then he rushed to the window and grabbed a matchbox. It turned out to be empty. He ran to the sideboard and found another matchbox with a single match, and he whispered, smiling, "Spirits of my ancestors, help me. You used to worship fire! Don't let me down in this last deed of mine! An instruction is not a law; a law is not God!"

The captain smelled something and muttered warily, "Where is that smell of gas coming from?"

Realizing what must be happening, he pushed Nasyr out of the way and ran to the house. He pulled the door open only to be driven back by a wave of flame. As the captain staggered back, he tripped and fell over. At that moment, huge tongues of fire rushed from the windows as the whole house became engulfed in flames.

"Dad!" Berish shouted. "Dad!"

He fell on the sand and rolled on the sand shouting, "Dad! Dad!" And the sand burned his arms and face . . . The sand . . .

Epilogue

Non bene pro toto libertas venditur auro.
"Liberty cannot be sold for all the gold of the world."

—Motto of the Dalmatian Republic of Ragusa
(now Dubrovnik, Croatia)

An animal looks beautiful even when it's old.
So why does clay, from which man is molded,
become so ugly?

—Antoine de Saint-Exupéry, twentieth century

The old police car rattled along the sand-strewn road toward Shumgen. Everyone in the car was silent, their faces covered with scarves.

The moment Nasyr realized that his son had burned alive in his house, he fell on the sand and could not get up again. He was crushed under the weight of what had happened. Berish and the policemen lifted him up, but Nasyr could hear nothing they said to him, as if he were deaf; he could see nothing happening around him and to him, as if he were blind. He wanted to see Korlan, to tell her about the death of their son, comfort the pain in her heart, stroke her bent back, and look into her eyes for the last time, then he could go to his grave. He didn't know yet that his beloved Korlan was already gone.

He sat, staring straight ahead. White hills stretched in front of him, monotonous, endless, and dreary. Where the sea—which was created with the rest of the world at the time of creation—was, there were long miles of white dust. It was stuffy in the hot car; everybody felt sick with the gas stench and the salt, which was getting jammed in every pore. They were truly driving on the road of hell.

"Boys, I see a rain cloud!" exclaimed the captain, who was sitting in the front seat. "There'll be rain! There it is, flying toward us!"

Nasyr also saw the black cloud, rapidly billowing in the air. But he didn't rejoice. His heart flinched. "Ah, Allah, you didn't hear my prayers, did you? You turned away from Nasyr." Even back then on the island, Nasyr realized, he had turned away. "You have not answered Nasyr's prayer from back on the island, where he took Nurdaulet."

"Here it comes!" The captain kept rejoicing.

Nasyr, looking at him, recounted the Surah of The Wind-Curved Sandhills, The Dunes[1] from the Quran.

> *Bismillahi ar-Rahmani ar-Rahim! Then, when they saw the (Penalty in the shape of) a cloud traversing the sky, coming to meet their valleys, they said, "This cloud will give us rain!" "Nay, it is the (Calamity) ye were asking to be hastened!" A wind wherein is a Grievous Penalty! "Everything will it destroy by the command of its Lord!" Then by the morning they—nothing was to be seen but (the ruins of) their houses! thus do We recompense those given to sin! And We had firmly established them in a (prosperity and) power which We have not given to you (ye Quraish!) and We had endowed them with (faculties of) hearing, seeing, heart and intellect: but of no profit to them were their (faculties of) hearing, sight, and heart and intellect, when they went on rejecting the Signs of Allah. and they were (completely) encircled by that which they used to mock at! We destroyed aforetime populations round about you; and We have shown the Signs in various ways, that they may turn (to Us).*
>
> *Why then was no help forthcoming to them from those whom they worshipped as gods, besides Allah, as a means of access to Allah? Nay, they left them in the lurch: but that was their falsehood and their invention.*[2]

The captain scratched the back of his head when Nasyr explained to him the meaning of this warning.

"But doesn't your Allah speak too much?" He grinned and winked at the sergeants. "We will find out soon enough. The cloud is almost here!"

Victor, whose hands had been tied at the order of the captain for his failure to apprehend Kakharman, looked gloomily at his senior. The captain looked back and him and then ordered the other policeman to untie Victor.

Victor, rubbing his numb hands, looked at Nasyr sympathetically. "Aqsaqal, read us more from the Quran."

Nasyr was filled with gratitude for this gentle young man. Ever since he had taken on the responsibly of being mullah, he had lifted the great book from its place on the chest every day and read deeply into each line. He was quietly reassured that the last years he had lived in this world were not in vain. This book had opened his eyes to many things. He looked with distaste at the captain, who was insulting Allah in such a ridiculous way. He tapped the captain on the shoulder. When the captain turned around, he said:

Verily Allah will admit those who believe and do righteous deeds, to Gardens beneath which rivers flow; while those who reject Allah will enjoy (this world) and eat as cattle eat; and the Fire will be their abode.

It is He Who gave you life, will cause you to die, and will again give you life: Truly man is a most ungrateful creature!

Berish nestled up to his granddad, trying to grasp the meaning of what he was saying. They had spent a lot of time together in the summer, and Nasyr had begun to educate him in his own way, teaching Berish to read and write Arabic. Berish turned out to be a good pupil, and Nasyr was happy that his grandson was equally fluent in both Russian and Kazakh. Berish could now read the Quran, although it was slow going for him. The more he read of the great book, the more the teenager's heart became responsive to the worries and troubles of other people. He asked Lena and Sergey to find him a Bible and began to read both great books, finding much in common between them. The books were lying next to each other in his old bag, which had been sewn out of fish skin long ago by Korlan. The Quran was the one his father had ordered him to take from the house before his death.

As the rain cloud drew nearer, the air became cooler, and the first gusts of wind slapped against the windows. Very quickly, it became dark. The driver stopped the car and looked at everyone. They had all fallen silent. Soon it was as dark as night. Sand whipped and hissed against the windows.

Not so long ago, Berish had read the revelations of Saint John with a beating heart. The text had sunk instantly into his memory. And now, comparing the words from the Bible with the Surah of Sandhills, which his granddad had just read, he thought that both the Bible and Quran could not be the creations of ordinary people. The words of Revelation, which he cited from memory, became words of tragedy for him:

My word is truth! And I saw the seven angels who stand before God . . . Then the seven angels who had the seven trumpets prepared to sound them . . .

The first angel sounded his trumpet, and there came hail and fire mixed with blood, and it was hurled down on the earth. A third of the earth was burned up, a third of the trees were burned up, and all the green grass was burned up.

The second angel sounded his trumpet, and something like a huge mountain, all ablaze, was thrown into the sea. A third of the sea turned into blood. A third of the living creatures in the sea died, and a third of the ships were destroyed.

The third angel sounded his trumpet, and a great star, blazing like a torch, fell from the sky on a third of the rivers and on the springs of water.

The name of the star is Wormwood. A third of the waters became wormwood, and many people died from the water, because it had been made bitter.

And I beheld, and heard an angel flying through the midst of heaven, saying with a loud voice, Woe, woe, woe, to the inhabiters of the earth by reason of the other voices of the trumpet of the three angels, which are yet to sound!

"We should take care not to get lost," the driver said.

"Head west," the captain instructed nervously.

"Which way is west?" Victor asked. "We can't see anything, comrade captain!"

"Shut up!" the captain barked. "Or I'll put you on trial as soon as we're back!"

"We'll need to make it back first," Victor joked.

Berish closed his eyes. "What came next? I remember now!"

And the fifth angel sounded, and I saw a star fall from heaven unto the earth: and to him was given the key of the bottomless pit. And he opened the bottomless pit; and there arose a smoke out of the pit, as the smoke of a great furnace; and the sun and the air were darkened by reason of the smoke of the pit. And there came out of the smoke locusts upon the earth: and unto them was given power, as the scorpions of the earth have power. And it was commanded them that they should not hurt the grass of the earth, neither any green thing, neither any tree; but only those men which have not the seal of God in their foreheads. And to them it was given that they should not kill them but that they should be tormented five months. And in those days shall men seek death, and shall not find it; and shall desire to die, and death shall flee from them. And thus I saw the horses in the vision, and them that sat on them, having breastplates of fire, and of jacinth, and brimstone: and the heads of the horses were as the heads of lions; and out of their mouths issued fire and smoke and brimstone. By these three was the third part of men killed, by the fire, and by the smoke, and by the brimstone, which issued out of their mouths . . .

They drove another forty minutes, stopping frequently—sometimes turning to the right, sometimes to the left—until the engine sneezed a few times and then died. The car stopped. Nasyr was confused; he had no idea where they were or in what direction they should go. The gas fumes and suffocating air had become unbearable.

"Are we going to die in the sand, then?" the captain asked in a surprisingly timid voice. He turned to Nasyr for reassurance.

"Patience!" Nasyr pushed open the car door and got out. His face was instantly scorched by a blast of hot sand. "Do you have a rope? I need a very long rope."

They had a heavy coil of wire. Nasyr wrapped the loose end of the wire around himself and gave the coil to the captain to hold. He dived into the white wraith, and the coil began to unwind. Nasyr moved slowly, bent low, stopping frequently to examine the sand. For a while, he came across nothing. His idea was simple: if they had gone too deep into the desert, he would find the skeletons of saigas or dogs or, at the very least, their excrement. Nasyr was suffocating in the white salt, which beat him on the face. It was good that at least they had this wire; otherwise, he would not have been able to take even a few steps away from the car. How long was this wire? About a third of a mile, no more. Soon he was almost crawling forward. Then his feet stumbled across a piece of metal. Soon, he was coming across jagged shards frequently. He lifted one up to his eyes to get a better look. He had often come across this kind of metal in the sands of Kyzylkum and Moiynkum; Musa, who used to collect whole bags of them, explained to him that they were from rockets or satellites. Their presence in the sand could only mean that they were very near the military zone—and maybe even inside it. How had they managed that? No one had set foot inside the zone since the Cosmodrome was built.

Thirty years ago, before Gagarin's flight, he had visited Baikonur. Now he couldn't even remember how he got into the outskirts of the Cosmodrome. It must've happened purely by accident; though back then, Baikonur was not as well protected as it was now. He saw the launch of a rocket with his own eyes and since then swore to himself: God forbid I ever see it again! Nasyr's horse had shied from the heaven-splitting roar and the pillars of fire and had fallen and crushed him beneath it. Nasyr's leg was broken. The animal lost its mind with fear and had to be shot. Nasyr had buried its corpse deep in the ground.

The wind was rising, and the fog was beginning to lift. Nasyr stretched his arm out and felt his hand touch something hard. He felt along what seemed to be brickwork. A wall. His fingers searched as he muttered fearfully, "It can't be true . . . No . . . Oh Almighty!" The wall began to curve, and the wire stretched taut. Nasyr hurriedly untied the wire. Soon his hands ran over a cast iron door embossed with a spiral pattern. He pushed hard, and the door opened inward.

"Bismillahi, ar-Rahmani, ar-Rahim!" Nasyr whispered. "Ya, Allah! Save and protect me."

He stepped cautiously through the door and under a high dome. Right at the center of the mausoleum, he saw a granite slab with Arabic writing on it—the headstone of Holy Imanbek. Nasyr fell on his knees and folded his arms in prayer.

"Almighty Allah! Thousands of gratitudes to you! You have sent the grave of the holy man to help us! Us . . . all of us . . ."

He lowered his head and began to pray. Back in the car, the captain was alarmed. "Something must have happened to the old man."

He pulled the wire; it was slack. Berish jumped out of the car right away.

"And I'll go with him!" Victor followed Berish.

"Stop! What's in your bag?" he shouted to Berish.

"The Quran and the Bible."

"They must be confiscated immediately! A teenager doesn't need things like this!" the captain spat.

Berish found Nasyr sitting on his chapan.

"For thirty-six years, not a single Kazakh could visit the grave of Holy Imanbek! It's an insult, a shame! And ahead of us, Berish, there're another thirty-six years of shame, maybe even more!" Nasyr coughed heavily, then continued. "Is it life, if we can't worship our holy man? Do these people, who fenced off the grave of Holy Imanbek, who left it without attention, have a conscience?"

His angry voice echoed in the dome of the mausoleum. When they reached this strange building, the policemen looked inside apprehensively, not daring to enter.

Nasyr turned to them.

"Why are you standing there? Come in! There's nothing tougher and more durable than these walls. What is this storm to them? Even if the storm heralds the end of the world—even then, these walls won't falter. On the Baikonur steppe, there was no man holier than Imanbek! There is no mausoleum more beautiful than Imanbek's! Don't stand there. Come in! The steppe is burning, but here under the dome, there is peace and coolness. Come in. Let your bodies rest in here. Your thoughts will calm down, your soul will relax, and your hearts will open."

The policemen took another step back.

The old fisherman stood up, leaned back against the cool wall, and spoke the thoughts he had carried with him in the last unhappy years of his life: "Ya, Allah! The sea is gone. It died. May it be your will, I'm not complaining. But why are you still keeping me alive? When will my last hour come? I beg you, come before me, give me your answer."

A white cloud that faintly resembled a human figure appeared in front of Nasyr. He fell on his knees.

"I prayed to you for ten long years, oh Creator!"

"That was your choice. Did you feel worse from praying?"

"No . . ."

"Did I treat you badly?"

Nasyr considered and then said quietly, "Oh Almighty, I don't know how you treated me."

"I created the world and man. I also created you, old fisherman. I foreordained for man to continue the human race. Am I lying?"

"No, Almighty. No!"

"I gave you strength so you could work and live in abundance. I gave you a mind so you could think and acquire knowledge . . . Ingrates! How did you spend the strength and mind that were given to you? You directed your strength and your mind to defile what I created! You forgot that God exists. You forgot that an hour will come when I will pay you back for this evil, mercilessly and cruelly!"

"Almighty! The desire for richness and his own well-being ruins man. By creating wealth and poverty, you cut the paths that lead toward you, oh Allah!"

"It's not my fault that people separated the rich and the poor. It's man's! It's not me who forces you to suffer from poverty and illnesses."

"Almighty! Who, if not you, sent these misfortunes to the earth? Who else is as powerful as you are to throw so much evil on man every day?"

The mist began to clear up, and now the voice came from inside the dome.

"Calm your anger, old man! It's only Satan that rages! I alone fight for good. And you have turned away from me. It's hard for me to fight him without your faith. You, man, have sold your soul to him! And here's the punishment! Goodbye, old man!"

"I'm not scared of death or hell's fire, Almighty! But could you help my poor nation, Allah? Our sea has died. Lake Balkhash is dying. Tomorrow the earth and man himself will die. Is this what you want?" Nasyr exclaimed.

But there was no answer.

"What's wrong with you, Granddad? You're shivering." Berish bent over Nasyr.

"Man is worthless," Nasyr muttered. "He's shit . . . Punishment for him . . . punishment . . ."

It was hard for him to breathe. He suddenly remembered Nurdaulet and Kyzbala and grew cold with fear. He was moving his lips, trying to say something, but he couldn't make a sound. His lips went white, and in their whisper came either curses or the words of the Quran—Berish couldn't tell.

Suddenly Berish remembered and shouted, "Ata, we forgot to take Uncle Nurdaulet and Aunt Kyzbala!"

Nasyr very slowly nodded and began to slide over on his side, still moving his lips. Berish rushed to him.

But it was too late.

Nasyr was breathing no more.

Rollan Seisenbayev

Aralsk, Balkhash, Alma-Ata, Zaysan, and Semipalatinsk:
1983–1988

Moscow: October, November, and December, 1989

Afterword

The Ghost of Existentialism Walks on the Sands in Rollan Seisenbayev's The Dead Wander in the Desert

This novel is about how Russians from the north reached the nomads. They brought scientific knowledge, the stability of settled life, and written literature instead of folklore. They brought the novel form instead of epic poetry and the writer instead of a zhyrau. But they brought lasting trouble to the lives of the free sons of the grass, who followed the sun with their herds throughout the year. The northern Russian civilization beat down the destined historical path of the Kazakh horse people. It led the Kazakhs to the brink of spiritual death, the ruin of the steppe, and the environmental disaster of the Aral Sea.

The novel is convincing, powerful, fearless, ruthless, desperate, and rebellious.

Despair is familiar in the spirituality of Europe and is expressed in the philosophy of existentialism. Despair came to the human soul and mind because man found himself in the eternal loneliness of his existence in the universe, abandoned without any hope and in a place of absolute helplessness before the fatal circumstances of his being.

It might seem that knowledge, science, and the accumulated experience of mankind is a blessing. The northern civilization of Russia, the eastern civilization of China, the southern Arabian civilization, and the western European civilization surrounded Sary-Arka and the endless steppes of Kazakhstan and could have swallowed up this vast land of nomads to dissolve its small people. But the northern Russian civilization was the nearest and the only one to swallow the free steppe, extending its imperial power among all the peoples surrounding Sary-Arka.

And the great genius of the Kazakh people, the spiritual leader, poet, and teacher, Abai Qunanbaiuly, from the Tobykty family, called them to turn to the north for Russian science and knowledge to enable them to survive in the civilized world in a way so much more successful than the world of nomadic horsemen that has no cities, libraries, museums, and all-powerful scientific thought.

But Abai's descendant, the Tobyktian with the exotic French name Rollan, wrote *The Dead Wander in the Desert* in Russian.'In it, Abai's descendant appears as the author of *The Book of Prosecution*, as if repeating the feat of his ancestor, who wrote *The Book of Words* but with a completely opposite goal.

As Abai wrote his merciless book, he strove to bring all the most obvious and secret sins of his people and himself into the court of reason and the spotlight of conscience. He revealed the unattractiveness of his beloved people and himself in the eyes of the High Judge, who alone knows the ideals of truly high, truly happy existence in this human world.

And Abai's *The Book of Words* showed how far the Kazakh is from perfection—steeped in flesh-eating, gluttony, ignorance, cunning, deceit, betrayal, cruelty, and bloodthirstiness.

Abai accused his people because he loved them desperately and wanted to put them on the true path to the highest levels of world civilization. He wanted to see with brutal clarity the reasons that prevent the Kazakhs from reaching these levels. And he found these reasons in the lives of his people.

But his descendant, Rollan Seisenbayev, looks for explanations of the Kazakh's misfortunes not in their inner qualities and the deadly squeeze of nature but in their relationship to the outside world and their geopolitical situation.

The novel *The Dead Wander in the Desert* does not blame the Kazakhs for how they work and exist in their steppe home. They exist in complete totality with their horses, sheep, camels, steppe expanses, desert mirages, and ancient legends. For Rollan Seisenbayev, the terrible disasters and sufferings that befell his people did not come from the ugliness of their behavior. No, the Kazakhs have a thousand-year-old culture and are descended from horse nomads who walked with their herds year after year, following the sun. They created their own culture—musical, poetic—in the lap of nature and cannot but be as beautiful as nature itself. The structure of the Kazakh soul is filled by the sun and is given air and refreshment by the grassy steppe, the great waters, and the great mountains—these are the spiritual qualities of the Kazakhs, living close to nature. Their life was beautiful and perfectly predisposed to a happy existence in Sary-Arka.

Then suddenly, it hit: "We are slaves since birth, and our generation will remain like that until the end." These are the last words of Kakharman, a true Kazakh who is already very civilized, and, following the precepts of the great Abai, knew fully knew the mind, science, and history of the great Russian north, as well as its social and political culture. Why did Abai offer such terrible words about the slave origin and for the slave position in order to unite with Russia in a common political fate?

"We are not slaves."

So why did the people and country of Kazakhia allow vast areas of the Aral Sea shoreline to dry up; the vital water arteries, the Amu Darya and Syr Darya, to be cut off; and the dead wind to blow clouds of salt dust over the once-blooming Aral valleys?

Environmental disaster. Whose evil will turn the steppe near Semey into the death zone? The Baikonur test site. These have become a symbol of the downfall of the great nomads in the Kazakh Sary-Arka.

One of the characters in Seisenbayev's novel kills himself, saying to his son, "Son! I just want to tell you one thing: don't give up! If there's no road, go off road! As long as you have energy, keep going!"

There is something painfully familiar in these words, something from the world context, from the epochal experience . . .

Such a desperate, nihilistic philosophical position was reached by European people in the middle of the last century. "If there's no road, go off road!" French writers like Albert Camus, Jean-Paul Sartre—bright people, talented writers—could see no solution to the contemporary impasse of global evil and the impending doom of humanity and expressed their despair in works such as *The Plague* and *The Myth of Sisyphus*. There is no solution. There is no way to overcome the world's evil, and man has only one thing in the face of his fatal evil and worthless virtue: his undoubtedly real and unconditional existence. This existence has no high evolutionary goal and ends meaninglessly in death. Yet despite this mass of hopelessness, a man has a quivering flame in the soul. It says no to the whole world evil. It is a resistance and struggle with evil without any hope of victory.

"Don't give up! If there's no road, go off road!" is the philosophy of despair.

It is a stoic position when confronted with the total black, hopeless meaninglessness of human existence. It is the fight against the world's evil and evil principles without any hope of victory.

The only sustenance is the fact that for some unexplainable reason, a man carries the Primordial Conscience.

Over a hundred years before European existentialism, this philosophy was laid out in Abai Kunanbaev's *The Book of Words* by an author who was born and died in the ancestral village of Zidebai, in the Semey district.

So world existentialism was defined on the steppe in Kazakhstan, where the nuclear test site near Semipalatinsk was created. This was the ominous symbol, proof of the Philosophy of Despair.

The ghost of existentialism has long wandered in the sands of Sary-Arka. Maybe it happened when a horse nomad, who suddenly found himself in the endless hot steppe, asked the questions: Who am I? Where I am from? Where am I going? And the colossal mirages of the desert over a wide sky answered him with images of fabulous high-rise cities with minarets and towers.

The great Abai wrote his final treatise in Kazakh in *The Book of Words*. His Tobyktian descendant, Rollan Seisenbayev, wrote his novel in Russian. *The Dead Wander in the Desert* is an existentialistic folk epic.

It reminds us of the Apocalypse or Revelation of John the Divine.

It is a disaster book about the death of the Aral Sea because of human intervention; about the degeneration of life on the steppes because of the radiation of the Semipalatinsk, Baikonur, and nuclear testing sites; and it is about all these signs of advancing Armageddon: with gradual degeneration, death, and the disappearance of all life on earth. The world problem that came to the steppe.

Thank God that the Armageddon, the total death of the world foretold by John the Divine, even after two thousand years, has not happened. And there are even clear signs that the human world thrives, armed with the achievements in science and technical civilization. And we live on, enjoying the benefits of civilization.

But can we relax and blissfully enjoy it all, tasting abundant genetically modified products, flying around the world, and flying into space in anticipation of its exploration by the power of the human mind?

Do we understand our phenomenon, and do we know who we are and where are we going?

And could we be mistaken in thinking that all our sins in the past and present will be forgiven?

This book from extraordinary Kazakh author Rollan Seisenbayev tells us.

Anatoly Kim, author
Moscow

Endnotes

Prologue

1. A colorful kaftanlike coat.

2. A shepherd.

3. A term of respect for an elder, a little like "sir" and a little like "uncle."

Book One
Chapter I

1. A collective farm.

2. Collective farmers.

3. *Zhyraus* were the traditional warrior bards of Kazakhstan, heroes who would put aside their instruments to fight battles whenever needed. In Kazakh lore, they are characterized by superhuman strength, bravery, and incorruptible honor. One of the most famous was Akhtamberdy, whose poetry was gloried even when he was young, but he still spent much of his time on the battlefield.

4. The Kokteniz fishery.

5. A ritual feast with food ranging from tea and bread to soup, meat, salads, nuts, and sweets that is a key part of Central Asian hospitality. It takes its name from the cloth that was once spread out for the feast.

6. In Kazakhstan, a *baibishe* is traditionally a man's first wife; a *tokal* is the younger of two wives. Technically, bigamy was illegal in Soviet times, but it never entirely disappeared here, and in 1998, it was decriminalized. But Nasyr has only one wife.

7. A headscarf.

8. In other words, when he married a daughter in the village, he not only became a son-in-law to her father but also to the entire village, so dearly was he held in their affections.

9. A Muslim prayer.

10. A traditional horseman or just a brave young man.

11. Literally meaning "white beard," an *aqsaqal* is a village elder.

12. A term of respect for an old man, meaning "Grandfather" or "Father."

13. There is now a plan to properly reintroduce the Caspian tiger to the *tugai*.

Chapter II

1. A jute is a massive die-off of nomad's cattle when pastures ice over.

2. The *khojas* were Sufi masters, descendants of the great Sufi teacher, Ahmad Kasani (1461–1542).

3. A kind of *koshma*, or patterned felt carpet made of sheep or camel wool.

4. Feasts.

5. Blood brother.

Chapter III

1. "Green Valley."

2. "Deep Lake."

3. Fermented camel's milk.

4. A long-necked Turkic lute.

5. *Paluan* is a suffix meaning "warrior."

6. A Kazakh flask made of leather.

Book Two
Chapter IV

1. *Kokpar*, or *Kok-boru*, literally means "cook forest," and it is a very ancient and tough game played by the horsemen of Central Asia in which two teams compete to drag a goat carcass to a target. It's known as *buzkashi* in Afghanistan.

2. An ancient Kazakh instrument with two horsehair strings and a cavity covered in goatskin.

3. A four-wheeled horse cart with sides, a little like a wagon.

4. The name for the nuclear weapon test ground at Semipalatinsk.

5. The *kyui* is a key form of Kazakh traditional music. It is a short piece, just two to three minutes long, and is played on an instrument such as the

dombra with a theme, such as the wide steppe (as in Kurmangazi's "Sary-Arka"), animals such as "Boz Ingen" (The Camel), events in the musician's life like Tattimbet's "The Secret," or in Kazakh history.

6. The *baiga* is a long and tough endurance race over rough terrain that dates back to ancient times. It's now run on a proper course, but in the past, it was run on land, like an extreme steeplechase.

7. A game where horse riders have to pick up a coin from the ground.

8. *Kures*, or *korash*, is an ancient bare-armed wrestling contest. Wrestlers use belts to grab their opponents and hurl them off their feet.

9. *Kyz kuu* is the kissing game and means "girl chase." Each young man races after a girl on horseback and tries to steal a kiss. If he fails to catch her, the girl chases him and tries to whip him.

10. Old friend.

11. The professor gets his facts slightly wrong. *The Creation of the World* is not a book but cuneiform tablets, and the story is commonly known as the Eridu Genesis. The Sumerian epic of Gilgamesh tells of a great flood that engulfed the world.

12. He is talking about *qanats*, the gently sloping tunnels created to bring water from the hills to irrigate the plains.

13. Al-Biruni (973–1048) was one of the greatest Islamic scholars. He came from the Khorezm region to the south of the Aral Sea, now on the borders of northern Uzbekistan, Turkmenistan, and Kazakhstan. Al-Karaji was a tenth-century Iranian scholar and engineer who lived in Baghdad and wrote an important treatise on qanats, only recently discovered.

Chapter V

1. A term of respect for old women, literally meaning "mother."

2. As part of a forced drive to create land for raising crops, the farming program devised by Lysenko in the 1930s led to mass confiscation and slaughter of the Kazakhs' herds.

3. Khan's wife—i.e., what a princess.

4. *Bogatyrs* were warrior-knights.

5. Until well into the 1970s, many villages heard news announcements on loudspeakers set up by Stalin, and were later replaced by radio, wired into every household.

6. A bowl for drinking tea.

7. A huge amount.

Chapter VI

1. That is, Nasyr's son.

2. Dimash Kunaev (Dinmukhamed Konayev) (1912–1993) was a leading Kazakh politician under the Communists. He was First Secretary of the Communist Party of Kazakhstan for twenty-two years, from 1964 until 1986, when he was removed under pressure from Gorbachev, who believed he was corrupt. When a Russian outsider, Gennady Kolbin, was installed in his place, it sparked the Jeltoqsan (December) riots by Kazakhs in Alma-Ata.

3. The nationally preferred name for Kazakhstan.

4. The quote is from Chekhov's play *Uncle Vanya*, and the professor slightly misquotes. The real quote is "Everything in a man should be beautiful: his face, clothes, soul, and thoughts."

5. Saken Seifullin (1894–1939) was one of the most influential of all twentieth-century Kazakh writers. He argued for greater independence for Kazakhs and was arrested, tortured, and executed by the NKVD in 1939. He was subsequently rehabilitated during de-Stalinization under Khrushchev.

Chapter VII

1. Nicolae Ceaușescu (1918–1989) was Romanian president and dictator from 1965 to 1989. He was the only Communist leader removed and executed by violent revolution in 1989. Gorbachev described him as "the Romanian führer."

2. Prayer.

3. Daughter-in-law.

4. These are the official notices sent to the soldier's family. They list the date and location where a soldier was killed.

5. Cheers.

6. A meat dish.

7. Bauyrzhan Momyshuly (1910–1982) a Hero of the Soviet Union, was the World War II Kazakh military officer who took part in the defense of Moscow against the German advance in 1942 at the city of Volokolamsk. It was there he met the war correspondent Alexander Bek, and Bek persuaded Momyshuly to collaborate with him in writing a novel about the fighting. Bek's novel, *Volokolamsk Highway*, made Momyshuly famous, but Momyshuly felt it was a huge distortion of events. He was

put forward for the titles Hero of the Soviet Union and People's Hero of Kazakhstan, but denied them at the time because of his overt Kazakh nationalism. He was eventually awarded them posthumously.

8. A naval mothership for unmanned underwater vehicles (UUV) robot subs.

Book Three
Chapter VIII

1. State collective farms.

2. Moneybags.

3. Ata-Balyk literally means "father fish" and is the name of the mythical father of all fish in Sinemorye.

4. There are uncorroborated tales of giant catfish occasionally attacking humans from around the world. Catfish have been known to feed on human corpses, and a very few times, catfish have been found with human bodies inside. Whether the victim was pulled under and drowned by the catfish or simply swallowed when already dead, no one knows. But giant catfish are big and powerful fish easily able to take a child.

5. A healer.

6. In Kazakh culture, when someone passes away, there is a special memorial gathering forty days after death.

7. Uniform tunic.

8. The executive committee in Communist countries.

9. The Kapchagay Reservoir near Almaty was created by damming the Ili River in 1969, something that has come under severe criticism for its environmental impact. It diverted water from Lake Balkhash, causing it to shrink

by nearly ten cubic miles in volume and grow much more saline. It also raised groundwater levels in the surrounding land, making agriculture impossible.

10. A muskrat.

11. The area around Balkhash.

12. Kara-Bogaz-Gol (literally "mighty straight lake") is a lagoon on the east side of the Caspian that acts as an overflow for it, with water draining into the lagoon from the sea through a narrow rocky channel. When the channel was blocked by the dam in 1980 in a misguided attempt to maintain water levels in the Caspian, the lake entirely dried out, letting salt blow across pastureland for hundreds of miles to the east, poisoning the soil and causing health problems. The dam was finally destroyed in 1992, allowing the lake to refill.

13. In the 1928 novel *Amphibian Man* by Alexander Belyaev, a scientist gives his son Ichtiander shark gills, and thereafter the boy has to live much of his life underwater. The 1962 film based on the book was a huge box office success in Russia.

14. The central board responsible for planning the Soviet Union's economy, known as Gosplan.

15. Leonid Brezhnev.

16. A mineral water brand from Georgia.

17. Vladimir Vysotsky (1938–1980) was an actor and poet and the most famous Russian singer and songwriter of the 1960s and '70s.

18. This is a Russian phrase—these are just flowers, berries are still to come—meaning that things are not that bad yet; the worst is still to come.

19. Korkut Ata is a legend throughout the Turkic world, and there is a huge new monument to him out in the middle of the dry plain between Kyzylorda and Baikonur. He may have been a historical figure, living around the eighth century, or he may be just a myth. He was said to have invented the *kobyz*, the bowed string instrument that is at the heart of Kazakh storytelling traditions, and one famous Kazakh melody is said to have been composed by Korkut Ata.

20. The *kobyz* is an ancient Kazakh stringed instrument played with a bow and with two horsehair strings. They were traditionally sacred instruments played by shamans and are said to be able to drive out evil spirits. A modern four-stringed version was developed in the 1920s.

21. Zidebai is one of the key sites in Kazakh cultural history. It is the country's Stratford-upon-Avon, the last home of the great national poet and mystic Abai, far out in the steppe. His humble cottage is here, along with a vast new memorial to him and his nephew, the poet Shakarim.

22. Abai Qunanbaiuly (1845–1904), known in Russian as Abai Kunanbaev, is Kazakhstan's greatest poet and looms large in Kazakh culture and thinking. He was the first national poet, famous for his *Book of Words*. Before him, most Kazakh poetry was oral, but Abai was the first Kazakh poet whose poetry was widely read. There is a famous opera about him written by the playwright Auezov and the composers Akhmet Zhubanov and Latif Khamidi.

23. During the last years of his life, Abai retreated to the remote steppes near the Chingistau hills to live in a humble cottage. The cottage is now preserved as a museum, and nearby is a giant modern mausoleum in concrete and marble, a monument to the poet and his nephew, the poet Shakarim Khudayberdieva (1858–1931).

24. The Konyr-Aulie cave is huge cave in the limestone hills next to the Shagan River in the Abai steppe district. The cave, visited by Abai and the playwright Auezov, has a large pear-shaped hall with two huge domes. It has

a freshwater lake with clear water. The temperature inside the cave never rises above fifty degrees Fahrenheit, even in high summer.

25. An epic Kazakh traditional song/poem sung by zhyraus.

26. The name of the nuclear testing site at Semipalatinsk, where the USSR conducted 456 explosions between 1949 and 1989 with little regard to their effects on the people and environment. Only since 1991 have their damaging effects been recognized.

27. The Nevada Semipalatinsk movement was the first nuclear protest group in the USSR, named in solidarity with antinuclear movements in the USA. It was set up in 1989 and by 1991 succeeded in getting tests stopped.

Chapter IX

1. The *Tuvans* are a Turkic ethnic group of nomads from southern Siberia, known in the past as one of the Uriankhai groups of Mongols.

2. Advection fogs form when warm, moist air blows across a cooler surface, typically water. The air cools until droplets of moisture condense.

3. A *topchan* is a giant bedlike sofa with a low table in the middle.

4. Hashish (cannabis) is usually chewed rather than smoked.

5. The people who settled on the coast.

6. A hand tool like a hoe, used in Central Asia.

7. Arabic greeting: Peace be on you.

8. *Bobik*, or "pup," is one of the many affectionate nicknames for the UAZ-452, a four-wheel drive utility vehicle used by the military and police from the 1960s and '70s.

9. An isolated valley between high mountains in Kyrgyzstan, said to be the birthplace of the legendary Kyrgyz hero Manas, subject of a half-million-verse epic of the eighteenth century. Talas was also the scene in 751 of the only battle between Arab and Chinese forces and between the Abbasid caliphates and the Tang dynasty. The Arab forces won, and so, the story goes, learned the Chinese secret of paper.

10. A Kyrgyz tribal chieftain, like an *akzaqal* in Kazakhstan.

11. Improvising poets and singers, rather different from zhyraus like Akbalak who perform epic stories and songs. Aqyns competed at aitys (like rap battles) to come up with witty instant responses to tricky questions.

12. One of the forms of improvisational song, along with *tolgau*.

13. One of the most famous kinds of saddle horse, ridden in Uzbekistan since ancient times.

14. One of the highest ranges in the Tian Shan mountains.

15. The singing competitions between aqyns and zhyraus.

Chapter X

1. Now known as Atyrau.

2. A brave warrior.

3. Now Astana, the new Kazakhstan capital. It was called Tselinograd between 1961 and 1992.

4. On April 19, 1989, the number two gun turret on the USS *Iowa* exploded, killing forty-seven crewmen. One report said it was deliberate and another said it was due to overramming of the gun barrel.

5. The *khojas* were Sufi masters, descendants of the great Sufi teacher, Ahmad Kasani (1461–1542).

6. Kazakhstan is thought to be the birthplace of cannabis, and although it is illegal, vast quantities grow in the Chuy Valley on the Kazakh-Kyrgyz border.

7. A VHS video player.

8. The Russian James Bond, Max Otto von Stierlitz, from the 1960s books by Yulian Semyonov.

9. Fermented mare's milk.

10. The Twentieth Congress of the Communist Party of the Soviet Union, 1956. In the 1920s and 1930s, there were at least seven million *besprizornye* (the "unattended"), orphaned or abandoned children, in the USSR due to famine and war. But between 1936 and 1938, many hundreds of thousands more were left to their fate as children of "enemies of the people," whose parents were killed or taken to the Gulags in the Great Purge. Adult family members of enemies of the people were deemed guilty by association and subject to execution or imprisonment. Criminality was thought to be inherited, so young children of enemies of the people were treated very harshly in orphanages, while those over fifteen were dispatched to labor camps to be reeducated. No wonder, then, that countless orphan children went on the run like Semeon tried to. The Twentieth Congress in 1956 marked a partial turning point as Khrushchev broke the link between enemies of the people and their children and urged that orphanages should be regarded as boarding schools where good Soviet citizens could be nurtured.

11. The wife of his older brother.

12. The Salang Pass is the main route from Kabul to the north and a focus of the Soviet war in Afghanistan. A fire in the tunnel on the pass in 1982 killed a huge but unknown number of Soviet soldiers.

13. Mukhtar Auezov (1897–1961) was a great Kazakh scholar and writer, one of the nation's leading playwrights, famous for his libretto for the opera *Abai* with the composer Zhubanov.

14. A collection of short pieces, fiction and nonfiction, from between 1873 and 1881, written by Dostoevsky for the periodical he ran.

15. A seducer.

16. Pyotr Chaadayev (1794–1856), an intellectual and writer whose view of Russian history set off the intellectual conflict between Slavophiles and Westernizers.

17. The Khakas are a tribe of Turkic people from Khakassia in southern Siberia.

18. A golden eagle.

19. An industrial city in central Kazakhstan set up to exploit the nearby coal mines, which were worked mainly with slave labor from the labor camps.

20. One of the transit points for the labor camps in the Stalin era and the site of gold mines worked by brutally forced labor.

21. A sheepyard.

22. A way of fortune-telling.

23. Dung fuel.

Book Four

1. Dear God, don't let me lose my mind.
No, better leave all wealth behind.
No, better be a slave and hungry—
Not that my reason I would I cost
So high, nor were it ever lost
Would I be too unhappy

If I was simply undisturbed,
Running wild and unperturbed
Into the deepest, darkest woods!
I'd sing out in a feverish daze,
I'd daydream in a blissful haze
Songs to suit my crazy moods.

I'd hear waves break and roughly fly,
And gaze up in an empty sky,
In an utter frenzy of delight.
I'd be strong and I'd be free,
Like a whirlwind rooting up a tree
And blasting every hedge in sight.

But here's the snag; if you go mad
It's like the plague or just as bad.
They put you under lock and key.
They bind these iron chains upon you.
Through the bars they daily taunt you
Like some wretched beast, unfree.

And then at night, the only noise
Is not the nightingale's sweet voice,
Nor rustling leaves in summer rains—

Just the inmates' piteous cries,
And the wardens' bitter sighs,
And shrieks and groans and rattling chains.

2. Gregory of Narek (951–1003), a monk and mystic, was Armenia's first great poet.

Chapter XI

1. Al-Baqra verse 164, in the translation by Abdullah Yusuf Ali.

2. Nartai Bekzhanov (1890–1954) was one of the most famous *aqyns* of the early twentieth century.

3. A type of song.

4. The salination of the land caused by the exploitation of the rivers has made the local grass very salty, giving poor hay.

5. One of the great early poets and philosophers of Kazakhstan, who lived in the fourteenth and fifteenth centuries. He was one of the key advisers to Janibek Khan when he set up the Kazakh Khanate.

6. Known by Kazakhs as the Great Jute (killing), or Holodomor, it was when Stalin enforced the confiscation and slaughter of thirty-six million of the Kazakh's forty million cattle as part of the collectivization program of the early 1930s. The animals that weren't slaughtered fell victim of the disease that spread from the makeshift abattoirs.

7. Gorbachev's replacement of Kunaev as first secretary of the Kazakh CC with the Russian Gennady Kolbin sparked the Jeltoqsan (December) riots of December 16 through 19 in 1986 in Alma-Ata, the first ethnic protests against Gorbachev's leadership.

8. Nursultan Nazarbayev (b. 1940), president of Kazakhstan since 1990.

9. The famous and much loved Kazakh opera and folk singer Bibigul Tulegenova, who played a key part in establishing an independent Kazakhstan as a supporter of Nazarbayev.

10. He means the labor camps.

11. Nobel-prize winning writer Aleksandr Solzhenitsyn (1918–2008) was famous for raising awareness of the terrors of the Gulag system in the West. Only one of his books was published in the USSR at the time, *One Day in the Life of Ivan Denisovitch* (1962). All others, such as *Cancer Ward* (1968), *August 1914* (1971), and *The Gulag Archipelago* (1973) had to be smuggled out and published in the West.

12. The hamlets of nomadic people, traditionally wintering places.

13. In the 1970s, wolves were hunted from helicopters, with devastating effects—a shocking development captured memorably when Russian singer Vladimir Vysotsky revisited his famous "Wolf Hunt" song quoted earlier. The author writes this scene with the knowledge that his readers will know this song.

"Hunting from Helicopters (to Mikhail Shemyakin)"
or "The End to the Wolf Hunt"

Like a razor, the sunrise slashes into our eyes
Like magic, triggers silently snap their ties
Talk of the devil, these snipers draw level.
From some rank stream rise these sharp dragonflies.
So with a wild will we'll drive in, into this revel.

We lie down on our fronts, our teeth out of sight
Even those who don't dive through the red flags in fright
Seek hidden wolf holes with sensitive footsoles;
Even those who can outrun the shot from a gun
Are shivering and sweating as fear takes control.

Life smiles at wolves? Where do I begin?
We just can't love life—the love is one way!
But death of course has a lovely, wide grin
And strong, healthy teeth on ready display.

So let's smile at the foe, with our wide wolf-grin.
The dogs aren't yet beaten, we're still not done for
Tattooed on the snow, in blood therein:
Our signature—we're not wolves anymore.

Tails tucked in like dogs, we crawl slowly on
Lifting surprised snouts to the sky, we move on.
Maybe harsh reprisals have poured from the skies—
Or it's the end of the world and our minds have been curled—
But we're knocked flat by lead dragonflies.

We're drenched in blood as the lead rains down.
We accept our fate; yes, we'll stand our ground.
The heat of our bellies melts the frozen snow.
This carnage began not with God but with man!
Some are flying. Some are running. Let them go. Let them go!

Don't mess with my pack, dogs—that understood?
In a fair fight, we'd beat you to the last breath.
Yes, we are wolves, and our wolves' life is good:
You are dogs and, for you, it will be a dog's death.

So let's smile at the foe, with our wide wolf-grin—
To scotch the gossip in this canine war.
Tattooed on the snow, in blood therein:
Our signature—we're not wolves anymore.

To the forest—we'll save at least some of you!
Run, run fast, then it's harder to kill you!

Run fast, run like hell, save the wolf cubs as well
I'm on a mad run past half-drunk men's guns
And I cry for the lost souls of wolves with each shell.

Those still alive, beyond the bank lying low.
What can I do alone? Nothing, I know.
My vision is grey. My instincts fade away.
Oh wolves, where are you? Forest beasts, where are you?
Where are you, my yellow-eyed braves?

I'm alive, yes—but now I'm boxed in
By those beasts that never heard a wolf's cry
They are canines, hounds—our distant kin.
They were once our prey, you know, by and by.

So I smile at them all with my wide wolf grin
Baring my rotten teeth in my rotting maw
But tattooed on the snow, in blood therein:
My signature melts—we're not wolves anymore . . .

1978

Chapter XII

1. The father of the famous poet Abai Kunanbaev.

2. Welcome rugs laid out for honored guests.

3. *"Remember, man, that you are dust. And unto dust you shall return."* The words with which Catholics begin Lent on Ash Wednesday as the ashes are touched to the forehead.

4. August Weismann was a German biologist working toward the end of the nineteenth century, and Thomas Hunt Morgan was an American geneticist working in the first part of the twentieth century. Weismann

developed the idea of the germ plasm—the unit of heredity passed on from generation to generation, unchanged by life and by anything but chance variations. Morgan promoted Mendel's basic ideas about heredity to develop the idea of the gene. Together these ideas form the basis of classical genetics, and the term "Weismannism-Morganism" was used pejoratively by supporters of the notorious agronomist Trofim Lysenko to ridicule and isolate his opponents.

5. Andrei Sakharov (1921–1989) was a Russian nuclear scientist and dissident in Soviet times. He was famous for his part in developing thermonuclear weapons and for being an activist for disarmament and human rights, for which he won the Nobel Prize for Peace in 1975.

6. Freedom cannot be sold for any amount of money.

7. Yuri Kuznetsov (1941–2003) was a Russian poet born during the war and famous for his war poetry.

Chapter XIII

1. Fasting.

2. The Autonomous Republic of Naxcivan is a landlocked exclave of Azerbaijan, stuck between Armenia and Iran. It was the first part of the Soviet Union to declare independence, in January 1990, following unrest as the Republic's Azeri people tried to dismantle the Soviet border and join their Azeri cousins in Iran, provoking the Soviet leadership and media to denounce the Azeris as embracing Islamic fundamentalism.

3. Aport apples have an almost legendary status in Kazakhstan, especially in Alma-Ata. The city's very name means "father of apples," and it is believed that the very first apples grew in the region. But in Soviet times, and since, many of the orchards were destroyed, and the aport all but disappeared. So the

commissar's gift was indeed a rare treasure. There are now efforts to restore some of the orchards and bring the aport back as a symbol of Kazakh culture.

4. Rocket launch site.

Chapter XIV

1. Shakarim Khudayberdieva (1858–1931) was one of Kazakhstan's greatest poets. After his father died when he was seven, he grew up in the remote steppe home of his uncle Abai, the giant of Kazakh poetry. It was from Abai, he later said, that he came to see that "learning taught him to see and feel the colors, scents, and sounds of the earth, to fathom secrets of the world." He believed that the three key qualities in life are honesty, common sense, and a pure and sincere heart, saying that without them you cannot live in peace and harmony. When the Bolsheviks came to power, they began the destruction of the Kazakh traditional way of life. Shakarim could not accept the new conditions for art and retreated to the Chingistau hills to live alone. But his work and his alleged links with counterrevolutionaries made him a target for the NKVD, who had him executed in 1931, as this scene from Korlan's childhood recalls. Today, his memorial stands alongside Abai's in the steppes. He is one of the author's ancestors.

2. Moscow.

3. *Buran* was the Soviet equivalent of the American space shuttle—and its name means "storm."

4. Insane.

5. This is the night of December 17, 1989, the key night in the Romanian Revolution that saw citizens defying the curfew and the military defect to ensure the overthrow of the Communist leader Nicolae Ceaușescu.

6. The Ceaușescus escaped by helicopter only for them to be recaptured and later brought to trial when they landed in a field outside Bucharest.

7. The last leader of Communist East Germany.

8. A saddle bag.

Epilogue

1. Surah 46: 24–28.

2. Translation by Abdullah Yusuf Ali.

About the Author

Rollan Seisenbayev is Kazakhstan's most celebrated and honored author. He played a prominent role in the emergence of Kazakh independence in the aftermath of the breakup of the Soviet Union and was a personal advisor to President Nazarbayev in the crucial early years of the 1990s. He is the author of *The Return of Kazybek*, *Throne of Satan*, and *The Day the World Collapsed*. Considered the founding novel of independent Kazakhstan, where it has sold over a million copies, *The Dead Wander in the Desert* marks the author's English-language debut.

About the Translators

London-based John Farndon is a bestselling nonfiction author, playwright, poet, composer, and translator of literary works. Although he does not speak Slavic or Turkic languages himself, he works in close collaboration with native speakers. He has translated poets such as Uzbek Chol'pon, Kazakh Galym Mutanov, and Russians Alexander Pushkin and Vladimir Vysotsky. He translated the verse in Uzbek author Hamid Ismailov's *The Devils' Dance*, winner of the 2019 European Bank for Reconstruction and Development (EBRD) Literature Prize, as well as books such as Anatoly Kucharena's *Time of the Octopus*, inspired by the story of Edward Snowden.

Born in St. Petersburg, Olga Nakston is a native Russian speaker who now lives in London. She has collaborated with John Farndon on many translations of Russian literature, including *Letters to Another Room* by Ravil Bukharaev, the poems of Lidia Grigorieva, Tatyana Moskvina's *The Life of a Soviet Girl*, and Rollan Seisenbayev's *The Dead Wander the Desert*.